*The Retrospective*
*& Other Phantasmagorical Stories by*
# Ramsey Campbell

*The Retrospective*

*& Other Phantasmagorical Stories by*

# RAMSEY CAMPBELL

VOLUME II

DIP

*The Retrospective & Other Phantasmagorical Stories*
*by* RAMSEY CAMPBELL
VOLUME II


2 4 6 8 10 9 7 5 3 1

978-1-80394-547-7

*Design & Layout by Michael Smith*
*Printed and bound by CPI Group (UK) Ltd, Croydon, CR0 4YY*

PS PUBLISHING LTD
Grosvenor House, 1 New Road
Hornsea, HU18 1PG, UK
editor@pspublishing.co.uk
www.pspublishing.co.uk

*Represented by*
Authorised Rep Compliance Ltd.
Ground Floor, 71 Lower Baggot Street
Dublin, D02 P593, Ireland
www.arccompliance.com

# Contents

# *Introduction*
# Part Secundus

PEOPLE, SEE HOW I PURSUE SOME PERNICIOUS SENSElessness that I previously set out to produce, solely from perverse self-regard or possibly senility. Mind you, Pete—satrap of PS—pitched such a book to me, celebrating twenty years of the publisher and promoting sixty years of its author, though he couldn't have predicted some of my tricks.

A passing seed of thought can often generate a tale, and the notion that there must be a story about pop-ups (the style of book, not the numbingly numerous sort of shock to be found in recent horror films) produced "Meeting the Author". The film *The Babadook*, refreshingly free of that kind of predictable scare, uses such a book, which eventually saw publication.

I suspect "The Alternative" may have had its beginnings in the structure of some dreams, where you believe you've wakened only to experience no such release. "A Street was Chosen" chose its own style, even if it reads like the kind of experiment I sometimes make—seeing what happens if I write a tale without using some element I routinely depend on. It's the only fictional first draft I've ever produced straight onto the computer, because I couldn't make it work longhand. Somehow this process seemed entirely appropriate.

"The Same in Any Language" and "Where They Lived" arose from our many Mediterranean holidays, Greek in the first instance, Turkish in the latter. Spinalonga exists—indeed, it gave its name to a tale in a *Pan Book of Horror*—and was very much as I described it at the time. "The Word" dealt with the millennium, and has dated in the way past visions of the future do, although perhaps solely in the sense that the book taking over the world would be published online these days, hence more powerful still. I class "The Dead Must Die" as a comedy, but not everyone was amused. "Going Under" was commissioned for an anthology about obsessions, but by the time the book appeared its theme had metamorphosed into dark love, practically stranding my story amidst the contents. "Never to be Heard" tried to conjure some sense of the classics of our field, as many of my tales do, while at times "The Entertainment" felt as if my old friend Robert Aickman hovered over it, although despite his interest in the psychic he has refrained from appearing since his death. "No Strings" is one of quite a few tales or more commonly sections of novels that were written during a Greek holiday, in this case on the balcony of an apartment near Tavronitis in Crete. For all the Mediterranean sunlight, it was darker inside my head.

If "No Story in It" is a kind of science fiction, it's one of my few successful attempts in the field. I thought I was inventing or at least exaggerating how book sales would dwindle, but no such luck. The general sense of a writer's decline wasn't invented, alas, and was based on John Brunner's career. "The Retrospective" proceeded simply from the notion of a museum in an unfamiliar town, while "Feeling Remains" was conceived in response to a commission by Ellen Datlow for a tale of supernatural terror. More than forty years after my first attempt, "The Place of Revelation" tries to capture some of Arthur Machen's insidious sense of the uncanny, using a naïve voice somewhat reminiscent of his masterpiece "The White People", perhaps the greatest of all supernatural tales. Recently a writer disparaged that story on the basis that a teenage girl wouldn't write prose such as it contains—plain silly as an observation, I'd say, and a poor substitute for criticism. The story is the work of a poetic sensibility, and shouldn't that be respected? "Hey, Bill, Romeo's supposed to be a teenager. Can't he just say 'Shut up! There's Juliet at the window and she's like the sun'?"

I've written quite a bunch of Yuletide tales, and one such was "The Decorations", composed as a sumptuous Alpenhouse Apparitions limited edition for Christmas. Gary Fry prompted "Just Behind You", my contribution to his anthology tracing the traditions of our field. "Skeleton Woods" began life as a sign I saw in the 1990s while driving through Leeds, Skelton Woods—not, as I thought, the name of a firm but a district near the city. Just then proper supernatural horror had been sent to its grave, and I recall mourning the potential story that would have borne the title. I'm a pragmatic soul and a persistent survivor, and set about preparing something that might sell. I put some years into producing suspense novels with psychological scenarios but no perceptible supernatural elements, and didn't write "Skeleton Woods" until a decade later. I might placate sceptics by suggesting that paranoid schizophrenia explains the narrator's peculiar state—a plausible situation and possible solution—but I hope this postponed story offers psychic sensations too.

Ra Page of Comma Press asked me into an anthology of phobic stories, and "Digging Deep" was the result, based on a Radio 4 report of precisely such a use of mobile phones. "Respects" had its roots in the media too, specifically the obituary pages of the local paper, where a teenager who'd crashed the latest vehicle he'd stolen was celebrated by family and friends as a loss to the world. I thought his departure, and those of any of his like, would be more of a reason to celebrate.

By the time "Passing Through Peacehaven" was published I'd forgotten where it came from—a preposterous statement, you may think, but my memory remains unhelpful. Which deserted station may have lodged in my mind to grow into the story? Perhaps some night you'll find yourself there and realise which it is. "Double Room" is an elderly man's tale, based on overhearing someone in the hotel bathroom next to mine at an American convention (I forget which). I owe "The Long Way" to an anecdote Kim Greyson told at breakfast with Tom Doherty at the

World Fantasy Convention in Saratoga Springs, about a reputedly haunted house he avoided in his childhood by taking the long way round. Among Jenny's and my favourite walks are the pinewoods surrounding Freshfield, which have produced several stories of mine. During one walk we encountered searchers looking for a party of young teenagers. They were found, having gone home without telling anyone, but "The Moons" is what my imagination made of them.

I always think doors communicating between hotel rooms have ominous possibilities—back in the eighties, touring the States for the Tor edition of *The Hungry Moon*, we stayed in a Florida room where the door to the next one, occupied by at least one oddly noisy guest, didn't lock—and I suspect this was the starting point of "The Room Beyond". Jonathan Oliver asked a number of us for an underground railway tale, and "The Rounds" was my result, where I fear that in reality the paranoid situation is less fantastic than the denouement allows. "With the Angels" stems from the sight of a party guest at the 2010 World Horror Convention in Brighton flinging a toddler high in the air to catch, and no doubt from the kind of parental scare this revived. "Holding the Light" relocates to England an underground irrigation tunnel constructed by Italians while they occupied the island of Rhodes, where it is now a feature on a guided tour. The English setting let me develop the situation of the characters, but the darkness they explore is no more total than that offered on the tour, which I found so appealing that I made a return visit. "Getting It Wrong"—I wonder if I even need to say that *Who Wants to Be A Millionaire?* was its source? If I can't have a million, I'll take the inspiration for a tale.

I never use the phones some tours offer in lieu of a living guide, but they suggested the theme of "At Lorn Hall". Do I spend too much time watching television, not least the trashy kind? Perhaps so, but the Jeremy Kyle circus gave me the opening of *Ghosts Know*, and its one-time Bingo sponsor sent me on the train of thought that ended with "The Callers". Incidentally, does television offer a more grotesque regular spectacle than the sight of the entire audience standing up to greet Kyle as though a teacher has come into a classroom? On drives Jenny and I often play at creating phrases from the number plates of passing cars, and the pastime suggested "Reading the Signs". "The Wrong Game" was commissioned by Conrad Williams for an anthology, and otherwise explains itself.

For Pete's sake (and Nicky's too), I have come to an end. Praise saints! Peruse sagely! May at least some of these pages satisfy you, and you may perhaps study my playful scheme throughout these ponderous sallies at prefatory sermons. I pray sincerely that it won't preclude solace or prompt somnolence.

Ramsey Campbell
Wallasey, Merseyside
15 November 2019

*The Retrospective*
*& Other Phantasmagorical Stories by*

# RAMSEY CAMPBELL

# Meeting the Author

I WAS YOUNG THEN. I WAS EIGHT YEARS OLD. I THOUGHT adults knew the truth about most things and would own up when they didn't. I thought my parents stood between me and anything about the world that might harm me. I thought I could keep my nightmares away by myself, because I hadn't had one for years—not since I'd first read about the little match girl being left alone in the dark by the things she saw and the emperor realising in front of everyone that he wasn't wearing any clothes. My parents had taken me to a doctor who asked me so many questions I think they were what put me to sleep. I used to repeat his questions in my head whenever I felt in danger of staying awake in the dark.

As I said, I was eight when Harold Mealing came to town. All my parents knew about him was what his publisher told the paper where they worked. My mother brought home the letter she'd been sent at the features desk. "A celebrity's coming to town," she said, or at least that's what I remember her saying, and surely that's what counts.

My father held up the letter with one hand while he cut up his meat with his fork. "'Harold Mealing's first book *Beware of the Smile* takes its place among the classics of children's fiction,'" he read.

"Well, that was quick. Still, if his publishers say so that's damn near enough by itself to get him on the front page in this town."

"I've already said I'll interview him."

"Robbed of a scoop by my own family." My father struck himself across the forehead with the letter and passed it to me. "Maybe you should see what you think of him too, Timmy. He'll be signing at the bookshop."

"You might think of reviewing his book now we have children writing the children's page," my mother added. "Get some use out of that imagination of yours."

The letter said Harold Mealing had written "a return to the old-fashioned moral tale for children—a story which excites for a purpose." Meeting an author seemed an adventure, though since both my parents were journalists, you could say I already had. By the time he was due in town I was so worked up I had to bore myself to sleep.

In the morning there was an accident on the motorway that had taken the traffic away from the town, and my father went off to cover the story. Me and my mother drove into town in her car that was really only big enough for two. In some of the streets the shops were mostly boarded up, and people with spray paint who always made my father angry had been writing on them. Most of the town worked at the toy factory, and dozens of their children were queueing outside Books & Things. "Shows it pays to advertise in our paper," my mother said.

Mrs Trend, who ran the shop, hurried to the door to let my mother in. I'd always been a bit afraid of her, with her pins bristling like antennae in her buns of hair that was black as the paint around her eyes, but her waiting on us like this made me feel grown up and superior. She led us past the toys and stationery and posters of pop stars to the bookshop part of the shop, and there was Harold Mealing in an armchair behind a table full of his book.

He was wearing a white suit and bow tie, but I thought he looked like a king on his throne, a bit petulant and bored. Then he saw us. His big loose face that was spidery with veins started smiling so hard it puffed his cheeks out, and even his grey hair that looked as if he never combed it seemed to stand up to greet us.

"This is Mary Duncan from the *Beacon*," Mrs Trend said, "and her son Timothy who wants to review your book."

"A pleasure, I'm sure." Harold Mealing reached across the table and shook us both by the hand at once, squeezing hard as if he didn't want us to feel how soft his hands were. Then he let go of my mother's and held on to mine. "Has this young man no copy of my book? He shall have one with my inscription and my blessing."

He leaned his elbow on the nearest book to keep it open and wrote "To Timothy Duncan, who looks as if he knows how to behave himself: best wishes from the author." The next moment he was smiling past me at Mrs Trend. "Is it time for me to meet the little treasures? Let my public at me and the register shall peal."

I sat on the ladder people used to reach the top shelves and started reading his book while he signed copies, but I couldn't concentrate. The book was about a smiling man who went from place to place trying to tempt children to be naughty and then punished them in horrible ways if they were. After a while I sat and watched Harold Mealing smiling over all the smiles on the covers of the books. One of the children waiting to have a book bought for him knocked a plastic letter-rack off a shelf and broke it, and got smacked by his mother and dragged out while nearly everyone turned to watch. But I saw Harold Mealing's face, and his smile was wider than ever.

When the queue was dealt with, my mother interviewed him. "A writer has to sell himself. I'll go wherever my paying public is. I want every child who will enjoy my book to be able to go into the nearest bookshop and buy one," he said, as well as how he'd sent the book to twenty publishers before this one had bought it and how we should all be grateful to his publisher. "Now I've given up teaching I'll be telling all the stories I've been saving up," he said.

The only time he stopped smiling was when Mrs Trend wouldn't let him sign all his books that were left, just some in case she couldn't sell the rest. He started again when I said goodbye to him as my mother got ready to leave. "I'll look forward to reading what you write about my little tale," he said to me. "I saw you were enjoying it. I'm sure you'll say you did."

"Whoever reviews your book won't do so under any coercion," my mother told him, and steered me out of the shop.

That evening at dinner my father said "So how did it feel to meet a real writer?"

"I don't think he likes children very much," I said.

"I believe Timmy's right," my mother said. "I'll want to read this book before I decide what kind of publicity to give him. Maybe I'll just review the book."

I finished it before I went to bed. I didn't much like the ending, when Mr Smiler led all the children who hadn't learned to be good away to his land where it was always dark. I woke in the middle of the night, screaming because I thought he'd taken me there. No wonder my mother disliked the book and stopped just short of saying in her review that it shouldn't have been published. I admired her for saying what she thought, but I wondered what Harold Mealing might do when he read what she'd written. "He isn't entitled to do anything, Timmy," my father said. "He has to learn the rules like the rest of us if he wants to be a pro."

The week after the paper printed the review we went on holiday to Spain, and I forgot about the book. When we came home I wrote about the parts of Spain we'd been to that most visitors didn't bother with, and the children's page published what I'd written, more or less. I might have written other things, except I was too busy worrying what the teacher I'd have when I went back to school might be like and trying not to let my parents see I was. I took to stuffing a handkerchief in my mouth before I went to sleep so they wouldn't hear me if a nightmare woke me up.

At the end of the week before I went back to school, my mother got the first phone call. The three of us were doing a jigsaw on the dining table, because that was the only place big enough, when the phone rang. As soon as my mother said who she was, the voice at the other end got so loud and sharp I could hear it across the room. "My publishers have just sent me a copy of your review. What do you mean by saying that you wouldn't give my book to a child?"

"Exactly that, Mr Mealing. I've seen the nightmares it can cause."

"Don't be so sure," he said, and then his voice went from crafty to pompous. "Since all they seem to want these days are horrors, I've invented one that will do some good. I suggest you give some thought to what children need before you presume to start shaping their ideas."

My mother laughed so hard it must have made his earpiece buzz. "I must say I'm glad you aren't in charge of children any longer. How did you get our home number, by the way?"

"You'd be surprised what I can do when I put my mind to it."

"Then try writing something more acceptable," my mother said, and cut him off.

She'd hardly sat down at the table when the phone rang again. It must have been my imagination that made it sound as sharp as Harold Mealing's voice. This time he started threatening to tell the paper and my school who he was convinced had really written the review. "Go ahead if you want to make yourself look more of a fool," my mother said.

The third time the phone rang, my father picked it up. "I'm warning you to stop troubling my family," he said, and Harold Mealing started wheedling: "They shouldn't have attacked me after I gave them my time. You don't know what it's like to be a writer. I put myself into that book."

"God help you, then," my father said, and warned him again before cutting him off. "All writers are mad," he told us, "but professionals use it instead of letting it use them."

After I'd gone to bed I heard the phone again, and after my parents were in bed. I thought of Harold Mealing lying awake in the middle of the night and deciding we shouldn't sleep either, letting the phone ring and ring until one of my parents had to pick it up, though when they did nobody would answer.

Next day my father rang up Harold Mealing's publishers. They wouldn't tell him where Harold Mealing had got to on his tour, but his editor promised to have a word with him. He must have, because the phone calls stopped, and then there was nothing for days until the publisher sent me a parcel.

My mother watched over my shoulder while I opened the padded bag. Inside was a book called *Mr Smiler's Pop-Up Surprise Book* and a letter addressed to nobody in particular. "We hope you are as excited by this book as we are to publish it, sure to introduce Harold Mealing's already famous character Mr Smiler to many new readers and a state-of-the-art example of pop-up design" was some of what it said. I gave the letter to my mother while I looked inside the book.

At first I couldn't see Mr Smiler. The pictures stood to attention as I opened the pages, pictures of children up to mischief, climbing on each other's shoulders to steal apples or spraying their names on a wall or making faces behind their teacher's back. The harder I had to look for Mr Smiler, the more nervous I became of seeing him. I turned back to the first pages and spread the book flat on the table, and he jumped up from behind the hedge under the apple tree, shaking his long arms. On every two pages he was waiting for someone to be curious enough to open the book that little bit further. My mother watched me, and then she said "You don't have to accept it, you know. We can send it back."

I thought she wanted me to be grown-up enough not to be frightened by the book. I also thought that if I kept it Harold Mealing would be satisfied, because he'd meant it as an apology for waking us in the night. "I want to keep it. It's good," I said. "Shall I write and say thank you?"

"I shouldn't bother." She seemed disappointed that I was keeping it. "We don't even know who sent it," she said.

Despite the letter, I hoped Harold Mealing might have. Hoped! Once I was by myself I kept turning the pages as if I would find a sign if I looked hard enough. Mr Smiler jumped up behind a hedge and a wall and a desk, and every time his face reminded me more of Harold Mealing's. I didn't like that much, and I put the book away in the middle of a pile in my room. After my parents had tucked me up and kissed me good night, early because I was starting school in the morning, I wondered if it might give me nightmares, but I slept soundly enough. I remember thinking Mr Smiler wouldn't be able to move with all those books on top of him.

My first day at school made me forget him. The teacher asked about my parents, who she knew worked on the paper, and wanted to know if I was a writer too. When I said I'd written some things she asked me to bring one in to read to the class. I remember wishing Harold Mealing could know, and when I got home I pulled out the pop-up book as if that would let me tell him.

At first I couldn't find Mr Smiler at all. I felt as if he was hiding to give me time to be scared of him. I had to open the book still wider before he came up from behind the hedge with a kind of shivery wriggle that reminded me of a dying insect. Once was enough. I pushed the book under the bottom of the pile and looked for something to read to the class.

There wasn't anything I thought was good enough, so I wrote about meeting Harold Mealing and how he'd kept phoning, pretty well as I've written it now. I finished it just before bedtime. When the light was off and the room began to take shape out of the dark, I thought I hadn't closed the pop-up book properly, because I could see darkness inside it that made me think of a lid, especially when I thought I could see a pale object poking out of it. I didn't dare get up to look. After a while I got so tired of being frightened I must have fallen asleep.

In the morning I was sure I'd imagined all that, because the book was shut flat on the shelf. At school I read out what I'd written. The children who'd been at Books & Things laughed as if they agreed with me, and the teacher said I wrote like someone older than I was. Only I didn't feel older, I felt as I used to feel when I had nightmares about books, because the moment I started reading aloud I wished I hadn't written about Harold Mealing. I was afraid he might find out, though I didn't see how he could.

When I got home I realised I was nervous of going to my room, and yet I felt I had to go there and open the pop-up book. Once I'd finished convincing my mother that I'd enjoyed my day at school I made myself go upstairs and pull it from under the pile. I thought I'd have to flatten it even more to make Mr Smiler pop up. I put it on the quilt and started leaning on it, but it wasn't even open flat when he squirmed up from behind the hedge, flapping his arms, as if he'd been waiting all day for me. Only now his face was Harold Mealing's face.

It looked as if part of Mr Smiler's face had fallen off to show what was underneath, Harold Mealing's face gone grey and blotchy but smiling harder than ever, straight at me. I wanted to scream and rip him out of the book, but all I could do was fling the book across my bed and run to my mother.

She was sorting out the topics she'd be covering for next week's paper, but she dropped her notes when she saw me. "What's up?"

"In the book. Go and see," I said in a voice like a scream that was stuck in my throat, and then I was afraid of what the book might do to her. I went up again, though only fast enough that she would be just behind me. I had to wait until she was in the room before I could touch the book.

It was leaning against the pillow, gaping as if something was holding it open from inside. I leaned on the corners to open it, and then I made myself pick it up and bend it back until I heard the spine creak. I did that with the first two pages and all the other pairs. By the time I'd finished I was nearly sobbing, because I couldn't find Mr Smiler or whatever he looked like now. "He's got out," I cried.

"I knew we shouldn't have let you keep that book," my mother said. "You've enough of an imagination without being fed nonsense like that. I don't care how he tries to get at me, but I'm damned if I'll have him upsetting any child of mine."

My father came home just then, and joined in. "We'll get you a better book, Timmy, to make up for this old rubbish," he said, and put the book where I couldn't reach it, on top of the wardrobe in their bedroom.

That didn't help. The more my mother tried to persuade me that the pop-up was broken and so I shouldn't care about not having the book, the more I thought about Mr Smiler's face that had stopped pretending. While we were having dinner I heard scratchy sounds walking about upstairs, and my father had to tell me it was a bird on the roof. While we were watching one of the programmes my parents let me watch on television a puffy white thing came and pressed itself against the window, and I almost wasn't quick enough at the window to see an old bin-liner blowing away down the road. My mother read to me in bed to try and calm me down, but when I saw a figure creeping upstairs beyond her that looked as if it hadn't much more to it than the dimness on the landing, I screamed before I realised it was my father coming to see if I was nearly asleep. "Oh dear," he said, and went down to get me some of the medicine the doctor had prescribed to help me sleep.

My mother had been keeping it in the refrigerator. It must have been years old. Maybe that was why, when I drifted off to sleep although I was afraid to in case anything came into my room, I kept jerking awake as if something had wakened me, something that had just ducked out of sight at the end of the bed. Once I was sure I saw a blotchy forehead disappearing as I forced my eyes open, and another time I saw hair like cobwebs being pulled out of sight over the footboard. I was too afraid to scream, and even more afraid of going to my parents, in case I hadn't really seen anything in the room and it was waiting outside for me to open the door.

I was still jerking awake when the dawn came. It made my room even more threatening, because now everything looked flat as the hiding places in the pop-up book. I was frightened to look at anything. I lay with my eyes squeezed shut until I heard movements outside my door and my father's voice convinced me it was him. When he inched the door open I pretended to be asleep so that he wouldn't think I needed more medicine. I actually managed to sleep for a couple of hours before the smell of breakfast woke me up.

It was Saturday, and my father took me fishing in the canal. Usually fishing made me feel as if I'd had a rest, though we never caught any fish, but that day I was too worried about leaving my mother alone in the house or rather, not as alone as she thought she was. I kept asking my father when we were going home, until he got so irritable that we did.

As soon as he was in his chair he stuck the evening paper up in front of himself. He was meaning to show that I'd spoiled his day, but suddenly he looked over the top of the paper at me. "Here's something that may cheer you up, Timmy," he said. "Harold Mealing's in the paper."

I thought he meant the little smiling man was waiting in there to jump out at me, and I nearly grabbed the paper to tear it up. "Good God, son, no need to look so timid about it," my father said. "He's dead, that's why he's in. Died yesterday of too much dashing about in search of publicity. Poor old twerp, after all his self-promotion he wasn't considered important enough to put in the same day's news."

I heard what he was saying, but all I could think was that if Harold Mealing was dead he could be anywhere—and then I realised he already had been. He must have died just about the time I'd seen his face in the pop-up book. Before my parents could stop me, I grabbed a chair from the dining suite and struggled upstairs with it, and climbed on it to get the book down from the wardrobe.

I was bending it open as I jumped off the chair. I jerked it so hard as I landed that it shook the little man out from behind the hedge. I shut my eyes so as not to see his face, and closed my hand around him, though my skin felt as if it was trying to crawl away from him. I'd just got hold of him to tear him up as he wriggled like an insect when my father came in and took hold of my fingers to make me let go before I could do more than crumple the little man. He closed the book and squeezed it under his arm as if he was as angry with it as he was with me. "I thought you knew better than to damage books," he said. "You know I can't stand vandalism. I'm afraid you're going straight to bed, and think yourself lucky I'm keeping my temper."

That wasn't what I was afraid of. "What are you going to do with the book?"

"Put it somewhere you won't find it. Now, not another word or you'll be sorry. Bed."

I turned to my mother, but she frowned and put her finger to her lips. "You heard your father."

When I tried to stay until I could see where my father hid the book, she pushed me into the bathroom and stood outside the door and told me to get ready for bed. By the time I came out, my father and the book had gone. My mother tucked me into bed and frowned at me, and gave my forehead a kiss so quick it felt papery. "Just go to sleep now and we'll have forgotten all about it in the morning," she said.

I lay and watched the bedroom furniture begin to go flat and thin as cardboard as it got dark. When either of my parents came to see if I was asleep I tried to make them think I was, but before it was completely dark I was shaking too much. My mother brought me some of the medicine and wouldn't go away until I'd swallowed it, and then I lay there fighting to stay awake.

I heard my parents talking, too low for me to understand. I heard one of them go out to the dustbin, and eventually I smelled burning. I couldn't tell if that was in our yard or a neighbour's, and I was too afraid to get up in the dark and look. I lay feeling as if I couldn't move, as if the medicine had made the bedclothes heavier or me weaker, and before I could stop myself I was asleep.

When I jerked awake I didn't know what time it was. I held myself still and tried to hear my parents so that I'd know they hadn't gone to sleep and left me alone. Then I heard my father snoring in their room, and I knew they had, because he always went to bed last. His snores broke off, probably because my mother had nudged him in her sleep, and for a while I couldn't hear anything except my own breathing, so loud it made me feel I was suffocating. And then I heard another sound in my room.

It was a creaking as if something was trying to straighten itself. It might have been cardboard, but I wasn't sure, because I couldn't tell how far away from me it was. I dug my fingers into the mattress to stop myself shaking, and held my breath until I was almost sure the sound was ahead of me, between me and the door. I listened until I couldn't hold my breath any longer, and it came out in a gasp. And then I dug my fingers into the mattress so hard my nails bent, and banged my head against the wall behind the pillow, because Harold Mealing had risen up in front of me.

I could only really see his face. There was less of it than last time I'd seen it, and maybe that was why it was smiling even harder, both wider and taller than a mouth ought to be able to go. His body was a dark shape he was struggling to raise, whether because it was stiff or crippled I couldn't tell. I could still hear it creaking. It might have been cardboard or a corpse, because I couldn't make out how close he was, at the end of the bed and big as life or standing on the quilt in front of my face, the size he'd been in the book. All I could do was bruise my head as I shoved the back of it against the wall, the furthest I could get away from him.

He shivered upright until his face was above mine, and his hands came flapping towards me. I was almost sure he was no bigger than he'd been in the book, but that didn't help me, because I could feel myself shrinking until I was small enough for him to carry away into the dark, all of me that mattered. He leaned towards me as if he was toppling over, and I started to scream.

I heard my parents waken, far away. I heard one of them stumble out of bed. I was afraid they would be too late, because now I'd started screaming I couldn't stop, and the figure that was smaller than my head was leaning down as if it meant to crawl into my mouth and hide there or drag what it wanted out of me. Somehow I managed to let go of the mattress and flail my hands at him. I hardly knew what I was doing, but I felt my fist close around something that broke and wriggled, just as the light came on.

Both my parents ran in. "It's all right, Timmy, we're here," my mother said, and to my father "It must be that medicine. We won't give him any more."

I clenched my fist harder and stared around the room. "I've got him," I babbled. "Where's the book?"

They knew which one I meant, because they exchanged a glance. At first I couldn't understand why they looked almost guilty. "You're to remember what I said, Timmy," my father said. "We should always respect books. But listen, son, that one was bothering you so much I made an exception. You can forget about it. I put it in the bin and burnt it before we came to bed."

I stared at him as if that could make him take back what he'd said. "But that means I can't put him back," I cried.

"What've you got there, Timmy? Let me see," my mother said, and watched until I had to open my fist. There was nothing in it except a smear of red that she eventually convinced me was ink.

When she saw I was afraid to be left alone she stayed with me all night. After a while I fell asleep because I couldn't stay awake, though I knew Harold Mealing was still hiding somewhere. He'd slipped out of my fist when I wasn't looking, and now I'd lost my chance to trap him and get rid of him.

My mother took me to the doctor in the morning and got me some new medicine that made me sleep even when I was afraid to. It couldn't stop me being afraid of books, even when my parents sent *Beware of the Smile* back to the publisher and found out that the publisher had gone bankrupt from gambling too much money on Harold Mealing's books. I thought that would only make Harold Mealing more spiteful. I had to read at school, but I never enjoyed a book again. I'd get my friends to shake them open to make sure there was nothing inside them before I would touch them, only before long I didn't have many friends. Sometimes I thought I felt something squirming under the page I was reading, and I'd throw the book on the floor.

I thought I'd grown out of all this when I went to college. Writing what I've written shows I'm not afraid of things just because they're written down. I worked so hard at college I almost forgot to be afraid of books. Maybe that's why he kept wakening me at night with his smile half the height of his face and his hands that feel like insects on my cheeks. Yes, I set fire to the library, but I didn't know what else to do. I thought he might be hiding in one of those books.

Now I know that was a mistake. Now you and my parents and the rest of them smile at me and say I'll be better for writing it down, only you don't realise how much it's helped me see things clear. I don't know yet which of you smilers Harold Mealing is pretending to be, but I will when I've stopped the rest of you smiling. And then I'll tear him up to prove it to all of you. I'll tear him up just as I'm going to tear up this paragraph.

# The Alternative

HIGHTON WAS DRIVING PAST THE DISUSED HOSPITAL when the car gave up. On the last fifty miles of motorway he had taken it slow, earning himself glances of pity mingled with hostility from the drivers of the Jaguars and Porsches. As he came abreast of the fallen gates the engine began to grate as though a rusty chunk of it were working itself loose, and the smell of fumes grew urgently acrid. The engine died as soon as he touched the brake.

A wind which felt like shards of the icy sun chafed the grass in the overgrown grounds of the hospital as he climbed out of the Vauxhall, rubbing his limbs. He was tempted to leave the car where it was, but the children who smashed windows were likely to set fire to it if he abandoned it overnight. Grasping the wheel with one hand and the crumbling edge of the door with the other, he walked the car home through the housing estate.

All the windows closest to the hospital were boarded up. Soon he encountered signs of life, random windows displaying curtains or, where the glass was broken, cardboard. A pack of bedraggled dogs roamed the estate, fighting over scraps of rotten meat, fleeing yelping out of the communal entrances of the two-storey concrete blocks.

His skin felt grubby with exertion when at last he reached his block. A drunk with an eyeshade pulled down to his brows was lolling at the foot of the concrete stairs. As Highton approached, he staggered away into the communal yard strewn with used condoms and syringes. Someone had recently urinated at the bend of the staircase, and the first flat on the balcony had been broken into; a figure was skulking in the dark at the far side of the littered front room. Highton was opening his mouth to shout when he saw that the man at the wall wasn't alone: bare legs emerging from a skirt as purple as a flower were clasped around his waist above his fallen trousers. The couple must have frozen in the act, hoping Highton wouldn't notice them. "Have fun," he muttered, and hurried past six doors to his.

The 9 on the door, where the red paint had been sunbleached almost pink, had lost one of its screws and hung head downwards from the other, like a noose. When he pushed it upright, it leaned drunkenly against the 6 as he let himself into the flat. The dim narrow corridor which led past three doors to the kitchen and the bathroom smelled of stale carpet and overcooked vegetables. He closed the front door quietly and eased open the first inner door.

Valerie was lying on the bed which they had moved into the living-room once the children needed separate bedrooms. Apart from the bed and the unmatched chairs the room contained little but shadowy patches lingering on the carpet to show where furniture had stood. At first he thought his wife was asleep, and then, as he tiptoed through the pinkish light to part the curtains, he saw that she was gazing at the corner which had housed the television until the set was repossessed. She gave a start which raised the ghost of a ring from the disconnected telephone. Tossing back her lank hair, she smiled shakily at him. "Just remembering," she said.

"We've plenty to remember." When her smile drooped he added hastily "And we'll have more."

"You got the job?"

"Almost."

She sighed as if letting go of the strength which had helped her to wait for him. As her shoulders sagged, she appeared to dwindle. "We'll have to manage."

He lowered himself into a chair, which emitted a weary creak. He ought to go to her, but he knew that if he held her while they were both depressed she would feel like a burden, not like a person at all. "Sometimes I think the bosses choose whoever travelled furthest because that shows how much they want the job," he said. "I was thinking on the way back, I should have another try at getting jobs round here."

Valerie was flicking a lock of hair away from her cheek. "If I can rewire a few properties," he went on, "so people know they shouldn't associate me with those cowboys just because I was fool enough to work for them, the work's bound to build up and we'll move somewhere better. Then we can tell Mr O'Mara that he's welcome to his ratholes."

She was still brushing at her greying hair. "Where are Daniel and Lucy?" he said.

"They said they wouldn't be long," she responded as if his query were an accusation, and he saw her withdraw into herself. He was trying to phrase a question which he wouldn't be afraid to ask when he heard the door creep open behind him. He turned and saw Lucy watching him.

He might have assumed Valerie was mistaken—that their fourteen-year-old had been in her room and was on her way out, since the front door was open—if it weren't for her stance and her expression. She was ready to take to her heels, and her look betrayed that she was wondering how much he knew—whether he recognised her cheap new dress as purple as a flower. She saw that he did, and her face crumpled. The next moment she was out of the flat, slamming the door.

As he shoved himself off the chair, his heart pulsating like a wound, Valerie made a grab at him. How could she think he would harm their daughter? "I only want to bring her back so we can talk," he protested.

She shrank against the headboard of the bed and tried to slap away the lock of hair, her nails scratching her cheek. "Don't leave us again," she said in a low dull voice.

"I'll be as quick as I can," he promised, and had a fleeting impression, which felt like a stab of panic, that she meant something else entirely. The clatter of Lucy's high heels had already reached the staircase. He clawed the front door open and sprinted after her.

He reached ground level just in time to see her disappearing into the identical block on the far side of the littered yard. The drunk with the eyeshade flung an empty bottle at him, and Highton was afraid that the distraction had lost him his daughter. Then he glimpsed a flash of purple beyond a closing door on the balcony, and he ran across the yard and up the stairs, on tiptoe now. As he reached the balcony he heard Lucy's voice and a youth's, muffled by the boards nailed over the window. He was at the door in two strides, and flung it open. But his words choked unspoken in his throat. The youth on the floor was his son Daniel.

The fifteen-year-old blinked at him and appeared to recognise him, for a vague grin brought some animation to his face as he went back to unwinding the cord from his bruised bare scrawny arm. Highton stared appalled at the hypodermic lying beside him on the grimy floorboards, at the money which Lucy was clutching. He felt unable to move and yet in danger of doing so before he could control himself. He heard Valerie pleading "Don't leave us again," and the memory seemed to release him. "No," he tried to shout, and woke.

He was alone in bed, and surrounded by some indeterminate distance by a mass of noises: a hissing and bubbling which made his skin prickle, a sound like an endless expelled breath, a mechanical chirping. When he opened his eyes, the room looked insufficiently solid. "Valerie," he managed to shout.

"Coming." The hissing and bubbling grew shriller and became a pouring sound. As he sat himself up she brought him a mug of coffee. "Don't dawdle in the bathroom or your father will be late for work," she called, and told him "You seemed to want to sleep."

"I'm just drying my hair," Lucy responded above the exhalation.

"Finish on the computer now, Daniel. You know not to start playing before school."

"It's not a game," Daniel called indignantly, but after a few seconds the chirping ceased.

Valerie winked at Highton. "At least all that should have woken you up."

"Thank God for it."

She stooped and, holding back her long black hair with one hand, kissed each of his eyes. "Have your shower while I do breakfast."

He sipped the coffee quickly, feeling more present as the roof of his mouth began to peel. The dream had been worse this time, and longer; previously it had been confined to the flat. It must have developed as it had because he would be seeing O'Mara this morning.

As usual when Lucy had used it, the bath was full of foam. Highton cleared the mirror and tidied away Daniel's premature electric razor before sluicing the foam down the plughole with the shower. By the time he went downstairs, Valerie was waving the children off to school. When the microwave oven beeped he grabbed his breakfast and wolfed it, though Valerie wagged a finger at him. "You'll be giving yourself indigestion and nightmares," she said, and he thought of telling her about his recurrent dream. Doing so seemed like inviting bad luck, and he gave her a long kiss to compensate for his secrecy as he left the house.

All along the wide suburban street the flowering cherry was in bloom. Highton inhaled the scent before he drove the Jaguar out of the double garage. He had an uninterrupted run along the dual carriageway into town until the traffic lights halted him at the junction with the road which led to the disused hospital past the flats O'Mara had bought from the council. When the lights released him Highton felt as if he were emerging from a trance.

The only spaces in the car park were on the ninth floor. Beyond the architectural secrets which the top storeys of the business district shared with the air he saw the old council estate. He put the sight out of his mind as he headed for his office, mentally assembling issues for discussion with O'Mara.

O'Mara was late as usual, and bustled into Highton's office as if he had been kept waiting. He plumped himself on the chair in front of the desk, slung one leg over the other, rubbed his hands together loudly and folded them over his waistcoated stomach, flashing a fat gold ring. Throughout this performance he stared at Highton's chair as if both men were on the wrong sides of the desk. "Tell me all the good news," he demanded, beginning to tap the carpet with the toecaps of his brogues.

"We've identified a few points you overlooked in your accounts."

A hint of wariness disturbed the heavy blandness of O'Mara's round face. "So long as you'll be making me more than I'm paying you."

"It depends whether you decide to follow our advice." Highton picked up the sheet on which he'd made notes for discussion, and blurted out a thought which seemed just to have occurred to him. "You might consider a programme of repairs and improvements to your properties as a tax expense."

O'Mara's face reddened and appeared to puff up. "I can't afford to splash money around now I'm no longer on the council."

"But surely—" Highton said, and heard his voice grow accusing. How could he forget himself like that? It wasn't his job to moralise, only to stay within the law. The dream must have disturbed him more than he knew for him to risk betraying to O'Mara his dislike of the man. "Let me guide you through your accounts," he said.

Half an hour later the landlord was better off by several thousand pounds, but Highton couldn't take much pleasure in it; he kept seeing how exorbitant the rents were. He showed O'Mara to the lift and made himself shake hands, and wiped off the man's sweat with his handkerchief as soon as the lift door closed. The sympathetic grins his partners and the secretaries gave him raised his spirits somewhat, and so did the rest of the day: he set up a company for a client, argued the case of another with the Inland Revenue, helped a third choose a pension plan. He had almost forgotten O'Mara until he returned to his car.

He leaned on the Jaguar and gazed towards O'Mara's streets. Could they really be as bad as he'd dreamed? He felt as if he wasn't entitled to go home until he had seen for himself. When he reached the junction at the edge of the estate he steered the car off the dual carriageway.

Concrete surrounded him, identical streets branching from both sides of the road like a growth which had consumed miles of terraced streets. The late afternoon sky was the same dull white. From the air the place must resemble a huge ugly crystal of some chemical. Perhaps half the windows he passed were boarded up, but he didn't know if he was more disturbed by the spectacle of so many disused homes or the thought of tenants having to live among the abandoned flats. The few people he passed—children who looked starved or unhealthily overweight, teenagers with skin the colour of concrete, older folk hugging bags tightly for fear of being mugged—either glared at him or dodged out of sight. They must take him for someone on O'Mara's payroll, since the landlord never visited his properties in person, and he was uncomfortably aware that his wallet contained a hundred pounds which he'd drawn from the bank at lunchtime. He'd seen enough to show him the district was all that he'd imagined it to be; but when he turned off the main road it was to drive deeper into the maze.

Why should he assume that he was following the street along which he'd turned in his dream? Apart from the numbers on the doors and over the communal entrances, there was little to distinguish one street from another. He was driving past the low nine hundreds; the block on the far side of a junction scattered with broken glass should contain the flat whose number he had dreamed of. He avoided the glass and cruised past the block, and then the car shuddered to a standstill beside a rusty Vauxhall as his foot faltered on the accelerator.

It was by no means the only faded red door he'd seen since leaving the dual carriageway, nor the only door on which a number was askew; but the sight of the 9 dangling upside-down as if the final 3 had been subtracted from it seemed disconcertingly familiar. He switched off the ignition and got clumsily out of the car. Glancing around to reassure himself that nobody was near, he ran across the road and up the stairs.

Of course the concrete staircase looked familiar, since he had already driven past a host of them. He peered around the corner at the top and hurried along the balcony as fast as he could creep. There were seven doors between the stairway and the door with the inverted 9. One glance through the gap between the curtains next to the door would quieten his imagination, he promised himself. He ducked his head towards the gap, trying to fabricate an explanation in case anyone saw him. Then he froze, his fingers digging into the rotten wood of the windowsill. On the carpet a few feet from the window was a telephone, and he'd recognised the number on the dial.

Even stronger than the shock which caused him to gasp aloud was the guilt which overwhelmed him at the sight of the room, the ragged pinkish curtains, the double bed against the wall beyond the unmatched chairs. He felt responsible for all this, and unable to retreat until he'd done his best to change it. He groped for his wallet and counted out fifty pounds, which he stuffed through the slot in the front door. Having kept half the cash made him feel unforgivably mean. He snatched the rest of the notes from his wallet and shoved them into the flat, where they flopped on the hall floor.

The sound, and the prospect of confronting anyone from the flat, sent Highton fleeing like a thief. How could he explain to Valerie what he'd just done when he could hardly believe that he'd done it? He swung the car screeching towards the dual carriageway and drove back to the business district, where he withdrew another hundred pounds from the dispenser in the wall outside the bank.

As he let himself into the house Valerie was coming downstairs laden with the manuals she employed to teach her students word processing. "Hello, stranger," she said.

Highton's stomach flinched. "How do you mean?"

"Just that you're late. Though now you mention it, you do look a bit strange."

"I'm home now," Highton said, feeling even more accused. "I had something to tidy up."

"You can't fool me, you've been visiting your mistress," Valerie said smiling. "I've had to eat so I can run. Everything for you three is by the microwave."

He was relieved not to have to face her while his thoughts were in turmoil, but his relief felt like disloyalty. He listened as the dreamy hum of her car receded, fading sooner than he was expecting. When the oven peeped he called the children downstairs. Lucy came at once, her extravagant earrings jangling; Daniel had to be shouted for three times, and would have worn his personal stereo at the dinner-table if Highton hadn't frowned at him. "Let's hear about your day instead," Highton appealed to both of them.

Daniel had scored a goal in a football match against a rival school and been praised for his science project, Lucy's work on local history had been singled out to be shown to the headmistress. "Now you have to tell us about your day," Lucy said.

"Just the usual, trying to balance the books." Feeling trapped, Highton went on quickly: "So are you both happy?"

Daniel looked puzzled, almost resentful. "Expect so," he said and shrugged.

"Of course we are. You and mummy see that we are."

Highton smiled at her and wondered if she was being sensitive to his emotional needs rather than wholly honest; perhaps it had been an unreasonably direct question to ask people of their ages. Once the dinner things were in the dishwasher Daniel lay on his bed with his headphones on while Lucy finished the homework her class had been set in advance to give them more time at the school disco, and Highton poured himself a large Scotch and put a compact disc of Mozart piano sonatas on the player.

The stream of music and the buzzing in his skull only unsettled him. Had he really donated a hundred pounds to someone he didn't know, with as little thought as he might have dropped a coin beside any of the beggars who were becoming an everyday sight in the downtown streets? In retrospect the gesture seemed so flamboyant as to be offensive. At least the money had been in old notes, and couldn't be traced to him; the idea that whoever lived in the flat might come to the house in search of an explanation terrified him. Worse still was the thought of their asking Valerie or the children. His growing confusion exhausted him, and he would have gone to bed if that hadn't seemed like trying to avoid Valerie when she came home. He refilled his glass and switched on the television, which was more likely than the music to keep him awake, but he found all the programmes discomforting: newscasts and documentaries about poverty and famine and a millionaire who had never paid tax, a film in which a policeman had to hunt down a jewel thief who had been his best friend when they were children in the slums. He turned off the set and waited for the financial report on the radio, in case the broadcast contained information he should know. The programme wasn't over when he fell asleep in the chair.

The next he knew, Valerie was shaking him. "Wake up, I want to talk to you. Why won't you wake up?"

He found himself clinging to the arms of the chair as if by staying immobile he could hold on to his slumber. One of his fingers poked through a tear in the fabric, into the spongy stuffing of the chair. The sensation was so disagreeable that it jerked his eyes open. Valerie was stooping to him, in danger of losing her balance and falling back on the bed. "Don't keep going away from me," she begged.

Highton grabbed her wrists to steady her. "What's wrong now? Is it the children?"

"Lucy's in her room. I've spoken to her. Leave her alone, Alan, or she'll be running off again. She only wanted to give Daniel what she could because she can't bear to see him suffer."

Highton blinked at Valerie as she tried to toss back her greying hair. The light from the overhead bulb glared from the walls of the room, except where the shadow of the lampshade lay on them like grime, yet he felt as if they or he weren't fully present. "Where is he?"

"Gone."

"Where?"

"Oh, where do you think?" Her resignation gave way momentarily to anger, and Highton felt deeply ashamed of having left her to fend for herself. "There was some money in the hall," she said as though she was trying to clarify her thoughts. "A hundred pounds that must have been put through our door by mistake. Whoever did that can't be up to any good, and they'll turn nasty if they don't get it back, but Daniel wouldn't listen. He was away with it before we could stop him."

Highton felt that he ought to know where the money had come from, as if he had foreseen it in a dream. The impression was too vague to grasp, and in any case he hadn't time to do so. "How long ago?"

"Ten minutes, maybe quarter of an hour. We didn't see which way he went," Valerie said like an accusation.

"You wouldn't be safe out there this late." Highton squeezed her shoulders through the faded grey checked dress and stood up. "You look after Lucy. I'll find him."

He wouldn't return until he had, he vowed to himself. He closed the front door and picked his way along the unlit balcony to the head of the stairs. Through the windy aperture in the rear wall he could see across the yard. Some of the windows that were lit shouldn't be; he glimpsed the glow of an upturned flashlight beyond one set of makeshift shutters, the flicker of candlelight through another. Daniel and youngsters like him would be in one or more of the abandoned rooms while their suppliers hid at home behind reinforced doors and windows. The knowledge enraged Highton, who launched himself at the stairs, too hastily. His foot missed the step it was reaching for, and he fell headlong.

He was bracing himself to hit concrete, but his impact with the carpet was a greater shock. His fists and his knees wobbled, and the crouch he had instinctively adopted almost collapsed. He stared bewildered at the chair from which he'd toppled forwards, the radio whose voice had grown blurred and distant, the glass of Scotch which seemed exactly half empty, half full. The room and its contents made him feel dislocated, unable to think. He stumbled to the telephone and dialled the number which had lingered in his head.

The number was disconnected. Its monotonous wail reached deep into him. He was pressing the receiver against his ear, and feeling as if he couldn't let go until he had conceived a response to the wail for help, when Valerie came into the room. "Who are you calling so late?"

He hadn't realised she was home. He clutched at the earpiece to muffle the wail and fumbled the receiver onto its rest. "Nobody. Nobody's there," he gabbled. "I mean, just the speaking clock."

"Don't look so disconcerted or you'll have me thinking you're being unfaithful." She gazed at him for several protracted seconds, then she winked. "Only teasing. I know you've just woken up," she said, and went upstairs.

Her affectionateness made him feel guiltier. He switched off the mumbling radio and sat trying to think, until he realised how long he had been sitting and followed Valerie. He was hoping they could make love—at least then he might feel closer to her without having to talk—but she was asleep.

He lay beside her and stared up at the dark. His desire for sleep felt like a compulsion to dream. He didn't know which disturbed him more, his fear of finding out what happened next or his need to do so. Why couldn't he accept that he had simply acted on impulse this afternoon—that he'd donated his cash to some of O'Mara's tenants to compensate for his involvement with the man? Given how cramped the flats were, the presence of a bed as well as a few worn-out chairs in the front room didn't require much imagining, and was he really certain that he had dreamed anything more specific about the place before he had looked in the window today? Had he genuinely recognised the phone number? The memory of seeing it through the window was vivid as a photograph—so vivid that it blotted out any memory of his having seen it before. Trying to recall the dream felt like slipping back into it, and he kept recoiling from the promise of sleep.

When at last he dozed off, the alarm seemed to waken him so immediately that he could hardly believe he was awake. As long as sleep had caught up with him, why couldn't the dream have reached a conclusion? He dozed again, and when he was roused by Daniel and Lucy calling their goodbyes he thought he was dreaming. He sprawled on the floor in his haste to be out of bed and under a reviving shower.

Whatever temperature he set it to, the downpour felt more distant than he would have liked. The breakfast Valerie put in front of him was almost too hot to taste, but he mustn't linger or he would be late for work. He kissed her cheek and ran to the car, feeling obscurely treacherous. Because of his unsettled night he drove as slowly as the traffic would allow. At the junction from which the concrete flats were visible he felt in danger of forgetting which way to go, and had to restrain himself from driving townwards while the lights were against him.

Julie brought him a mug of coffee and the news that a client had cancelled that morning's appointment because one of her boutiques had been looted overnight. Highton set about examining a hairdresser's accounts, but he didn't feel safe with them: in his present state he might overlook something. He dictated letters instead, trusting the secretaries to spot mistakes. Since he had no appointments, should he take the afternoon off and catch up on his sleep? Once Rebecca had collected the tape of his dictation he cleared a space among the files on the desk and propped his hand against his mouth.

The phone jolted him awake. He wondered how they had been able to afford to have it reconnected until he saw that he was in the office. "It's Mrs Highton," Julie's voice told him.

"Yes, I want to talk to her."

A moment later Valerie's breathing seemed to nestle against his cheek. "Next time it will be," he said.

"What's that, Alan?"

"I was talking to someone here." Despite his confusion he could lie about that, and say "What can I do for you?"

"Do I have to make an appointment? I was going to ask if you wanted to meet for lunch."

He couldn't say yes when he hadn't had time to think. "I'm already booked," he lied. "I'm awfully sorry."

"So you should be," Valerie retorted, and laughed. "I just thought when you went out you looked as if you could do with easing up on yourself."

"I will when I can."

"Do, for all our sakes. See you this evening. Don't be late."

"Why should I be?" Highton demanded, hoping that didn't sound guilty. He dropped the receiver onto its cradle and pinched his forehead viciously to quicken his thoughts. He knew why he'd greeted Valerie as he had: because on wakening he'd found himself remembering the last words she had addressed to him. "Why did it have to be money? Why couldn't it have been something that might have meant something to him?"

She meant the cash Daniel had taken from the flat. Highton must have dreamed her words at the moment of wakening, but he couldn't recall doing so, which made them seem unassailably real. He wouldn't be able to function until he had proved to himself that they weren't. He told the secretaries that he wouldn't be more than an hour, and hurried to his car.

By the time he reached the junction he had a plan. He needed only to be shown that the tenants of the flat weren't the victims of his dream. If sounding his horn didn't bring someone to the window he would go up and knock. He could always say he had mistaken the address, and surely nobody would take him for a thief.

The pavements were scattered with chunks of rubble. Icy winds ambushed him at intersections and through gaps in the architecture, carrying tin cans and discarded polystyrene into the path of the Jaguar, dislodging an empty liquor bottle from a balcony. As he came in sight of the block where he'd posted the notes, a wind raised washing on the line outside the flat as if the clothes were welcoming him. Closest to the edge of the balcony was a dress as purple as a flower.

He clung to the wheel and sent the car racing onwards. Not only the purple dress was familiar; beside it was a grey checked dress, more faded by another wash. He trod on the brake at last, having realised that he was speeding through the duplicated streets with no idea of where he was. Before he found a route to the dual carriageway his head was brimming with panic. He succeeded in returning to the car park without mishap, though he couldn't recall driving there. He strode almost blindly into his office, shouting "Leave me alone for a while." But when Julie tapped on the glass to inform him that the rest of the office was going home he was no closer to understanding what had happened or where it might lead.

He depressed the accelerator hard when the lights at the junction with the dual carriageway turned amber, and was dismayed to find that he wasn't so much anxious to be home as even more nervous of being sidetracked. He steered the car into the driveway and was unlocking the garage when Valerie opened the French windows and stepped onto the back patio. "You may as well leave your car out, Alan."

"Why, are we going somewhere?"

"You haven't forgotten. You're teasing." Her amused expression disguised a plea. "You're getting worse, Alan. I've been saying for months that you need to take it easier."

When he didn't respond she marched into the house, and he could only follow her. The sight of Lucy still in her school uniform released his thoughts. "I was joking, you know," he called after Valerie. "It's time to meet Lucy's teachers again."

"Don't bother if it's that much trouble," Lucy said.

"Of course it isn't," Highton replied automatically, hearing Valerie tell Daniel "Make sure you're home by nine."

As the family sat down to dinner Highton said to Lucy "You know I like seeing your schoolwork." He saw that she guessed this was a preamble, and he hurried on: "But your mother's right, I've been having to push myself lately. Better too much work than none, eh? Would you mind if I stayed home tonight and had a rest? I can catch up on your achievements next time."

She suppressed her disappointment so swiftly he might almost have believed he hadn't glimpsed it. "I don't mind," she said, and Valerie refrained from saying whatever she had been about to say to him, rationing herself to a frown.

She and Lucy drove away before Daniel made for the youth club. Now that Highton had created a chance for himself—the only time he could foresee when he was certain to be alone in the house—he felt both anxious to begin and nervous of betraying his eagerness to Daniel. Hadn't he time to conduct an investigation which should already have occurred to him? He leafed through the phone directory to the listing for Highton, but none of the numbers alongside the column of names was the one he'd seen in the flat. Nor could Directory Enquiries help him; a woman with a persistent dry cough explained patiently that she couldn't trace the number, and seemed to suspect he'd made it up.

Whatever he'd been hoping the search would prove, it left him even more confused. As soon as Daniel had left the house, Highton ran Valerie's Toyota out of the garage and unlocked the boot, then he carried Daniel's computer out to the car. The boy wouldn't be without it for long, he told himself, and the insurance money might pay for an upgraded model. He felt unexpectedly mean for removing only the computer, and so he rushed through the house, collecting items which he felt ashamed to be able to afford: the telephone extension in his and Valerie's bedroom, the portable television in the guest room. Dumping them in the boot, he ran back to the house, trying to decide which window to smash.

A burglar would enter through the French windows, but the prospect of so much breakage dismayed him. The thief or his accomplice could have been small enough to climb through the kitchen window. He was picking up a tenderiser mallet to break the glass, and a towel to help muffle the sound, before he realised that he couldn't use anything in the house. He dashed out, locking the front door behind him, and ran on tiptoe around the house.

He mustn't take long. He had to leave the items on the balcony outside the flat and drive to the school in time to appear to have decided to see Lucy's work after all. Once they were home he would discover that he'd been in such a hurry to get to the school that he had forgotten to switch on the burglar alarm. There were tools in the garden shed which an unprepared burglar might use, but how would the burglar open the padlock on the door? Highton had been straining for minutes to snap the hasp, using a branch which he'd managed to twist off the apple tree, when he wondered if he could say that he had left the shed unlocked, though wouldn't he be claiming to have been too careless for even pressure of work to explain? He ran to the garage for a heavy spanner, with which he began to lever at the hasp and then to hammer at it, afraid to make much noise in case it attracted attention. He was still attacking the padlock when the Jaguar swung into the drive and spotlighted him.

Lucy was first out of the car. “They couldn’t turn off the fire alarm, so everyone had to go home,” she called; then her cheerfulness wavered. “What are you doing?”

He felt paralysed by the headlights. He couldn’t hide the spanner. “I lost the key,” he said, and remembered that Valerie knew it was on the ring with his keys to her car. “I mean, I snapped it. Bent it. Had to throw it away,” he babbled. “I was going to come to the school after all when I—” He had no idea how he would have continued if he hadn’t been interrupted, but the interruption was anything but welcome. A police car had drawn up behind the Jaguar.

Valerie climbed out of his car as the two policemen approached. “I wasn’t speeding, was I?”

“We weren’t following you, madam,” the broader of the pair assured her, staring at Highton. “We received a report of someone behaving suspiciously around this house.”

“There must be some mistake. That’s my husband.” But as she laughed, Valerie’s gaze strayed to the open boot of her car. “It’s all right, Lucy,” she said—too late, for the girl was already blurting “What are you doing with Daniel’s computer?”

“I’m sure there’s a perfectly reasonable explanation,” Valerie said in a tone so clear that she might have been addressing not only Lucy and the policemen but also the neighbours who had appeared at several windows. “In any case, it’s a domestic matter.”

The police stood their ground. “Perhaps the gentleman would like to explain,” the thickset policeman said.

“I was just pottering. Can’t I potter around my own property?” Highton felt as if the lights were exposing his attempt at humour for the defensiveness it was, and the police obviously thought so; they stepped forward, the man who was built like a bouncer declaring “We’ll have a look around if you don’t mind, to make sure everything’s in order.”

They stared hard at the spanner and the padlock, they examined all the downstairs locks and bolts. They lingered over the contents of the boot of the Toyota. "These are yours, are they, madam?" the wiry policeman enquired, and looked ready to ask Valerie to produce receipts. Eventually the police left, having expressed dissatisfaction by their ponderousness. "There won't be any reason for us to come back, I hope," the broad policeman commented, and Highton knew that they'd concluded they had cut short an insurance fraud.

Once they had driven away, Valerie glared at the neighbouring houses until the pairs of curtains fell into place. "Don't say anything, Lucy. Help me carry these things into the house." To Highton she said "You look terrible. For God's sake try and get some sleep. Tomorrow we'll talk about what has to be done. We can't go on like this."

He felt too exhausted to argue, too exhausted even to be afraid of sleep. He fumbled through washing his face and brushing his teeth, and crawled into bed. Sleep held itself aloof from him. In a while he heard Daniel and Lucy murmuring in the back garden, obviously about him. The unfamiliar smell of smoke made him flounder to the window, from which he saw them sharing a cigarette. "Don't start smoking or you won't be able to give it up," he cried, and they fled around the house.

Later, as he lay feeling that sleep was gathering just out of reach, Valerie came to bed. When he tried to put an arm round her she moved away, and he heard muffled sobs. He had the notion that somehow her grief wouldn't go to waste, but before he succeeded in grasping the idea, sleep blotted out his thoughts.

Then she was leaning over him and whispering in his ear. "Come and see," she repeated.

Her voice was too low for him to distinguish its tone, but when he opened his eyes he saw she had been crying. He swung his legs off the bed, on which he had been lying fully dressed. "What is it?"

"Nothing bad," she assured him, and he realised that her tears had been of relief. "Come and see."

He followed her into the hall of the flat and saw a portable television near the front door. "Where did that come from?"

"That's part of it. Have you really been asleep in there all this time?" She was too full of her news to wait for an answer. "He didn't spend that money on drugs. That's why you couldn't find him. He bought the television for us and something for himself to keep him straight."

She put a finger to her lips and beckoned him to the door of Daniel's room. Daniel and Lucy were sitting together on the chair in front of the rickety dressing-table, which bore a computer with a small monochrome screen. Both of them were engrossed in the calculations which it was displaying. "I'm teaching them how to use it," Valerie said in his ear. "Once they're old enough to get a job doing it, maybe I can go back to mine."

Though Highton recognised that he shouldn't enquire too closely into how or where Daniel had been able to buy both a computer and a television for a hundred pounds, it looked like a miracle. "Thank God," he said under his breath.

She squeezed his arm and led him back to the front room. "It won't be easy," she said with a strength which he'd feared had deserted her. "The next few days are going to be awful for him. He swears he'll straighten himself out so long as we don't leave him alone for a moment. He means you particularly, Alan. He needs you to be here."

She wasn't referring only to the present, Highton knew. "I will be, I promise," he said, trying to grasp why he felt less sure of himself than he sounded. "Do you mind if I go out for a stroll and a think, seeing as I won't be going anywhere for a while? I won't be long."

"Don't be," she said, and hugged him fiercely.

He would go back to her, he vowed as he descended the dark concrete stairs, just as soon as he understood why he was harbouring any doubt that he would. Not far now, not much further, he kept telling himself as he tramped through the dark between the broken streetlamps, trying to relax enough to think. When at last he turned and saw only darkness and looming blocks of flats he was seized by panic. Before he could run back to the flat, he awoke.

Valerie had wakened him by sitting up. When he reached for her, desperate to feel that she was there, she slid out of bed without looking at him. "I'm sorry," he mumbled, rubbing his eyes.

She gave him a wavering glance and sat on the far end of the bed. "I don't even want to know what you thought you were doing, but I need to know what's wrong."

"It's as you've been saying, pressure of work."

"You're going to have to tell me more than that, Alan."

He couldn't tell her the truth, but what else might convince her? "I'm not happy about some of the clients I have to work for. One in particular, a landlord called O'Mara."

"You used to talk to me about anything like that," Valerie said as if he had confirmed his disloyalty. She nodded at the open door, past which Lucy was padding on her way to the bathroom. "Wait until we're alone."

Once the bathroom was free Highton made for the shower. If he closed his eyes he could imagine that the water was lukewarm rain, surging at him on a wind between the blocks of flats. He hurried downstairs as soon as he was dressed, not wanting the children to leave the house until he'd bidden them goodbye.

They were still at the table. They stared at their food and then smiled at him, so brightly yet so tentatively that he felt like an invalid whose condition was obvious to everyone except himself. As Valerie put his plate in front of him with a kind of resentful awkwardness, Lucy said "Don't worry about Mr O'Mara."

The side of Highton's hand brushed against the hot plate. The flare of pain was too distant to bother him. "What do you know about O'Mara?"

"Only that he says you're the best accountant in town," she said, flinching from his roughness. "I didn't mean to listen to what you and mummy were saying."

"Never mind that. Where have you come across him?"

"I haven't yet. His son Lionel told me what he said. Lionel goes to our school." She lifted a forkful of scrambled egg to her lips before adding defiantly "He's taking me to the disco."

Highton could see that she was expecting an argument, but he didn't want to upset her now, particularly since there was no need. He finished his breakfast and waited near the front door to give her and Daniel a hug. "Don't let life get you down," he told them, and watched as they walked away beneath the sunlit cherry trees and turned the corner.

Valerie was switching on the dishwasher. "So tell me about this O'Mara," she said with more than a hint of accusation.

"You look after Lucy. I'll deal with him."

"Not in your present state of mind you won't. You need to see someone, Alan. Maybe they'll prescribe some time off work, which we can afford."

That was true, especially since she was a director of the firm. "At the very least I have to tidy things up," he said.

She seemed resigned, even relieved. "Shall I drive you to the office?"

A surge of love almost overwhelmed him, and he would have pulled her to him if he hadn't been afraid that the violence of his emotion would rouse her suspicions. "I don't know how long I'll be," he said. "I'll come back as soon as I can."

Having to be so careful of his words to her distressed him. He yearned to linger until he had somehow communicated his love for her, except that if he stayed any longer he might be unable to leave. He grabbed his overcoat and made for the front door. "We want you back," she said, and for a moment he was certain that she had an inkling of his plan; then he realised that she was referring to the way he had become unfamiliar. He gave her a wordless smile which he just managed to hold steady, and hurried out to the car.

The lights at the junction on the road into town remained green as he approached them, and he drove straight through. For years he had driven through without considering where the side road led, but now there was barely room for anything else in his mind. It wasn't the money he'd left at the flat which had changed the situation, he thought; it was the balance of fortune. Life at the flat had started to grow hopeful because life at the house had taken a turn for the worse. He parked the car and marched himself to the office, thinking how to restore the balance.

"I'm going to have to take some time off. I wish I could be more definite." His partners reassured him that they could handle the extra workload; they didn't seem surprised by his decision. He discussed with them the cases about which they needed information, and when they left him he grabbed the phone. "No, I can't leave a message. I want to speak to Mr O'Mara in person."

Eventually the landlord picked up the car phone. "I hope I'm going to like what you have to tell me, Alan."

"You won't," Highton said, savouring the moment. "I want you to tell your son to stop sniffing around my daughter. I won't have her feeling that she needs to prostitute herself for the family's sake."

For some time O'Mara only spluttered, so extravagantly that Highton imagined being sprayed in the face with saliva. "He won't be going near her again," O'Mara shouted, "but I'll be wanting a few words with her father in private."

"Just so long as you don't send your thugs to do your talking. I'm not one of your tenants," Highton said, and felt reality lurch. "And if you come anywhere near my house the police will want to know why."

When O'Mara began spluttering obscenities Highton cut him off and kept hold of the receiver as if he couldn't bear to let go until he'd placed one last call. He dialled and closed his eyes, waiting for Valerie's voice. "Look after one another," he said, and set the receiver on its cradle before she could respond. Snatching a fistful of old financial journals from the table in the reception area, he headed for his car.

The lights at the junction seemed almost meaningless. He had to remind himself not to turn left while they were against him. As soon as they changed he drove through the rubbly streets until he found a courtyard entirely surrounded by boarded-up flats. With the tyre-iron he wrenched the number-plates off the Jaguar, then he thrust the rolled-up magazines into the petrol tank. Once they were all soaked he piled them under the car and set fire to them with the dashboard lighter. As he ran out of the courtyard he shoved the plates between the planks over a window, and the numbers fell into the dark.

He was nearly at the flat when he heard the car explode. Surely that would be enough misfortune for his family to suffer. The sound of the explosion spurred him onwards, up the smelly concrete steps, along the balcony. The door of the flat swung inwards as he poked a key from his ring at the lock. "I'm home," he called.

Silence met him. The cramped kitchen and bathroom were deserted, and so were the untidy bedrooms and the front room. The small television in the latter, and the computer in the boy's room next to it, were switched off. He prayed that he wasn't too late—that Daniel had gone wherever Lucy and his mother were so that they could watch over him. Thank heaven the phone wasn't working, or he might have been tempted to make a call which could only confuse and distract him. He lay down on the bed and closed his eyes, wondering if he might dream of his life in the house while he waited for his family to come to him.

# The Wrong Game

Conrad, I'd better say at once that I don't think this is for your book. It isn't fiction, even though I've given it that kind of title, and so I don't imagine it will fit in. I hope at least you may feel able to respond to it—perhaps even help me understand what happened to me. Please be aware that I'm not blaming you. Perhaps I should blame myself.

You'll recall that I was one of the writers you invited into an anthology of tales based on items returned to the dead letter office. I liked the idea and was eager to contribute, but by the time the proposal found a publisher I'd been overtaken by several projects of my own, and so I had to let you down. Other work put the anthology out of my mind, and when I received a package a couple of months ago I didn't think of your idea at all.

While I don't generally examine mail before I open it, this item put me on guard. It was a white Jiffy bag—to be precise, a MailLite manufactured by Sealed Air—with a price sticker on the back, 39p from Osborne Office. The packaging looked unusually pristine, as if it might be designed to seem innocent. The First Class Large stamp wasn't franked, and my address had been written by more than one person. Most of it was in bold capitals inscribed with a black marker pen, but the postcode had been corrected with a ballpoint. You may understand why I was growing suspicious, unless you think it doesn't take much to rouse my paranoia. The contents might have made you feel that way as well.

Inside I found a small white envelope on which several people appeared to have written. It was addressed to Roland Malleson at 1 Harvell Crescent in London (West Heath, SE2), but all this had been crossed out and marked **NOT KNOWN AT THIS ADDRESS**. Someone else had written *Postage unpaid* where a stamp should have been. On the back I read NO FORWARD ADDRESS in yet another script, and "return to sender" in a fifth one, using a pink marker. Was all this meant to confuse me so that I wouldn't think what I was taking out of the envelope? One point in particular made me cautious. Although the **NOT KNOWN** message was printed with a blue marker, it was unquestionably in the same hand that had addressed the entire package to me. Roland Malleson's mail hadn't been returned to the post office, though I was meant to think it had.

Other aspects didn't ring true either. The envelope had been roughly opened, but if the addressee was indeed not known, why had the recipient looked inside? At least this let me do so. The envelope contained a pair of cardboard rectangles approximately two and a half inches by four and a half, crudely cut out of a larger piece of card and taped together so closely that there wasn't space between them for much more than a scrap of paper. It occurred to me that in the days of LSD on blotting paper this might have been how people sent it through the mail. Call me paranoid again if you like, Conrad, but I was afraid that somebody had set me up—that if I opened the cardboard packet I would incriminate myself or be accused of having done so. I even wondered if the post office was involved in the operation.

It was a Saturday, the 24th of April, and the sorting office was still open. I spent some time at the bathroom sink—my hands felt grimy, and I remember peering at them to convince myself they weren't—and then I went to the sorting office. It's fifteen minutes' walk from this house, three minutes' drive at my age. A number of women were waiting to collect their post, and I've seen faster queues outside a toilet, since there was just one postman behind the counter. When at last I reached the window I showed him the package but kept hold of it. "Who do I need to speak to about this?"

"Depends what it is. Won't I do?"

His smooth round face looked as if he'd tried to scrub it younger, and I thought I smelled soap through the gap under the window; there might even have been slivers of pink soap beneath some of his fingernails. "Is the supervisor available?" I said.

"She's busy right now." Professionalism didn't entirely disguise his resentment as he added "I can help."

"If you can tell me why I've received this."

He stared at the words on the front of the package I pushed under the window. "Is that you? Then that's why."

As he slid the package back across the counter I thought he was a little too eager to return it. "Have a look inside," I said.

Did I glimpse a hint of reluctance? He poked the padded bag open with a finger and thumb and squinted inside before shaking out the smaller envelope onto the counter. He read both sides of it and then turned Malleson's address to face me. "Did you send him this?"

"Of course I didn't. I've never even heard of him."

"Well, whoever forwarded it to you must think you have."

"And why should they think I want what's in there?"

The postman looked inside the envelope but left the cardboard packet where it was. "What is?"

"I think you ought to check. It's still your responsibility, isn't it? Property of Royal Mail."

"Not once it's been delivered," he said and slipped the envelope under the window. "It's yours to do what you want with."

I couldn't help thinking he was as wary as I had every right to feel. Was he trying to pretend he thought the packet could be lethal? "I'll open it here," I said, "if you'll be a witness."

I could have fancied he was trying to compete with me at cautiousness. "A witness to what?" he objected.

"To the fact that I'm only just opening it now."

"You could have done it once and stuck it back together."

"I've done nothing of the kind," I said with far less ire than I was experiencing. "I give you my word."

He stared at that as if it was nowhere to be seen. He rubbed his hands together, apparently feeling they weren't clean enough, while I removed the packet from the envelope. I made sure he saw how fragments of the cardboard stuck to the tape as I peeled it off. I opened up one long side of the packet and a short one, and fished out the contents. If I'd been alone I might have laughed at the anticlimax. My prize was a grubby pair of playing cards, a two of clubs and a six of hearts. "Using the mail for a game?" the postman suggested.

"At my expense, you'd have to mean."

"Some people play chess through the mail, don't they? Maybe someone's having a game of cards."

"I shouldn't think so." In case he meant me I told him "I haven't played cards since I was your age."

"So what do you want to do with those?"

"I'll take them home. As you say, they were sent to me."

Had I begun to wonder if they might give me an idea for your anthology, Conrad? If you're like me you never waste material, however trivial it may seem. I put the cards in the envelope and returned that to the padded bag, and was on my way past the queue that had gathered behind me until the postman called "Don't you want this?"

He was brandishing the empty cardboard packet. "Bin it for me," I said, and now I wonder if I should have taken it with me, though I've no idea what difference it could have made.

I found myself rubbing my thumb and finger together as I headed for the car. It felt like a tic, especially since I could see no reason for it, and it distracted me from thinking about Malleson. Was the name wholly unfamiliar? Was it somehow associated with a convention I'd attended long ago? Surely I must have Miles Malleson in mind. He'd been in many of the Hammer horror films I'd sought out as soon as I was able to pass for sixteen, and decades later I'd seen him interviewed at the Festival of Fantastic Films in Manchester. All the same, this didn't help me grasp an impression that was loitering just beyond reach in my mind. It seemed too vague to be related to the actor.

Once I was home I emailed you, Conrad, asking if you'd sent me the package even though I'd had to turn down your invitation. I don't know if you received my message, since I never saw a reply. Of course you did say at the outset that you wouldn't enter into any correspondence about the items you sent your contributors. I didn't wait too long to hear from you before I did what I should have done in the first place. I searched online for Roland Malleson and his address.

I couldn't find his name, and the address didn't exist in the form that was on the envelope. While there is a Harvell Crescent in SE2, West Heath is in Birmingham. That district does include a Horwell Crescent, however. After more research and some expenditure I managed to obtain the names and phone numbers of the occupier of the London house and of 1 Horwell Crescent as well. Neither name was Malleson. The London number didn't answer, and so I tried the one in Birmingham, where the phone rang eight times before a woman said "Yes?"

She sounded less affirmative than the word did. I was about to begin explaining my call when it occurred to me to say just "Malleson."

After a silence she spoke, but not to me. "Someone's saying Malleson."

"I'll speak to them." In a moment the man's voice came as close as my ear and grew sharper. "Hello, what do you want?"

"Whatever you can tell me about Roland Malleson."

"Who wants to know?"

"I believe you sent me a package that was meant for him."

"Right." Though the man seemed reluctant to admit this made any difference, his Midland accent had turned shriller. "It's, don't tell me," he said to me or his companion. "It's, I'll have it in a sec. Ramsay somebody. Ramsay Macdonald, that's who you are, right?"

"He's dead." It was by no means the first time someone had tried to give me the name; I've even been introduced that way as a speaker. "I'm from the other clan," I said. "Ramsey Campbell."

"So I wasn't too far off, right."

He sounded as if he thought I was being unreasonable, which provoked me to retort "You managed to get it right when you sent the package."

"That was her." Without discovering any enthusiasm he said "So what are you after now?"

"For a start I'd like to know why you sent it to me."

"Roland said he played with you."

My memory had let me down a few times, but for some reason I hoped this wasn't such a case. "When?"

"When he saw some of your books in the shops. That was years back."

I didn't need to be told that, however resigned to the situation I've grown. "I'm asking when I'm meant to have played whatever I'm supposed to have played. I certainly don't remember."

"Cards." If it's possible for triumph to be apathetic, the man brought off the trick by saying "Mally said it was a long time back, before you ever got yourself in the shops."

I seemed to experience the faintest stirring of memory, like a glimpse of movement in a virtually lightless place. I won't pretend it was welcome, but I was going to ask for more detail until another question jumped the queue. "Who opened the envelope? I'm guessing it wasn't him."

"He couldn't have even when he was here." Before I could pursue this the man said "We did, right? We needed to find out why we were still getting post for him."

"And was there anything else in the envelope?"

"Just what you've got. Don't you think we'd have sent you anything there was?"

His tone seemed so inappropriate that I almost laughed. "I still don't understand why you sent it at all."

"Because he said he helped you with the cards."

"Helped me do what with them?"

"No, I'm saying he said they helped you, right?" As I prepared to enquire into this if not simply to deny it the man said "Can we leave it now? She's getting upset with all this talking about her brother."

"I'm sorry, but I'd like this to make more sense. Who sent him the cards? I hope you don't imagine I did."

"You could have." More magnanimously than he had any right to sound the man conceded "If it wasn't you, maybe it was someone who didn't like how Mally played cards."

Something like a memory seemed to loom in my mind, but the man disrupted it. "I'm putting this down now, right," he said. "We've resurrected him enough."

"Don't say that," I heard the woman cry, and that was the end of the call. I sat here at my desk and gazed out at the river, where a stubborn length of fog stood for the condition of my brain. I could only examine the cards once more. Though their backs showed an identical picture, they might not have belonged to the same pack, since the two was red as blood while the heart was a pallid amalgam of blue and green, a colour I don't think I've seen anywhere in life. Each bore a slim female silhouette that was leaning against a palm tree beneath a supine crescent moon. The figure might have been dressed in a grass skirt—the tendrils dangling from one bent leg resembled the tufts that sprouted from the black earth—and she was playing with a necklace. Why should I have thought the object at the end of the necklace was an amulet rather than a locket? The entire image brought a phrase to mind, and I didn't know why. "There's magic underneath."

I hadn't time to ponder it. I'd been overtaken by the nervousness I'm prone to suffer when I have to speak in public on a topic I haven't previously addressed—in this case the generation of ideas and how to develop them. Much of the time I've no idea where they come from, but months earlier I'd agreed to talk on the subject at the Bournemouth Festival of Book and Film, and all of a sudden—that's always how it happens—the date of the booking was tomorrow. As usual I felt disgracefully unprepared, and I still did next morning as I rehearsed some of my speech in the shower. I was leaving the house when I decided to take the Malleson package with me, telling myself I might be able to work it into my talk.

I didn't have much of a chance to think how on the drive down to Bournemouth. That took most of Sunday, starting at dawn.

Once I'd checked into my hotel room I had time for just a quick shower before I had to hurry to the evening's venue, a hall with far more seats in it than audience. The organisers delayed the event for several minutes, nearly always an ominous sign, but eventually they put me on for the benefit of a dozen listeners. At least the lady who announced me got my name right and wasn't too inaccurate about my career. I read a couple of extracts from tales of mine and went some way towards analysing how the stories came to be, after which I took half a dozen questions from the audience. Throughout the talk the Malleson business had been loitering in my brain, and the session still had more than ten minutes to run. On an impulse I took the package out of the laptop case that serves me as a briefcase and produced the cards, feeling like a magician who'd neglected to plan a trick. "Sometimes something ought to give you an idea," I said, "but you can't think what it might be. Someone sent me these the other day. What do we think they could mean?"

Everyone looked wary, perhaps just of being singled out. After quite a pause a man said "Did that really happen or are you saying it did?"

"Both. There's no difference." I might have said more to prove I can distinguish reality from my own imaginings if I hadn't been driven to ask "Why would you send anyone a couple of old cards?"

"Maybe—" A woman seemed to wish she hadn't spoken, and cleared her throat twice before saying "Maybe they're meant for your fortune."

"I don't know what that means."

"Maybe they're trying to tell you."

I could have said this was impossible, since they hadn't been sent to me in the first place, but it would have called for too much explanation. More disconcertingly, I felt as if she'd let me glimpse some kind of truth. An impression had lodged in my head—the image of a figure watching me across a table spread with cards. The figure wasn't just indistinct but unstable, as if it was composed of the kind of restless darkness you may see where there's no source of illumination. The idea bewildered me much more than it inspired me; in fact, I couldn't say it appealed to me at all. All the same, I told the woman that there might be a story in it and thanked her, and asked for any last questions. When nobody obliged, the organisers brought the event to an end.

I autographed a handful of books and then dined with some of the festival folk, but had difficulty concentrating on the table talk or even savouring the Cantonese banquet. The image of a figure at a table surrounded by oppressive darkness had begun to feel like a memory or a distortion of one, but did this simply mean I was recalling the moment when it had entered my mind at the festival event? As soon as I politely could I said goodnight to my hosts and went back to the hotel, where I felt the need for yet another shower. After that I would have gone to bed if I hadn't been troubled by wondering where to put the Malleson package. I stowed it in the drawer that contained the obligatory Bible, in a chest some distance from the bed.

I must have dozed despite the image that wouldn't leave my mind or grow clearer, because I awoke at a few minutes past two. I had a sense that I'd heard something not especially substantial on the move in the dark. The only light came from the scrawny digits of the bedside clock, which aggravated the darkness. As I groped for the cord above the bed I felt as if the gloom was gathering like soot on my fingers. By the time I located the cord I'd begun rubbing them together. The light showed that I hadn't closed the drawer of the chest as tight as I'd imagined, since it displayed a shadow like a thin strip of earth. Surely it was just because I hadn't fully wakened that the sliver of blackness looked restive. Lurching out of bed, I slammed the drawer and found myself staring at the room. What should it remind me of? Then I knew, and rather more than that. It brought to mind the first time I'd stayed by myself at a hotel.

I'd been in Harrogate, at a science fiction convention more than half a century ago. For decades I'd gone almost every Easter, wherever in Britain the annual convention might be. I would pass these weekends listening to programme items and meeting increasingly old friends, usually in the bar. After the programme was done for the day there would be parties in the bedrooms and often a card game somewhere in the hotel. Recalling this unlocked my memory, and with a shock that felt as if a dark part of my mind had given way I realised I had indeed met Malleson at one such Easter weekend. The people I'd phoned about him had been right after all.

He didn't go by that name at the convention. When he turned up at the poker game he was Malleficus on his badge. "Just call me Mally," he said, having peered at everybody else's badges, and shouldn't I have recognised the nickname when I heard it over the phone? Perhaps the memory was blurred by how he'd seemed to feel I should appreciate the word on his badge. As he sat opposite me across the large round table he caught my eye and indicated the name with his left little finger, which was as pale and thick as his lips and didn't look much firmer. With its cobweb strands of greying hair his big-eyed long-nosed oval face put me in mind of an egg well past its best. He kept up a loose-lipped grin at me until the dealer began laying out the cards. In those days I was only starting to manufacture the personality I use as armour for shyness, and so I tried to ignore Malleson.

I don't think his playing style went down too well. Whenever it was his turn to open he would say "What the prince wears," a joke that soon grew tedious and then irritating. It meant half a crown, not a negligible amount of money at the time. When he followed someone else's bid he would wave his hand over the cards in his left one, a gesture that might have signified indecision or a silent wish. "Waving goodbye to your money?" an opponent fell to saying, which didn't deter Malleson, especially once it became clear that he was winning many of the pots and losing only the smaller ones. By midnight several players had thrown in their hands and gone in search of other diversions, and soon an especially competitive round gave Malleson his most substantial win with a full house. This proved too much for the owner of the pack of cards, who took them and himself off. As the other players wandered away, Malleson detained me by saying "Aren't you a writer?"

I hadn't much to show for it compared to the authors on the convention programme—Moorcock, Brunner, Bulmer, Tubb. I had just a single book and a few short stories to my name, and so I couldn't help feeling flattered when Malleson said "I've been looking for someone like you."

"There's a few here this weekend."

"Not like you." As I prepared to feel more acclaimed he said "They're here for science fiction, not the occult."

I did feel somewhat outcast at the convention. I'd found one book dealer who stocked fantasy as well as science fiction—Sci Fi Fo Fum—but he scarcely touched horror. It would be years before an Eastercon saw its first dealer in my field, the Horrid Variorum, sadly short-lived even once it changed its name to Rarum Scarum. All the same, I was about to establish that I never mistook my fiction for reality when Malleson pointed at his badge. "You know what that means, don't you?"

I wasn't sufficiently sure of myself to tell him the word was misspelled. "Wasn't it some kind of criminal in Latin?"

"That's been dead a long time. I thought you'd know better." Having stared at me as though to give me a chance to redeem myself, he said "What's malefica mean?"

In those days it was easy to make me feel I was being quizzed by a schoolteacher, and I was forced to guess. "A witch?"

"That's it, a sorceress. I knew you'd know your occult history. It's where they got the title of that vile book from, the *Malleus Maleficarum*. As you see, I've taken the word back."

All I could produce in the way of an answer was "Well, good."

"I knew you'd think so. Our type need to stick together."

This struck me as ominous, especially in a dimly illuminated lounge late at night with nobody else nearby. "Anyway," I said, "if you'll excuse me."

"Wait there." Malleson stood up, pushing the table towards me so that it came close to pinning me against the shabby upholstered chair. "I want to do something for you," he said.

His approach shook the floorboards and seemed to do that to his lips, which quivered into an ingratiating smile. "What?" I demanded and caught hold of the edge of the table, ready to shove myself back.

"Only to show you what you ought to see." Malleson rested his hands on the table as he sat next to me, extracting a creak from his chair. He dragged the chair around so that he was facing me and lifted his hands with a flourish. "Those are yours," he said.

He'd revealed a pair of cards lying face down. No doubt leaning on the table had let him plant them unobserved. They must have been hidden in the sleeves of his black turtleneck or of his tweed jacket, which was even more voluminous than he seemed this close. "That's a good trick," I admitted. "You're that kind of magician."

"They were there all the time," he said and unfolded his left hand above the cards. "You see, there's magic underneath."

I thought he meant on the backs of the cards, but now I wonder. Perhaps he was talking about the world. At this remove I've no idea whether the backs showed the sylph beneath the tree. I flipped them over, and I don't need to tell you what I saw, Conrad. I didn't know how useful they might have been to me in the final round of poker, but I said "If these are my cards they're a bit late."

"We aren't playing that game any more. We're concerned with your life."

I found this unnervingly intrusive. "Who is?"

"I hope you are." With a winning smile or rather a triumphant grin Malleson said "You could make your name."

"How are these going to help?"

"They can point the way. They'll be part of you. That's why cards were made in the first place. Once they've been read to you they'll direct you."

Of course I didn't believe any of this—I didn't even think I could get a story out of it—which was why I said "So that's what you'd like to do?"

"To read you? I already am." He'd lowered his voice when he joined me, and now it grew so muted that it made me strain to grasp it. "Would you like to hear?" he said.

"If I can."

"Oh, you will." This sounded less promissory than ominous, not least since it seemed to have become more audible by creeping inside my head. "The deuce of wands," he said and rested his left forefinger on the two of clubs. "I give you power and boldness and originality."

"Well, thank you," I said with some irony, since I imagined I already had them.

"The six of cups." He transferred the finger to the other card, and I saw a moist print fade from the two like ripples sinking into a pond. "I take innocence and childhood," he said. "I leave nostalgia and the influence of the past."

I didn't learn for years how unlike an ordinary tarot reading this was. Shouldn't that have fixed it in my mind? I'm disturbed to think I could have forgotten all about it until that night in the Bournemouth hotel. Malleson lifted his finger from the six, leaving a second sweaty mark, and I couldn't help asking "Is that all?"

"It will be all you need. It can be your life."

At least this seemed to end the session. "Well, thank you," I found myself repeating like a response in church.

As I pushed back my chair Malleson said "Don't you want to hear the price?"

I felt I should have known there would be something of the sort. "You won all my money," I tried protesting.

"It should never be that kind of price." When he rose to his feet he might have been recoiling in distaste. "The price is no more than an acknowledgement," he said, and the trembling of the floor receded as he moved towards the corridor. "Just remember."

He must have raised his voice, because it didn't grow distant as soon as he did. I felt as though it had taken root in my head, and in the Bournemouth hotel room I fancied I could hear its soft insinuating hiss: "the price..." I left the cards on the table in the lounge and didn't follow Malleson until I was sure of not catching up with him. For fear of encountering him at a party I retreated to my room and went to bed. During the rest of the weekend I kept an eye out for him, but I never saw him again—not at an Easter gathering, at any rate.

Could he have meant that remembering was the acknowledgement—the price? In that case I've paid it here and am liable to carry on. Or if he was asking for an acknowledgement in my work, surely this account fits that bill too. I was already striving for originality and boldness, and I hope those lend my stuff some power, but it's also founded on the traditions of my field; you could say I'm nostalgic for them. I haven't been innocent for a long time, and I trust I'm not childish either. Mustn't saying all this settle whatever debt I owed him? What else could he want of me?

It took me a while to recapture sleep in Bournemouth. I wakened just after six with several ideas in my head. This very often happens—sometimes it's a stray phrase or image, more frequently material for the piece I'm writing—but these words seemed more pointed than usual. *Take what's on offer, friends. Cards let us be shrewd. Symbolic images ("X") offer foresight, however enigmatic and random they seem.* Perhaps you find all that as meaningful as I do, Conrad, or your readers would, though if you interpret an oracle it becomes part of you, just as employing any form of magic is said to do. I didn't spend much time on the sentences, because I'd had another waking notion. I thought it might lead to a story, perhaps for your book. On my way home I could revisit the hotel where I'd met Malleson.

I won't name it, though it isn't listed online. I remembered where it had been, which looked as if it was about half an hour's drive from the motorway. By the time I reached the junction I'd been delayed by several traffic queues, all of which seemed to be caused solely by signs warning of a queue ahead. I considered driving straight on, but it felt too much like cowardice. Perhaps I ought to have wondered why I should be nervous, instead of which I made for the hotel.

I didn't recognise the road. It wound through a couple of elongated villages kept apart by miles of fields, and then it wandered between trees that added to the gloom beneath the sunless April sky. To begin with I drove past a side road, which didn't appear to be signposted. Backing up, I saw there was a post after all, though its top was raggedly rotten. The long grass around the post came close to hiding several fragments of a wooden pointer, but I spotted the remains of a word, **OTEL**, and gave in to fancying that it sounded like an instruction as I turned along the road.

This wasn't as wide as it used to be. The hedges on both sides had swelled up, stretching out thorny branches. Tufts of grass and weeds were well on the way to reclaiming the road for an older landscape. Beyond the hedges trees elaborately cabled with vines blocked most of the view until the road bent, revealing the hotel, a three-storey crescent composed of twin curves on either side of a straight midsection framing a wide pair of doors above six broad steps. At first I thought it was blackened just by the low unbroken clouds, but as I drove closer I saw that the building couldn't have been cleaned for decades. By the time it hosted Eastercon the hotel had been dilapidated, offering discounts to conventions and the like in an attempt to prolong its life. This obviously hadn't worked, since it was clear that the hotel had been boarded up years ago.

The curving drive in front of the hotel was deserted. The splintered concrete was strewn with rubble, shattered slates from the roof, fragments of brick, a board so rotten it had fallen from the window across which it had been nailed. None of the windows above the ground floor was boarded up, and all of them were encrusted with windblown grime. I parked in front of the main entrance, and as I climbed the cracked steps the ends of the building loomed at the edges of my vision like a claw poised to close around me. I nearly slipped on a patch of moss, and the claw lurched closer. I might have fancied that my approach had been greeted in another way—that the left-hand door had crept open to invite me in. I mustn't have noticed it was ajar.

When I pushed the door it lumbered inwards, grinding debris into the carpet. I had to lean against it to make a gap I could fit through. Beyond it I saw the lobby, or rather a few sooty outlines—the reception counter, a dead chandelier. The flashlight on my phone gradually revealed section after section of the extravagantly large high-ceilinged room, where shadows dodged behind everything that stood in the dark. They brought to life the pale child perched on the end of a stone banister. I was crossing the threshold when I thought better of it; at least, I went back to the car to find the Malleson package in my overnight case. I slipped the cards into my pocket as I returned to the hotel. Perhaps I still thought I was creating a tale for you, Conrad.

The floor of the lobby gave as I trod on it, or at any rate the discoloured carpet did. The heavy fabric was sodden with however many years of rain had leaked through holes in the roof above the stairwell. As I advanced towards the counter I felt boards shift beneath the carpet, blundering sluggishly together like blind creatures under earth. That must have been why the rusty bell on the counter emitted a dull muffled note, and I needn't have felt it was summoning anyone. In response to my approach all the denizens of the pigeonholes behind the counter stirred in unison—just shadows roused by the flashlight, which also made the grime on the counter seem to swarm. I halted under the chandelier, in which the blackened bulbs only served to solidify the dark, and swung the flashlight beam around me while I tried to recall the layout of the hotel.

As the stone child stretched its arms out to the light I saw its eyes were caked with grime. Beyond the wide stairs over which it was standing some kind of guard, a pair of lifts began to inch their doors open. The shadows of the bars were shifting, not the grilles themselves, but the beam also found a collapsed face on the floor of the lift, peering out at me with its crumpled eyes. I had to pace a good deal closer to be certain that the face was on an abandoned poster for some forgotten event at the hotel. At least I was heading in the right direction, because I'd remembered passing the lifts on my way to the poker game.

Are you beginning to wonder what I thought I was doing? I had the ill-defined notion that putting the cards back where I'd left them might bring some form of resolution, perhaps just to the tale I imagined I was in. As I stepped into the corridor beyond the lifts the walls appeared to lunge towards me, not least because whole sections of the wallpaper were drooping towards the floor, exposing their fungoid undersides. A board shivered underfoot, and I couldn't tell whether its muffled clatter obscured a sound somewhere ahead, a whisper or a faint restlessness. It seemed likely that there would be mice or other vermin in the hotel, and

I didn't halt too long while I tried to hear. Staying still for any length of time made me feel as if the grime that constituted a good deal of the dark was settling on my skin.

The floor wasn't holding up well. It felt like treading on planks in a marsh. A doorway gaped on my left, and I saw that both of the doors were held open by the carpet, which appeared to have burgeoned around their lowest edges. Beyond the doorway a cavernous darkness was emphasised more than relieved by glimmers of light through chinks in the boards over the windows, but I glimpsed a crouching shape that looked poised for a leap. It was a chair crippled by a broken leg and discarded in the empty dining-room, and I told myself it was the only reason why I felt awaited in the dark.

As I passed the bar I saw fragments of a figure keeping pace with me, my reflection dodging across a long mirror and visible only where the glass wasn't black. Next to the bar the outer doors of both toilets were caught permanently open by the carpet and whatever had taken root in it. Through one doorway I thought I heard a whisper of water, but it fell silent the instant I paused, and so it could hardly have been the plumbing. Might it have been somewhere ahead, around the curve of the corridor? I did my best to assume I'd heard mice again, although now that I tried to grasp the sound, it seemed to have been unnecessarily surreptitious. In a story I might have made it suggest that the dark was taking on more substance—settling together into a more solid form.

I sent myself along the corridor, since otherwise my detour from the motorway would have been pointless. An oval mirror partly draped with sagging wallpaper blinded me with my own flashlight, and I had to halt again while my eyesight seeped back. My vision hadn't entirely returned when the sensation of gathering grime urged me onwards, and so at first I didn't notice the figure behind me in the mirror. Its face looked not merely black with dirt, as though it had just risen from the earth, but composed of it if not fattened by it. The flashlight beam swung around faster than I did, which meant that it took altogether too long to locate the occupant of the corridor. It was a portrait opposite the mirror, its face masked by a stain that had attracted a good deal of grit. Identifying it might have reassured me more if the beam hadn't illuminated something else. The lounge where I'd encountered Malleson was just along the corridor.

It was on the left: a wide space without doors, where I could see a segment of the edge of the round table. By now I'd decided on my course, whether as an incident in the tale I planned to tell or simply to rid myself of the cards in the way that seemed most appropriate. I believed—still believe—that I'd worked out why they had been sent to Malleson. One of the poker players had found them where I'd left them and assumed they were evidence of cheating, which indeed they could have been; after all, what had Malleson been doing with them before he read them to me? Why the sender had waited so long, I couldn't say. Perhaps, having failed to track Malleson down at the convention, they'd been frustrated all these years until they stumbled on his address or thought to search online. Now I proposed to leave the cards on the table once again. If anybody found them—if rubble hadn't hidden them by the time the hotel was renovated or more likely demolished—they would mean nothing. This felt like a conclusion to me.

I took the cards out of my pocket as I advanced towards the lounge. I wasn't intending to linger, especially since I'd heard the noise in the dark again. It was somewhere in the lounge beyond the table, which was scaly with scraps of fallen plaster. It might have been a furtive movement or a bid to whisper or even an attempt to draw a breath through some suffocating medium, if not a combination of them all. As I came abreast of the lounge I couldn't help lowering the flashlight beam. It showed the near edge of the table, which had been divested of its chairs, unless one had been left on the far side, where part of the darkness seemed more solid. I kept the flashlight low while I made for the table, holding out the cards, which felt unpleasantly slippery and gritty into the bargain. As soon as I was close enough I dropped them on the table, where they landed like part of a poker hand, the club peeking out from behind the heart. The impact seemed too negligible to affect the other contents of the table, and the scraps of plaster didn't stir. All the same, there was another movement in the dark.

I raised the flashlight beam with a good deal of reluctance. The grime on the table scurried away from the light, or shadows did, and came not quite to rest on a pair of objects on the far side of the table. Surely they were just a pair of artificial hands, broken off a statue if not sculpted in that fashion. I couldn't identify the material, since they were caked with grime. In fact they appeared to be at least partly composed of it, and it wasn't as tranquil as it ought to have been. It was shifting almost imperceptibly, which put me in mind of a multitude of insects hatching or otherwise coming to life.

I tried to blame this on the shaky flashlight. The spectacle was so disagreeably fascinating that it distracted me from a movement I should have noticed sooner. Almost too gradually for it to be evident, the hands were creeping across the table towards the cards—towards me. Before I could prevent myself I jerked up the flashlight beam.

What did I see? Not much for long, but far too much. The hands belonged to a shape that occupied all the space on a solitary dilapidated chair. Like the hands, the shape appeared to owe its substance to the grime that was everywhere in the dark. Perhaps the soft insidious sound I heard was demonstrating how restless that substance was, but I had the awful idea that it could be an attempt to breathe. I just had time to glimpse a face—eyes as black and unstable as the rest of the lopsided bulk, nostrils desperately dilating, lips that sagged into a helpless grimace and then struggled to produce another expression if not to speak—before the figure collapsed.

The hands stayed on the table. I could have thought they'd been severed for a crime. I don't know whether they continued to move, but the rest of the presence did. Beyond the table I heard a soft dismayingly widespread mass start to crawl across the floor towards me. In the midst of this I thought I heard another sound or a variation on the same one, as if the crawler had begun to regain something like a voice. I didn't wait to make sure. I fled so fast that the corridor appeared to be caving in as the flashlight beam reeled from wall to wall, and I had the nightmare notion that the hotel might indeed give way around me, trapping me with its denizen. By the time I staggered into the lobby I couldn't tell how fast the soft dogged sounds behind me were, or how close. As I dashed towards the way out of the hotel I risked sending the flashlight beam into the corridor, and thought I glimpsed a disintegrating figure heave itself up to summon me back.

I ran to the car and drove away, not slowing for the overgrown road. The car still bears scratches from the hedge. I didn't stop until I reached the nearest motorway services, where I spent so long washing my hands that several people stared at me. I always keep a bottle of antiseptic gel in the car, but it was used up by the time I arrived home. Besides the crawling sensation of grime on my skin I took with me the word I'd seemed to hear in the abandoned hotel. "Cheat," the voice might have whispered as its source recovered some shape.

Perhaps the speaker meant the accusation for himself, in which case the admission may have brought closure, but I fear it was aimed at me. If neglecting to acknowledge my debt was how I cheated, haven't I repaid the debt now? Or perhaps my career has been the cheat, in which case this account disguised as fiction is the latest proof. Writing it has left me feeling grimy, desperate to clean myself up, and I only hope it hasn't invited anything out of my past, let alone given it more substance. Surely reading it can't make you in any way complicit. I hope you and any other readers won't feel the need to wash your hands now that you've finished it, Conrad.

# A Street was Chosen

A STREET WAS CHOSEN. WITHIN ITS PARAMETERS, HOMES were randomly selected. Preliminary research yielded details of the occupants as follows:

A (husband, insurance salesman, 30; wife, 28; infant daughter, 18 months)

B (widow, 67)

C (husband, 73; wife, 75; son, library assistant, 38

D (mother, bank clerk, 32; daughter, 3)

E (husband, social worker, 35; wife, social worker, 34)

F (electrician, male, 51; assistant, male, 25)

G (husband, 42; wife, industrial chemist, 38; son, 4; infant son, 2)

H (mother, 86; son, teacher, 44; son's wife, headmistress, 41; granddaughter, 12; grandson, 11)

I (window-cleaner, male, 53)

J (tax officer, female, 55)

K (milkman, male, 39)

L (waiter, 43)

It was noted that subjects I-L occupied apartments in the same house.

Further preliminary observation established that

(a) subject B wrote letters to newspapers

(b) the children of couples A and G visited each other's homes to play

(c) granddaughter H sat with child D while mother D was elsewhere on an average of 1 evening per week

(d) husband G experienced bouts of temporary impotence lasting between 6 and 8 days

(e) elder F performed sexual acts with his partner in order to maintain the relationship

(f) subject L had recently been released into the community after treatment for schizophrenia

It was decided that stimuli should be applied gradually and with caution. During an initial 8-night period, the following actions were taken:

(1, i) each night a flower was uprooted from the garden of subject B, and all evidence of removal was erased

(1, ii) the lights in house H were caused to switch on at random intervals for periods of up to 5 minutes between the hours of 3 and 6 in the morning

(1, iii) on alternate nights, subject J was wakened shortly after entering deep sleep by telephone calls purporting to advertise life insurance

(1, iv) the tinfoil caps of milk-bottles delivered to subject D were removed after delivery, and feeding nipples substituted

At the end of 8 days, it was noted that subject B was less inclined than previously to engage her neighbours in conversation, and more prone to argue or to take offence. From the 7th day onwards she was seen to spend extended periods at the windows which overlooked her garden.

Subjects F were employed by couple H to trace the source of an apparent electrical malfunction. It was observed that mother H became increasingly hostile to her son's wife both during this process and after electricians F had failed to locate any fault in the wiring. Observations suggested that she blamed either her daughter-in-law or her grandchildren for tampering with the electricity in order to disturb her sleep.

Subject J was observed to approach subject A in order to obtain names and addresses of insurance companies which advertised by telephone. It was noted that when the list provided by A failed to yield the required explanation, A undertook to make further enquiries on J's behalf.

It was observed that subject D initially responded to the substitution of nipples as if it were a joke. After 2 days, however, she was seen to accuse subject K of the substitution. At the end of the 8-day period she cancelled the delivery and ordered milk from a rival company. It was decided to discontinue the substitution for an indefinite period.

After observations were completed, the following stimuli were applied during a period of 15 days:

(2, i) an anonymous letter based on a computer analysis of B's prose style was published in the free newspaper received by all subjects, objecting to the existence of househusbands and claiming that the writer was aware of two people who committed adultery while their children played together

(2, ii) every third night as subject L walked home, he was approached by religious pamphleteers whose faces had been altered to resemble the other tenants of his building in the order I, K, J, I, K

(2, iii) the dustbin of subjects F was overturned, and pages from a magazine depicting naked prepuberal boys were scattered around it

(2, iv) the figure of subject I was projected on the bedroom window of subjects E and caused to appear to pass through it while husband E was alone in the room

(2, v) brochures advertising old folks' homes were sent on alternate days to son C

(2, vi) telephone calls using a simulation of the voice of subject J were made between 3 and 5 in the morning on 6 occasions to house A, complaining that J had just received another advertising call

At the end of the second period of stimuli, the following observations were made:

After the appearance of the letter in the newspaper, husband

G was observed to suffer a bout of impotence lasting 11 days. It was also noted that subject D attempted to befriend wives A and G, who appeared to be suspicious of her motives. As a result of this encounter, increasing strain was recorded within couples A and G.

Subject L was seen to examine the mail addressed to subjects I, J, and K, and also to attempt to view the apartments of these subjects through the keyholes. Whenever any two of these subjects began a conversation while L was in the building, attempts by L to overhear were observed. Also noted was the growing tendency of L to scrutinise the faces of diners while he waited on them in the restaurant.

After the elder of subjects F discovered the pages which had apparently been hidden in the dustbin, several disagreements of increasing length and violence between subjects F were recorded, both subjects accusing the other of responsibility for the material. At the end of 11 days, the younger of the subjects was seen to take up residence beyond the parameters of the present experiment. It was further observed that mother G required her sons to promise to inform her or their father if they were approached in any way by subjects F.

It was noted that subject E did not mention the apparition of subject I to his wife.

After the first delivery of brochures to their son, parents C were observed to cease speaking to him, despite his denial of responsibility for the receipt of the material. It was noted that parents C opened and destroyed all brochures subsequently delivered. Hot meals prepared for son C were left on the table for him for up to 1 hour before his consumption of them.

Husband A was seen twice to request subject J not to telephone his house after 11 o'clock at night. When the calls continued, wife A was observed to threaten J with legal action, despite J's denial of all knowledge. During this confrontation, subject L was seen to accuse J of attempting to distress both himself and wife A. It was recorded that wife A advised him to take up the matter with the landlord of the apartments.

A decision was reached to increase the level of stimuli. The following actions were taken during a 6-day period:

(3, i) in the absence of subject B, all the furniture in her house was dismantled

(3, ii) several brochures concerning euthanasia and the right to die were addressed to son C

(3, iii) whenever husband G succeeded in achieving an erection, the car alarm of subjects A was made to sound

(3, iv) a box of fireworks labelled as a free sample was delivered to children H. Several fireworks were later removed and were exploded inside the house of subject F

(3, v) the face of subject B was made to appear above the beds of children G. When infant G fled, he was caused to fall downstairs. Snapping of the neck was observed to occur

(3, vi) live insects were introduced into meals which subject L was about to serve to diners

(3, vii) the outer doors of apartments I and K were painted crimson overnight

During and after this period, the following observations were made:

After parents C were seen to examine the brochures addressed to their son, it was noted that they placed his belongings outside the house and employed a neighbour to change the external locks. It was observed that when on his return son C attempted to protest that he owned the house, he was refused any response. Later he was found to be sleeping in a public park. Information was received that when his workmates attempted to help him he quit his job. It was observed that although mother C wished to take the son's belongings into the house, father C insisted on their remaining outside.

Grandmother H was seen to attack grandchildren H under the impression that they were responsible for the damage to house F, although the police had accepted evidence that the children could not have been involved. When mother H defended her children from their grandmother, it was noted that she was accused of having succeeded professionally at the expense of her husband. A protracted argument between all five subjects H was observed, after which increases in tension between all subjects were recorded, the greatest increase being between son and wife. It was observed that when granddaughter H offered to sit with child D, mother D refused to employ her. Mother H was later seen to accuse mother D of attempting to befriend families in the hope of developing a sexual relationship with the father.

Husband G was observed to smash the headlights of car A with a hammer. The ensuing altercation was seen to be terminated when wife G reported that infant G had been injured on the stairs. It was noted that infant G died en route to the nearest hospital.

It was recorded that subject L was unable to determine whether or not the insects placed in the meals he was about to serve were objectively real. It was noted that this confusion caused L to lose his job. Subsequently L was observed to attempt to persuade several of the other subjects that a pattern was discernible in the various recent events, without success. It was noted that L overheard subjects I and K suggesting that L had repainted their doors.

Surviving child G was seen to inform its parents that subject B had driven infant G out of the children's room. It was observed that when mother G confronted B with this, B accused G of having caused the apparition by experimenting on the children with drugs produced in the laboratory where G worked. It was further noted that subjects E attempted to intervene in the argument but were met with hostility bordering on accusation, both by B and G and by several bystanders. When subject I was attracted by the confrontation, husband E was observed to retreat at speed.

It was noted that subject L approached his landlord and tried to persuade him that subjects I, J, and K were conspiring against L. It was further observed that when L was given notice to quit the apartment, L set fire to the building in the absence of the other tenants. Temperatures in excess of 450 degrees Celsius were recorded, and it was observed that L was trapped beneath a fallen lintel. Melting of the flesh was recorded before the subject lost consciousness, and death was subsequently observed.

Husband E was seen to propose a separation from wife E while refusing to explain his motives. The separation was observed to take place and to become permanent.

Preparations for suicide by subject B were observed. It was noted that the previously dismantled chair used by B for support gave way as the subject was seen to decide against this course of action. Dislocation of the neck by hanging was recorded, and death from strangulation ensued after a period of 53 minutes. It was further observed that after 8 days subject F entered house B and discovered the corpse of subject B.

Because of the risk of discovery, it was decided to discontinue the experiment at this stage. Since the results were judged to be inconclusive, it is proposed that several further experiments on larger groups of subjects should be conducted simultaneously. Communities have been chosen at random, and within them a further random selection of streets has been made.

# The Same in Any Language

THE DAY MY FATHER IS TO TAKE ME WHERE THE lepers used to live is hotter than ever. Even the old women with black scarves wrapped around their heads sit inside the bus station instead of on the chairs outside the tavernas. Kate fans herself with her straw hat like a basket someone's sat on and gives my father one of those smiles they've made up between them. She's leaning forward to see if that's our bus when he says "Why do you think they call them lepers, Hugh?"

I can hear what he's going to say, but I have to humour him. "I don't know."

"Because they never stop leaping up and down."

It takes him much longer to say the first four words than the rest of it. I groan because he expects me to, and Kate lets off one of her giggles I keep hearing whenever they stay in my father's and my room at the hotel and send me down for a swim. "If you can't give a grin, give a groan," my father says for about the millionth time, and Kate pokes him with her freckly elbow as if he's too funny for words. She annoys me so much that I say "Lepers don't rhyme with creepers, dad."

"I never thought they did, son. I was just having a laugh. If we can't laugh we might as well be dead, ain't that straight, Kate?" He winks at her thigh and slaps his own instead, and says to me "Since you're so clever, why don't you find out when our bus is coming."

"That's it now."

"And I'm Hercules." He lifts up his fists to make his muscles bulge for Kate and says "You're telling us that tripe spells A Flounder?"

"Elounda, dad. It does. The letter like a Y upside down is how they write an L."

"About time they learned how to write properly, then," he says, staring around to show he doesn't care who hears. "Well, there it is if you really want to trudge round another old ruin instead of having a swim."

"I expect he'll be able to do both once we get to the village," Kate says, but I can tell she's hoping I'll just swim. "Will you two gentlemen see me across the road?"

My mother used to link arms with me and my father when he was living with us. "I'd better make sure it's the right bus," I say and run out so fast I can pretend I didn't hear my father calling me back.

A man with skin like a boot is walking backwards in the dust behind the bus, shouting "Elounda" and waving his arms as if he's pulling the bus into the space in line. I sit on a seat opposite two Germans who block the aisle until they've taken off their rucksacks, but my father finds three seats together at the rear. "Aren't you with us, Hugh?" he shouts, and everyone on the bus looks at him.

When I see him getting ready to shout again I walk down the aisle. I'm hoping nobody notices me, but Kate says loudly "It's a pity you ran off like that, Hugh. I was going to ask if you'd like an ice cream."

"No thank you," I say, trying to sound like my mother when she was only just speaking to my father, and step over Kate's legs. As the bus rumbles uphill I turn as much of my back on her as I can, and watch the streets.

Aghios Nikolaos looks as if they haven't finished building it. Some of the tavernas are on the bottom floors of blocks with no roofs, and sometimes there are more tables on the pavements outside than in. The bus goes downhill again as if it's hiccupping, and when it reaches the bottomless pool where young people with no children stay in the hotels with discos, it follows the edge of the bay. I watch the white boats on the blue water, but really I'm seeing the conductor coming down the aisle and feeling as if a lump is growing in my stomach from me wondering what my father will say to him. The bus is climbing beside the sea when he reaches us. "Three for leper land," my father says.

The conductor stares at him and shrugs. "As far as you go," Kate says and rubs herself against my father. "All the way."

When the conductor pushes his lips forward out of his moustache and beard my father begins to get angry, unless he's pretending. "Where you kept your lepers. Spiny Lobster or whatever you call the damned place."

"It's Spinalonga, dad, and it's off the coast from where we're going."

"I know that, and he should." My father is really angry now. "Did you get that?" he says to the conductor. "My ten-year-old can speak your lingo, so don't tell me you can't speak ours."

The conductor looks at me, and I'm afraid he wants me to talk Greek. My mother gave me a little computer that translates words into Greek when you type them, but I've left it at the hotel because my father said it sounded like a bird which only knew one note. "We're going to Elounda, please," I stammer.

"Elounda, boss," the conductor says to me. He takes the money from my father without looking at him and gives me the tickets and change. "Fish is good by the harbour in the evening," he says, and goes to sit next to the driver while the bus swings round the zigzags of the hill road.

My father laughs for the whole bus to hear. "They think you're so important, Hugh, you won't be wanting to go home to your mother."

Kate strokes his head as if he's her pet, then she turns to me. "What do you like most about Greece?"

She's trying to make friends with me like when she kept saying I could call her Kate, only now I see it's for my father's sake. All she's done is make me think how the magic places seemed to have lost their magic because my mother wasn't there with me, even Knossos where Theseus killed the Minotaur. There were just a few corridors left that might have been the maze he was supposed to find his way out of, and my father let me stay in them for a while, but then he lost his temper because all the guided tours were in foreign languages and nobody could tell him how to get back to the coach. We nearly got stuck overnight in Heraklion, when he'd promised to take Kate for dinner that night by the bottomless pool. "I don't know," I mumble, and gaze out the window.

"I like the sun, don't you? And the people when they're being nice, and the lovely clear sea."

It sounds to me as if she's getting ready to send me off swimming again. They met while I was, our second morning at the hotel. When I came out of the sea my father had moved his towel next to hers and she was giggling. I watch Spinalonga Island float over the horizon like a ship made of rock and grey towers, and hope she'll think I'm agreeing with her if that means she'll leave me alone. But she says "I suppose most boys are morbid at your age. Let's hope you'll grow up to be like your father."

She's making it sound as if the leper colony is the only place I've wanted to visit, but it's just another old place I can tell my mother I've been. Kate doesn't want to go there because she doesn't like old places—she said if Knossos was a palace she was glad she's not a queen. I don't speak to her again until the bus has stopped by the harbour.

There aren't many tourists, even in the shops and tavernas lined up along the winding pavement. Greek people who look as if they were born in the sun sit drinking at tables under awnings like stalls in a market. Some priests who I think at first are wearing black hatboxes on their heads march by, and fishermen come up from their boats with octopuses on sticks like big kebabs. The bus turns round in a cloud of dust and petrol fumes while Kate hangs on to my father with one hand and flaps the front of her flowery dress with the other. A boatman stares at the tops of her boobs which make me think of spotted fish and shouts "Spinalonga" with both hands round his mouth.

"We've hours yet," Kate says. "Let's have a drink. Hugh may even get that ice cream if he's good."

If she's going to talk about me as though I'm not there I'll do my best not to be. She and my father sit under an awning and I kick dust on the pavement outside until she says "Come under, Hugh. We don't want you with sunstroke."

I don't want her pretending she's my mother, but if I say so I'll only spoil the day more than she already has. I shuffle to the table next to the one she's sharing with my father and throw myself on a chair. "Well, Hugh," she says, "do you want one?"

"No thank you," I say, even though the thought of an ice cream or a drink starts my mouth trying to drool.

"You can have some of my lager if it ever arrives," my father says at the top of his voice, and stares hard at some Greeks sitting at a table. "Anyone here a waiter?" he says, lifting his hand to his mouth as if he's holding a glass.

When all the people at the table smile and raise their glasses and shout cheerily at him, Kate says "I'll find someone and then I'm going to the little girls' room while you men have a talk."

My father watches her crossing the road and gazes at the doorway of the taverna once she's gone in. He's quiet for a while, then he says "Are you going to be able to say you had a good time?"

I know he wants me to enjoy myself when I'm with him, but I also think what my mother stopped herself from saying to me is true—that he booked the holiday in Greece as a way of scoring off her by taking me somewhere she'd always wanted to go. He stares at the taverna as if he can't move until I let him, and I say "I expect so, if we go to the island."

"That's my boy. Never give in too easily." He smiles at me with one side of his face. "You don't mind if I have some fun as well, do you?"

He's making it sound as though he wouldn't have had much fun if it had just been the two of us, and I think that was how he'd started to feel before he met Kate. "It's your holiday," I say.

He's opening his mouth after another long silence when Kate

comes out of the taverna with a man carrying two lagers and a lemonade on a tray. "See that you thank her," my father tells me.

I didn't ask for lemonade. He said I could have some lager. I say "Thank you very much," and feel my throat tightening as I gulp the lemonade, because her eyes are saying that she's won.

"That must have been welcome," she says when I put down the empty glass. "Another? Then I should find yourself something to do. Your father and I may be here for a while."

"Have a swim," my father suggests.

"I haven't brought my cossy."

"Neither have those boys," Kate says, pointing at the harbour. "Don't worry, I've seen boys wearing less."

My father smirks behind his hand, and I can't bear it. I run to the jetty the boys are diving off, and drop my T-shirt and shorts on it and my sandals on top of them, and dive in.

The water's cold, but not for long. It's full of little fish that nibble you if you only float, and it's clearer than tap water, so you can see down to the pebbles and the fish pretending to be them. I chase fish and swim underwater and almost catch an octopus before it squirms out to sea. Then three Greek boys about my age swim over, and we're pointing at ourselves and saying our names when I see Kate and my father kissing.

I know their tongues are in each other's mouths—getting some tongue, the kids at my school call it. I feel like swimming away as far as I can go and never coming back. But Stavros and Stathis and Costas are using their hands to tell me we should see who can swim fastest, so I do that instead. Soon I've forgotten my father and Kate, even when we sit on the jetty for a rest before we have more races. It must be hours later when I realise Kate is calling "Come here a minute."

The sun isn't so hot now. It's reaching under the awning, but she and my father haven't moved back into the shadow. A boatman shouts "Spinalonga" and points at how low the sun is. I don't mind swimming with my new friends instead of going to the island, and I'm about to tell my father so when Kate says "I've been telling your dad he should be proud of you. Come and see what I've got for you."

They've both had a lot to drink. She almost falls across the table as I go to her. Just as I get there I see what she's going to give me, but it's too late. She grabs my head with both hands and sticks a kiss on my mouth.

She tastes of old lager. Her mouth is wet and bigger than mine, and when it squirms it makes me think of an octopus. "Mmm*mwa*," it says, and then I manage to duck out of her hands, leaving her blinking at me as if her eyes won't quite work. "Nothing wrong with a bit of loving," she says. "You'll find that out when you grow up."

My father knows I don't like to be kissed, but he's frowning at me as if I should have let her. Suddenly I want to get my own back on them in the only way I can think of. "We need to go to the island now."

"Better go to the loo first," my father says. "They wouldn't have one on the island when all their willies had dropped off."

Kate hoots at that while I'm getting dressed, and I feel as if she's laughing at the way my ribs show through my skin however much I eat. I stop myself from shivering in case she or my father makes out that's a reason for us to go back to the hotel. I'm heading for the toilet when my father says "Watch out you don't catch anything in there or we'll have to leave you on the island."

I know there are all sorts of reasons why my parents split up, but just now this is the only one I can think of—my mother not being able to stand his jokes and how the more she told him to finish the more he would do it, as if he couldn't stop himself. I run into the toilet, trying not to look at the pedal bin where you have to drop the used paper, and close my eyes once I've taken aim.

Is today going to be what I remember about Greece? My mother brought me up to believe that even the sunlight here had magic in it, and I expected to feel the ghosts of legends in all the old places. If there isn't any magic in the sunlight, I want there to be some in the dark. The thought seems to make the insides of my eyelids darker, and I can smell the drains. I pull the chain and zip myself up, and then I wonder if my father sent me in here so we'll miss the boat. I nearly break the hook on the door, I'm so desperate to be outside.

The boat is still tied to the harbour, but I can't see the boatman. Kate and my father are holding hands across the table, and my father's looking around as though he means to order another drink. I squeeze my eyes shut so hard that when I open them everything's gone black. The blackness fades along with whatever I wished, and I see the boatman kneeling on the jetty, talking to Stavros. "Spinalonga," I shout.

He looks at me, and I'm afraid he'll say it's too late. I feel tears building up behind my eyes. Then he stands up and holds out a hand towards my father and Kate. "One hour," he says.

Kate's gazing after a bus that has just begun to climb the hill. "We may as well go over as wait for the next bus," my father says, "and then it'll be back to the hotel for dinner."

Kate looks sideways at me. "And after all that he'll be ready for bed," she says like a question she isn't quite admitting to.

"Out like a light, I reckon."

"Fair enough," she says, and uses his arm to get herself up.

The boatman's name is Iannis, and he doesn't speak much English. My father seems to think he's charging too much for the trip until he realises it's that much for all three of us, and then he grins as if he thinks Iannis has cheated himself. "Heave ho then, Janice," he says with a wink at me and Kate.

The boat is about the size of a big rowing-boat. It has a cabin at the front and benches along the sides and a long box in the middle that shakes and smells of petrol. I watch the point of the boat sliding through the water like a knife and feel as if we're on our way to the Greece I've been dreaming of. The white buildings of Elounda shrink until they look like teeth in the mouth of the hills, and then Spinalonga floats up ahead.

It makes me think of an abandoned ship bigger than a liner, a ship so dead that it's standing still in the water without having to be anchored. The evening light seems to shine out of the steep rusty sides and the bony towers and walls high above the sea. I know it was a fort to begin with, but I think it might as well have been built for the lepers. I can imagine them trying to swim to Elounda and drowning because there wasn't enough left of them to swim with, if they didn't just throw themselves off the walls because they couldn't bear what they'd turned into. If I say these things to Kate I bet more than her mouth will squirm—but my father gets in first. "Look, there's the welcoming committee."

Kate gives a shiver that reminds me I'm trying not to feel cold. "Don't say things like that. They're just people like us, probably wishing they hadn't come."

I don't think she can see them any more clearly than I can. Their heads are poking over the wall at the top of the cliff above the little pebbly beach which is the only place a boat can land. There are five or six of them, only I'm not sure they're heads; they might be stones someone has balanced on the wall—they're almost the same colour. I'm wishing I had some binoculars when Kate grabs my father so hard the boat rocks and Iannis waves a finger at her, which doesn't please my father. "You keep your eye on your steering, Janice," he says.

Iannis is already taking the boat towards the beach. He didn't seem to notice the heads on the wall, and when I look again they aren't there. Maybe they belonged to some of the people who are coming down to a boat bigger than Iannis's. That boat chugs away as Iannis's bumps into the jetty. "One hour," he says. "Back here."

He helps Kate onto the jetty while my father glowers at him, then he lifts me out of the boat. As soon as my father steps onto the jetty Iannis pushes the boat out again. "Aren't you staying?" Kate pleads.

He shakes his head and points hard at the beach. "Back here, one hour."

She looks as if she wants to run into the water and climb aboard the boat, but my father shoves his arm round her waist. "Don't worry, you've got two fellers to keep you safe, and neither of them with a girl's name."

The only way up to the fort is through a tunnel that bends in the middle so you can't see the end until you're nearly halfway in. I wonder how long it will take for the rest of the island to be as dark as the middle of the tunnel. When Kate sees the end she runs until she's in the open and stares at the sunlight, which is perched on top of the towers now. "Fancying a climb?" my father says.

She makes a face at him as I walk past her. We're in a kind of street of stone sheds that have mostly caved in. They must be where the lepers lived, but there are only shadows in them now, not even birds. "Don't go too far, Hugh," Kate says.

"I want to go all the way round, otherwise it wasn't worth coming."

"I don't, and I'm sure your father expects you to consider me."

"Now, now, children," my father says. "Hugh can do as he likes as long as he's careful and the same goes for us, eh, Kate?"

I can tell he's surprised when she doesn't laugh. He looks unsure of himself and angry about it, the way he did when he and my mother were getting ready to tell me they were splitting up. I run along the line of huts and think of hiding in one so I can jump out at Kate. Maybe they aren't empty after all; something rattles in one as if bones are crawling about in the dark. It could be a snake under part of the roof that's fallen. I keep running until I come to steps leading up from the street to the top of the island, where most of the light is, and I've started jogging up them when Kate shouts "Stay where we can see you. We don't want you hurting yourself."

"It's all right, Kate, leave him be," my father says. "He's sensible."

"If I'm not allowed to speak to him I don't know why you invited me at all."

I can't help grinning as I sprint to the top of the steps and duck out of sight behind a grassy mound that makes me think of a grave. From up here I can see the whole island, and we aren't alone on it. The path I've run up from leads all round the island, past more huts and towers and a few bigger buildings, and then it goes down to the tunnel. Just before it does it passes the wall above the beach, and between the path and the wall there's a stone yard full of slabs. Some of the slabs have been moved away from holes like long boxes full of soil or darkness. They're by the wall where I thought I saw heads looking over at us. They aren't there now, but I can see heads bobbing down towards the tunnel. Before long they'll be behind Kate and my father.

Iannis is well on his way back to Elounda. His boat is passing one that's heading for the island. Soon the sun will touch the sea.

If I went down to the huts I'd see it sink with me and drown. Instead I lie on the mound and look over the island, and see more of the boxy holes hiding behind some of the huts. If I went closer I could see how deep they are, but I quite like not knowing—if I was Greek I expect I'd think they lead to the underworld where all the dead live. Besides, I like being able to look down on my father and Kate and see them trying to see me.

I stay there until Iannis's boat is back at Elounda and the other one has almost reached Spinalonga, and the sun looks as if it's gone down to the sea for a drink. Kate and my father are having an argument. I expect it's about me, though I can't hear what they're saying; the darker it gets between the huts the more Kate waves her arms. I'm getting ready to let my father see me when she screams.

She's jumped back from a hut which has a hole behind it. "Come out, Hugh. I know it's you," she cries.

I can tell what my father's going to say, and I cringe. "Is that you, Hugh? Yoo-hoo," he shouts.

I won't show myself for a joke like that. He leans into the hut through the spiky stone window, then he turns to Kate. "It wasn't Hugh. There's nobody."

I can only just hear him, but I don't have to strain to hear Kate. "Don't tell me that," she cries. "You're both too fond of jokes."

She screams again, because someone's come running up the tunnel. "Everything all right?" this man shouts. "There's a boat about to leave if you've had enough."

"I don't know what you two are doing," Kate says like a duchess to my father, "but I'm going with this gentleman."

My father calls me twice. If I go to him I'll be letting Kate win. "I don't think our man will wait," the new one says.

"It doesn't matter," my father says, so fiercely that I know it does. "We've our own boat coming."

"If there's a bus before you get back I won't be hanging around," Kate warns him.

"Please yourself," my father says, so loud that his voice goes into the tunnel. He stares after her as she marches away; he must be hoping she'll change her mind. But I see her step off the jetty into the boat, and it moves out to sea as if the ripples are pushing it to Elounda.

My father puts a hand to his ear as the sound of the engine fades. "So every bugger's left me now, have they?" he says in a kind of shout at himself. "Well, good riddance."

He's waving his fists as if he wants to punch something, and he sounds as if he's suddenly got drunk. He must have been holding it back while Kate was there. I've never seen him like this. It frightens me, so I stay where I am.

It isn't only my father that frightens me. There's only a little bump of the sun left above the water now, and I'm afraid how dark the island may be once that goes. Bits of sunlight shiver on the water all the way to the island, and I think I see some heads above the wall of the yard full of slabs, against the light. Which side of the wall are they on? The light's too dazzling, it seems to pinch the sides of the heads so they look thinner than any heads I've ever seen. Then I notice a boat setting out from Elounda, and I squint at it until I'm sure it's Iannis's boat.

He's coming early to fetch us. Even that frightens me, because I wonder why he is. Doesn't he want us to be on the island now he realises how dark it's getting? I look at the wall, and the heads have gone. Then the sea puts the sun out, and it feels as if the island is buried in darkness.

I can still see my way down—the steps are paler than the dark—and I don't like being alone now I've started shivering. I back off from the mound, because I don't like to touch it, and almost back into a shape with bits of its head poking out and arms that look as if they've dropped off at the elbows. It's a cactus. I'm just standing up when my father says "There you are, Hugh."

He can't see me yet. He must have heard me gasp. I go to the top of the steps, but I can't see him for the dark. Then his voice moves away. "Don't start hiding again. Looks like we've seen the last of Kate, but we've got each other, haven't we?"

He's still drunk. He sounds as if he's talking to somebody nearer to him than I am. "All right, we'll wait on the beach," he says, and his voice echoes. He's gone into the tunnel, and he thinks he's following me. "I'm here, dad," I shout so loud that I squeak.

"I heard you, Hugh. Wait there. I'm coming." He's walking deeper into the tunnel. While he's in there my voice must seem to be coming from beyond the far end. I'm sucking in a breath that tastes dusty, so I can tell him where I am, when he says "Who's that?" with a laugh that almost shakes his words to pieces.

He's met whoever he thought was me when he was heading for the tunnel. I'm holding my breath. I can't breathe or swallow, and I don't know if I feel hot or frozen. "Let me past," he says as if he's trying to make his voice as big as the tunnel. "My son's waiting for me on the beach."

There are so many echoes in the tunnel I'm not sure what I'm hearing besides him. I think there's a lot of shuffling, and the other noise must be voices, because my father says "What kind of language do you call that? You sound drunker than I am. I said my son's waiting."

He's talking even louder as if that'll make him understood. I'm embarrassed, but I'm more afraid for him. "Dad," I nearly scream, and run down the steps as fast as I can without falling.

"See, I told you. That's my son," he says as if he's talking to a crowd of idiots. The shuffling starts moving like a slow march, and he says "All right, we'll all go to the beach together. What's the matter with your friends, too drunk to walk?"

I reach the bottom of the steps, hurting my ankles, and run along the ruined street because I can't stop myself. The shuffling sounds as though it's growing thinner, as if the people with my father are leaving bits of themselves behind, and the voices are changing too—they're looser. Maybe the mouths are getting bigger somehow. But my father's laughing, so loud that he might be trying to think of a joke. "That's what I call a hug. No harder, love, or I won't have any puff left," he says to someone. "Come on then, give us a kiss. They're the same in any language."

All the voices stop, but the shuffling doesn't. I hear it go out of the tunnel and onto the pebbles, and then my father tries to scream as if he's swallowed something that won't let him. I scream for him and dash into the tunnel, slipping on things that weren't on the floor when we first came through, and fall out onto the beach.

My father's in the sea. He's already so far out that the water is up to his neck. About six people who look stuck together and to him are walking him away as if they don't need to breathe when their heads start to sink. Bits of them float away on the waves my father makes as he throws his arms about and gurgles. I try to run after him, but I've got nowhere when his head goes underwater. The sea pushes me back on the beach, and I run crying up and down it until Iannis comes.

It doesn't take him long to find my father once he understands what I'm saying. Iannis wraps me in a blanket and hugs me all the way to Elounda, and the police take me back to the hotel. Kate gets my mother's number and calls her, saying she's someone at the hotel who's looking after me because my father's drowned, and I don't care what she says, I just feel numb. I don't start screaming until I'm on the plane back to England, because then I dream that my father has come back to tell a joke. "That's what I call getting some tongue," he says, leaning his face close to mine and showing me what's in his mouth.

# Reading the Signs

When Vernon came to a roundabout with no diversion sign he saw he'd gone wrong. He lowered his window in the hope of hearing where the motorway was, but the night was as silent as the February sky that looked close to sagging onto the roofs of all five streets. He drove back to the last sign, which stood on another roundabout, and then he noticed what he'd previously overlooked. The four metal legs supporting the sign had gouged erratic tracks through the dewy grass. Plainly someone had thought it would be fun to move the sign.

Five roads met at this intersection too. Vernon had been driving for at least ten minutes through the moorland town, and surely he ought to be close to the route back to the motorway. He might have phoned Emma to say he was delayed, except that she was generally asleep by midnight; he hoped she was now. Instead he turned along the road between the pair he'd already followed. If it didn't bring him to a sign he would come back.

The terraced streets were deserted. The low sky appeared to have squashed every colour besides grey out of the ranks of narrow houses. The wan glare of the streetlamps blackened the window-frames and the curtains that blinded the panes, the front doors that opened onto the street. He glimpsed movement among the vehicles parked half on the pavement, but it was only a cloud of fumes seeping from under the hood of a car. Beyond the car the road bent sharply, and when it straightened he saw somebody trudging ahead.

Even from several hundred yards away Vernon saw the walker was unusually tall. As he put on speed for fear that the man might turn aside before Vernon could ask for directions, he became aware that the fellow's head was disconcertingly small. It turned to peer towards the car, and the upper portion of the body slipped askew. The light of the next streetlamp found it as it righted itself, and Vernon realised that a child was perched on the man's shoulders. He was relieved to see it but unnerved by having imagined anything else. He could only hope that he was safe to drive—that he wasn't too much in need of sleep.

The boy had regained his hold on the man's shoulders by the time Vernon drew alongside. The small face looked scrubbed shiny, gleaming under the streetlamp, and the wide eyes were alert despite the hour. His long nose twitched, perhaps with nerves, as his lips pinched inwards. The father's long face had been dragged thinner by the weight of his jowls, and his dull tired eyes were underscored by skin that looked bruised, while his loose lips drooped under a bulbous nose. In his indeterminately coloured suit and with his shirt collar open he scarcely seemed dressed for the night, and the boy's outfit wasn't much more suitable—a waspishly striped jumper inside a dark overall, both of them a size too large. Vernon lowered the passenger window and shivered at the chill that met him. "Will this bring me back to the motorway?" he called.

The man sidled between two parked cars and stooped to the window, but didn't speak until he'd lowered himself almost to his knees as if his burden had brought him to them. Vernon heard the boy's hands thump the roof, presumably for support. The man's breath glimmered in the wintry air as he said "What are you asking for?"

"I'm looking for the motorway. I was wondering if I've gone wrong."

If the man seemed unhappy with this, perhaps that was his habitual condition—the flatness of his voice would be a local trait. As the boy's hands clutched at his shoulders, he gave the road ahead a dull glance. "You're no more wrong than me."

"We were going that way, weren't we?" The boy's voice was shrill and rendered tinny by the roof. "You have to say," he said.

The skin beneath the man's eyes twitched while his lips chafed each other. No doubt he was embarrassed to be prompted to hitch. "Look for a lift by all means," Vernon said, and when the fellow's face grew blanker still "I mean with me."

The boy kicked up his legs, displaying trainers that reminded Vernon how much Tom's used to cost, and as the cuffs of the overalls flapped they revealed the boy wasn't wearing socks. "I'll give you a ride, son," Vernon called and told the man "You don't want him out like that at this time of night in this weather."

Even if this was presumptuous, he thought it needed to be said. The man's face stayed expressionless as the boy leapt down from his shoulders like an acrobat. The trainers struck the pavement with a plump thud that set a dog barking in a house, and the boy released one of the man's hands. "Where you going?" the man said.

Did he think the boy was about to run off? The man had straightened up, and Vernon couldn't see his face. Perhaps Vernon had misunderstood the question, since the man added "You can't stay sat on me."

The boy's thin lips sucked inwards, losing any colour, as if his teeth or something else had pained him. "Would you like to sit in front?" Vernon said.

The man ducked to stare at Vernon. "Who'll be telling you the way?"

"I expect you should." Vernon leaned over to tip the passenger seat forward. "You do as your dad says," he said. "Better sit in the back."

As the boy clambered in he gave Vernon quite a look. Vernon remembered earning glares whenever he told Tom not to do something at that age. When he pushed the seat upright the boy made a face, though in the dimness Vernon couldn't see what kind. Once the man had slumped onto the seat and fumbled the safety belt into its socket Vernon said "Straight on?"

"That's where."

The man seemed to resent having to say so. No doubt he was as weary as he looked. As he shut the window Vernon sent the car forward. Talking ought to help him stay wakeful, and he said "What's kept you both out so late?"

The man's breath clouded the air as he muttered "Broke down."

"Was that your car I saw back there?"

"No idea what you've seen."

Perhaps the boy would be better company. As Vernon glanced at the small indistinct face he saw the empty street fleeing backwards. "Have you been somewhere good?"

"Playing."

Vernon took that for an affirmative. He tried giving the man the kind of look adults shared on the subject of children, but the fellow was staring dully through the windscreen. It was hardly polite to seem amused by how the boy took after him, and Vernon stayed quiet until the street ended at a junction. "Left?" he suggested.

"That's us," the man just about said.

From previous journeys Vernon had a sense that the motorway curved in this direction several miles ahead. The road he turned along was wider than the one he left but no less deserted. Cars occupied the concrete drives of houses frozen by the frigid light. He saw the boy's eyes flickering from side to side as though to take everything in, which prompted him to say "I'll bet my son would have thought this was an adventure at your age."

A shadow fluttered over the boy's face as he peered out of the mirror. "How old's that?"

"You tell him."

Vernon thought the man was addressing the boy, then wondered if he was. "Eight?" Vernon said, which was apparently an insult, given how blank the small face grew. "His name's Tom," Vernon said in an attempt to placate him. "What's yours?"

"Tell the man your name, son."

"I'm me."

"I'm sure you are and nobody else." Vernon made another bid to share the adult viewpoint, but the man was keeping his thoughts to himself. "I'm Jack," Vernon said.

Neither of his passengers responded with a name, though the man uttered a breath that bloomed grey. Vernon thumbed the button on his side of the car to ensure the passenger window was shut and turned the heating up to full. The man's gaze had begun to dodge back and forth as though he was imitating his son, and his thick tongue poked his lips apart. "Time to play," he said.

The boy sat forward. "Try telling, pop," he said and grinned as if he was no less proud of his teeth than of the answer.

"Sit back, son," Vernon told him. "You need to put your belt on."

As the boy's face withdrew into the dimness, his grin was the first thing to vanish. "That's no fun."

"I can't drive unless everyone is strapped in. I don't want the police telling me I can't, do I?"

"You don't."

Perhaps the man's voice was so toneless because he didn't like to see his son rebuked, in which case he should have done the parental job, though Vernon felt guilty for neglecting to check the boy had used the belt. He braked and waited for the boy to yank it across himself in a mime of resentment. As the car regained speed he said "Time to play what?"

The man's eyes flickered, but not in his direction. "You'll see."

"If it's a secret just say so."

"Don't be like that."

Could the fellow actually think Vernon was being unreasonable? Before Vernon could make his feelings even plainer the man turned his head away from him. "See the signs," he mumbled.

Vernon saw the small head swing that way too. "So that's safe," the boy said.

In a moment Vernon thought he understood, but said only "Intelligent chap, isn't he?"

The man expelled another ashen breath. "Likes to think so."

Did he resent his own son's intellect? That might explain why the boy seemed somehow to be holding back, but Vernon wasn't about to be daunted from showing concern. "Are you cold there in the back?" he said. "I've a blanket in the boot if you'd like to wrap up."

"Last thing he wants," the man declared.

"It really won't be any trouble."

"You're right, it won't."

Vernon was ready to ignore if not to argue with the man until the boy spoke up, shriller than ever. "I'm how I like."

"If you say so," Vernon said but felt inadequate. "If there's anything else I can do for you, just let me know."

"No call for that." The man nodded at the windscreen as though to indicate he was leaving the subject behind. "I'm miserable tired," he said.

The boy was looking where the man had looked. "It's my turn."

"I believe I see what you're up to," Vernon said.

"Is that a fact."

It sounded like a question the man lacked the energy to raise. "Can anybody play?" Vernon said.

"Depends." Even less encouragingly the man added "Depends what you reckon the game is."

"I'll make tea." As the man gave him a look that might have been convicting him of feeblemindedness Vernon found the next number-plate ahead. "Owls own banks," he suggested.

"You're as clever as him." This didn't much resemble praise, but the man contributed "Our own business."

"Out of bounds," the boy said.

Vernon felt oddly relieved to have identified the game, as if he'd recovered some kind of control. "Do you play it whenever you're on the road?" he asked the man.

"Got to keep your brain going somehow."

"So you don't nod off at the wheel, you mean." When the fellow kept any response to himself Vernon found inspiration on a number-plate. "Weariness is fiendish."

The man thumped his forehead with the fingertips of one hand as though to enliven his mind. "What it's for."

The boy seemed to need no time to ponder. "What I found."

Was the man scowling at his quickness? Perhaps it was up to Vernon to carry on the game, and a registration number let him say "Gee up, Trigger."

The boy's giggle was even higher than his voice. His father glowered at it, unless he was making sure his turn came next. He looked away from the mirror before he said "Get us thinking."

"Gone up there," the boy said at once.

Vernon had the odd notion that the game had turned into a dialogue from which he was excluded. He was glad to see they'd reached the edge of town. The houses ended several hundred yards ahead, and beyond them the road stretched into empty darkness. "Where shall I drop you?" he said.

The man shook his head as if to rouse himself or to dislodge some unwelcome burden. "Not round here."

"I thought you said you were on my way."

"Never said different. Not yet, that's all."

Vernon almost laughed aloud at the man's brusqueness, since there seemed to be no other way to take it. "So long as you let me know when you're where you want to be," he said as the last of the light slipped from the boy's face in the mirror.

The streetlamps receded while the moor loomed around the car. The long low slopes were in no hurry to reveal themselves, and even once they gained some definition the ragged crests were scarcely distinguishable from the drooping sky. Although they hid the motorway, the strip of illuminated road that ran between the sprawling verges led in the direction where Vernon assumed it to be. Otherwise the headlamp beams only blurred the dark that hunched around and ahead of the specimen of road. He needed more than the monotonous sight to keep him vigilant, and he tried saying "So what do you do, Mr…"

"Mister is right." Just as dully the man added "You've seen."

"That's what we get for being fathers, isn't it?" When his bid for good humour fell short of the man Vernon said "I was thinking of the other kind of job."

"After one of them, are you?"

Even by the man's standards the retort seemed unnecessarily

harsh, and then Vernon wondered if he was unemployed. "Isn't there much work hereabouts?"

"Here?" The man waved a hand so sluggishly that it looked hampered by the darkness. "See if you can think."

Vernon might have countered that the man didn't seem especially capable of it. Instead he concentrated on the lit stretch of road as it veered from side to side. A protracted curve led so far out of the way he thought he should be taking that he let out a dimly luminous breath when another elongated bend corrected the deviation. All this made him say "Don't you mind leaving your car all that way back?"

"Doesn't matter what I mind."

"Couldn't you call someone?"

Presumably he didn't belong to a motoring organisation, and the local garages would have shut down hours ago. Vernon was aware of talking for the sake of it as he said "I wouldn't like to break down out here and not be able to get help."

"Better hadn't, then."

"No, I mean if I did I'd be able to call."

"Not here you'd not. Nothing gets out," the man said with morose triumph.

"I think my phone would. It's pretty well up to date, not like its owner."

Vernon slowed the car to a walking pace and found his mobile in the fat pocket of his padded coat. As he touched the illuminated screen he glimpsed the boy's face blanching in the mirror. "Expect you've never seen the like, son," the man muttered.

Vernon blinked at the phone and brought it closer to his face before pocketing it. "I'm afraid your dad was right. I can't pick anything up."

"Want to watch out what you're picking," the man said so indistinctly that he might almost have been talking in his sleep.

"He's right again, son," Vernon said, the only way he could make sense of the remark. "Be careful."

The boy lurched forward, not far enough for the dashboard lights to illuminate his face. "What about?"

"Who you get involved with," Vernon said and glanced at the

man for agreement. When the fellow kept his gaze on the dark Vernon added "What they're up to as well."

The boy fell back as if the belt had recaptured him. If his father had glanced at him in the mirror, the man's expression was too fleeting for Vernon to catch. As the car put on speed once more, the grass and weeds that framed the headlight beams twitched to greet them. The dim outlines of the slopes shifted as a wind rattled the passenger window, emphasising the chill. "Would you really have walked all the way up here?" Vernon said.

The man shrugged as if trying to work off the last traces of his burden. "No choice."

"Well, I think we always have those. It's up to us to decide what's best to do."

That was aimed at the boy, even if Vernon couldn't have explained precisely why—it was the kind of thing he still said to Tom—but the man mumbled "Try saying that round here."

Vernon might have pointed out that he just had. He assumed the man was referring to the kind of life he had to lead, the poverty he believed he'd made plain. He was relieved to see a pair of headlamp beams sprout above a slope against the sky ahead; at least the number-plate would provide a distraction. The beams groped back and forth as if they were reaching vainly for the lightless clouds, and then they fell to the road as the car appeared around a bend. Vernon sensed his passengers readying themselves, but it seemed he was the first to read the plate. "Three nice eggs," he said.

He heard the man part his sticky lips, but the boy was faster. "That's not easy."

"There's no escape," the man said and stared at the mirror.

The other car sped past, and the boy's face went out like a dead bulb. It was dimly silhouetted by a pair of red lights that shrank to embers before the darkness doused them. Vernon was realising how devious a route the other vehicle had followed. "This can't be the only road, can it?" he said.

"It's that all right," the man said without looking away from the mirror. "You'll see."

In that case it must be the diversion, and Vernon had to admit he wouldn't be unhappy to leave his passengers along the way, together with the tension they'd brought with them. It and the chill were afflicting him with shivers, and he was tempted to offer the blanket again. Perhaps the boy was inured to the local weather, and as the headlights revealed yet another extended bend Vernon said "Are there still schools round here, then?"

"Still."

The man might have been aiming the word at the reflection in the mirror. "I was wondering where he goes to school," Vernon said.

"Try asking."

Though this sounded quite unlike an invitation, Vernon said "Where do you, son?"

As the boy inched forward the man demanded "Who's saying he does?"

Improbable as it seemed, could the boy have been taught at home? At least that might explain the man's resentment. "I'm saying he seems educated," Vernon said. "Literate for his age."

"He's good at that. Good at a lot else as well."

This seemed more discontented than Vernon understood. How could anyone deplore their own child's intelligence? He was determined to involve the boy now, and as the road straightened out further than the headlamp beams could reach he said "What should I be looking for, son?"

"Don't know."

"What sign, I mean."

"Sign."

Was the boy imitating his father to placate him? "For your village if that's what it is," Vernon said.

"There's none."

Vernon wished he could make out the boy's face. Might the child be afraid to display too much intelligence around his father? "Your house, then," Vernon said.

"Can't see."

Perhaps he was protesting about having to sit in the back, and yet Vernon wondered if he'd misunderstood. "Will I know it when I come to it?"

"You'll be put right," the man said.

He sounded weary of the conversation if not resolved to end it. Vernon wasn't going to be silenced, and not just because chatting would help him to stay awake. "I'm guessing you're a reader, son."

"Reader."

"Of books, yes. Is that where you've picked up some of your way with words?"

"Here's where."

If he was trying to sound like his father it didn't quite come off, and the uninhabited night all around them didn't lend his answer much credibility. "I'm asking because I travel in books," Vernon said as much to the man as to the child.

"Thought you were travelling in a car."

Vernon couldn't judge from the boy's shrill tone whether this was a joke, and the man's dull face gave no assistance. "The publishers send me around to show the shops their books," Vernon said doggedly. "A few of us still do that even with all the modern developments."

The boy leaned forward far enough that Vernon saw his indistinct face was blank. Surely no child could be unaware of computers and the internet and how they'd changed the world. Perhaps, having grown up with it, the boy simply took it all for granted. "I've some books in the boot you might like," Vernon said. "The kind my son used to."

"He'll want none of them," the man said so fiercely that his breath glimmered with each word. "Nobody's getting out."

"I didn't mean up here. Hardly the right place."

"Right for some things."

Vernon wasn't about to enquire which. For several reasons he welcomed the sight of headlamp beams ahead. They ranged about beneath the clouds until the night appeared to cut them down, and he felt as if more than the dark and the huge smudges of moorland had closed in. Only the moor had obscured the beams, and soon they were brandished above a lower slope. As the lorry swung into view around a bend he grew tense, surely just anticipating the game. The headlamp beams dropped to the tarmac as his did, and he squinted at the registration number. "Call general assembly," he said.

"Child goes a-roving."

Vernon was reflecting that the boy had proved his point about literacy when the man said "Can't get away."

The lorry roared past, and Vernon glanced at the mirror. Had just the headlamps turned the boy's face so white? As the rear lights shrank into the darkness the boy sank back as though he wanted to emulate them. Vernon didn't like to think the child could be so afraid of his father—and then a worse notion came to him.

He could only drive while he struggled to think. His mind felt frozen by the chill and weighed down by the dark, as if he mightn't be able to use it until he left the desolate emptiness behind. A wind blundered against the car and set the passenger window jittering, and he found he didn't want to look towards the man beside him. The dim slopes of the moor were trembling, and he wondered if the boy was fighting to restrain a shiver, just as Vernon was. He did his best to peer into the mirror without betraying that he was, but the boy's face had retreated into indistinctness. He was trying to discern its expression when he glimpsed a light ahead, and then another and a third—an irregular series of them following a line beyond a gap between the slopes. He didn't dare hope too much until the car was nearly at the gap, through which he saw more lights speeding both ways on a straight road close to the uneven horizon. They were on the motorway, and the intervening land was almost flat. He took a breath and swallowed, and then he had to speak. "I don't think I'm seeing a house."

The man stared ahead. "Keep looking."

"What am I likely to see?"

The man seemed no more eager to respond than Vernon had been to ask. It was the boy who said "Nothing you'd call one."

What was he trying to convey? Even by narrowing his eyes Vernon still couldn't see the boy's face. He might have thought the child was trying to stay out of reach of the man's gaze. Before Vernon could think of a comment to risk, the man muttered "You'll have us for a way yet."

Vernon saw the miles of deserted moorland he had yet to cross, and the lights shuttling along the motorway as if to remind him how distant they were, and then he saw another light, a dim but undeniable glow on the clouds beyond the spot where the motorway disappeared rightwards over the horizon. He was sure the glow denoted a service area, and it prompted him to say "I can take you to the services and then you're on your own."

He sensed unease so palpable it sent a shiver through him. The man raised his sluggish head as if he was confronting the mirror. "Depends what happens on the way," he said.

Too late Vernon realised he shouldn't have spoken. His first mistake had been to bring his passengers up here, where nobody else could see them. Now he would have been taking them among other people, but what chance had he left himself? Why had he taken so long to grasp how little the man knew about the child he pretended was his son? Not his name or his age, not where he lived or went to school...No wonder he hadn't owned up to a name either, although perhaps that gave Vernon some faint hope, since it suggested that the man might leave him capable of talking. Then the hope went out as if the darkness had seized it, and the car seemed to grow cold as the depths of a cave. The man had withheld his name before Vernon's phone had turned out not to work.

He was overtaken by a shiver so convulsive that his foot slipped off the accelerator. The car lost speed at once, and the man's head swung towards him. "What are you trying to do?"

"I'm not trying anything," Vernon protested, and instantly knew what he should. Using just his toes while he dug his heel into the rubber mat on the floor of the car, he pressed the pedal down. He let the car surge forward and then lifted his foot from the accelerator. His ankle and his shin ached from the strain, but his leg hadn't moved, and surely the man couldn't see what Vernon was doing. The head at the edge of his vision loomed towards him once more, and he didn't dare meet the fellow's eyes. "What's happened now?" the man demanded.

"I don't know. I'm not sure." Vernon managed not to grit his teeth at the pain in his leg before he'd finished speaking. He waited for the speed to drop so far that the car began to judder, and then he went down a gear, and another. He inched his foot higher, slowing the car enough to turn it shaky again. Before he could speak he had to swallow a cry at the dull agony in his leg. "Something's wrong with the engine. I don't know the first thing about them. Do you?"

He hadn't said half of that when he realised how useless his plan was. If the man was able to fix cars he would have fixed his own. The pain made his foot lurch off the accelerator, and the car wavered to a halt and stalled. The man was staring at him, but it took Vernon some seconds to turn his head. The man's eyes were so dull that his emotions were unreadable, even when he spoke. "I'll give it a look."

"I'll need to open the bonnet."

The man's sagging face came so close that his greyish breath settled on Vernon's skin. "How'll you do that?"

"I'm doing it now," Vernon said and leaned towards the floor in front of his seat. "It's done."

He was unable to breathe until the man had sprung the buckle of the belt out of its socket and scrabbled at the handle to open the door and sidled in a crouch onto the road. The fellow twisted around in that position and stared into the car. "Shut the door for heaven's sake," Vernon urged. "It's cold enough in here."

The man slammed the door hard enough to shake the car. Vernon had been afraid he would demur. As the man tramped into the headlight beams Vernon said low but urgently "Is your dad—"

"He's not my dad."

That was all the confirmation Vernon needed, and he blurted "What can you tell me about him?"

The boy leaned forward as the man stooped to the bonnet, and Vernon saw that the child's face was pale as ice. "Never mind," Vernon murmured. "You're safe now. Where do you want me to take you?"

"Over there," the boy said and pointed beyond the man, who was attempting to lift the bonnet that Vernon hadn't actually released. "Past all the lights."

Vernon was distressed to think that the child might be almost too scared to breathe; certainly his breaths weren't visible. "The far side of the motorway, you mean."

"That's where he got me from."

The man thrust his head towards the windscreen and thumped on the bonnet. "Can't get in."

"Stand back a moment. Let me try the engine again," Vernon shouted before lowering his voice. "Sit back, son. Hold on tight."

As the man straightened up, the boy did the same. "Have you got your belt on?" Vernon was anxious to learn.

"Never took it off."

How had he managed to crane forward so far? Vernon hadn't time to think about it now. The glare of the headlights mounted the man's body as he retreated several steps, which left his face harder to read. "Stay there," Vernon shouted and twisted the key in the ignition.

The starter motor rasped, and the engine emitted a shrill stuttering cough, but that was all. He felt the key grow slippery with perspiration as his mouth grew dry as ash. He mustn't release the key yet, you could keep it turned for ten seconds before you had to leave the engine dead for thirty more—and then the engine sputtered into life. He seized the gear lever and struggled to manipulate it into reverse, but it only jerked into the slot for fourth gear. The man was growing restless, swaying forward in the headlights, and Vernon realised that he hadn't locked the passenger door in case the fellow heard. Even if he did, what could he do about it? Vernon thumbed the button, and the door locked with a loud click just as the lever found reverse gear. The car lurched backwards with a squeal of the tyres, and as Vernon threw it into first gear to swerve around the man the headlights illuminated his entire figure. His hands were jerking towards his face, and Vernon thought he was miming dismay until the man cupped them around his mouth to yell a solitary word. "Moorchild."

For a confused moment Vernon thought the fellow was giving his name at last. The hands sank, and he saw the man's expression. If the long face had slumped even further, it was with relief; he looked as though he could scarcely believe his own good fortune. Perhaps that was what seized Vernon with an icy chill, unless it was the sight of his small passenger escaping the restraint of the safety belt with a sinuous reptilian motion, or even just the way the temperature dropped with the cavernous iciness the boy brought with him. His neck was owning up to its length as his head swayed towards the man, who had retreated to the verge of the road and was thrusting out his hands to fend off whatever he saw. "He's yours now," he yelled. "You chose him. You're welcome to him."

He sounded hysterical with delight, and perhaps this was too much for Vernon's passenger. Before Vernon could flinch the boy scrambled over the back of the empty seat and slithered head down to unlock the door. He darted out of the car on all fours and leapt to his feet with a cry that sounded less like a child than a night bird. All the same, it was a word. "Carry," he was demanding.

Vernon had a last glimpse of his face, which was as white as the underside of a slug. The eyes dwindled as the lips gaped with a grin that reached around the sides of the head. The man had staggered backwards as the door swung wide, and now he whirled around to dash along the road. He hadn't reached the limits of the headlights when the pursuer caught him. Clothes flapping about its elongated limbs, it sprang onto his shoulders and dug its fingers into the top of his head.

Vernon didn't know if the shrill sound was a cry of triumph or the man's wail of despair or both. He saw the man flee out of the headlamp beams as if he could somehow outdistance the burden on his back. Then the man stumbled off the road and rushed into the night as the rider kicked his chest to spur him onwards. It was a game, Vernon thought wildly—a childish game if not a senile one. Quite some time after the figure pranced helplessly into the wilderness Vernon managed to shut the passenger door and lock it, and eventually his shaking fingers let him control the car. He eased it forward and then drove as fast as he dared, because the lights on the motorway seemed as distant as stars. Until he reached them, if he ever did, he would be more aware of the darkness at his back.

# Where They Lived

The Hatchards had just crossed Ataturk Bulvari when a shoeshine boy commenced rubbing the straps of Don's sandals with a cloth. "Your shoes very dirty, sir."

"'All right, son, they're only sandals. He'll be polishing my feet next, Maggie. Not the kind of feet you'd want in bed with you." As he walked faster towards the sun-bleached concrete seafront the boy pursued him like a terrier, and Don felt the cloth catch the nail of one big toe. "That's all, son, would you mind? They're going in the sea, so you might as well not bother."

"He has to make a living somehow, Don. If he was a beggar you'd only look away from him."

"You know I hadn't any Turkish money until we went to the bank. What did you want me to give that woman, a travellers' cheque?" He dug in the pocket of his shorts for change, muttering "Have this if it'll help you mind your own business," and jangled the coins for Maggie's benefit before he dropped them into the small thin grubby hand. "I hope you heard that," he said as he tramped puffing after her.

She pulled her sun-hat lower, netting her forehead with

shadows. "Oh yes, I'm getting expert at hearing what you don't want me to hear."

"I meant the donation, and you know I— We'll look for her on the way back to the hotel if you like." He was reaching out a hand for one of Maggie's, and about to say "Let's start again like we said we would" when a man shouted at his back "Hey, English."

Only a policeman took that tone, Don thought—one of the policemen he'd seen strolling through the town as if all they needed to keep order were the guns they wore. This one must have observed Don appearing to taunt the shoeshine boy, or assumed he was pestering Maggie, and if Don couldn't clarify the situation, where might he end up? "Wait," he called, images of a communal jail-cell with plumbing even worse than the hotel provided crowding into his overheated head. When he turned, however, he saw two tourists bearing down on him.

They might have spent their marriage growing more alike. They looked like body-builders who had settled at some point for plumpness. They had identical pale blue eyes and marble grins, and over their swimwear both wore open buttonless shirts printed with cartoon figures brandishing bubbling cocktails. Their peeling skins were all the colours of new plaster, and oily with lotion. The woman's cropped hair was the same greying red as the strips under the man's nose and above his ears. Cameras bounced on their stomachs as they overtook the Hatchards. "Thank all the saints for someone who speaks English like a native," the woman said in a voice that would have carried across the street. "We were beginning to think we were the only people in town."

Her husband's shout had expressed enthusiasm, Don gathered now, because the man said in the same tone "Gareth and Trixie Lunt. Hotel's just as bad. Run by characters who bring you boiled fruit juice if you ask for tea, that's if you can make yourself heard above the Huns and God knows what else the hotel's full of."

"My friends call me Trick."

"We're Don Hatchard and—"

Maggie swung round from watching a man in an embroidered cap leading a bear on a chain up the dusty slope beyond the promenade. "'I'm Maggie," she said, and when Trixie Lunt tittered behind her hand, added with the ostentatious patience she ordinarily reserved for Don "Did I miss something?"

"Just how you can tell you're married, having to fight to get a word past the old man. Don't tell me, china. No, silver."

"'I'm afraid I don't—"

"Never only crystal."

"I'm still not—"

"Are you saying ivory? Look at them, Gar, ivory. You wouldn't think it in a million years."

"If you mean anniversaries," Maggie said, "I wouldn't know. It's been nearly twenty."

"Then Don should be ashamed of himself. If Gar missed any he'd know about it till the next one. When was the last time Don bought you something nice?"

"Oh, he has his moments."

"We'll make this one then, won't we, Gar?"

"Actually," Don said, "we were just—"

Trixie retreated a step and seized her husband's arm and rubbed her left cheek as though Don had slapped it. "Don't let us interrupt anything, I'm sure. We were going to ask you to take our photograph."

"Den's better with technology than I am."

"Mine's so simple even a man can't get it wrong. Just look through my hole, Don, and find us in the little lit-up bit, then you squeeze my button till you feel it stick and poke it down."

While the Lunts posed, intensifying their grins and plumping their arms around each other, Don surreptitiously wiped the sweaty back of the camera on his shorts, earning himself a sympathetic grimace from Maggie. He moved so as to frame the Lunts against a rank of bootblacks sitting on low stools behind elaborate brass stands and a stallholder brushing peaches with a small birch broom. The shutter release gave before he thought it would, and he was considering a retake when Trixie strode up to him and bumped him with her leopard-skinned breasts as she retrieved the camera. "Now we'll get you."

Don stood beside Maggie and took her hand, and realised he'd forgotten how it felt—slim and smooth and cooler than the relentlessly hot day. As he stroked it with his thumb she responded with a squeeze which he was almost sure was more affectionate than a request for him to stop. The camera clicked, and Lunt produced a notebook. "We'll need your address."

Maggie relinquished Don's hand at once, from which he assumed she was telling him to give the information. "Well, would you believe it," Trixie said when he had. "You don't live far from us at all. We'll have to deliver your snap personally."

Several seconds later Lunt broke the silence. "First time?"

"I'm the only one who'd put up with him," Maggie said.

"Ha," Lunt commented, and after a pause, "ha. I'm sure Don knows I was asking if you'd been before."

"We've wanted to, but the children never did. This year we decided they were old enough to go off on their own, so we have."

"You ought to have let them know who's in charge," Lunt told him. "So you won't know the best place to eat in town."

"We only flew in yesterday."

"Then we'll show you," Trixie cried. "We'll take you now."

"Actually, we were going—"

"I wouldn't mind some lunch."

"You tell him, Maggie," Trixie said. "Come with us and you'll never eat anywhere else."

Her husband led the way, and whenever anyone looked like approaching them—proprietors of the seafood restaurants by the harbour, stallholders selling imitation Rolexes and Gucci T-shirts in the pedestrian precinct near the mosque, owners of leather shops seeking customers in the crowds constricted by the arches flanking a mediaeval tower—he said "No thank you" with such authority that those addressed fell back. The narrow street beyond the arches was the Old Bazaar, and Don thought Lunt was conducting them along it towards the market area, where kebabs lay on grills outside restaurants which Maggie had proposed visiting. Instead Lunt marched up an alley. "I bet you're thanking us already," Trixie said.

It was full of would-be English restaurants. Nearest was the Englisch Pub, outside which a blackboard advertised Watneys Red Baral and rost beef and Yorkschire pudding. "Can't expect them to spell when half the yobs at home can't either," Lunt thundered, having caught Don's eye. "They do food that isn't only fit for pigs, that's the appeal."

"Actually, I'm not as hungry as I thought I was."

"We like trying the local cuisine," Don said.

"We'll see how long that lasts. Turkey, isn't that what the Yanks call a dead loss?" Lunt said loudly as a young man with large eyes the same deep brown as his skin opened the door of the pub. "You'll want a drink at least. Is it gin for the ladies? Two of them with tonic, and two pints of your best for the lads."

By the time the drinks were brought to the outside table Trixie had ascertained the name of the Hatchards' hotel. "What are you doing tomorrow?" she enquired, ice-cubes clicking against her display of teeth.

"Taking it easy by the pool," Maggie said at once.

"If you're after conversation, we're at the Turkish Paradise, ha ha. Or are you here on your own so you'll stay together?"

"Does it show?"

"When you've seen as many marriages fall apart as Gar and me have it does. We've found it helps for the hens to go off for a natter, and the same for the cocks if they're that way inclined."

"I expect Don and I will discuss it."

The Lunts had a good deal more to say, but nothing which Don thought he needed to be aware of. When he and Maggie had downed their drinks he felt justified in not offering to buy another round. They left the Lunts groaning and yawning and complaining at the non-appearance of the waiter, and when they were alone in the crowd Maggie said "Suddenly I like you better."

"In that case I'm glad we met them."

"Just let's make sure we never do again."

She took his hand as they arrived at the road beyond the funfair with which the market merged. Once they were across the dual carriageway, which was divided by cacti and interrupted by a roundabout where rights of way seemed chancy as roulette, she kept hold of his hand for long enough to convince him that things might be improving. They plodded up the slope of the pulverised pavement to their hotel, above which horses grazed within the frameworks of new buildings, the most nearly completed of which sprouted concrete weeds bristling with cables, the pillars of unbuilt walls. Don expected Maggie to head for the poolside bar, but she collected their key from Reception. "Coming up?"

"Try and stop me." As she let them into the small sparsely furnished room he added "Maybe all we need is time to get used to being just us again."

"Forever hopeful," she said, less encouragingly than he would have liked. Nevertheless she wriggled out of her swimsuit and lay on her bed and gazed at him, so that he undressed and pushed his bed against hers. He knelt between her legs and kissed her mottled breasts, and experienced a surge of affection for their wrinkles. Beyond foreplay, however, the situation was as frustrating as it had been all year: both he and Maggie had put on too much weight for him to be able to reach as deep into her as he used to. Before long he was aware only of their stomachs smacking together and the sweat pouring off him. "Never mind," Maggie said as, having fallen out of her a second time, he began to manipulate himself.

"I won't if you don't."

"It's something else we have to see if we can get used to. Come again?"

Don refrained from saying "I wish I could", but "And if we can't?" or "Such as what else?" seemed equally inadvisable. "So long as we're used to each other," he said.

After they'd taken turns to stand on the tiled bathroom floor to use the curtainless shower, they dozed on their united beds, their bodies touching carelessly, until a huge blurred recorded voice singing the praises of Allah wakened them. They ate in a restaurant where a boy in a fez turned a spit with one hand and clattered a bell to attract customers with the other. During the meal all the power failed for hundreds of yards, and in the moments before waiters lit candles on the tables the only light came from the sun drowning in the Aegean. "I wonder what we can do tomorrow to top this," Don said.

"Anything except what I told them we'd do," Maggie responded, more sharply than he thought was called for.

The muezzin roused them before dawn, and a morning chorus of nausea resounding through the pipes kept them awake. They were alone on the patio for breakfast of boiled eggs and goat's cheese. Don sensed she was holding him responsible for something, but if he asked what was wrong she would blame him for not knowing. Over his second apple tea he risked saying "So..."

"I fancy one of those boat trips out of the harbour."

Skewered chickens drooped on spits outside restaurants; a teenage youth with a hint of muscles was brushing a poster for a Schwarzenegger film in Turkish onto the mediaeval tower. Don dropped a coin on the plate in front of a young mother sitting cross-legged in the dust beside the tower, but when he said "No thank you" as a man with silk scarves draped over his arm commenced an approach, Maggie shot a frown at him.

Several medium-sized motorboats were swaying not quite in unison a few yards out from the pebbly beach. The boat Maggie chose because all the people queuing for it were Turkish was the last to leave. They'd waded through the shallows and were being helped under the awning onto the bench that surrounded the deck when a voice shouted "Hold the boat. You with the boat, wait for us."

"Don't look," Don muttered. "They'll see it's not their sort of day out."

He heard a concerted wallowing behind him, and then the boat lurched. "Here, here, don't go starting your engine till we've parked ourselves," Lunt yelled. "We've paid your feller, your partner, whatever the two of you are."

"Make room for two big ones," Trixie bellowed.

Don and Maggie sat still, hoping that the other passengers would close the gaps on either side of them, making space elsewhere on the bench. When the family beside Don backed away from him his mouth opened, and he found himself addressing Maggie, more loudly when she gave him an uncomprehending look. "Garababry splento," he persisted. "Parrawarra akkabroddle prothny binoth."

He was praying that the Lunts would take him for a foreigner, but his performance brought him a scowl from a Turk with a rectangular ebony moustache, who appeared to suspect Don of mocking his countrymen. That dismayed Don less than being joined by the Lunts. "Don't bother trying to learn that jabber," Lunt advised him. "They understand our lingo fast enough when they want to fleece us of our shekels."

Though the boat was already a hundred yards into the deeper water Don might have asked to disembark or even swum for the shore with Maggie, except that she had turned her back on him to watch the captain while he manoeuvred the boat out of the bay and spoke extensively in Turkish. "I speak English," he promised at last. "Name is Bekir."

"What's he on about now?" Trixie demanded, gazing straight at him.

"He's telling us his name," Don said.

"He'd be better off keeping quiet about it," Lunt declared. "Sounds a bit too much like bugger for my taste. I've never seen such a lot as these for pawing other men. You could get a few sly fingers up your arse round here if you ask me."

"'I'll bet you're thanking the saints we came, or by the look of it you'd have had no-one to talk to. Except each other, and we'll see you do that, won't we, Gar?"

So the Lunts did as the boat chugged fuming through the uneven sea, until Don felt that the sunlight, like their questions, was probing for him. He assumed Maggie shared the feeling, but she kept her hand away from him. Two protracted hours later, as an island rose into view, Trixie wanted to know if he and Maggie still made love. "Why on earth should you assume any different?" he blurted.

"We've heard that before, haven't we, Gar? A man who doesn't want to own up there's a problem. Some friendly advice, Mag—sometimes it takes more than one to solve it."

"Really."

Don told himself that she was inching away from the Lunts, not from him. He was almost relieved when Lunt set about haranguing the captain, who had substituted a cassette of Turkish music for the collection of American hits which had just ended.

"Can't we do without that heathen racket? Our friends won't like it any more than we do."

"Perhaps you wouldn't mind just speaking for yourself," Maggie said.

"Well, pardon us, I'm sure," Trixie said, and as loudly to the captain '"As long as it's a barbecue I hope we're getting good plain food. I don't want to end up using your excuse for a toilet, thank you very much."

"A waiter was saying it's too many cold drinks in the heat that upsets people's stomachs," Maggie said with a pointed glance at the latest bottle of beer in Trixie's fist. "He said you should hold it in your mouth before you swallow it."

"Gar said they were dirty buggers," Trixie squealed, wincing in delight, and nudged Don with a quivering elbow.

Several passengers dived off the boat as it glided into a cove, one of them catching the rope thrown by the captain and tying it to a ring embedded in the rocky beach. "Shall we?" Don suggested, first turning away from the Lunts, and had to swivel his gaze twice towards the water before Maggie deigned to understand.

The shock of his plunge was assuaged in seconds. He swam near the Turks, thinking their presence should keep the Lunts away, then realised that Maggie was staying at a distance from him too. He swam with his face in the gentle waves, hearing the constant undertone of pebbles grinding together on the seabed, and was almost in a trance when he felt her hand lay itself on his spine and trail between his legs as he moved. Was it the water that made it seem plumper than usual? As it wriggled like an octopus he turned over and came face to face with Trixie Lunt, whose hand floated up and bumped its knuckles against his flattened crotch. "What do you— Where's Maggie?" he spluttered.

Trixie wiped her grin with the back of her hand. "She's all right, she's with my big feller."

Don's question had been provoked to some extent by guilt, and that was one of the emotions which sent him floundering past the seaward side of the boat. Against the silent chatter of sunlight on the waves he saw Lunt standing waist-deep in the sea and shouting over Maggie as she heaved herself to her knees. "You keep your eyes for your own women," Lunt was shouting at the moustached Turk. "I know you. I've seen you hanging round the hotel."

As the man and his two friends stepped forward, kicking waves aside, the captain called to them in a tone which Don thought sounded altogether too encouraging. His stomach felt inextricably knotted by the time he grasped that the captain was summoning everyone to the barbecue. He stayed in the water with Maggie, wishing she would look at him, until the Lunts and all the Turks had been served, then he paddled ashore with her to collect bread and salad and half a chicken each. As soon as they were seated on a rock the Lunts came over. "Try not to look so nervous. If things turn ugly I'll deal with them," Lunt said. "I've handled a good few men in my time."

"He used to drill them in the army. You never saw such a knees-up."

For a while the Hatchards used their food as an excuse not to talk, and then Maggie dropped her greasy paper plate and shoved herself to her feet. "I'm going to lie down."

"See, you should have eaten where we told you," Trixie said.

"Nothing to do with it," Don retorted, and tore at the remains of Maggie's chicken with his teeth to demonstrate.

"You can have mine to chew if you're that starved."

"I've got all I want, thank you," Don said, and devoted himself to gnawing. On his way to the boat he complimented the captain loudly on the food, realising too late that his comment could be interpreted as a rebuke to Maggie as well as to the Lunts. "Let me be," she groaned when he tried to stroke her forehead, and stretched her body away from him along the bench.

She had to sit up when the rest of the passengers boarded. Don could tell she was determined not to be sick while the Lunts were watching, but it was an impossible resolve; she spent much of the last hour of the voyage with her head over the side of the boat. The Lunts took a great deal of persuading not to assist her to the hotel, but Don managed to do so alone, almost losing the way in the littered side streets Maggie insisted on keeping to. In their room she lowered herself onto her bed and looked as if she meant to wave the entire world away with one hand.

That was her for the next day as well. Don ate at the hotel and confined himself to the pool area, where waiters asked after Maggie and sketched sun-hats with their fingers above their heads. She had him bring her bottles of water, but whenever he asked if he could do anything else for her, he received at best a stare.

A cock-crow woke him next day to find her giving him the same look. "What's wrong?" he said through the night's accumulation in his mouth. "How are you feeling?"

"Can't you tell?"

"You sound better," he risked saying. "Shall we do something today?"

"What are you suggesting?"

"What would you like to do besides avoiding you know who?"

"You think that'll take care of it, do you?"

"Unless you've a better idea."

"My idea would have been not to let them take our photograph."

"We didn't know what they were like then."

"Precisely." After a pause she said even more accusingly "Didn't we?"

"Do you want me to tell them to have it developed here and, I don't know, leave it at Reception for us?"

"Oh yes, I'm sure they'd trust the locals with their film."

"We could say, we could say there was a film place another Yorkshire pudding fan had recommended to us."

"What good would that do? They'll still have our address."

"Not much we can do about that, unless you feel like asking for it back."

"It wasn't me who was so anxious to give it to them."

"I didn't notice you trying to stop me," he said, and was tempted to add that he hadn't noticed her trying to avoid Lunt in the sea. "You can't expect me to ask for it. It isn't done."

"It's been a while since I've expected much of you at all."

The dawn showed him her face slackening under the weight of their marriage, wrinkles multiplying as he watched. He must look the same to her. "If there's nothing we can do there's nothing we can do," she said and turned towards the wall.

What she meant was clear enough to him. It hung unspoken between them as they explored the market which had sprung up overnight in all the streets around the hotel. At Ephesus, where the marble of the ruins hurled back the sunlight, he thought of phoning the Lunts' hotel to discover how long they were staying. At Didyma the stumps of columns leading to the temple of the oracle towered over him as he considered venturing to the hotel instead of attempting to conquer the local phone system. At Pamukkale, where they swam in fizzing water which had drowned an ancient portico, he felt all Maggie's silences weighing him down, and vowed to present her with a plan at dinner.

He was sitting on the narrow concrete balcony outside their room that evening, and watching an old man lead his camel up the road which became a rubbly path, when he saw the Lunts marching towards the hotel. "Thank God for a civilised face," Gareth bellowed, and Trixie yelled "What have you done with her? Don't tell us she's still heaving."

"My wife's in the shower."

"Well, when she comes out," Trixie shouted despite having strode closer, "tell her you're both joining us for dinner."

"I'm afraid we've already booked a table at a Turkish place."

"So if you don't show up," Lunt roared, "they'll think it was the will of Allah. It's our last night. We thought you'd want to help us celebrate."

"I promised Maggie we'd go to her favourite restaurant," Don said, wondering how many lies that encompassed. "While you're here I don't suppose you've got our photograph."

"I haven't finished my roll yet. We didn't find much else worth taking."

"We told you we'd bring it to you at home."

Looking down on them emboldened Don. "No, don't do that. Just send it if you want us to have it."

Lunt fixed him with a stare Don could imagine him thrusting in the faces of new recruits. "If you think again we'll be drinking till the bus leaves for the airport. You know where we'll be."

Don watched them tramp away, swinging their arms, dwindling, gone for good. He felt able to indulge in some pity for them. Now he had plenty to tell Maggie, and he saved it until they were in the restaurant where the boy with the fez rang the bell—saved it until they'd ordered a second bottle of the special reserve, which cost all of five pounds. "Did you hear me talking when you were in the shower?" he asked as the waiter pulled the cork.

"If I had I'd have answered, wouldn't I?"

"Not to you, to guess who. Guess who's going home tonight so we won't need to spend next week watching for them."

"Did you ask?"

Don had raised his glass for hers to chime against, but when she didn't respond he half emptied it. "Ask?"

"For God's sake, Don. For our address."

"Of course I—would have if I'd needed to. I got him to promise they wouldn't come, just send the picture."

"'And you believed him."

"What's your reason not to trust him?"

"How much reason do you need? You can tell just by looking at them."

Don could have probed further, but his anger was growing more diffuse. "So what do you want me to make him do, tear it up in front of us?"

"I'm not making anyone do anything. It wasn't me who handed them our address on a plate in the first place."

The remainder of their conversation consisted of the scraping of utensils on china and the thumps of glasses on the table. They had another week together here, Don told himself as they trudged to the hotel, but he could see that wouldn't be enough. As Maggie pulled off her dress in the room he thought of making love to her, and knew that he would fail, not only because he was too drunk. "I'm going for a walk," he blurted.

"I notice you wait until I can't."

"What's stopping you?" he would have retorted, except that an argument now would solve even less than usual. He stalked out, holding his head erect as if to keep his rage steady, and down the randomly lamplit road to the side turning which led to the Turkish Paradise Hotel.

The coach to the airport wouldn't be making its rounds for hours. The forecourt surrounded on three sides by single-storey concrete blocks was empty even of the luggage of the departing guests. Don could hear the murmur of an open-air restaurant beyond the rooms. He went straight to the Reception window at the near end of the left-hand concrete block, and had to slap a bell to summon a large bald Turk from an inner office. "Are Mr and Mrs Lunt here?"

The man touched the dangling key to room 18 and shook his head. "Back later."

"Can I wait for them in the restaurant?"

"Round there," the man said, indicating the end of the right-hand block, and withdrew into the office.

It occurred to Don that the man was loath to spend any more time with a friend of the Lunts than was absolutely necessary. Don reached across the sill and, grasping the key and its brass persuader, lifted them off the hook. The bunch of his shadows fanned out and merged like the props in an obscure magic trick as he crossed to room 18, which was directly opposite Reception. He remembered looking down on Lunt, the wallet in the man's breast pocket leaving no room for a notebook. Before his sense of the impossibility of what he planned to do overtook him, he poked the key in the lock and turned it. Glancing back, he stepped in and closed the door behind him. "Attaboy," he muttered, "or maybe Ataturk." An object crouching at the level of his shins tripped him and sent him sprawling into the dark.

He landed face down on a bed whose crumpled sheets smelled thickly of perfume and felt sodden with sweat. He writhed upright and sat on the edge, rubbing his shins and brandishing the brass club of the key, until he could see around the dim room. It was empty except for two suitcases, one of which had tripped him. By stooping until his face was inches from them he ascertained that neither label identified which Lunt each case belonged to. He heaved his assailant onto the bed, jarring a protest out of the sketches of hangers in the doorless wardrobe, and fumbled for the zipper.

At first he thought the case was locked, the zipper was so stiff. Abruptly it tore along half the length of its track, opening the case as far as the handle. Shirts bulged out of the gap, releasing such a smell of lotion that he thought the Lunts had crept into the room behind him. He flexed his shoulders and dragged the zipper all the way. The canvas lid reared up, exposing Lunt's stale underwear. Don was rubbing his fingers on his shirt preparatory to rummaging when he saw the notebook peeking out of a nest of used socks. He fished it out between finger and thumb and hurried to the window.

The margins of the pages were a staircase of initial letters, and it took him mere seconds to locate H. That page and its reverse were full of names and addresses, but he only had time to observe that they didn't include his and Maggie's. Theirs was all by itself on the next page, which he ripped out at once. Doing so revealed that what he'd almost noticed about the names and addresses on the previous page was equally true of those on the I pages, and of as much of the book as he dared linger to examine. Virtually every address, including those listed only under first names, had been crossed out.

Shame at having torn out the page almost made him replace it, but he stuffed it into his pocket. He returned the book to its sweaty niche and struggled to zip the case shut, and had to reopen it so as to extract an escaping arm from the teeth. Hauling the case off the bed, he dumped it where it had lain in wait for him. The memory, and his growing need to urinate, revived his anger. He kicked open the bathroom door and, unzipping himself, aimed into the glimmering pedestal. "This'll teach you to keep whatever you didn't keep off my wife," he snarled.

It didn't work. He inched forward and stood wider-legged, but couldn't produce a drop. He smelled the Lunts in the dark and felt as though they'd seized him by his useless crotch. He packed himself away and waddled aching to the door. Sneaking into the deserted forecourt, he hurried bow-legged to Reception, where he craned over the sill and hooked the key into place with an expertness born of urgency. He limped out of the gate as if the pain in his bladder was a leash and swerved away from the main road. Once he was beyond the glow of the forecourt he bowed over a lump of rubble shaped like an ancient helmet and let himself out, but the pressure in his bladder was its own defeat. He clenched his eyelids and gritted his teeth, and at last was rewarded by a jet so fierce it splashed his ankles. He was luxuriating in the sensation of release when he heard footsteps closing in on him.

If the Lunts had returned, they couldn't touch him. Surely they wouldn't recognise his back view in the gloom. The footsteps continued to approach, and he had to look, still spouting. Behind him were the moustached Turk and his two friends from the boat.

Don felt his buttocks squeezing together, his mouth opening helplessly. He was about to burst into the gibberish he'd spoken on the boat. He'd lost his balance, and as his shoulder bruised itself against the forecourt wall his penis and its jet swung towards them. "Yes, look at it," he heard himself yelling in a parade-ground voice. "Hardly worth having, is it? Might as well be a woman. Tom Thumb, she used to call it when she wanted it, and that was a long time ago."

He felt sick, tingling with nervousness, and hadn't the least idea what he might do next. He could see only the watching faces and eyes, darkened further by the shadow of the wall. He felt his penis trying to shrink as it worked. Then the three brayed wordlessly in contempt and strolled into the forecourt. Don leaned his forehead against the wall and vomited, and remembered Lunt wielding his ballpoint in the notebook like a weapon. He should have torn out the next page too in case it retained an impression of his and Maggie's address.

"Don Hatchard?"

"Who wants him?"

"The name's Lunt. We met this year in Turkey. I've got something for him and his wife."

"You'll need the new address. Are you ready?"

"Fire away." A sound of scribbling fierce enough to be audible over the phone responded to the details. "That's close enough to drive to," Lunt declared.

"'I'm glad to hear that. Is it something Mrs Hatchard asked for?"

"Now you mention it, I wouldn't be surprised."

Don broke the connection. "It'll be something for her to remember me by," he said in a voice that sounded very much like Lunt's, and as grim.

# The Word

NOBODY TRIES TO SPEAK TO ME WHILE I'M WAITING for the lift, thank Sod. Whenever you want to go upstairs at a science fiction convention the lift is always on the top floor, and by the time it arrives it'll have attracted people like a dog-turd attracts flies. There'll be a woman whose middle is twice as wide as the rest of her, and someone wearing no sleeves or deodorant, and at least one writer gasping to be noticed, and now there's a vacuumhead using a walkie-talkie to send messages to another weekend deputy who's within shouting distance. Here comes a clump wearing convention badges with names made up out of their own little heads, N. Trails and Elfan and Si Fye, and I amuse myself trying to decide which of them I'd least like to hear from. Here's the lift at last, and I shut the doors before some bald woman with dragons tattooed on her scalp can get in as well, but a thin boy in a suit and tie manages to sidle through the gap. He sees my Retard T-shirt, then he reads my badge. "Hi there," he says. "I'm—"

"Jess Kray," I tell him, since he seems to think I can't read, "and you sent me the worst story I ever read in my life."

The

He sucks in his lips as if I've punched him in the mouth. "Which one was that?"

"How many have you written that are that bad?"

"None that I know of."

Everyone's pretending not to watch his face doing its best not to wince. "You sent me the one about Frankenstein and the dead goat and the two nuns," I say for everyone to hear.

"I've written lots since."

"Just don't send any to *Retard*."

My fanzine isn't called that now, but I'm not telling him. I leave him to ride to the top with our audience while I lock myself in my room. I was going to write about the Sex, Sects and Subtexts in Women's Horror Fiction panel, which showed me why I've never been able to read a book by the half of the participants I'd heard of, but now I've too much of a headache. I lie on the bed for as long as I can stand being by myself, then I look for someone I can bear to dine with.

We're at Contraception in Edinburgh, but it could be anywhere a mob of fans calling themselves fen take over a hotel for the weekend. As I step into the lobby I nearly bump into Hugh, a writer who used to have tons of books in the shops, maybe because nobody was buying them. Soon books will all be games you play on screens, but I'll bet nobody will play with his. "How are you this year, Jeremy?" he booms.

"Dying like everyone else."

He emits a sound as if he's trying not to react to being poked in the ribs, and the rest of his party comes out of the bar. One of them is Jess Kray, who says "Join us, Jeremy, if you're free for dinner."

He's behaving like the most important person there, grinning with teeth that say we're real and a mouth that says you can check if you like and eyes with a message just for me. I'd turn him down to see how that makes him look, except Hugh Zit says "Do by all means" so his party knows he means the opposite, and it's too much fun to refuse.

Hugh Know's idea of where to eat is a place called Godfathers. I sit next to his Pakistani wife and her friend who isn't even a convention member, and ignore them so they stop talking English. I've already heard Hugh Ever say on panels all the garbage he's recycling, about how it's a writer's duty to offer a new view of the world, as if he ever did, and how the most important part of writing is research. He still talks like the fan he used to be, like all the fen I know talk, either lecturing straight in your face or staring over your shoulder as though there's a mirror behind you. Only Kray couldn't look more impressed. Hugh Cares finishes his pizza at last and says "I feel better for that."

I say "You must have felt bloody awful before."

Kray actually laughs at that while grimacing sympathetically at Hugh, and I can't wait to go back to my room and write a piece about the games he's playing. I write until I can't see for my headache, and after I've managed to sleep I write about the rest of the clowns at Contraception, until I've almost filled up the first issue of *Parade of the Maladjusted and Malformed*, which is what conventions are. On the last day I see Kray buying a publisher's editor a drink, which no doubt means he'll sell at least a trilogy. At least that's what I write once I'm home.

Then it's back to wearing a suit at the bank in Fulham and having people line up for me on the far side of a window, which at least keeps them at a distance while I turn them and their lives into numbers on a screen. But there's the smell of the people on my side of the glass, and sometimes the feel of them if I don't move fast enough. Playing the game of never saying what I think just about sees me through the day, and the one after that, and the one after that. I print my fanzine in my room and mail it and wait for the clowns I've written about to threaten to sue me or beat me up. The year isn't over when among the review copies and the rest of the unnecessaries publishers send to fanzines I get a sheet about Jess Kray, the most exciting new young writer of the decade, whose first three novels are going to give a new meaning to fantasy.

Sod knows I thought I was joking. I ask for copies to see how bad they are, and they're worse. They're about an alternate world where everyone becomes their sexual opposite, so a gay boy turns into a barbarian hero and a dyke becomes his lover, and some of the characters remember when they return to the real world and most of them try to remind the rest, except one thinks it's meant to be forgotten, and piles of similar crap. I just skim a few chapters of the first book to get a laugh at the idea of people buying a book called *A Touch of Other* under the impression that it's a different kind of junk. Apparently the books go on to be about some wimp who teaches himself magic in the other world and gets to be leader of this one. It's nine months since I saw Kray talking to the editor, so either he writes even more glibly than he comes on to people or he'd already written them. One cover shows a woman's face turning into a man's, and the second has a white turning black, and the third's got a tinfoil mirror where a face should be. That's the one I throw hardest across the room. Later I put them in the pile to sell to Everybody's Fantasy, the skiffy and comics shop near the docks, and then I hear Kray will be there signing books.

How does a writer nobody's heard of put that over on even a shop run by fen? I'm beginning to think it's time someone exposed him. That Saturday I take the books with me, leaving the compliments slips in so he'll see I haven't bought them. Maybe I'll let him see me selling them as soon as he's signed them. But the moment I spot him at the table with his three piles on it he jumps up. "Jeremy, how are you! This is Jeremy Bates, everyone. He was my first critic."

Sod knows who he's trying to impress. The only customers are comics readers, that contradiction in terms, who look as if they're out without their mothers to buy them their funnies. And the proprietor, who I call Kath on account of his kaftan and long hair, doesn't seem to think much of Kray trying to hitch a ride on my reputation, not that he ever seems to think of much except where the next joint's coming from. I give Kray the books with the slips sticking up, but he carries on grinning. "My publishers haven't sent me your review yet, Jeremy."

I should tell him that's because I won't be writing one, but I'm mumbling like a fan, for Sod's sake. "Write something in them for me."

In the first book he writes For Jeremy who knew me

*before I was good*, and *To our future* in the second, and *For life* in what I hope's the last. When he hands them back like treasure I stuff them in my armpit and leaf through some tatty fanzines so I can see how many people he attracts.

Zero. Mr Nobody and all his family. A big round hole without a rim. Some boys on mountain bikes point at him through the window until Kath chases them, and once a woman goes to Kray, but only to ask him where the Star Trek section is. Kath's wife brings him a glass of herbal tea, which isn't even steaming, and with the bag drowning in it, and it's fun to watch him having to drink that. We all hang around for the second half of the hour, then Kath says in the drone that always sounds as if he's talking in his sleep "Maybe you can sign some stock for us."

I can hear he doesn't mean all the books on the table, but that doesn't stop our author. When Kray's defaced every one he says "How about that lunch?"

Kath and Mrs Kath glance at each other, and Jess Kidding gives them an instant grin each. "I understand. Don't even think of it. You can buy lunch next time, after I've made you a bundle. Let me buy this one."

They shake their heads, and I see them thinking there'll never be a next time, but Jess Perfect flashes them an even more embracing grin before he turns to me. "If you want to interview me, Jeremy, I'll stand lunch. You can be the one who tells the world."

"About what?"

"That'd be telling."

I want the next *PotMaM* to spill a lot more blood and besides, nobody's ever bought me lunch. I take him round the corner to Le Marin Qui Rit, which some French chef with too much money built in an old warehouse by the Thames. "This is charming," Kray says when he sees the nets full of crabs hanging from the beams and the waiters in their sailor suits, though I bet he doesn't think so when he sees the prices on the menu. As soon as we've ordered he hurries through the door that says Matelots, maybe to be sick over the prices, and I rip through his books until he comes back with his grin and says "Ask me anything." But I've barely opened my mouth when he says "Aren't you recording?"

"Didn't know I'd need to. Don't worry, I remember everything. My ex could tell you."

He digs a pocket tape-recorder out of his trench coat. "Just in case you need to check. I always carry one for my thoughts."

He heard an ex-success say that at Contraception. A sailor brings us a bottle of sheep juice, Mutton Cadet, and I switch on. "What's a name like Kray supposed to mean to the world?"

"It's my father's name," he says, then proves I was right to be suspicious, because it turns out his father was a Jewish Pole who was put in a camp and left the rest of his surname behind when he emigrated with the remains of his family after the war.

"Speaking of prejudice, what's with the black guy calling himself Nigger when he gets to be the hero?"

"A nigger is someone who minds being called one. Either you take hold of words or they take hold of you."

"Which do you think your books do?"

"A bit of both. I'm learning. I want to be an adventurer on behalf of the imagination."

I can hardly wait to write about him, except here's my poached salmon. He waits until I've taken a mouthful and says "What did you like about the books?"

I'm shocked to realise how much of them has stuck in my mind—lines like "AIDS is such a hell you'll go straight to heaven." I want to say "Nothing," but his grin has got to me. "Where you say that being born male is the new original sin."

"Well, that's what one of my characters says."

What does he mean by that? His words keep slipping away from me, and I've no idea where they're going. By the time we finish I'm near to nodding in my pudding, his refusal to be offended by anything I say has taken so much out of me. The best I can come up with as a final question is "Where do you think you're going?"

"To Florida for the summer with my family. That's where the ideas are."

"Here's hoping you get some."

He doesn't switch off the recorder until we've had our coffee, then he gives me the tape. "Thanks for helping," he says, and insists on shaking hands with me. It feels like some kind of Masonic trick, trying to find out if I know a secret—either that or he's working out the best way to shake hands. He pays the bill without letting his face down and says he's heading for the station, which is on my way home, but I don't tell him. I turn my back on him and take the long way through the streets I always like, with no gardens and no gaps between the houses and less sunlight than anywhere else in town. While I'm there I don't need to think, and I feel as if nothing can happen in me or outside me. Only I have to go home to deal with the tape, which is itching in my hip pocket like a tapeworm.

I'm hoping he'll have left some thoughts on it by mistake, but there's just our drivelling. So either he brought the machine to make sure I could record him or more likely wanted to keep a copy of what we said. Even if he didn't trust me, it's a struggle to write about him in the way I want to. It takes me days and some of my worst headaches. I feel as if he's stolen my energy and turned it into a force that only works on his behalf.

When I seem to have written enough for an issue of *PotMaM* I print out the pages. I have to pick my way around them or tread on them whenever I get up in the night to be sick. I send out the issue to my five subscribers and anyone who sent me their fanzine, though not many do after what I write about their dreck. I take copies to Constipation and Convulsion and sell a few to people who haven't been to a convention before and don't like to say no. When I start screaming at the fanzine in the night and kicking the piles over I pay for a table in the dealers' room at Contamination. But on the Saturday night the dealers' room is broken into, and in the morning every single copy's gone.

It isn't one of my better years. My father dies and my mother tells me my ex-wife went to the funeral. The branch of the bank closes down because of the recession, and it looks as if I'll be out of a job, only luckily one of the other clerks gets his back broken in a hit and run. They move me to Chelsea, where half the lunchtime crowd looks like plain-clothes something and all the litter bins are sealed up so nobody can leave bombs in them. At least the police won't let marchers into the district, though you can hear them shouting for employment or life sentences for pornography or Islamic blasphemy laws or a curfew for all males as soon as they reach puberty or all tobacco and alcohol profits to go to drug rehabilitation or churchgoing to be made compulsory by law… Some writers stop their publisher from sending me review copies, so at least I've bothered them. I give up going to conventions for almost a year, until I forget how boring they are, so that staying in my room seems even worse. And at Easter I set out to find myself a ride to Consternation in Manchester.

I wait most of an hour at the start of the motorway and see a car pick up two girls who haven't waited half as long, so I'm in no mood for any crap from the driver who finally pulls over. He asks what I'm doing for Easter and I think he's some kind of religious creep, but when I tell him about Consternation he starts assuring me how he used to enjoy H. G. Wells and Jules Verne, as if I gave a fart. Then he says "What would you call this new johnny who wrote *The Word*? Is he sci-fi or fantasy or what?"

"I don't know about any word."

"I thought he might be one of you chaps. Went to a publisher and told him his ideas for the book and came away with a contract for more than I expect to make in a lifetime."

"How come you know so much about it?"

"Well, I am a bookseller. Those on high want us to know in advance this isn't your average first novel. Let me cudgel the old brains and I'll give you his name."

I'm about to tell him not to bother when he grins. "Don't know how I could forget a name like that, except it puts you in mind of the Kray brothers, if you're not too young to remember their reign of terror. The last thing he sounds like is a criminal. Jess Kray, that's the phenomenon."

I'd say I knew him if I could be sure of convincing this caricature that he isn't worth knowing. I bite my tongue until it feels as if my teeth are meeting, then I realise the driver has noticed the tears that have got away from me, and I could scream.

He says no more until he stops to let me out of the car. "You ought to tell your people about this Kray. Sounds as if he has some ideas that bear thinking about."

The last thing I'll do is tell anyone about Kray, particularly when I remember him saying I should. I wait in my hotel room for my headache to let me see, then I go down to the dealers' room. Instead of books a lot of the tables are selling virtual reality viewers or pocket CD-ROM players. I can't find anything by Kray, and some of the dealers watch me as if I'm planning to steal from them, which makes me feel like throwing their tables over. Then the fat one who always wears a sombrero says "Can I do something for you?"

"Not by the look of it." That doesn't make him go away, and all I can think of is to confuse him. "You haven't got *The Word*."

"No, but Jess sent us each a copy of the cover," he says, and props up a piece of cardboard with letters in the middle of its right-hand side:

**JESS KRAY**
**THE WORD**

I can't tell if they're white on a black background or black on white, because as soon as I move an inch they turn into the opposite. I shut my eyes once I've seen it's going to be published by the dump that stopped sending me review copies. "What do you mean, he sent you it? He's just a writer."

"And he designed the cover, and he wants everyone to know what's coming, so he got the publisher to print enough cover proofs for us all in the business."

I'm not asking what Kray said about his book. When Fat in the Hat says "You can't keep your eyes shut forever" I want to shut his, especially when as soon as I open mine he says "Shall we put you down for a copy when it's published?"

"They'll send me one."

"I doubt it," he says, and he'll never know how close he came to losing the bone in his nose, except I have to take my head back to my room.

Maybe he wasn't just getting at me. Once I'm home I ring Kray's new publisher for a review copy. I call myself Jay Battis, the first name that comes into my head, and say I'm the editor of *Psychofant* and no friend of that total cynic Jeremy Bates. But the publicity girl says Kray's book isn't genre fiction, it's literature and they aren't sending it to fanzines.

So why should I care? Except I won't have her treating me as though I'm not good enough for Kray after I gave him more publicity than he deserved when he needed it most. And I remember him thanking me for helping—did he mean with this book? I ask the publicity bitch for his address, but she expects me to believe they don't know it. I could ask her who his agent is, but I've realised how I'd most like to get my free copy of his world-shaking masterpiece.

I don't go to Kath's shop, because I'd be noticed. On the day the book is supposed to come out I go to the biggest bookshop in Chelsea. There's a police car in front, and the police are making them move out of the window a placard that's a big version of the cover of *The Word*—I hear the police say it has been distracting drivers. I walk to a table with a pile of *The Word* on it and straight out with one in my hand, because the staff are busy with the police. Only I feel as if Kray's forgiving me for liberating his book, and it takes all my strength not to throw it away.

Even when I've locked my apartment door I feel watched. I hide the book under the bed while I fry some spaghetti and open a tin of salmon for dinner. Then I sit at the window and watch the police cars hunting and listen to the shouts and screams until it's dark. When I begin to feel as if the headlights are searching for me I close the curtains, but then I can't think of anything to do except read the book.

Only the first few pages. Just the prospect of more than a thousand of them puts me off. I can't stand books where the dialogue isn't in quotes and paragraphs keep beginning with "And". And I'm getting the impression that the words are slipping into my head before I can grasp them. Reading the book makes me feel I'm hiding in my room, shutting myself off from the world. I stuff *The Word* down the side of the bed where I can't see the cover playing its tricks, and switch on the radio.

Kray's still in my head. I'm hoping that since it's publication day I'll hear someone tearing him to bits. There isn't a programme about books any longer on the radio, just one about what they call the arts. They're reviewing an Eskimo rock band and an exhibition of sculptures made out of used condoms and a production of *Jesus Christ Superstar* where all the performers are women in wheelchairs, and I'm sneering at myself for imagining they would think Kray was worth their time and at the world for being generally idiotic when the presenter says "And now a young writer whose first novel has been described as a new kind of book. Jess Kray, what's the purpose behind *The Word*?"

"Well, I think it's in it rather than behind it if you look. And I'd say it may be the oldest kind of book, the one that's been forgotten."

At first I don't believe it's him, because he has no accent at all. I make my head throb trying to remember what accent he used to have, and when I give up the presenter is saying "Is the narrator meant to be God?"

"I think the narrator has to be different for everyone, like God."

"You seem to want to be mysterious."

"Don't you think mystery has always been the point? That isn't the same as trying to hide. We've all read books where the writer tries to hide behind the writing, though of course it can't be done, because hiding reveals what you thought you were hiding…"

"Can you quote an example?"

"I'd rather say that every book you've ever read has been a refuge, and I don't want mine to be."

"Every book? Even the Bible? The Koran?"

"They're attempts to say everything regardless of how much they contradict themselves, and I think they make a fundamental error. Maybe Shakespeare saw the problem, but he couldn't quite solve it. Now it's my turn."

I'm willing the presenter to lose her temper, and she says "So to sum up, you're trying to top Shakespeare and the Bible and the rest of the great books."

"My book is using up a lot of paper. I think that if you can't put more into the world than you take out of it you shouldn't be here at all."

"As you say somewhere in *The Word*. Jess Kray, thank you."

Then she starts talking to a cretic—which is a cretin who thinks they're a critic, such as everyone who attacks my fanzines—about Kray and his book. When the cretic says she thinks the narrator might be Christ because of a scene where he sees the light beyond the mountain through the holes in his hands I start shouting at the radio for quite a time before I turn it off. I crawl into bed and can't stop feeling there's a light beside me to be seen if I open my eyes. I keep them closed all night and wake up with the impression that some of Kray's book is buried deep in my head.

For the first time since I can remember I'm looking forward to a day at the bank. I may even be able to stand the people on my side of the glass without grinding my teeth. But that afternoon Mag, one of the middle-aged girls, waddles in with an evening paper and nearly slaps me in the face with it as though it's my fault. "Will you look at this. Where will it stop. I don't know what the world is coming to."

**CALL FOR BAN ON "BLASPHEMOUS" BOOK.** I don't want to read any more, yet I grab the paper. It says that on the radio programme I heard, Kray said his book was better than the Bible and people should read it instead. A bishop is calling for the police to prosecute, and some mob named Christ Will Rise is telling Christians to destroy *The Word* wherever they find it. So I can't help walking past the shop my copy came from, even though it isn't on my way home. And on the third day half a dozen Earnests with placards saying **CHRIST NOT KRAY** are picketing the shop.

The police apparently don't think they're worth more than cruising past, and I hope they'll get discouraged, because they're giving Kray publicity. But the next day there are eight of them, and twelve the day after, and at the weekend several Kray fans start reading *The Word* to the pickets to show them how they're wrong. And I feel as though I've had no time to breathe before there's hardly a shop in the country without clowns outside it reading *The Word* and the Bible or the Koran at one another. And then Kray starts touring all the shops and talking to the pickets.

I keep switching on the news to check if he's been scoffed into oblivion, but no such luck. All the time in my room I'm aware of his book in there with me. I'd throw it away except someone might end up reading it—I'd tear it up and burn it except then I'd be like the Christ Will Risers. The day everyone at the bank is talking about Kray being in town during my lunch hour I scrape my brains for something else to do, anything rather than be one of the mob. Only suppose this is the one that stops him? That's a spectacle I'd enjoy watching, so off I limp.

There must be at least a hundred people outside the bookshop. Someone's given Kray a chair to stand on, but Sod knows who's arranged for a beam of sunlight to shine on him. He's answering a question, saying "If you heard the repeats of my interview you'll know I didn't say my book was better than the Bible. I'm not sure what better means in that context. I hope my book contains all the great books."

And he grins, and I wait for someone to attack him, but nobody does, not even verbally. I feel my voice forcing its way out of my mouth, and all I can think of is the question vacuumheads ask writers at conventions. "Where did you get your ideas?"

So many people stare at me I think I've asked the question he didn't want asked. I feel as if he's using more eyes than a spider to watch me, more than a whole nest of spiders—more than there are people holding copies of his drivel. Kray himself is only looking in my general direction, trying to make me think he hasn't recognised me or I'm not worth recognising. "They're in my book."

I want to ask why he's pretending not to know me, except I can't be sure it'll sound like an accusation, and the alternative makes me cringe with loathing. But I'm not having any of his glib answers, and I shout "Who are?"

The nearest Kray fan stops filming him with a steadycam video and turns on me. "His ideas, he means. You're supposed to be talking about his ideas."

I won't be told what I'm supposed to be saying, especially not by a never-was who can't comb her hair or keep her lips still, and I wonder if she's trying to stop me asking the question I hadn't realised I was stumbling on. "Who did you meet in Florida?" I shout.

Kray looks straight at me, and it's as if his grin is carving up my head. "Some old people with some old ideas that were about to be lost. They're in my book. Everyone is in any book that matters."

Maybe he sees me sucking in my breath to ask about the three books he wants us to forget he wrote, because he goes on. "As I was about to say, all I'm asking is that we should respect one another. Do me the honour of not criticising *The Word* until you've read it. If anyone feels harmed by it, I want to know."

I might have vanished or never been there at all. When he pauses for a response I feel as if his grin has got stuck in my mouth. The mob murmurs, but nobody seems to want to speak up. Any protest is being swallowed by vagueness. Then two minders appear from the crowd and escort Kray to a limo that's crept up behind me. I want to reach out to him and— I don't know what I want, and one of the minders pushes me out of the way. I see Kray's back, then the limo is speeding away and all the mob are talking to one another, and I have to take the afternoon off because I can't see the money at the bank.

Whenever the ache falters my head fills up with thoughts of Kray and his book. When I sense his book by me in the dark I can't help wishing on it—wishing him and it to a hell as everlasting as my headache feels. It's the first time I've wanted to believe in hell. Not that I'm so far gone I believe wishes work, but I feel better when the radio says his plan's gone wrong. Some Muslim leaders are accusing him of seducing their herd away from Islam.

I keep looking in the papers and listening in the night in case an ayatollah has put a price on his head. Some bookshops in cities that are overrun with Muslims are either hiding their copies of *The Word* or sending them back, and I wish on it that the panic will spread. But the next headline says he'll meet the Muslim leaders in public and discuss *The Word* with them.

A late-night so-called arts programme is to broadcast the discussion live. I don't watch it, because I don't know anyone who would let me watch their television, but when it's on I switch out my light and sit at my window. More and more of the windows out there start to flicker as if the city is riddled with people watching to see what will happen to Kray. I open my window and listen for shouting Muslims and maybe Kray screaming, but I've never heard so much quiet. When it starts letting my head fill up with thoughts I don't want to have, I go to bed and dream of Kray on a cross. But in the morning everyone at the bank is talking about how the Muslims ended up on Kray's side and how one of them from a university is going to translate *The Word* into whatever language Muslims use.

And everyone, even Mag who didn't know what the world was coming to with Kray, is saying how they admire him or how they've fallen in love with him and the way he handled himself, and wish they'd gone to see him when he was in town. When I say I've got *The Word* and can't read it they all look as though they pity me. Three of them ask to borrow it, and I tell them to buy their own because I never paid for mine, which at least means nobody speaks to me much after that. I can still hear them talking about Kray and feel them thinking about him, and in the lunch hour two of them buy *The Word* and the rest, even the manager, want a read. I'm surrounded by Kray, choked by a mass of him. I'm beginning to wonder if anyone in the world besides me knows what he's really like. The bank shuts at last, and when I leave the building two Christ Will Risers are waiting for me.

Both of them wear suits like civil servants and look as though they spend half their lives scrubbing their faces and polishing the crosses at their throats. They both step forward as the sunlight grabs me, and the girl says "You knew him."

"Me, no, who? Knew who?"

Her boyfriend or whatever touches my arm likes a secret sign. "We saw you making him confess who he'd met."

"Let's sit down and talk," says the girl.

Every time they move, their crosses flash until my eyes feel like a whole graveyard of burnt crosses. At least the couple haven't swallowed *The Word*, and talking to them may be better than staying in my room. We find a bench that isn't full of unemployed and clear the McDonald's cartons off it, and the Risers sit on either side of me even though I've sat almost at the end of the bench. "Was he a friend of yours?" the girl says.

"Seems like he wants to be everyone's friend," I say.

"Not God's."

It doesn't matter which of them said that, it could have come from either. "So how much do you know about what happened in Florida?"

"As much as he said when I asked him."

"You must be honest with us. We can't do anything about him if we don't put our faith in the truth."

"Why not?"

That throws them, because they're obviously not used to thinking. Then they say "We need to know everything we can find out about him."

"Who's we?"

"We think you could be one of us. You're of like mind, we can tell."

That's one thing I'll never be with anyone. I nearly jump up and lean on their shining shampooed heads so they won't follow me, but I want to know what they know about Kray that I don't. "Then that must be why I asked him about Florida. All I know is that last time I met him he was going there and he wrote *The Word* when he came back. So what happened?"

They look at each other across me and then swivel their eyes to me. "There are people who came down a mountain almost a hundred years ago. We know he met them or someone connected with them. That has to be the source of his power. Nothing else could have let him win over Islam."

I wouldn't have believed anyone could talk less sense than Kray. "He was like that when he was just a fantasy fan. He's got a genius for charming everyone he meets and promoting himself."

"That must be how he learned the secret that came down the mountain. What else can you tell us?"

I don't mind making them more suspicious of Kray, but I won't have them thinking I tried to help them. "Nothing," I say, and get up.

They both reach inside their jackets for pamphlets. "Please

take these. Our address is on the back whenever you want to get in touch."

I could tell them that's never and stuff their pamphlets in their faces, but at least while I've the pamphlets in my fist nobody can take me for a Jess Kray fan. At home I glance at them to see they're as stupid as I knew they would be, full of drone out of the Bible about the Apocalypse and the Antichrist and the Antifreeze and Sod knows what else. I shove them down the side of the bed and try to believe that I've helped the Risers get Kray. And I keep hoping until I see *Time* magazine with him on the cover.

By then half the bank has read *The Word*. I've seen them laughing or crying or going very still when they read it in their breaks, and when they finish it they look as if they have a secret they wish they could tell everyone else. I won't ask, I nearly chew my tongue off. Anyone who asks them about the book gets told "Read it" or "You have to find out for yourself", and I wonder if the book tells you to make as many people read it as you can, like they used to tell you on posters not to give away the end of films. I won't touch my copy of *The Word*, but one day I sneak into a bookshop to read the last page. Obviously it makes no sense, only I feel that if I read the page before it I'll begin to understand, because maybe it can be read backwards as well as forwards. I throw the book on the table and run out of the shop.

At least they've taken *The Word* out of the window to make room for another pound of fat in a jacket, but I keep seeing people reading it in the streets. Whenever I see anything flash in a crowd I'm afraid it's another copy drawing attention to itself. At home I feel it beginning to surround me in the night out there, and I tell myself I've one copy nobody is reading. But I have to take train rides into the country for walks to get away from it—they're the only way I can be certain I'm nowhere near anyone who's read it. And coming back from one of those rides, I see him watching me from the station bookstall.

He looks like a recruiting poster for himself that doesn't need to point a finger. While I'm pretending to flip through the magazine I knock all the copies of *Time* onto the floor of the booking hall, except for the one I shove down the front of my trousers. All the way home I feel my peter wiping itself on his mouth, and in my room I have a good laugh at my stain on his face before I turn to the pages about him.

The headline says **WHAT IS THE WORD**? in the same typeface as the cover of his book. Maybe the article will tell me what I need to put him out of my mind for good. But it says how he bought his parents a place in Florida with part of his advances, and how *The Word* is already being translated into thirteen languages, and I'm starting to puke. Then the hack tries to explain what makes *The Word* such a publishing phenomenon, as she calls it. And by the time I've finished nearly going blind with reading what she wrote I think it's another of Kray's tricks.

It says too much and nothing at all. She doesn't know if the word is the book or the narrator or the words that keep looking as if they've been put in by mistake. Kray told her that if a book wasn't language it was nothing. "So perhaps we should take him at his, you should forgive it, word." He said he just put the words on paper and it's for each reader to decide what they add up to. So she collected a gaggle of cretics and fakes who profess and that old joke "leading writers" and got them to discuss *The Word.*

If I'd been there I'd have mashed all their faces together. It was the funniest book someone had ever read, and the most moving someone else had, and everyone agreed with both of them. One woman thought it was like *The Canterbury Tales*, and then there's a discussion about whether it's told by one character or several or whether all the characters might be the same one in some sort of mental state or it's showing a new kind of relationship between them all. A professor points out that the Bible was written by a crowd of people but when you read it in translation you can't tell, whereas she thinks you can identify to the word where Kray's voices change, "as many voices as there are people who understand the book". That starts them talking about the idea in *The Word* that people in Biblical times lived longer because they were closer in time to the source, as if that explains why some people are living longer now and the rest of what's happening to us, the universe drifting closer to the state it was in before it formed. And there's crap about people sinning more so their sins will reach back to the Crucifixion because otherwise Christ won't come back, or maybe the book says people have to know when to stop before they have the opposite effect and throw everything off balance, only by now I'm having to run my finger under the words and read them out loud, though my voice makes my head worse. There are still columns to go, the experts saying how if you read *The Word* aloud it's poetry and how you'll find passages almost turning into music, and how there are developments of ideas from Sufism and the Upanishads and Buddhism and Baha'i and the Cabbala and Gnosticism, and Greek and Roman and older myths, and I scrape my fingernail over all this until I reach the end, someone saying "I think the core of this book may be the necessary myth for our time." And everyone agrees, and I tear up the magazine and try to sleep.

I can still hear them all jabbering as if Kray is using their voices to make people read his book to discover what they were raving about. I hear them in the morning on my way to the bank, and I wonder how many of them his publisher will quote on the paperback, and that's when I realise I'm dreading the paperback because so many more people will be able to afford it. I'm dreading being surrounded by people with Kray in their heads, because then the world will feel even more like somewhere I've wandered into by mistake. It almost makes me laugh to find I didn't want to be shown that people are as stupid as I've always thought they were.

When posters for the paperback start appearing on bus shelters and hoardings I have to walk about with my eyes half shut. The posters don't use the trick the cover did, but that must mean the publishers think that just the title and his name will sell the book. At the bank I keep being asked if I don't feel well, until I say I'm not getting my Sunday dinner any more since my mother had a heart attack and died in hospital, not that it's anyone's business, but as well as that I can hardly eat for waiting for the paperback.

The day I catch sight of one there's a march of lunatics demanding that the hospitals they've been thrown out of get reopened, and in the middle of all this a woman's sitting on a bench reading *The Word* as though she can't see or hear what's going on around her for the book. And then the man she's waiting for sits down by her and squashes his wet mouth on her cheek, and leans over to see what she's reading, and I see him start to read as if it doesn't matter where you open the book, you'll be drawn in. And when I run to the bank one of the girls asks me if I know when the paperback is coming out, and saying I don't know makes me feel I'm trying to stop something that can't be stopped.

Or am I the only one who can? I spend the day trying to remember where I put the interview with him. Despite whoever stole all the copies of *PotMaM* at Contamination, I should still have the tape. I look under my clothes and the plates and the tins and in the tins as well, and under the pages of the magazine I tore up, and under the towels on the floor in the corner, and among the bits of glasses I've smashed in the sink. It isn't anywhere. My mother must have thrown it out one of the days she came to clean my room. I start screaming at her until I lose my voice, by which time I've thrown just about everything movable out of the window. They're demolishing the houses opposite, so some more rubbish in the street won't make any difference, and my fellow rats in the building must be too scared to ask what I'm doing, unless they're too busy reading *The Word.*

By the end of the week, two of the slaves at the bank have the paperback and will lend it to anyone who asks. And I don't know when they start surrounding me with Kray's words. Most of the time—Sod, all the time—I know they're saying things they've heard someone else say, but after a while I notice they've begun speaking in a way that's meant to show they're quoting. Like the girl at the window by mine would start talking about a murder mystery on television and the one next to her would say "The mystery is around you and in you" and they'd laugh as if they were sharing a secret. Or one would ask the time and her partner in the comedy team would say "Time is as soon as you make it." And all sorts of other crap: "Look behind the world" or "You're the shadow of the infinite," which the manager says once as if he's topping everyone else's quotes. And before I know it at least half the slaves don't say "Good morning" any more, they say "What's the word?"

That makes the world feel like a headache. People say it in the street too, and when they come up to my window, until I wonder if I was wrong to blame my mother for losing the tape, if someone else might have got into my room. By the time the next catch-phrase takes root in the dirt in people's heads I can't control myself—when I hear one of the girls respond to another "As Kray would say."

"Is there anything he doesn't have something to say about?"

I think I'm speaking normally enough, but they cover their ears before they shake their heads and look sad for me and chorus "No."

"Sod, listening to you is like listening to him."

"Maybe you should."

"Maybe he will."

"Maybe everyone will."

"Maybe is the future."

"As Kray would say."

"Do you know you're the only one who hasn't read him, Jeremy?"

"Thank Sod if it keeps me different."

"Unless we find ourselves in everybody else . . . "

"As fucking Kray would say."

A woman writing a cheque gasps, and another customer clicks his tongue like a parrot, and I'm sure they're objecting to me daring to utter a bad word about their idol. None of the slaves speaks to me all day, which would be more of a relief if I couldn't feel them thinking Kray's words even when they don't speak them. I assume the manager didn't hear me, since he was in his office telling someone the bank is going to repossess their house. But on Monday morning he calls me in and says "You'll have been aware that there's been talk of further rationalisation."

He was talking before that, only I was trying to see where he's hidden *The Word.* At least he doesn't sound like Kray. "Excuse me, Mr Bates, but are there any difficulties you feel I should know about?"

"With what?"

"I'd like to give you a chance to explain your behaviour. You're aware that the bank expects its staff to be smart and generally presentable."

I hug myself in case that hides whatever he's complaining about and hear my armpits squelch, and me saying "I thought you were supposed to see yourself in me."

"That was never meant to be used as an excuse. Have you really nothing more to say?"

I can't believe I tried to defend myself by quoting Kray. I chew my tongue until it hurts so much I have to stick it out. "I should advise you to seek some advice, Mr Bates," says the manager. "I had hoped to break this to you more gently, but I must say I can see no reason to. Due to the economic climate I've been asked to propose further cuts in staff, and you will appreciate that your attitude has aided my decision."

"Doesn't Kray have anything to say about fixing the economy?"

"I believe he does in world terms, but I fail to see how that helps our immediate situation."

The manager's beginning to look reluctantly sympathetic—he must think I've turned out to be one of them after all, and I won't have him thinking that. "If he tried I'd shove his book back where it came from."

The manager looks as if I've insulted him personally. "I can see no profit in prolonging this conversation. If you wish to work your notice I must ask you to take more care with your appearance and, forgive my bluntness, to treat yourself to a bath."

"How often does he say I've got to have one?" I mean that as a sneer, but suppose it sounds like a serious question? "Not that I give a shit," I say, which isn't nearly enough. "And when I do I can use his book to wipe my arse on. And that goes for your notice as well, because I don't want to see any of you again or anyone else who's got room in their head for that, that . . . " I can't think of a word bad enough for Kray, but it doesn't matter, because by now I'm backing out of the office. "Just so everyone knows I know I'm being fired because of what I say about him," I add, raising my voice so they'll hear me through their hands over their ears. Then I manage to find my way home, and the locks to stick the keys in, and my bed.

There's almost nothing else in my room except me and *The Word*. So I still have a job, to stay here to make sure it's the copy nobody reads. I do that until the bank sends me a cheque for the money they must wish they didn't owe me, and I remember all my money I forgot to take with me when I escaped from the bank.

I'm waiting when they open. At first I think the slaves are pretending not to know me, then I wonder if they're too busy thinking Kray's thoughts. A slave takes my cheque and my withdrawal slip and goes away for longer than I can believe it would take even her to think about it, then I see the manager poke his head out of his office to spy on me while I'm tearing up a glossy brochure about how customers can help the bank to help the Third World. I see him tell the clerk to give me what I want, then he pulls in his head like a tortoise that's been kicked, and it almost blinds me to realise he's afraid of what I am. Only what am I?

The slave stuffs all my money in an envelope and drops it in the trough under the window, the trough that always made me wonder which side the pigs were on. I shove the envelope into my armpit and leave behind years of my life. I'm walking home as fast as I can, through the streets where every shop either has a sale on or is closing down or both, when I see Kray's face.

It's a drawing on the cover of just about the only magazine that is still about books. I have to find out what he's up to, but with the money like a cancer under my arm I can't be sure of liberating the magazine without people noticing. I go into the bookshop and grab it off the rack, and people backing away make me feel stronger. I've only read how *The Word* is shaping up to outsell the Bible worldwide, and how some campus cult is saying there's a different personal message in it for everybody and anyone who can't read it should have it read to them, when a bouncer trying to look like a policeman tells me to buy the rag or leave. I've read all I need to, and I have all I need. The money is to give me time to do what I have to do.

Only I'm not sure what that is. The longer I stay in my room, the more I'm tempted to look in *The Word* for a clue. It's trying to trick me into believing there's no help outside its pages, but I've something else to read. I find the Christ Will Rise pamphlets that *The Word* has done its best to tear up and shove out of my reach, and when I've dragged them and my face out of the dust under the bed I manage to smooth out the address.

It's down where most of the fires in the streets are and the police drive round in armoured cars when they go there at all, and no cameras are keeping watch, and hardly any helicopters. By now it's dark. People are doing things to each other standing up in doorways if they aren't prowling the streets in dozens searching for less than themselves. I'm afraid they may set fire to me, because I see dogs pulling apart something charred that looks as if it used to be someone, but nobody seems to think I'm worth bothering with, which is their loss.

The Risers' sanctuary is in the middle of a block of hundred-year-old houses, some of which have roofs. Children are running into one house holding a cat by all its legs, but I can't see anyone else. I feel the front steps tilt and crunch together as I climb to the Risers' door, and I hold onto the knocker to steady myself, though it makes my fingers feel as if they're crumbling. I'm about to slam the knocker against the rusty plate when a fire in a ruin across the street lights up the room inside the window next to me.

It's full of chairs around a table with pamphlets on it. Then the fire jerks higher, and I see they aren't piles of pamphlets, they're two copies of *The Word*. The books start to wobble like two blocks of gelatin across the table towards me, and I nearly wrench the knocker off the door with trying to let go of it. I fall down the steps and don't stop running until I'm locked in my room.

I watch all night in case I've been followed. Even after the last television goes out I can't sleep. And when the dawn brings the wagons to clean up the blood and vomit and empty cartridges I don't want to sleep, because I've remembered that the Risers aren't the only other people who know what Kray was.

I go out when the streets won't be crawling—when the taken care of have gone to work and the beggars are counting their pennies. When I reach Everybody's Fantasy it looks as if the books in the window and the Everything Half Price sign have been there for months. The rainy dirt on the window stops me reading the spines on the shelf where Kray would be. I'm across the road in a burned-out house, waiting for a woman with three Dobermans to pass so I can smash my way into the shop with a brick, when Kath arrives in a car with bits of it scraping the road. He doesn't look interested in why I'm there or in anything else, especially selling books, so I say "You're my last hope."

"Yeah, okay." It takes him a good few seconds to get around to saying "What?"

"You've got some books I want to buy."

"Yeah?" He comes to as much life as he's got and wanders into the shop to pick up books strewn over the floor. "There they are."

I think he's figured out which books I want and why until I realise he means everything in the shop. I'm heading for the shelf when I see *The Word, The Word, The Word, The Word*... "Where's *A Touch of Other*?" I nearly scream.

"Don't know it."

"Of course you do. Jess Kray's first novel and the two that go with it. He signed them all when you didn't want him to. You can't have sold them, crap like them."

"Can't I?" Kath scratches his head as if he's digging up thoughts. "No, I remember. He bought the lot. Must have been just about when *The Word* was due."

"You realise what he was up to, don't you?"

"Being kind. Felt guilty about leaving us with all those books after nobody came, so he bought them back when he could afford to. Wish we still had them. I've never even seen them offered for sale."

"That's because he doesn't want anyone to know he wrote them, don't you see? Otherwise even the world might wonder how someone like that could have written the thing he wants everyone to buy."

"You can't have read *The Word* if you say that. It doesn't matter what came before it, only what will happen when everyone's learned from it."

He must have stoned whatever brains he had out of his head. "I felt like you do about him," he's saying now, "but then I got to know him."

"You know him? You know where I can find him?"

"Got to know him in his book."

"But you've got the address where you sent him his books."

"Care of his publishers."

"He didn't even give you his address and you think he's your friend?"

"He was moving. He's got nothing to hide, you have to believe that." Having to give me so many answers so fast seems to have used Kath up, then his face rouses itself. "If you want to get to know him as he is, he's supposed to be at Consummation."

"I've given up on fans. The people I meet every day are bad enough."

Kath's turning over magazines on the counter like a cat trying to cover its turds. "There'll be readings from *The Word* for charity and a panel about it, and he's meant to be there. We'd go, only we've not long had a kid."

"Don't tell me there'll be someone growing up without *The Word*."

"No, we'd like her to see him one day. I was just telling you we can't afford to go." He shakes two handfuls of fanzines until a flyer drops out of one. "See, there he is."

The flyer is for Consummation, which is two weeks away in Birmingham, and it says the Sunday will be Jess Kray Day. I manage not to crumple much of it up. "Can I have this?"

"I thought you didn't want to know him."

"You've sold me." I shove the flyer into my pocket. "Thanks for giving me what I was looking for," I say, and leave him fading with his books.

I don't believe a whole sigh fie convention can be taken in by Kray. Fen are stupid, Sod knows, but in a different way—thinking they're less stupid than everyone else is. I'll know what to do when I see them and him. The two weeks seem not so much to pass as not to be there at all. On the Friday morning I have a bath so I won't draw attention to myself until I want to. For the first time ever I don't hitch to a convention, I go by train to be in time to spy out the situation. Once I'm in my seat I stay there, because I've seen one woman reading *The Word* and I don't want to see how many other passengers are. I stare at streets of houses with steel shutters over the windows and rivers covered with chemicals and forests that children keep setting fire to, but I can feel Kray's words hatching in all the nodding heads around me.

The convention hotel is five minutes' walk from the station. After about ten beggars I pretend I'm alone in the street. The hotel is booked solid as a fan's cranium, and the hotel next to it, and I have to put up with one where the stairs lurch as if I'm drunk and my room smells of someone's raincoat and old cigarettes. It won't matter, because I'll be spending as much time with the fen as I can bear. I go to the convention hotel while it's daylight and there are police out of their vehicles. And the first thing the girl at the registration desk with a ring in her nose and six more in her ears says is "Have you got *The Word*?"

My face goes hard, but I manage to say "It's at home."

"If you'd like one to have with you, they're free with membership."

It'll be another nobody else can read. I tell her my name's Jay Batt and pin my badge on when she's written it, and squeeze the book in my right hand so hard I can almost feel the words mashing together. "Is he here yet?"

"He won't be."

"But he's why I'm here. I was promised he was coming."

She must think I sound the same kind of disappointed as her. "He said he would be when we wrote to him, only now he has to be in the film about him they'll be televising next month. Shall I tell you what he said? That now we've got *The Word* we don't need him."

I know that's garbage, but I'm not sure why. I bite my tongue so I won't yell, and when I see her sympathising with the tears in my eyes I limp off to the bar. It's already full of more people than seats, and I know most of them—I've written about them in my fanzines. I'm wondering how I can get close enough to find out what they really think about *The Word* when they start greeting me like an old friend. Two people have offered to buy me a drink before I realise why they're behaving like this—because I've got *The Word*.

I down the drinks, and more when they're offered, and make sure everyone knows I won't buy a round. I'm trying to infuriate someone as much as their forgiveness infuriates me, because then maybe they'll argue about Kray. But whatever I say about him and his lies they just look more understanding and wait patiently for me to understand. The room gets darker as my eyes fill up with the dirt and smoke in the air, and faces start to melt as if *The Word* has turned them into putty. Then I'm screaming at the committee members and digging my nails into the cover of the book. "Why would anyone be making a film about him? More likely he was afraid he'd meet someone here who knows what he wants us to forget he wrote."

"You mustn't say that. He sent us this, look, all about the film." The chairman takes a glossy brochure out of his briefcase. The sight of Kray grinning on the cover almost blinds me with rage, but I manage to read the name of the production company. "And they're going to do a live discussion with him after the broadcast," the chairman says.

I run after my balance back to my hotel. I can hear machine-guns somewhere, and I have to ring the bell three times before the armed night porter lets me in, but they can't stop me now. I haul myself up to my room, snapping a banister in the process, and fall on the bed to let my headache come. Whenever it lessens I think of another bit of the letter I'm going to write. The night and the sounds of gunfire falter at last, and the room fades into some kind of reality. It's like being part of the cover of a book nobody wants to take out of a window, but they won't be able to ignore me much longer.

I write the letter and check out of the hotel, telling the receptionist I've been called away urgently, and fight my way through the pickpockets to the nearest post office, where I get the address of the television channel. Posting the letter reminds me of going to church when I had to live with my parents, where they used to put things in your mouth in front of the altar. As soon as the letter is out of my hands I don't know if I feel empty or unburdened, and I can't remember exactly what I wrote.

I spend Sunday at home trying to remember. Did I really claim I was the first to spread the word about Kray? Did I really call myself Jude Carrot because I was afraid he'd remember the interview and tell the producer not to let me anywhere near? Won't he just say he's never heard of me? I can't think how that idea makes me feel. I left the other copy of *The Word* in my hotel room as if it was the Bible, and I have to stop myself from throwing the one under the bed out of the window to give them something to fight over besides the trash in the street.

On Monday I know the letter has arrived. Maybe it'll take a few hours to reach the producer of the discussion programme, since I didn't know his name. By Tuesday it must have got to him, and by Wednesday he should have written to me. But Thursday comes, and I watch the postman dodging in and out of his van while his partner rides shotgun, and there's no letter for me.

Twice I hear the phone in the hall start to ring, but it could just be army trucks shaking the house. I start trying to think of a letter I could write under another name, saying I know things about Kray nobody else does, only I can't think of a letter that's different enough. I go to bed to think, then I get up to, and keeping doing those is Thursday and Friday morning. Then I hear the van screech to a halt just long enough for the postman to stick a letter through the door without getting out of his cabin, because presumably they can't afford to pay his partner any more, then it screeches away along the sidewalk. And when I look down the stairs I see the logo of the television company on the envelope.

I'd open it in the hall except I find I'm afraid to read what it says. I remember I'm naked and cover my peter with it while I run upstairs, though everyone in the house is scared to open their door if they hear anyone else. I lock all my locks and hook up the chains and wipe my hands on my behind so the envelope won't slip out of them, then I tear it almost in half and shake the letter flat.

Dear Mr "Carrot"
Jess Kray says

Suddenly my hands feel like gloves someone's just pulled their hands out of, and when I can see again I have to fetch the letter from under the bed. I'm already struggling to think of a different name to sign on the next letter I send, though since now I'll know who the producer is, should I phone them? I poke at my eyes until they focus enough that I can see her name is Tildy Bacon, then I make them see what she wrote.

Dear Mr "Carrot"
Jess Kray says he will look forward to seeing you and including you in our discussion on the 25th.

There's more about how they'll pay my expenses and where I'm to go, but I fall on the bed, because I've just discovered I don't know what to do after all. It doesn't matter, I'll know what to say when the cameras are on and the country's watching me. Only something's missing from that idea and the absence keeps pecking at my head. It feels like an intruder in my room, one I can't see that won't leave me alone. Maybe I know what I'm trying not to think, but a week goes by before I realise: I can't be certain of exposing Kray unless I read *The Word.*

I spend a day telling myself I have to, and the next day I drag the book out of its hiding place and claw off the dusty cobwebs. I stare at the cover until it feels as if it's stuck behind my eyes, then I scream at myself to make me open it. As soon as I can see the print I start reading, but it feels as if Kray's words and the noises of marching drums and sirens and gunfire are merging into a substance that's filling up my head before I can stop it, and I have to shut the book. There's less than a week before I'm on television, and all I can think of that may work is being as far away from people as I can get when I read the book.

The next day is Sunday, which makes no difference, since there are as many people wandering around the countryside with nothing else to do any day of the week. I tear the covers off a Christ Will Rise pamphlet and wrap them round *The Word* before I head for Kings Cross, and I'm sure some of the people I avoid look at it to see if it's *The Word*. I thump on the steel shutter until the booking clerk sells me a ticket. While I'm waiting for the train I see through the reinforced glass of the bookstall that most of the newspapers are announcing a war that's just begun in Africa. I catch myself wondering if *The Word* has been translated in those countries yet, and then I imagine a world where there are no wars because everyone's too busy reading *The Word* and thinking about it and talking about it, and my fingernails start aching from gripping the book so I won't throw it under a train.

When my train leaves I'm almost alone on it, but I see more people than I expect in the streets. Quite a few seem to be gathering in a demolished church, and I see a whole crowd scattered over a park, being read to from a book—I can't decide whether it's black or white. All their faces are turned to the sun as if they don't know they're being blinded. As the city falls away I'm sure I can feel all those minds clogged with Kray trying to drag mine back and having to let go like old tasteless chewing gum being pulled out of my head. Then there are only fields made up of lines waiting to be written on, and hedges blossoming with litter, and hours later mountains hack their way up through fields and forests as if the world is still crystallising. In the midst of the mountains I get off at a station that's no more than two empty platforms, and climb until I'm deep in a forest and nearly can't breathe for climbing. I sit on a fallen tree, and there's nothing to do except read. And I make myself open *The Word* and read as fast as I can.

I won't look up until I've finished. I can feel his words crowding into my head and breeding there, but I have to understand what he's put into the world before I confront him. The only sound is of me turning pages and ripping each one out as I finish it, but I sense the trees coming to read over my shoulder, and moss oozing down them to be closer to the book, and creatures running along branches until they're above my head. I won't look; I only read faster, so fast that the book is in my head before I know. However much there is of it, I'm stronger—out here it's just me and the book. I wonder suddenly if the pages may be impregnated with some kind of drug, but if they are I've beaten it by throwing away the pages, because you must have to be holding the whole book for the drug to work. I've no idea how long I've been reading the book aloud, but it doesn't matter if it helps me see what Kray is up to. Though my throat is aching by the time I've finished, I manage a laugh that makes the trees back away. I fall back with my face to the clouds and try to think what the book has told me that he wouldn't want anyone to know.

My body's shaking inside and out, and I feel as if my brain is too. There was something about panic in *The Word*, but if I think of it, will that show me how the book is causing it, or won't I be able to resist swallowing *The Word* as the cure? I'm already remembering, and digging my fingernails into my temples can't crush the thought. Kray says we'll all experience a taste of the panic Christ experienced as we approach the time when the world is changed. I feel the idea cracking open in my brain, and as I fight it I see in a flash what he was trying not to admit by phrasing it that way. He wanted nobody to know that he is panicking—that he has something to be afraid of.

I sit up and crouch around myself until I stop shaking, then I go down through the forest. The glade papered with *The Word* seems to have a meaning I no longer need to understand. Some of the pages look as if they're reverting to wood. The night comes down the forest with me, and in a while a train crawls out of it. I go home and lock myself in.

Now it takes me all my time to hold *The Word* still in my head. The only other thing I need to be aware of is when the television company sends me my train ticket, but everything around me seems on the point of making a move. Whenever I hear a car it sounds about to reveal it's a mail-van. At least that helps me ignore my impression that all I can see of the world is poised to betray itself. If this is how having read *The Word* feels…

The next day the mail-van screeches past my building, and the day after that. Suppose the letter to me has been stolen, or someone at the television company has stopped it from being sent? I'll pay my own fare and get into the discussion somehow. But the ticket finally arrives, which may mean they'll try and steal it from my room.

I sit with the ticket between my teeth and watch the street and listen for them setting up whatever they may use to smash my door in. Suppose the room itself is the trap? Or am I being made to think that so I'll be driven out of it? I wrap the ticket in some of a Christ Will Rise pamphlet so that the ink won't run when I take it with me to the bathroom, and on the last morning I have a long bath that feels like some kind of ritual. That would be a good time for them to come for me, but they don't, nor on my way to the station, though I'm sure I notice people looking at me as if they know something about me. For the first time since I can remember there are no sounds of violence in the streets, and that makes me feel there are about to be.

On the train I sit where I can watch the whole compartment, and see the other passengers pretending not to watch me. All the way to Hyde Park Corner I expect to be headed off. I'm trudging up the slope to the hotel when a limo pulls up in front of the glass doors and two minders climb out before Kray does. As he unbends he looks like a snake standing on its tail. I pretend to be interested in the window of a religious bookshop in case he tries to work on me before the world is watching. I see copies of *The Word* next to the Bible and the Koran, and Kray's reflection merging with his book as he goes into the hotel. He must have noticed me, so why is he leaving me alone? Because passiveness is the trick he's been playing on me ever since I read *The Word*—doing nothing so I'll be drawn towards him and his words. It's the trick he's been playing on the world.

Knowing that makes me impatient to finish. I wait until I see him arrive in the penthouse suite, then I check in. My room is more than twice the size of the one I left at home. The world is taking notice of me at last. I drink the liquor in the refrigerator while I have another bath, and ignore the ringing of the phone until I think there's only just time to get to the studio before the discussion starts.

A girl's face on the phone screen tells me my taxi's waiting. As soon as we're in it she wants to know everything about me, but I won't let her make me feel I don't know what I am. I shrug at her until she shuts up. There are no other cars on the road, and I wonder if there's a curfew or everyone's at home waiting for Kray and me.

Five minutes later the taxi races into the forecourt of the television studios. The girl with not much breath rushes me past a guard at the door and another one at a desk and down a corridor that looks as if it never ends. I think that's the trick they were keeping in store for me, but then she steers me left into a room, and I'm surrounded by voices and face to face with Kray.

There are about a dozen other people in the room. The remains of a buffet are on a table and scattered around on paper plates. A woman with eyes too big for her face says she's Tildy Bacon and hands me a glass of wine while a girl combs my hair and powders my face, and I feel as if they're acting out some ritual from *The Word*. Kray watches me as he talks and grins at some of his cronies, and once the girl has finished with me he puts a piece of cake on a plate and brings it over. "You must have something, Jeremy. You look as if you've been fasting for the occasion."

So does he. He looks thinner and older, as if he's put almost all of himself into his book, or is he trying to trick me into thinking he'll be easy to deal with? I take the plate and wash a bite of the cake down with some wine, and he gives me the grin. "It's nearly time."

Is he talking about the programme I can see behind him on a monitor next to a fax machine? Someone who might be a professor or a student is saying that nobody he's met has been unchanged by *The Word* and that he thinks it promises every reader the essential experience of their life. Kray's watching my face, but I won't let him see I know how much crap the screen is talking until we're on the air. Then Tildy Bacon says to everyone "Shall we go up? Bring your drinks."

As the girl who ought to learn how to breathe ushers people towards the corridor, Tildy Bacon steps in front of me and looks me in the face. So they've saved stopping me until the last possible moment. I'll wait until everyone else is out of the room, then I'll do whatever needs to be done to make certain she can't follow me and throw me off the air. But she says "We had to ask Jess how to bill you on screen since you weren't here."

If she thinks I'm going to ask what he said I was, she can go on thinking. "I'm sure he knows best," I tell her with a grin that may look like his for all I care, and dodge around her before she can delay me any further, and follow the procession along the corridor.

At first the set-up in the studio looks perfect. The seven of us, including Kray, will sit on couches around a low table with glasses and a jug of water on it while Kray's minders have to stay on the far side of a window. Only I haven't managed to overtake the procession, so how can I get close to him? Then he says "Sit next to me, Jeremy," and pats a leather cushion, and before I have time to wonder what he's up to I've joined him.

Everyone else sitting down sounds like something leathery stirring in its sleep. The programme about Kray is on a monitor in a corner of the studio. A priest says he believes the secret of *The Word* needs to be understood, then the credits are rolling, and a woman who I hadn't even realised was going to run the discussion leans across the table and waits for a red light to signal her. Then she says "So, Jess Kray, what's your secret?"

He grins at her and the world. "If I have one it must be in my book."

A man with holes in his purple face where spots were says "In other words, if you revealed the secret it wouldn't sell."

Is there actually someone here besides me who doesn't believe in *The Word?* Kray grins at him. "No, I'm saying the secret must be different for everyone. It isn't a question of commerce. In some parts of the world I'm giving the book away."

The holey man seems satisfied, but a woman with almost more hair on her upper lip than on her scalp says "To achieve what?"

"Peace?"

Good Sod, Kray really does believe his book can put a stop to wars. Or does he mean he won't be peaceful until the whole world has *The Word* inside them? The woman who was given the signal leans across the table again, reaching for Kray with her perfume and her glittering hands and her hair swaying like oil on water. She means to turn the show into a discussion, which will give him the chance not to be watched all the time by the camera. I'll say anything to bother him, even before I know what. "It's supposed to be…"

That heads her off, and everyone looks at me. Then I hear what I'm going to say—that the secret of *The Word* is supposed to be some kind of eternal life. But there is no secret in *The Word*, that's why I'm here. "Jeremy?" Kray says.

I'm wondering if *The Word* has got inside me without my knowing—if it was making me say what I nearly said and that's why he is encouraging me. He wants me to say that for him, and he's talking about peace, which I already knew was his weapon, and suddenly I see what everything has been about. It's as if a light is shining straight into my eyes, and I don't care if it blinds me. "He's supposed to be Christ," I shout.

There's some leathery movement, then someone I don't need to see says "All the characters are clearly aspects of him."

"We're talking about the narrator of *The Word*," the television woman explains to the camera, and joins in. "I took him to be some kind of prophet."

"Christ was a prophet," says a man who I can just about see is wearing a turban.

"Are we saying—" the television woman begins, but she can't protect Kray from me like that. "He knows I didn't mean anyone in his book," I shout. "I mean him."

The words are coming out faster than I can think, but they feel right. "If people don't believe in him they won't believe in his book. And they won't believe in him unless he can save himself."

Ideas are fighting in my head as if *The Word* is trying to come clear. If Christ came back now he'd have to die to make way for a religion that works better than his did, or would it be the opposite of Christ who'd try to stop all the violence and changes in the world? Either way… I'm going blind with panic, because I can feel Kray close to me, willing me to… He wants me to go on speaking while my words are out of control—because they're his, or because I won't be able to direct them at him? Then I realise how long he's been silent, and I think he wants me to speak to him so he can speak to me. Is the panic I'm suffering his? He's afraid—afraid of me, because I'm...

"I think it's time we moved on," the television woman says, but she can't make anything happen now. I turn and look at him.

He's waiting for me. His grin is telling me to speak—to say whatever I have to say, because then he'll answer and all that the world will remember hearing is him. It's been that way ever since the world heard of him. I see that now, but he's let me come too close. As I open my mouth I duck my head towards him.

For a moment it seems I'm going to kiss him. I see his lips parting, and his tongue feeling his teeth, and the blood in his eyes, and the fear there at last. I duck lower and go for his throat. I know how to do it from biting my tongue, and now I don't need to restrain myself or let go. Someone is screaming, it sounds as if the world is, but it can't be Kray, because I've torn out his voice. I lift my head and spit it back into his face.

It doesn't blot out his eyes. They meet mine, and there's forgiveness in them, or something even worse—fulfilment? Then his head falls back, opening his throat so I'm afraid he'll try and talk through it, and he throws his arms wide for the cameras. That's all I see, because there's nothing in my eyes now except light. But it isn't over, because I can still taste his voice like iron in my mouth.

Words are struggling to burst out of my head, and I don't know what they are. Any moment Kray's minders or someone will get hold of me, but if I can just...I bang my knees against the table to find it, and hear the glasses clash against the jug. I throw myself forwards and find one, and a hand grabs my arm, but I wrench myself free and shove the glass against my teeth until it breaks. Now the light feels as if it's turning into pain that is turning into the world, but whose pain is it—Kray's or mine? Hands are pulling at me, and I've no more time to think. As I make myself chew and swallow, at least I'm sure I'll never say another word.

# The Dead Must Die

As soon as I push the doors open I know I am in the presence of evil. The lobby walls are white as innocence, but the place stinks of deceit. It is crowded with lost souls who wander aimlessly or talk to one another in low voices as though they are in church. Sensitivity to atmospheres is yet another gift which the mass of mankind has abandoned. I breathe a prayer and cross the threshold, steeling myself against the unhealthy heat which refutes the pretence of healing, the disinfectant stench bespeaking the presence of corruption, the closeness of so much unredeemed flesh.

Except I single myself out I may pass unnoticed. I silently intone the Twenty-third Psalm, and am halfway through the fifth verse when I reach the lifts. I step into the nearest, thumbing the number of the floor to which I have been called. The doors are closing when they spring back as if possessed, and two men dressed like choirboys push in a trolley laden with a draped form that is sucking up blood.

The doors shut, embracing the heat which now I understand is meant to dull the senses, and the lift shudders as though revolted by the burden it is being made to carry. But the cage rises,

humming smugly to itself, and I close my eyes and attempt not to breathe in the stink of devil's incense that reminds me I am in a place which might be a chapel of rest if it were not teeming with unholy corrupt life. "Aren't you well?" one of the surpliced attendants says.

His clammy breath in my ear is like a shameful kiss. I step back from him and shake one finger at the thing on the trolley, mumbling "Can't stand..."

"You get used to it," he says with a laugh which I gather is intended to express sympathy but which shows me that he sees no deeper into me than I desire. I pray God that all his kind here will be as gullible, as indeed their employment in this place suggests.

The lift stops, and I button the doors open, resisting the instinct to let them close and burst the dangling sac of blood. The temptation to perform good works in haste, at the expense of the greater good, is one of the Adversary's subtlest tricks. As the attendants rush the trolley away the other lift releases a stream of visitors in the direction I am pointed by an arrow on the wall. I let them pass so as to move more swiftly to my goal; but when I emerge I see the way is guarded.

A uniformed woman sits like a wicked child cast out of a schoolroom at a desk in the corridor. She is playing the scribe, noting on a clipboard the names of all who pass. Some she appears to have turned back, for they are slumped against the walls, their faces sagging with the heat. I grip my case more firmly and stride forward, silently repeating the psalm, and the woman raises first her face and then her eyebrows. "Visiting?"

"As you see."

She shakes her head like a beast that has been struck across the face. "Whom?"

"Paul Vincent."

"Relative?"

"A *caring* relative."

She lowers her gaze to her list as though my emphasis has crushed her. "Name?"

"George Saint."

Presumably this is as nothing to her, for she merely grunts and sets it down. When I make to pass, however, she emits a more bestial grunt and bars my way with a hand luxurious with fat and jewellery. "Two visitors maximum even in the private rooms. You'll have to wait."

I see myself driving a nail through her outstretched palm, and I press my free hand against my thigh. "I have come a long way to be here."

"Then I imagine you'll be staying for a while." When I refrain from contradicting her she says "You needn't be afraid you won't see Mr Vincent again. He's our star patient, getting better every day."

That is a taunt even if she is unaware the Adversary is using her voice. "When his wife wrote to me," I say loudly, "she said he was not expected to live."

"These days we can perform miracles."

Perhaps the triumph in her voice means only that she suspects I would have profited by my brother's death. I retreat for fear of venting my wrath upon her, and I am beyond the lolling visitors when the door of Paul's room opens and my niece Mary looks around for me. "Yes, it was him," she calls into the room. "Hello, Uncle—"

I interrupt before she can arouse suspicion by pronouncing my name from my former life. "Mary. I must wait until someone makes way for me."

"I'll stay out here if you want to see dad."

The guardian of the corridor turns to ensure that she refrains from returning to the room, and I wait until Mary comes forward. I have not set eyes on her for fifteen years—not since she would sit on my lap while I told her about Our Lord—and if I had any doubts about my mission they vanish at the sight of her. She is paler and thinner than she ought to be, and I believe I glimpse a knowing look in her eyes before she says "Dad will be pleased you've come to see him."

I detect no guile in this, and pray that knowingness is only a façade which she feels bound to present to the world. "I hope he can find it in his heart to welcome me."

"He says it's up to the individual what they believe."

For a moment I assume she is defending her father out of misplaced loyalty, and then I grasp that she thinks I was apologising for my faith, though she has no idea of its strength. I must surmise that she is not beyond redemption, however insidious are the influences which surround her. When she says "I'll wait here" I stride past the desk of the false scribe, repeating the fourth verse of the psalm under my breath, and enter the room.

My brother is lying in a bed, his eyes upturned to Heaven. His wife Penelope sits beside him, holding his hand. Their stillness almost persuades me that I am not needed here, and I succumb to a craven feeling of relief. Then my brother's head wavers up from the pillow, and his eyes, which are watery and veinous, light up with a blasphemous parody of intelligence and life. "Thomas," he whispers.

I want to proclaim my outrage with all my voice, but instead I advance to the foot of the bed and gaze solemnly at him. That appears to satisfy him, and his head sinks back. "Thank you for coming, Thomas," says his wife.

Her gratitude is as bogus as everything else in this evil chamber. She must have felt bound to contact me when my brother was at death's door. His eyes close, and he expels a long slow breath. "He waited for you," Penelope tells me.

Though that sounds as if she is holding me responsible for the unnatural prolongation of his life, I am filled with a hope that it has come to an end. His wide pasty face has collapsed as though it is no longer anything but a mask, and he has folded his hands on his chest. Then his hands stir, betraying their mockery of piety, as his chest rises and falls. He is dead, yet he breathes. He has joined the Undead.

How can God's daylight allow such a thing to be? When I attempt to recall how long it has been since I last saw the sun, it seems to me that the sky has been overcast for weeks before I was called to my brother. And the sun and the air were darkened by reason of the smoke of the pit, and there is no sunlight to combat the room's Godless light, which celebrates the flush of my brother's cheeks that gives him the appearance of a whore rouged with the blood of her victims. I turn away in revulsion and confront his wife, who says "I didn't know if you would come. I wasn't even sure we had your right address."

Nor have they, God be thanked. "I felt I had to," I confess.

"You're still born again, then. You're still of the same mind."

"We are all of His mind, however we regard ourselves. There is no birth nor death but proceeds from Him."

At least she has the grace to look embarrassed, though only because in these faithless days God is the dirtiest of words. "We've become quite friendly with the Beynons," she says defensively. "The donor's family."

The heat and stink coagulate in my throat, and for some seconds I cannot swallow for the thought of my brother with part of a corpse sewn up inside him. "Have you visited the grave?" I croak.

"Whose?"

"What you call the donor."

"Why, no," she says as though it is I who am in the wrong. "We don't want to intrude."

"Where is he buried?"

"She. Kidneys don't have a sex, you know. She's in the churchyard near where you used to have your flat."

"A short walk from where I am staying. If there is no objection I shall pay my respects."

"I expect you'll do whatever you think is right," she says in a tone which suggests I ought to be ashamed of doing so. "I hope you don't mind staying in a hotel, by the way. I've my hands full getting the house ready for Paul to come home."

She must take me for a fool if she imagines I assume that otherwise I would be welcome in her house when everything about myself is a reproach. I succeed in sounding casual. "When is that to be?"

"The doctors say Sunday."

The word should choke them. "I shall be in church."

"Come over afterwards to say goodbye to Paul if you have time."

She clearly hopes the opposite, and I may let her think her wish is granted. Sometimes a venial sin is justified in the prosecution of His work. “I have troubled you enough for the nonce,” I tell her. “Beynon, you said. What Christian name?”

She seems reluctant to answer, but perhaps she senses that I am prepared to demand the information of my brother, for she replies “Bernadette.”

It is indeed Christian—the name of the saint to whom His Blessed Mother chose to appear—which makes the mutilation yet more blasphemous. “May God watch over you and Paul,” I curse, and retreat into the corridor.

Only Mary and the guard remain. The guard is studying her clipboard as though it holds a sacred text, while Mary leans against the wall. As I approach, her eyes open and her pale undernourished face attempts to counterfeit a smile. “How was dad?”

I needn’t lie. “I am more concerned with how you are, Mary.”

“I’m all right. I’m fine,” she says, failing to conceal her evasiveness.

I raise my case against my chest so that neither she nor the guard can see what I am carrying, and reach in. “Will you wear this to please me?” I say, and hand Mary the twin of the cross which I never remove.

She hesitates, and I feel as if the Adversary has seized me by the throat. If she is unable to take hold of the cross I shall know she is already a victim of the Undead. Then she holds out a hand palm upwards and suffers me to lay the cross on it. “It’s a bit heavy,” she complains.

The childishness of her protest convinces me that she is still fundamentally innocent, and I offer up a silent prayer of thanks. “Wear it always,” I exhort her. “If anyone tries to dissuade you, do not hesitate to contact me.”

“I like wearing pretty things.”

I am taken unawares by a wave of grief for her. “I’ll buy you a pretty cross if you promise to wear this one at night until I do, and say your prayers.”

“Do I really have to, Unc—”

I interrupt her, though the guard appears to be trying not to overhear, by taking the cross from her hand and touching it to her lips before lifting the cord over her head. "Wear it until you get home at least, for His sake."

She looks rebellious, as children can be. I walk quickly to the lifts and step into the nearest before she has time to argue. Perhaps if my brother or his wife attempts to influence her not to wear the cross she will turn her rebelliousness against them. I say another prayer for her as I pass through the lobby and out of that place.

As I entered it had seemed an anteroom to Hell, but now I find it little different from its surroundings. In less time than it takes me to repeat the psalm I am in the shadow of chemical factories discharging their poisons into a sky the colour of sin. Behind them, on the bank of a filthy river, chimneys spout flames that dance and struggle, and I think of machines that begin to consume souls at the hour of death. Opposite the tract of factories gaunt terraces like cellblocks extending as far as the eye can see face one another across pinched streets with narrow pavements unrelieved except by tainted plots of grass. Broken glass surrounds every streetlamp, and I see that the denizens of these streets abhor the light. How many of them may be Undead, freed by the shrouding of the sun to walk by day?

It takes me half an hour's unbroken march to come in sight of the hotel near the factories. I comfort myself by repeating the psalm aloud, and whenever anyone approaches within earshot they pass by on the other side. I raise my voice to let them know they have betrayed themselves. Their dull self-absorbed faces are pale as tissue paper—a tissue of lies.

A few cheap shops huddle opposite the hotel, and I buy vegetables from a greengrocer whose hands are calloused with toil and who wears a small cross at her throat. As I enter the hotel's dim and dismal hall, where the walls are a mass of advertisements for gluttony and other forms of self-indulgence, the landlady accosts me. "I'm afraid cooking isn't allowed in the rooms, Mr Saint," she says, slowly wringing her colourless hands in a pretence of regret.

"Nor do I propose it, Mrs Trollope."

"And I still have to charge for meals even if you don't take them."

"We must all be guided by our consciences, Mrs *Trollope.*" Since she has no answer to this I say "If I may have my key I need trouble you no further."

She thrusts at me the cudgel to which the key is attached, and I climb the shabby stairs to my cheerless room, which smells of must and stale smoke and nights of solitary lechery. I hang my overcoat in the nondescript wardrobe and fall to my knees between the sink and the bed. When I feel I have prayed out the evils of the day I eat half a cabbage and two raw potatoes, savouring the taste of God's earth and the gritting of it between my teeth. The vegetables are as wholesome as can be expected in this place, and at least they were sold to me by a believer. Anything that is served in the hotel will have been touched by blood.

Night has fallen. The factories howl and glare with evil light. Hordes who have squandered their day in the factories shuffle into the narrow streets as if their shadows are dragging them home, while their neighbours swarm to take their places in the workshops of pollution. Then the land is quiet until the young begin to prowl, quaffing wine and smashing bottles in the roadways, if indeed the wine has not undergone some sacrilegious transubstantiation. After a time the corpse-lights of the factories show only lost souls fleeing after their shadows through a lurid icy rain, and I have prayed enough that I crave sleep.

I use the communal bathroom, which is full of warm fog and a suggestive smell of perfumed soap, and then I set about defending my room. I rub garlic around the inside of the door and windows, and employ the cloves to plug the taps and the sink. I hang a cross above the bed and another at its foot, and lay a cross on the frayed carpet at each side. Though thus protected, I am reluctant to switch off the lamp while I sense the land is teeming with corruption. Even the miserly light of the room seems preferable to the unholy glow outside the faded curtains. I kneel to recite Psalm 130, pummelling my breasts and temples as

I raise my voice, and when I feel Him answer me in my depths I lay me down to sleep.

But the Adversary has sent his minions to beset me. As I cried out my left-hand neighbour buffeted the wall in a vain attempt to interrupt my supplication, and now I hear Mrs Trollope's voicc, first beneath my window and then much closer. I think that she has scaled the outer wall, as the Undead are known to do, until I realise that she is at my door. "I hope you won't be keeping that light on much longer, Mr Saint," she says.

I hold my peace, hoping that she will conclude I am not to be awakened by trifles. Then she begins to smite the door with a clumsiness which suggests to me that she is the worse, if such is possible, for drink. "I know you're in there, Mr Saint," she bawls. "Put that light out or I'll put you out."

When I tire of her blustering I grasp the cord above the bed. As I pull it, darkness descends like the outpouring of a cloaca. A muffled discussion ensues in the corridor outside my room; no doubt the Adversary's minions are plotting further ways to disturb me. Let them seek to enter—they will find me armed. But nothing transpires except the closing of several doors, and so I lie on my back and take a cross in each hand.

In the fullness of time I slumber, as best I can while maintaining a vigil over my hands for fear that the Adversary may endeavour to loosen their grasp and trick them into repudiating the cross. When the sky begins to pale with the dawn I rise and pray that the sun may sear away the pall which darkens the land. Hours later only an enfeebled glow has seeped through the shroud, which I see is the colour of the corpse-lights, as though some poisonous exhalation has grown solid overnight to snuff out the day.

I venture to the bathroom in order to do the penance of voiding myself, then I scour my body at the sink in my room. I plan to spend the greater portion of the day in prayer. The Adversary will have none of this, however. I have scarcely fallen to my knees when he sends his trollop to besiege me. "I want a word with you, Mr Saint," she shouts.

"Have it, then."

"I can't hear you. I won't talk through a door."

"I thought that was a favourite pastime of yours," I say, and fling the door open. "Now you see me, madam."

I have revealed only my right-hand side when she falls back and shields her eyes like Eve after eating the apple. "For God's sake, Mr Saint, cover yourself up."

"We are all naked before Him." Smirking at her hypocrisy, I hold a cross in front of myself. "Now I am as clothed as any man need be."

She stays out of sight and raises her voice. "I'm afraid I must ask you to leave at once."

"May I ask who requires it of you?"

She stamps her foot, shaking the floor. "Let me remind you this is my house."

"It's worthy of your name."

"I don't know what this room smells of, but I want it out, and you. I've had complaints about the row you made all night, snoring and carrying on like I don't know what."

"Why, madam, I took you as my model."

She stamps so hard that the crosses on the floor spring up. "I'm giving you ten minutes to pay up and get out and then I'm calling the police."

So the scheme is to have me cast out before I can fulfil my mission. It would be the work of moments to pursue her and cut her down, but how many of her creatures might I have to put an end to, thereby perhaps drawing unwelcome attention to myself? Shall I abase myself and plead to be allowed to stay two further nights? The notion sticks in my gullet, and then I know that He has not forsaken me, for all at once I see where I may take refuge.

My cases are packed in five minutes, and in less than ten I am downstairs, jangling the bell of ill repute which stands on the counter. When Mrs Trollope pokes her face through the hole in the wall above it I cast my coins before her. "I think you will find that fits the bill."

"Haven't you any notes?"

"I thought silver more appropriate. Please count it."

She glowers and with a Jew's gesture scoops the coins together so as to pick them up with both thumbs and forefingers and drop them onto two piles. "That seems to be right," she grudgingly admits.

Can she really not have noticed there are thirty coins? "Wholly," I assure her, and depart out of that house, shaking off the dust from my feet.

The railway station where I arrived is five minutes' forced march distant, up a steep hill between extravagant windows choked with finery. The flesh of the crowds around me seems no less discoloured and artificial than that of the cheap sculptures modelling luxury in the stores which steep the pavements in alluring light. In the station the voice of a false oracle echoes through the vault, sending the lost fleeing hither and thither. As I slide my suitcase into a locker I am reminded of the ungodly practice of cremation. The thought fuels my anger as I set out on the first stage of my task.

The churchyard crowns a hill ribbed with mean streets. While the spire still points to Heaven, many of the gravestones have been overturned, perhaps by the revels of the Undead. Stone angels display mutilated wrists, as thieves in heathen countries do, so that I wonder if this may be yet another symptom of the undermining of our Christian ways by the influx of the heathen. Let it never be forgotten that the Undead originated in lands less Christian than ours.

A few mourners, if that is what they are, loiter morosely near wreaths, and a pair of silent workmen are spading out a grave. Rather than draw attention to myself by enquiring of the labourers where I should go I play the aimless visitor, wandering the stone rows, at whose junctions wire baskets are piled with empty bottles and withered flowers. I am halfway across the churchyard when a funeral arrives at the new grave, and I watch the mourners weep more copiously than is Christian. By the time I reach my goal, a family grave near the top of the churchyard, a vicious wind has cleared the place except for myself.

The Beynon plot is marked by a granite obelisk. Gilded names and dates are etched on the shaft, and the lowest name is Bernadette. As I would expect of a family which allowed her helpless body to be violated, no prayer has been inscribed on her behalf. Her yearning to be hallowed is as clear to me as though she is murmuring a plea in my ear. I kick the pharisaical wreath away from the obelisk and grind the flowers underfoot before falling to my knees on her mound. "The Day of Judgement shall find thee whole," I vow, and immediately I sense her gratitude. I grub her mound open with my hands and bury a cross as deep as I can to keep her safe.

I stay at prayer until the hellish lights of the town begin to waken; then I make for the church. I know that tonight the Undead must exert all their powers against me. I pass through the porch and open my flask to collect holy water from the font, and my heart quails within me. The church is starkly furnished with thin pews and an altar. How shall I go unnoticed when the priest locks the church for the night?

As I stopper the flask I hear footsteps on the gravel path outside the porch. I run to the sole refuge the place affords and crouch behind the altar. The inner door opens, and footsteps approach. Should I not declare myself and my mission, and crave sanctuary against the Undead? If the priest doubts my mission he is no priest, and I must strike him down before the altar he has desecrated. Yet I have little stomach for such an act in God's house, and breathe a prayer as the footsteps halt at the altar.

In a very few minutes the priest, having presumably breathed a perfunctory prayer, retreats along the aisle; then I hear him stop at the font and mutter what sounds all too like profanity. How can a man of the cloth let slip such a word, above all in church? I prepare to follow him and cut him down like the fig tree that beareth no fruit but cumbereth the ground. But darkness falls inside the church, the inner door closes, and I hear the false priest lock the outer door.

At once the church is no longer dark. A faint evil glow rises from the town, transforming the saints in the window above me into swarthy heathens and encrusting the pews with a dimness that appears to crawl. I should be safest where I am, guarded by the altar. I grasp two crosses and lie down on stone with my case for a pillow, and try to pray myself to sleep in order to be ready for the morrow's task. Out of the depths have I cr

A crash of glass! I leap up, brandishing the crosses, and stumble against the altar. The sainted window is intact. I have slumbered; was the sound only in my dream? No, for there comes an outburst of bestial yelling beyond the window, and the thump of gravestones on the earth. The Undead are abroad to trouble my sleep.

When I begin to pronounce an exorcism with all my voice the clamour falters momentarily, then redoubles. The Undead dance and jeer while their hands, if hands they are, belabour the wall of the church. More glass shatters, and I replace the cross in my right hand with my blade. If anything enters the building I shall shed its foul gore.

Perhaps the church is secure against evil, however, because the Undead content themselves with lupine baying in a vain bid to blot out my exorcism. When I grow so hoarse that I can barely whisper, their uproar subsides. I hear them shambling away, toppling gravestones as perhaps they seep back into their graves. I am seized by a fit of coughing, and when at last I am able to contain myself I strain my ears, distrusting the silence. Much later I sink to the floor behind the alt

"Who's there? Is someone there?"

The voice is in the church. The door has been unlocked. I have slept longer than I meant to, until a snore wakened me. Too late I understand that the Undead have achieved their purpose after all. I try to remain absolutely still, praying silently that I need not use my blade, as the priest comes up the aisle. He is almost at the altar—he has only to lean over it to see me. Then he turns on his heel and trots away, and I hear him on the gravel that surrounds the church.

I drop the blade into my case as I run on tiptoe to the porch. The priest has yet to reappear around the building; he must be searching among the graves beyond the far end of the church for the sleeper he overheard. I dart over the grass and crouch behind an angel, only to be overwhelmed by the sense that I am in a position for my bowels to betray me. I hear the priest marching over the gravel, muttering and rubbing his hands together, having presumably righted the gravestones. As he arrives at the porch, a loud and lengthy noisome wind escapes me. The pollution of the land must have inured him, for without hesitation he re-enters the church.

I compose myself and follow him. I mean to spend my time in prayer and fasting until I must be about my mission. The priest is replenishing the font, and gives me a sharp glance. "God be with you," I bid him as I cross myself.

Perhaps he recognises that I feel it to be more appropriate that I should wish him this than the reverse; he can hardly bring himself to respond "And with you." I make my way to the foremost pew and kneel, scorning the luxury of the kneeler. I shall pray silently until the priest says Mass, and th

Something is thrust between my ribs. The Undead have invaded the church and turned my weapons against me. "Retro me, Satanas!" I scream, and find myself surrounded by churchgoers, one of whom has elbowed me. All of them, and the priest in the pulpit, are staring at me. If his sermon and his celebration of the Mass had been sincere I would not have slumbered. "Pray continue," I say with a wave of my hand.

When he tires of striving to force me to avert my gaze he recommences prating to the congregation on the subjects of forgiveness and tolerance. In this land there is far too much of both, and almost all of it misdirected. I keep myself awake by gripping crosses so that their corners dig into my palms, though the false priest appears to frown on crosses. The Mass ends and the congregation straggles out while I remain on my knees. I have by no means done praying when the priest sidles up to me. "Are you in need of help, my son?"

"Psalm Twenty-eight, verse seven."

"I'm sorry, I'm not too familiar—"

"The Lord is my strength and my shield. My heart trusted in him, and I am helped."

He scowls at the rebuff or at having revealed his ignorance, and stalks off to gather prayer-books; then he loiters about the church until I finish praying, although I continue until it is almost dark. It seems that, like the landlady, he is being used to drive me out and rob me of a day's grace, and there are moments when I have to struggle to contain my wrath. When at last I succeed in relaxing my grip on the crosses and return them to my case I perform a solemn obeisance before the altar; then I glare so fiercely at the priest that he feigns a sudden interest in the contents of a hymnal as I stride out of the church.

The grubby light is draining into the vile landscape. As I make my way downhill through the blackened furtive terraces the tethered flames jerk above the soiled roofs, and I see I am descending into Hell. The light of a telephone box diverts me along a terrace whose windows are shrouded with net curtains like the dusty webs of a dozen or more enormous spiders. The box is derelict; holes gape where its instrument and light should be. No doubt the denizens of the land are anxious to prevent anyone less irredeemable than themselves from communicating with the outside world, though surely I saw telephones in use when I arrived at the railway station.

As I enter its vault the voice of the oracle proclaims the name of the town where I live. This is so transparently intended as a temptation that I scoff aloud. Few are there to hear me, and most of them are supine on benches after some debauch. I walk to the nearest telephone and dial the number of my brother's house before turning my back to the wall. The bell ceases its measured tolling. "Vincent," says Paul's wife.

"It is I."

"Oh yes," she says discouragingly. "Calling to say goodbye?"

"That is what I understand you wanted me to do."

"Did I? Paul's home, but he's in bed resting. I'll tell him you rang."

"Perhaps," I suggest after mouthing a prayer, "I could say goodbye to Mary."

"She isn't here. She's at a friend's, watching videos."

My prayer is answered. I need not wait until tomorrow, when Mary will be at college. Nevertheless Penelope's tone is too defiant for me to allow it to pass unreproved. "On a Sunday?" I rebuke her.

"She's been working hard all day helping me to get the house ready for her father."

"Working on the Sabbath is a poor excuse for self-indulgence,"

I declare, and am abruptly overwhelmed by the panic I experienced on Mary's behalf at the hospital. "Besides, when I last saw her she hardly looked fit for work."

"I suppose you think that's funny."

"I assure you I am not smiling."

"Do you ever?" Penelope says, and with a sudden weariness which I suspect is counterfeit: "This sort of conversation's why I'm glad Paul's in bed. I don't want you upsetting him, or Mary either."

"I fail to see how one can upset somebody by enquiring after their health."

"You know perfectly well what I mean. Or if you don't I'll tell you, because I'm proud of her. She's become a lot more responsible since she nearly lost her father. When you saw her she'd just given a pint of blood."

I shudder so violently that I almost kick my case away, and my knees scrape together. Even worse than the revelation is my sense that I ought to have known—that only my fears on Mary's behalf had prevented me from realising the Undead were already battening on her. I sway against the wall, and the oracle names my home again. "It sounds as if it's time to go," Penelope says in my ear.

If there is one thing the Father of Lies can be trusted sooner or later to do, it is to contradict himself. The attempt to lure me home has rebounded on my enemies. I hang up the receiver as a response to her and, snatching my case, leave the station at a run.

My brother's house is hidden among the terraces opposite the factories. As I stride up the street which leads to it, my shadow lengthens ahead of me. I will not allow myself to feel that it is leading me into darkness; rather am I forcing it onwards between windows black as the pit or flickering with light from screens around which pallid faces cluster. Some of the faces rise as though from feeding and gaze dead-eyed at me. Each step I take brings me closer to a black panic which, it appears, I can fend off only by outrunning it. I force myself to slow down and intone the psalms until their rhythm imparts discipline to my walk.

My brother lives in our parents' old house. It, and the square of which it is a part, seemed like a haven to me until I began to perceive the errors of my life. Now I see it is an unhallowed sepulchre concealed deep in a monstrous graveyard. I unlatch the gate and venture past the willow into the garden, where the cloying scent of flowers cannot disguise the tell-tale smell of turned earth. I have taken out my largest cross, and I hammer with it on the front door. In a moment my brother's voice, feeble when it should be mute, calls out "Who's that, love?"

"I'll see. You rest," Penelope says beyond the door. At once it is flung open, and her frown multiplies at the sight of me. "I thought you—"

"Is Mary home yet?"

"No, I told you—"

I need hear no more. I raise the cross above my head. If I had any doubts, the fear which immediately fills her eyes would show me what she is. I bring the cross down with all my force, and one arm of it strikes her left temple, which splinters and begins to leak. A second blow shatters her throat as she attempts to cry out. She is already falling to her knees like a slaughtered beast, making obeisance too late, and I slam the door as I step into the hall. I am raising the cross to deliver a final blow when her eyes go out, and she topples over backwards, still kneeling, so that I hear her knees creak and then snap like pistol shots. If she were alive I am sure she would scream. I stoop to wipe the bloodied cross on her breast, and then I hear the voice of my dead brother. "Penelope? Penelope?"

The sound infects me with terror, but also rekindles my wrath. As I straighten my back I repeat the Twenty-third Psalm aloud. I have just reached the foot of the stairs when my brother's walking corpse gropes out of his room and advances to the banister on legs that should no longer move. Grotesquely, it is wearing pyjamas instead of a shroud. "Thomas, what are you—" it says in a voice like a wind in a churchyard, and its eyes focus, though they must be rotting from within, on what is left of Paul's wife. "My God, what's happened to— Thomas, what have you—"

I am not interrupting. Its brain must be rotting too, and able to recall only fragments of living speech. The thing is no longer my brother, although may I be right to have heard a plea when it took His name in vain? "God help you, Paul, if you can understand me. I'll save you," I cry, and spring up the stairs.

The suffused remains of its eyes turn to me as if they can hardly focus. I hope it will welcome the end, or else I expect it to recoil before the advance of the cross in my hand. The Adversary has clouded my thoughts, so that I am unprepared when the face of the thing that was once my brother darkens as though all the blood it has consumed is rushing to its brain, and it flies at me, snarling like a wild beast, seeking whom it may devour.

My case is open. I drop it beside me on the stair and snatch out the flask of holy water. I barely have time to unscrew the cap when the Undead thing is upon me. I retreat a step and dash holy water into its eyes. It staggers, moaning, and falls on its back on the stairs. Before it can recover I seize my blade from the case and plunge the point deep between the thing's ribs.

The stolen blood gushes high as though grateful for release. I lean all my weight on the blade, and feel it penetrate the stair beneath as the Undead corpse writhes like an impaled insect, fluttering its hands. When at last it ceases moving I withdraw the blade and hammer the stake in its place, hearing ribs splinter.

The foul but necessary work is not yet done. I unbutton the thing's jacket and, cutting open the flesh beneath the lower ribs, widen the incision with my hands. By digging with the blade I am able to lay bare the kidneys. One is slightly smaller, and my instincts tell me this belongs to the victim of the Undead. I hack it free and prise it out of its raw nest, and pray over it before wrapping it in the bag which contained the potatoes. I place the bag in my case and trudge downstairs, bearing the cross before me.

I am almost at the front door when I catch sight of the directory beside the telephone. I leave my gory fingerprints on the page that lists Blood. Long before the prints can be identified my task will be done. The key to a mortise lock protrudes from a keyhole inside the front door, and I lock the door behind me as I leave, then I break off the shaft of the key in the lock. Now Mary must seek help with entering the house, and I pray she will not be the first to see how my brother and his wife have been redeemed. I should like to be with her when she sees them, but there is still much to do. In the morning I shall ask the greengrocer where I can buy a pretty cross to have sent to my niece.

My shadow follows me out of the dead terraces and turns ahead of me. It leads me past the station and uphill to the church. It seems to me that the shadow is my own black soul, urging me to redeem it with further good works. For the moment the churchyard is silent; the Undead must be elsewhere. I make my way swiftly to the Beynon grave and, withdrawing the cross from the mound, place the stolen organ in the hole before covering it with the cross and with earth.

Now I shall keep watch here until the morning. I could go now and destroy the house of vampirism, but I mean to strike down those who administer this iniquity. Whatsoever soul it shall be that eateth any manner of blood, even that soul shall be cut off. The victims such as Mary I shall spare, and the town of the Undead shall rise up against me, nor shall I escape. Let my exploit and my martyrdom act as a sign to the righteous, that they may destroy the false healers, the vampires whose uniforms mock sanctity, the halls of intensive care which are factories of mutilation. I am not alone. Our time has come.

# GOING UNDER

BLYTHE HAD SHUFFLED ALMOST TO THE TICKET BOOTH when he knew he should have sent Lydia her money. Beyond the line of booths another phalanx of walkers, some of them wearing slogans and some not a great deal else, advanced towards the tunnel under the river. While he'd failed to pocket the envelope, he never left his phone at home, and given the pace at which walkers were being admitted to the tunnel, which was closed to traffic for its anniversary, he should have plenty of time to complete a call before he reached the wide semicircular concrete mouth, rendered whiter by the July sun. As he unfolded the phone and tapped his home number on the keyboard the men on either side of him began jogging on the spot, an action which the left-hand man accompanied with a series of low hollow panting hoots. The phone rang five times and addressed Blythe in his own voice.

"Valerie Mason and Steve Blythe. Whatever we're doing, it's keeping us away from the phone, so please leave your name and number and the date and time and we'll tell you what we were up to when we call you back..." Though the message was less than six months old, it and Valerie's giggle at the end of it sounded

worn by too much playback. Once the beep had stuttered four times on the way to uttering its longer tone, he spoke.

"Val? Valerie? It's me. I'm just about to start the tunnel walk. Sorry we had a bit of a tiff, but I'm glad you didn't come after all. You were right, I should send her the maintenance and then object. Let them have to explain to the court instead of me. Are you in the darkroom? Come and find out who this is, will you? Don't just listen if you're hearing me. Be fair."

Quite a pack jogged between the booths at that moment, the man to his immediate left taking time to emit a triumphal hoot before announcing to the ticket seller "Aids for AIDS." Blythe turned his head and the phone to motion the woman behind him to pass, because if he stopped talking for more than a couple of seconds the machine would take him to have rung off, but the official in the booth ahead of him poked out his head, which looked squashed flat by his peaked cap. "Quick as you can. Thousands more behind you."

The woman began jogging to encourage Blythe, shaking both filled bags of her ample red singlet. "Get a move on, lover. Give your stocks and shares a rest."

Her companion, who seemed to have donned a dwarf's T-shirt by mistake, entered the jogging competition, her rampant stomach bobbing up and down more than the rest of her. "Put that back in your trousers or you'll be having a heart attack."

At least their voices were keeping the tape activated. "Hold on if you're there, Val. I hope you'll say you are," Blythe said, using two fingers to extract a fiver from the other pocket of his slacks. "I'm just going through the booth."

The official frowned his disagreement, and Blythe breathed hard into the phone while he selected a charity to favour with his entrance fee. "'Are you sure you're fit?" the official said.

Blythe imagined being banned on the grounds of ill health from the walk when it was by far his quickest route home. "Fitter than you sitting in a booth all day," he said, not as lightly as he'd meant to, and smoothed the fiver on the counter. "Families in Need will do me."

The official wrote the amount and the recipient on a clipboard with a slowness which suggested he was still considering whether to let Blythe pass, and Blythe breathed harder. When the official tore most of a ticket off a roll and slapped it on the counter Blythe felt released, but the man stayed him with a parting shot. "You won't get far with that, chum."

The phone had worked wherever Blythe had taken it, just as the salesman had promised. In any case, he was still two hundred yards short of the tunnel entrance, into which officials with megaphones were directing the crowd. "Just had to get my ticket, Val. Listen, you've plenty of time to post the cheque, you've almost an hour. Only call me back as soon as you hear this so I know you have, will you? Heard it, I mean. That's if you don't pick it up before I ring off, which I hope you will, answer, that's to say, that's why I'm droning on. I should tell you the envelope's inside my blue visiting suit, not the office suit, the one that says here's your accountant making a special effort so why haven't you got your accounts together. Can you really not hear it's me? You haven't gone out, have you?"

By now his awareness was concentrated in his head, so that he didn't notice that his pace had been influenced by the urgency of his speech until the upper lip of the tunnel swayed to a halt above him. Hot bare arms brushed his in passing as the megaphones began to harangue him. "Keep it moving, please," one crackled, prompting its mate to declare "No stopping now till the far side." An elderly couple faltered and conferred before returning to the booths, but Blythe didn't have that option. "That's you with the phone," a third megaphone blared.

"I know it's me. I don't see anybody else with one." This was meant to amuse Blythe's new neighbours, none of whom betrayed any such response. Not by any means for the first time, though less often since he'd met Valerie, he wished he'd kept some words to himself. "I'm starting the walk now. Please, I'm serious, ring me back the moment you hear this, all right? I'm ringing off now. If I haven't heard from you in fifteen minutes I'll call back," he said, and was in the tunnel.

Its shadow was a solid chill at which his body was uncertain whether to shiver, considering the heat which was building up in the tunnel. At least he felt cool enough to itemise his surroundings, something he liked to do whenever he was confronted by anywhere unfamiliar, though he'd driven through the tunnel several times a week for most of twenty years. Its two lanes accommodated five people abreast now, more or less comfortably if you discounted their body heat. Six feet above them on either side was a railed-off walkway for the use of workmen, with no steps up to either that Blythe had ever been able to locate. Twenty feet overhead was the peak of the arched roof, inset with yard-long slabs of light randomly punctuated with slabs off sick. No doubt he could count them if he wanted to calculate how far he'd gone or had still to go, but just now the sight of several hundred heads bobbing very slowly towards the first curve summed up the prospect vividly enough. Apart from the not quite synchronised drumming of a multitude of soles on concrete and their echoes, the tunnel was almost silent except for the squawks of the megaphones beyond the entrance and the occasional audible breath.

The two women who'd addressed Blythe at the booths were ahead of him, bouncing variously. Maybe they'd once been as slim as his wife Lydia used to be, he thought, not that there was much left of the man she'd married either, or if there was it was buried under all the layers of the person he'd become. The presence of the women, their abundant sunlamped flesh and determined perfume and their wagging buttocks wrapped in satin, reminded him of too much it would do him no good to remember, and he might have let more walkers overtake him if it hadn't been for the pressure looming at his back. That drove him to step up his pace, and he'd established a regular rhythm when his trousers began to chirp.

More people than he was prepared for stared at him, and he felt bound to say "Just my phone" twice. So much for the ticket seller's notion that it wouldn't work in the tunnel. Blythe drew it from his pocket without breaking his stride and ducked one ear to it as he unfolded it. "Hello, love. Thanks for saving my—"

"Less of the slop, Stephen. It's a long time since that worked."

"Ah." He faltered, and had to think which foot he was next putting forward. "Lydia. Apologies. My mistake. I thought—"

"I had enough of your mistakes when we were together, and your apologies, and what you think."

"That pretty well covers it, doesn't it? Were you calling to share anything else with me, or was that it?"

"I wouldn't take that tone with me, particularly now."

"Don't, then," Blythe said, a form of response he remembered as having once amused her. "If you've something to say, spit it out. I'm waiting for a call."

"Up to your old tricks, are you? Can't she stand you never going anywhere without that thing either? Where are you, in the pub as usual trying to calm yourself down?"

"I'm perfectly calm. I couldn't be calmer," Blythe said as though this might counteract the effect she was having on him. "And I may tell you I'm on the charity walk."

Was that a chorus of ironic cheers behind him? Surely they weren't aimed at him, even if they sounded as unimpressed as Lydia, who said "Never did begin at home for you, did it? Has your fancy woman found that out yet?"

He could have pounced on Lydia's syntax again, except that there were more important issues. "I take it you've just spoken to her."

"I haven't and I've no wish to. She's welcome to you and all the joy you bring, but she won't hear me sympathising. I didn't need to speak to her to know where you'd be."

"Then you were wrong, weren't you? And as long as we're discussing Valerie, maybe you and your solicitor friend ought to be aware she makes a lot less than he does now he's a partner in his firm."

"Watch it, big boy."

That was the broader-buttocked of the women. He'd almost trodden on her heels, his aggressiveness having communicated itself to his stride. "Sorry," he said, and without enough thought "Not you, Lyd."

"Don't you dare start calling me that again. Who've you been talking to about his firm? So that's why I haven't had my cheque this month, is it? Let me tell you this from him. Unless that cheque is postmarked today you'll find yourself in prison for non-payment, and that's a promise from both of us."

“Well, that’s the first—” Her rising fury had already borne her off, leaving him with a drone in his ear and hot plastic stuck to his cheek. He cleared the line as he tramped around more of the prolonged curve, which showed him thousands of heads and shoulders bobbing down a slope to the point almost a mile away from which, packed closer and closer together, they streamed sluggishly upwards. On some days that midpoint was hazy with exhaust fumes, but the squashed crowd there looked distinct except for a slight wavering which must be an effect of the heat; he wasn’t really smelling a faint trace of petrol through the wake of perfume. He bent a fingernail against the keys on the receiver, and backhanded his forehead as drops of sweat full of a fluorescent glare swelled the numbers on the keypad. His home phone had just rung when a man’s voice said loudly “They’re all the same, these buggers with their gadgets. Can’t be doing with them, me.”

There was surely no reason for Blythe to feel referred to. “Pick it up, Val,” he muttered. “I said I’d ring you back. It’s been nearly fifteen minutes. You can’t still be doing whatever you were doing. Come out, there’s a love.” But his voice greeted him again and unspooled its message, followed by Valerie’s giggle, which under the circumstances he couldn’t help feeling he’d heard once too often. “‘Are you really not there? I’ve just had Lydia on, ranting about her maintenance. Says if it isn’t posted today her boyfriend the solicitor who gives new meaning to the word solicit will have me locked up. I suppose technically he might be able to, so if you can make absolutely certain you, I know I should have, I know you said, but if you can do that for me, for both of us, nip round the corner and get that bloody envelope in the shit.”

The last word came out loudest, and three ranks in front of him glanced back. Of them, only the woman whose T-shirt ended halfway up her midriff retained any concern once she saw him. “Are you all right, old feller?”

“Yes, I’m…No, I’m…Yes, yes.” He shook his free hand so extravagantly he saw sweat flying off it, his intention being to wave away his confusion more than her solicitude, but she advanced her lips in a fierce grimace before presenting her substantial rear view to him. He hadn't time to care if she was offended, though she was using the set of her buttocks to convey that she was, exactly as Lydia used to. The ticket seller had been right after all. The tunnel had cut Blythe off, emptying the receiver except for a faint distant moan.

It could be a temporary interruption. He pressed the recall button so hard it felt embedded in his thumb and was attempting to waft people past him when a not unfamiliar voice protested "Don't go standing. There's folk back here who aren't as spry as some."

"When you're my dad's age maybe you won't be so fond of stopping and starting."

Either might be the disliker of gadgets, though both appeared to have devoted a good deal of time and presumably machinery to the production of muscles, not only beneath shoulder level. Blythe tilted his head vigorously, almost losing the bell which was repeating its enfeebled note at his ear. "Don't mind me, just go round me. Just go, will you?"“

"Put that bloody thing away and get on with what we're here for," the senior bruiser advised him. "We don't want to be having to carry you. We had his mother conk out on us once through not keeping the pace up."

"Don't mind me. Don't bother about me."

"We're bothered about all the folk you're holding up and putting the strain on."

"We'll be your trainers till we all finish," the expanded youth said.

"Then I ought to stick my feet in you," Blythe mumbled as those very feet gave in to the compulsion to walk. The phone was still ringing, and now it produced his voice. "Valerie Mason and Steve Blythe," it said, and at once had had enough of him.

All the heat of the tunnel rushed into him. He felt his head waver before steadying in a dangerously fragile version of itself, raw with a smell which surely wasn't of exhaust fumes, despite the haze into which the distant walkers were descending. He had to go back beyond the point at which his previous call had lost its hold. He peeled the soggy receiver away from his face and swung round, to be confronted by a mass of flesh as wide and as long as the protracted curve of the tunnel. He could hear more of it being tamped into the unseen mouth by the jabbing of the megaphones. Of the countless heads it was wagging at him, every one that he managed to focus looked prepared to see him trampled underfoot if he didn't keep moving. He could no more force his way back through it than through the concrete wall, but there was no need. He would use a walkway as soon as he found some steps up.

Another wave of heat which felt like the threat of being overwhelmed by the tide of flesh found him, sending him after the rhythmically quivering women. As far ahead as he could see there were no steps onto the walkways, but his never having noticed them while driving needn't mean steps didn't exist; surely a trick of perspective was hiding them from him. He narrowed his eyes until he felt the lids twitch against the eyeballs and his head ache more than his feet were aching. He poked the recall button and lifted the receiver above his head in case that might allow him to hook a call, but the phone at home hadn't even doubled its first ring when his handful of technology went dead as though suffocated by the heat or drowned in the sweat of his fist. As he let it sink past his face, a phone shrilled further down the tunnel.

"They're bloody breeding," the old man growled behind him, but Blythe didn't care what he said. About three hundred yards ahead he saw an aerial extend itself above a woman's scalp as blonde as Lydia's. Whatever had been interfering with his calls, it apparently wasn't present in that stretch of the tunnel. He saw the aerial wag a little with her conversation as she walked at least a hundred yards. As he tramped towards the point where she'd started talking he counted the slabs of light overhead, some of which appeared to be growing unstable with the heat. He had only half as far to go now, however much the saturated heat might weigh him down. It must be his eyes which were flickering, not as many of the lights as seemed to be. He needn't wait until he arrived at the exact point in the tunnel. He only wanted reassurance that Valerie had picked up his message. He thumbed the button and flattened his ear with the receiver. The tone had barely invited him to dial when it was cut off.

He mustn't panic. He hadn't reached where phones worked, that was all. On, trying to ignore the sluggishly retreating haze of body heat which smelled increasingly like exhaust fumes, reminding himself to match the pace of the crowd, though the pair of walkers on each side of him made him feel plagued by double vision. Now he was where the woman's phone had rung, beneath two dead fluorescents separated by one which looked as though it had stolen its glare from both. All three were bumped backwards by their fellows as he jabbed the button, bruised his ear with the earpiece, snatched the receiver away and cleared it, supported it with his other hand before it could slide out of his sweaty grip, split a fingernail against the button, bruised his ear again... Nothing he did raised the dialling tone for longer than it took to mock him.

It couldn't be the phone itself. The woman's had worked, and his was the latest model. He could only think the obstruction was moving, which meant it had to be the crowd that was preventing him from acting. If Lydia's replacement for him took him to court he would lose business because of it, probably the confidence of many of his clients too because they wouldn't understand he took more care with their affairs than he did with his own, and if he went to prison... He'd closed both fists around the phone, because the plastic and his hands were aggravating one another's slippiness, and tried not to imagine battering his way through the crowd. There were still the walkways, and by the time he found the entrance to one it might make sense to head for the far end of the tunnel. He was trudging forward, each step a dull ache which bypassed his hot swollen body wrapped in far too much sodden material and searched for a sympathetic ache in his hollowed-out head, when the phone rang.

It was so muffled by his grip that he thought for a moment it wasn't his. Ignoring the groans of the muscled duo, he nailed the button and jammed the wet plastic against his cheek. "Steve Blythe. Can you make it quick? I don't know how long this will work."

"It's all right, Steve. I only called to see how you were surviving. Sounds as if you're deep in it. So long as you're giving your brain a few hours off for once. You can tell me all about it when you come home."

"Val. Val, wait. Val, are you there?" Blythe felt a mass of heat which was nearly flesh lurch at him from behind as he missed a step. "Speak to me, Val."

"Calm down, Steve. I'll still be here when you get back. Save your energy. You sound as though you need it."

"I'll be fine. Just tell me you got the message."

"Which message?"

The heat came for him again—he couldn't tell from which direction, nor how fast he was stumbling. "Mine. The one I left while you were doing whatever you were doing."

"I had to go out for some black and white. The machine can't be working properly. There weren't any messages on the tape when I came in just now."

That halted Blythe as if the phone had reached the end of an invisible cord. The vista of walkers wavered into a single flat mass, then steadied and regained some of its perspective. "Never mind. Plenty of time," he said rapidly. "All I wanted—"

A shoulder much more solid than a human body had any right to be rammed his protruding elbow. The impact jerked his arm up, and the shooting pain opened his fist. He saw the phone describe a graceful arc before it clanged against the railing of the right-hand walkway and flew into the crowd some thirty yards ahead. Arms flailed at it as though it was an insect, then it disappeared. "What was that for?" he screamed into the old man's face as it bobbed alongside his. "What are you trying to do to me?"

The son's face crowded Blythe's from the other side, so forcefully it sprayed Blythe's cheek with sweat. "Don't you yell at him, he's got a bad ear. Lucky you weren't knocked down, stopping like that. Better believe you will be if you mix it with my dad."

"Can someone pick up my phone, please?" Blythe called at the top of his voice.

The women directly in front of him added winces to their

quivering and covered their ears, but nobody else acknowledged him. "My phone," he pleaded. "Don't step on it. Who can see it? Look for it, can you all? Please pass it back."

"I said about my dad's ear," the man to his left rumbled, lifting a hammer of a fist which for the present he used only to mop his forehead. Blythe fell silent, having seen a hand raised some yards ahead of him to point a finger downwards where the phone must be. At least it was in the middle of the road, in Blythe's immediate path. A few raw steps brought him a glimpse of the aerial, miraculously intact, between the thighs of the singleted woman. He stooped without breaking his stride, and his scalp brushed her left buttock. His finger and thumb closed on the aerial and drew it towards him—only the aerial. He was staggering forward in his crouch when he saw most of the keypad being kicked away to his left, and several other plastic fragments skittering ahead.

As he straightened up, a grasp as hot and soft as flesh yet rough as concrete seemed to close around his skull. The singleted woman had turned on him. "Whose bum do you think you're biting?"

Any number of hysterical replies occurred to him, but he managed to restrain himself. "I'm not after any of that, I'm after this." The words sounded less than ideally chosen once they were out, especially since the aerial in his hand was rising between her legs as though magnetised by her crotch. He whipped it back, the grip on his skull threatening to blind him, and heard himself shouting. "Look at it. Who did this? Who smashed my phone? Where are your brains?"

"Don't look at us," said the woman with the increasingly bare and moist midriff, while the son leaned his dripping face into Blythe's: "Keep the row up if you're after an ear like my dad's." All at once they were irrelevant, and he let the aerial slip from his hand. There was at least one working phone in the tunnel.

As soon as he attempted to edge forward the crowd swung its nearest heads towards him, its eyes blinking away sweat, its mouths panting hotly at him, and started to mutter and grumble. "What's the panic? Wait your turn. We all want to get there. Keep your distance. There's people here, you know," it warned him in several voices, and raised one behind him. "Now where's he scuttling off to? Must be afraid I'll report him for going for my bum."

The obstruction to his calls was about to turn physical if he couldn't find a way to fend it off. "Emergency," he murmured urgently in the nearest unmatched pair of ears, which after hesitating for a second parted their bodies to let him through. "Excuse me. Emergency. Excuse," he repeated, stepping up the intensity, and was able overtake enough people that he must be close to the phone. Which of the clump of blonde heads belonged to it? Only one looked real. "Excuse me," he said and, realising that sounded as if he wanted to get by, took hold of its unexpectedly thin and angular shoulder. "You had the phone just now, didn't you? I mean, you have—"

"Let go."

"Yes. What I'm saying is, you've got—"

"Let go."

"There. I have. Excuse me. My hand's in my pocket, look. What I'm trying to say—"

The woman turned away as much of her sharp face as she'd bothered to incline towards him. "Not me."

"'I'm sure it was. Not my phone, not the one that was trodden on, but weren't you talking on the phone before? If it wasn't yours—"

She was surrounded by female heads, he saw, all of them preserving a defiant blankness. Without warning she snapped her head round, her hair lashing his right eye. "Who let you out? Which madhouse have they closed down now?"

"Excuse me. I didn't mean to…" That covered more than he had time to put into words, not least the inadvertent winks which his right eye must appear to be sharing with her. "It's an emergency, you see. If it wasn't you you must have seen who it was with the phone. She was somewhere round here."

All the heads in her clump jeered practically in unison, then used her head to speak. "It's an emergency all right, an emergency that you need locking up. Just you wait till we get out of here and talk to someone."

That made Blythe peer at his watch. Sweat or a tear from his stinging eye bloated the digits, and he had to shake his wrist twice before he was able to distinguish that he would never reach the tunnel exit in time to find a phone outside. The crowd had beaten him—or perhaps not yet, unless he'd failed to notice it sending a message ahead that he was to be stopped. "Emergency. Emergency," he said in a voice whose edge the heat seemed determined to blunt, and when he thought he'd sidled far enough away from the woman who wanted to persuade him he was going mad, let his desperation grow louder. "Emergency. Need to phone. Has anyone a phone? Emergency." A shake or a wave of the heat passed through bunch after bunch of heads, and each time it did so his right eye blinked and smarted. He was trying to sound more official and peremptory when his voice trailed off. At the limit of his vision the packed flesh beneath the unsteady lights had come to a complete stop.

He could only watch the stasis creeping towards him, wavering into place in layer after layer of flesh. It was his worst possible future racing to meet him, and the crowd had been on its side all along. As he heard a murmur advancing down the tunnel from the direction of the unseen exit, he strained his ears to hear what it was saying about him. He was feeling almost calm—for how long, he couldn't predict—when words in an assortment of voices grew distinct. The message was past him before he succeeded in piecing it together. "Someone's collapsed in the middle of the tunnel. They're clearing the way for an ambulance."

"Bastard," Blythe snarled, not knowing if he meant the casualty or the crowd or the ambulance—and instantly knew he should mean none of them, because he was saved from the future he'd almost wished on himself. He began to shoulder his way forward. "Emergency. Make way, please. Make way," he was able to say more officiously, and when that failed to clear his route fast enough "Let me through. I'm a doctor."

He mustn't let himself feel guilty. The ambulance was coming—he could see the far end of the tunnel beginning to turn blue and shiver—and so he was hardly putting the patient at risk. The ambulance was his only hope. Once he was close enough he would be injured, he would be however disabled he needed to seem in order to persuade the crew to take him out of the crowd. "I'm a doctor," he said louder, wishing he was and unmarried too, except that his life was controllable again, everything was under control. "'I'm the doctor," he said, better yet, strong enough to part the flesh before him and to blot out the voices that were discussing him. Were they trying to confuse him by dodging ahead of him? They had to be echoes, because he identified the voice of the woman who'd pretended she had no phone. "What's he babbling about now?"

"He's telling everyone he's a doctor."

"I knew it. That's what they do when they're mad."

He needn't let her bother him; nobody around him seemed to hear her—maybe she was fishing for him with her voice. "'I'm the doctor," he shouted, seeing the ambulance crawling towards him at the end of the visible stretch of tunnel. For a moment he thought it was crushing bruised people, exhaust fumes turning their pulse blue, against the walls, but of course they were edging out alongside it, making way. His shout had dislodged several voices from beneath the bleary sweat-stained lights. "What did she say he's saying, he's a doctor?"

"Maybe he wanted to examine your bum."

"I know the kind of consultation I'd like to have with him. It was a quack made my dad's ear worse."

Could the crowd around Blythe really not hear them, or was it pretending ignorance until it had him where it wanted him? Wasn't it parting for him more slowly than it should, and weren't its heads only just concealing its contempt for his imposture? The mocking voices settled towards him, thickening the heat which was putting on flesh all around him. He had to use one of the walkways. Now that he had to reach the ambulance as speedily as possible, he was entitled to use them. "'I'm the doctor," he repeated fiercely, daring anyone to challenge him, and felt his left shoulder cleaving the saturated air. He'd almost reached the left-hand walkway when a leotarded woman whose muscles struck him as no more likely than her deep voice moved into his path. "Where are you trying to get to, dear?"

"Up behind you. Give me a hand, would you?" Even if she was a psychiatric nurse or warder, he had seniority. "I'm needed. I'm the doctor."

Only her mouth moved, and not much of that. "Nobody's allowed up there unless they work for the tunnel."

He had to climb up before the heat turned into sweaty voices again and trapped him. "I do. I am. There's been a collapse, the tunnel's made them collapse, and they need me."

He'd seen ventriloquists open their mouths wider. Her eyes weren't moving at all, though a drop of sweat was growing on her right eyelashes. "I don't know what you're talking about."

"That's all right, nurse. You aren't required to. Just give me a hand. Give me a leg up," Blythe said, and saw the drop swelling on her untroubled eyelid, swelling until he could see nothing else. If she was real she would blink, she wouldn't stare at him like that. The mass of flesh had made her out of itself to block his plan, but it had miscalculated. He flung himself at her, dug his fingers into her bristly scalp and heaved himself up with all the force his arms could muster.

His heels almost caught her shoulders. They scraped down to her breasts, which gave them enough leverage for him to vault over her. His hands grabbed at the railing, caught it, held on. His feet found the edge of the walkway, and he hauled one leg over the railing, then the other. Below him the nurse was clutching her breasts and emitting a sound which, if it was intended as a cry of pain, failed to impress him. Perhaps it was a signal, because he'd taken only a few steps along the way to freedom when hands commenced trying to seize him.

At first he thought they meant to injure him so that the ambulance would take him, and then he saw how wrong he was. He had an unobstructed view of the ambulance as it rammed its way through the crowd, its blue light pounding like his head, the white arch flaring blue above it as he felt the inside of his skull flaring. There was no sign of anyone collapsed ahead. The ambulance had been sent for Blythe, of course; the message had been passed along that they'd succeeded in driving him crazy. But they couldn't conceal their opinion of him, hot oppressive breathless waves of which rose towards him and would have felt like shame if he hadn't realised how they'd given themselves away: they couldn't hold him in such contempt unless they knew more about him than they feigned to know. He kicked at the grasping fingers and glared about in search of a last hope. It was behind him. The woman with Lydia's hair had abandoned her pretence of having no phone, and he had only to grab the aerial.

He dashed back along the walkway, hanging onto the rail and kicking out at anyone within reach, though his feet so seldom made contact that he couldn't tell how many of the hands and heads were real. The woman who was still trying to convince him he'd injured her breasts flinched, which gratified him. She and the rest of the mob could move when they wanted to, they just hadn't done so for him. The beckoning aerial led his gaze to the face dangling from it. She was staring at him and talking so hard her mouth shaped every syllable. "Here he comes now," she mouthed.

She must be talking to the ambulance. Of course, she'd used the phone before to summon it, because she was another of the nurses. She'd better hand over the phone if she didn't want worse than he was supposed to have done to her colleague. "Here I come all right," he yelled, and heard what sounded like the entire crowd, though perhaps only the tunnel that was his head, echoing him. As he ran the tunnel widened, carrying her further from the walkway, too far for him to grab the aerial over the crowd. They thought they'd beaten him, but they were going to help him again. He vaulted the railing and ran across the mass of flesh.

It wasn't quite as solid as he had assumed, but it would do. The heat of its contempt streamed up at him, rebounding from the dank concrete of his skull. Was it contemptuous of what he was doing or of his failure to act when he could have? He had a sudden notion, so terrible it almost caused him to lose his footing, that when he raised the phone to his ear he would discover the woman had been talking to Valerie. It wasn't true, and only the heat was making him think it. Stepping-stones turned up to him and gave way underfoot—there went some teeth and there, to judge by its yielding, an eye—but he could still trample his way to the phone, however many hands snatched at him.

Then the aerial whipped up out of his reach like a rod that had caught a fish. The hands were pulling him down into their contempt, but they weren't entitled to condemn him: he hadn't done anything they weren't about to do. "I'm you," he screamed, and felt the shoulders on which he'd perched move apart further than his legs could stretch. He whirled his arms, but this wasn't a dream in which he could fly away from everything he was. Too late he saw why the woman had called the ambulance for him. He might have screamed his thanks to her, but he could make no words out of the sounds which countless hands were dragging from his mouth.

# The Callers

MARK'S GRANDMOTHER SEEMS BARELY TO HAVE LEFT the house when his grandfather says "Can you entertain yourself for a bit? I could do with going to the pub while I've got the chance."

Mark wonders how much they think they've entertained him, but he only says "Will grandma be all right coming home on her own?"

"Never fret, son. They can look after theirselves." The old man's hairy caterpillar eyebrows squirm as he frowns at Mark and blinks his bleary eyes clear. "No call for you to fetch her. It's women's stuff, the bingo." He gives the boy's shoulder an unsteady squeeze and mutters "You're a good sort to have around."

Mark feels awkward and a little guilty that he's glad he doesn't have to meet his grandmother. "Maybe I'll go to a film."

"You'd better have a key, then." His grandfather rummages among the contents of a drawer of the shaky sideboard—documents in ragged envelopes, rubber bands so desiccated they snap when he takes hold of them, a balding reel of cotton, a crumpled folder stuffed with photographs—and hauls out a key on a frayed noose of string. "Keep hold of that for next time you come," he says.

Does he mean Mark will be visiting by himself in future? Was last night's argument so serious? His mother objected when his grandfather offered him a glass of wine at dinner, and then her mother accused her of not letting Mark grow up. Before long the women were shouting at each other about how Mark's grandmother had brought up her daughter, and the men only aggravated the conflict by trying to calm it down. It continued after Mark went to bed, and this morning his father informed him that he and Mark's mother were going home several days early. "You can stay if you like," she told Mark.

Was she testing his loyalty or hoping he would make up for her behaviour? While her face kept her thoughts to itself his father handed him the ticket for the train home like a business card, one man to another. Mark's mother spent some time in listing ways he shouldn't let anyone down, but these didn't include going to the cinema. Wearing his coat was among the requirements, and so he takes it from the stand in the hall. "Step out, lad," his grandfather says as Mark lingers on the pavement directly outside the front door. "You don't want an old crock slowing you down."

At the corner of the street Mark glances back. The old man is limping after him, resting a hand on the roof of each car parked with two wheels on the pavement. Another narrow similarly terraced street leads into the centre of the small Lancashire town, where lamps on scalloped iron poles are stuttering alight beneath a congested late April sky. Many of the shops are shuttered, and some are boarded up. Just a few couples stroll past deserted pristine kitchens and uninhabited items of attire. Most of the local amusements have grown too childish for Mark, though he might still enjoy bowling or a game of indoor golf if he weren't by himself, and others are years out of bounds—the pubs, the clubs waiting for the night crowds while doormen loiter outside like wrestlers dressed for someone's funeral. Surely the cinema won't be so particular about its customers. More than one of Mark's schoolmates has shown him the scene from *Facecream* where the girl gets cream squirted all over her face.

As he hurries past the clubs he thinks a doorman is shouting behind him, but the large voice is down a side street full of shops that are nailed shut. At first he fancies that it's chanting inside one of them, and then he sees an old theatre at the far end. While he can't distinguish the words, the rhythm makes it clear he's hearing a bingo caller. Mark could imagine that all the blank-faced doormen are determined to ignore the voice.

The Frugoplex is beyond the clubs, across a car park for at least ten times as many vehicles as it presently contains. The lobby is scattered with popcorn, handfuls of which have been trodden into the purple carpet. A puce rope on metal stilts leads the queue for tickets back and forth and twice again on the way to the counter. When Mark starts to duck under the rope closest to the end of the queue, a man behind the counter scowls at him, and so he follows the rope all the way around, only just heading off two couples of about his own age who stoop under. He's hoping to avoid the disgruntled man, but the queue brings Mark to him. "*Facecream*, please," Mark says and holds out a ten-pound note.

"Don't try it on with me, laddie," the man says and turns his glare on the teenagers who have trailed Mark to the counter. "And your friends needn't either."

"He's not our friend," one of the boys protests.

"I reckon not when he's got you barred."

Mark's face has grown hot, but he can't just walk away or ask to see a film he's allowed to watch. "I don't know about them, but I'm fifteen."

"And I'm your sweet old granny. That's it now for the lot of you. Don't bother coming to my cinema." The manager tells his staff at the counter "Have a good look at this lot so you'll know them."

Mark stumbles almost blindly out of the multiplex. He's starting across the car park when somebody mutters behind him "He wants his head kicked in."

They're only words, but they express his feelings. "That's what he deserves," Mark agrees and turns to his new friends.

It's immediately clear that they weren't thinking of the manager. "You got us barred," says the girl who didn't speak.

"I didn't mean to. You oughtn't to have stood so close."

"Doesn't matter what you meant," she says, and the other girl adds "We'll be standing a lot closer. Standing on your head."

Mark can't take refuge in the cinema, but running would look shameful and invite pursuit as well. Instead he tramps at speed across the car park. His shadow lurches ahead, growing paler as it stretches, and before long it has company, jerking forward to catch up on either side of him. He still stops short of bolting but strides faster. He's hoping passers-by will notice his predicament, but either they aren't interested or they're determined not to be. At last he reaches the nightclubs, and is opening his mouth to appeal to the nearest doorman when the fellow says "Keep walking, lad."

"They're after me."

The doorman barely glances beyond Mark, and his face stays blank. "Walk on."

It could be advice, though it sounds like a dismissal. It leaves Mark feeling that he has been identified as an outsider, and he thinks the doormen's impassive faces are warning him not to loiter. He would make for the police station if he knew where it is. He mustn't go to his grandparents' house in case they become scapegoats as well, and there's just one sanctuary he can think of. He dodges into the side street towards the bingo hall.

The street looks decades older than the main road and as though it has been forgotten for at least that long. Three streetlamps illuminate the cracked roadway bordered by grids that are clogged with old leaves. The glow is too dim to penetrate the gaps between the boards that have boxed up the shopfronts, because the lanterns are draped with grey cobwebs laden with drained insects. The only sign of life apart from a rush of footsteps behind Mark is the amplified voice, still delivering its blurred chant. It might almost be calling out to him, and he breaks into a run.

So do his pursuers, and he's afraid that the bingo hall may be locked against intruders. Beyond the grubby glass of three pairs of doors the foyer is deserted; nobody is in the ticket booth or behind the refreshment counter. His pursuers hesitate as he sprints to the nearest pair of doors, but when neither door budges, the gang closes in on him. He nearly trips on the uneven marble steps as he stumbles along them. He throws all his weight, such as it is, against the next set of doors, which give so readily that he almost sprawls on the threadbare carpet of the foyer.

The caller seems to raise his voice to greet him. "Sixty-three," he's announcing, "just like me." The pursuers glare at Mark from the foot of the shallow steps. "You can't stay in there," one girl advises him, and the other shouts "Better not try."

All the gang look determined to wait for him. If they don't tire of it by the time the bingo players go home, surely they won't dare to let themselves be identified, and so Mark shuts the doors and crosses the foyer. The entrance to the auditorium is flanked by old theatrical posters, more than one of which depicts a plump comedian with a sly schoolboyish face. Mark could imagine they're sharing a joke about him as he pushes open the doors to the auditorium.

The theatre seats have been cleared out, but the stage remains. It faces a couple of dozen tables, most of which are surrounded by women with score cards in front of them and stumpy pencils in their hands. The stage is occupied by a massive lectern bearing a large transparent globe full of numbered balls. Mark might fancy that he knows why the posters looked secretly amused, because the man in them is behind the lectern. He looks decades older, and the weight of his face has tugged it piebald as well as out of shape, but his grin hasn't entirely lost its mischief, however worn it seems. Presumably his oversized suit and baggy shirt are meant to appear comical rather than to suggest a youngster wearing cast-off clothes. He examines a ball before returning it to the globe, which he spins on its pivot. "Three and three," he says as his eyes gleam blearily at Mark. "What do you see?" he adds, and all the women eye the newcomer.

At first Mark can't see his grandmother. He's distracted by a lanky angular woman who extends her speckled arms across the table nearest to him. "Lost your mammy, son?" she cries. "There's plenty here to tend to you."

For an uneasy moment he thinks she has reached for her breast to indicate how motherly she is, but she's adjusting her dress, her eagerness to welcome him having exposed a mound of wrinkled flesh. Before he can think of an answer his grandmother calls "What are you doing here, Mark?"

She's at a table close to the stage. He doesn't want to make her nervous for him if there's no need, and he's ashamed of having run away. The uncarpeted floorboards amplify every step he takes, so that he feels as if he's trying to sound bigger than he is. All the women and the bingo caller watch his progress, and he wonders if everybody hears him mutter "I went to the cinema but they wouldn't let me see the film."

As his grandmother makes to speak one of her three companions leans forward, flattening her forearms on the table to twice their width. "However old are you, son?"

"Mark's thirteen," says his grandmother.

Another of her friends nods vigorously, which she has been doing ever since Mark caught sight of her. "Thirteen," she announces, and many of the women coo or hoot with enthusiasm.

"Looks old enough to me," says the third of his grandmother's tablemates, who is sporting more of a moustache than Mark has achieved. "Enough of a man."

"Well, we've shown you off now," Mark's grandmother tells him. "I'll see you back at home."

This provokes groans throughout the auditorium. The woman who asked his age raises her hands, and her forearms sag towards the elbows. "Don't keep him to yourself, Lottie."

The nodding woman darts to grab a chair for him. "You make this the lucky table, Mark."

He's disconcerted to observe how frail his grandmother is by comparison with her friends, though they're at least as old as she is. The bingo caller gives him a crooked grin and shouts "Glad to have another feller here. Safety in numbers, lad."

Presumably this is a joke of some kind, since quite a few women giggle. Mark's grandmother doesn't, but says "Can he have a card?"

This prompts another kind of laughter, and the nodding

woman even manages to shake her head. "It's the women's game, lad," the caller says. "Are you ladies ready to play?"

"More than ever," the moustached woman shouts, which seems somehow to antagonise Mark's grandmother. "Sit down if you're going to," she says. "Stop drawing attention to yourself."

He could retort that she has just done that to him. He's unable to hide his blazing face as he crouches on the spindly chair while the bingo caller elevates the next ball from the dispenser. "Eighty-seven," he reads out. "Close to heaven."

The phrase earns mirth and other noises of appreciation as the women duck in unison to their cards. They chortle or grunt if they find the number, grimacing if they fail. Nobody at Mark's table has located it when the man at the lectern calls "Number forty, old and naughty."

"That's us and no mistake," the moustached woman screeches before whooping at the number on her card.

"Number six, up to tricks."

"That's us as well," her friend cries, but all her nodding doesn't earn her the number.

"Forty-nine, you'll be fine."

The third woman crosses out the number, and flesh cascades down her arm as she lifts the pencil. "He's that with bells on," she says, favouring Mark with a wink.

He has to respond, though the smile feels as if his swollen lips are tugging at his hot stiff face. "Three and twenty," the man at the lectern intones. "There'll be plenty."

Mark's grandmother hunches over the table. He could think she's trying to evade the phrase or the coos of delight it elicits from the rest of the players, but she's marking the number on her card. She seems anxious to win, staying bent close to the card as the bingo caller consults the next ball. "Six and thirty," he says, and a roguish grin twists the left side of his mouth. "Let's get dirty."

He pokes at the grin with a finger as if he wants to push the words back in, although they've raised appreciative squeals throughout the auditorium. The fleshy woman falls to her card so eagerly that every visible part of her wobbles. "That'll do me," she cries.

Presumably she means his suggestion, since she hasn't completed her card. Mark sees his grandmother glance nervously at it and then stare at her own as though striving to conjure up a number. "Four and four," the caller says and almost at once "There's the door."

The moustached woman rubs her upper lip so hard that Mark fancies he hears the hairs crackle. "Never mind that," she tells the caller.

He blinks at her and stares around the hall. Mark feels more out of place than ever, as though he's listening to jokes too old for him—beyond his comprehension, at any rate. The caller's drooping face grows defiant as he identifies the next ball. "Ninety-five," he says. "Leave alive."

This brings no laughter, just a murmur that falls short of words. At least Mark's grandmother has found the number on her card. She needs three more to win, and he's surprised by how much he hopes she will. He puts the wish into his eyes as he gazes up at the stage. "Number fifty," the caller says in a tone that seems almost as mechanical as the dispenser. "He'll be nifty."

"Aye," several women respond, and the quivering woman gives Mark another wink.

"Eighty-one, nearly done."

"That's me," the nodding woman agrees, bowing to her card as if the motion of her head has overtaken the rest of her.

Perhaps she means her age, since the irregular cross she makes doesn't finish off the card. "Twenty-nine," the caller says, keeping his eyes on the ball he's raised between the fingertips of both hands. "See the sign."

If the players do so, they keep quiet about it, not even greeting the number or bemoaning their luck. The caller displays the next ball like a magician and puts a finger to the edge of a grin that's meant to appear mysterious. "Sixty-three," he says. "Time to flee."

The murmur this provokes is unamused, and he concentrates on the ball that rolls out of the dispenser. "Twenty-four," he says. "Can't do more."

His gaze is drifting towards Mark when the fleshy woman emits a shriek that jabs deep into the boy's ears. "We're done," she cries. "It's mine."

The caller shuts the globe and extends a hand. "Give us a look."

As she mounts the steps to the stage a series of tremors passes through her body, starting at her veinous legs. Having checked her numbers against those that came up, the caller says "We've a winner."

She snatches the card and plods back to the table, where Mark sees how the crosses resemble sketches of gravestones, at least until she turns the card the right way up. She lowers herself onto her creaking chair and says "I claim the special."

The caller doesn't look at her or anywhere near her. "It's not time yet," he tells whoever needs to hear.

While he leans on the lectern to say so he puts Mark in mind of a priest in a pulpit, though the comparison seems wrong in some way Mark doesn't understand. He's distracted by his grandmother, who lays down her pencil next to the card scattered with the kind of crosses all the women have been drawing. "I'll do without my luck tonight," she says and grasps his arm to help her stand up. "Time someone was at home."

"Don't be like that," the fleshy woman says. "You can't just go running off."

"I won't be running anywhere." As Mark wonders whether that's defiance or the painful truth his grandmother says "I'll see you all another night."

"See us now and see yourself." The speaker nods so violently that her words grow jagged. "You're still one of us."

"I'm not arguing," Mark's grandmother says and grips his arm harder. "Come along now, Mark."

He doesn't know how many women murmur as she turns towards the exit. While he can't make out their words, they sound unhappy if not worse, and all of them are closer than the exit. Nobody moves as long as he can see them, and he finds he would rather not look back. His grandmother has almost led him out, clutching his arm so tightly that it throbs, when the lanky woman who first greeted him plants a hand on her breast again. Though she could be expressing emotion, Mark has the unwelcome fancy that she's about to bare the wizened breast to him. His grandmother hurries him past, and the doors to the foyer are lumbering shut behind them when a woman says "We aren't done."

Mark hopes she's addressing the man on the stage—urging him to start the next game—but he hasn't heard the caller by the time he and his grandmother emerge onto the steps. The street is deserted, and he suspects that the couples who followed him from the cinema are long gone. Outside the clubs the doormen keep their faces blank at the sight of him and his escort, who is leaning on him as much as leading him. She's quiet until they reach the shops, where she mutters "I wish you hadn't gone there tonight, Mark. We're meant to be responsible for you."

He feels guiltier than he understands. She says nothing more while they make their increasingly slow way home. She's about to ring the doorbell with her free hand when Mark produces the key. "Isn't he in?" she protests.

"He went to the pub."

"Men," she says so fiercely that Mark feels sentenced too. She slams the door by tottering against it and says "I think you should be in your bed."

He could object that it isn't his bedtime—that he doesn't know what offence he's committed—but perhaps he isn't being punished, in which case he isn't sure he wants to learn her reason for sending him to his room. He trudges up the narrow boxed-in stairs to the decidedly compact bathroom, where every item seems too close to him, not least the speckled mirror that frames his uneasy face. The toothpaste tastes harsher than usual, and he does his best to stay inaudible while spitting it into the sink. As he dodges into the smaller of the two front bedrooms he sees his grandmother sitting at the bottom of the stairs. He retreats under the quilt of the single bed against the wall beneath the meagre window and listens for his grandfather.

He doesn't know how long he has kept his eyes shut by the time he hears the front door open below him. His grandmother starts to talk at once, and he strains to catch her words. "Did you send Mark to fetch me tonight?"

"I told him to stay clear," Mark's grandfather says not quite as low. "What did he see?"

"It isn't what he saw, it's what they did."

"Are you still up to that old stuff? Makes you all feel powerful, does it?"

"I'll tell you one thing, Len—you don't any more." Just as righteously she says "I don't remember you crying about it too much when it was your turn."

"Well, it's not now."

"It shouldn't be our house at all." This sounds accusing, especially when she adds "If there's any talking to be done you can do it."

Apparently that's all. Mark hears his grandparents labour up the stairs and take turns to make various noises in the bathroom that remind him how old they are. He finds himself wondering almost at random whether they'll take him to the celebrations tomorrow on the town green; they have on other May Days. The prospect feels like a reward if not a compensation for some task. The door of the other front bedroom shuts, and he hears a series of creaks that mean his grandparents have taken to their bed.

For a while the night is almost quiet enough to let him drift into sleep, except that he feels as if the entire house is alert. He's close to dozing when he hears a distant commotion. At first he thinks a doorman outside a club is shouting at someone, perhaps a bunch of drunks, since several people respond. There's something odd about the voice and the responses too. Mark lifts his head from the lumpy pillow and strives to identify what he's hearing, and then he realises his efforts are unnecessary. The voice and its companions are approaching through the town.

Mark does his best to think he's misinterpreting what he hears. The voices sound uncomfortably close by the time he can't mistake them. "Seventy-four," the leader calls, and the ragged chorus answers "Knock on his door." Mark is additionally disconcerted by recognising that the caller isn't the man who was on the stage. However large and resonant it is, it's a woman's voice.

"Number ten," it calls, and the chant responds "Find the

men." The chorus is nearly in unison now, and the performance puts Mark in mind of a priest and a congregation—some kind of ritual, at any rate. He kicks the quilt away and kneels on the yielding mattress to scrag the curtain and peer through the window. Even when he presses his cheek against the cold glass, all of the street that he can see is deserted. His breath swells up on the pane and shrinks as the first voice cries "Sweet thirteen" and the rest chant "While he's green."

They sound surer of themselves with every utterance, and they aren't all that troubles Mark. Although he knows that the houses opposite are occupied, every window is dark and not a single curtain stirs. Is everyone afraid to look? Why are his grandparents silent? For a few of Mark's breaths the nocturnal voices are too, but he can hear a muffled shuffling—the noise of a determined march. Then the caller announces "Pair of fives," and as her followers chant "We're the wives" the procession appears at the end of the road.

It's led by the fleshy woman. As she advances up the middle of the street she's followed by her moustached friend and the nodding one, and then their fellow players limp or trot or hobble in pairs around the corner. The orange glow of the streetlamp lends them a rusty tinge like an unnatural tan. Mark doesn't need to count them to be certain that the parade includes everybody from the bingo hall except the man who was onstage and Mark's grandmother. As his grip on the windowsill bruises his fingers the fleshy woman declares "Ninety-eight."

She has a handful of bingo cards and is reading out the numbers. "We're his fate," the procession declares with enthusiasm, and Mark sees eyes glitter, not only with the streetlight. The moustached woman wipes her upper lip with a finger and thumb while her partner in the procession nods so eagerly that she looks in danger of succumbing to a fit. "Eighty-nine," their leader intones as if she's reading from a missal, and the parade almost as long as the street chants "He'll be mine."

They're close enough for Mark to see the fleshy woman join in the response. He sees her quivering from head to foot with every step she takes towards him, and then his attention is caught by the lanky woman in the middle of the procession. She's by no means alone in fumbling at a breast as though she's impatient to give it the air. That's among the reasons why Mark lets go of the curtain and the windowsill to huddle under the quilt. Once upon a time he might have believed this would hide him, but it doesn't even shut out the voices below the window. "Twenty-four," the caller shouts and joins in the chant of "Here's the door."

This is entirely too accurate for Mark's liking. It's the number of the house. As he hugs his knees with his clasped arms and grinds his spine against the wall he hears a muffled rumble close to him. Someone has opened the window of the next bedroom. Mark holds his breath until his grandfather shouts "Not here. Like Lottie says, you've been here once."

"That was a long time ago, Len." Mark can't tell whether this is reminiscent or dismissive, but the tone doesn't quite leave the fleshy woman's voice as she says "It's either you or him."

After a pause the window rumbles shut, and Mark finds it hard to breathe. He hears footsteps padding down the stairs—whose, he doesn't know—and the front door judders open. This is followed by an outburst of shuffling, first in the street and almost at once to some extent inside the house. As it begins to mount the stairs Mark hears the caller's voice, though it's little more than a whisper. "Number one," she prompts, and a murmuring chorus responds "Let's be mum." Is it proposing a role to play or enjoining secrecy? Mark can't judge, even when the procession sets about chanting in a whisper "Mum, mum, mum…" The repetition seems to fill the house, which feels too small for it, especially once the front door closes behind the last of the procession. The chorus can't blot out the shuffling, which sounds like the restlessness of an impatient queue. All Mark can do is squeeze his eyes so tight that the darkness throbs in time with his pulse, and he manages not to look until he hears a door creep open.

# The Entertainment

By the time Shone found himself back in Westingsea he was able to distinguish only snatches of the road as the wipers strove to fend off the downpour. The promenade where he'd seen pensioners wheeled out for an early dose of sunshine, and backpackers piling into coaches that would take them inland to the Lakes, was waving isolated trees that looked too young to be out by themselves at a grey sea baring hundred of edges of foam. Through a mixture of static and the hiss on the windscreen a local radio station advised drivers to stay off the roads, and he felt he was being offered a chance. Once he had a room he could phone Ruth. At the end of the promenade he swung the Cavalier around an old stone soldier drenched almost black and coasted alongside the seafront hotels.

There wasn't a welcome in sight. A sign in front of the largest and whitest hotel said NO, apparently having lost the patience to light up its second word. He turned along the first of the narrow streets of boarding houses, in an unidentifiable one of which he'd stayed with his parents most of fifty years ago, but the placards in the windows were just as uninviting. Some of the streets he remembered having been composed of small hotels had fewer buildings now, all of them care homes for the elderly. He had to lower his window to read the signs across the roads, and before he'd finished his right side was soaked. He needed a room for the night—he hadn't the energy to drive back to London. Half an hour would take him to the motorway, near which he was bound to find a hotel. But he had only reached the edge of town, and was braking at a junction, when he saw hands adjusting a notice in the window of a broad three-storey house.

He squinted in the mirror to confirm he wasn't in anyone's way, then inched his window down. The notice had either fallen or been removed, but the parking area at the end of the short drive was unoccupied, and above the high thick streaming wall a signboard that frantic bushes were doing their best to obscure appeared to say most of HOTEL. He veered between the gateposts and came close to touching the right breast of the house.

He couldn't distinguish much through the bay window. At least one layer of net curtains was keeping the room to itself. Beyond heavy purple curtains trapping moisture against the glass, a light was suddenly extinguished. He grabbed his overnight bag from the rear seat and dashed for the open porch.

The rain kept him company as he poked the round brass bellpush next to the tall front door. There was no longer a button, only a socket harbouring a large bedraggled spider that recoiled almost as violently as his finger did. He hadn't laid hold of the rusty knocker above the neutral grimace of the letter-slot when a woman called a warning or a salutation as she hauled the door open. "Here's someone now."

She was in her seventies but wore a dress that failed to cover her mottled toadstools of knees. She stooped as though the weight of her loose throat was bringing her face, which was almost as white as her hair, to meet his. "Are you the entertainment?" she said.

Behind her a hall more than twice his height and darkly papered with a pattern of embossed vines not unlike arteries led to a central staircase that vanished under the next floor up. Beside her a long-legged table was strewn with crumpled brochures for local attractions; above it a pay telephone with no number in the middle of its dial clung to the wall. Shone was trying to decide if this was indeed a hotel when the question caught up with him. "Am I…"

"Don't worry, there's a room waiting." She scowled past him and shook her head like a wet dog. "And there'd be dinner and a breakfast for anyone who settles them down."

He assumed this referred to the argument that had started or recommenced in the room where the light he'd seen switched off had been relit. Having lost count of the number of arguments he'd dealt with in the Hackney kindergarten where he worked, he didn't see why this should be any different. "I'll have a stab," he said, and marched into the room.

Despite its size, it was full of just two women—of the breaths of one at least as wide as her bright pink dress, who was struggling to lever herself up from an armchair with a knuckly stick and collapsing red-faced, and of the antics of her companion, a lanky woman in the flapping jacket of a dark blue suit and the skirt of a greyer outfit, who'd bustled away from the light-switch to flutter the pages of a television listings magazine before scurrying fast as the cartoon squirrel on the television to twitch the cord of the velvet curtains, an activity Shone took to have dislodged whatever notice had been in the window. Both women were at least as old as the person who'd admitted him, but he didn't let that daunt him. "What seems to be the problem?" he said, and immediately had to say "I can't hear you if you both talk at once."

"The light's in my eyes," the woman in the chair complained, though of the six bulbs in the chandelier one was dead, another missing. "Unity keeps putting it on when she knows I'm watching."

"Amelia's had her cartoons on all afternoon," Unity said, darting at the television, then drumming her knuckles on top of an armchair instead. "I want to see what's happening in the world."

"Shall we let Unity watch the news now, Amelia? If it isn't something you like watching you won't mind if the light's on."

Amelia glowered before delving into her cleavage for an object that she flung at him. Just in time to field it he identified it as the remote control. Unity ran to snatch it from him, and as a newsreader appeared with a war behind him Shone withdrew. He was lingering over closing the door while he attempted to judge whether the mountainous landscapes on the walls were vague with mist or dust when a man at his back murmured "Come out, quick, and shut it."

He was a little too thin for his suit that was grey as his sparse hair. Though his pinkish eyes looked harassed, and he kept shrugging his shoulders as though to displace a shiver, he succeeded in producing enough of a grateful smile to part his teeth. "By gum, Daph said you'd sort them out, and you have. You can stay," he said.

Among the questions Shone was trying to resolve was why the man seemed familiar, but a gust of rain so fierce it strayed under the front door made the offer irresistible. "Overnight, you mean," he thought it best to check.

"That's the least," the manager presumably only began, and twisted round to find the stooped woman. "Daph will show you up, Mr…"

"Shonc."

"Who is he?" Daph said as if preparing to announce him.

"Tom Shone," Shone told her.

"Mr Thomson?"

"Tom Shone. First name Tom."

"Mr Tom Thomson."

He might have suspected a joke if it hadn't been for her earnestness, and so he appealed to the manager. "Do you need my signature?"

"Later, don't you fret," the manager assured him, receding along the hall.

"And as for payment…"

"Just room and board. That's always the arrangement."

"You mean you want me to…"

"Enjoy yourself," the manager called, and disappeared beyond the stairs into somewhere that smelled of an imminent dinner.

Shone felt his overnight bag leave his shoulder. Daph had relieved him of the burden and was striding upstairs, turning in a crouch to see that he followed. "He's forever off somewhere, Mr Snell," she said, and repeated "Mr Snell."

Shone wondered if he was being invited to reply with a joke until she added "Don't worry, we know what it's like to forget your name."

She was saying he, not she, had been confused about it. If she hadn't cantered out of sight his response would have been as sharp as the rebukes he gave his pupils when they were too childish. Above the middle floor the staircase bent towards the front of the house, and he saw how unexpectedly far the place went back. Perhaps nobody was staying in that section, since the corridor was dark and smelled old. He grabbed the banister to speed himself up, only to discover it wasn't much less sticky than a sucked lollipop. By the time he arrived at the top of the house he was furious to find himself panting.

Daph had halted at the far end of a passage lit, if that was the word, by infrequent bulbs in glass flowers sprouting from the walls. Around them shadows fattened the veins of the paper. "This'll be you," Daph said and pushed open a door.

Beside a small window under a yellowing light bulb the ceiling angled almost to the carpet brown as mud. A narrow bed stood in the angle, opposite a wardrobe and dressing-table and a sink beneath a dingy mirror. At least there was a phone on a shelf by the sink. Daph passed him his bag as he ventured into the room. "You'll be fetched when it's time," she told him.

"Time? Time..."

"For dinner and all the fun, silly," she said, with a laugh so shrill his ears wanted to flinch.

She was halfway to the stairs when he thought to call after her "Aren't I supposed to have a key?"

"Mr Snell will have it. Mr Snell," she reminded him, and was gone.

He had to phone Ruth as soon as he was dry and changed. There must be a bathroom somewhere near. He hooked his bag over his shoulder with a finger and stepped into the twilight of the corridor. He'd advanced only a few paces when Daph's head poked over the edge of the floor. "You're never leaving us."

He felt absurdly guilty. "Just after the bathroom."

"It's where you're going," she said, firmly enough to be commanding rather than advising him, and vanished down the hole that was the stairs.

She couldn't have meant the room next to his. When he succeeded in coaxing the sticky plastic knob to turn, using the tips of a finger and thumb, he found a room much like his, except that the window was in the angled roof. Seated on the bed in the dimness on its way to dark was a figure in a toddler's blue overall—a Teddy bear with large black ragged eyes or perhaps none. The bed in the adjacent room was strewn with photographs so blurred that he could distinguish only the grin every one of them bore. Someone had been knitting in the next room, but had apparently lost concentration, since one arm of the mauve sweater was at least twice the size of the other. A knitting needle pinned each arm to the bed. Now Shone was at the stairs, beyond which the rear of the house was as dark as that section of the floor below. Surely Daph would have told him if he was on the wrong side of the corridor, and the area past the stairs wasn't as abandoned as it looked: he could hear a high-pitched muttering from the dark, a voice gabbling a plea almost too fast for words, praying with such urgency the speaker seemed to have no time to pause for breath. Shone hurried past the banisters that enclosed three sides of the top of the stairs, and pushed open the door immediately beyond them. There was the bath, and inside the plastic curtains that someone had left closed would be a shower. He elbowed the door wide, and the shower curtains shifted to acknowledge him.

Not only they had. As he tugged the frayed cord to kindle the bare bulb, he heard a muffled giggle from the region of the bath. He threw his bag onto the hook on the door and yanked the shower curtains apart. A naked woman so scrawny he could see not just her ribs but the shape of bones inside her buttocks was crouching on all fours in the bath. She peered wide-eyed over one splayed knobbly hand at him, then dropped the hand to reveal a nose half the width of her face and a gleeful mouth devoid of teeth as she sprang past him. She was out of the room before he could avoid seeing her shrunken disused breasts and pendulous grey-bearded stomach. He heard her run into a room at the dark end of the corridor, calling out "For it now" or perhaps "You're it now." He didn't know if the words were intended for him. He was too busy noticing that the door was boltless.

He wedged his shoes against the corner below the hinges and piled his sodden clothes on top, then padded across the sticky linoleum to the bath. It was cold as stone, and sank at least half an inch with a loud creak as he stepped into it under the blind brass eye of the shower. When he twisted the reluctant squeaky taps it felt at first as though the rain had got in, but swiftly grew so hot he backed into the clammy plastic. He had to press himself against the cold tiled wall to reach the taps, and had just reduced the temperature to bearable when he heard the doorknob rattle. "Taken," he shouted. "Someone's in here."

"My turn."

The voice was so close the speaker's mouth must be pressed against the door. When the rattling increased in vigour Shone yelled "I won't be long. Ten minutes."

"My turn."

It wasn't the same voice. Either the speaker had deepened his pitch in an attempt to daunt Shone or there was more than one person at the door. Shone reached for the sliver of soap in the dish protruding from the tiles, but contented himself with pivoting beneath the shower once he saw the soap was coated with grey hair. "Wait out there," he shouted. "I've nearly finished. No, don't wait. Come back in five minutes."

The rattling ceased, and at least one body dealt the door a large soft thump. Shone wrenched the curtains open in time to see his clothes spill across the linoleum. "Stop that," he roared, and heard someone retreat—either a spectacularly crippled person or two people bumping into the walls as they carried on a struggle down the corridor. A door slammed, then slammed again, unless there were two. By then he was out of the bath and grabbing the solitary bath-towel from the shaky rack. A spider with legs like long grey hairs and a wobbling body as big as Shone's thumbnail scuttled out of the towel and hid under the bath.

He hadn't brought a towel with him. He would have been able to borrow one of Ruth's. He held the towel at arm's length by two corners and shook it over the bath. When nothing else emerged, he rubbed his hair and the rest of him as swiftly as he could. He unzipped his case and donned the clothes he would have sported for dining with Ruth. He hadn't brought a change of shoes, and when he tried on those he'd worn, they squelched. He gathered up his soaked clothes and heaped them with the shoes on his bag, and padded quickly to his room.

As he kneed the door open he heard sounds beyond it: a gasp, another, and then voices spilling into the dark. Before he crossed the room, having dumped his soggy clothes and bag in the wardrobe that, like the rest of the furniture, was secured to a wall and the floor, he heard the voices stream into the house. They must belong to a coach party—brakes and doors had been the sources of the gasps. On the basis of his experiences so far, the influx of residents lacked appeal for him, and made him all the more anxious to speak to Ruth. Propping his shoes against the ribs of the tepid radiator, he sat on the underfed pillow and lifted the sticky receiver.

As soon as he obtained a tone he began to dial. He was more than halfway through Ruth's eleven digits when Snell's voice interrupted. "Who do you want?"

"Long distance."

"You can't get out from the rooms, I'm afraid. There's a phone down here in the hall. Everything else as you want it, Mr Thomson? Only I've got people coming in."

Shone heard some of them outside his room. They were silent except for an unsteady shuffling and the hushed sounds of a number of doors. He could only assume they had been told not to disturb him. "There were people playing games up here," he said.

"They'll be getting ready for tonight. They do work themselves up, some of them. Everything else satisfactory?"

"There's nobody hiding in my room, if that's what you mean."

"Nobody but you."

That struck Shone as well past enough, and he was about to

make his feelings clear while asking for his key when the manager said "We'll see you down shortly, then." The line died at once, leaving Shone to attempt an incredulous grin at the events so far. He intended to share it with his reflection above the sink, but hadn't realised until now that the mirror was covered with cracks or a cobweb. The lines appeared to pinch his face thin, to discolour his flesh and add wrinkles. When he leaned closer to persuade himself that was merely an illusion, he saw movement in the sink. An object he'd taken to be a long grey hair was snatched into the plughole, and he glimpsed the body it belonged to squeezing itself out of sight down the pipe. He had to remind himself to transfer his wallet and loose coins and keys from his wet clothes to his current pockets before he hastened out of the room.

The carpet in the passage was damp with footprints, more of which he would have avoided if he hadn't been distracted by sounds in the rooms. Where he'd seen the Teddy bear someone was murmuring "Up you come to mummy. Gummy gum." Next door a voice was crooning "There you all are", presumably to the photographs, and Shone was glad to hear no words from the site of the lopsided knitting, only a clicking so rapid it sounded mechanical. Rather than attempt to interpret any of the muffled noises from the rooms off the darker section of the corridor, he padded downstairs so fast he almost missed his footing twice.

Nothing was moving in the hall except rain under the front door. Several conversations were ignoring one another in the television lounge. He picked up the receiver and thrust coins into the box, and his finger faltered over the zero on the dial. Perhaps because he was distracted by the sudden hush, he couldn't remember Ruth's number.

He dragged the hole of the zero around the dial as far as it would go in case that brought him the rest of the number, and as the hole whirred back to its starting point, it did. Ten more turns of the dial won him a ringing padded with static, and he felt as if the entire house was waiting for Ruth to answer. It took six pairs of rings—longer than she needed to cross her flat—to make her say "Ruth Lawson."

"It's me, Ruth." When there was silence he tried reviving their joke. "Old Ruthless."

"What now, Tom?"

He'd let himself hope for at least a dutiful laugh, but its absence threw him less than the reaction from within the television lounge: a titter, then several. "I just wanted you to know—"

"You're mumbling again. I can't hear you."

He was only seeking to be inaudible to anyone but her. "I say I wanted you to know I really did get the day wrong," he said louder. "I really thought I was supposed to be coming up today."

"Since when has your memory been that bad?"

"Since, I don't know, today, it seems like. No, fair enough, you'll be thinking of your birthday. I know I forgot that too."

A wave of mirth escaped past the ajar door across the hall. Surely however many residents were in there must be laughing at the television with the sound turned down, he told himself as Ruth retorted "If you can forget that you'll forget anything."

"I'm sorry."

"I'm sorrier."

"I'm sorriest," he risked saying, and immediately wished he hadn't completed their routine, not only since it no longer earned him the least response from her but because of the roars of laughter from the television lounge. "Look, I just wanted to be sure you knew I wasn't trying to catch you out, that's all."

"Tom."

All at once her voice was sympathetic, the way it might have sounded at an aged relative's bedside. "Ruth," he said, and almost as stupidly "What?"

"You might as well have been."

"I might . . . you mean I might . . ."

"I mean you nearly did."

"Oh." After a pause as hollow as he felt he repeated the syllable, this time not with disappointment but with all the surprise he could summon up. He might have uttered yet another version of the sound, despite or even because of the latest outburst of amusement across the hall, if Ruth hadn't spoken. "I'm talking to him now."

"Talking to who?"

Before the words had finished leaving him Shone understood that she hadn't been speaking to him but about him, because he could hear a man's voice in her flat. Its tone was a good deal more than friendly to her, and it was significantly younger than his. "Good luck to you both," he said, less ironically and more maturely than he would have preferred, and snagged the hook with the receiver.

A single coin trickled down the chute and hit the carpet with a plop. Amidst hilarity in the television lounge several women were crying "To who, to who" like a flock of owls. "He's good, isn't he," someone else remarked, and Shone was trying to decide where to take his confusion bordering on panic when a bell began to toll as it advanced out of the dark part of the house.

It was a small but resonant gong wielded by the manager. Shone heard an eager rumble of footsteps in the television lounge, and more of the same overhead. As he hesitated Daph dodged around the manager towards him. "Let's get you sat down before they start their fuss," she said.

"I'll just fetch my shoes from my room."

"You don't want to bump into the old lot up there. They'll be wet, won't they?"

"Who?" Shone demanded, then regained enough sense of himself to answer his own question with a weak laugh. "My shoes, you mean. They're the only ones I've brought with me."

"I'll find you something once you're in your place," she said, opening the door opposite the television lounge, and stooped lower to hurry him. As soon as he trailed after her she bustled the length of the dining-room and patted a small isolated table until he accepted its solitary straight chair. This faced the room and was boxed in by three long tables, each place at which was set like his with a plastic fork and spoon. Beyond the table opposite him velvet curtains shifted impotently as the windows trembled with rain. Signed photographs covered much of the walls—portraits of comedians he couldn't say he recognised, looking jolly or amusingly lugubrious. "We've had them all," Daph said. "They kept us going. It's having fun keeps the old lot alive." Some of this might have been addressed not just to him, because she was on her way out of the room. He barely had time to observe that the plates on the Welsh dresser to his left were painted on the wood, presumably to obviate breakage, before the residents crowded in.

A disagreement over the order of entry ceased at the sight of him. Some of the diners were scarcely able to locate their places for gazing at him rather more intently than he cared to reciprocate. Several of them were so inflated that he was unable to determine their gender except by their clothes, and not even thus in the case of the most generously trousered of them, whose face appeared to be sinking into a nest of flesh. Contrast was provided by a man so emaciated his handless wristwatch kept sliding down to his knuckles. Unity and Amelia sat facing Shone, and then, to his dismay, the last of the eighteen seats was occupied by the woman he'd found in the bath, presently covered from neck to ankles in a black sweater and slacks. When she regarded him with an expression of never having seen him before and delight at doing so now he tried to feel some relief, but he was mostly experiencing how all the diners seemed to be awaiting some action from him. Their attention had started to paralyse him when Daph and Mr Snell reappeared through a door Shone hadn't noticed beside the Welsh dresser.

The manager set about serving the left-hand table with bowls of soup while Daph hurried over, brandishing an especially capacious pair of the white cloth slippers Shone saw all the residents were wearing. "We've only these," she said, dropping them at his feet. "They're dry, that's the main thing. See how they feel."

Shone could almost have inserted both feet into either of them. "I'll feel a bit of a clown, to tell you the truth."

"Never mind, you won't be going anywhere."

Shone poked his feet into the slippers and lifted them to discover whether the footwear had any chance of staying on. At once all the residents burst out laughing. Some of them stamped as a form of applause, and even Snell produced a fleeting grateful smile as he and Daph retreated to the kitchen. Shone let his feet drop, which was apparently worth another round of merriment. It faded as Daph and Snell came out with more soup, a bowl of which the manager brought Shone, lowering it over the guest's shoulder before spreading his fingers on either side of him. "Here's Tommy Thomson for you," he announced, and leaned down to murmur in Shone's ear "That'll be all right, won't it? Sounds better."

At that moment Shone's name was among his lesser concerns. Instead he gestured at the plastic cutlery. "Do you think I could—"

Before he had time to ask for metal utensils with a knife among them, Snell moved away as though the applause and the coos of joy his announcement had drawn were propelling him. "Just be yourself," he mouthed at Shone.

The spoon was the size Shone would have used to stir tea if the doctor hadn't recently forbidden him sugar. As he picked it up there was instant silence. He lowered it into the thin broth, where he failed to find anything solid, and raised it to his lips. The brownish liquid tasted of some unidentifiable meat with a rusty undertaste. He was too old to be finicky about food that had been served to everyone. He swallowed, and when his body raised no protest he set about spooning the broth into himself as fast as he could without spilling it, to finish the task.

He'd barely signalled his intentions when the residents began to cheer and stamp. Some of them imitated his style with the broth while others demonstrated how much more theatrically they could drink theirs; those closest to the hall emitted so much noise that he could have thought part of the slurping came from outside the room. When he frowned in that direction, the residents chortled as though he'd made another of the jokes he couldn't avoid making.

He dropped the spoon in the bowl at last, only to have Daph return it to the table with a briskness not far short of a rebuke. While she and Snell were in the kitchen everyone else gazed at Shone, who felt compelled to raise his eyebrows and hold out his hands. One of the expanded people nudged another, and both of them wobbled gleefully, and then all the residents were overcome by laughter that continued during the arrival of the main course, as if this was a joke they were eager for him to see. His plate proved to bear three heaps of mush, white and pale green and a glistening brown. "What is it?" he dared to ask Daph.

"What we always have," she said as if to a child or to someone who'd reverted to that state. "It's what we need to keep us going."

The heaps were of potatoes and vegetables and some kind of mince with an increased flavour of the broth. He did his utmost to eat naturally, despite the round of applause this brought him. Once his innards began to feel heavy he lined up the utensils on his by no means clear plate, attracting Daph to stoop vigorously at him. "I've finished," he said.

"Not yet."

When she stuck out her hands he thought she was going to return the fork and spoon to either side of his plate. Instead she removed it and began to clear the next table. While he'd been concentrating on hiding his reaction to his food the residents had gobbled theirs, he saw. The plates were borne off to the kitchen, leaving an expectant silence broken only by a restless shuffling. Wherever he glanced, he could see nobody's feet moving, and he told himself the sounds had been Daph's as she emerged from the kitchen with a large cake iced white as a memorial. "Daph's done it again," the hugest resident piped.

Shone took that to refer to the portrait in icing of a clown on top of the cake. He couldn't share the general enthusiasm for it; the clown looked undernourished and blotchily red-faced, and not at all certain what shape his wide twisted gaping lips should form. Snell brought in a pile of plates on which Daph placed slices of cake, having cut it in half and removed the clown's head from his shoulders in the process, but the distribution of slices caused some debate. "Give Tommy Thomson my eye," a man with bleary bloodshot eyeballs said.

"He can have my nose," offered the woman he'd seen in the bath.

"I'm giving him the hat," Daph said, which met with hoots of approval. The piece of cake she gave him followed the outline almost precisely of the clown's sagging pointed cap. At least it would bring dinner to an end, he thought, and nothing much could be wrong with a cake. He didn't expect it to taste faintly of the flavour of the rest of the meal. Perhaps that was why, provoking a tumult of jollity, he began to cough and then choke on a crumb. Far too eventually Daph brought him a glass of water in which he thought he detected the same taste. "Thanks," he gasped anyway, and as his coughs and the applause subsided, managed to say "Thanks. All over now. If you'll excuse me, I think I'll take myself off to bed."

The noise the residents had made so far was nothing to the uproar with which they greeted this. "We haven't had the entertainment yet," Unity protested, jumping to her feet and looking more than ready to dart the length of the room. "Got to sing for your supper, Tommy Thomson."

"We don't want any songs and we don't want any speeches," Amelia declared. "We always have the show."

"The show," all the diners began to chant, and clapped and stamped in time with it, led by the thumping of Amelia's stick. "The show. The show."

The manager leaned across Shone's table. His eyes were pinker than ever, and blinking several times a second. "Better put it on for them or you'll get no rest," he muttered. "You won't need to be anything special."

Perhaps it was the way Snell was leaning down to him that let Shone see why he seemed familiar. Could he really have run the hotel where Shone had stayed with his parents nearly fifty years ago? How old would he have to be? Shone had no chance to wonder while the question was "What are you asking me to do?"

"Nothing much. Nothing someone of your age can't cope with. Come on and I'll show you before they start wanting to play their games."

It wasn't clear how much of a threat this was meant to be. Just now Shone was mostly grateful to be ushered away from the stamping and the chant. Retreating upstairs had ceased to tempt him, and fleeing to his car made no sense when he could hardly shuffle across the carpet for trying to keep his feet in the slippers. Instead he shambled after the manager to the doorway of the television lounge. "Go in there," Snell urged, and gave him a wincing smile. "Just stand in it. Here they come."

The room had been more than rearranged. The number of seats had been increased to eighteen by the addition of several folding chairs. All the seats faced the television, in front of which a small portable theatre not unlike the site of a Punch and Judy show had been erected. Above the deserted ledge of a stage rose a tall pointed roof that reminded Shone of the clown's hat. Whatever words had been inscribed across the base of the gable were as faded as the many colours of the frontage. He'd managed to decipher only ENTER HERE when he found himself hobbling towards the theatre, driven by the chanting that had emerged into the hall.

The rear of the theatre was a heavy velvet curtain, black where it wasn't greenish. A slit had been cut in it up to a height of about four feet. As he ducked underneath, the mouldy velvet clung to the nape of his neck. A smell of damp and staleness enclosed him when he straightened up. His elbows knocked against the sides of the box, disturbing the two figures that lay on a shelf under the stage, their empty bodies sprawling, their faces nestling together upside down as though they had dragged themselves close for companionship. He turned the faces upwards and saw that the figures, whose fixed grins and eyes were almost too wide for amusement, were supposed to be a man and a woman, although only a few tufts of grey hair clung to each dusty skull. He was nerving himself to insert his hands in the gloves of the bodies when the residents stamped chanting into the room.

Unity ran to a chair and then, restless with excitement, to another. Amelia dumped herself in the middle of a sofa and inched groaning to one end. Several of the jumbo residents lowered themselves onto folding chairs that looked immediately endangered. At least the seating of the audience put paid to the chant, but everyone's gaze fastened on Shone until he seemed to feel it clinging to the nerves of his face. Beyond the residents Snell mouthed "Just slip them on."

Shone pulled the open ends of the puppets towards him and poked them gingerly wider, dreading the emergence of some denizen from inside one or both. They appeared to be uninhabited, however, and so he thrust his hands in, trying to think which of his kindergarten stories he might adapt for the occasion. The brownish material fitted itself easily over his hands, almost as snug as the skin it resembled, and before he was ready each thumb was a puppet's arm, the little fingers too, and three fingers were shakily raising each head as if the performers were being roused from sleep. The spectators were already cheering, a response that seemed to entice the tufted skulls above the stage. Their entrance was welcomed by a clamour in which requests gradually became audible. "Let's see them knock each other about like the young lot do these days."

"Football with the baby."

"Make them go like animals."

"Smash their heads together."

They must be thinking of Punch and Judy, Shone told himself—and then a wish succeeded in quelling the rest. "Let's have Old Ruthless."

"Old Ruthless" was the chant as the stamping renewed itself—as his hands sprang onto the stage to wag the puppets at each other. All at once everything he'd been through that day seemed to have concentrated itself in his hands, and perhaps that was the only way he could be rid of it. He nodded the man that was his right hand at the balding female and uttered a petulant croak. "What do you mean, it's not my day?"

He shook the woman and gave her a squeaky voice. "What day do you think it is?"

"It's Wednesday, isn't it? Thursday, rather. Hang on, it's Friday, of course. Saturday, I mean."

"It's Sunday. Can't you hear the bells?"

"I thought they were for us to be married. Hey, what are you hiding there? I didn't know you had a baby yet."

"That's no baby, that's my boyfriend."

Shone twisted the figures to face the audience. The puppets might have been waiting for guffaws or even groans at the echo of an old joke: certainly he was. The residents were staring at him with, at best, bemusement. Since he'd begun the performance the only noise had been the sidling of the puppets along the stage and the voices that caught harshly in his throat. The manager and Daph were gazing at him over the heads of the residents; both of them seemed to have forgotten how to blink or grin. Shone turned the puppets away from the spectators as he would have liked to turn himself. "What's up with us?" he squeaked, wagging the woman's head. "We aren't going down very well."

"Never mind, I still love you. Give us a kiss," he croaked, and made the other puppet totter a couple of steps before it fell on its face. The loud crack of the fall took him off guard, as did the way the impact trapped his fingers in the puppet's head. The figure's ungainly attempts to stand up weren't nearly as simulated as he would have preferred. "It's these clown's shoes. You can't expect anyone to walk in them," he grumbled. "Never mind looking as if I'm an embarrassment."

"You're nothing else, are you? You'll be forgetting your own name next."

"Don't be daft," he croaked, no longer understanding why he continued to perform, unless to fend off the silence that was dragging words and antics out of him. "We both know what my name is."

"Not after that crack you fetched your head. You won't be able to keep anything in there now."

"Well, that's where you couldn't be wronger. My name…" He meant the puppet's, not his own: that was why he was finding it hard to produce. "It's, you know, you know perfectly well. You know it as well as I do."

"See, it's gone."

"Tell me or I'll thump you till you can't stand up," Shone snarled in a rage that was no longer solely the puppet's, and brought the helplessly grinning heads together with a sound like the snapping of bone. The audience began to cheer at last, but he was scarcely aware of them. The collision had split the faces open, releasing the top joints of his fingers only to trap them in the splintered gaps. The clammy bodies of the puppets clung to him as his hands wrenched at each other. Abruptly something gave, and the female head flew off as the body tore open. His right elbow hit the wall of the theatre, and the structure lurched at him. As he tried to steady it, the head of the puppet rolled under his feet. He tumbled backwards into the mouldy curtains. The theatre reeled with him, and the room tipped up.

He was lying on his back, and his breath was somewhere else. In trying to prevent the front of the theatre from striking him he'd punched himself on the temple with the cracked male head. Through the proscenium he saw the ceiling high above him and heard the appreciation of the audience. More time passed than he thought necessary before several of them approached.

Either the theatre was heavier than he'd realised or his fall had weakened him. Even once he succeeded in peeling Old Ruthless off his hand he was unable to lift the theatre off himself as the puppet lay like a deflated baby on his chest. At last Amelia lowered herself towards him, and he was terrified that she intended to sit on him. Instead she thrust a hand that looked boiled almost into his face to grab the proscenium and haul the theatre off him. As someone else bore it away she seized his lapels and, despite the creaking of her stick, yanked him upright while several hands helped raise him from behind. "Are you fit?" she wheezed.

"I'll be fine," Shone said before he knew. All the chairs had been pushed back against the windows, he saw. "We'll show you one of our games now," Unity said behind him.

"You deserve it after all that," said Amelia, gathering the fragments of the puppets to hug them to her breasts.

"I think I'd like—"

"That's right, you will. We'll show you how we play. Who's got the hood?"

"Me," Unity cried. "Someone do it up for me."

Shone turned to see her flourishing a black cap. As she raised it over her head, he found he was again robbed of breath. When she tugged it down he realised that it was designed to cover the player's eyes, more like a magician's prop than an element of any game. The man with the handless watch dangling from his wrist pulled the cords of the hood tight behind her head and tied them in a bow, then twirled her round several times, each of which drew from her a squeal only just of pleasure. She wobbled around once more as, having released her, he tiptoed to join the other residents against the walls of the room.

She had her back to Shone, who had stayed by the chairs, beyond which the noise of rain had ceased. She darted away from him, her slippered feet patting the carpet, then lurched sideways towards nobody in particular and cocked her head. She was well out of the way of Shone's route to the door, where Daph and the manager looked poised to sneak out. He only had to avoid the blinded woman and he would be straight up to his room, either to barricade himself in or to retrieve his belongings and head for the car. He edged one foot forward into the toe of the slipper, and Unity swung towards him. "Caught you. I know who that is, Mr Tommy Thomson."

"No you don't," Shone protested in a rage at everything that had led to the moment, but Unity swooped at him. She closed her bony hands around his cheeks and held on tight far longer than seemed reasonable before undoing the bow of the hood with her right hand while gripping and stroking his chin with the other. "Now it's your turn to go in the dark."

"I think I've had enough for one day, if you'll excuse—"

This brought a commotion of protests not far short of outrage. "You aren't done yet, a young thing like you." "She's older than you and she didn't make a fuss." "You've been caught, you have to play." "If you don't it won't be fair." The manager had retreated into the doorway and was pushing air at Shone with his outstretched hands as Daph mouthed "It's supposed to be the old lot's time." Her words and the rising chant of "Be fair" infected Shone with guilt, aggravated when Unity uncovered her reproachful eyes and held out the hood. He'd disappointed Ruth, he didn't need to let these old folk down too. "Fair enough, I'll play," he said. "Just don't twist me too hard."

He hadn't finished speaking when Unity planted the hood on his scalp and drew the material over his brows. It felt like the clammy bodies of the puppets. Before he had a chance to shudder it was dragging his eyelids down, and he could see nothing but darkness. The hood moulded itself to his cheekbones as rapid fingers tied the cords behind his head. "Not too—" he gasped at whoever started twirling him across the room.

He felt as if he'd been caught by a vortex of cheering and hooting, but it included murmurs too. "He played with me in the bath." "He wouldn't let us in there." "He made me miss my cartoons." "That's right, and he tried to take the control off us." He was being whirled so fast he no longer knew where he was. "Enough," he cried, and was answered by an instant hush. Several hands shoved him staggering forward, and a door closed stealthily behind him.

At first he thought the room had grown colder and damper. Then, as his giddiness steadied, he understood that he was in a different room, further towards the rear of the house. He felt the patchy lack of carpet through his slippers, though that seemed insufficient reason for the faint scraping of feet he could hear surrounding him to sound so harsh. He thought he heard a whisper or the rattling of some object within a hollow container level with his head. Suddenly, in a panic that flared like white blindness inside the hood, he knew Daph's last remark hadn't been addressed to him, nor had it referred to anyone he'd seen so far. His hands flew to untie the hood—not to see where he was and with whom, but which way to run.

He was so terrified to find the cord immovably knotted that it took him seconds to locate the loose ends of the bow. A tug at them released it. He was forcing his fingertips under the edge of the hood when he heard light dry footsteps scuttle towards him, and an article that he tried to think of as a hand groped at his face. He staggered backwards, blindly fending off whatever was there. His fingers encountered ribs barer than they ought to be, and poked between them to meet the twitching contents of the bony cage. The whole of him convulsed as he snatched off the hood and flung it away.

The room was either too dark or not quite dark enough. It was at least the size of the one he'd left, and contained half a dozen sagging armchairs that glistened with moisture, and more than twice as many figures. Some were sprawled like loose bundles of sticks topped with grimacing masks on the chairs, but nonetheless doing their feeble best to clap their tattered hands. Even those that were swaying around him appeared to have left portions of themselves elsewhere. All of them were attached to strings or threads that glimmered in the murk and led his reluctant gaze to the darkest corner of the room.

A restless mass crouched in it—a body with too many limbs, or a huddle of bodies that had grown inextricably entangled by the process of withering. Some of its movement, though not all, was of shapes that swarmed many-legged out of the midst of it, constructing parts of it or bearing away fragments or extending more threads to the other figures in the room. It took an effort that shrivelled his mind before he was able to distinguish anything else: a thin gap between curtains, a barred window beyond—to his left, the outline of a door to the hall. As the figure nearest to him bowed so close he saw the very little it had in the way of eyes peering through the hair it had stretched coquettishly over its face, Shone bolted for the hall.

The door veered aside as his dizziness swept it away. His slippers snagged a patch of carpet and almost threw him on his face. The doorknob refused to turn in his sweaty grasp, even when he gripped it with both hands. Then it yielded, and as the floor at his back resounded with a mass of uneven yet purposeful shuffling, the door juddered open. He hauled himself around it and fled awkwardly, slippers flapping, out of the dark part of the hall.

Every room was shut. Other than the scratching of nails or of the ends of fingers at the door behind him, there was silence. He dashed along the hall, striving to keep the slippers on, not knowing why, knowing only that he had to reach the front door. He seized the latch and flung the door wide and slammed it as he floundered out of the house.

The rain had ceased except for dripping of foliage. The gravel glittered like the bottom of a stream. The coach he'd heard arriving—an old private coach spattered with mud—was parked across the rear of his car, so close it practically touched the bumper. He could never manoeuvre out of that trap. He almost knocked on the window of the television lounge, but instead limped over the gravel and into the street, towards the quiet hotels. He had no idea where he was going except away from the house. He'd hobbled just a few paces, his slippers growing more sodden and his feet sorer at each step, when headlamps sped out of the town.

They belonged to a police car. It halted beside him, its hazard lights twitching, and a uniformed policeman was out of the passenger seat before Shone could speak. The man's slightly chubby concerned face was a wholesome pink beneath a streetlamp. "Can you help me?" Shone pleaded. "I—"

"Don't get yourself in a state, old man. We saw where you came from."

"They boxed me in. My car, I mean, look. If you can just tell them to let me out—"

The driver moved to Shone's other side. He might have been trying to outdo his colleague's caring look. "Calm down now. We'll see to everything for you. What have you done to your head?"

"Banged it. Hit it with, you wouldn't believe me, it doesn't matter. I'll be fine. If I can just fetch my stuff—"

"What have you lost? Won't it be in the house?"

"That's right, at the top. My shoes are."

"Feet hurting, are they? No wonder with you wandering around like that on a night like this. Here, get his other arm." The driver had taken Shone's right elbow in a firm grip, and now he and his partner easily lifted Shone and bore him towards the house. "What's your name, sir?" the driver enquired.

"Not Thomson, whatever anyone says. Not Tommy Thomson or Tom either. Or rather, it's Tom all right, but Tom Shone. That doesn't sound like Thomson, does it? Shone as in shine. I used to know someone who said I still shone for her, you still shine for me, she'd say. Been to see her today as a matter of fact." He was aware of talking too much as the policemen kept nodding at him and the house with its two lit windows—the television lounge's and his—reared over him. "Anyway, the point is the name's Shone," he said. "Ess aitch, not haitch as some youngsters won't be told it isn't, oh en ee. Shone."

"We've got you." The driver reached for the empty bellpush, then pounded on the front door. It swung inwards almost at once, revealing the manager. "Is this gentleman a guest of yours, Mr Snell?" the driver's colleague said.

"Mr Thomson. We thought we'd lost you," Snell declared, and pushed the door wide. All the people from the television lounge were lining the hall like spectators at a parade. "Tommy Thomson," they chanted.

"That's not me," Shone protested, pedalling helplessly in the air until his slippers flew into the hall. "I told you—"

"You did, sir," the driver murmured, and his partner said even lower "Where do you want us to take you?"

"To the top, just to—"

"We know," the driver said conspiratorially. The next moment Shone was sailing to the stairs and up them, with the briefest pause as the policemen retrieved a slipper each. The chant from the hall faded, giving way to a silence that seemed most breathlessly expectant in the darkest sections of the house. He had the police with him, Shone reassured himself. "I can walk now," he said, only to be borne faster to the termination of the stairs. "Where the door's open?" the driver suggested. "Where the light is?"

"That's me. Not me really, anything but, I mean—"

They swung him through the doorway by his elbows and deposited him on the carpet. "It couldn't be anybody else's room," the driver said, dropping the slippers in front of Shone. "See, you're already here."

Shone looked where the policemen were gazing with such sympathy it felt like a weight that was pressing him into the room. A photograph of himself and Ruth, arms around each other's shoulders with a distant mountain behind, had been removed from his drenched suit and propped on the shelf in place of the telephone. "I just brought that," he protested, "you can see how wet it was," and limped across the room to don his shoes. He hadn't reached them when he saw himself in the mirror.

He stood swaying a little, unable to retreat from the sight. He heard the policemen murmur together and withdraw, and their descent of the stairs, and eventually the dual slam of car doors and the departure of the vehicle. His reflection still hadn't allowed him to move. It was no use his telling himself that some of the tangle of wrinkles might be cobwebs, not when his hair was no longer greying but white. "All right, I see it," he yelled—he had no idea at whom. "I'm old. I'm old."

"Soon," said a whisper like an escape of gas in the corridor, along which darkness was approaching as the lamps failed one by one. "You'll be plenty of fun yet," the remains of another voice said somewhere in his room. Before he could bring himself to look for its source, an item at the end of most of an arm fumbled around the door and switched out the light. The dark felt as though his vision was abandoning him, but he knew it was the start of another game. Soon he would know if it was worse than hide and seek—worse than the first sticky unseen touch of the web of the house on his face.

# NO STRINGS

"GOOD NIGHT TILL TOMORROW," PHIL LINFORD SAID, having faded the signature tune of *Linford Till Midnight* up under his voice, "and a special good night to anyone I've been alone with." As he removed his headphones, imitated by the reverse of himself in the dark beyond the inner window, he felt as if he was unburdening himself of all the voices he'd talked to during the previous two hours. They'd been discussing the homeless, whom most of the callers had insisted on describing as beggars or worse, until Linford had declared that he respected anyone who did their best to earn their keep, to feed themselves and their dependants. He hadn't intended to condemn those who only begged, if they were capable of nothing else, but several of his listeners did with increasing viciousness. After all that, the very last caller had hoped aloud that nobody homeless had been listening. Maybe Linford oughtn't to have responded that if they were homeless they wouldn't have anywhere to plug in a radio, but he always tried to end with a joke.

There was no point in leaving listeners depressed: that wasn't the responsibility he was paid for. If he'd given them a chance to have their say and something to carry on chewing over, he'd done what was expected of him. If he weren't doing a good job he wouldn't still be on the air. At least it wasn't television—at least he wasn't making people do no more than sit and gawk. As the second hand of the clock above the console fingered midnight he faded out his tune and gave up the station to the national network.

The news paced him as he walked through the station, killing lights. This year's second war, another famine, a seaboard devastated by a hurricane, a town buried by a volcano—no room for anything local, not even the people who'd been missing for weeks or months. In the deserted newsroom computer terminals presented their blank bulging profiles to him. Beyond the unstaffed reception desk a solitary call was flashing like a warning on the switchboard. Its glow and its insect clicking died as he padded across the plump carpet of the reception area. He was reaching for the electronic latch to let him into the street when he faltered. Beyond the glass door, on the second of the three concrete steps to the pavement, a man was seated with his back to him.

Had he fallen asleep over the contents of his lap? He wore a black suit a size too large, above which peeked an inch of collar gleaming white as a vicar's beneath the neon streetlights, not an ensemble that benefited from being topped by a dark green baseball cap pulled as low as it would stretch on the bald neck. If he was waiting for anyone it surely couldn't be Linford, who nonetheless felt as if he had attracted the other somehow, perhaps by having left all the lights on while he was alone in the station. The news brought itself to an end with a droll anecdote about a music student who had almost managed to sell a forged manuscript before the buyer had noticed the composer's name was spelled Beathoven, and Linford eased the door open. He was on the way to opening enough of a gap to sidle through, into the stagnant July heat beneath the heavy clouds, when *Early Morning Moods* commenced with a rush of jaunty flourishes on a violin. At once the figure on the steps jerked to his feet as though tugged by invisible strings and joined in.

So he was a busker, and the contents of his lap had been a violin and its bow, but the discovery wasn't the only reason why

Linford pulled the door wide. The violinist wasn't merely imitating the baroque solo from the radio; he was copying every nuance and intonation, an exact echo no more than a fraction of a second late. Linford felt as though he'd been selected to judge a talent show. "Hey, that's good," he said. "You ought—"

He had barely started speaking when the violinist dodged away with a movement that, whether intentionally or from inability, was less a dance than a series of head-to-toe wriggles that imparted a gypsy swaying to the violin and bow. Perhaps to blot out the interference Linford's voice represented, he began to play louder, though as sweetly as ever. He halted in the middle of the pedestrianised road, between the radio station and a department store lit up for the night. Linford stayed in the doorway until the broadcast melody gave way to the presenter's voice, then closed the door behind him, feeling it lock. "Well done," he called. "Listen, I wonder—"

He could only assume the musician was unable to hear him for playing. No sooner had the melody ended than it recommenced while the player moved away as though guided by his bunch of faint shadows that gave him the appearance of not quite owning up to the possession of several extra limbs. Linford was growing frustrated with the behaviour of someone he only wanted to help. "Excuse me," he said, loud enough for the plate glass across the street to fling his voice back at him. "If it's an audition you need I can get you one. No strings. No commission."

The repetition of the melody didn't falter, but the violinist halted in front of a window scattered with wire skeletons sporting flimsy clothes. When the player didn't turn to face him, Linford followed. He knew talent when he heard it, and local talent was meant to be the point of local radio, but he also didn't mind feeling like the newsman he'd been until he'd found he was better at chatting between his choices of music too old to be broadcast by anyone except him. Years of that had landed him the late-night phone-in, where he sometimes felt he made less of a difference than he had in him. Now here was his chance to make one, and he wasn't about to object if putting the violinist on the air helped his reputation too, not when his contract was due for renewal. He was almost alongside the violinist—close enough to glimpse a twitching of the pale smooth cheek, apparently in time with a mouthing that accompanied the music—when the other danced, if it could be called a dance, away from him.

Unless he was mute—no, even if he was—Linford was determined to extract some sense from him. He supposed it was possible that the musician wasn't quite right in some way, but then it occurred to him that the man might already be employed and so not in need of being discovered. "Do you play with anyone?" he called at the top of his voice.

That seemed to earn him a response. The violinist gestured ahead with his bow, so tersely that Linford heard no break in the music. If the gesture hadn't demonstrated that the player was going Linford's way, he might have sought clarification of whatever he was meant to have understood. Instead he went after the musician, not running or even trotting, since he would have felt absurd, and so not managing to come within arm's length.

The green glow of a window display—clothed dummies exhibiting price tags or challenging the passer-by to guess their worth, their blank-eyed faces immobile and rudimentary as death-masks moulded by a trainee—settled on the baseball cap as the player turned along the side street that led to the car park, and the cap appeared to glisten like moss. A quarter of a mile away down the main road, Linford saw a police car crested with lights speed across a junction, the closest that traffic was allowed to approach. Of course the police could drive anywhere they liked, and their cameras were perched on roofs: one of his late-night partners in conversation had declared that these days the cameras were the nearest things to God. While Linford felt no immediate need of them, there was surely nothing wrong with knowing you were watched. Waving a hand in front of his face to ward off a raw smell the side street had enclosed, he strode after the musician.

The street led directly into the car park, a patch of waste ground about two hundred yards square, strewn with minor chunks of rubble, empty bottles, squashed cans. Only the exit barrier and the solitary presence of Linford's Peugeot indicated that the square did any work. Department stores backed onto its near side, and to its right were restaurants whose bins must be responsible for the wafts of a raw smell. To the left a chain fence crowned with barbed wire protected a building site, while the far side was overlooked by three storeys of derelict offices. The musician was prancing straight for these beneath arc-lights that set his intensified shadows scuttling around him.

He reached the building as Linford came abreast of the car. Without omitting so much as a quaver from the rapid eager melody, the violinist lifted one foot in a movement that suggested the climax of a dance and shoved the back door open. The long brownish stick of the bow jerked up as though to beckon Linford. Before he had time to call out, if indeed he felt obliged to, he saw the player vanish into a narrow oblong black as turned earth.

He rested a hand on the tepid roof of the car and told himself he'd done enough. If the musician was using the disused offices as a squat he was unlikely to be alone, and perhaps his thinness was a symptom of addiction. The prospect of encountering a roomful of drug addicts fell short of appealing to Linford. He was fishing out his keys when an abrupt silence filled the car park. The music, rendered hollow by the dark interior, had ceased in the midst of a phrase, but it hadn't entirely obscured a shrill cry from within—a cry, Linford was too sure to be able to ignore it, for help.

Five minutes—less if he surprised himself by proving to be in a condition to run—would take him back to the radio station to call the police. The main street might even feature a phone booth that accepted coins rather than cards. Less than five minutes could be far too long for whoever needed help, and so Linford stalked across the car park, waving his arms at the offices as he raised his face to mouth for help at the featureless slate sky. He was hoping some policeman was observing him and would send reinforcements—he was hoping to hear a police car raise its voice on its way to him. He'd heard nothing but his own dwarfed isolated footsteps by the time he reached the ajar door.

Perhaps someone had planned to repaint it and given up early in the process. Those patches of old paint that weren't flaking were blistered. The largest blister had split open, and he saw an insect writhe into hiding inside the charred bulge as he dealt the door a slow kick to shove it wide. A short hall with two doors on each side led to a staircase that turned its back on itself halfway up. The widening glare from the car park pressed the darkness back towards the stairs, but only to thicken it on them and within the doorways. Since all the doors were open, he ventured as far as the nearest pair and peered quickly to either side of him.

Random shapes of light were stranded near the windows, all of which were broken. The floorboards of both rooms weren't much less rubbly than the car park. In the room to his left two rusty filing cabinets had been pulled fully open, though surely there could have been nothing to remove from them, let alone to put in. To his right a single office desk was leaning on a broken leg and grimacing with both the black rectangles that used to contain drawers. Perhaps it was his tension that rendered these sights unpleasant, or perhaps it was the raw smell. His will to intervene was failing as he began to wonder if he had really heard any sound except music—and then the cry was repeated above him. It could be a woman's voice or a man's grown shrill with terror, but there was no mistaking its words. "Help," it pleaded. "Oh God."

No more than a couple of streets away a nightclub emitted music and loud voices, followed by an outburst of the slamming of car doors. The noises Linford feel less alone: there must be at least one bouncer outside the nightclub, within earshot of a yell. Perhaps that wasn't as reassuring as he allowed it to seem, but it let him advance to the foot of the stairs and shout into the dimness that was after all not quite dark. "Hello? What's happening up there? What's wrong?"

His first word brought the others out with it. The more of them there were, the less sure he was how advisable they might be. They were met by utter silence except for a creak of the lowest stair, on which he'd tentatively stepped. He hadn't betrayed his presence, he told himself fiercely: whoever was above him had already been aware of him, or there would have been no point to the cry for help. Nevertheless once he seized the splintered banister it was on tiptoe that he ran upstairs. He was turning the bend when an object almost tripped him—the musician's baseball cap.

The banister emitted a groan not far short of vocal as he leaned on it to steady himself. The sound was answered by another cry of "Help", or most of it before the voice was muffled by a hand over the mouth. It came from a room at the far end of the corridor ahead. He was intensely aware of the moment, of scraps of light that clung like pale bats to the ceiling of the corridor, the rat's tails of the flexes that had held sockets for light bulbs, the blackness of the doorways that put him in mind of holes in the ground, the knowledge that this was his last chance to retreat. Instead he ran almost soundlessly up the stairs and past two rooms that a glance into each appeared to show were empty save for rubble and broken glass. Before he came abreast of the further left-hand room he knew it was where he had to go. For a moment he thought someone had hung a sign on the door.

It was a tattered office calendar dangling from a nail. Dates some weeks apart on it—the most recent almost a fortnight ago—were marked with ovals that in daytime might have looked more reddish. He was thinking that the marks couldn't be fingerprints, since they contained no lines, as he took a step into the room.

A shape lay on the area of the floor least visited by daylight, under the window amid shards of glass. A ragged curtain tied at the neck covered all of it except the head, which was so large and bald and swollen it reminded him of the moon. The features appeared to be sinking into it: the unreadably shadowed eyes and gaping whitish lips could have passed for craters, and its nostrils were doing without a nose. Despite its baldness, it was a woman's head, since Linford distinguished the outline of breasts under the curtain—indeed, enough bulk for an extra pair. The head wobbled upright to greet him, its scalp springing alight with the glare from the car park, and large hands whose white flesh was loose as oversized gloves groped out from beneath the curtain. He could see no nails on them. The foot he wasn't conscious of holding in mid-air trod on a fragile object he'd failed to notice—a violinist's bow. It snapped and pitched him forward to see more of the room.

Four desk drawers had been brought into it, one to a corner. Each drawer contained a nest of newspapers and office scrap. Around the drawers were strewn crumpled sheets of music, stained dark as though—Linford thought and then tried not to—they had been employed to wipe mouths. Whatever had occurred had apparently involved the scattering about the bare floor of enough spare bows to equip a small string orchestra. By no means anxious to understand any of the contents of the room until he was well clear of it, Linford was backing away when the violin recommenced its dance behind him.

He swung around and at once saw far too much. The violinist was as bald as the figure under the window, but despite the oddly temporary nature of the bland smooth face, particularly around the nose, it was plain that the musician was female too. The long brown stick she was passing back and forth over the instrument had never been a bow—not that one would have made a difference, since the cracked violin was stringless. The perfect imitation of the broadcast melody was streaming out of her wide toothless mouth, the interior of which was at least as white as the rest of her face. Despite her task she managed a smile, though he sensed it wasn't for him but about him. She was blocking the doorway, and the idea of going closer to her—to the smell of rawness, some of which was certainly emerging from her mouth—almost crushed his mind to nothing. He had to entice her away from the doorway, and he was struggling to will himself to retreat into the room—struggling to keep his back to it—when a voice cried "Help."

It was the cry he'd come to find: exactly the cry, and it was behind him in the room. He twisted half round and saw the shape under the window begin to cover her mouth, then let her hand fall. She must have decided there was no longer any reason to cut the repetition short. "Oh God," she added, precisely as she had before, and rubbed her curtained stomach.

It wasn't just a trick, it was as much of an imitation as the music had been. He had to make more of an effort than he could remember ever having used to swallow the sound the realisation almost forced out of his mouth. For years he'd earned his living by not letting there be more than a second of silence, but could staying absolutely quiet now save him? He was unable to think what else to do, not that he was anything like sure of being capable of silence. "Help, oh God," the curtained shape repeated, more of a demand now, and rubbed her stomach harder. The player dropped the violin and the other item, and before their clatter faded she came at Linford with a writhing movement that might have been a jubilant dance—came just far enough to continue to block his escape.

His lips trembled, his teeth chattered, and he couldn't suppress his words, however idiotic they might be. "My mistake. I only—"

"My mistake. I only." Several voices took up his protest at once, but he could see no mouths uttering it, only an agitation of the lower half of the curtain. Then two small forms crawled out from underneath, immediately followed by two more, all undisguised by any kind of covering. Their plump white bodies seemed all the more wormlike for the incompleteness of the faces on the bald heads—no more than nostrils and greedily dilated mouths. Just the same they wriggled straight to him, grabbing pointed fragments of glass. He saw the violinist press her hands over her ears, and thought that she felt some sympathy for him until he grasped that she was ensuring she didn't have to imitate whatever sound he made. The window was his only chance now: if the creature beneath it was as helpless as she seemed, if he could bear to step over or on her so as to scream from the window for somebody out there to hear—But when he screamed it was from the floor where, having expertly tripped him, the young were swarming up his legs, and he found he had no interest in the words he was screaming, especially when they were repeated in chorus to him.

# Getting it Wrong

Edgeworth was listening to a reminiscence of the bus ride in Hitchcock's *Lucky Jim* when the phone rang. He switched off the deluxe anniversary special collector's edition of *Family Plot* and raised the back of his armchair to vertical. As he grabbed the receiver he saw the time on his watch jerk even closer to midnight. "Hello?" he said and in less than a second "Hello?"

"Is this Mr Edgeworth?"

He didn't recognise the woman's voice, not that he knew any women he could imagine ringing him. "That's who you've got," he said.

"Mr Eric Edgeworth?"

"You're not wrong yet."

"Have you a few minutes, Mr Edgeworth?"

"I don't want anybody fixing my computer. I haven't had an accident at work or anywhere else either. I'm not buying anything and I'm not going to tell you where I shop or what I shop for. My politics are my affair and so's the rest of what I think right now. I've never won a competition, so don't bother saying I have. I don't go on holiday abroad, so you needn't try to sell me anything over there. I don't go away here either, not that it's any of your business. Anything else you want to know?"

"That isn't why we're calling, Mr Edgeworth." In the same brisk efficient tone she said "Will you be a friend of Mary Barton?"

At first Edgeworth couldn't place the name, and then it brought him an image from work—a woman heaping cardboard tubs of popcorn while she kept up a smile no doubt designed to look bright but more symptomatic of bravery. "I wouldn't go that far," he said, although the call had engaged his interest now: it might be the police. "Is she in trouble?"

"She's in inquisition." This might well have meant yes until the woman added "She'd like you to be her expert friend."

"Never heard of it." Having deduced that they were talking about a quiz show, Edgeworth said "Why me?"

"She says she's never met anyone who knows so much about films."

"I don't suppose she has at that." All the same, he was growing suspicious. Could this be a joke played by some of his workmates? "When's she going to want me?" Edgeworth said.

"Immediately if you're agreeable."

"Pretty late for a quiz, isn't it?"

"It's not a show for children, Mr Edgeworth."

"Aren't I supposed to be asked first?"

"We're doing that now."

If all this was indeed a joke, he'd turn it on them. "Fair enough, put her on," he said as he stood up, retrieving his dinner container and its equally plastic fork from beside the chair.

"Please stay on the line."

As Edgeworth used his elbow to switch on the light in the boxy kitchen off the main room of the apartment, a man spoke in his ear. "Eric? Good to have you on. Terry Rice of *Inquisition* here."

He sounded smug and amused, and Edgeworth had no doubt he was a fake. The kitchen bin released a stagnant tang of last night's Chinese takeaway while Edgeworth shoved the new container down hard enough to splinter it and snap the fork in half. "Mary's hoping you'll give her an edge," the man said. "Do you know the rules?"

"Remind me."

"There's only one you should bother about. You're allowed to get three answers wrong."

"If we're talking about films I'm not bothered at all."

"You don't need any more from me, then. Mary, talk to your friend."

"Eric? I'm sorry to trouble you like this so late. I couldn't think of anybody else."

That was a laugh when she'd hardly ever spoken to him. It was the first time she'd even used his name, at least to him. From her tone he could tell she was wearing her plucky smile. "What channel are you on?" he said.

He was hoping to throw her, but she barely hesitated. "Night Owl."

The hoaxers must have thought this up in advance. Edgeworth would have asked how he could watch the channel, but he didn't want to end the game too soon. He'd begun to enjoy pretending to be fooled, and so he said "What have you brought me on for?"

"Because I don't know what a film is."

He thought this was true of just about all his workmates—a good film, at any rate. He'd imagined a job in a cinema would mean working with people who loved films as much as he did. Had she tried to put a tremble in her voice just now? She'd got that wrong; contestants on quiz shows weren't supposed to sound like that. "Give me a go, then," he said.

"What's the film where James Dean has a milkshake?"

Edgeworth waited, but that was all. She ought to be telling him how little time he had, and shouldn't there be some kind of urgent music? "*East of Eden*," he said.

"That's a twist," said whoever was calling himself Terry Rice.

"Mr Rice is saying you're not right, Eric."

It was a funny way of saying so, even by the standards of a prank. Perhaps that was why she sounded nervous. "Then it'll be *Rebel without a Cause*," Edgeworth said with a grin but no mirth.

"That's another."

"Mr Rice says that's not right either."

She sounded close to desperation. However far they took the pretence, Edgeworth could go further. "It's *Giant* for sure, then," he said. "They're the only films he starred in."

"That's one more."

Did Edgeworth hear a faint suppressed shriek? Perhaps one of Mary Barton's accomplices had poked her to prompt her to speak. "That can't be right, Eric," she said high enough to irritate his ear.

"Give up," the supposed quizmaster said or asked, though Edgeworth wasn't sure who was being addressed. "Eric can't have heard of *Has Anyone Seen My Gal?*"

"Of course I have. I've seen it. James Dean has a milkshake at the soda fountain." In case this failed to restore his own reputation Edgeworth added "I knew it was the answer."

"Were you fancying a bit of fun? You should play seriously even if you think it's just a game." To Edgeworth's disbelief, this sounded like a rebuke. "I expect your friend has something to say about it," the man said.

"She's not my friend and none of you are." Edgeworth confined himself to mouthing this, if only to hear what comment she would have to manufacture. He heard her draw an unsteady breath and say "Thanks for coming on, Eric. I wish—"

"No point in wishing here. You know that isn't how we play. Thank you for entering into the spirit, Eric," the man said and, along with Mary and the girl who'd called, was gone.

Surely his last words contradicted his rebuke, which had to mean he couldn't even keep the hoax up. Of course the number he'd called from had been withheld. It was too late for Edgeworth to go back to the commentary on the disc, and he returned the film to the shelf before tramping to the bathroom and then to bed.

With all his films he didn't need to dream. In the morning he ate off a tray in front of *Third Time Sucky*, a Stooges short just the right length for breakfast. "I wish I knew what to wish for." "I wish I had one of your wishes." "I wish you two would shut up," Moe retorted, the effects of which made Edgeworth splutter a mouthful of Sticky Rotters over his dressing-gown. He showered and donned his uniform, which said Frugotomovies on the sweater, and headed for the Frugoplex.

The cinema was an extensive concrete block that resembled the one where he lived. The February sky was just as flat and white. He'd chosen the apartment because he could walk to the cinema, but there were increasingly fewer new films that he wanted to watch; he hardly used his free pass any more. At least he didn't have to enthuse about them to the public. He was gazing with disfavour at the titles outside when the manager let him in. "Any problem?" Mr Gittins said, and his plump smooth face displayed a smile too swift and sketchy to be identified as such. "I hope you can leave it at home."

Rather than retort that some of his workmates were to blame, Edgeworth made for the anonymous concrete staffroom. Soon the rest of the staff began to show up, some of them not far from late. Without exception they were decades younger than he was. As he took his place behind a ticket desk Larry Rivers came over. "What were you watching last night, Eric?" Larry said with a grin as scrawny as his face.

Had he called himself Terry Rice last night? His name was similar, and he liked quizzing Edgeworth, who said "I was listening."

"What were you listening to, Eric?"

He was using the name like a quizmaster. Edgeworth was tempted to confront him, but perhaps that was exactly what he and the rest of them wanted. "The man who wrote *North by Northwest*," Edgeworth said.

"Don't know it. Is it a film?"

Edgeworth suspected this wasn't even meant as a joke. "Cary Grant," he said. "James Mason."

"Don't know them either."

"Hitch, for heaven's sake."

"Is that the film with Will Smith?" one of the girls seemed to feel it would be helpful to suggest.

"Hitchcock, love."

"Sounds a bit mucky to me."

"Sounds a bit like sexual harassment," another girl warned Edgeworth.

"Alfred Hitchcock," he said in desperation. "*Psycho*."

"Was that the one with Vince Vaughn?" Larry said.

Did they all think the past—anything older than them—was a joke? No wonder Timeless Video had failed when there were so many people like them. Edgeworth had lost all the money he'd sunk in the video library, which was why he'd been glad of the job at the Frugoplex. Some old things wouldn't go away, not least him. He was about to say at least some of this when Mr Gittins opened the door once again. "Only just in time," he said like a head teacher at a school gate.

Mary Barton ducked as if her apologetic smile had dragged her head down. Did she glance at Edgeworth or just towards all the staff around the ticket counter? She seemed wary of being seen to look. She hurried to the staffroom and scampered back to the lobby as Mr Gittins addressed the staff. "Let's keep the public happy and coming back for more."

Edgeworth might have wished to be a projectionist if the job wouldn't have involved watching too many films that bored him if not worse. He was reduced to noticing which film attracted the most customers, a dispiriting observation. Today it was the latest 3-D film, *Get Outta My Face*. Whenever there was a lull he watched Mary Barton at the refreshments counter opposite. Had her left little finger been bandaged yesterday? It looked significantly bigger than its twin. Her smile was if possible braver than ever, especially if she caught him watching, though then he stared at her until her eyes flinched aside. At times he thought her thin prematurely lined face was trying to look even older than it was, almost as old as him. He wasn't going to accuse her and give everyone a chance to scoff at him; he wouldn't put it past them to accuse him of harassing her. Instead he made sure she never had an opportunity to speak to him away from the public—she clearly didn't have the courage or the gall to approach him in front of anyone who wasn't privy to last night's witless joke.

When he left for home she was besieged by a queue, but as she filled a popcorn tub that she was holding gingerly with her left hand she sent him an apologetic look. If they'd been alone it might well have goaded him to respond. He had to be content with stalking next door to Pieca Pizza, where he bought a Massive Mighty Meat that would do for tomorrow's dinner as well.

He downed two slices in the kitchen and took another three into the main room, one for each version of *Touch of Evil*. He was halfway through Orson Welles' preferred cut when the phone rang. He paused the manic gangling hotel clerk and prepared to say a very few short words to the uninvited caller. "It's that time again, Eric," said a voice he could hardly believe he was hearing.

"My God, you're worse than a joke." Edgeworth almost cut him off, but he wanted to learn how long they could keep up the pretence. "Can't you even get your own rules right?" he jeered.

"Which rules are those, Eric?"

"Three mistakes and I was supposed to be out of your game."

"You haven't quite got it, my friend. Last night was just one question you couldn't answer."

"Trust me, I could. I was having a laugh just like you."

"Please don't, Eric."

Mary Barton sounded so apologetic it was painful, which he hoped it was for her. He could almost have thought she'd been forced against her will to participate in the hoax, but any sympathy he might have felt she lost by adding "Don't make any more mistakes. It's serious."

"He sounds it."

"We get this problem sometimes." The man's amusement was still plain. "Listen to your friend," he said. "See how she sounds."

"I'm truly sorry to be pestering you again, Eric. Hand on heart, you're my only hope."

Edgeworth didn't know which of them angered him more. Her pathetic attempt to convince him she was desperate made her sound as though she was trying to suppress the emotion, and he was provoked to demand "Where are you on the television? I want to watch."

"We're on the radio." With a giggle all the more unpleasant because it had to be affected the man said "You wouldn't want to, trust me."

Edgeworth agreed, having left out the comma. What radio show would have inflicted this kind of conversation on its audience? All that interested him now, though not much, was learning what question they'd come up with this time. They must have been reading a film guide to have thought of last night's. "Go on then, Mr Terry Rice," he said, baring his teeth in a substitute for a grin. "Terrorise me again."

"Do your best, Mary."

"What's the Alfred Hitchcock film where you see him miss a bus?"

Someone stupider than Edgeworth might have imagined she was pleading with him. Did they genuinely expect him not to realise they were mocking what he'd said today to Larry Rivers? "*Strangers on a Train*," he said at once.

"Have a closer look."

He didn't know if this was meant for him or the Barton woman, but her voice grew shrill and not entirely firm. "Not that one, Eric."

"Must have been *The Birds*, then."

"Closer."

"Please, Eric," Mary Barton blurted, and he was disgusted to hear her attempting to sound close to tears. "You must know. It's your kind of thing."

"I know," Edgeworth said with a vicious grin. "I'll give it to you. *Rope*."

"Not close enough yet."

"Please!"

Edgeworth jerked the receiver away from his aching ear. "What are you supposed to be doing?"

"It's my eye."

Was he also meant to hear a stifled sob? "That's what my grandma used to say," he retorted. "She'd say it to anyone talking rubbish." Nevertheless he wasn't going to seem ignorant. "Here's your answer since you're making such a fuss about it, as if you didn't know. It's—"

"Too late, Eric," the man said without concealing his delight. "You've had your second chance."

"Please…"

Edgeworth could only just hear Mary Barton's voice, as if it was no longer directed at him. He was right to hold the phone at arm's length to protect his eardrum from any surprises they had in mind, because he heard a shrill metallic sound before the line went dead. It was ridiculous even to think of searching the airwaves for Night Owl. He did his best to pick up the Welles film where he'd left off, but the twitching maniac in charge of the motel disturbed him more than he liked. He put the film back in its place among the dozens of Ts before tramping angrily to bed.

He lurched awake so often, imagining he'd heard the phone, that not just his eyes were prickly with irritation by the time he had to get up for work. He was going to let Mary Barton know he'd had more than enough, and he wouldn't give the rest of them the chance to enjoy the show. "Eager to get going?" the manager said by way of greeting.

"I'm eager all right," Eric said and grinned as well.

He clocked on and hurried to the ticket counter, hoping Mary Barton would be first to arrive so that he could follow her to the staffroom. She'd been warned yesterday about timekeeping, after all. He watched the manager let in their workmates and grew more frustrated every time the newcomer wasn't her. Larry Rivers was among the last to join Edgeworth at the counter. "What were you up to last night, Eric?" he said.

Edgeworth almost turned on him, but he could play too. "Nothing you've ever seemed interested in."

Somebody more gullible than Edgeworth might have thought the fellow felt rebuffed. No doubt he was disappointed that Edgeworth hadn't taken the bait, and some of their audience looked as if they were. There was still no sign of Mary Barton by opening time. "Meet the public with a smile," Mr Gittins said.

Perhaps the woman had stayed home because she was too embarrassed to face Edgeworth, unless it was her day off. "Isn't Mary Barton coming in?" he said before he knew he meant to.

"She's called in sick." Mr Gittins seemed surprised if not disapproving that Edgeworth felt entitled to ask. As he made for the doors he added "Some trouble with her eye."

Edgeworth struggled to think of a question. "She'll have had it for a while, won't she?"

"She's never said so." Mr Gittins stopped short of the doors to say "Her mother hasn't either."

"What's she got to do with anything?"

"She's looking after Mary's children while Mary's at the hospital. Happy now, Eric? Then I hope we can crack on with the job."

As Mr Gittins let the public in, one of the girls alongside Edgeworth murmured "You'll have to send her a Valentine, Eric. She isn't married any longer."

"Keep your gossiping tongues to yourselves." He glared at her and her friends who'd giggled, and then past them at Rivers. "I'm putting you on your honour," he said as his grandmother often had. "You and your friends have been ringing me up at night, haven't you?"

"What?" Once Rivers finished the laugh that underlined the word he said "We get more of you here than we want as it is, Eric."

After that nobody except the public spoke to Edgeworth, and he couldn't even interest himself in which films they were unwise enough to pay for. Of course there was no reason to believe Rivers was as ignorant as he'd pretended—not about the late-night calls, at any rate. Edgeworth felt as if the long slow uneventful day were a curtain that would soon be raised on a performance he had no appetite for. At last he was able to leave behind everyone's contemptuous amusement, which felt like a threat of worse to come. When he shut himself in his apartment he found that he hoped he was waiting for nothing at all.

The pizza tasted stale and stodgy, an unsuccessful attempt to live up to itself. He tried watching classic comedies, but even his favourites seemed unbearably forced, like jokes cracked in the midst of a disaster or anticipating one. They hardly even passed the time, never mind distracting him from it. He was gazing in undefined dismay at the collapse of a dinosaur skeleton under Cary Grant and Katherine Hepburn when the phone went off like an alarm.

He killed the film and stared at the blank screen while the phone rang and rang again. He left it unanswered until a surge of irrational guilt made him grab it. "What is it now?" he demanded.

"Someone was scared you weren't playing any more, Eric."

"I thought your friend was meant to be in hospital," Edgeworth said in triumph.

"She's your friend, Eric, only yours. You're the only one she can turn to about films."

"Can't she even speak for herself now?"

"I'm here, Eric." Mary Barton's voice had lost some strength or was designed to sound as feeble as the prank. "They've fixed me up for now," she said. "I had to come back tonight or I'd have lost everything."

"Trying to make a bit extra for your children, are you?"

"I'm trying to win as much as we need."

Was she too preoccupied to notice his sarcasm, or wouldn't that fit in with her game? Could she really be so heartless that she would use her children to prolong a spiteful joke? His grandmother never would have—not even his mother, though she'd had plenty to say about any of Edgeworth's shortcomings that reminded her of his unidentified father. "Ready to help?" the man with Mary Barton said.

"What will you do if I don't?"

Edgeworth heard a suppressed moan that must be meant to sound as terrified as pained. "Up to you if you want to find out," the man said.

"Go on then, do your worst." At once Edgeworth was overtaken by more panic than he understood. "I mean," he said hastily, "ask me about films."

"Be careful, Mary. See he understands."

The man seemed more amused than ever. Did he plan to ask about some detail in the kind of recent film they knew Edgeworth never watched? Edgeworth was ready with a furious rejoinder by the time Mary Barton faltered "Which was the film where Elisha Cook played a gangster?"

There were three possibilities; that was the trick. If she and Rivers hoped to make Edgeworth nervous of giving the wrong answer, they had no chance. "*The Maltese Falcon*," he said.

"Wider, Mary."

"That's not right, Eric."

Her voice had grown shriller and shakier too, and Edgeworth was enraged to find this disturbed him. "He was a gangster in that," he objected.

"It isn't what they want."

"Then I expect they're thinking of *The Killing*."

"Wider again," the man said as if he could hardly bear to put off the end of the joke.

"No, Eric, no."

It occurred to Edgeworth that the actor had played a criminal rather than a gangster in the Kubrick film. The piercing harshness of the woman's ragged voice made it hard for him to think. "Just one left, eh?" he said.

"Please, Eric. Please be right this time."

She might almost have been praying. Far from winning Edgeworth over, it embarrassed him, but he wasn't going to give a wrong answer. "No question," he said. "It's *Baby Face Nelson*."

"Wider still."

"What are you playing at?" Edgeworth protested. "He was a gangster in that."

"No, it was his son," the man said. "It was Elisha Cook Junior."

"That's what you've been working up to all along, is it?" Edgeworth wiped his mouth, having inadvertently spat with rage. "What a stupid trick," he said, "even for you." He would have added a great deal if Mary Barton hadn't cried "No."

It was scarcely a word. It went on for some time with interruptions and rose considerably higher. Before it had to pause for breath Edgeworth shouted "What are you doing?"

"It's a good thing we aren't on television." By the sound of it, the man had moved the phone away from her. "We couldn't show it," he said gleefully, "and I don't think you'd want to see."

"Stop it," Edgeworth yelled but failed to drown out the cry.

"Relax, Eric. That's all for you for now," Terry Rice said and left silence aching in Edgeworth's ear.

The number was withheld again. Edgeworth thought of calling the police, but what could that achieve? Perhaps it would just prove he'd fallen for a joke after all. Perhaps everything had been recorded for his workmates to hear. He grabbed the remote control and set about searching the audio channels on the television. He thought he'd scanned through every available radio station, since the identifications on the screen had run out, when a voice he very much wished he couldn't recognise came out of the blank monitor. "This is Night Owl signing off," Terry Rice said, and Edgeworth thought he heard a muffled sobbing. "Another night, another game."

Edgeworth gazed at the silent screen until he seemed to glimpse a vague pale movement like a frantic attempt to escape. He turned off the set, nearly breaking the switch in his haste, and sought refuge in bed. Very occasionally his thoughts grew so exhausted that they almost let him doze. He did without breakfast—he couldn't have borne to watch a film. Once the shower had made him as clean as he had any chance of feeling he dressed and hurried to work.

He had to ring the bell twice at length to bring Mr Gittins out of his office. The manager's plump smooth face set not much less hard than marble as he saw Edgeworth. He was plainly unimpressed by Edgeworth's timeliness; perhaps he thought it was a ruse to gain his favour. "I hope you'll be doing your best to get on with your colleagues," he said.

"Why, who's said what?"

Mr Gittins didn't deign to answer. He was turning away until Edgeworth blurted "Do we know if Mary Barton's coming in today?"

"What concern is it of yours?" Having gazed at Edgeworth, Mr Gittins said "She won't be in for some time. I'm told she can't walk."

Edgeworth swallowed, but his voice still emerged as a croak. "Do we know why?"

"It really isn't something I'm prepared to discuss further."

Mr Gittins looked disgusted by Edgeworth's interest and whatever it revived in his mind. Edgeworth gave him a grimace that felt nothing like apologetic and dashed to the staffroom. For once the list of staff and their phone numbers on the notice board was of some use. He keyed Mary Barton's number on his mobile and made the call before he had time to grow any more fearful. Well ahead of any preparation he could make for it a woman's tightened weary voice said "Hello, yes?"

"I'm one of Mary's friends at work. I was wondering how she is." With more of an effort he managed to add "Just wondering what's wrong with her."

"Has it got something to do with you?"

The woman's voice was loud and harsh enough to start two children crying, and Edgeworth felt as if the sounds were impaling his brain. "I wouldn't say it has exactly, but—"

"If I thought you were the man who did that to Mary I'd find you and make sure you never went near a woman again. Just you tell me your name or I'll—"

Edgeworth jabbed the key to terminate the call and shoved the mobile in his pocket. As soon as it began to ring he switched it off. He couldn't loiter in the staffroom in case Mr Gittins wondered why, and so he ventured into the lobby, where a stray lump of popcorn squeaked piteously underfoot and then splintered like an insect. He'd hardly reached the ticket counter when the phones on it began to ring in chorus. "See who it is," Mr Gittins said.

Edgeworth clutched at the nearest receiver and hoisted it towards his face. "Frugoplex Cinemas," he said, trying not to sound like himself.

When he heard the woman's voice he turned his back on the manager. While she wasn't the caller he'd been afraid to hear or the one he might have hoped for, she was all too familiar. "Congratulations, Eric," she said. "Three wrong means you're our next contestant. Someone will pick you up tonight."

He dropped the phone, not quite missing its holder, and turned to find Mr Gittins frowning at him. "Was that a personal call?"

"It was wrong. Wrong number," Edgeworth said and wished he could believe. Mr Gittins frowned again before making for the doors as some of Edgeworth's workmates gathered outside. Edgeworth searched their faces through the glass and struggled to think what he could say to them. Just a few words were repeating themselves in his head like a silent prayer. "You're my friend, aren't you?" he would have to say to someone. "Be my friend."

# Holding the Light

As his cousin followed him into the Frugoplex lobby Tom saw two girls from school. Out of uniform and in startlingly short skirts they looked several years older. He hoped his leather jacket performed that trick for him, in contrast to the duffle coat Lucas was wearing. Since the girls were giggling at the cinema staff dressed as Halloween characters, he let them see him laugh too. "Hey, Lezly," he said in his deepest voice. "Hey, Dianne."

"Don't come near us if you've got a cold," Lezly protested, waving a hand that was bony with rings in front of her face.

"It's just how boys his age talk," Dianne said far too much like a sympathetic adult and blinked her sparkly purple eyelids. "Who's your friend, Tom?"

"It's my cousin Lucas."

"Hey, Luke."

Lezly said it too and held out her skull-ringed hand, at which Lucas stared as if it were an inappropriate present. "He's like that," Tom mumbled but refrained from pointing at his own head. "Don't mind him."

"Maybe he doesn't want to give you his germs, Lezly." To the boys Dianne said "What are you going to see?"

"*Vampire Dating Agency*," Lucas said before Tom could make a choice.

"That's for kids," Lezly objected. "We're not seeing any films with them."

"We don't have to either, do we, Lucas?" Tom said in a bid to stop his face from growing hotter. "What are you two seeing?"

"*Cheerleaders with Guts*," Dianne said with another quick glittery blink.

"We can't," Lucas informed everyone. "Nobody under fifteen's allowed."

Tom glared at him as the girls did. At least none of the staff dealing with the noisy queues appeared to have heard the remark. Until that moment Tom had been able to prefer visiting the cinema to any of the other activities their parents had arranged for the boys over the years—begging for sweets at neighbours' houses, ducking for apples and a noseful of water, carving pumpkins when Lucas's received most of the praise despite being so grotesque only out of clumsiness. Now that the parents had reluctantly let them outgrow all this Tom seemed to be expected to take even more care of his cousin. Perhaps Lucas sensed his resentment for once, because he said "We don't have to go to a film."

"Who doesn't?" said Dianne.

Tom wanted to say her and Lezly too, but first he had to learn "Where, then?"

"The haunted place." When nobody admitted to recognising it Lucas said "Grinfields."

"Where the boy and girl killed themselves together, you mean," Lezly said.

"No, he did first," Dianne said, "and she couldn't live without him."

It was clear that Lucas wasn't interested in these details, and he barely let her finish. "My mum and dad say they did it because they watched films you aren't supposed to watch."

"My parents heard they were always shopping," Tom made

haste to contribute. "Them and their families spent lots of money they didn't have and all it did was leave them thinking nothing was worth anything."

That was his father's version. Perhaps it sounded more like a gibe at the girls than he was afraid Lucas's comment had. "Why do you want us to go there, Luke?" Dianne said.

"Who's Luke?"

"I told you," Tom said in some desperation, "he's like that."

"No I'm not, I'm like Lucas."

At such times Tom understood all too well why his cousin was bullied at school. There was also the way Lucas stared at anybody unfamiliar as if they had to wait for him to make up his mind about them, and just now his pasty face—far spottier than Tom's and topped with unruly red hair—was a further drawback. Nevertheless Dianne said "Are you sure you don't want to see our film?"

She was speaking to Tom, but Lucas responded. "We can't. We've been told."

"I haven't," Tom muttered. He watched the girls join the queue for the ticket desk manned by a tastefully drooling vampire in a cloak, and then he turned on Lucas. "We need to switch our phones off. We're in the cinema."

Accuracy mattered most to Lucas. Once he'd done as he was told Tom said "Let's go, and not to the kids' film either."

A frown creased Lucas's pudgy forehead. "Which one, then?"

"None of them. We'll go where you wanted," Tom said, leading the way out into the Frugall retail park. More vehicles than he thought he could count in a weekend were lined up beneath towering lamps as white as the moon. In that light people's faces looked as pallid as Lucas's, but took on colour once they reached the shops, half a mile of which surrounded the perimeter. As Tom came abreast of a Frugelectric store he said "We'll need a light."

Lucas peered at the lanky lamps, and yet again Tom wondered what went on inside his cousin's head. "A torch," he resented having to elucidate.

"There's one at home."

"That's too far." Before Lucas could suspect he didn't want their parents learning where the boys would be Tom said "You'll have to buy one."

He was determined his cousin would pay, not least for putting the girls off. He watched Lucas select the cheapest flashlight and load it with batteries, then drop a ten-pound note beside the till so as to avoid touching the checkout girl's hand. He made her place his change there for him to scoop up while Tom took the flashlight wrapped in a flimsy plastic bag. "That's mine. I bought it," Lucas said at once.

"You hold it then, baby." Tom stopped just short of uttering the last word, though his face was hot again. "Look after it," he said and stalked out of the shop.

They were on the far side of Frugall from their houses and the school. An alley between a Frugranary baker's and a Frugolé tapas bar led to a path around the perimeter. A twelve-foot wall behind the shops and restaurants cut off most of the light and the blurred vague clamour of the retail park. The path was deserted apart from a few misshapen skeletal loiterers nuzzling the wall or propped against the chain-link fence alongside Grinfields Woods. They were abandoned shopping trolleys, and the only sound apart from the boys' padded footsteps was the rustle of the plastic bag.

Tom thought they might have to follow the path all the way to the housing estate between Grinfields and the retail park, but soon they came to a gap in the fence. Lucas dodged through it so fast that he might have forgotten he wasn't alone. As Tom followed he saw his own shadow emerge from a block of darkness fringed with outlines of wire mesh. The elongated shadows of trees were reaching for the larger dark. By the time the boys found the official path through the woods they were almost beyond the glare from the retail park, and Lucas switched on the flashlight. "That isn't scary," he declared as Tom's shadow brandished its arms.

Tom was simply frustrated that Lucas hadn't bothered to remove the flashlight from the bag. He watched his cousin peer both ways along the dim path like a child showing how much care he took about crossing a road, and then head along the stretch that vanished into darkness. The sight of Lucas swaggering off as though he didn't care whether he was followed did away with any qualms Tom might have over scaring him more than he would like. He tramped after Lucas through the woods that looked as if the dark had formed itself into a cage, and almost collided with him as the blurred jerky light swerved off the path to flutter across the trees to the left. "What's pulling something along?" Lucas seemed to feel entitled to be told.

"It's got a rope," Tom said, but didn't want to scare Lucas too much too soon. "No, it's only water."

He'd located it in the dried-up channel out of sight below the slope beyond the trees. It must be a lingering trickle of rain, which had stopped before dark, unless it was an animal or bird among the fallen leaves. "Make your mind up," Lucas complained and swung the light back to the path.

The noise ceased as Tom tramped after him. Perhaps it had gone underground through the abandoned irrigation channel. Without warning—certainly with none from Lucas—the flashlight beam sprang off the ragged stony path and flew into the treetops. "Is it laughing at us?" Lucas said.

Tom gave the harsh shrill sound somewhere ahead time to make itself heard. "What do you think?"

"Of course it's not," Lucas said as if his cousin needed to be put right. "Birds can't laugh."

Once more Tom suspected Lucas wasn't quite as odd as he liked everyone to think, although that was odd in itself. When the darkness creaked again he said "That's not a bird, it's a tree."

Lucas might have been challenging someone by striding up the path to jab the beam at the treetops. As he disappeared over a ridge the creaking of the solitary branch fell silent. Though he'd taken the light with him, Tom wasn't about to be driven to chase it. He hadn't quite reached the top of the path when he said "No wonder aunt and uncle say you can't make any friends."

He hadn't necessarily intended his cousin to hear, but Lucas retorted "I've got one."

Tom was tempted to suggest that Lucas should have brought

this unlikely person instead of him. His cousin was taking the light away as though to punish Tom for his remark. Having left the path, he halted under an outstretched branch. "You can see where they did it," he said.

The flashlight beam plunged into the earth—into a circular shaft that led down to the middle of the irrigation tunnel. At some point the entrance had been boarded over, but now the rotten wood was strewn among the trees. Tom peered into the opening, from which a rusty ladder descended into utter darkness. "You can't see if you don't take the bag off."

As darkness raced up the ladder, chasing the light out of the shaft, Lucas said "What do you think is laughing now?"

"Maybe you should go down and find out."

Another hollow liquid giggle rose out of the unlit depths, and Tom thought of convincing his cousin it wasn't water they were hearing. Lucas crumpled the bag in his hand and sent the light down the shaft again. The beam just reached the foot of the ladder, below which Tom seemed to glimpse a dim sinuous movement before Lucas snatched the beam out of the shaft and aimed it at the branch overhead. "He hung himself on that, didn't he, and then she threw herself down there."

He sounded little more than distantly interested, which wasn't enough for Tom. "Aren't you going down, then? I thought you wanted a Halloween adventure."

The glowing leafless branch went out as Lucas swung the light back to the path. "All right," he said and made for the opposite side of the ridge.

Did he really need absolute precision or just demand it? As Tom trudged after him he heard a rustling somewhere near the open shaft. "I thought you never left litter," he called. "How about that bag?"

"It's here," Lucas said and tugged it half out of his trouser pocket before stuffing it back in.

When Tom glanced behind him the Frugall floodlights glared in his eyes, and he couldn't locate what he'd heard—perhaps leaves stirring in a wind, although he hadn't felt one. Of course there must be wildlife in the woods, even if he'd yet to see any. He followed Lucas down the increasingly steep path and saw the flashlight beam snag on the curve of a stone arch protruding from the earth beside the track. It was the end of the tunnel, which had once helped irrigate the fields beyond the ridge. Now the fields were overgrown and the tunnel was barricaded, or rather it had been until somebody tore the boards down. As Lucas poked the flashlight beam into the entrance he said "Where's the bell?"

Tom thought the slow dull metallic notes came from a car radio in the distance, but said "Is it in the tunnel?"

Lucas stooped under the arch, which wasn't quite as tall as either of the boys. "Listen," he said. "That's where."

Tom heard a last reverberation as he stepped off the path. Surely it was just his cousin's gaze that made him wonder if the noise had indeed come from the tunnel, unless someone was playing a Halloween joke. Suppose the girls had followed them from the cinema and were sending the sound down from the ridge? In his hopelessly limited experience this didn't seem the kind of thing girls did, especially while keeping quiet as well. The thought of them revived his discontent, and he said "Better go and see."

Lucas advanced into the tunnel at once. His silhouette blotted out most of the way ahead, the stone floor scattered with sodden leaves, the walls and curved roof glistening with moss, a few weeds drooping out of cracks. The low passage was barely wider than his elbows as he held them at his sides—so narrow that the flashlight bumped against one wall with a soft moist thud as he turned to point the beam at Tom. "What are you doing?"

"Get that out of my face, can you?" As the light sank into the cramped space between them Tom said "I'm coming too."

"I don't want you to."

Tom backed out, almost scraping his scalp on the arch. "Now you've got what you want as usual. Just you remember you did."

"It won't be scary if we both go in." This might have been an effort to placate his cousin—as much of one as Lucas was likely to make—but Tom suspected it was just a stubborn statement of fact. "I'm not scared yet," Lucas complained. "It's Halloween."

"Want me to make sure?"

"I know it is." Before Tom could explain, if simply out of frustration, Lucas said "You've got nothing to do."

He sounded intolerably like a teacher rebuking an idle pupil. As Tom vowed to prove him wrong in ways his cousin wouldn't care for, Lucas ducked out of the tunnel and thrust the flashlight at him. "You can hold this while I'm in there."

Tom sent the beam along the tunnel. It fell short of the ladder, which was a couple of hundred yards in. Once Lucas returned to the tunnel the light wouldn't even reach past him. Tom was waiting to watch his reaction to this when Lucas said "I don't mean here."

He might have been criticising Tom's ability to understand, a notion that was close to more than Tom could take. "Where?" he demanded without at all wanting to know.

"Go up and shine it down the hole, then I can see where halfway is. Shout when you get to the hole."

"And you answer." In case this wasn't plain enough Tom added "So I can hear."

"Course I will."

Tom could have done without the haughtiness. He made off with the flashlight, swinging it from side to side of the deserted woods. As he reached the top of the path the lights above the distant retail park glared in his eyes, and he had a momentary impression that a rounded object was protruding just above the shaft at the midpoint of the tunnel. He squeezed his eyes shut, widening them as he stepped onto the ridge. Perhaps he'd seen an exposed root beyond the shaft, but he couldn't see it now. He marched to the opening and sent the beam down to the tunnel, where he seemed to glimpse movement—a dim shape like a scrawny limb or an even thinner item retreating at speed into the dark. It must have been a shadow cast by the ladder. "Come on," he called. "I'm here."

"I'm coming."

Tom was disconcerted to hear his cousin's shout resound along the tunnel while it also came from beyond the ridge. Despite straining his eyes he couldn't judge how far the flashlight beam reached; the glare from the retail park was still hindering his vision. He dodged around the shaft to turn his back on the problem, and saw that the beam of the cheap flashlight fell short of illuminating the tunnel itself. "Can you see the light?" he called.

"I see something."

Tom found this wilfully vague. "What?" he yelled.

"Must be you."

This was vaguer still, particularly for Lucas. Was he trying to unnerve his cousin? Tom peered into the shaft, waiting for Lucas to dart into view in a feeble attempt to alarm him. Or did Lucas mean to worry him by staying out of sight? Tom vowed not to call out again, but he was on the edge of yielding to the compulsion when an ill-defined figure appeared at the bottom of the shaft. He didn't really need it to turn its dim face upwards to show it was Lucas. "What am I doing now?" Tom grudged having to ask.

"Holding the light."

"I'm saying," Tom said more bitterly still, "what do you want me to do?"

"Stay there till I say," Lucas told him and stooped into the other section of the tunnel.

Tom tried to listen to his receding footsteps but soon could hear nothing at all—or rather, just the sound he'd previously ascribed to plastic. Perhaps the bag in his cousin's pocket was brushing against the wall, except that Tom seemed to hear the noise behind him. Had Lucas sneaked out of the far end of the tunnel to creep up and pounce on him? Surely his shadow would give him away, and when Tom swung around, only the trees were silhouetted against the glare from the retail park. He'd kept the flashlight beam trained down the shaft on the basis that he might have misjudged Lucas, but how long would he have to wait to hear from him? He had a sudden furious idea that, having left the tunnel, Lucas was on his way home. "Where are you now?" he shouted.

"Here," Lucas declared, appearing at the foot of the shaft.

So he'd been playing a different trick—staying out of sight until Tom grew nervous. "Finished with the light?" Tom only just bothered to ask.

"Go and meet me at the end," Lucas said before ducking into the dark.

Tom felt juvenile for using the flashlight to search among the trees around him—he wasn't the one who was meant to be scared—and switched it off as he hurried down the path. He was waiting at the mouth of the tunnel by the time his cousin emerged. Lucas looked dully untroubled, unless the darkness was obscuring his expression, and Tom wished he'd hidden long enough to make his cousin nervous. "What's it like?" he tried asking.

"Like I wasn't alone."

"You weren't."

"That's scary."

Tom thought he'd been more than sufficiently clear. He was feeling heavy with resentment when Lucas said "Now it's your turn."

As Tom switched on the flashlight, darkness shrank into the tunnel. "You can't do that," Lucas protested. "I'm supposed to go on top with it so you'll be in the dark."

Was he planning some trick of the kind Tom had spared him? When Tom hesitated while the unsteady shadows of weeds fingered the moss on the walls of the tunnel, Lucas said "I have to say what we do with it. It's mine."

Tom was so disgusted that he almost dropped the flashlight because of his haste to be rid of it. "I'll have to shout," Lucas told him. "You won't see."

He hadn't extinguished the light, which scrambled up the path ahead of him, leaving Tom to wonder if Lucas was uneasy after all. Suppose that distracted him from keeping the beam down the shaft? Once his cousin vanished over the ridge Tom peered along the tunnel, but it might as well have been stuffed with earth. He hadn't distinguished even a hint of light when Lucas called "It's waiting."

His voice was in more than one place again—somewhere down the tunnel and on the ridge as well. It occurred to Tom that he should have extracted a promise, and he cupped his hands around his mouth to yell "Say you'll wait there for me."

"That's what I'm doing."

Tom could have fancied he was hearing another voice imitate Lucas. "Say you will," he insisted, "as long as I want the light."

"I will as long as you want the light."

This had to be precise enough, and surely Lucas was incapable of acting other than he'd said he would. Wasn't his saying it in more than one voice like a double promise? Tom had no reason to hesitate, even if he wished Dianne were with him to be scared and then comforted. He wouldn't be comforting Lucas, and he ducked into the tunnel.

The darkness fastened on his eyes at once. They felt coated with it, a substance like the blackest paint. It hindered his feet too, as if they had to wade through it, shuffling forward an inch at a time, which was all he felt able to risk. He extended his arms in front of him to avoid touching the slimy walls, though he could have imagined his fingertips were about to bump into the dark. Of course there was nothing solid in front of him. Lucas hadn't switched off the flashlight and sneaked down the ladder to stand in the blackness until Tom's outstretched fingers found him. Just the same, the thought made Tom bring his hands back and lower his arms. "Are you really up there?" he shouted.

"You'll see."

His cousin's voice was somewhere ahead and above the tunnel. Otherwise the exchange didn't reassure Tom as much as he would have hoped if he'd needed reassurance. It wasn't simply that his shout had been boxed in by the walls and the roof that forced his head down; his voice had seemed muffled by some obstacle in front of him. Was he about to see it? There appeared to be a hint of pallor in the blackness, if that wasn't just an effect of straining his eyes or of hoping to locate the flashlight beam. When he edged forward the impression didn't shift, and he kept his gaze fixed on the promise of light until his foot nudged an object on the floor of the tunnel.

He heard it stir and then subside. He had no room to sidle around it, and he didn't care to turn his back. By resting his foot on it and trampling on it he deduced that it was a mass of twigs and dead leaves. He trod hard on it on his way past, and worked out that the material must have fallen down the shaft, which was just visible ahead by the light that nearly reached down to the tunnel roof. He could scarcely believe how long he'd taken to walk halfway; it felt as if the darkness had weighed down the passing of time. A few waterlogged leaves slithered underfoot as he reached the shaft and was able to raise his head. "See me?" he called.

Lucas was an indefinite silhouette against the night sky beyond the flashlight, which almost blinded Tom even though the beam on the wall opposite the ladder was so dim. "You were a long time," Lucas protested.

An acoustic quirk made versions of his voice mutter in both sections of the tunnel. Before Tom could reply, less irately than the complaint deserved, Lucas said "When you've been through the rest you have to come back this way."

That he had needn't mean Tom should. Lucas wasn't frightened yet, which was among the reasons why Tom intended to leave the tunnel by the far end so as to tiptoe up behind him. He shut his eyes to ready them for the darkness as far as he could. He hadn't opened them when Lucas enraged him by calling "Are you scared to go in?"

Tom lowered his head as if he meant to butt the dark and advanced into the tunnel. He wouldn't have believed the blackness could grow thicker, but now it didn't just smother his eyes—it filled them to the limit. He'd taken a very few steps, which felt shackled by his wariness, when his foot collided with another heap of leaves. He heard twigs if not small branches snap as he trod several times on the yielding heap, which must be almost as long as he was tall. Once he was past it the floor seemed clear, but how far did he have to shuffle to catch his first glimpse of the night outside? It couldn't be so dark out there that it was indistinguishable from the underground passage. He was stretching his eyes wide, which only served to let more of the darkness into them, when his foot struck a hindrance more solid than leaves—an object that his groping fingers found to be as high and wide as the tunnel. The entrance was boarded up.

So Lucas hadn't just been setting out the rules of the game.

Perhaps he'd believed he was making it plain that Tom couldn't leave the tunnel at this end. Tom thumped the boards with his fists and tried a few kicks as well, but the barrier didn't give. When he turned away at last he had to touch the cold fur of the wall with his knuckles to be certain he was facing down the tunnel. He shuffled forward as if he were being dragged by his bent head, and his blacked-out eyes were straining to find the light when his toe poked the mass of leaves and wood on the floor. If he was so close to the shaft, why couldn't he make out even a hint of the flashlight beam? "What are you playing at?" he shouted.

There was no response of any kind. Perhaps Lucas had decided to alarm him. He dealt the supine heap a kick, but it held more or less together. He tramped on it a number of times while edging forward. It was behind him, though not far, when something moved under his feet—a large worm, he thought, or a snake. As he stumbled clear of it he heard scattered leaves rustle with its movement, and recognised the sound he'd attributed to plastic on his way to the tunnel. He needn't think about it further—he only wanted to reach the light. That still wasn't visible, and he wasn't eager to shout into the dark again, surely just because Lucas might think he was scared. He had no idea how many timid paces he'd taken before he was able to lift his head.

For a moment this felt like nothing but relief, and then he saw that the top of the shaft was deserted. "Lucas," he yelled. "Lucas." He was trying just to feel furious, but the repetition unnerved him—it seemed too close to doing his best to ensure that only his cousin would respond. He was about to call once more when Lucas appeared above him, at least fifty feet away, and sent the flashlight beam down the highest rungs of the ladder. Tom would have shouted at him except for being assailed by a sudden unwelcome thought. He knew why he'd seemed to take too long to return to the shaft: because the supine mass on which he'd trodden was further from it than before. While he'd been trying to find his way out, it had crawled after him in the dark.

He twisted around to peer behind him, but the blackness was impenetrable. Although he was afraid to see, not seeing might be worse. "Lucas," he blurted, and then forced himself to raise his voice. "Send the light down here."

The response was a noise very much like one he'd previously heard—a clang like the note of a dull bell. Now he realised it had been the sound of an object swinging against the ladder, repeatedly colliding with the upper rungs. This time the flashlight was making the noise, and struck another rung as it plummeted down the shaft. The lens smashed on the tunnel floor, and the light went out at once.

"What have you done now," Tom almost screamed, "you stupid useless retard?" He dropped into a crouch that felt as if a pain in his guts had doubled him over. His fingers groped over the cold wet stone and eventually closed around the flashlight. He pushed the switch back and forth, but the bulb must be broken too. When he jerked his head back to yell at Lucas he saw that the dim round hole at the top of the shaft was empty once more. He staggered to his feet and threw out a hand to help him keep his balance, and clutched an object that was dangling beside him in the tunnel. It was the rope he'd wanted to think was a worm or a snake.

A mindless panic made him haul at the bedraggled rope, and an object nuzzled the back of his hand. It was a face, though not much of one, and as he recoiled with a cry he felt it sag away from the bone. He was backing away so fast he almost overbalanced when he heard sounds in the other section of the tunnel. Between him and the way out, someone was running through the absolute blackness as if they had no need of light—as if they welcomed its absence.

For a moment that seemed endless Tom felt the darkness claim him, and then he shied the flashlight in the direction of the sodden flopping footsteps. He clutched at the ladder and hauled himself desperately upwards. He mustn't think about climbing towards the outstretched branch that had creaked as the boys made for the ridge. Perhaps nobody had killed themselves—perhaps that was just a story made up by adults to scare children away from any danger. He could no longer hear the loose footsteps for all the noise he was making on the shaky ladder.

Lucas must be waiting by the shaft—he'd promised to—and of course he'd turned the light away when he'd heard Tom thumping the boards that blocked the tunnel. The thought gave Tom the chance to realise who the friend Lucas said he had must be. "I'm still your friend," he called, surely not too late, as he clambered up the rusty ladder. He didn't dare to look down, and he was just a few rungs from the top when he lost his footing. His foot flailed in the air and then trod on the head of whatever was climbing after him.

It moved under his foot—moved more than any scalp ought to be able—as he kicked it away. He was terrified what else he might tread on, but he only found the rung again. His head was nearly level with the exit from the shaft before a pulpy grasp closed around his ankle. However soft they were, the swollen fingers felt capable of dragging him down into the blackness to share it with its residents. He thrust his free hand above the shaft in a desperate appeal. Surely Lucas hadn't felt so insulted that he'd abandoned his cousin—surely only he was out there. "Get hold of me," Tom pleaded, and at once he had his answer.

# No Story in It

"GRANDAD."

Boswell turned from locking the front door to see Gemima running up the garden path cracked by the late September heat. Her mother April was at the tipsy gate, and April's husband Rod was climbing out of their rusty crimson Nissan. "Oh, dad," April cried, slapping her forehead hard enough to make him wince. "You're off to London. How could we forget it was today, Rod."

Rod pursed thick lips beneath a ginger moustache broader than his otherwise schoolboyish plump face. "We must have had other things on our mind. It looks as if I'm joining you, Jack."

"You'll tell me how," Boswell said as Gemima's small hot five-year-old hand found his grasp.

"We've just learned I'm a cut-back."

"More of a set-back, will it be? I'm sure there's a demand for teachers of your experience."

"I'm afraid you're a bit out of touch with the present."

Boswell saw his daughter willing him not to take the bait. "Can we save the discussion for my return?" he said. "I've a bus and then a train to catch."

"We can run your father to the station, can't we? We want to tell him our proposal." Rod bent the passenger seat forward. "Let's keep the men together," he said.

As Boswell hauled the reluctant belt across himself he glanced up. Usually Gemima reminded him poignantly of her mother at her age—large brown eyes with high startled eyebrows, inquisitive nose, pale prim lips—but in the mirror April's face looked not much less small, just more lined. The car jerked forward, grating its innards, and the radio announced "A renewed threat of war—" before Rod switched it off. Once the car was past the worst of the potholes in the main road Boswell said "So propose."

"We wondered how you were finding life on your own," Rod said. "We thought it mightn't be the ideal situation for someone with your turn of mind."

"Rod. Dad—"

Her husband gave the mirror a look he might have aimed at a child who'd spoken out of turn in class. "Since we've all over-extended ourselves, we think the solution is to pool our resources."

"Which are those?"

"We wondered how the notion of our moving in with you might sound."

"Sounds fun," Gemima cried.

Rod's ability to imagine living with Boswell for any length of time showed how desperate he, if not April, was. "What about your own house?" Boswell said.

"There are plenty of respectable couples eager to rent these days. We'd pay you rent, of course. Surely it makes sense for all of us."

"Can I give you a decision when I'm back from London?" Boswell said, mostly to April's hopeful reflection. "Maybe you won't have to give up your house. Maybe soon I'll be able to offer you financial help."

"Christ," Rod snarled, a sound like a gnashing of teeth.

To start with the noise the car made was hardly harsher. Boswell thought the rear bumper was dragging on the road until tenement blocks jerked up in the mirror as though to seize the vehicle, which ground loudly to a halt. "Out," Rod cried in a tone poised to pounce on nonsense.

"Is this like one of your stories, grandad?" Gemima giggled as she followed Boswell out of the car.

"No," her father said through his teeth and flung the boot open. "This is real."

Boswell responded only by going to look. The suspension had collapsed, thrusting the wheels up through the rusty arches. April took Gemima's hand, Boswell sensed not least to keep her quiet, and murmured "Oh, Rod."

Boswell was staring at the tenements. Those not boarded up were tattooed with graffiti inside and out, and he saw watchers at as many broken as unbroken windows. He thought of the parcel a fan had once given him with instructions not to open it until he was home, the present that had been one of Jean's excuses for divorcing him. "Come with me to the station," he urged, "and you can phone whoever you need to phone."

When the Aireys failed to move immediately he stretched out a hand to them and saw his shadow printed next to theirs on a wall, either half demolished or never completed, in front of the tenements. A small child holding a woman's hand, a man slouching beside them with a fist stuffed in his pocket, a second man gesturing empty-handed at them... The shadows seemed to blacken, the sunlight to brighten like inspiration, but that had taken no form when the approach of a taxi distracted him. His shadow roused itself as he dashed into the rubbly road to flag the taxi down. "I'll pay," he told Rod.

"Here's Jack Boswell, everyone," Quentin Sedgwick shouted. "Here's our star author. Come and meet him."

It was going to be worth it, Boswell thought. Publishing had changed since all his books were in print—indeed, since any were. Sedgwick, a tall thin young but balding man with wiry veins exposed by a singlet and shorts, had met him at Waterloo, pausing barely long enough to deliver an intense handshake before treating him to a headlong ten-minute march and a stream of enthusiasm for his work. The journey ended at a house in the midst of a crush of them resting their fronts on the pavement. At least the polished nameplate of Cassandra Press had to be visible to anyone who passed. Beyond it a hall that smelled of curried vegetables was occupied by a double-parked pair of bicycles and a steep staircase not much wider than their handlebars. "Amazing, isn't it?" Sedgwick declared. "It's like one of your early things, being able to publish from home. Except in a story of yours the computers would take over and tell us what to write."

"I don't remember writing that," Boswell said with some unsureness.

"No, I just made it up. Not bad, was it?" Sedgwick said, running upstairs. "Here's Jack Boswell, everyone..."

A young woman with a small pinched studded face and glistening black hair spiky as an armoured fist emerged from somewhere on the ground floor as Sedgwick threw open doors to reveal two cramped rooms, each featuring a computer terminal, at one of which an even younger woman with blonde hair the length of her filmy flowered blouse was composing an advertisement. "Starts with C, ends with e," Sedgwick said of her, and of the studded woman "Bren, like the gun. Our troubleshooter."

Boswell grinned, feeling someone should. "Just the three of you?"

"Small is sneaky, I keep telling the girls. While the big houses are being dragged down by excess personnel, we move into the market they're too cumbersome to handle. Carole, show him his page."

The publicist saved her work twice before displaying the Cassandra Press catalogue. She scrolled past the colophon, a C with a P hooked on it, and a parade of authors: Ferdy Thorn, ex-marine turned ecological warrior; Germaine Gossett, feminist fantasy writer; Torin Bergman, Scandinavia's leading magic realist... "Forgive my ignorance," Boswell said, "but these are all new to me."

"They're the future." Sedgwick cleared his throat and grabbed Boswell's shoulder to lean him towards the computer. "Here's someone we all know."

**BOSWELL'S BACK!** the page announced in letters so large they left room only for a shout line from, Boswell remembered, the *Observer* twenty years ago—"Britain's best sf writer since Wyndham and Wells"—and a scattering of titles: *The Future Just Began*, *Tomorrow Was Yesterday*, *Wave Goodbye To Earth*, *Terra Spells Terror*, *Science Lies In Wait*... "It'll look better when we have covers to reproduce," Carole said. "I couldn't write much. I don't know your work."

"That's because I've been devouring it all over again, Jack. You thought you might have copies for my fair helpers, didn't you?"

"So I have," Boswell said, struggling to spring the catches of his aged briefcase.

"See what you think when you've read these. Some for you as well, Bren," Sedgwick said, passing out Boswell's last remaining hardcovers of several of his books. "Here's a Hugo winner, and look, this one got the Prix du Fantastique Écologique. Will you girls excuse us now? I hear the call of lunch."

They were in sight of Waterloo Station again when he seized Boswell's elbow to steer him into the Delphi, a tiny restaurant crammed with deserted tables spread with pink and white checked cloths. "This is what one of our greatest authors looks like, Nikos," Sedgwick announced. "Let's have all we can eat and a litre of your red if that's your style, Jack, to be going on with."

The massive dark-skinned variously hairy proprietor brought them a carafe without a stopper and a brace of glasses Boswell would have expected to hold water. Sedgwick filled them with wine and dealt Boswell's a vigorous clunk. "Here's to us. Here's to your legendary unpublished books."

"Not for much longer."

"What a scoop for Cassandra. I don't know which I like best, *Don't Make Me Mad* or *Only We Are Left*. Listen to this, Nikos. There are going to be so many mentally ill people they have to be given the vote and everyone's made to have one as a lodger. And a father has to seduce his daughter or the human race dies out."

"Very nice."

"Ignore him, Jack. They couldn't be anyone else but you."

"I'm glad you feel that way. You don't think they're a little too dark even for me."

"Not a shade, and certainly not for Cassandra. Wait till you read our other books."

Here Nikos brought meze, an oval plate splattered with varieties of goo. Sedgwick waited until Boswell had transferred a sample of each to his plate and tested them with a piece of lukewarm bread. "Good?"

"Most authentic," Boswell found it in himself to say.

Sedgwick emptied the carafe into their glasses and called for another. Blackened lamb chops arrived too, and prawns dried up by grilling, withered meatballs, slabs of smoked ham that could have been used to sole shoes... Boswell was working on a token mouthful of viciously spiced sausage when Sedgwick said "Know how you could delight us even more?"

Boswell swallowed and had to salve his mouth with half a glassful of wine. "Tell me," he said tearfully.

"Have you enough unpublished stories for a collection?"

"I'd have to write another to bring it up to length."

"Wait till I let the girls know. Don't think they aren't excited, they were just too overwhelmed by meeting you to show it. Can you call me as soon as you have an idea for the story or the cover?"

"I think I may have both."

"You're an example to us all. Can I hear?"

"Shadows on a ruined wall. A man and woman and her child, and another man reaching out to them, I'd say in warning. Ruined tenements in the background. Everything overgrown. Even if the story isn't called *We Are Tomorrow*, the book can be."

"Shall I give you a bit of advice? Go further than you ever have before. Imagine something you couldn't believe anyone would pay you to write."

Despite the meal, Boswell felt too elated to imagine that just now. His capacity for observation seemed to have shut down too, and only an increase in the frequency of passers-by outside the window roused it. "What time is it?" he wondered, fumbling his watch upward on his thin wrist.

"Not much past five," Sedgwick said, emptying the carafe yet again. "Still lunchtime."

"Good God, if I miss my train I'll have to pay double."

"Next time we'll see about paying for your travel." Sedgwick gulped the last of the wine as he threw a credit card on the table to be collected later. "I wish you'd said you had to leave this early. I'll have Bren send copies of our books to you," he promised as Boswell panted into Waterloo, and called after him down the steps into the Underground "Don't forget, imagine the worst. That's what we're for."

For three hours the worst surrounded Boswell. **SIX NATIONS CONTINUE REARMING... CLIMATE CHANGES ACCELERATE, SAY SCIENTISTS... SUPERSTITIOUS FANATICISM ON INCREASE... WOMEN'S GROUPS CHALLENGE ANTI-GUN RULING... RALLY AGAINST COMPUTER CHIPS IN CRIMINALS ENDS IN VIOLENCE: THREE DEAD, MANY INJURED**... Far more commuters weren't reading the news than were: many wore headphones that leaked percussion like distant discos in the night, while the sole book to be seen was *Page Turner*, the latest Turner adventure from Midas Paperbacks, bound in either gold or silver depending, Boswell supposed, on the reader's standards. Sometimes drinking helped him create, but just now a bottle of wine from the buffet to stave off a hangover only froze in his mind the image of the present in ruins and overgrown by the future, of the shapes of a family and a figure poised to intervene printed on the remains of a wall by a flare of painful light. He had to move on from thinking of them as the Aireys and himself, or had he? One reason Jean had left him was that she'd found traces of themselves and April in nearly all his work, even where none was intended; she'd become convinced he was wishing the worst for her and her child when he'd only meant a warning, by no means mostly aimed at them. His attempts to invent characters wholly unlike them had never convinced her and hadn't improved his work either. He needn't consider her feelings now, he thought sadly. He had to write whatever felt true—the best story he had in him.

It was remaining stubbornly unformed when the train stammered into the terminus. A minibus strewn with drunks and defiant smokers deposited him at the end of his street. He assumed his house felt empty because of Rod's proposal. Jean had taken much of the furniture they hadn't passed on to April, but Boswell still had seats where he needed to sit and folding canvas chairs for visitors, and nearly all his books. He was in the kitchen, brewing coffee while he tore open the day's belated mail, when the phone rang.

He took the handful of bills and the airmail letter he'd saved for last into his workroom, where he sat on the chair April had loved spinning and picked up the receiver. "Jack Boswell."

"Jack? They're asleep."

Presumably this explained why Rod's voice was low. "Is that an event?" Boswell said.

"It is for April at the moment. She's been out all day looking for work, any work. She didn't want to tell you in case you already had too much on your mind."

"But now you have."

"I was hoping things had gone well for you today."

"I think you can do more than that."

"Believe me, I'm looking as hard as she is."

"No, I mean you can assure her when she wakes that not only do I have a publisher for my two novels and eventually a good chunk of my backlist, but they've asked me to put together a new collection too."

"Do you mind if I ask for her sake how much they're advancing you?"

"No pounds and no shillings or pence."

"You're saying they'll pay you in euros?"

"I'm saying they don't pay an advance to me or any of their authors, but they pay royalties every three months."

"I take it your agent has approved the deal."

"It's a long time since I've had one of those, and now I'll be ten per cent better off. Do remember I've plenty of experience."

"I could say the same. Unfortunately it isn't always enough."

Boswell felt his son-in-law was trying to render him as insignificant as Rod believed science fiction writers ought to be. He tore open the airmail envelope with the little finger of the hand holding the receiver. "What's that?" Rod demanded.

"No panic. I'm not destroying any of my work," Boswell told him, and smoothed out the letter to read it again. "Well, this is timely. The Saskatchewan Conference on Prophetic Literature is giving me the Wendigo Award for a career devoted to envisioning the future."

"Congratulations. Will it help?"

"It certainly should, and so will the story I'm going to write. Maybe even you will be impressed. Tell April not to let things pull her down," Boswell said as he rang off, and "Such as you" only after he had.

Boswell wakened with a hangover and an uneasy sense of some act left unperformed. The image wakened with him: small child holding woman's hand, man beside them, second man gesturing. He groped for the mug of water by the bed, only to find he'd drained it during the night. He stumbled to the bathroom and emptied himself while the cold tap filled the mug. In time he felt equal to yet another breakfast of the kind his doctor had warned him to be content with. Of course, he thought as the sound of chewed bran filled his skull, he should have called Sedgwick last night about the Wendigo Award. How early could he call? Best to wait until he'd worked on the new story. He tried as he washed up the breakfast things and the rest of the plates and utensils in the sink, but his mind seemed as paralysed as the shadows on the wall it kept showing him. Having sat at his desk for a while in front of the wordless screen, he dialled Cassandra Press.

"Hello? Yes?"

"Is that Carole?" Since that earned him no reply, he tried "Bren?"

"It's Carole. Who is this?"

"Jack Boswell. I just wanted you to know—"

"You'll want to speak to Q. Q, it's your sci-fi man."

Sedgwick came on almost immediately, preceded by a creak of bedsprings. "Jack, you're never going to tell me you've written your story already."

"Indeed I'm not. Best to take time to get it right, don't you think? I'm calling to report they've given me the Wendigo Award."

"About time, and never more deserved. Who is it gives those again? Carole, you'll need to scribble this down. Bren, where's something to scribble with?"

"By the phone," Bren said very close, and the springs creaked.

"Reel it off, Jack."

As Boswell heard Sedgwick relay the information he grasped that he was meant to realise how close the Cassandra Press personnel were to one another. "That's capital, Jack," Sedgwick told him. "Bren will be lumping some books to the mail for you, and I think I can say Carole's going to have good news for you."

"Any clue what kind?"

"Wait and see, Jack, and we'll wait and see what your new story's about."

Boswell spent half an hour trying to write an opening line that would trick him into having started the tale, but had to acknowledge that the technique no longer worked for him. He was near to being blocked by fearing he had lost all ability to write, and so he opened the carton of books the local paper had sent him to review. *Sci-Fi On The Net*, *Create Your Own* Star Wars™ *Character*, *1000 Best Sci-Fi Videos*, *Sci-Fi From Lucas To Spielberg*, *Star Wars™: The Bluffer's Guide*... There wasn't a book he would have taken off a shelf, nor any appropriate to the history of science fiction in which he intended to incorporate a selection from his decades of reviews. Just now writing something other than his story might well be a trap. He donned sandals and shorts and unbuttoned his shirt as he ventured out beneath a sun that looked as fierce as the rim of a total eclipse.

All the seats of a dusty bus were occupied by pensioners, some of whom looked as bewildered as the young woman who spent the journey searching the pockets of the combat outfit she wore beneath a stained fur coat and muttering that everyone needed to be ready for the enemy. Boswell had to push his way off the bus past three grim scrawny youths bare from the waist up, who boarded the vehicle as if they planned to hijack it. He was at the end of the road where the wall had inspired him—but he hadn't reached the wall when he saw Rod's car.

It was identifiable solely by the charred number plate. The car itself was a blackened windowless hulk. He would have stalked away to call the Aireys if the vandalism hadn't made writing the new story more urgent than ever, and so he stared at the incomplete wall with a fierceness designed to revive his mind. When he no longer knew if he was staring at the bricks until the story formed or the shadows did, he turned quickly away. The shadows weren't simply cast on the wall, he thought; they were embedded in it, just as the image was embedded in his head.

He had to walk a mile homeward before the same bus showed up. Trudging the last yards to his house left him parched. He drank several glassfuls of water, and opened the drawer of his desk to gaze for reassurance or perhaps inspiration at his secret present from a fan before he dialled the Aireys' number.

"Hello?"

If it was April, something had driven her voice high. "It's only me," Boswell tentatively said.

"Grandad. Are you coming to see us?"

"Soon, I hope."

"Oh." Having done her best to hide her disappointment, she added "Good."

"What have you been doing today?"

"Reading. Dad says I have to get a head start."

"I'm glad to hear it," Boswell said, though she didn't sound as if she wanted him to be. "Is mummy there?"

"Just dad."

After an interval Boswell tried "Rod?"

"It's just me, right enough."

"I'm sure she didn't mean— I don't know if you've seen your car."

"I'm seeing nothing but. We still have to pay to have it scrapped."

"No other developments?"

"Jobs, are you trying to say? Not unless April's so dumbstruck with good fortune she can't phone. I was meaning to call you, though. I wasn't clear last night what plans you had with regard to us."

Rod sounded so reluctant to risk hoping that Boswell said "There's a good chance I'll have a loan in me."

"I won't ask how much." After a pause presumably calculated to entice an answer Rod added "I don't need to tell you how grateful we are. How's your new story developing?"

This unique display of interest in his work only increased the pressure inside Boswell's uninspired skull. "I'm hard at work on it," he said.

"I'll tell April," Rod promised, and left Boswell with that—with hours before the screen and not a word of a tale, just shadows in searing light: child holding woman's hand, man beside, another gesturing…He fell asleep at his desk and jerked awake in a panic, afraid to know why his inspiration refused to take shape.

He seemed hardly to have slept in his bed when he was roused by a pounding of the front-door knocker and an incessant shrilling of the doorbell. As he staggered downstairs he imagined a raid, the country having turned overnight into a dictatorship that had set the authorities the task of arresting all subversives, not least those who saw no cause for optimism. The man on the doorstep was uniformed and gloomy about his job, but brandished a clipboard and had a carton at his feet. "Consignment for Boswell," he grumbled.

"Books from my publishers."

"Wouldn't know. Just need your autograph."

Boswell scrawled a signature rendered illegible by decades of autographs, then bore the carton to the kitchen table, where he slit its layers of tape to reveal the first Cassandra Press books he'd seen. All the covers were black as coal in a closed pit except for bony white lettering not quite askew enough for the effect to be unquestionably intentional. **GERMAINE GOSSETT, *Women Are The Wave.*** **TORIN BERGMAN, *Oracles Arise!*** **FERDY THORN, *Fight Them Fisheries*** . . . Directly inside each was the title page, and on the back of that the copyright opposite the first page of text. Ecological frugality was fine, but not if it looked unprofessional, even in uncorrected proof copies. Proofreading should take care of the multitude of printer's errors, but what of the prose? Every book, not just Torin Bergman's, read like the work of a single apprentice translator.

He abandoned a paragraph of Ferdy Thorn's blunt chunky style and sprinted to his workroom to answer the phone. "Boswell," he panted.

"Jack. How are you today?"

"I've been worse, Quentin."

"You'll be a lot better before you know. Did the books land?"

"The review copies, you mean."

"We'd be delighted if you reviewed them. That would be wonderful, wouldn't it, if Jack reviewed the books?" When this received no audible answer he said "Only you mustn't be kind just because they're ours, Jack. We're all in the truth business."

"Let me read them and then we'll see what's best. What I meant, though, these aren't finished books."

"They certainly should be. Sneak a glance at the last pages if you don't mind knowing the end."

"Finished in the sense of the state that'll be on sale in the shops."

"Well, yes. They're trade paperbacks. That's the book of the future."

"I know what trade paperbacks are. These—"

"Don't worry, Jack, they're just our first attempts. Wait till you see the covers Carole's done for you. Nothing grabs the eye like naïve art, especially with messages like ours."

"So," Boswell said in some desperation, "have I heard why you called?"

"You don't think we'd interrupt you at work without some real news."

"How real?"

"We've got the figures for the advance orders of your books. All the girls had to do was phone with your name and the new titles till the batteries went flat, and I don't mind telling you you're our top seller."

"What are the figures?" Boswell said, and took a deep breath.

"Nearly three hundred. Congratulations once again."

"Three hundred thousand. It's I who should be congratulating you and your team. I only ever had one book up there before. Shows publishing needs people like yourselves to shake it up." He became aware of speaking fast so that he could tell the Aireys his—no, their—good fortune, but he had to clarify one point before letting euphoria overtake him. "Or is that, don't think for a second I'm complaining if it is, but is that the total for both titles or each?"

"Actually, Jack, can I just slow you down a moment?"

"Sorry. I'm babbling. That's what a happy author sounds like. You understand why."

"I hope I do, but would you mind— I didn't quite catch what you thought I said."

"Three hundred—"

"Can I stop you there? That's the total, or just under. As you say, publishing has changed. I expect a lot of the bigger houses are doing no better with some of their books."

Boswell's innards grew hollow, then his skull. He felt his mouth drag itself into some kind of a grin as he said "Is that three hundred, sorry, nearly three hundred per title?"

"Overall, I'm afraid. We've still a few little independent shops to call, and sometimes they can surprise you."

Boswell doubted he could cope with any more surprises, but heard himself say, unbelievably, hopefully "Did you mention *We Are Tomorrow*?"

"How could we have forgotten it?" Sedgwick's enthusiasm relented at last as he said "I see what you're asking. Yes, the total is for all three of your books. Don't forget we've still the backlist to come, though," he added with renewed vigour.

"Good luck to it." Boswell had no idea how much bitterness was audible in that, nor in "I'd best be getting back to work."

"We all can't wait for the new story, can we?"

Boswell had no more of an answer than he heard from anyone else. Having replaced the receiver as if it had turned to heavy metal, he stared at the uninscribed slab of the computer screen. When he'd had enough of that he trudged to stare into the open rectangular hole of the Cassandra carton. Seized by an inspiration he would have preferred not to experience, he dashed upstairs to drag on yesterday's clothes and marched unshaven out of the house.

Though the library was less than ten minutes' walk away through sunbleached streets whose desert was relieved only by patches of scrub, he'd hardly visited it for the several years he had been too depressed to enter bookshops. The library was almost worse: it lacked not just his books but practically everyone's except for paperbacks with injured spines. Some of the tables in the large white high-windowed room were occupied by newspaper readers. **MIDDLE EAST WAR DEADLINE EXPIRES**...**ONE IN TWO FAMILIES WILL BE VICTIMS OF VIOLENCE, STUDY SHOWS**...**FAMINES IMMINENT IN EUROPE**...**NO MEDICINE FOR FATAL VIRUSES**...Most of the tables held Internet terminals, from one of which a youth whose face was red with more than pimples was being evicted by a librarian for calling up some text that had offended the black woman at the next screen. Boswell paid for an hour at the terminal and began his search.

The only listings of any kind for Torin Bergman were the publication details of the Cassandra Press books, and the same was true of Ferdy Thorn and Germaine Gossett. When the screen told him his time was up and began to flash like lightning to alert the staff, the message and the repeated explosion of light and the headlines around him seemed to merge into a single inspiration he couldn't grasp. Only a hand laid on his shoulder made him jump up and lurch between the reluctantly automatic doors.

The sunlight took up the throbbing of the screen, or his head did. He remembered nothing of his tramp home other than that it tasted like bone. As he fumbled to unlock the front door the light grew audible, or the phone began to shrill. He managed not to snap the key and ran to snatch up the receiver. "What now?"

"It's only me, dad. I didn't mean to bother you."

"You never could," Boswell said, though she just had by sounding close to tears. "How are you, April? How are things?"

"Not too wonderful."

"Things aren't, you mean. I'd never say you weren't."

"Both." Yet more tonelessly she said "I went looking for computer jobs. Didn't want all the time mummy spent showing me how things worked to go to waste. Only I didn't realise how much more there is to them now, and I even forgot what she taught me. So then I thought I'd go on a computer course to catch up."

"I'm sure that's a sound idea."

"It wasn't really. I forgot where I was going. I nearly forgot our number when I had to ring Rod to come and find me when he hasn't even got the car and leave Gemima all on her own."

Boswell was reaching deep into himself for a response when she said "Mummy's dead, isn't she?"

Rage at everything, not least April's state, made his answer harsh. "Shot by the same freedom fighters she'd given the last of her money to in a country I'd never even heard of. She went off telling me one of us had to make a difference to the world."

"Was it years ago?"

"Not long after you were married," Boswell told her, swallowing grief.

"Oh." She seemed to have nothing else to say but "Rod."

Boswell heard him murmuring at length before his voice attacked the phone. "Why is April upset?"

"Don't you know?"

"Forgive me. Were you about to give her some good news?"

"If only."

"You will soon, surely, once your books are selling. You know I'm no admirer of the kind of thing you write, but I'll be happy to hear of your success."

"You don't know what I write, since you've never read any of it." Aloud Boswell said only "You won't."

"I don't think I caught that."

"Yes you did. This publisher prints as many books as there are orders, which turns out to be under three hundred."

"Maybe you should try and write the kind of thing people will pay to read."

Boswell placed the receiver with painfully controlled gentleness on the hook, then lifted it to redial. The distant bell had started to sound more like an alarm to him when it was interrupted. "Quentin Sedgwick."

"And Torin Bergman."

"Jack."

"As one fictioneer to another, are you Ferdy Thorn as well?"

Sedgwick attempted a laugh, but it didn't lighten his tone much. "Germaine Gossett too, if you must know."

"So you're nearly all of Cassandra Press."

"Not any longer."

"How's that?"

"Out," Sedgwick said with gloomy humour. "I am. The girls had all the money, and now they've seen our sales figures they've gone off to set up a gay romance publisher."

"What lets them do that?" Boswell heard himself protest.

"Trust."

Boswell could have made plenty of that, but was able to say merely "So my books…"

"Must be somewhere in the future. Don't be more of a pessimist than you have to be, Jack. If I manage to revive Cassandra you know you'll be the first writer I'm in touch with," Sedgwick said, and had the grace to leave close to a minute's silence unbroken before ringing off. Boswell had no sense of how much the receiver weighed as he lowered it—no sense of anything except some rearrangement that was aching to occur inside his head. He had to know why the news about Cassandra Press felt like a completion so imminent the throbbing of light all but blinded him.

It came to him in the night, slowly. He had been unable to

develop the new story because he'd understood instinctively there wasn't one. His sense of the future was sounder than ever: he'd foreseen the collapse of Cassandra Press without admitting it to himself. Ever since his last sight of the Aireys the point had been to save them—he simply hadn't understood how. Living together would only have delayed their fate. He'd needed time to interpret his vision of the shadows on the wall.

He was sure the light in the house was swifter and more intense than dawn used to be. He pushed himself away from the desk and worked aches out of his body before making his way to the bathroom. All the actions he performed there felt like stages of a purifying ritual. In the mid-morning sunlight the phone on his desk looked close to bursting into flame. He winced at the heat of it before, having grown cool in his hand, it ventured to mutter "Hello?"

"Good morning."

"Dad? You sound happier. Are you?"

"As never. Is everyone up? Can we meet?"

"What's the occasion?"

"I want to fix an idea I had last time we met. I'll bring a camera if you can all meet me in the same place in let's say half an hour."

"We could except we haven't got a car."

"Take a cab. I'll reimburse you. It'll be worth it, I promise."

He was on his way almost as soon as he rang off. Tenements reared above his solitary march, but couldn't hinder the sun in its climb towards unbearable brightness. He watched his shadow shrink in front of him like a stain on the dusty littered concrete, and heard footsteps attempting stealth not too far behind him. Someone must have seen the camera slung from his neck. A backward glance as he crossed a deserted potholed junction showed him a youth as thin as a puppet, who halted twitching until Boswell turned away, then came after him.

A taxi sped past Boswell as he reached the street he was bound for. The Aireys were in front of the wall, close to the sooty smudge like a lingering shadow that was the only trace of their car. Gemima clung to her mother's hand while Rod stood a little apart, one fist in his hip pocket. They looked posed and uncertain why. Before anything had time to change, Boswell held up his palm to keep them still and confronted the youth who was swaggering towards him while attempting to seem aimless. Boswell lifted the camera strap over his tingling scalp. "Will you take us?" he said.

The youth faltered barely long enough to conceal an incredulous grin. He hung the camera on himself and snapped the carrying case open as Boswell moved into position, hand outstretched towards the Aireys. "Use the flash," Boswell said, suddenly afraid that otherwise there would be no shadows under the sun at the zenith—that the future might let him down after all. He'd hardly spoken when the flash went off, almost blinding its subjects to the spectacle of the youth fleeing with the camera.

Boswell had predicted this, and even that Gemima would step out a pace from beside her mother. "It's all right," he murmured, unbuttoning his jacket, "there's no film in it," and passed the gun across himself into the hand that had been waiting to be filled. Gemima was first, then April, and Rod took just another second. Boswell's peace deepened threefold as peace came to them. Nevertheless he preferred not to look at their faces as he arranged them against the bricks. He had only seen shadows before, after all.

Though the youth had vanished, they were being watched. Perhaps now the world could see the future Boswell had always seen. He clawed chunks out of the wall until wedging his arm into the gap supported him. He heard sirens beginning to howl, and wondered if the war had started. "The end," he said as best he could for the metal in his mouth. The last thing he saw was an explosion of brightness so intense he was sure it was printing their shadows on the bricks for as long as the wall stood. He even thought he smelled how green it would grow to be.

TICKET

# The Retrospective

Trent had no idea how long he was unable to think for rage. The guard kept out of sight while she announced the unscheduled stop, and didn't reappear until the trainload of passengers had crowded onto the narrow platform. As the train dragged itself away into a tunnel simulated by elderly trees and the low March afternoon sky that was plastered with layers of darkness, she poked her head out of the rearmost window to announce that the next train should be due in an hour.

The resentful mutters of the crowd only aggravated Trent's frustration. He needed a leisurely evening and, if he could manage it for a change, a night's sleep in preparation for a working breakfast. If he'd known the journey would be broken, he could have reread his paperwork instead of contemplating scenery he couldn't even remember. No doubt the next train would already be laden with commuters—he doubted it would give him space to work. His skull was beginning to feel shrivelled and hollow when it occurred to him that if he caught a later train he would both ensure himself a seat and have time to drop in on his parents. When had he last been home to see them? All at once he felt so guilty that he preferred not to look anyone in the face as he excused his slow way to the ticket office.

It was closed—a board lent it the appearance of a frame divested of a photograph—but flanked by a timetable. Stoneby to London, Stoneby to London... There were trains on the hour, like the striking of a clock. He emerged from the short wooden passage into the somewhat less gloomy street, only to falter. Where was the sweet shop whose window used to exhibit dozens of glass-stoppered jars full of colours he could taste? Where was the toyshop fronted by a headlong model train that had never stopped for the travellers paralysed on the platform? What had happened to the bakery displaying tiered white cakes elaborate as Gothic steeples, and the bridal shop next door, where the headless figures in their pale dresses had made him think of Anne Boleyn? Now the street was overrun with the same fast-food eateries and immature clothes shops that surrounded him whenever he left his present apartment, and he couldn't recall how much change he'd seen on his last visit, whenever that had been. He felt suddenly so desperate to be somewhere more like home that he almost didn't wait for twin green men to pipe up and usher him across the road.

The short cut was still there, in a sense. Instead of separating the toyshop from the wedding dresses, it squeezed between a window occupied by a regiment of boots and a hamburger outlet dogged by plastic cartons. Once he was in the alley the clamour of traffic relented, but the narrow passage through featureless discoloured concrete made him feel walled in by the unfamiliar. Then the concrete gave way to russet bricks and released him into a street he knew.

At least, it conformed to his memory until he looked closer. The building opposite, which had begun life as a music hall, had ceased to be a cinema. A pair of letters clung to the whitish border of the rusty iron marquee, two letters N so insecure they were on the way to being Zs. He was striving to remember if the cinema had been shut last time he'd seen it when he noticed that the boards on either side of the lobby contained posters too small for the frames. The neighbouring buildings were boarded up. As he crossed the deserted street, the posters grew legible. MEMORIES OF STONEBY, the amateurish printing said.

The two wide steps beneath the marquee were cracked and chipped and stained. The glass of the ticket booth in the middle of the marble floor was too blackened to see through. Behind the booth the doors into the auditorium stood ajar. Uncertain what the gap was showing him, he ventured to peer in.

At first the dimness yielded up no more than a strip of carpet framed by floorboards just as grubby, and then he thought someone absolutely motionless was watching him from the dark. The watcher was roped off from him—the several indistinct figures were. He assumed they represented elements of local history: there was certainly something familiar about them. That impression, and the blurred faces with their dully glinting eyes, might have transfixed him if he hadn't remembered that he was supposed to be seeing his parents. He left the echo of his footsteps dwindling in the lobby and hurried around the side of the museum.

Where the alley crossed another he turned left along the rear of the building. In the high wall to his right a series of solid wooden gates led to back yards, the third of which belonged to his old house. As a child he'd used the gate as a short cut to the cinema, clutching a coin in his fist, which had smelled of metal whenever he'd raised it to his face in the crowded restless dark. His parents had never bolted the gate until he was home again, but now the only effect of his trying the latch was to rouse a clatter of claws and the snarling of a neighbour's dog that sounded either muzzled or gagged with food, and so he made for the street his old house faced.

The sunless sky was bringing on a twilight murky as an unlit room. He could have taken the street for an aisle between two blocks of dimness so lacking in features they might have been identical. Presumably any children who lived in the terrace were home from school by now, though he couldn't see the flicker of a single television in the windows draped with dusk, while the breadwinners had yet to return. Trent picked his way over the broken upheaved slabs of the pavement, supporting himself on the roof of a lone parked car until it shifted rustily under his hand, to his parents' front gate.

The small plot of a garden was a mass of weeds that had spilled across the short path. He couldn't feel it underfoot as he tramped to the door, which was the colour of the oncoming dark. He was fumbling in his pocket and then with the catches of his briefcase when he realised he would hardly have brought his old keys with him. He rang the doorbell, or at least pressed the askew pallid button that set off a muffled rattle somewhere in the house.

For the duration of more breaths than he could recall taking, there was no response. He was about to revive the noise, though he found it somehow distressing, when he heard footsteps shuffling down the hall. Their slowness made it sound as long as it had seemed in his childhood, so that he had the odd notion that whoever opened the door would tower over him.

It was his mother, and smaller than ever—wrinkled and whitish as a figure composed of dough that had been left to collect dust, a wad of it on top of and behind her head. She wore a tweed coat over a garment he took to be a nightdress, which exposed only her prominent ankles above a pair of unmatched slippers. Her head wavered upwards as the corners of her lips did. Once all these had steadied she murmured "Is it you, Nigel? Are you back again?"

"I thought it was past time I was."

"It's always too long." She shuffled in a tight circle to present her stooped back to him before calling "Guess who it is, Walter."

"Hess looking for a place to hide," Trent's father responded from some depth of the house.

"No, not old red-nosed Rudolph. Someone a bit younger and a bit more English."

"The Queen come to tea."

"He'll never change, will he?" Trent's mother muttered and raised what was left of her voice. "It's the boy. It's Nigel."

"About time. Let's see what he's managed to make of himself."

She made a gesture like a desultory grab at something in the air above her left shoulder, apparently to beckon Trent along the hall. "Be quick with the door, there's a good boy. We don't want the chill roosting in our old bones."

As soon as the door shut behind him he couldn't distinguish whether the stairs that narrowed the hall by half were carpeted only with dimness. He trudged after his mother past a door that seemed barely sketched on the crawling murk and, more immediately than he expected, another. His mother opened a third, beyond which was the kitchen, he recalled rather than saw. It smelled of damp he hoped was mostly tea. By straining his senses he was just able to discern his father seated in some of the dark. "Shall we have the light on?" Trent suggested.

"Can't you see? Thought you were supposed to be the young one round here." After a pause his father said "Come back for bunny, have you?"

Trent couldn't recall ever having owned a rabbit, toy or otherwise, yet the question seemed capable of reviving some aspect of his childhood. He was feeling surrounded by entirely too much darkness when his mother said "Now, Walter, don't be teasing" and clicked the switch.

The naked dusty bulb seemed to draw the contents of the room inwards—the blackened stove and stained metal sink, the venerable shelves and cabinets and cupboards Trent's father had built, the glossy pallid walls. The old man was sunk in an armchair, the least appropriate of an assortment of seats surrounding the round table decorated with crumbs and unwashed plates. His pear-shaped variously reddish face appeared to have been given over to producing fat to merge with the rest of him. He used both shaky inflated hands to close the lapels of his faded dressing-gown over his pendulous chest cobwebbed with grey hairs. "You've got your light," he said, "so take your place."

Lowering himself onto a chair that had once been straight, Trent lost sight of the entrance to the alley—of the impression that it was the only aspect of the yard the window managed to illuminate. "Will I make you some tea?" his mother said.

She wasn't asking him to predict the future, he reassured himself. "So long as you're both having some as well."

"Not much else to do these days."

"It won't be that bad really, will it?" Trent said, forcing a guilty laugh. "Aren't you still seeing…"

"What are we seeing?" his father prompted with some force.

"Your friends," Trent said, having discovered that he couldn't recall a single name. "They can't all have moved away."

"Nobody moves any longer."

Trent didn't know whether to take that as a veiled rebuke. "So what have you two been doing with yourselves lately?"

"Late's the word."

"Nigel's here now," Trent's mother said, perhaps relevantly, over the descending hollow drum-roll of the kettle she was filling from the tap.

More time than was reasonable seemed to have passed since he'd entered the house. He was restraining himself from glancing even surreptitiously at his watch when his father quivered an impatient hand at him. "So what are you up to now?"

"He means your work."

"Same as always."

Trent hoped that would suffice until he was able to reclaim his memory from the darkness that had gathered in his skull, but his parents' stares were as blank as his mind. "And what's that?" his mother said.

He felt as though her forgetfulness had seized him. Desperate to be reminded what his briefcase contained, he nevertheless used reaching for it as a chance to glimpse his watch. The next train was due in less than half an hour. As Trent scrabbled at the catches of the briefcase, his father said "New buildings, isn't it? That's what you put up."

"Plan," Trent said, clutching the briefcase on his lap. "I draw them."

"Of course you do," said his mother. "That's what you always wanted."

It was partly so as not to feel minimised that Trent declared "I wouldn't want to be responsible for some of the changes in town."

"Then don't be."

"You won't see much else changing round here," Trent's mother said.

"Didn't anyone object?"

"You have to let the world move on," she said. "Leave it to the young ones."

Trent wasn't sure if he was included in that or only wanted to be. "How long have we had a museum?"

His father's eyes grew so blank Trent could have fancied they weren't in use. "Since I remember."

"No, that's not right," Trent objected as gently as his nerves permitted. "It was a cinema and before that a theatre. You took me to a show there once."

"Did we?" A glint surfaced in his mother's eyes. "We used to like shows, didn't we, Walter? Shows and dancing. Didn't we go on all night sometimes and they wondered where we'd got to?"

Her husband shook his head once slowly, whether to enliven memories or deny their existence Trent couldn't tell. "The show you took me to," he insisted, "I remember someone dancing with a stick. And there was a lady comedian, or maybe not a lady but dressed up."

Perhaps it was the strain of excavating the recollection that made it seem both lurid and encased in darkness—the outsize figure prancing sluggishly about the stage and turning towards him a sly greasy smile as crimson as a wound, the ponderous slap on the boards of feet that sounded unshod, the onslaughts of laughter that followed comments Trent found so incomprehensible he feared they were about him, the shadow that kept swelling on whatever backdrop the performer had, an effect suggesting that the figure was about to grow yet more gigantic. Surely some or preferably most of that was a childhood nightmare rather than a memory. "Was there some tea?" Trent blurted.

At first it seemed his mother's eyes were past seeing through their own blankness. "In the show, do you mean?"

"Here." When that fell short of her he said more urgently "Now."

"Why, you should have reminded me," she protested and stood up. How long had she been seated opposite him? He was so anxious to remember that he didn't immediately grasp what she was doing. "Mother, don't," he nearly screamed, flinging himself off his chair.

"No rush. It isn't anything like ready." She took her hand out of the kettle on the stove—he wasn't sure if he glimpsed steam trailing from her fingers as she replaced the lid. "We haven't got much longer, have we?" she said. "We mustn't keep you from your duties."

"You won't do that again, will you?"

"What's that, son?"

He was dismayed to think she might already have forgotten. "You won't put yourself in danger."

"There's nothing we'd call that round here," his father said.

"You'll look after each other, won't you? I really ought to catch the next train. I'll be back to see you again soon, I promise, and next time it'll be longer."

"It will."

His parents said that not quite in chorus, apparently competing at slowness. "Till next time, then," he said and shook his father's hand before hugging his mother. Both felt disconcertingly cold and unyielding, as if the appearance of each had hardened into a carapace. He gripped the handle of his briefcase while he strove to twist the rusty key in the back door. "I'll go my old way, shall I? It's quicker."

When nobody answered he hauled open the door, which felt unhinged. Cobwebbed weeds sprawled over the doorstep into the kitchen at once. Weedy mounds of earth or rubble had overwhelmed the yard and the path. He picked his way to the gate and with an effort turned his head, but nobody was following to close the gate: his mother was still at her post by the stove, his father was deep in the armchair. He had to use both hands to wrench the bolt out of its socket, and almost forgot to retrieve his briefcase as he stumbled into the alley. The passage was unwelcomingly dark, not least because the light from the house failed to reach it—no, because the kitchen was unlit. He dragged the gate shut and took time to engage the latch before heading for the rear of the museum.

Damp must be stiffening his limbs. He hoped it was in the air, not in his parents' house. Was it affecting his vision as well? When he slogged to the end of the alley the street appeared to be composed of little but darkness, except for the museum. The doors to the old auditorium were further ajar, and as he crossed the road Trent saw figures miming in the dimness. He hadn't time to identify their faces before panting down the alley where brick was ousted by concrete.

Figures sat in the stark restaurants and modelled clothes in windows. Otherwise the street was deserted except for a man who dashed into the station too fast for Trent to see his face. The man let fly a wordless plea and waved his briefcase as he sprinted through the booking hall. Trent had just begun to precipitate himself across the road when he heard the slam of a carriage door. He staggered ahead of his breath onto the platform in time to see the last light of a train vanish into the trees, which looked more like a tunnel than ever.

His skull felt frail with rage again. Once he regained the ability to move he stumped to glower at the timetable next to the boarded-up office. His fiercest glare was unable to change the wait into less than an hour. He marched up and down a few times, but each end of the platform met him with increasing darkness. He had to keep moving to ward off a chill stiffness. He trudged into the street and frowned about him.

The fast-food outlets didn't appeal to him, neither their impersonal refreshments nor the way all the diners faced the street as though to watch him, not that doing so lent them any animation. He couldn't even see anyone eating. Ignoring the raw red childishly sketched men, he lurched across the road into the alley.

He oughtn't to go to his parents. So instant a return might well confuse them, and just now his own mind felt more than sufficiently unfocused. The only light, however tentative, in the next street came from the museum. He crossed the roadway, which was as lightless as the low sky, and climbed the faint steps.

Was the ticket booth lit? A patch of the blackened glass had been rubbed relatively clear from within. He was fumbling for money to plant on the sill under the gap at the foot of the window when he managed to discern that the figure in the booth was made of wax. While it resembled the middle-aged woman who had occupied the booth when the building was a cinema, it ought to look years—no, decades—older. Its left grey-cardiganed arm was raised to indicate the auditorium. He was unable to judge its expression for the gloom inside the booth. Tramping to the doors, he pushed them wide.

That seemed only to darken the auditorium, but he felt the need to keep on the move before his eyes had quite adjusted. The apparently sourceless twilight put him in mind of the glow doled out by the candle that used to stand in an encrusted saucer on the table by his childhood bed. As he advanced under the enormous unseen roof, he thought he was walking on the same carpet that had led into the cinema and indeed the theatre. He was abreast of the first of the figures on either side of the aisle before he recognised them.

He'd forgotten they were sisters, the two women who had run the bakery and the adjacent bridal shop. Had they really been twins? They were playing bridesmaids in identical white ankle-length dresses—whitish, rather, and trimmed with dust. Presumably it was muslin as well as dust that gloved their hands, which were pointing with all their digits along the aisle. The dull glints of their grimy eyes appeared to spy sidelong on him. He'd taken only a few steps when he stumbled to a halt and peered about him.

The next exhibits were disconcerting enough. No doubt the toyshop owner was meant to be introducing his model railway, but he looked as if he was crouching sideways to grab whatever sought refuge in the miniature tunnel. Opposite him the sweet shop man was enticing children to his counter, which was heaped with sweets powdered grey, by performing on a sugar whistle not entirely distinguishable from his glimmering teeth. Trent hadn't time to ascertain what was odd about the children's wide round eyes, because he was growing aware of the extent of the museum.

Surely it must be a trick of the unreliable illumination, but the more he gazed around him, the farther the dimness populated with unmoving figures seemed to stretch. If it actually extended so far ahead and to both sides, it would encompass at least the whole of the street that contained his parents' house. He wavered forward a couple of paces, which only encouraged figures to solidify out of that part of the murk. He swivelled as quickly as he was able and stalked out of the museum.

The echoes of his footsteps pursued him across the lobby like mocking applause. He could hear no other sound, and couldn't tell whether he was being watched from the ticket booth. He found his way down the marble steps and along the front of the museum. In a few seconds he was sidling crabwise along it in order to differentiate the alley from the unlit façade. He wandered further than he should have, and made his way back more slowly. Before long he was groping with his free hand at the wall as he ranged back and forth, but it was no use. There was no alley, just unbroken brick.

He was floundering in search of a crossroads, from which there surely had to be a route to his old house, when he realised he might as well be blind. He glanced back, praying wordlessly for any relief from the dark. There was only the glow from the museum lobby. It seemed as feeble as the candle flame had grown in the moment before it guttered into smoke, and so remote he thought his stiff limbs might be past carrying him to it. When he retreated towards it, at first he seemed not to be moving at all.

More time passed than he could grasp before he felt sure the light was closer. Later still he managed to distinguish the outstretched fingertips of his free hand. He clung to his briefcase as though it might be snatched from him. He was abreast of the lobby, and preparing to abandon its glow for the alley that led to the station, when he thought he heard a whisper from inside the museum. "Are you looking for us?"

It was either a whisper or so distant that it might as well be one. "We're in here, son," it said, and its companion added "You'll have to come to us."

"Mother?" It was unquestionably her voice, however faint. He almost tripped over the steps as he sent himself into the lobby. For a moment, entangled in the clapping of his footsteps on the marble, he thought he heard a large but muted sound as of the surreptitious arrangement of a crowd. He blundered to the doors and peered into the auditorium.

Under the roof, which might well have been an extension of the low ponderous black sky, the aisle and its guardians were at least as dim as ever. Had things changed, or had he failed to notice details earlier? The bridal sisters were licking their lips, and he wasn't sure if they were dressed as bridesmaids or baked into giant tiered cakes from which they were trying to struggle free. Both of the toyshop owner's hands looked eager to seize the arrested train if it should try to reach the safety of the tunnel, and the bulging eyes of the children crowded around the man with the sugar whistle—were those sweets? Trent might have retreated if his mother's voice hadn't spoken to him. "That's it, son. Don't leave us this time."

"Have a thought for us. Don't start us wondering where you are again. We're past coming to find you."

"Where are you? I can't see."

"Just carry on straight," his parents' voices took it in turns to murmur.

He faltered before lurching between the first exhibits. Beyond them matters could hardly be said to improve. He did his best not to see too much of the milkman holding the reins of a horse while a cow followed the cart, but the man's left eye seemed large enough for the horse, the right for the cow. Opposite him stood a rag and bone collector whose trade was apparent from the companion that hung onto his arm, and Trent was almost glad of the flickering dimness. "How much further?" he cried in a voice that the place shrank almost to nothing.

"No more than you can walk at your age."

Trent hung onto the impression that his father sounded closer than before and hugged his briefcase while he made his legs carry him past a policeman who'd removed his helmet to reveal a bald ridged head as pointed as a chrysalis, a priest whose smooth face was balanced on a collar of the same paleness and no thicker than a child's wrist, a window cleaner with scrawny legs folded like a grasshopper's, a bus conductor choked by his tie that was caught in his ticket machine while at the front of the otherwise deserted vehicle the driver displayed exactly the same would-be comical strangled face and askew swollen tongue... They were nightmares, Trent told himself: some he remembered having suffered as a child, and the rest he was afraid to remember in case they grew clearer. "I still can't see you," he all but wailed.

"Down here, son."

Did they mean ahead? He hoped he wasn't being told to use any of the side aisles, not least because they seemed capable of demonstrating that the place was even vaster than he feared. The sights they contained were more elaborate too. Off to the right was a brass band, not marching but frozen in the act of tiptoeing towards him: though all the players had lowered their instruments, their mouths were perfectly round. In the dimness to his left, and scarcely more luminous, was a reddish bonfire surrounded by figures that wore charred masks, unless those were their faces, and beyond that was a street party where children sat at trestle tables strewn with food and grimaced in imitation of the distorted versions of their faces borne by deflating balloons they held on strings... Trent twisted his stiff body around in case some form of reassurance was to be found behind him, but the exit to the lobby was so distant he could have mistaken it for the last of a flame. He half closed his eyes to blot out the sights he had to pass, only to find that made the shadows of the exhibits and the darkness into which the shadows trailed loom closer, as if the dimness was on the point of being finally extinguished. He was suddenly aware that if the building had still been a theatre, the aisle would have brought him to the stage by now. "Where are you?" he called but was afraid to raise his voice. "Can't you speak?"

"Right here."

His eyes sprang so wide they felt fitted into their sockets. His parents weren't just close, they were behind him. He turned with difficulty and saw why he'd strayed past them. His mother was wearing a top hat and tails and had finished twirling a cane that resembled a lengthening of one knobbly finger; his father was bulging out of a shabby flowered dress that failed to conceal several sections of a pinkish bra. They'd dressed up to cure Trent of his nightmare about the theatre performance, he remembered, but they had only brought it into his waking hours. He backed away from it—from their waxen faces greyish with down, their smiles as fixed as their eyes. His legs collided with an object that folded them up, and he tottered sideways to sit helplessly on it. "That's it, son," his mother succeeded in murmuring.

"That's your place," his father said with a last shifting of his lips.

Trent glared downwards and saw he was trapped by a school desk barely large enough to accommodate him. On either side of him sat motionless children as furred with grey as their desks, even their eyes. Between him and his parents a teacher in a gown and mortarboard was standing not quite still and sneering at him. "Mr Bunnie," Trent gasped, remembering how the teacher had always responded to being addressed by his name as though it was an insult. Then, in a moment of clarity that felt like a beacon in the dark, he realised he had some defence. "This isn't me," he tried to say calmly but firmly. "This is."

His fingers were almost too unmanageable to deal with the briefcase. He levered at the rusty metal buttons with his thumbs until at last the catches flew open and the contents spilled across the desk. For a breath, if he had any, Trent couldn't see them in the dimness, and then he made out that they were half a dozen infantile crayon drawings of houses. "I've done more than that," he struggled to protest, "I am more," but his mouth had finished working. He managed only to raise his head, and never knew which was worse: his paralysis, or his parents' doting smiles, or the sneer that the teacher's face seemed to have widened to encompass—the sneer that had always meant that once a child was inside the school gates, his parents could no longer protect him. It felt like an eternity before the failure of the dimness or of Trent's eyes brought the dark.

# The Room Beyond

As soon as Todd drove off the motorway it vanished from the mirror, and so did the sun across the moor. On both sides of the street the slender terraced houses huddled together like old folk afraid of descending the precipitous slope. Most of the shops in the town at the foot of the street were illuminated, but the streetlamps seemed oblivious of the September dusk. As he braked and braked again he saw the hotel sign across the maze of roofs.

The middle was blocked by the spire of a church, but **BEL** and the final **E** were visible. He hadn't realised that the hotel was on the far side of town. Whenever he stayed with his uncle and aunt he'd come by train, from which they had escorted him through the back streets to their house, interrogating him and talking at him so incessantly that he'd had little chance to learn the route. It had been the same on Sundays, when they'd walked to the Bellevue for a dauntingly formal lunch. Now the town hardly seemed large enough to accommodate either route.

More than this had changed in fifty years. While the clock from beneath which figures emerged on the hour was still outside the jewellers on the High Street, the road was one way only now. It turned away from the hotel, and all the side streets leading there displayed No Entry signs. Most of the shops were either new or disused, and the Apollo, where he'd once seen an airman climbing steps to heaven, had become the Valley Bottom pub. In a few minutes Todd found himself back at the clock, which hadn't moved on from twenty-five to six. The tarnished figures were paralysed on their track, and one stood in a miniature doorway as if he were loath to venture beyond. Shops were being shuttered, and at last the streetlamps came on, illuminating virtually deserted streets. This time Todd left the High Street ahead of the bend, but the lane he followed returned to the clock. He glimpsed Christ the Redeemer down a narrow alley, though the church was dark. He had to drive along the High Street yet again to discover that a road around the outside of the town led towards the hotel.

Was the park beside the road the one where his relatives had taken him to hear a brass band? He wouldn't have placed it so close to the hotel. The doctor's surgery must have been in one of the derelict houses facing the park, but Todd couldn't identify which. He hadn't thought of it for all these years, and he would have been happy to forget it now. He hadn't passed a single inhabited house by the time the road brought him to the hotel.

He had to laugh, as his uncle liked him to. The long black building was less than half the size he seemed to remember. While it might have been designed to resemble a mansion, he could have taken it for some kind of institution now. A wind blundered off the moor and flapped a torn section of the canvas awning across most of the unilluminated name. A couple of cars were parked on the forecourt, under a solitary orange floodlight that turned his blue Passat as black as they appeared to be. Dead windblown vegetation splintered beneath the wheels as he parked in front of a tall window blacked out by heavy curtains. His boxy suitcase was resting on the back seat, and he trundled it to the hotel.

No uniformed doorman was waiting to sweep the massive glass door wide, and Todd might have imagined that the door itself had shrunk. Its metal corner scraped over the tiled floor with an excruciating screech that made the receptionist glower. She was a brawny broad-shouldered woman with gilded spectacles as narrow as her eyes. Her grey hair was severely waved, and the glasses seemed to pinch her features small and sharp. She kept up her frown as Todd crossed the lobby, which was lit to some extent by a few bulbs of the dusty chandelier. More than just her attitude reminded him of someone else, so that he blurted "Excuse me, did you have a mother?"

She pursed her lips so hard that the surrounding skin turned grey along with them. "I beg your pardon," she said while doing nothing of the kind.

Her voice was hoarse and blurred, like a smoker's who was also somewhat drunk. "Sorry," Todd said and risked a laugh, only to wish he'd kept it to himself. "Does it run in the family, I meant to say."

"I'm sure I don't know what you mean."

"What you do. Admitting. Admission." Todd's words seemed to be straying out of his control, an unwelcome reminder of his age. "What I'm trying to say," he said, "was she a receptionist? The one in the practice by the park round the corner."

"That's a graveyard, not a park."

He could only assume she had somewhere else in mind. "Anyway," he said, "can I have my room?"

"Have you booked?"

"I rang," Todd said and wondered if the woman who'd taken the call had been her in a more hospitable mood. "Jacob Todd."

"Todd." His uncle used to greet him with a cry of "Now it's all jake," but Todd felt as if the receptionist had dropped his name with a dull thud. She dragged a ledger bound in black from under the counter and plucked at the pages before repeating "Todd" like an accusation. He might have thought the pages at the back were loose with age until he realised they were registration forms, one of which she laid before him on the counter. "Fill yourself in," she said.

Discolouration had lent the form a dark border. The print was both small and smudged, and squinting at it only left Todd more frustrated with the task it set him. "Who needs all this?"

The receptionist raised her spectacles to train her gaze on him. Her fingertips looked as earthy as the edges of the form. "You might be taken ill," she said.

"Suppose I am, who'll want all this information?"

"The authorities," she said and stared unblinkingly at him.

The solitary writing instrument on the counter was a ballpoint splintered like a bone and bandaged with sticky plastic tape. As Todd strove to fit his details into narrow boxes on the form, the inky tip stumbled about like a senile limb. Last name, first name, address, date of birth, place of birth... "What's your business in our town?" the receptionist said.

"A funeral."

"You'll be just round the corner."

Even if that was indeed a graveyard, it needn't be the only one in town. Christ the Redeemer hadn't appeared to be anywhere near the hotel. Todd could go for a walk and find his way to the church once he'd checked into his room. Profession, driving licence number, car registration number, telephone number, email... "Will you be taking the dinner?" the receptionist said.

Todd was distracted by someone's attempts to enter the hotel or even to locate the handle of the door. He turned to see that the door was shaking just with rain, which was surging across the moor. "When do you need to know?" he said.

"As soon as you like." This plainly meant as soon as she did. "Cook wants to get away."

Perhaps at least the meal would be up to the standard Todd remembered, and he could save his walk in case the rain ceased. "Put me down, then," he said.

The receptionist vanished like a shadow into a small office behind the counter. Presumably the dim light from the lobby was all she required, for Todd heard the rattle of a telephone receiver. "One for dinner," she said, and somewhere in the building a distant version of her voice joined in. Another hollow rattle was succeeded by a metallic one, and she reappeared with a key attached to a tarnished baton. "Are you written up yet?" she said.

Towards the bottom of the form the print was almost too indistinct to read. Method of payment, onward destination, next of kin... "That's a blank, I'm afraid," Todd said. He scrawled his signature, in which age had reduced the first name to resembling Jab, and unstuck his discoloured fingers from the pen while the receptionist pored over the form.

He'd had more than enough of the sight of her greyish scalp through her irregular parting—it put him in mind of a crack in weedy stone—by the time she raised her head. "Retired from what?" she apparently felt entitled to learn.

"Education." When this didn't lessen her scrutiny Todd added "Teaching them their sums."

This failed to earn him even a blink. "Will you be dressing?" she said.

"For dinner, you mean?" She'd begun to remind him of his aunt, who had always found some element of his appearance to improve—a collar to tug higher on his neck, a tie to yank tighter, a handkerchief that was either lying too low in his breast pocket or standing too impolitely erect. "I'll be changing," he said.

"Better look alive, then. It's nearly eight, you know."

"Nowhere near," said Todd, shaking the cuff of his heavy sweater back from his thin wrist. He was about to brandish the time—not much after half past five—when he saw his watch had stopped. His aunt and uncle had sent it for his twenty-first, and it had never let him down before. He drew his cuff over its battered face and found the receptionist frowning at him as if he'd betrayed some innumeracy. "Let's have my key, then," he said, "and I'll be down as soon as I'm fit to kill."

Whenever she'd finished sprucing him Todd's aunt used to say that was how he was dressed, but perhaps the receptionist didn't know the phrase. "You're number one," she informed him, planting the brass club on the counter with a blow like the stroke of a hammer. "You'll have to work the lift yourself."

Todd couldn't tell whether she was apologising for the attendant's absence or reminiscing about the hotel's better days. As he headed for the gloomy alcove that housed the entrance to the single lift, a wheel of his suitcase dislodged a loose tile. The receptionist watched with disfavour while he replaced it in its gritty niche, and he didn't linger over deciphering the blurred letters on the underside of the tile—presumably some firm's trademark. Once he dragged open both latticed doors of the lift he struggled over shutting them. The wall of the lift shaft inched past the rusty mesh, and at last the floor of a grudgingly illuminated corridor sank into view, although the lift fell short of aligning with it. Todd had to clamber up and haul his suitcase after him before he could make for his room.

It was at the far end of the left-hand stretch of corridor, where a window above a fire escape showed the town reduced to runny mud by the rain on the glass. The feeble lamps on the corridor walls resembled glazed flames, all the more by flickering. The number on Todd's door was dangling head down from its one remaining screw. He twisted the key in the aged shaky lock and pushed the leaden door open, to be met by a smell of old fabric. It made Todd feel enclosed, invisibly and impalpably but oppressively, even after he switched on the miniature chandelier.

The small room was darkened by the furniture—a black wardrobe with a full-length mirror in its narrow door, an ebony dressing-table, a squat chest of drawers that looked stunted by age, a bed that wasn't quite single or double, with a hint of an indentation underneath a shaggy blanket as brown as turned earth. A door led to a shower and toilet, while another would have communicated with the next bedroom but was blocked by a luggage stand. Behind the heavy curtains at the foot of the bed Todd found a window that showed him darkness raging above the moor. He was unpacking his case when he heard what could have been the fall of several pans in the kitchen. As he changed into his dark suit—the only one he'd brought—a phone rang.

At first he thought it was in the next room. It shrilled at least a dozen times before he traced the dusty wire from the skirting board to the upper compartment of the wardrobe. When he swung the door open, the receiver toppled off the hook, starting to speak as he fumbled it towards his face. "The gong's gone, Mr Todd."

The receptionist's tone seemed capable of stripping Todd of all the years since his last visit. "Oh, is that what it was?" he retorted. "I'll be with you as soon as I can."

He would have liked to shower and shave, but the hotel could take the blame, even if the man in the black frame of the mirror would never have passed his aunt's inspection. Todd had always felt on probation, never quite knowing if his visits were treats or punishments. "If you won't behave you can go to your aunt's," his mother used to say, and he'd suspected she was a little afraid of her older sister. His uncle hadn't seemed to be, and made a joke wherever he could find one, but then he'd done so at the surgery as well. Todd didn't need to be alone with those memories, and hurried out of the room.

If he'd been able to locate the stairs he would have used them, but the corridor offered him just the silent doors, bearing numbers like steps in a child's first arithmetic lesson. He was close to hearing them chanted in his skull. He stepped gingerly down into the lift and pushed the marble button, only to leave a blotchy print on it. He hadn't even washed his hands. "Not my fault," he muttered, feeling threatened by a second childhood.

The lobby was deserted except for a sign on a stand outside a room Todd hadn't previously noticed. The plastic numbers separated by a hyphen weren't years, they were hours with just sixty minutes between them. The words above them would have said **DINING ROOM** if they hadn't lost a letter. Todd found the **N** on the carpet in the doorway—carpet trampled as flat and black as soil. As he attempted to replace the letter between the **I** and its twin he felt as if he were playing an infantile game. He hadn't succeeded when he grew aware of being watched from the room beyond the sign. "Just putting you together," he said.

The waiter was dressed even more sombrely than Todd. He stepped back a silent pace and indicated the room with a sweep of one white-gloved hand. The room was nowhere near as daunting as Todd recalled. While the tables were still draped like altars, and the place was certainly as hushed as a church, it was scarcely big enough for a chapel. Even if it had always sported chandeliers, he didn't remember them as being so ineffectual. He had to squint to be sure of the burly waiter's small sharp face, the eyes narrowed as though in need of spectacles, the brow that he could have imagined had been tugged unnaturally smooth by the removal of a wig from the clipped grey hair. He was disconcerted enough to blurt "Has your sister gone off?"

The waiter paced to the farthest table and drew back its solitary chair. "Who was that, sir?"

His voice was as unctuously slow as a priest's at a pulpit, and might have been striving for hoarseness and depth. "Aren't you related to the lady at reception?" Todd said.

"They say we're all related, don't they?" Before Todd could give this whatever response it deserved, the waiter said "Will you be taking the buffet?"

Todd sat down as the waiter slipped the chilly leather seat beneath him. "Can I see the menu?" he said.

He never had while he was visiting—he'd only watched his aunt and uncle leafing through leather-bound volumes and then ordering for him. "I wouldn't recommend it, sir," the waiter said.

Todd was starting to feel as he'd felt as a child—that everyone around him knew a secret he wouldn't learn until he was older. "Why not?" he demanded.

"We're just providing the buffet option on this occasion. Chef had to leave us."

"Then I haven't much choice, have I?"

"We always have while we're alive."

The waiter sounded more priestly than ever, and his pace was deliberate enough for a ritual as he approached the lengthy table that stood along the left side of the room. He uncovered every salver and tureen before extending a hand towards them. "Enough for a large party, sir."

When waiters used to say things like that, Todd had expected his uncle to respond with a witticism. The hotel seemed to be turning into a joke Todd didn't understand. As he crossed the shiny blackened carpet to the buffet, the waiter raised a cloth from an elongated heap at the end of the table and handed him a plate. The buffet offered chicken legs and slices of cold meat, potatoes above which a fog hovered or at least a stagnant cloud of steam, a mound of chips that reminded him of extracting sticks from a haphazard pile in a game for which his aunt had never had the patience. Last came salads, and as he loaded his plate a lettuce leaf attempted a feeble crawl before subsiding on the salver. The movement might have betrayed the presence of an insect, but it was the work of a wind that had moved the floor-length curtain away from a window behind the table as though somebody was lurking there. As a child Todd had somehow been led to believe that God lived behind the curtains above the altar in the church. The curtains on the far side of the table veiled only a vast darkness tossing restlessly as a sleeper in a nightmare. He did his best to ignore the impression while remarking "At least I'm the first one down."

"The only one," the waiter said and found utensils under the cloth for him. "It's all been put on for you, Mr Todd."

Was this meant to shame him into taking more? Todd might have wondered if his fellow guests knew better than to eat at the hotel, but he was more inclined to ask how the waiter knew his name. The man spoke before Todd could. "Will you be having the house?"

"I'll try a bottle. Make it red." In a further attempt to recapture some sense of maintaining control Todd said "And a jug out of the tap."

The waiter gave a priestly bow before gliding through a doorway to the left of the buffet, and Todd heard him droning to himself under his breath. Any response was in the same voice, and monotonous enough to suggest that the man was murmuring a ritual. After some sounds of pouring the waiter reappeared with a tray that bore an unstoppered carafe and a jug. He served Todd water and wine and stepped back. "Can you taste it, sir?" he murmured.

Todd took a mouthful of the wine, which seemed oddly lifeless, like some kind of token drink. "It'll do," he said, if only to make the waiter step back.

The man continued loitering within rather less than arm's length. He'd clasped his hands together on his chest, which put Todd in mind of someone praying beside a bed. When he tried to concentrate on his meal the hands glimmered so much at the edge of his vision that he might have imagined the gloves were plastic. "I'll be fine now," he said as persuasively as he could.

The waiter seemed reluctant to part his hands or otherwise move. At last he retreated, so slowly that he might have felt he didn't exist apart from his job. "Call me if there's anything you need," he said as he replaced the covers on the buffet before withdrawing into the inner room. He began murmuring again at once, which made it hard for Todd to breathe. It reminded him too much of the voice he used to hear beyond the doctor's waiting-room.

"Go to the doctor's with your uncle," his aunt would say, and Todd had never known whether she disliked having him in the house by herself or was providing her husband with company if not distraction, unless it had been her way of making certain that Todd's uncle saw the doctor yet again. Every time he'd filled the wait with jokes at which Todd had felt bound to laugh, although neither the quips nor his mirth had seemed to please the other patients. He'd felt not just embarrassed but increasingly aware that the joking was designed to distract someone—himself or his uncle or both—from the reason they were waiting in the room. He had never ventured to ask, and his uncle hadn't volunteered the information. It had been the secret waiting beyond the door through which his uncle would disappear with a last wry grin at Todd, after which Todd would gaze at the scuffed carpet while he tried to hear the discussion muffled by the wall. Eventually his uncle would return, looking as if he'd never given up his grin. While Todd had seldom managed to distinguish even a word, he'd once overheard his uncle protest "This isn't much of a joke."

Todd knew the secret now, but he preferred not to remember. He was even glad to be distracted by the waiter, who had stolen at some point back into the dining-room. Todd seemed to have been so preoccupied that he might have imagined somebody else had eaten his dinner, which he couldn't recall tasting. The jug and carafe were empty too. He'd barely glanced at his plate when the waiter came swiftly but noiselessly to him. "Do go back, Mr Todd."

The subdued light and the oppressive silence, not to mention the buffet, were making Todd feel as if he were already at a wake.

"I've finished, thank you," he said. "The doctor says I have to watch my food."

When his uncle used to say that, Todd could never tell if it was a joke. Certainly his uncle had gazed at his food until his wife protested "Don't put ideas in the boy's head, Jack." Since the waiter seemed ready to persist, Todd said "I'll be down in the morning. I have to be ready for a funeral."

The waiter looked lugubriously sympathetic, but Todd was thrown by the notion that the man already had. "Whose is that, sir?"

"I'd rather not talk about it if you don't mind." Todd regretted having brought the subject up. "I'm on my own now," he said as he made his way between the empty tables, which had begun to remind him of furniture covered with dustsheets in an unoccupied house. When he glanced back from the lobby the waiter was nowhere to be seen, and Todd's place was so thoroughly cleared that he might never have been there. A curtain stirred beside the long uneven mound draped from head to foot on the buffet table, and Todd discovered he would rather not see the mound stir too. He made some haste to leave before he realised that he didn't know when breakfast was served. Calling "Hello?" brought him no response, neither from the dining-room nor from the impenetrably dark office beyond the reception counter. He'd arrange to be wakened once he was in his room.

Why did he expect to be met in the lift? He was close to fancying there was no room for anyone but him as soon as he returned to the panelled box. He fumbled the gates shut and watched the wall ooze past them like a mudslide. He was anxious for light to appear above it well before that happened, and as soon as the lift wobbled to a halt he clambered up into the corridor.

It was as silent as ever. The sombre doors between the dim glazed flames could easily have reminded him of a mausoleum. The rain on the window at the end was borrowing colours from the lights of the town. The storm was slackening, and Todd was able to read some of the illuminated signs. Beneath the race of headlamps on the motorway he made out several letters perched on a high roof—**ELLE** and also **U**. An unwelcome thought took him to the window, on which he couldn't distinguish his breath from the unravelling skeins of rain. The sign swam into focus as if he were regaining his vision, and he saw it belonged to the Bellevue Hotel.

If anybody heard his gasp of disbelief, they gave no response. For a moment he had no idea where he was going, and then he found his numbered baton and jammed the key into the lock. A few bulbs flared in the dwarfish chandelier—not as many as last time, but they showed him the shabby leather folder on the dressing-table. He threw the folder open on the bed, revealing a few dog-eared sheets of notepaper and a solitary envelope. While he couldn't tell how much of their brownishness the items owed to age, there was no mistaking the name they bore. He was in the Belgrave Hotel.

It might have been yet another element of a joke that somebody was playing on him, unless he was playing it on himself. He was too late to change hotels, whatever time it was—"too late, Kate," as his uncle liked to say even when Todd's aunt wasn't there. Just now Todd wanted nothing more than to lie down, but first he needed to arrange his morning call.

He retrieved the phone from the upper cupboard of the wardrobe, only to find no instructions on the yellowed paper disc in the middle of the dial. When he picked up the bony receiver he heard a sound not unlike a protracted breathless gust of wind, presumably the Belgrave's version of a dialling tone. 9 seemed the likeliest number, but when he tried it Todd heard a phone begin to ring along the corridor. He was tempted to speak to his fellow guest, if only to establish there was one, but the hollow muffled note tolled until he cut it off. Dialling 1 brought him only the empty tone, and so he tried the zero. A bell went off in the depths of the building and was silenced, and a slow hoarse blurred voice in his ear said "Mr Todd."

"Can you get me up for eight?"

"For how many would that be, sir?"

"I'm saying can you see I'm down for breakfast. What time's that?"

"Eight will do it, Mr Todd."

Had the receptionist heard his first question after all? Todd was too weary to say any more—almost too exhausted to stand up. He stumbled to the token bathroom, where he lingered as briefly as seemed polite. The shower cubicle put him in mind of a cramped lift that had somehow acquired plumbing, while the space outside it was so confined it almost forced the toilet under the sink. Another reason for him to leave the windowless room was the mirror, but the wardrobe door showed him more of the same, displaying how age had shrunken and sharpened his face. He switched off the light and clambered into bed.

The indentation in the mattress made it easiest for him to lie on his back, hands crossed on his breastbone. He heard a hollow plop of rain on wood and then an increasingly sluggish repetition of the sound, which put him in mind of heartbeats. The wind was more constant, keeping up an empty drone not unlike the voiceless noise of the receiver. Though he'd remembered one of his uncle's favourite turns of phrase—the comment about lateness—it didn't revive as many jokes as Todd hoped. It only brought back his uncle's response to hearing the doctor's receptionist call his name. "That's me," he would say, "on my tod."

It wasn't even true. His nephew had been with him, sharing the apprehension the man had been anxious if not desperate to conceal. None of these were memories Todd wanted to keep close to him in the dark. With an effort he recalled names his uncle had dug up from history: Addled Hitler, Guiser Wilhelm, Josef Starling, Linoleum Bonypart, Winsome Churchill... For years Todd had believed they had all been alive at the same time. Now the names seemed more like evidence of senility than jokes—blurred versions of the past that put him in mind of the way the rain on the window had twisted the world into a different shape. They left him unsure of himself, so that he was grateful to hear a voice.

It was next door. No, it was beyond the other room, though not far, and apparently calling a name. Presumably the caller wanted to be let in, since Todd heard a door open and shut. For a while there was silence, and then someone came out of the adjoining bathroom—a door opened, at any rate. As Todd tried to use the hint of companionship to help him fall asleep, he grew aware of more sounds in the next room.

His neighbour must be drunk. They seemed to be doing their utmost to speak—to judge by their tone, striving to voice some form of protest—but so unsuccessfully that Todd might have imagined they had no means of pronouncing words. He was struggling to make sense of it, since it was impossible to ignore, when someone else spoke. Was it the voice he'd first heard? Or perhaps the guest in the next room but one was calling for quiet. In a moment a door opened and closed. Todd willed the silence to let him sleep, but he was still awake when he heard the door again, followed by activity in the other room. His neighbour seemed to be in a worse state than ever, and had given up any attempt to speak while bumping into all the furniture. After some time the ungainly antics subsided, letting Todd hope his neighbour had found the bed or at least fallen asleep. But a voice was calling a name, and the door was audible again. By now Todd knew the silence wouldn't last, and he reared up from the trough of the mattress. "What are you doing in there?" he shouted.

The darkness engulfed his protest as somebody came back into the next room. They no longer sounded able to walk. They were crawling about on the floor, so effortfully that Todd fancied he heard them thumping it with their hands if not clawing at it. He'd had enough, and he lurched off the bed, groping at the dark until he found the light-switch. As soon as a couple of bulbs flickered in the chandelier he stumbled along the corridor to knock on the door of his neighbour's room.

The huge indifferent voice of the dark answered him—the wind. He pounded on the door until the number shivered on its loose screw, but nobody responded. The nearest glazed flame lent the digit a vague shadow that came close to transforming it into an 8, although Todd was reminded of a different symbol. It would have needed to be lying down, as he did. He thumped on the door again as a preamble to tramping back to his room. He parted his thin dry lips as he snatched the receiver off the hook and heard its empty sound. It was the wind, and the instrument was dead as a bone.

As he let the receiver drop into its cradle he heard the door in the next room. He couldn't take a breath while he listened to the noises that ensued. His neighbour was crawling about as blindly as before but less accurately than ever. It took them a considerable time to progress across the room. Todd would have preferred them not to find the connecting door, especially once he heard a fumbling at the bottom of it, a rudimentary attempt that sounded too undefined to involve fingers. As the door began to shake, a rage indistinguishable from panic swept away Todd's thoughts. Grabbing the suitcase, he flung it on the bed and dragged the luggage stand aside. He heard a series of confused noises in the other room, as if somebody were floundering across it, retreating in an agony of embarrassment at their own state. The connecting door wasn't locked, and he threw it wide open.

The next room was deserted, and it wasn't a bedroom. By the light from his own room Todd made out two low tables strewn with open books and magazines. Against the walls stood various chairs so decrepit that they seemed to need the dimness to lend them more substance. If the room hadn't been deserted he might not have ventured in, but he felt compelled to examine the items on the tables, like a child determined to learn a secret. He was halfway across the stained damp carpet when he wished he hadn't left his room.

The books were textbooks, in so many pieces that they might have been dismantled by someone's fumbling attempts to read them. There were no magazines, just scattered pages of the oversized books. Despite the dimness, Todd was able to discern more about the illustrations than he even slightly liked. All of them depicted surgical procedures he wanted to believe could never have been put into practice, certainly not on anyone alive or still living afterwards. Mixed up with the pages were sheets of blank paper on which someone had drawn with a ballpoint pen, perhaps the taped-up pen that lay among them. Its unsteadiness might explain the grotesque nature of the drawings, which looked like a child's work or that of someone unusually crippled. In a way Todd was grateful that he couldn't judge whether the drawings were attempts to reproduce the illustrations from the textbooks or to portray something even worse. He was struggling to breathe and to retreat from the sight of all the images, not to mention everything they conjured up, when he heard the door shut behind him.

He whirled around to find he could still see it—could see it had no handle on this side. He only had to push it open, or would have except that it was locked. He was throwing all his weight against it, the very little weight he seemed to have left, when a voice at his back said "Mr Todd."

It was the voice he'd been hearing, as hoarse and practically as blurred as it had sounded through the wall. "You don't want me," he pleaded, "you want someone else," but the silence was so eloquent that he had to turn. He still had one hope—that he could flee into the corridor—but the door to it had no handle either. The only open door was on the far side of the room.

The doorway was admitting the light, such as it was. When he trudged across the waiting-room he saw that the source of the dim glow was a solitary bare bulb on a tattered flex. It illuminated a room as cramped as a trench. The bare rough walls were the colour of earth, which might be the material of the floor. The room was empty apart from a long unlidded box. Surely the box might already contain someone, and Todd ventured forward to see. He had barely crossed the threshold when a voice behind him murmured "He's gone at last." They switched off the power and shut him in, and the light left him so immediately that he had no time to be sure that the room was another antechamber.

# Feeling Remains

I'M WATCHING MRS HAMMOND'S EMPTY HOUSE WHILE I try to think of anything interesting about myself to write for my English homework when I see my mother. She's walking down the street with two people in track suits, a woman and a boy. I know my mother says you have to see the spirit inside everyone, but any time there are track suits in our part of town it means trouble. The other night a gang of girls in them kept jumping on the cars in our street, but by the time the police came and my parents finished discussing whose fault it was the girls behaved like that, they'd gone. I hope my mother's showing the people the way out of our suburb, but she holds the front gate open and the boy in roller boots clumps under the rosy arch. I save my homework on the screen and wait till she unlocks the front door and calls "Jeremy, come and say hello."

I go to the top of the stairs. When she gives me her look that says she trusts me not to disappoint her, I have to go down. "Jane and Brad, I told you about Jeremy. He'll be a friend for you, Brad," she says. "Jane's one of my students, Jeremy."

That needn't mean she's an addict like the women my mother brought home from the refuge where she used to work. I thought

Brad was bald and my mother would expect me to be sorry about that, but he's only shaved so he'll have even less hair than his mother. Mine is saying "I should take off your boots in the house, Brad. I expect we can find you some old Christmas slippers of Jeremy's."

Brad makes his mouth thinner, but Jane grabs his shoulder when he starts clumping out of the porch into the hall. "Do what Willa tells you. Act like you deserve to be let in a house like this."

"You'll have to pay for new ones if they're nicked," he tells my mother.

"We promise they'll be safe, don't we, Jeremy? We understand if people who haven't been as lucky as us value what they have. Of course you're making your own luck now, Jane, by coming to night class."

"They should have made me stay at school when I was these ones' ages. The advice centre says I should be able to sue the education."

"Will you look after your new friend, Jeremy, while Jane and I work out what schedule's best for her?"

"I was doing my English."

"I'm certain Brad wishes he had homework. You don't want him and Jane to think we've no time for people who need us."

I can't see why they'd think that or feel entitled either. Brad sits on the doormat and yanks his boots off and jumps up to shove past me and sprint upstairs. "Show him your room, Jeremy," my mother says. "Perhaps he can give you some ideas to write."

At least he isn't wearing any shoes. When he's finished using the toilet without shutting the door or flushing he steps in the bath and the bidet and then the shower stall in the guest room. He looks around my parents' room as if he's memorising everything and runs into mine. I knew he'd head for the computer, but he sticks two fingers up at it when he sees there's only writing on the screen. He holds on to my desk to poke his face at the window. "There's the house your mam said some old twat lived in."

"It's where an old lady used to live."

"Where's she now?"

"Gone."

"Where? She live by herself?" Brad says and starts typing on my keyboard. All the words have four letters, and some of them are spelt right. "Leave it alone," I shout, hoping they can hear me downstairs. "That's for school."

"Your mam said you had to let me do some." He rests a thumb on the power button and watches me nearly get to him before he switches the computer off. He dodges me and runs downstairs yelling "He won't tell me about the old woman and he won't let me go on his pee see."

I switch it back on and wait for it to scan the drives. I'd pray if I knew what to pray to. When the screen shows I haven't lost anything I shut down properly, because my mother's calling "Come and talk to us, Jeremy. We don't hide from our guests."

They're in the front room. Mother and Jane are drinking coffee out of Empowered Woman mugs while Brad wanders about picking things up. "You'll break that," Jane keeps saying as if she wants him to prove she's right, and he nearly drops the carving of a goddess my father bought at the African craft shop.

"You're supposed to be paying attention to your guest, Jeremy. You're thirteen and he's not even at secondary school."

"He nearly wrecked my computer."

"Things are only things and we shouldn't get attached to them," my mother says, though she doesn't seem too happy with Brad handling her Muslim pictures on the mantelpiece. "People are what matters. Why wouldn't you tell Brad about Mrs Hammond? I'm sure he'd enjoy hearing how you took care of her."

"He likes to know about people," Jane said. "He never knew his dad before the scum went off and left us."

"Tell Brad how you were Mrs Hammond's little helper after Mr Hammond died."

Suddenly Brad's interested. "How'd he die?"

"Fluid retention," my mother tells Jane as if she's the only one that's listening. "His heart gave up."

"Too much booze, you mean? Sounds like a man."

I'm remembering how Mr Hammond's legs swelled up till they were twice as wide—I used to think they were like balloons and the ankles were knots you could untie to let everything out. "I don't think his wife ever recovered from," my mother stops saying, "it took him most of a year. But you did everything you could for her, didn't you, Jeremy?"

Brad is opening and shutting the doors of an icon as if he hopes it'll change into something better than a Greek saint with gold around his head. "Just you listen, you," Jane says. "This is how you're meant to behave. What did he do, Willa?"

My mother opens her eyes wide at me to make me answer and looks disappointed when I can't. "Shopping and housework and just sitting and talking to her," she says.

That was the worst part—listening to her and feeling how afraid she was. It felt as if all the dimness of her house had crawled inside my head and started filling up my chest as well. Maybe the dark was meant to help her stop seeing herself, but I thought it made things worse. I'm willing my mother not to go on about Mrs Hammond, and surely Jane and Brad have to leave soon, because I can smell dinner, lentils again. But my mother says "Our guests are dining with us, Jeremy, and then I said you'd keep Brad with you while Jane and I go to my class."

"I haven't finished my homework."

"You didn't seem too busy when we came along. You seemed to be concentrating on Mrs Hammond's house."

Maybe Brad will be so rude about dinner she won't want him to stay. He stares at his chunk of her lentil loaf and says he wants a burger. Jane isn't too impressed either when she hears how we never eat anything that injures the rainforest or puts us higher up the food chain than anybody else or with additives in. She tells Brad to be grateful and get on with eating, though she doesn't do too much of that herself. When he won't, my mother makes him a sandwich of the ham my father says he needs for a balanced diet, but Brad hasn't finished his first bite when he starts wanting to watch television and not sit at the table. My mother persuades him to take his plate with him and sends me after him without mine. I'm watching him spill crumbs from his plate and his mouth while he plays with the remote control and keeps asking why we've got no sex channels when my father comes in.

He gives Brad the kind of blink he's started giving anyone my mother brings home, the kind that says he's tired and now he'll be more so. She meets him in the hall and just about puts a kiss on his cheek, as if she doesn't want Jane to see. "Jane, this is Leslie," she says, and tells him "Plenty left for you in the oven. We're off to my class now and the boys are staying here."

"There aren't likely to be ructions, are there? Only I've brought home quite a wodge of work."

"I'm certain you're man enough for everything," she says with a wink at Jane. "Are we ready? The boys can wash up."

"You do what Leslie says since they've let you in their nice house," Jane tells Brad.

"What does Jane stand for?" my mother asks her as they walk arm in arm along the hall.

"I don't stand for anything."

"Darn right, and what does your name stand for?"

"Justice Against Naked Exploitation."

"That's what we need. I got all my students to empower their names," my mother tells my father as she leaves.

I wonder if he's thinking they're all women when he comes to frown at me and Brad at the kitchen sink. The second time Brad drops a plate in it to see how much noise it makes if it won't smash, my father hurries to him. "Please, allow me."

Brad flinches out of the way in case he's touched. "Willa said I could watch your telly."

"Then you must, of course," my father says and helps me finish washing up. By then Brad is turning the sound up and down and changing channels as fast as he can. My father goes in the office, where his desk is smaller than my mother's, but soon he opens the door and calls me. "Do you think you might take your friend along to the play area for a while?"

"I didn't want to stay here anyway," Brad shouts and runs out of the house.

"Go with him, Jeremy," my father says with even more of his usual worried look. "He's our responsibility."

I don't see why he has to be, but if I say I'll get a disappointed lecture and a worse one from my mother. I go after Brad as my father shuts himself in the office. Brad's across the road in Mrs Hammond's front garden. "You can't go in there," I tell him.

"You mean you can't, soft twat," he says and dodges round the back.

There's nothing to be afraid of, I try and think. There never really was for Mrs Hammond, so how can there be for me? I don't want Brad doing anything I'll be blamed for not stopping. I hurry down the path with weeds sticking out of all its cracks into the back garden, where the hedge hides me and Brad from the neighbours. He's trying to see into the kitchen. "Dirty cow, was she?" he says.

He means the way the windows look black with grime, though they aren't. He points at the top of the kitchen window, at a gap big enough for him to put his skinny arm through. "Give us a step up."

"You mustn't go inside."

"Give us one or I'll say your dad kept feeling me and that's why I ran off."

"Nobody'd believe you."

His face squashes itself thinner at me, and then he sees a lawnmower lying on its back in the long grass. He tips it up and drags it to the house and wedges the handle under the windowsill. There's a bar under the handle, and he stands one foot on that. "If I fall through the glass I'll say you pushed me," he says.

I'm almost sure nobody will believe him except maybe Jane, but being so close to Mrs Hammond's house is making me nervous. He levers himself up and grabs the top of the sash and plants his other grubby foot on the windowsill. He wobbles as he shoves his arm through the gap, and I wonder whether he'll say I felt him if I get hold of him. Then he twists the catch and the sash rattles down. He steps over and lands with a clang in the sink and pokes his head out of the window. "What are you going to do now, soft twat?"

There's nothing to be afraid of in there except what he might do. I know that's what I'm most afraid of when he jumps down onto the kitchen floor. "Wait," I plead. "I'll come."

I'm not as used to getting into other people's houses as him. I haul myself up to the sill from the bar of the mower and swing one leg through the window to try and stand in the sink. It's further down than I like, and when I drag my other leg over the sash I nearly lose my balance. I feel as if I'm falling into somewhere deep and dark. I manage to grab hold of the taps, and when I'm steady I shut the window and fix the catch. Brad is staring at the windows painted black inside as high as Mrs Hammond could reach. "Mad old bitch then, was she?" he says.

"Just didn't like seeing herself in anything."

"Mad old bitch," he says as though I agreed with him. He stares at the scratches she made all over the metal sink with a fork, and then I have to chase after him into the hall. He touches the switch for the jangly chandelier and leaves it alone in case people see he's in the house. He scowls at the walls—at the patches that look painted with how dark it'll be very soon. "Who got all her pictures?" he says as if it should have been him.

"They weren't pictures, they were mirrors. She took them down."

I remember them lying on their faces on one of her spare beds that was covered with broken glass. Brad's throwing all the doors open. The rooms sound too big and empty, though they've still got furniture that looks fat and sagging out of shape with the dimness the black windows make. "Be a good fire," Brad mutters to himself, but then he runs upstairs.

The bathroom mirrors are smashed in the bath. "Said she was a dirty cow," Brad sniggers, and I can't tell him it was where she was most afraid to see herself. He probably wouldn't listen anyway. He's too busy heading for her room, where I used to hear her begging and praying when I had to let myself into the house with the keys she gave my parents. She wasn't answering the doorbell any more, and she didn't answer when I called up the stairs—maybe she didn't hear me for talking, or maybe she couldn't stop. "That's some sponge that's gone bad," I heard once. "That's a stick with some old rubber round it. That's a claw, I don't know what it belongs to. That's a nasty mask someone's wearing. It's not me. It's not me."

She hadn't smashed the bedroom mirrors then. She'd wedged

the wardrobe door open with some shoes to hide the glass on it, and she'd covered up the dressing-table mirror with a dress. Now they're just bare wood that makes me think bits of a coffin have got into the room. "Feels squelchy," Brad says, and I think he's imitating Mrs Hammond somehow till I see he means the carpet under his bare feet. "Nothing worth a turd in here," he complains and runs to push up the painted-over window.

He kneels on the floor and squints through the slit at the backs of the houses across the garden. "Bet they've got stuff we ought to have," he mumbles. As he's getting up he points at the bed. "Is that her?"

I feel as if the dimness is a crawling lump of soot that fills my head. I'm not just afraid to look, I can't even see. Then Brad picks up what he was talking about—Mrs Hammond's photograph album that was shoved under the pillow. A photograph of her being not much older than me falls out and he treads on it while he turns the pages, not caring if he tears them. "It's just her old pictures," I say to make him stop.

I wish I hadn't said it. Surely Mrs Hammond couldn't hear me, but I feel guilty anyway, because it was the album she kept hold of when she was trying to hide from herself in the bed. "Which one do I look like?" she kept pleading the last time I let myself into the house. "Do I still look like this?" Now Brad picks up the photograph she was talking about and throws it in the album. "Got any matches?" he says.

"I never have any."

"Sad soft twat then, aren't you?" he says and runs downstairs.

I'd leave the album if I didn't think he might come back and use it to set fire to the house. I tuck it under my arm and go after him. When he sidles out of the front door I copy him and shut it so gently it feels as if it's turned into rubber. Brad sneaks out of the gate but waits to mutter "If you say we went in there I'll say you made me go in so you could have a feel of me."

I won't be saying we went in. I'd take Mrs Hammond's album to my room if I didn't have to follow him while he spies on houses. More than once he wants me to keep watch while he prowls into someone's garden or round the back of their house, but I won't do that however many names he calls me. We go through the whole suburb that way in the dark till we come round again to my house.

I let myself in and have to let Brad in as well. I'm glad he goes straight to the television, because it means he doesn't see me putting the album under my bed. I'm hurrying to tell him to turn the television down when mother and Jane come in. "Jane wrote nearly a whole paragraph," my mother tells anyone who's listening, "didn't you, Jane? You'll be wearing a white collar at your factory at this rate, if you even stay. I know you'll do everything you can for your workmates."

Jane doesn't seem to like being talked about so much. "Have you been behaving?" she shouts at Brad over the television. "Get home now and turn that off. You can't take it with you even if it's bigger than ours."

"He hasn't been much trouble, has he, Jeremy?" my father wants me to agree.

"He didn't stop you working."

"Luckier than me, then," Jane tells my father.

Brad switches off the television and sprints to pick his boots up. He's sitting on the doorstep to pull them on when my father says "Excuse me, young man, but could that be our remote control that's slipped into your pocket by mistake?"

"Give it here," Jane yells at Brad, and nearly hits him across the head with it except he ducks. She jabs it at my mother and says "I'm sorry that's all you get for helping."

"You've given me and more importantly yourself a lot more than that." As Jane drags Brad out of the gate my mother calls "Looking forward to next week."

My father makes a noise like humming a question and says "Bedtime for our youngest member unless he wants to finish his homework."

That's all they say till I'm out of the bathroom and in bed, but the silence feels like my mother getting ready to tramp into the office and start. "So the best you can offer one of my students is calling her child a thief."

"Well, hold on, I don't think we can honestly say I quite—"

"Diet's all that's wrong with him, the kind the multinationals won't be happy until everybody's eating. That and wanting to be a man. Couldn't you and Jeremy deal with him for even a couple of hours? His mother has to all the time."

"I wonder if we saw much evidence that she—"

"There's lots of evidence anybody but a man could see that she's as brave as every one of my mature students. They need to be, not having the gender advantage. They work as hard as I do, but perhaps you don't think that's hard enough."

"Of course I do. I really wish you wouldn't teach at night if it leaves you on edge like this."

"You'd rather we both left all the people we've failed to sink further, would you?"

"I'm not sure you can say it's us who've failed—"

"Our whole class has," my mother cries, and a lot more as well.

When my parents come upstairs at last I still can't sleep. My father says we always have to leave our bedroom windows open at night so the central heating doesn't make us vulnerable to all the germs that are developing or being developed. The gap must be letting a wind in my room, because there's a noise under the bed as if something's got hold of Mrs Hammond's album but can't quite open it. I'm not going to look. I'm almost asleep when I hear the fumbling creep away, and then I am.

In the morning my parents aren't speaking much to each other, more at me instead. I'm almost glad to head for the school I have to go to because everyone else is as deserving of an education as I am and it wouldn't be fair to the others to put all the best children together. I don't think I'm one of them even if my dad does, just one of the few that go in uniform. Shaun's been sniffing glue again and starts dancing on his desk, and Cindy keeps screaming at people because she says they're staring at her, till they do to make her scream. Only those aren't the main reasons I can't do my work properly. Even when the teacher gets Shaun and Cindy taken off to the disruption room I can't stop trying to think what to do with Mrs Hammond's album.

I don't want to hear something moving in my room at night again. I never have before even when there was a wind. There's nowhere to put the album except back where I found it—if my parents see it they'll know I sneaked into Mrs Hammond's house. Only we gave her keys to her son after she died even though he hadn't been visiting her, so how can I get back in? I nearly think of asking Brad, though there are plenty of children at my school who'd be the same kind of help. I'll have to climb up to her bedroom window he left open at the bottom if I can carry the album and a ladder across the road without being seen. Maybe I can climb without a ladder. I'm trying to remember the back of her house as I walk home with the homework half the class never bothers doing. By the time I reach my street I'm sure there's a drainpipe close to her window. But there's no drainpipe—there isn't even a house.

All that's left is a huge lump of black smoke squirming every way as if it wants to dodge the water three fire engines are squirting at it. The house has fallen in with just some bricks of the ground floor and half a window left standing. It looks as if the house has been pulled out of shape by the smoke that's black as tonight will be. I'm watching it and feeling Mrs Hammond's nightmare is holding me there when my parents drive up in my mother's car.

When she climbs out her head goes up as if her open mouth is pulling it till her chin points at where the house was. "How on earth has that managed to happen?" she says as if whoever's responsible is listening, and I do my best not to.

"At least Mrs Hammond's gone, thank heaven," says my father.

"The late owner," my mother tells a fireman. "We did think she might cause a fire when there's so little care for the elderly in their own homes, but do you know what actually happened here?"

"The lady who reported it said some boys were seen going in there recently," the fireman says, rubbing some black onto his forehead with the back of his hand.

"That's the least we can expect when child care for single parents is so inadequate."

He gives her quite a look and says "You'll have to excuse me" as he strides off to his engine. Maybe he doesn't realise that leaves my mother with an argument still to have, or maybe that's what he's avoiding. I watch the smoke trying to stand up as if it's desperate to find the shape the house used to be. When my mother says "Come along, Jeremy, we don't stare" I hurry after her.

All the way through our Indian dinner that's mostly rice so we remember how other people have to eat, I'm afraid someone will ask me if the boys were me and Brad. Instead she talks about her students so hard I can tell my father doesn't dare to mention the children at his school. I wonder if she can't let herself believe I got into Mrs Hammond's house, but I think it's more she won't believe Brad did. As soon as all the dinner's eaten my father says to me "I'll see to the washing up and I should be about your homework."

I can't open my window in case the smoke that's left gets in. It feels as if its dark is trying to—I keep feeling its dark has crept behind me. Whenever I look round there's nothing I haven't always seen except Mrs Hammond's album lying under the bed. I push it further under to make sure my parents won't see it, but when I try and concentrate on my homework I can't help seeing bits of the smoke heaving themselves about and turning into the night. As soon as I've finished my work, which isn't much good, I go to the bathroom again and make myself switch off the light and get in bed.

I seem to wake up more often than I sleep, but I suppose I do some of that as well, because I keep thinking something wants to catch hold of me in the dark. I try to stay close to the side of the bed near the window, but that means the dark is behind me. Before I came to bed I must have pushed Mrs Hammond's album too hard, because in the morning I see a picture of her when she was a few years older than me has come out on the far side. It's crumpled up as if someone tried to get hold of it, and most of its yellow has turned black—it looks as if the blackness is turning her into a shape I'd rather not see. I pinch the photograph between my nails and wriggle it into the album and drop the album in my school-bag.

I just want the only thing that's left of Mrs Hammond's to go somewhere it'll be safe. I'd ask my parents to give it to her son if

I wouldn't have to tell them I was keeping it away from Brad—I'd ask where the son lives if they wouldn't make me tell them why I want to know. I can't eat much breakfast for being afraid they'll see the album before I can leave, and my father has to eat what I don't or my mother would tell us how many people could live on it for a week. I try not to look as if I'm carrying anything I shouldn't in my bag when my mother puts her mouth on my forehead and my father shakes my hand before I can run out of the house.

I wonder if I'll have to keep the album away from people, but the girls and boys who might add it to the litter everybody drops at school are after anyone who doesn't look English because the papers say the country's letting too many asylum seekers in. At lunchtime I go upstairs to the library, where I often hide though there aren't many books I want to read or many I don't either. The librarian who's always blinking and patting her foggy hair as if she's making sure nothing has jumped into it off anyone is at the desk. "Hello, er," she says when I start taking out the album. "Did you enjoy it?"

"It's an old lady's photos I wondered if you'd want to have."

"Oh," she says the way people sigh at babies, "er. Is she your grandma?"

I haven't seen either of my grandmothers for years, because my mother argues with them about everything, which she says means they're victims of their class. "She was just a lady who lived near us," I say.

"And how did it come your way, er?"

"She died. She didn't want anything to happen to it," I say and wonder if that's true—I somehow think it is.

"I don't see it as material for us," the librarian says without even looking inside it. "I expect you should give it to a parent or whoever you live with to look after, er."

"Jeremy," I tell her, but she's at her hair again as if I might have brought her more than a book.

There's a history lesson after lunch, and I try to give the album to the teacher. "That's not the kind of history we teach," he says without looking in it, and lifts his top lip with his bottom one as if he'd like to plug his nose up, "even if any of you little charmers wanted to learn." He oughtn't to mean me, and it's so unfair I don't think about the album for the rest of the afternoon. I don't start feeling nervous till I'm halfway home, but when I let myself in there's another reason. My mother's waiting with something to say and a blank face.

The longer she doesn't say it, the worse I think it's going to be. I'm sure I'm being blamed but I don't know for what. I hide in my room and try to work till my father comes home. At first she only sends him up to tell me dinner's ready. She ladles out her carrot casserole before she dumps herself on her chair. "Well, I hope everyone's satisfied," she says to the ceiling.

"It's quite tasty and filling, thank you, dear."

If I were my father I wouldn't have said that. I can tell she wasn't talking about dinner. She makes us wait for her to say "My student Jane's son has been arrested."

"No great surprise, perhaps. What's the offence?"

"Supposedly he was found in a house up the street, and the couple who live next door to it are claiming he robbed them. I don't know how someone his size would be capable of taking everything they say he took."

"Perhaps it was inevitable. You shouldn't blame yourself."

She lets her eyes and then her face down to him. "They're saying they saw him near their house the night before last. Presumably nobody who hasn't had their advantages is allowed near."

I see my father wants to think she's stopped accusing us, but he doesn't dare. "You were taking him to the park, weren't you, Jeremy?" he says.

"I said I would."

If she asks whether I did I'll tell them everything. Maybe that will stop me feeling that it's getting darker inside me than it is yet outside. But all my mother says is "I'm going to Jane's to see what I can do for her. I've no idea when I'll be back."

"I've got my parents' evening at school," my father tells me. "I'll try not to be too late. You won't mind being on your own, will you?"

"There's nothing round here to be scared of," my mother says. "You aren't a woman living by herself."

I know she means most of her students, but I feel as if she's talking about Mrs Hammond. I don't want to remember how being alone in her house filled Mrs Hammond up with fear. I pretend I don't mind being left by myself at night. I keep on trying to pretend once my parents leave.

I spend all the time I can at washing up the dinner things till the window shows me it'll soon be dark. I start watching television, but there's nothing on that can reach inside my head. Running through the channels twice makes me feel I'm trying to be like Brad, and I think how my mother would blame me but not him. I know I ought to be doing my homework, though when so many people at my school don't, sometimes I wonder why I should. My mother would make me feel guilty for wasting my advantages, that's mostly why. There's no reason for me to be scared of going in my room.

I switch on the light and the one on my desk as well before I take my books out of my bag and shut Mrs Hammond's album in it. Even when I turn the computer on I feel there isn't enough light in the room. Outside the window it looks as if the dark is spreading out of the black place where Mrs Hammond used to live. When I start thinking the blackness or something in it wants to get hold of me I pull the curtains together.

For history we have to write what it was like to live in England in the years leading up to the Second World War. I take everything I can find in my schoolbooks and type it on the screen, but it doesn't feel as if it was ever alive. Mrs Hammond would have been about my age at the beginning of the thirties, and I try to think if she told me about them. I can't remember anything she said, but my thoughts seem to start using her voice. I keep thinking I ought to look in her album.

I'm not sure I want to while I'm by myself, even if it helps me do the kind of homework my mother always says I can. I do my best to let the stuff I've copied tell me more to write, but trying makes the inside of my head feel as if it's turning black. I almost type the only thing that's in there, which is "See my pictures", even if it sounds like Mrs Hammond's voice that's left its mouth somewhere. I don't want to hear it. I jump up and pull the album out and put it on my desk.

It falls open, and a photograph tries to stand up. It's the one I found crumpled on the floor, which must be why it's moving, only it looks as if someone's trying to get hold of it without much of a hand. I squash it between the cover and the first cardboardy page, which doesn't have strips cut out of it to hold photographs. I wish I'd shut the album instead, because I don't like the look of any of the photographs at all.

They're in the order of how old Mrs Hammond was. The baby ones are nearly black like fruit that's shrunk—all you can see are little eyes trying to peer out of the blackness. I start hoping they've all gone like that, because the bits of her as a girl that the blackness hasn't covered up look so thin I think it's taken their flesh off. But those aren't as bad as the ones where she's grown up. Maybe the blackness is some kind of mould, because the parts of her it's left white look swollen like toadstools that burst if you poke them. I get as far as a picture of her and Mr Hammond with their eyes staring out of two fat raw white blobs. I shut the album tight, which feels as if I'm not squashing only pictures. I don't want it in my room.

I don't even want it in the house, not when it's keeping Mrs Hammond's voice inside my head. "See the rest," I think she's pleading. "See all of me." I'd leave the album outside and wait till tomorrow to think what to do if I wasn't afraid it might rain. I find three plastic bags in a kitchen cupboard and put the album inside one and the others too. There's a wind, and if I leave the album behind the house my parents may hear the plastic rustling and find out what it is. I hurry out the front instead, across the road.

Half Mrs Hammond's front door is lying on its back beyond some coaly bricks. Bits of burnt wood flake off and grit under my nails when I lift the door enough to slide the album under. Tomorrow I'll pretend to find the album on my way to school and give it to my parents to pass on to Mrs Hammond's son. I try to imagine her voice being muffled by the door when I drop it, except that's like imagining her trapped in her coffin, not able to see. The wind stirs up the patch where she lived, and the choking smell feels as if the dark is rising up to wall me in. I dash across the road into not enough light, but I'm only at the gate when I hear our phone ringing.

I have to get the key out of my pocket and push it in the lock the right way up and turn it, and all the while I'm afraid the phone will stop or won't. I shut the dark out and run to grab the phone out of its plastic nest on the wall. "Hello?" I call louder than the voice in my head.

"Are you there at last? I was starting to think you were doing a Brad. Don't tell Willa I said that. Were you asleep?"

"Not yet."

"Glad I didn't wake you, then, but time for bed all the same. I'm just in discussion with some colleagues."

I can hear the kind they're having and the other noises of the pub. "Will you be home soon?" I plead.

"Not while you're conscious, I shouldn't think. I do need to relax occasionally, you know. Just get your head on the pillow and before you know it you'll be gone. Willa and her women may have got themselves some strength, but that doesn't have to mean they've taken ours away." I don't think he meant me to hear the last part, or maybe he doesn't care. "See you in the morning, Jeremy," he says.

I ram the phone into its nest and run upstairs to the bathroom. I stay in there till I realise I'm staring at my face in the mirror. That reminds me how Mrs Hammond couldn't look in one. I'm afraid something like her face will wobble up over the edge, trying to see me instead of itself. I'd rather be in my room than think about that, and I dash across the landing.

There's too much of a mirror in my room. I keep my back to it while I undress for bed and hurry to the switch by the door. I turn the light off and on again at once. I've never seen my room so dark. I run over to the window and open the curtains without looking at the glass that might as well be a mirror. Either the streetlamp outside Mrs Hammond's garden isn't working—maybe somebody like Brad has broken it—or the blackness from where she lived has caught it somehow, because when I switch the light off it's as dark as it was. It's so dark I'm afraid switching the light back on won't make any difference. But it does, and I leave it on and hide in my bed.

At least I've stopped having thoughts that sound like Mrs Hammond. Maybe it's too light for her, that's if I ever really heard her. I don't mind when it starts getting dark inside my eyelids, since that means I'm falling asleep and I know it's light in the room. Then I'm asleep, and I don't like it, because I'm groping about in a place with no light till I stick my fingers in a toadstool. That feels so bad it jerks my eyes open and me awake.

I'm still in the dark, and my hand feels the same. I hope I've only dreamed I'm awake, but then I feel how I'm lying at the edge of the bed with one arm hanging nearly to the floor. I hear something dragging on the carpet, and there's a tug at my arm. What I thought was a toadstool I'd poked my hand into are fingers holding mine.

My thoughts start talking in Mrs Hammond's voice. There's nothing in my head except them and terror, and I don't even know how much of that is hers. "Touch more of me," I think or hear. "I can't feel like this. This can't be me. It's just all this dark making me worse."

I'm desperate to get free, but I'm afraid if I tear myself loose her hand will come with me, or some of it will. I make myself roll closer to the edge and reach down with my other hand. I touch hers that's holding mine and run my fingers up her arm. "That's it," her voice says in my head. "Find my face."

I think I'd stop living if I did that. The rest is bad enough. Her hand is too big for the arm that feels thinner than its bones used to and made of spongy putty. There's just one thing I can think of to do if my mouth will work. I push my tongue between my lips to open them and oil them. "I can feel you're all right," I say, though my words don't want to leave my mouth. "You're like your favourite photo when you weren't much older than me."

"Am I really?" I think her voice is going away and then I hear it's only sunk. I stop touching her arm and inch back onto the bed and pray she'll let go of my hand before I have to pull it out of her squashy one. But I'm leaning off the edge of the bed as if I may fall instead of creeping out of reach when she says "See me, then" not in my head but in the room and not using much I'd call a voice.

I'm not sure what comes then. Maybe it isn't light even if I can see by it—maybe it's her hope. For however long it takes me to start seeing her I can't breathe. I see her arm first, then how it stretches all the way across the room to the rest of her. She's the lumpy white heap against the wall, because I can just make out a thing on top like a soft balloon with hardly any face. I don't know if she's lost her eyes or if what it's made of has swollen over them.

I feel a tug at my hand. There's a noise like a stuffed wet sack dragging along the wall as she tries to get up and come across the room to let me see her clearer. I wrench myself loose and press my back and my head against the wall above the pillow, and rub my hands together in case any of her has stuck to them. Squeezing my eyes shut doesn't feel safe enough, so I grip my hands over them. In case it helps to keep her off I scream.

I'm doing all that when my parents get home. My mother must have picked my father up on the way, because I hear her car and then they both come into the house. "That's never Jeremy, is it?" my father doesn't quite shout.

"I hope you won't try to suggest it's my fault if it is."

They have a competition over who'll be upstairs first, and my father wins. "Whatever's the matter, Jeremy?" he says in his pub voice, and clicks the switch a few times. "Why is it so dark in here?"

I want to be taken out of the room into the light where Mrs Hammond will be afraid to come and see herself. "Too dark," I try to say. When hands take hold of me I scream louder till I'm sure they aren't hers. I keep mine over my eyes as my parents argue while they lead me out. I don't know when I'll dare to open my eyes again, and even if I do I know the darkest place will be inside my head. Maybe Mrs Hammond will wait in there for me to see her. Maybe I'll have to till I'm afraid to see myself, and then I'll be on my way to her place. Maybe till then I won't really know what screaming is.

# The Rounds

As the train arrives at James Street one of the women behind me in the carriage murmurs "They're talking about us again."

"What's somebody saying this time?" her friend protests, but I miss the answer in the midst of a recorded warning not to leave luggage unattended. The amplified voice seems to herd commuters off the underground platform onto the train, and an Asian woman in a headscarf black enough for a funeral takes a seat at the far end of the carriage. Perhaps she's a lawyer from the courts at the top of James Street, since she's carrying a briefcase. The voice falls silent as the train heads into the tunnel.

There's just a solitary track on the loop under Liverpool, where the tunnel shrinks to half its previous width. Lights embedded in the walls flash out of the dark every few seconds like some kind of signal. In about a minute, more passengers board at Moorfields; it's the start of the rush hour. I'm at the nearest doors well before the train pulls into Lime Street, where the Muslim woman alights further down the carriage. As I make to step onto the platform I notice she's without her briefcase.

"Excuse me," I call, but she doesn't seem to hear. Several

people look up or around and then lose interest as I dash along the carriage. The case is on the floor by the seat she vacated, and I grab it before struggling between the last of the commuters boarding the train. The woman isn't on the platform. She could have used the lift, but the escalators are closer, and I sprint for the exit that leads to them.

Is she late for a main line train? By the time I reach the bank of escalators her strides have taken her almost to the top. I'd try and overtake her on the other upward escalator, but it isn't moving. "Excuse me," I shout, "you dropped this."

She turns with one hand on the banister and smiles, though the expression looks a little automatic. I'm hurrying towards her when she sails out of view. The briefcase is so shabby that I might conclude she meant to dump it if it weren't also heavy with documents. I assume that's what the contents are, but the lock is jammed; it's so distorted that someone might already have tried to force it—perhaps she has lost the key. I admit I'm glad to find her waiting beyond the escalator, this side of the ticket barrier. "Oh, thank you," she says and makes her smile rueful. "I don't know what I could have been thinking of."

I'm at least equally ashamed of having thought she might be up to no good. It shows how prejudiced we've all grown, how inclined to think in today's stereotypes. I pass her the briefcase with both hands, and she grasps the scruffy handle as she shows her ticket at the barrier. I flash my pass and am following her along the passage to the escalators that lead up to the main station when my breast pocket emits a series of piercing clanks that put me in mind of a faulty pacemaker.

I read the message on my mobile as the escalator lifts me into the glare of sunlight through the glass roof. Have to cancel, it says. No train. Beneath the huge cautionary voice of the station there's the babble of a crowd that's hurrying to the platforms while at least as many people stream out onto the concourse. The Muslim woman has disappeared among them. I pocket the mobile without sending a response and tramp down the descending escalator. As I display my pass the ticket collector says "You look familiar."

"I expect there's plenty more like me."

I'd say that was as witty as her quip, but she doesn't bother laughing. She seems to feel it's her duty to ask "Weren't you here just now?"

"If you say so."

"Did you forget something?"

"That's not me. I thought I was meeting someone but I'm not after all."

"You want to be sure what's happening another time."

The pointless exchange has delayed me so much that as I step on the underground escalator I hear a squeal of wheels—the arrival of the train I meant to catch. I clutch at the unsynchronised banisters and dash down two sinking steps at a time, to reach the platform just as the train sets about shutting its doors. With a leap that leaves me feeling rejuvenated I jam my foot between the nearest pair, which flinch apart, raising an alarm that all the others take up. "I've still got it," I declare as I board the train.

Nobody seems interested. One man lowers his head as though his tweed hat is weighing it down. A younger man is leafing through a cardboard folder full of documents, and a girl is lost in the world of her personal stereo, while a woman in a coat patterned like a chessboard frowns at a Mtogo poster as if she thinks an African restaurant has no right to advertise on the train. I find a seat near the doors as the train heads for Central Station, where it swaps commuters for commuters before following the loop back to James Street. Just one passenger alights there, hurrying behind the crowd on the platform. She's the Muslim with the briefcase.

She must have used the lift at Lime Street while I was held up at the barrier. I've a reason to have caught the first train back, but what's hers? However prejudiced it makes me feel, I can't help lurching to my feet and forcing my way onto the platform. She's already past the nearest exit—she isn't even on the stairs to which it leads. If I find she's returning to the courts, where she could perfectly well have left some item, I hope I'll be cured of making suspicious assumptions. If she sees me I'll be more embarrassed still. I sprint up the boxed-in stairs and reach the top just in time to see her leaving the enclosed bridge across the underground tracks. She isn't bound for the outside world. She's on her way down to the platform for the trains around the loop.

I hear a train approaching, and her running down to meet it. I can't see her as I dash down the steps, and she isn't on the platform scattered with commuters. I'm opposite the last carriage of the train. I could try to reach the driver or attract their attention, but what would I say? All I know is that if the woman plans to abandon the briefcase again, we should all be safe until she's well away from it. The thought sends me onto the train.

This time I don't trigger the alarm, and the train moves off at once. The carriage is crowded, but I can see every head, and there's no sign of a headscarf. Suppose she's so fanatical that she would take it off to be less obvious? I struggle through the crowd, peering at every face and at the floor beside and between and especially under the seats. All the people in the aisle would make a briefcase easier to hide, but it seems the woman wasn't in this carriage, or at least she hasn't left the case here. I haul open the door between the carriages, to see a man leaning against the next door. He's so bulky that he blocks the view into the other carriage, and he doesn't budge when I knock on the window. I make to shove the door at him, and then I'm overwhelmed by a blaze of light. It isn't an explosion, even if my innards wince. The train has emerged from the tunnel.

We're at Moorfields. The doors open to the platform, but I'm nowhere near any of them. When I push at the one between the carriages the man with his wide flabby shoulders against it doesn't shift an inch. More people squeeze onto the train, and I'm near to panicking. As it moves off I crane back to stare through a window at the platform. A woman is striding fast along a passage to the escalators. She's the headscarved passenger, and she doesn't have her briefcase.

My guts clench like a helpless fist, and a sour taste surges into my mouth. Until this moment I can't really have believed my own suspicions—I might as well have been enacting a scene from a cheap thriller based on the news. As the tunnel closes around the carriage I kick the connecting door and pound on it with both fists. When the hulking man turns his big stupid head to stare at me I flash my pass, too quickly for him to take issue with it. "Let me through," I shout and mime as well.

Even he must realise we all need to be concerned about security, though he makes it clear that he's doing me a favour by stepping aside. I brush past him and shoulder my way through the swaying crowd. The lights on the walls of the tunnel are hurtling towards me like the future. There's a bag of shopping between two seats, and there's another carrier bag on the floor, but where's the briefcase? Is it even in this carriage? How much distance may the woman want to put between herself and the case, or how little? I'm nearly at the first set of doors, and I'm shamefully tempted to make my escape, but we're still in the tunnel. The train lurches as if it has been derailed, and its hollow roar seems to grow louder. I seize the metal pole above the partition that separates the seats from the crowded space in front of a pair of doors. The carriage steadies, and as I grasp there was no explosion I see a briefcase on the floor, almost hidden by the legs of passengers. "Sir," I say urgently, "is that your case?"

The man who's closest to it glances down and then just as indifferently at my face. "Nothing to do with me."

His neighbours shake their heads, and I stoop to retrieve the case. I recognise it at once—recognise the warped lock, which I'm beginning to think might have been deliberately forced out of shape so that nobody can open it. I close my fist around the ragged handle and lift the case.

At once light flares all around me. I'm back at Lime Street. All along the carriage matrix signs spell it out, and a woman's amplified voice pronounces the words for anyone who can't read. As I make for the doors I'm frantically trying to decide where to take the briefcase. The train is coasting to a halt, and I'm still trapped by all the bodies pressing close around me, when someone taps me on the shoulder hard enough for a knock on a door. "That yours?" a man says in my ear.

"It isn't," I declare and struggle around to face him. He's a cleaner in a yellow jerkin. Usually the cleaners don't collect the rubbish from the trains during the rush hour, and his appearance is as unexpected as it's reassuring—even the Union Jack badge just visible on the lapel of his jacket. "It was left before," I murmur for only him to hear. "I think—"

"We saw," he says just as low and reaches for the briefcase. "Give it here."

However grateful I am to let it go, I want to be sure he understands. "You saw who left it," I mutter.

"We know all about those."

This could be prejudice symbolised by the badge. Under the circumstances I can't be choosy, and I hand him the briefcase. "Be careful with it," I whisper. "Whatever's inside—"

"It's seen to, granddad," he says and steps onto the platform.

As he strides towards the nearest exit a young woman offers me a seat. Perhaps I look shaken by having to deal with the briefcase, unless she heard what the cleaner called me. I sink onto the seat, but I can't begin to relax until the train leaves the station and is safely in the tunnel. "Thank God that's over," I say aloud.

I oughtn't to have spoken. At least nobody seems to want to enquire into my remark. One man clasps his hands and bows his head as if to dazzle everyone with the shine of his bald scalp. A girl in a sweater striped like a wasp stares out of the window at the repetition of the lights. A young businessman reads a magazine, and the woman next to him might almost be hypnotised by the swaying of her earrings, which are shaped like inverted question marks although she doesn't look remotely Spanish. More passengers manage to find room when we reach Central Station, and soon the voice of the train reads out the illuminated announcement about James Street. In a very few moments I'll be out of the loop at last. Just one person leaves the train and heads for the exit. He's wearing a yellow jerkin, and he's carrying a briefcase.

He's the man who spoke to me. It needn't be the same case, except that I can see the warped lock. Didn't he understand my warning? How could he risk bringing the case back on the train? The explanation makes my nerves yank me to my feet. "It's him as well," I gasp. "He's part of it."

Nobody appears to want to understand or to let me off the train. I have to shout in one man's ear before he gives an inch, followed by hardly any more as I struggle past him. I've barely staggered onto the platform when the train shuts its doors. I could shout to the driver, but if anyone else hears me, won't that cause a panic or worse? My heart thumps like a frenzied drum as I dash up the steps to the underground bridge.

I can't see the man in the yellow jerkin or the briefcase. Has he used one of the lifts up to street level? I could—there are always staff at the top—but that might take longer than it's safe to take. There's a more immediate way of communicating with the staff, and I sprint across the bridge to leap down two steps at a time to the other platform.

Passengers are waiting for a train around the loop, but I can't see what I'm afraid to see. An intercom is embedded in the wall. A blue button offers **Information**, but I jab the green one that says **Emergency**. My heart deals me a couple of irregular thumps that I hear as well as feel before the grille above the buttons speaks. "Hello?"

"I'm at James Street." Lurching close to the grille, I cup my hands around my mouth to murmur "I think—"

"Can't hear you."

"You won't want anybody else hearing." All the same, the man's voice is coarse with static, and suppose mine is even more distorted? I press the sides of my hands around the grille and shove my mouth closer. "Someone's up to something down here," I say as loud as I dare. "They keep trying to leave a case on the train."

"Who does?"

"I think they're Muslims, or they may not be. Maybe they're people who're against Muslims and trying to make it look as if it's them." The speaker has begun to remind me of a grille in the door of a cell. I strain my eyes as far to the side as their aching muscles will drag them. I can't see the man or the briefcase, but everyone nearby seems to be watching me until they look away. I'm the last person they ought to suspect, and they wouldn't find my behaviour odd if they knew I was acting on their behalf. "The one who's got the case now," I say urgently, "he's one of your cleaners or he's pretending to be."

"Where are you saying he is?"

"He just got off the train at James Street. I'm not sure where he went." I have to raise my voice to compete with the sounds of the latest train. Most of the people around me converge on the doors, and I'm so confused by nervousness that for a moment I think I'm about to miss the train. Of course I don't want to return to the loop, and I'm about to demand how the railway will be dealing with my information when a man darts off the stairs and onto the train.

He's wearing an unobtrusively dark suit. It's no longer hidden by the yellow jerkin, and I might not have recognised him except for the flag pinned to his lapel and the briefcase in his hand. "He's here," I shout, and my hands sprawl away from the grille. "He's got back on the train."

The only response from the grille is a blurred metallic clatter. I didn't say that the man has the case, and now I'm sure it's too late. My instincts send me to the train before I have a chance to think, and I dodge between the closing doors. "Let me through," I say at once.

I didn't have time to reach the carriage the man boarded. Nobody ahead of me seems to believe my mission is urgent. I have to thrust my pass over people's shoulders to flash it in their faces, just long enough to leave them with an impression of officialdom. I'm crawling with sweat from the closeness of so many bodies, whose softness feels horribly vulnerable, ready to be blown apart. The carriage seems little better than airless, and I feel walled in by the tunnel, not to mention my own scarcely rational decision to pursue the man onto the train. Now I'm at the door to the next carriage, and someone is lounging against it. As I pound on the glass my heart mimics the rhythm. At last the loafer turns his sluggish apathetic head. He stares at my pass and then at me as if I might be a patient posing as a nurse, and then he slouches aside just far enough to let me sidle around the door.

I can't see the man with the briefcase. His badge is too small to show up in the crowd, and what else is there to distinguish him?

Mousy hair, bland nondescript face, dark suit—none of these stands out. My heart counts the seconds like a clock or some more lethal mechanism as I force my way along the carriage. I peer at the floor but see only people's legs—bones that could shatter in a moment, flesh and muscles that would fill the air. I'm nearly at the first set of doors, and I crane around the partition behind the seats. There indeed is the briefcase.

I feel as though I've rehearsed the moment. I stoop and grab the handle, and I'm lifting the case when the train shudders in the midst of a burst of light. I'm almost used to that, because I know it means we've reached Moorfields. I still haven't located the man with the flag in his lapel, but it can't matter just now. The moment the door opens I struggle through the crowd and its reinforcements onto the platform. Where can I take the briefcase? I'm fleeing to the nearest exit when a hand grasps my shoulder. "Where do you think you're going with that?" says a voice.

It belongs to a tall man in an unobtrusively expensive suit. The lines on his high forehead and the hint of grey in his cropped black hair may be raising his apparent age, but he seems reassuringly official. "Where's safe?" I blurt.

"I'm asking what you're doing with it," he says and keeps hold of my shoulder.

"Trying to get rid of it, to dispose of it, I mean. Someone deliberately left it on the train, and not just once either. Don't you know what that means?" I'm so desperate that I shake the case at him, and it emits an ominous metallic rattle. "Just let me—"

"You made the call."

I don't see how this can be an accusation, and so I say "It was me, yes."

"Thank you, Mr Conrad."

I'm bemused by this, even though his grip on my shoulder has begun to feel more appreciative than custodial. "How do you know my name?"

"We know everything we have to know."

His eyes have grown so professionally blank that I say "You're not with the railway, are you?"

"We're responsible for this kind of situation. That's all I can tell you." He lets go of my shoulder and repeats "Thank you, Mr Conrad."

Even when he holds out his hand I don't immediately see he's asking for the briefcase. Its reappearances have left me wary, and I say "I wonder if you've got some identification."

"Don't you think we would have?" he says and produces a wallet almost as thin as a wafer. It contains a single card with his name and his likeness and some abbreviated information. "Is that good enough for you?" he wants to know.

"Thank you, Mr Joseph," I say and hand over the briefcase.

He doesn't move away at once. He has to know what he's about, which is why I didn't panic when he lingered over questioning me—he would hardly have been putting himself at risk. There may be a trace of doubt in my eyes, since he says "Are you sure that settles it? Would you like to be there when it's disposed of?"

"I'm sure." Indeed, I'm growing anxious for him and the case to be gone. "You're the authority," I tell him. "It's in safe hands now."

As he heads for the nearest stairway I hear a train. I'm eager to board, and more eager for it to leave any danger behind. The doors close as I find a seat and give in to expressing relief—shaking my head, mopping my brow, letting out a loud sigh that shudders with my heartbeat. "I've really done it this time," I declare.

Nobody responds except for glancing at me as if I might be a mental patient on the loose. I don't care what they think of me; I know I've kept them safe. A young man in a business suit returns to reading a comic book, and a girl gazes at her extravagantly large wristwatch, which shows seven minutes to six. A woman who pushed her thin spectacles high with a forefinger lets them subside, and a man lifts one foot after the other to rub the toecaps of his shoes even shinier on his trouser cuffs. None of the passengers might be able to do any of this without me. The idea accompanies me around the loop, past Lime Street and Central Station, and prompts me to stare along the James Street platform. I see nobody with a briefcase, but the absence isn't quite reassuring enough. As the doors start to close I jump off the train and run up the stairs to the underground bridge.

I still seem to have a task. When a train appears I stay on the platform until the doors begin to close, but I can't see anyone suspicious. As soon as I step aboard a girl gives me a seat, and everything seems settled as the train sets off around the loop. A bald man with a tweed hat on his lap gazes at the polished toecaps of his shoes before turning over his newspaper. A bespectacled woman in a checked overcoat and with queries dangling from her earlobes is reading another copy of the paper. A young man dressed for business takes a comic book from among the documents in a cardboard folder, and a young woman in a waspishly striped sweater pushes a headphone away from one ear while she consults her considerable wristwatch. As blackness closes around the train I see the time is seven minutes to six.

I could imagine the lights on the tunnel walls are signalling to me, and I search for some distraction inside the carriage. The headline on the front page of the bald man's newspaper says **ISLAMIC PANIC**, but I'm not sure if that's the name of a terrorist group. The bespectacled woman's paper has its letters page facing me. One letter is entitled **NO ASYLUM**, which seems to be the slogan of a party called Pure Brit, and the correspondent has suggested that the party is planting bombs so as to blame Muslims and provoke a backlash against immigrants. I grow aware of a voice too small to belong to any of the passengers. It isn't in my head; it's on the young woman's headphones—a recorded radio phone-in, where somebody is arguing that the bombs are the work not of Muslims or their foes but the first stages of a plan by the secret service to force the country to accept dictatorship. Another caller on the phone-in accuses the man who was credited with trying to save his fellow passengers of having planted the bomb himself. All these idle theories make me feel as if nothing is to be trusted, and I focus my attention on the young man's comic book. The cover shows a boffin grimacing in disbelief while he tells his colleagues "It's not that kind of time bomb. It's a bomb that destroys time. It'll blow the past to bits."

"It's nothing like that." The idea has gone too far, and I can't keep quiet any longer, especially since I've seen the truth at last. I can hear the women murmuring behind me like nurses, and I should have listened to them sooner. "That's right, someone's talking about us again," I tell everyone. "But don't you see, if they can keep changing it we can change it too."

Nobody appears to want to listen. They're all gazing at the floor, even those who've turned towards me. "It needn't be what any of them say happened to us," I insist—I feel as if a voice is speaking through me. "It needn't even be what did."

Everyone is staring at the floor beside me. I look at last and see the briefcase. "We don't have to be what people say just because of where we are," I vow as I take hold of the handle. A thunderous rumble swells in my ears, and brightness flares in my eyes, but it's on the wall of the tunnel. I mustn't be distracted by the absence of my shadow—of anyone's. I have to get my task right this time, and then we can head for the light, out of the tunnel.

# The Place of Revelation

At dinner Colin's parents do most of the talking. His mother starts by saying "Sit down," and as soon as he does his father says "Sit up." Auntie Dot lets Colin glimpse a sympathetic grin while Uncle Lucian gives him a secret one, neither of which helps him feel less nervous. They're eating off plates as expensive as the one he broke last time they visited, when his parents acted as if he'd meant to drop it even though the relatives insisted it didn't matter and at least his uncle thought so. "Delicious as always," his mother says when Auntie Dot asks yet again if Colin's food is all right, and his father offers "I expect he's just tired, Dorothy." At least that's an excuse, which Colin might welcome except it prompts his aunt to say "If you've had enough I should scamper off to bye-byes, Colin. For a treat you can leave us the washing up."

Everyone is waiting for him to go to his room. Even though his parents keep saying how well he does in English and how the art mistress said he should take up painting at secondary school, he's expected only to mumble agreement whenever he's told to speak up for himself. For the first time he tries arguing. "I'll do it. I don't mind."

"You've heard what's wanted," his father says in a voice that seems to weigh his mouth down.

"You catch up on your sleep," his mother says more gently, "then you'll be able to enjoy yourself tomorrow."

Beyond her Uncle Lucian is nodding eagerly, but nobody else sees. Everyone watches Colin trudge into the high wide hall. It offers him a light, and there's another above the stairs that smell of their new fat brown carpet, and one more in the upstairs corridor. They only put off the dark. Colin is taking time on each stair until his father lets him hear "Is he getting ready for bed yet?" For fear of having to explain his apprehensiveness he flees to the bathroom.

With its tiles white as a blizzard it's brighter than the hall, but its floral scent makes Colin feel it's only pretending to be a room. As he brushes his teeth the mirror shows him foaming at the mouth as though his nerves have given him a fit. When he heads for his room, the doorway opposite presents him with a view across his parents' bed of the hospital he can't help thinking is a front for the graveyard down the hill. It's lit up as pale as a tombstone, whereas his window that's edged with tendrils of frost is full of nothing but darkness, which he imagines rising massively from the fields to greet the black sky. Even if the curtains shut tight they wouldn't keep out his sense of it, nor does the flimsy furniture that's yellow as the wine they're drinking downstairs. He huddles under the plump quilt and leaves the light on while he listens to the kitchen clatter. All too soon it comes to an end, and he hears someone padding upstairs so softly they might almost not be there at all.

As the door inches open with a faint creak that puts him in mind of the lifting of a lid, he grabs the edge of the quilt and hauls it over his face. "You aren't asleep yet, then," his mother says. "I thought you might have drifted off."

Colin uncovers his face and bumps his shoulders against the bars behind the pillow. "I can't get to sleep, so can I come down?"

"No need for that, Colin. I expect you're trying too hard. Just think of nice times you've had and then you'll go off. You know there's nothing really to stop you."

She's making him feel so alone that he no longer cares if he gives away his secrets. "There is."

"Colin, you're not a baby any more. You didn't act like this when you were. Try not to upset people. Will you do that for us?"

"If you want."

She frowns at his reluctance. "I'm sure it's what you want as well. Just be as thoughtful as I know you are."

Everything she says reminds him how little she knows. She leans down to kiss each of his eyes shut, and as she straightens up, the cord above the bed turns the kisses into darkness with a click. Can he hold on to the feeling long enough to fall asleep? Once he hears the door close he burrows under the quilt and strives to be aware of nothing beyond the bed. He concentrates on the faint scent of the quilt that nestles on his face, he listens to the silence that the pillow and the quilt press against his ears. The weight of the quilt is beginning to feel vague and soft as sleep when the darkness whispers his name. "I'm asleep," he tries complaining, however babyish and stupid it sounds.

"Not yet, Colin," Uncle Lucian says. "Story first. You can't have forgotten."

He hasn't, of course. He remembers every bedtime story since the first, when he didn't know it would lead to the next day's walk. "I thought we'd have finished," he protests.

"Quietly, son. We don't want anyone disturbed, do we? One last story."

Colin wants to stay where he can't see and yet he wants to know. He inches the quilt down from his face. The gap between the curtains has admitted a sliver of moonlight that turns the edges of objects a glimmering white. A sketch of his uncle's face the colour of bone hovers by the bed. His smile glints, and his eyes shine like stars so distant they remind Colin how limitless the dark is. That's one reason why he blurts "Can't we just go wherever it is tomorrow?"

"You need to get ready while you're asleep. You should know that's how it works." As Uncle Lucian leans closer, the light tinges his gaunt face except where it's hollowed out with shadows, and Colin is reminded of the moon looming from behind a cloud.

"Wait now, here's an idea," his uncle murmurs. "That ought to help."

Colin realises he would rather not ask "What?"

"Tell the stories back to me. You'll find someone to tell one day, you know. You'll be like me."

The prospect fails to appeal to Colin, who pleads "I'm too tired."

"They'll wake you up. Your mother was saying how good you are at stories. That's thanks to me and mine. Go on before anyone comes up and hears."

A cork pops downstairs, and Colin knows there's little chance of being interrupted. "I don't know what to say."

"I can't tell you that, Colin. They're your stories now. They're part of you. You've got to find your own way to tell them."

As Uncle Lucian's eyes glitter like ice Colin hears himself say "Once..."

"That's the spirit. That's how it has to start."

"Once there was a boy..."

"Called Colin. Sorry. You won't hear another breath out of me."

"Once there was a boy who went walking in the country on a day like it was today. The grass in the fields looked like feathers where all the birds in the world had been fighting, and all the fallen leaves were showing their bones. The sun was so low every crumb of frost had its own shadow, and his footprints had shadows in when he looked behind him, and walking felt like breaking little bones under his feet. The day was so cold he kept thinking the clouds were bits of ice that had cracked off the sky and dropped on the edge of the earth. The wind kept scratching his face and pulling the last few leaves off the trees, only if the leaves went back he knew they were birds. It was meant to be the shortest day, but it felt as if time had died because everything was too slippery or too empty for it to get hold of. So he thought he'd done everything there was to do and seen everything there was to see when he saw a hole like a gate through a hedge."

"That's the way." Uncle Lucian's eyes have begun to shine like fragments of the moon. "Make it your story."

"He wasn't sure if there was an old gate or the hedge had grown like one. He didn't know it was one of the places where the world is twisted. All he could see was more hedge at the sides of a bendy path. So he followed it round and round, and it felt like going inside a shell. Then he got dizzy with running to find the middle, because it seemed to take hours and the bends never got any smaller. But just when he was thinking he'd stop and turn back if the spiky hedges let him, he came to where the path led all round a pond that was covered with ice. Only the pond oughtn't to have been so big, all the path he'd run round should have squeezed it little. So he was walking round the pond to see if he could find the trick when the sun showed him the flat white faces everywhere under the ice.

"There were children and parents who'd come searching for them, and old people too. They were everyone the maze had brought to the pond, and they were all calling him. Their eyes were opening as slow as holes in the ice and growing too big, and their mouths were moving like fish mouths out of water, and the wind in the hedge was their cold rattly voice telling him he had to stay for ever, because he couldn't see the path away from the pond—there was just hedge everywhere he looked. Only then he heard his uncle's voice somewhere in it, telling him he had to walk back in all his footprints like a witch dancing backwards and then he'd be able to escape."

This is the part Colin likes least, but his uncle murmurs eagerly "And was he?"

"He thought he never could till he remembered what his footprints looked like. When he turned round he could just see them with the frost creeping to swallow them up. So he started walking back in them, and he heard the ice on the pond start to crack to let all the bodies with the turned-up faces climb out. He saw thin white fingers pushing the edge of the ice up and digging their nails into the frosty path. His footprints led him back through the gap the place had tried to stop him finding in the hedge, but he could see hands flopping out of the pond like frogs. He still had to walk all the way back to the gate like that, and every step he took the hedges tried to catch him, and he heard more ice being pushed up and people crawling after him. It felt like the place had got hold of his middle and his neck and screwed them round so far he'd never be able to walk forward again. He came out of the gate at last, and then he had to walk round the fields till it was nearly dark to get back into walking in an ordinary way so his mother and father wouldn't notice there was something new about him and want to know what he'd been doing."

Colin doesn't mind if that makes his uncle feel at least a little guilty, but Uncle Lucian says "What happens next?"

Colin hears his parents and his aunt forgetting to keep their voices low downstairs. He still can't make out what they're saying, though they must think he's asleep. "The next year he went walking in the woods," he can't avoid admitting.

"What kind of a day would that have been, I wonder?"

"Sunny. Full of birds and squirrels and butterflies. So hot he felt like he was wearing the sun on his head, and the only place he could take it off was the woods, because if he went back to the house his mother and father would say he ought to be out walking. So he'd gone a long way under the trees when he felt them change."

"He could now. Most people wouldn't until it was too late, but he felt…"

"Something had crept up behind him. He was under some trees that put their branches together like hands with hundreds of fingers praying. And when he looked he saw the trees he'd already gone under were exactly the same as the ones he still had to, like he was looking in a mirror except he couldn't see himself in it. So he started to run but as soon as he moved, the half of the tunnel of trees he had to go through began to stretch itself till he couldn't see the far end, and when he looked behind him it had happened there as well."

"He knew what to do this time, didn't he? He hardly even needed to be told."

"He had to go forwards walking backwards and never look to see what was behind him. And as soon as he did he saw the way he'd come start to shrink. Only that wasn't all he saw, because leaves started running up and down the trees, except they weren't leaves. They were insects pretending to be them, or maybe they weren't insects. He could hear them scuttling about behind him, and he was afraid the way he had to go wasn't shrinking, it was growing as much longer as the way he'd come was getting shorter. Then all the scuttling things ran onto the branches over his head, and he thought they'd fall on him if he didn't stop trying to escape. But his body kept moving even though he wished it wouldn't, and he heard a great flapping as if he was in a cave and bats were flying off the roof, and then something landed on his head. It was just the sunlight, and he'd come out of the woods the same place he'd gone in. All the way back he felt he was walking away from the house, and his mother said he'd got a bit of sunstroke."

"He never told her otherwise, did he? He knew most people aren't ready to know what's behind the world."

"That's what his uncle kept telling him."

"He was proud to be chosen, wasn't he? He must have known it's the greatest privilege to be shown the old secrets."

Colin has begun to wish he could stop talking about himself as though he's someone else, but the tales won't let go of him—they've closed around him like the dark. "What was his next adventure?" it whispers with his uncle's moonlit smiling mouth.

"The next year his uncle took him walking in an older wood. Even his mother and father might have noticed there was something wrong with it and told him not to go in far." When his uncle doesn't acknowledge any criticism but only smiles wider and more whitely Colin has to add "There was nothing except sun in the sky, but as soon as you went in the woods you had to step on shadows everywhere, and that was the only way you knew there was still a sun. And the day was so still it felt like the woods were pretending they never breathed, but the shadows kept moving whenever he wasn't looking—he kept nearly seeing very tall ones hide behind the trees. So he wanted to get through the woods as fast as he could, and that's why he ran straight onto the stepping stones when he came to a stream."

Colin would like to run fast through the story too, but his uncle wants to know "How many stones were there again?"

"Ten, and they looked so close together he didn't have to stretch to walk. Only he was on the middle two when he felt them start to move. And when he looked down he saw the stream was really as deep as the sky, and lying on the bottom was a giant made out of rocks and moss that was holding up its arms to him. They were longer than he didn't know how many trees stuck together, and their hands were as big as the roots of an old tree, and he was standing on top of two of the fingers. Then the giant's eyes began to open like boulders rolling about in the mud, and its mouth opened like a cave and sent up a laugh in a bubble that spattered the boy with mud, and the stones he was on started to move apart."

"His uncle was always with him though, wasn't he?"

"The boy couldn't see him," Colin says in case this lets his uncle realise how it felt, and then he knows his uncle already did. "He heard him saying you mustn't look down, because being seen was what woke up the god of the wood. So the boy kept looking straight ahead, though he could see the shadows that weren't shadows crowding behind the trees to wait for him. He could feel how even the water underneath him wanted him to slip on the slimy stones, and how the stones were ready to swim apart so he'd fall between them if he caught the smallest glimpse of them. Then he did, and the one he was standing on sank deep into the water, but he'd jumped on the bank of the stream. The shadows that must have been the bits that were left of people who'd looked down too long let him see his uncle, and they walked to the other side of the woods. Maybe he wouldn't have got there without his uncle, because the shadows kept dancing around them to make them think there was no way between the trees."

"Brave boy, to see all that." Darkness has reclaimed the left side of Uncle Lucian's face; Colin is reminded of a moon that the night is squeezing out of shape. "Don't stop now, Colin," his uncle says. "Remember last year."

This is taking longer than his bedtime stories ever have. Colin feels as if the versions he's reciting may rob him of his whole night's sleep. Downstairs his parents and his aunt sound as if they need to talk for hours yet. "It was here in town," he says accusingly. "It was down in Lower Brichester."

He wants to communicate how betrayed he felt, by the city or his uncle or by both. He'd thought houses and people would keep away the old things, but now he knows that nobody who can't see can help. "It was where the boy's mother and father wouldn't have liked him to go," he says, but that simply makes him feel the way his uncle's stories do, frightened and excited and unable to separate the feelings. "Half the houses were shut up with boards but people were still using them, and there were men and ladies on the corners of the streets waiting for whoever wanted them or stuff they were selling. And in the middle of it all there were railway lines and passages to walk under them. Only the people who lived round there must have felt something, because there was one passage nobody walked through."

"But the boy did."

"A man sitting drinking with his legs in the road told him not to, but he did. His uncle went through another passage and said he'd meet him on the other side. Anyone could have seen something was wrong with the tunnel, because people had dropped needles all over the place except in there. But it looked like it'd just be a minute to walk through, less if you ran. So the boy started to hurry through, only he tried to be quiet because he didn't like how his feet made so much noise he kept thinking someone was following him, except it sounded more like lots of fingers tapping on the bricks behind him. When he managed to be quiet the noise didn't all go away, but he tried to think it was water dripping, because he felt it cold and wet on the top of his head. Then more of it touched the back of his neck, but he didn't want to look round, because the passage was getting darker behind him. He was in the middle of the tunnel when the cold touch landed on his face and made him look."

His uncle's face is barely outlined, but his eyes take on an extra gleam. "And when he looked… "

"He saw why the passage was so dark, with all the arms as thin as his poking out of the bricks. They could grow long enough to reach halfway down the passage and grope around till they found him with their fingers that were as wet as worms. Then he couldn't even see them, because the half of the passage he had to walk through was filling up with arms as well, so many he couldn't see out. And all he could do was what his uncle's story had said, stay absolutely still, because if he tried to run the hands would grab him and drag him through the walls into the earth, and he wouldn't even be able to die of how they did it. So he shut his eyes to be as blind as the things with the arms were, that's if there wasn't just one thing behind the walls. And after he nearly forgot how to breathe the hands stopped pawing at his head as if they were feeling how his brain showed him everything about them, maybe even brought them because he'd learned to see the old things. When he opened his eyes the arms were worming back into the walls, but he felt them all around him right to the end of the passage. And when he went outside he couldn't believe in the daylight any more. It was like a picture someone had put up to hide the dark."

"He could believe in his uncle though, couldn't he? He saw his uncle waiting for him and telling him well done. I hope he knew how much his uncle thought of him."

"Maybe."

"Well, now it's another year."

Uncle Lucian's voice is so low, and his face is so nearly invisible, that Colin isn't sure whether his words are meant to be comforting or to warn the boy that there's more. "Another story," Colin mumbles, inviting it or simply giving in.

"I don't think so any more. I think you're too old for that."

Colin doesn't know in what way he feels abandoned as he whispers "Have we finished?"

"Nothing like. Tomorrow, just go and lie down and look up."

"Where?"

"Anywhere you're by yourself."

Colin feels he is now. "Then what?" he pleads.

"You'll see. I can't begin to tell you. See for yourself."

That makes Colin more nervous than his uncle's stories ever did. He's struggling to think how to persuade his uncle to give him at least a hint when he realises he's alone in the darkness. He lies on his back and stares upwards in case that gets whatever has to happen over with, but all he sees are memories of the places his uncle has made him recall. Downstairs his parents and his aunt are still talking, and he attempts to use their voices to keep him with them, but feels as if they're dragging him down into the moonless dark. Then he's been asleep, because they're shutting their doors close to his. After that, whenever he twitches awake it's a little less dark. As soon as he's able to see he sneaks out of bed to avoid his parents and his aunt. Whatever is imminent, having to lie about where he's going would make his nerves feel even more like rusty wire about to snap.

He's as quick and as quiet in the bathroom as he can be. Once he's dressed he rolls up the quilt to lie on and slips out of the house. In the front garden he thinks moonlight has left a crust on the fallen leaves and the grass. Down the hill a train shakes itself awake while the city mutters in its sleep. He turns away and heads for the open country behind the house.

A few crows jab at the earth with their beaks and sail up as if they mean to peck the icy sky. The ground has turned into a single flattened greenish bone exactly as bright as the low vault of dull cloud. Colin walks until the fields bear the houses out of sight. That's as alone as he's likely to be. Flapping the quilt, he spreads it on the frozen ground. He throws himself on top of it and slaps his hands on it in case that starts whatever's meant to happen. He's already so cold he can't keep still.

At first he thinks that's the only reason he's shivering, and then he notices the sky isn't right. He feels as if all the stories he's had to act out have gathered in his head, or the way they've made him see has. That ability is letting him observe how thin the sky is growing, or perhaps it's leaving him unable not to. Is it also attracting whatever's looming down to peer at him from behind the sky? A shiver is drumming his heels on the ground through the quilt when the sky seems to vanish as though it has been clawed apart above him, and he glimpses as much of a face as there's room for—an eye like a sea black as space with a moon for its pupil. It seems indifferent as death and yet it's watching him. An instant of seeing is all he can take before he twists onto his front and presses his face into the quilt as though it's a magic carpet that will transport him home to bed and, better still, unconsciousness.

He digs his fingers into the quilt until he recognises he can't burrow into the earth. He stops for fear of tearing his aunt's quilt and having to explain. He straightens up in a crouch to retrieve the quilt, which he hugs as he stumbles back across the field with his head down. The sky is pretending that it never faltered, but all the way to the house he's afraid it will part to expose more of a face.

While nobody is up yet, Colin senses that his uncle isn't in the house. He tiptoes upstairs to leave the quilt on his bed, and then he sends himself out again. There's no sign of his uncle on the way downhill. Colin dodges onto the path under the trees in case his uncle prefers not to be seen. "Uncle Lucian," he pleads.

"You found me."

He doesn't seem especially pleased, but Colin demands "What did I see?"

"Not much yet. Just as much as your mind could take. It's like our stories, do you understand? Your mind had to tell you a story about what you saw, but in time you won't need it. You'll see what's really there."

"Suppose I don't want to?" Colin blurts. "What's it all for?"

"Would you rather be like my sister and only see what everyone else sees? She was no fun when she was your age, your mother."

"I never had the choice."

"Well, I wouldn't ever have said that to my grandfather. I was nothing but grateful to him."

Though his uncle sounds not merely disappointed but offended, Colin says "Can't I stop now?"

"Everything will know you can see, son. If you don't greet the old things where you find them they'll come to find you."

Colin voices a last hope. "Has it stopped for you?"

"It never will. I'm part of it now. Do you want to see?"

"No."

Presumably Colin's cry offends his uncle, because there's a spidery rustle beyond the trees that conceal the end of the path and then silence. Time passes before Colin dares to venture forward. As he steps from beneath the trees he feels as if the sky has lowered itself towards him like a mask. He's almost blind with resentment of his uncle for making him aware of so much and for leaving him alone, afraid to see even Uncle Lucian. Though it doesn't help, Colin starts kicking the stone with his uncle's name on it and the pair of years ending with this one. When he's exhausted he turns away towards the rest of his life.

# THE DECORATIONS

"HERE THEY ARE AT LAST," DAVID'S GRANDMOTHER cried, and her face lit up: green from the luminous plastic holly that bordered the front door and then, as she took a plump step to hug David's mother, red with the glow from the costume of the Santa in the sleigh beneath the window. "Was the traffic that bad, Jane?"

"I still don't drive, mummy. One of the trains was held up and we missed a connection."

"You want to get yourself another man. Never mind, you'll always have Davy," his grandmother panted as she waddled to embrace him.

Her clasp was even fatter than last time. It smelled of clothes he thought could be as old as she was, and of perfume that didn't quite disguise a further staleness he was afraid was her. His embarrassment was aggravated by a car that slowed outside the house, though the driver was only admiring the Christmas display. When his grandmother abruptly released him he thought she'd noticed his reaction, but she was peering at the sleigh. "Has he got down?" she whispered.

David understood before his mother seemed to. He retreated

along the path between the flower-beds full of grass to squint past the lights that flashed MERRY CHRISTMAS above the bedroom windows. The second Santa was still perched on the roof; a wind set the illuminated figure rocking back and forth as if with silent laughter. "He's there," David said.

"I expect he has to be in lots of places at once."

Now that he was nearly eight, David knew that his father had always been Santa. Before he could say as much, his grandmother plodded to gaze at the roof. "Do you like him?"

"I like coming to see all your Christmas things."

"I'm not so fond of him. He looks too empty for my liking." As the figure shifted in another wind she shouted "You stay up there where you belong. Never mind thinking of jumping on us."

David's grandfather hurried out to her, his slippers flapping on his thin feet, his reduced face wincing. "Come inside, Dora. You'll have the neighbours looking."

"I don't care about the fat old thing," she said loud enough to be heard on the roof and tramped into the house. "You can take your mummy's case up, can't you, David? You're a big strong boy now."

He enjoyed hauling the wheeled suitcase on its leash—it was like having a dog he could talk to, sometimes not only in his head—but bumping the luggage upstairs risked snagging the already threadbare carpet, and so his mother supported the burden. "I'll just unpack quickly," she told him. "Go down and see if anyone needs help."

He used the frilly toilet in the equally pink bathroom and lingered until his mother asked if he was all right. He was trying to stay clear of the argument he could just hear through the salmon carpet. As he ventured downstairs his grandmother pounced on some remark so muted it was almost silent. "You do better, then. Let's see you cook."

He could smell the subject of the disagreement. Once he'd finished setting the table from the tray with which his grandfather sent him out of the kitchen, he and his mother saw it too: a casserole encrusted with gravy and containing a shrivelled lump of beef. Potatoes roasted close to impenetrability came with it, and green beans from which someone had tried to scrape the worst of the charring. "It's not as bad as it looks, is it?" David's grandmother said through her first mouthful. "I expect it's like having a barbecue, Davy."

"I don't know," he confessed, never having had one.

"They've no idea, these men, have they, Jane? They don't have to keep dinner waiting for people. I expect your hubby's the same."

"Was, but can we not talk about him?"

"He's learned his lesson, then. No call to make that face at me, Tom. I'm only saying Davy's father— Oh, you've split up, Jane, haven't you. Sorry about my big fat trap. Sorry Davy too."

"Just eat what you want," his grandfather advised him, "and then you'd best be scampering off to bed so Santa can make his deliveries."

"We all want to be tucked up before he's on the move," said his grandmother before remembering to smile.

Santa had gone away like David's father, and David was too old to miss either of them. He managed to breach the carapace of a second potato and chewed several forkfuls of dried-up beef, but the burned remains of beans defeated him. All the same, he thanked his grandmother as he stood up. "There's a good boy," she said rather too loudly, as if interceding with someone on his behalf. "Do your best to go to sleep."

That sounded like an inexplicit warning, and was one of the elements that kept him awake in his bedroom, which was no larger than his room in the flat he'd moved to with his mother. Despite their heaviness, the curtains admitted a repetitive flicker from the letters ERR above the window, and a buzz that suggested an insect was hovering over the bed. He could just hear voices downstairs, which gave him the impression that they didn't want him to know what they were saying. He was most troubled by a hollow creaking that reminded him of someone in a rocking chair, but overhead. The Santa figure must be swaying in the wind, not doing its best to heave itself free. David was too old for stories: while real ones didn't always stay true, that wasn't an excuse to make any up. Still, he was glad to hear his mother and her parents coming upstairs at last, lowering their voices to compensate. He heard doors shutting for the night, and then a nervous question from his grandmother through the wall between their rooms. "What's he doing? Is he loose?"

"If he falls he falls," his grandfather said barely audibly, "and good riddance to him if he's getting on your nerves. For pity's sake come to bed."

David tried not to find this more disturbing than the notion that his parents had shared one. Rather than hear the mattress sag under the weight his grandmother had put on, he tugged the quilt over his head. His grasp must have slackened when he drifted off to sleep, because he was roused by a voice. It was outside the house but too close to the window.

It was his grandfather's. David was disconcerted by the notion that the old man had clambered onto the roof until he realised his grandfather was calling out of the adjacent window. "What do you think you're doing, Dora? Come in before you catch your death."

"I'm seeing he's stayed where he's meant to be," David's grandmother responded from below. "Yes, you know I'm talking about you, don't you. Never mind pretending you didn't nod."

"Get in for the Lord's sake," his grandfather urged, underlining his words with a rumble of the sash. David heard him pad across the room and as rapidly if more stealthily down the stairs. A bated argument grew increasingly stifled as it ascended to the bedroom. David had refrained from looking out of the window for fear of embarrassing his grandparents, but now he was nervous that his mother would be drawn to find out what was happening. He mustn't go to her; he had to be a man, as she kept telling him, and not one like his father, who ran off to women because there was so little to him. In time the muttering beyond the wall subsided, and David was alone with the insistence of electricity and the restlessness on the roof.

When he opened his eyes the curtains had acquired a hem of daylight. It was Christmas Day. Last year he'd run downstairs to handle all the packages addressed to him under the tree and guess at their contents, but now he was wary of encountering his grandparents by himself in case he betrayed he was concealing their secret. As he lay hoping that his grandmother had slept off her condition, he heard his mother in the kitchen. "Let me make breakfast, mummy. It can be a little extra present for you."

He didn't venture down until she called him. "Here's the Christmas boy," his grandmother shouted as if he was responsible for the occasion, and dealt him such a hug that he struggled within himself. "Eat up or you won't grow."

Her onslaught had dislodged a taste of last night's food. He did his best to bury it under his breakfast, then volunteered to wash up the plates and utensils and dry them as well. Before he finished she was crying "Hurry up so we can see what Santa's brought. I'm as excited as you, Davy."

He hoped she was only making these remarks on his behalf, not somehow growing younger than he was. In the front room his grandfather distributed the presents while the bulbs on the tree flashed patterns that made David think of secret messages. His grandparents had wrapped him up puzzle books and tales of heroic boys, his mother's gifts to him were games for his home computer. "Thank you," he said, sometimes dutifully.

It was the last computer game that prompted his grandmother to ask "Who are you thanking?" At once, as if she feared she'd spoiled the day for him, she added "I expect he's listening."

"Nobody's listening," his grandfather objected. "Nobody's there."

"Don't say things like that, Tom, not in front of Davy."

"That isn't necessary, mummy. You know the truth, don't you, David? Tell your grandmother."

"Santa's just a fairy tale," David said, although it felt like robbing a younger child of an illusion. "Really people have to save up to buy presents."

"He had to know when we've so much less coming in this Christmas," said his mother. "You see how good he's being. I believe he's taken it better than I did."

"I'm sorry if I upset you, Davy."

"You didn't," David said, not least because his grandmother's eyes looked dangerously moist. "I'm sorry if I upset you."

Her face was already quivering as if there was too much of it to hold still. When she shook her head her cheeks wobbled like a whitish rubber mask that was about to fall loose. He didn't know whether she meant to answer him or had strayed onto another subject as she peered towards the window. "There's nothing to him at all then, is there? He's just an empty old shell. Can't we get him down now?"

"Better wait till the new year," David's grandfather said, and with sudden bitterness "We don't want any more bad luck."

Her faded sunken armchair creaked with relief as she levered herself to her feet. "Where are you going?" her husband protested and limped after her, out of the front door. He murmured at her while she stared up at the roof. At least she didn't shout, but she began to talk not much less quietly as she returned to the house. "I don't like him moving about with nothing inside him," she said before she appeared to recollect David's presence. "Maybe he's like one of those beans with a worm inside, Davy, that used to jig about all the time."

While David didn't understand and was unsure he wanted to, his mother's hasty intervention wasn't reassuring either. "Shall we play some games? What would you like to play, mummy?"

"What do you call it, Lollopy. The one with all the little houses. Too little for any big fat things to climb on. Lollopy."

"Monopoly."

"Lollopy," David's grandmother maintained, only to continue "I don't want to play that. Too many sums. What's your favourite, Davy?"

Monopoly was, but he didn't want to add to all the tensions that he sensed rather than comprehended. "Whatever yours is."

"Ludo," she cried and clapped her hands. "I'd play it every Sunday with your granny and grandpa when I was Davy's age, Jane."

He wondered if she wasn't just remembering but behaving as she used to. She pleaded to be allowed to move her counters whenever she failed to throw a six, and kept trying to move more than she threw. David would have let her win, but his grandfather persisted in reminding her that she had to cast the precise amount to guide her counters home. After several games in which his grandmother squinted with increasingly less comical suspicion at her opponents' moves, David's mother said "Who'd like to go out for a walk?"

Apparently everyone did, which meant they couldn't go fast or far. David felt out of place compared with the boys he saw riding their Christmas bicycles or brandishing their Christmas weapons. Beneath a sky frosty with cloud, all the decorations in the duplicated streets looked deadened by the pale sunlight, though they were still among the very few elements that distinguished one squat boxy house from another. "They're not as good as ours, are they?" his grandmother kept remarking when she wasn't frowning at the roofs. "He's not there either," he heard her mutter more than once, and as her house came in sight "See, he didn't follow us. We'd have heard him."

She was saying that nothing had moved or could move, David tried to think, but he was nervous of returning to the house. The preparation of Christmas dinner proved to be reason enough. "Too many women in this kitchen," his mother was told when she offered to help, but his grandmother had to be reminded to turn the oven on, and she made to take the turkey out too soon more than once. Between these incidents she disagreed with her husband and her daughter about various memories of theirs while David tried to stay low in a book of mazes he had to trace with a pencil. At dinner he could tell that his mother was willing him to clean his plate so as not to distress his grandmother. He did his best, and struggled to ignore pangs of indigestion as he washed up, and then as his grandmother kept talking about if not to every television programme her husband put on. "Not very Christmassy," she commented on all of them, and followed the remark with at least a glance towards the curtained window. Waiting for her to say worse, and his impression that his mother and grandfather were too, kept clenching David's stomach well before his mother declared "I think it's time someone was in bed."

As his grandmother's lips searched for an expression he wondered if she assumed that her daughter meant her. "I'm going," he said and had to be called back to be hugged and kissed and wished happy Christmas thrice.

He used the toilet, having pulled the chain to cover up his noises, and huddled in bed. He had a sense of hiding behind the scenes, the way he'd waited offstage at school to perform a line about Jesus last year, when his parents had held hands at the sight of him. The flickers and the buzzing that the bedroom curtains failed to exclude could have been stage effects, while over the mumbling of the television downstairs he heard sounds of imminent drama. At least there was no creaking on the roof. He did his best to remember last Christmas as a sharp stale taste of this one continued its antics inside him, until the memories blurred into the beginnings of a dream and let him sleep.

Movements above his head wakened him. Something soft but determined was groping at the window—a wind so vigorous that its onslaughts made the light from the sign flare like a fire someone was breathing on. The wind must be swinging the bulbs closer to his window. He hadn't time to wonder how dangerous that might be, because the creaking overhead was different: more prolonged, more purposeful. He was mostly nervous that his grandmother would hear, but there was no sign of awareness in the next room, and silence downstairs. He pressed the quilt around his ears, and then he heard sounds too loud for it to fend off—a hollow slithering followed by a thump at the window, and another. Whatever was outside seemed eager to break the glass.

David scrambled onto all fours and backed away until the quilt slipped off his body, but then he had to reach out to part the curtains at arms' length. He might have screamed if a taste hadn't choked him. Two eyes as dead as pebbles were level with his. They didn't blink, but sputtered as if they were trying to come to a kind of life, as did the rest of the swollen face. Worse still, the nose and mouth surrounded by a dirty whitish fungus of beard were above the eyes. The inversion lent the unnecessarily crimson lips a clown's ambiguous grimace.

The mask dealt the window another blundering thump before a savage gust of wind seized the puffed-up figure. As the face sailed away from the glass, it was extinguished as though the wind had blown it out. David heard wires rip loose and saw the shape fly like a greyish vaguely human balloon over the garden wall to land on its back in the road.

It sounded as if someone had thrown away a used plastic bottle or an empty hamburger carton. Was the noise enough to bring his grandmother to her window? He wasn't sure if he would prefer not to be alone to see the grinning object flounder and begin to edge towards the house. As it twitched several inches he regretted ever having tipped an insect over to watch it struggle on its back. Then another squall of wind took possession of the dim figure, sweeping it leftwards out of sight along the middle of the road. David heard a car speed across an intersection, its progress hardly interrupted by a hollow thump and a crunch that made him think of a beetle crushed underfoot.

Once the engine dwindled into silence, nothing moved on the roads except the wind. David let the curtains fall together and slipped under the quilt. The drama had ended, even if some of its lighting effects were still operating outside the window. He didn't dream, and wakened late, remembering at once that there was nothing on the roof to worry his grandmother. Only how would she react to the absence?

He stole to the bathroom and then retreated to his bedroom. The muffled conversations downstairs felt like a pretence that all was well until his grandmother called "What are you doing up there?"

She meant David. He knew that when she warned him that his breakfast would go cold. She sounded untroubled, but for how long? "Eat up all the lovely food your mother's made," she cried, and he complied for fear of letting her suspect he was nervous, even when his stomach threatened to throw his efforts back at him. As he downed the last mouthful she said "I do believe that's the biggest breakfast I've ever had in my life. I think we all need a walk."

David swallowed too soon in order to blurt "I've got to wash up."

"What a good boy he is to his poor old granny. Don't worry, we'll wait for you. We won't run away and leave you," she said and stared at her husband for sighing.

David took all the time he could over each plate and utensil. He was considering feigning illness if that would keep his grandmother inside the house when he saw the door at the end of the back garden start to shake as if someone was fumbling at it. The grass shivered too, and he would have except for seeing why it did. "It'll be too windy to go for a walk," he told his grandmother. "It's like grandad said, you'll catch cold."

His mouth stayed open as he realised his mistake, but that wasn't the connection she made. "How windy is it?" she said, standing up with a groan to tramp along the hall. "What's it going to do to that empty old thing?"

David couldn't look away from the quivering expanse of grass while he heard her open the front door and step onto the path. His shoulders rose as if he fancied they could block his ears, but even sticking his fingers in mightn't have deafened him to her cry. "He's got down. Where's he hidden himself?"

David turned to find his mother rubbing her forehead as though to erase her thoughts. His grandfather had lifted his hands towards his wife, but they drooped beneath an invisible weight. David's grandmother was pivoting around and around on the path, and David was reminded of ballet classes until he saw her dismayed face. He felt that all the adults were performing, as adults so often seemed compelled to do, and that he ought to stop them if he could. "It fell down," he called. "It blew away."

His grandmother pirouetted to a clumsy halt and peered along the hall at him. "Why didn't you say? What are you trying to do?"

"Don't stand out there, Dora," his grandfather protested. "You can see he only wants—"

"Never mind what Davy wants. It can be what I want for a change. It's meant to be my Christmas too. Where is he, Davy? Show me if you think you know so much."

Her voice was growing louder and more petulant. David felt as if he'd been given the job of rescuing his mother and his grandfather from further embarrassment or argument. He dodged past them and the stranded sleigh to run to the end of the path. "It went along there," he said, pointing. "A car ran it over."

"You didn't say that before. Are you just saying so I won't be frightened?"

Until that moment he hadn't grasped how much she was. He strained his gaze at the intersection, but it looked as deserted as the rest of the street. "Show me where," she urged.

Might there be some trace? David was beginning to wish he hadn't spoken. He couldn't use her pace as an excuse for delay; she was waddling so fast to the intersection that her entire body wobbled. He ran into the middle of the crossroads, but there was no sign of last night's accident. He was even more disconcerted to realise that she was so frightened she hadn't even warned him to be careful on the road. He straightened up and swung around to look for fragments, and saw the remains heaped at the foot of a garden wall.

Someone must have tidied them into the side road. Most of the body was a shattered pile of red and white, but the head and half the left shoulder formed a single item propped on top. David was about to point around the corner when the object shifted. Still grinning, it toppled sideways as if the vanished neck had snapped. The wind was moving it, he told himself, but he wasn't sure that his grandmother ought to see. Before he could think how to prevent her, she followed his gaze. "It is him," she cried. "Someone else mustn't have liked him."

David was reaching to grab her hand and lead her away when the head shifted again. It tilted awry with a slowness that made its grin appear increasingly mocking, and slithered off the rest of the debris to inch along the pavement, scraping like a skull. "He's coming for me," David's grandmother babbled. "There's something inside him. It's the worm."

David's mother was hurrying along the street ahead of his grandfather. Before they could join his grandmother, the grinning object skittered at her. She recoiled a step, and then she lurched to trample her tormentor to bits. "That'll stop you laughing," she cried as the eyes shattered. "It's all right now, Davy. He's gone."

Was the pretence of acting on his behalf aimed at him or at the others? They seemed to accept it when at last she finished stamping and let them usher her back to the house, unless they were pretending as well. Though the adults had reverted to behaving as they were supposed to, it was too sudden. It felt like a performance they were staging to reassure him.

He must be expected to take part. He had to, or he wouldn't be a man. He pretended not to want to go home, and did his best to simulate enjoyment of the television programmes and the games that the others were anxious his grandmother should like. He feigned an appetite when the remnants of Christmas dinner were revived, accompanied by vegetables that his mother succeeded in rescuing from his grandmother's ambitions for them.

While the day had felt far too protracted, he would have preferred it to take more time over growing dark. The wind had dropped, but not so much that he didn't have to struggle to ignore how his grandmother's eyes fluttered whenever a window shook. He made for bed as soon as he thought he wouldn't be drawing attention to his earliness. "That's right, Davy, we all need our sleep," his grandmother said as if he might be denying them theirs. He suffered another round of happy Christmases and hugs that felt more strenuous than last night's, and then he fled to his room.

The night was still except for the occasional car that slowed outside the house—not, David had to remember, because there was anything on the roof. When he switched off the light the room took on a surreptitious flicker, as if his surroundings were nervous. Surely he had no reason to be, although he could have imagined that the irritable buzz was adding an edge to the voices downstairs. He hid under the quilt and pretended he was about to sleep until the sham overtook him.

A change in the lighting roused him. He was pushing the quilt away from his face so as to greet the day that would take him home when he noticed that the illumination was too fitful to be sunlight. As it glared under the curtains again he heard uncoordinated movement through the window. The wind must have returned to play with the lit sign. He was hoping that it wouldn't awaken his grandmother, or that she would at least know what was really there, when he realised with a shock that paralysed his breath how wrong he was. He hadn't heard the wind. The clumsy noises outside were more solid and more localised. Light stained the wall above his bed, and an object blundered as if it was limbless against the front door.

If this hadn't robbed David of the ability to move, the thought of his grandmother's reaction would have. It was even worse than the prospect of looking himself. He hadn't succeeded in breathing when he heard her say "Who's that? Has he come back?"

David would have blocked his ears if he had been capable of lifting his fists from beside him. He must have breathed, but he was otherwise helpless. The pause in the next room was almost as ominous as the sounds that brought it to an end: the rumble of the window, another series of light but impatient thumps at the front door, his grandmother's loose unsteady voice. "He's here for me. He's all lit up, his eyes are. The worm's put him back together. I should have squashed the worm."

"Stop wandering for God's sake," said David's grandfather. "I can't take much more of this, I'm telling you."

"Look how he's been put back together," she said with such a mixture of dismay and pleading that David was terrified it would compel him to obey. Instead his panic wakened him.

He was lying inert, his thoughts as tangled as the quilt, when he heard his grandmother insist "He was there."

"Just get back in bed," his grandfather told her.

David didn't know how long he lay waiting for her to shut the window. After that there seemed to be nothing to hear once her bed acknowledged her with an outburst of creaking. He stayed uneasily alert until he managed to think of a way to make sense of events: he'd overheard her in his sleep and had dreamed the rest. Having resolved this let him feel manly enough to regain his slumber.

This time daylight found him. It seemed to render the night irrelevant, at least to him. He wasn't sure about his grandmother, who looked uncertain of something. She insisted on cooking breakfast, rather more than aided by her husband. Once David and his mother had done their duty by their portions it was time to call a taxi. David manhandled the suitcase downstairs by himself and wheeled it to the car, past the decorations that appeared dusty with sunlight. His grandparents hugged him at the gate, and his grandmother repeated the gesture as if she'd already forgotten it. "Come and see us again soon," she said without too much conviction, perhaps because she was distracted by glancing along the street and at the roof.

David thought he saw his chance to demonstrate how much of a man he was. "It wasn't there, granny. It was just a dream."

Her face quivered, and her eyes. "What was, Davy? What are you talking about?"

He had a sudden awful sense of having miscalculated, but all he could do was answer. "There wasn't anything out here last night."

Her mouth was too nervous to keep hold of a smile that might have been triumphant. "You heard him as well."

"No," David protested, but his mother grabbed his arm. "That's enough," she said in a tone he'd never heard her use before. "We'll miss the train. Look after each other," she blurted at her parents, and shoved David into the taxi. All the way through the streets full of lifeless decorations, and for some time on the train, she had no more to say to him than "Just leave me alone for a while."

He thought she blamed him for frightening his grandmother. He remembered that two months later, when his grandmother died. At the funeral he imagined how heavy the box with her inside it must be on the shoulders of the four gloomy men. He succeeded in withholding his guilty tears, since his grandfather left crying to David's mother. When David tried to sprinkle earth on the coffin in the hole, a fierce wind carried off his handful as if his grandmother had blown it away with an angry breath. Eventually all the cars paraded back to the house that was only his grandfather's now, where a crowd of people David hadn't met before ate the sandwiches his mother had made and kept telling him how grown-up he was. He felt required to pretend, and wished his mother hadn't taken two days off from working at the nursery so that they could stay overnight. Once the guests left he felt more isolated still. His grandfather broke one of many silences by saying "You look as if you'd like to ask a question, Davy. Don't be shy."

David wasn't sure he wanted to be heard, but he had to be polite and answer. "What happened to granny?"

"People change when they get old, son. You'll find that out, well, you have. She was still your grandmother really."

Too much of this was more ominous than reassuring. David was loath to ask how she'd died, and almost to say "I meant where's she gone."

"I can't tell you that, son. All of us are going to have to wait and see."

Perhaps David's mother sensed this was the opposite of comforting, for she said "I think it's like turning into a butterfly, David. Our body's just the chrysalis we leave behind."

He had to affect to be happy with that, despite the memory it threatened to revive, because he was afraid he might otherwise hear worse. He apparently convinced his mother, who turned to his grandfather. "I wish I'd seen mummy one last time."

"She looked like a doll."

"No, while she was alive."

"I don't think you'd have liked it, Jane. Try and remember her how she used to be and I will. You will, won't you, Davy?"

David didn't want to imagine the consequences of giving or even thinking the wrong answer. "I'll try," he said.

This appeared to be less than was expected of him. He was desperate to change the subject, but all he could think of was how bare the house seemed without its Christmas finery. Rather than say so he enquired "Where do all the decorations go?"

"They've gone as well, son. They were always Dora's."

David was beginning to feel that nothing was safe to ask or say. He could tell that the adults wanted him to leave them alone to talk. At least they oughtn't to be arguing, not like his parents used to as soon as he was out of the way, making him think that the low hostile remarks he could never quite hear were blaming him for the trouble with the marriage. At least he wouldn't be distracted by the buzzing and the insistent light while he tried to sleep or hear. The wind helped blur the voices below him, so that although he gathered that they were agreeing, he only suspected they were discussing him. Were they saying how he'd scared his grandmother to death? "I'm sorry," he kept whispering like a prayer, which belatedly lulled him to sleep.

A siren wakened him—an ambulance. The pair of notes might have been crying "Davy" through the streets. He wondered if an ambulance had carried off his grandmother. The braying faded into the distance, leaving silence except for the wind. His mother and his grandfather must be in their beds, unless they had decided David was sufficiently grown-up to be left by himself in the house. He hoped not, because the wind sounded like a loose voice repeating his name. The noises on the stairs might be doing so as well, except that they were shuffling footsteps or, as he was able to make out before long, rather less than footsteps. Another sound was approaching. It was indeed a version of his name, pronounced by an exhalation that was just about a voice, by no means entirely like his grandmother's but too much so. It and the slow determined unformed paces halted outside his room.

He couldn't cry out for his mother, not because he wouldn't be a man but for fear of drawing attention to himself. He was offstage, he tried to think. He only had to listen, he needn't see more than the lurid light that flared across the carpet. Then his visitor set about opening the door.

It made a good deal of locating the doorknob, and attempting to take hold of it, and fumbling to turn it, so that David had far more time than he wanted to imagine what was there. If his grandmother had gone away, had whatever remained come to find him? Was something of her still inside her to move it, or was that a worm? The door shuddered and edged open, admitting a grotesquely festive glow, and David tried to shut his eyes. But he was even more afraid not to see the shape that floundered into the room.

He saw at once that she'd become what she was afraid of. She was draped with a necklace of fairy lights, and two guttering bulbs had taken the place of her eyes. Dim green light spilled like slimy water down her cheeks. She wore a long white dress, if the vague pale mass wasn't part of her, for her face looked inflated to hollowness, close to bursting. Perhaps that was why her mouth was stretched so wide, but her grin was terrified. He had a sudden dreadful thought that both she and the worm were inside the shape.

It blundered forward and then fell against the door. Either it had very little control of its movements or it intended to trap him in the room. It lurched at him as if it was as helpless as he was, and David sprawled out of bed. He grabbed one of his shoes from the floor and hurled it at the swollen flickering mass. It was only a doll, he thought, because the grin didn't falter. Perhaps it was less than a doll, since it vanished like a bubble. As his shoe struck the door the room went dark.

He might almost have believed that nothing had been there if he hadn't heard more than his shoe drop to the floor. When he tore the curtains open he saw fairy lights strewn across the carpet. They weren't what he was certain he'd heard slithering into some part of the room. All the same, once he'd put on his shoes he trampled the bulbs into fragments, and then he fell to his hands and knees. He was still crawling about the floor when his mother hurried in and peered unhappily at him. "Help me find it," he pleaded. "We've got to kill the worm."

# With the Angels

As Cynthia drove between the massive mossy posts where the gates used to be, Karen said "Were you little when you lived here, Auntie Jackie?"

"Not as little as I was," Cynthia said.

"That's right," Jacqueline said while the poplars alongside the high walls darkened the car, "I'm even older than your grandmother."

Karen and Valerie giggled and then looked for other amusement. "What's this house called, Brian?" Valerie enquired.

"The Populars," the four-year-old declared and set about punching his sisters almost before they began to laugh.

"Now, you three," Cynthia intervened. "You said you'd show Jackie how good you can be."

No doubt she meant her sister to feel more included. "Can't we play?" said Brian as if Jacqueline were a disapproving bystander.

"I expect you may," Jacqueline said, having glanced at Cynthia. "Just don't get yourselves dirty or do any damage or go anywhere you shouldn't or that's dangerous."

Brian and the eight-year-old twins barely waited for Cynthia to haul two-handed at the brake before they piled out of the Volvo and chased across the forecourt into the weedy garden. "Do try and let them be children," Cynthia murmured.

"I wasn't aware I could change them." Jacqueline managed not to groan while she unbent her stiff limbs and clambered out of the car. "I shouldn't think they would take much notice of me," she said, supporting herself on the hot roof as she turned to the house.

Despite the August sunlight, it seemed darker than its neighbours, not just because of the shadows of the trees, which still put her in mind of a graveyard. More than a century's worth of winds across the moors outside the Yorkshire town had plastered the large house with grime. The windows on the topmost floor were half the size of those on the other two storeys, one reason why she'd striven in her childhood not to think they resembled the eyes of a spider, any more than the porch between the downstairs rooms looked like a voracious vertical mouth. She was far from a child now, and she strode or at any rate limped to the porch, only to have to wait for her sister to bring the keys. As Cynthia thrust one into the first rusty lock the twins scampered over, pursued by their brother. "Throw me up again," he cried.

"Where did he get that from?"

"From being a child, I should think," Cynthia said. "Don't you remember what it was like?"

Jacqueline did, not least because of Brian's demand. She found some breath as she watched the girls take their brother by the arms and swing him into the air. "Again," he cried.

"We're tired now," Karen told him. "We want to see in the house."

"Maybe grandma and auntie will give you a throw if you're good," Valerie said.

"Not just now," Jacqueline said at once.

Cynthia raised her eyebrows high enough to turn her eyes blank as she twisted the second key. The door lumbered inwards a few inches and then baulked. She was trying to nudge the obstruction aside with the door when Brian made for the gap. "Don't," Jacqueline blurted, catching him by the shoulder.

"Good heavens, Jackie, what's the matter now?"

"We don't want the children in there until we know what state it's in, do we?"

"Just see if you can squeeze past and shift whatever's there, Brian."

Jacqueline felt unworthy of consideration. She could only watch the boy wriggle around the edge of the door and vanish into the gloom. She heard fumbling and rustling, but of course this didn't mean some desiccated presence was at large in the vestibule. Why didn't Brian speak? She was about to prompt him until he called "It's just some old letters and papers."

When he reappeared with several free newspapers that looked as dusty as their news, Cynthia eased the door past him. A handful of brown envelopes contained electricity bills that grew redder as they came up to date, which made Jacqueline wonder "Won't the lights work?"

"I expect so if we really need them." Cynthia advanced into the wide hall beyond the vestibule and poked at the nearest switch. Grit ground inside the mechanism, but the bulbs in the hall chandelier stayed as dull as the mass of crystal teardrops. "Never mind," Cynthia said, having tested every switch in the column on the wall without result. "As I say, we won't need them."

The grimy skylight above the stairwell illuminated the hall enough to show that the dark wallpaper was even hairier than Jacqueline remembered. It had always made her think of the fur of a great spider, and now it was blotchy with damp. The children were already running up the left-hand staircase and across the first-floor landing, under which the chandelier dangled like a spider on a thread. "Don't go out of sight," Cynthia told them, "until we see what's what."

"Chase me." Brian ran down the other stairs, one of which rattled like a lid beneath the heavy carpet. "Chase," he cried and dashed across the hall to race upstairs again.

"Don't keep running up and down unless you want to make me ill," Jacqueline's grandmother would have said. The incessant rumble of footsteps might have presaged a storm on the way to turning the hall even gloomier, so that Jacqueline strode as steadily as she could towards the nearest room. She had to pass one of the hall mirrors, which appeared to show a dark blotch hovering in wait for the children. The shapeless sagging darkness at the top of the grimy oval was a stain, and she needn't have waited to see the children run downstairs out of its reach. "Do you want the mirror?" Cynthia said. "I expect it would clean up."

"I don't know what I want from this house," Jacqueline said.

She mustn't say she would prefer the children not to be in it. She couldn't even suggest sending them outside in case the garden concealed dangers—broken glass, rusty metal, holes in the ground. The children were staying with Cynthia while her son and his partner holidayed in Morocco, but couldn't she have chosen a better time to go through the house before it was put up for sale? She frowned at Jacqueline and then followed her into the dining-room.

Although the heavy curtains were tied back from the large windows, the room wasn't much brighter than the hall. It was steeped in the shadows of the poplars, and the tall panes were spotted with earth. A spider's nest of a chandelier loomed above the long table set for an elaborate dinner for six. That had been Cynthia's idea when they'd moved their parents to the rest home; she'd meant to convince any thieves that the house was still occupied, but to Jacqueline it felt like preserving a past that she'd hoped to outgrow. She remembered being made to sit up stiffly at the table, to hold her utensils just so, to cover her lap nicely with her napkin, not to speak or to make the slightest noise with any of her food. Too much of this upbringing had lodged inside her, but was that why she felt uneasy with the children in the house? "Are you taking anything out of here?" Cynthia said.

"There's nothing here for me, Cynthia. You have whatever you want and don't worry about me."

Cynthia gazed at her as they headed for the breakfast room. The chandelier stirred as the children ran above it once again, but Jacqueline told herself that was nothing like her nightmares—at least, not very like. She was unnerved to hear Cynthia exclaim "There it is."

The breakfast room was borrowing light from the large back

garden, but not much, since the overgrown expanse lay in the shadow of the house. The weighty table had spread its wings and was attended by six straight-backed ponderous chairs, but Cynthia was holding out her hands to the high chair in the darkest corner of the room. "Do you remember sitting in that?" she apparently hoped. "I think I do."

"I wouldn't," Jacqueline said.

She hadn't needed it to make her feel restricted at the table, where breakfast with her grandparents had been as formal as dinner. "Nothing here either," she declared and limped into the hall.

The mirror on the far side was discoloured too. She glimpsed the children's blurred shapes streaming up into a pendulous darkness and heard the agitated jangle of the chandelier as she made for the lounge. The leather suite looked immovable with age, and only the television went some way towards bringing the room up to date, though the screen was as blank as an uninscribed stone. She remembered having to sit silent for hours while her parents and grandparents listened to the radio for news about the war—her grandmother hadn't liked children out of her sight in the house. The dresser was still full of china she'd been forbidden to venture near, which was grey with dust and the dimness. Cynthia had been allowed to crawl around the room—indulged for being younger or because their grandmother liked babies in the house. "I'll leave you to it," she said as Cynthia followed her in.

She was hoping to find more light in the kitchen, but it didn't show her much that she wanted to see. While the refrigerator was relatively modern, not to mention tall enough for somebody to stand in, it felt out of place. The black iron range still occupied most of one wall, and the old stained marble sink projected from another. Massive cabinets and heavy chests of drawers helped box in the hulking table scored by knives. It used to remind her of an operating table, even though she hadn't known she would grow up to be a nurse. She was distracted by the children as they ran into the kitchen. "Can we have a drink?" Karen said for all of them.

"May we?" Valerie amended.

"Please." Once she'd been echoed Jacqueline said "I'll find you some glasses. Let the tap run."

When she opened a cupboard she thought for a moment that the stack of plates was covered by a greyish doily. Several objects as long as a baby's fingers but thinner even than their bones flinched out of sight, and she saw the plates were draped with a mass of cobwebs. She slammed the door as Karen used both hands to twist the cold tap. It uttered a dry gurgle rather too reminiscent of sounds she used to hear while working in the geriatric ward, and she wondered if the supply had been turned off. Then a gout of dark liquid spattered the sink, and a gush of rusty water darkened the marble. As Karen struggled to shut it off Valerie enquired "Did you have to drink that, auntie?"

"I had to put up with a lot you wouldn't be expected to."

"We won't, then. Aren't there any other drinks?"

"And things to eat," Brian said at once.

"I'm sure there's nothing." When the children gazed at her with various degrees of patience Jacqueline opened the refrigerator, trying not to think that the compartments could harbour bodies smaller than Brian's. All she found were a bottle of mouldering milk and half a loaf as hard as a rusk. "I'm afraid you'll have to do without," she said.

How often had her grandmother said that? Supposedly she'd been just as parsimonious before the war. Jacqueline didn't want to sound like her, but when Brian took hold of the handle of a drawer that was level with his head she couldn't help blurting "Stay away from there."

At least she didn't add "We've lost enough children." As the boy stepped back Cynthia hurried into the kitchen. "What are you doing now?"

"We don't want them playing with knives, do we?" Jacqueline said.

"I know you're too sensible, Brian."

Was that aimed just at him? As Cynthia opened the cupboards the children resumed chasing up the stairs. Presumably the creature Jacqueline had glimpsed was staying out of sight, and so were any more like it. When Cynthia made for the hall Jacqueline said "I'll be up in a minute."

Although she didn't linger in the kitchen, she couldn't leave her memories behind. How many children had her grandmother lost that she'd been so afraid of losing any more? By pestering her mother Jacqueline had learned they'd been stillborn, which had reminded her how often her grandmother told her to keep still. More than once today Jacqueline had refrained from saying that to the twins and to Brian in particular. Their clamour seemed to fill the hall and resonate all the way up the house, so that she could have thought the reverberations were shaking the mirrors, disturbing the suspended mass of darkness like a web in which a spider had come to life. "Can we go up to the top now?" Brian said.

"Please don't," Jacqueline called.

It took Cynthia's stare to establish that the boy hadn't been asking Jacqueline. "Why can't we?" Karen protested, and Valerie contributed "We only want to see."

"I'm sure you can," Cynthia said. "Just wait till we're all up there."

Before tramping into the nearest bedroom she gave her sister one more look, and Jacqueline felt as blameworthy as their grandmother used to make her feel. Why couldn't she watch over the children from the hall? She tilted her head back on her shaky neck to gaze up the stairwell. Sometimes her grandfather would raise his eyes ceilingwards as his wife found yet another reason to rebuke Jacqueline, only for the woman to say "If you look like that you'll see where you're going." Presumably she'd meant heaven, and perhaps she was there now, if there was such a place. Jacqueline imagined her sailing upwards like a husk on a wind; she'd already seemed withered all those years ago, and not just physically either. Was that why Jacqueline had thought the stillbirths must be shrivelled too? They would have ended up like that, but she needn't think about it now, if ever. She glanced towards the children and saw movement above them.

She must have seen the shadows of the treetops—thin shapes that appeared to start out of the corners under the roof before darting back into the gloom. As she tried to grasp how those shadows could reach so far beyond the confines of the skylight, Cynthia peered out of the nearest bedroom. "Jackie, aren't you coming to look?"

Jacqueline couldn't think for all the noise. "If you three will give us some peace for a while," she said louder than she liked. "And stay with us. We don't want you going anywhere that isn't safe."

"You heard your aunt," Cynthia said, sounding unnecessarily like a resentful child.

As Brian trudged after the twins to follow Cynthia into her grandmother's bedroom Jacqueline remembered never being let in there. Later her parents had made it their room—had tried, at any rate. While they'd doubled the size of the bed, the rest of the furniture was still her grandmother's, and she could have fancied that all the swarthy wood was helping the room glower at the intrusion. She couldn't imagine her parents sharing a bed there, let alone performing any activity in it, but she didn't want to think about such things at all. "Not for me," she said and made for the next room.

Not much had changed since it had been her grandfather's, which meant it still seemed to belong to his wife. It felt like her disapproval rendered solid by not just the narrow single bed but the rest of the dark furniture that duplicated hers, having been her choice. She'd disapproved of almost anything related to Jacqueline, not least her husband playing with their granddaughter. Jacqueline avoided glancing up at any restlessness under the roof while she crossed the landing to the other front bedroom. As she gazed at the two single beds that remained since the cot had been disposed of, the children ran to cluster around her in the doorway. "This was your room, wasn't it?" Valerie said.

"Yours and our grandma's," Karen amended.

"No," Jacqueline said, "it was hers and our mother's and father's."

In fact she hadn't been sent to the top floor until Cynthia was born. Their grandfather had told her she was going to stay with the angels, though his wife frowned at the idea. Jacqueline would have found it more appealing if she hadn't already been led to believe that all the stillbirths were living with the angels. She hardly knew why she was continuing to explore the house. Though the cast-iron bath had been replaced by a fibreglass tub as blue as the toilet and sink, she still remembered flinching from the chilly metal. After Cynthia's birth their grandmother had taken over bathing Jacqueline, scrubbing her with such relentless harshness that it had felt like a penance. When it was over at last, her grandfather would do his best to raise her spirits. "Now you're clean enough for the angels," he would say and throw her up in the air.

"If you're good the angels will catch you"—but of course he did, which had always made her wonder what would happen to her if she wasn't good enough. She'd seemed to glimpse that thought in her grandmother's eyes, or had it been a wish? What would have caught her if she'd failed to live up to requirements? As she tried to forget the conclusion she'd reached Brian said "Where did they put you, then?"

"They kept me right up at the top."

"Can we see?"

"Yes, let's," said Valerie, and Karen ran after him as well.

Jacqueline was opening her mouth to delay them when Cynthia said "You'll be going up there now, won't you? You can keep an eye on them."

It was a rebuke for not helping enough with the children, or for interfering too much, or perhaps for Jacqueline's growing nervousness. Anger at her childish fancies sent her stumping halfway up the topmost flight of stairs before she faltered. Clouds had gathered like a lifetime's worth of dust above the skylight, and perhaps that was why the top floor seemed to darken as she climbed towards it, so that all the corners were even harder to distinguish—she could almost have thought the mass of dimness was solidifying. "Where were you, auntie?" Karen said.

"In there," said Jacqueline and hurried to join them outside the nearest room.

It wasn't as vast as she remembered, though certainly large enough to daunt a small child. The ceiling stooped to the front wall, squashing the window, from which the shadows of the poplars seemed to creep up the gloomy incline to acquire more substance under the roof at the back of the room. The grimy window smudged the premature twilight, which had very little to illuminate, since the room was bare of furniture and even of a carpet. "Did you have to sleep on the floor?" Valerie said. "Were you very bad?"

"Of course not," Jacqueline declared. It felt as if her memories had been thrown out—as if she hadn't experienced them—but she knew better. She'd lain on the cramped bed hemmed in by dour furniture and cut off from everyone else in the house by the dark that occupied the stairs. She would have prayed if that mightn't have roused what she dreaded. If the babies were with the angels, mustn't that imply they weren't angels themselves? Being stillbirths needn't mean they would keep still—Jacqueline never could when she was told. Suppose they were what caught you if you weren't good? She'd felt as if she had been sent away from her family for bad behaviour. All too soon she'd heard noises that suggested tiny withered limbs were stirring, and glimpsed movements in the highest corners of the room.

She must have been hearing the poplars and seeing their shadows. As she turned away from the emptied bedroom she caught sight of the room opposite, which was full of items covered with dustsheets. Had she ever known what the sheets concealed? She'd imagined they hid some secret that children weren't supposed to learn, but they'd also reminded her of enormous masses of cobweb. She could have thought the denizens of the webs were liable to crawl out of the dimness, and she was absurdly relieved to see Cynthia coming upstairs. "I'll leave you to it," Jacqueline said. "I'll be waiting down below."

It wasn't only the top floor she wanted to leave behind. She'd remembered what she'd once done to her sister. The war had been over at last, and she'd been trusted to look after Cynthia while the adults planned the future. The sisters had only been allowed to play with their toys in the hall, where Jacqueline had done her best to distract the toddler from straying into any of the rooms they weren't supposed to enter by themselves—in fact, every room. At last she'd grown impatient with her sister's mischief, and in a wicked moment she'd wondered what would catch Cynthia if she tossed her high. As she'd thrown her sister into the air with all her strength she'd realised that she didn't want to know, certainly not at Cynthia's expense—as she'd seen dwarfish shrivelled figures darting out of every corner in the dark above the stairwell and scuttling down to seize their prize. They'd come head first, so that she'd seen their bald scalps wrinkled like walnuts before she glimpsed their hungry withered faces. Then Cynthia had fallen back into her arms, though Jacqueline had barely managed to keep hold of her. Squeezing her eyes shut, she'd hugged her sister until she'd felt able to risk seeing they were alone in the vault of the hall.

There was no use telling herself that she'd taken back her unforgivable wish. She might have injured the toddler even by catching her—she might have broken her frail neck. She ought to have known that, and perhaps she had. Being expected to behave badly had made her act that way, but she felt as if all the nightmares that were stored in the house had festered and gained strength over the years. When she reached the foot of the stairs at last she carried on out of the house.

The poplars stooped to greet her with a wordless murmur. A wind was rising under the sunless sky. It was gentle on her face—it seemed to promise tenderness she couldn't recall having experienced, certainly not once Cynthia was born. Perhaps it could soothe away her memories, and she was raising her face to it when Brian appeared in the porch. "What are you doing, auntie?"

"Just being by myself."

She thought that was pointed enough until he skipped out of the house. "Is it time now?"

Why couldn't Cynthia have kept him with her? No doubt she thought it was Jacqueline's turn. "Time for what?" Jacqueline couldn't avoid asking.

"You said you'd give me a throw."

She'd said she wouldn't then, not that she would sometime. Just the same, perhaps she could. It might be a way of leaving the house behind and all it represented to her. It would prove she deserved to be trusted with him, as she ought not to have been trusted with little Cynthia. "Come on then," she said.

As soon as she held out her arms he ran and leapt into them. "Careful," she gasped, laughing as she recovered her balance. "Are you ready?" she said and threw the small body into the air.

She was surprised how light he was, or how much strength she had at her disposal. He came down giggling, and she caught him. "Again," he cried.

"Just once more," Jacqueline said. She threw him higher this time, and he giggled louder. Cynthia often said that children kept you young, and Jacqueline thought it was true after all. Brian fell into her arms and she hugged him. "Again," he could hardly beg for giggling.

"Now what did I just say?" Nevertheless she threw him so high that her arms trembled with the effort, and the poplars nodded as if they were approving her accomplishment. She clutched at Brian as he came down with an impact that made her shoulders ache. "Higher," he pleaded almost incoherently. "Higher."

"This really is the last time, Brian." She crouched as if the stooping poplars had pushed her down. Tensing her whole body, she reared up to fling him into the pendulous gloom with all her strength.

For a moment she thought only the wind was reaching for him as it bowed the trees and dislodged objects from the foliage—leaves that rustled, twigs that scraped and rattled. But the thin shapes weren't falling, they were scurrying head first down the tree-trunks at a speed that seemed to leave time behind. Some of them had no shape they could have lived with, and some might never have had any skin. She saw their shrivelled eyes glimmer eagerly and their toothless mouths gape with an identical infantile hunger. Their combined weight bowed the lowest branches while they extended arms like withered sticks to snatch the child.

In that helpless instant Jacqueline was overwhelmed by a feeling she would never have admitted—a rush of childish glee, of utter irresponsibility. For a moment she was no longer a nurse, not even a retired one as old as some of her patients had been.

She shouldn't have put Brian at risk, but now he was beyond saving. Then he fell out of the dark beneath the poplars, in which there was no longer any sign of life, and she made a grab at him. The strength had left her arms, and he struck the hard earth with a thud that put her in mind of the fall of a lid.

"Brian?" she said and bent groaning to him. "Brian," she repeated, apparently loud enough to be audible all the way up the house. She heard her old window rumble open, and Cynthia's cry: "What have you done now?" She heard footsteps thunder down the stairs, and turned away from the small still body beneath the uninhabited trees as her sister dashed out of the porch. Jacqueline had just one thought, but surely it must make a difference. "Nothing caught him," she said.

# Just Behind You

I'VE HARDLY SLAMMED THE CAR DOOR WHEN MR HOLT trots out of the school. "Sorry we're late, head," I tell him.

"Don't send yourself to my office, Paul. It was solid of you to show up." He elevates his bristling eyebrows, which tug his mottled round face blank. "I'd have laid odds on you if I were a betting man."

"You don't mean no one else has come."

"None of your colleagues. You're their representative. Don't worry, I'll make sure it goes on your record somehow."

I want to keep this job, whatever memories the school revives, but now it looks as if I'm attending his son's party to ingratiate myself rather than simply assuming it was expected; the invitations were official enough. I'm emitting a diffident sound when Mr Holt clasps his pudgy hands behind his back. "And let me guess, this is your son," he says, lowering his face at Tom as if his joviality is weighing it down. "What's the young man's name?"

I'm afraid Tom may resent being patronised, but he struggles to contain a grin as he says "Tom."

"Tom Francis, hey? Good strong name. You could go to bat for

England with a name like that. The birthday boy's called Jack. I expect you're eager to meet him."

Tom hugs the wrapped computer game as if he's coveting it all over again, and I give him a frown that's both a warning and a reminder that his mother promised we'd buy him one for Christmas. "I don't mind," he says.

"Not done to show too much enthusiasm these days, is it, Paul? Cut along there, Tom, and the older men will catch you up."

As Tom marches alongside the elongated two-storey red brick building as if he's determined to leave more of his loathed chubbiness behind, Mr Holt says "I think we can say it's a success. A couple of the parents are already talking about hiring the school for their parties. Do let me know if you have any wheezes for swelling the funds."

I'm distracted by the notion that a boy is pacing Tom inside the ground-floor classrooms. It's his reflection, of course, and now I can't even see it in the empty sunlit rooms. "It was tried once before," I'm confused enough to remark. "Hiring the place out."

"Before my time," the headmaster says so sharply he might be impressing it on someone who doesn't know. "There was a tragedy, I gather. Was it while you were a pupil here?"

Although I'm sure he doesn't mean to sound accusing, he makes me feel accused. I might almost not have left the school and grown up, and the prospect ahead doesn't help—the schoolyard occupied by people I've never seen before. The adults and most of the boys have taken plastic cups from a trestle table next to one laden with unwrapped presents. "I'm afraid I was," I say, which immediately strikes me as an absurd turn of phrase.

"Can we start now, dad?" the fattest boy shouts. "Who else are we supposed to be waiting for?"

"I think you've just got one new friend, Jack."

I hope it's only being told it that makes him scowl at Tom. "Who are you? Did you have to come?"

"I'm sure he wanted to," Mr Holt says, though I think he may have missed the point of the question, unless he's pretending. "This is Paul Francis and his son Tom, everyone. Paul is proving to be the loyallest of my staff."

Some of the adults stand their cups on the table to applaud while others raise a polite cheer. "Is that my present?" Jack Holt is asking Tom. "What have you got me?"

"I hope you like it," Tom says and yields it up. "I would."

Jack tears off the wrapping and drops it on the concrete. A woman who has been dispensing drinks utters an affectionate tut as she swoops to retrieve it and consign it to the nearest bin. "Thank you, dear," Mr Holt says, presumably identifying her as his wife. "Even if it's your birthday, Jack—"

"I'll see if it's any good later," Jack tells Tom, and as Tom's face owns up to hoping he can have a turn, adds "When I get home."

"Do pour Paul some bubbly, dear. Not precisely champers, Paul, but I expect you can't tell on your salary."

As a driver I should ask for lemonade, but I don't think I'll be able to bear much more of the afternoon without a stronger drink or several. As Mrs Holt giggles at the foam that swells out of my cup, her husband claps his hands. "Well, boys, I think it's time for games."

"I want to eat first." With a slyness I'm surely not alone in noticing Jack says "You wouldn't like all the food mother made to go stale."

I take rather too large a gulp from my cup. His behaviour reminds me of Jasper, and I don't care to remember just now, especially while Tom is on the premises. I look around for distraction, and fancy that I glimpsed someone ducking out of sight behind the schoolyard wall closest to the building. I can do without such notions, and so I watch Mrs Holt uncover the third table. The flourish with which she whips off its paper shroud to reveal plates of sandwiches and sausage rolls and a cake armed with eleven candles falters, however, and a corner of the paper scrapes the concrete. "Dear me," she comments. "Don't say this was you, Jack."

"It wasn't me," Jack protests before he even looks.

Someone has taken a bite out of a sandwich from each platter and sampled the sausage rolls as well, though the cake has survived the raid. Jack stares at Tom as if he wants to blame him, but must realise Tom had no opportunity. "Who's been messing with my food?" he demands at a pitch that hurts my ears.

"Now, Jack, don't spoil your party," his mother says. "Someone must have sneaked in when we all went to welcome your guests."

"I don't want it any more. I don't like the look of it."

"We'll just put the food that's been nibbled out for the birds, shall we? Then it won't be wasted, and I'm certain the rest will be fine."

I do my best to share her conviction for Tom's sake, although the bite marks in the food she lays on top of the wall closest to the sports field look unpleasantly discoloured. Jack seems determined to maintain his aversion until the other boys start loading their paper plates, and then he elbows Tom aside and grabs handfuls to heap his own plate. I tell myself that Tom will have to survive worse in his life as I promise mentally to make up to him for the afternoon. If I'd come alone I wouldn't be suffering quite so much.

I let Mrs Holt refill my cup as an aid to conversing with the adult guests. I've already spoken to a magistrate and a local councillor and an accountant and a journalist. Their talk is so small it's close to infinitesimal, except when it's pointedly personal. Once they've established that this is my first job at a secondary school, and how many years I attended night classes to upgrade my qualifications, and that my wife doesn't teach since she was attacked by a pupil, except I'd call her nursery work teaching, they seem to want me and Tom to feel accepted. "He certainly knows how to enjoy himself," says the magistrate, and the councillor declares "He's a credit to his parents." The accountant contributes "He's a generous chap," and it's only when the journalist responds "Makes everybody welcome even if he doesn't know them" that I realise they're discussing not my son but Jack. The relentlessly sparkling wine helps me also understand they're blind to anything here that they don't want to see. I refrain from saying so for Tom's sake and quite possibly my job's. I do my best not to be unbearably aware of Tom's attempts to stay polite while Jack boasts how superior his private school is to this one. When Jack asks Tom if his parents can't afford to send him to a better school than he's admitted to attending, my retort feels capable of heading off Tom's. It's Mrs Holt who interrupts, however. "If everyone has had sufficient, let's bring on the cake."

If she meant to cater for the adults, Jack has seen off their portions, either gobbling them or mauling them on his plate. He dumps it on the pillaged table as his mother elevates the cake and his father touches a lighter to the candles. Once all the pale flames are standing up to the July sun, Mr Holt sets about "Happy birthday to you" as if it's one of the hymns we no longer sing in school. Everybody joins in, with varying degrees of conviction; one boy is so out of tune that he might be poking fun at the song. At least it isn't Tom; his mouth is wide open, whereas the voice sounds muffled, almost hidden. The song ends more or less in unison before I can locate the mocking singer, and Jack plods to blow out the candles. As he takes a loud moist breath they flutter and expire. "Sorry," says his father and relights them.

Jack performs another inhalation as a prelude to lurching at the cake so furiously that for an instant I think his movement has blown out the candles. "Who's doing that?" he shouts.

He glares behind him at the schoolyard wall and then at his young guests. His gaze lingers on Tom, who responds "Looks like someone doesn't want you to have a birthday."

Jack's stare hardens further. "Well, they'd better play their tricks on someone else or my dad'll make them wish they had."

"I'm sure it's just these candles," Mrs Holt says with a reproachful blink at her husband and holds out the cake for him to apply the lighter. "Have another try, Jack. Big puff."

The boy looks enraged by her choice of words. He ducks to the candles the moment they're lit and extinguishes them, spraying the cake with saliva. I won't pretend I'm disappointed that the adults aren't offered a slice. I can tell that Tom accepts one out of politeness, because he dabs the icing surreptitiously with a paper napkin. Mrs Holt watches so closely to see all the cake is consumed that it's clear she would take anything less as an insult to her or her son. "That's the idea. Build up your vim," she says and blinks across the yard. "Those birds must have been quick. I didn't see them come or go, did you?"

Mr Holt hardly bothers to shake his head at the deserted field. "All right, boys, no arguments this time. Let's work off some of that energy."

I suspect that's a euphemism for reducing Jack's weight, unless Mr Holt and his wife are determined to be unaware of it. I'm wondering what I may have let Tom in for when Mr Holt says "Who's for a race around the field?"

"I don't mind," says Tom.

"Go on then. We'll watch," Jack says, and the rest of the boys laugh.

"How about a tug of war?" the magistrate suggests as if she's commuting a sentence.

"I don't think that would be fair, would it?" the councillor says. "There'd be too many on one side."

Jack's entourage all stare at Tom until the accountant says "How do you come up with that? Twelve altogether, that was twice six when I went to school."

"I mustn't have counted the last chap. I hope it won't lose me your vote," the councillor says to me and perhaps more facetiously to Tom, and blames her drink with a comical grimace.

"I don't care. It's supposed to be my party for me. It's like she said, if we have games it isn't fair unless I win," Jack complains, and I can't avoid remembering any longer. Far too much about him reminds me of Jasper.

I didn't want to go to Jasper's party either. I only accepted the invitation because he made me feel I was the nearest to a friend he had at his new school. I mustn't have been alone in taking pity on him, because all his guests turned out to be our classmates; there was nobody from his old school. His mother had remarried, and his stepfather had insisted on moving him to a state school, where he could mix with ordinary boys like us. I expected him to behave himself in front of his family, but whenever he saw the opportunity he acted even worse than usual, accusing the timidest boy of taking more than his share of the party food, and well-nigh wailing when someone else was offered whichever slices of the cake Jasper had decided were his, and arguing with his parents over who'd won the various games they organised unless he was the winner, and refusing to accept that he hadn't caught us moving whenever he swung around while we were trying to creep up on him unnoticed. Now I remember we played that game among ourselves when the adults went to search for him. As if I've communicated my thoughts Tom says "How about hide and seek?"

I could almost imagine that someone has whispered the suggestion in his ear. He looks less than certain of his inspiration even before Jack mimics him. "How about it?"

"Give it a try," Mrs Holt urges. "It'll be fun. I'm sure Mr Francis must have played it when he was your age. I know I did."

Why did she single me out? It brings memories closer and a grumble from Jack. As his allies echo him, his father intervenes. "Come on, chaps, give your new friend a chance. He's made an effort on your behalf."

I wonder whether Mr Holt has any sense of how much. Perhaps Jack takes the comment as an insult; he seems still more resentful. I can't help hoping he's about to say something to Tom that will provide us with an excuse to leave. Despite his scowl he says only "You've got to be It, then."

"You see, you did know how to play," his mother informs him.

This aggravates his scowl, but it stays trained on Tom. "Go over by the wall," he orders, "and count to a hundred so we can hear you. Like this. One. And. Two. And. Three, and don't dare look."

Tom stands where he's directed—overlooking the sports field—and rests his closed eyes on his folded arms on top of the bare wall. As soon as Tom begins to count, Jack waddles unexpectedly fast and with a stealth I suspect is only too typical of him out of the yard, beckoning his cronies to follow. There must be a breeze across the field; Tom's hair is standing up, and he seems restless, though I can't feel the wind or see evidence of it elsewhere. I'm distracted by Mr Holt's shout. "Boys, don't go—"

Either it's too late or it fails to reach them, unless they're pretending not to hear. All of them vanish into the school. Mrs Holt puts a finger to her lips and nods at Tom, who's counting in a loud yet muffled voice that sounds as if somebody is muttering in unison with him—it must be rebounding from the wall. I take Mrs Holt not to want the game to be spoiled. "They won't come to any harm in there, will they?" she murmurs.

Jasper didn't, I'm forced to recall: he was on the roof until he fell off. Mr Holt tilts his head as though his raised eyebrow has altered the balance. "I'm sure they know not to get into any mischief."

Tom shouts a triumphant hundred as he straightens up. He seems glad to retreat from the wall. Without glancing at anyone, even at me, he runs out of the yard. Either he overheard the Holts or his ears are sharper than mine, since he heads directly for the school. Someone peers out to watch his approach and dodges back in. I don't hear the door then, nor as Tom disappears into the school. It's as if the building has joined in the general stealth.

I remember the silence that met all the shouts of Jasper's name. For years I would wonder why he was so determined not to be found: because he didn't want to be It, or on the basis that we couldn't play any games without him? In that case he was wrong about us. As the calls shrank into and around the school, we played at creeping up on one another while he wasn't there to ruin it for us. It was my turn to catch the others out when I heard his mother cry "Jasper" in the distance—nothing else, not so much as a thud. The desperation in her voice made me turn to see what my friends made of it. Could I really have expected to find Jasper at my back, grinning at the trick he'd worked on us and on his parents, or was that only a dream that troubled my sleep for weeks?

He must have resolved not to be discovered even by his parents; perhaps he didn't want them to know he'd been on the roof. I assume he tried to scramble out of sight. We didn't abandon our game until we heard the ambulance, and by the time we reached the front of the school, Jasper was covered up on a stretcher and his parents were doing their best to suppress their emotions until they were behind closed doors. As the ambulance pulled away it emitted a wail that I didn't immediately realise belonged to Jasper's mother. The headmaster had emerged from his office, where no doubt he'd hoped to be only nominally in charge of events, and put us to work at clearing away the debris of the party and storing Jasper's presents in his office; we never knew what became of them. Then he sent us home without quite accusing us of anything, and on Monday told the school how it had lost a valued pupil and warned everyone against playing dangerous games. I couldn't help taking that as at least a hint of an accusation. If we hadn't carried on with our game, might we have spotted Jasper on the roof or caught him as he fell?

It seems unlikely, and I don't want to brood about it now. I attempt to occupy my mind by helping Mrs Holt clear up. This time she doesn't leave any food on the wall for whatever stole away with it, but drops the remains in the bin. From thanking me she graduates to saying "You're so kind" and "He's a treasure," none of which helps me stay alert. It's the magistrate who enquires "What do we think they're up to?"

"Who?"

She answers Mr Holt's tone with an equally sharp glance before saying "Shouldn't some of them have tried to get back to base by now?"

At once I'm sure that Jack has organised his friends in some way against Tom. I'm trying to decide if I should investigate when Mr Holt says "They should be in the fresh air where it's healthier. Come with me, Paul, and we'll flush them out."

"Shall we tag along?" says the journalist.

"Two members of staff should be adequate, thank you," Mr Holt tells her and trots to catch me up. We're halfway along the flagstoned path to the back entrance when he says "You go this way and I'll deal with the front, then nobody can say they didn't know the game was over."

As he rounds the corner of the building at a stately pace I make for the entrance through which all the boys vanished. I grasp the metal doorknob and experience a twinge of guilt: suppose we call a halt to the game just as Tom is about to win? He should certainly be able to outrun Jack. This isn't the thought that seems to let the unexpected chill of the doorknob spread up my arm and shiver through me. I'm imagining Tom as he finds someone who's been hiding—someone who turns to show him a face my son should never see.

It's absurd, of course. Just the sunlight should render it ridiculous. If any of the boys deserves such an encounter it's Jack, not my son. I can't help opening my mouth to say as much, since nobody will hear, but then I'm shocked by what I was about to do, however ineffectual it would be. Jack's just a boy, for heaven's sake—a product of his upbringing, like Jasper. He's had no more chance to mature than Jasper ever will have, whereas I've had decades and should behave like it. Indeed, it's mostly because I'm too old to believe in such things that I murmur "Leave Tom alone and the rest of them as well. If you want to creep up on anyone, I'm here." I twist the knob with the last of my shiver and let myself into the school.

The empty corridor stretches past the cloakroom and the assembly hall to the first set of fire doors, pairs of which interrupt it all the way to the front of the building. My thoughts must have affected me more than I realised; I feel as though it's my first day at school, whether as a pupil or a teacher hardly matters. I have a notion that the sunlight propped across the corridor from every window won't be able to hold the place quiet for much longer. Of course it won't if the boys break cover. I scoff at my nerves and start along the corridor.

Am I supposed to be making a noise or waiting until Mr Holt lets himself be heard? For more reasons than I need articulate I'm happy to be unobtrusive, if that's what I am. Nobody is hiding in a corner of the cloakroom. I must have glimpsed a coat hanging down to the floor, except that there aren't any coats—a shadow, then, even if I can't locate it now. I ease open the doors of the assembly hall, where the ranks of folding chairs resemble an uproar held in check. The place is at least as silent as the opposite of the weekday clamour. As the doors fall shut they send a draught to the fire doors, which quiver as though someone beyond them is growing impatient. Their panes exhibit a deserted stretch of corridor, and elbowing them aside shows me that nobody is crouching out of sight. The gymnasium is unoccupied except for an aberrant reverberation of my footsteps, a noise too light to have been made by even the smallest of the boys; it's more like the first rumble of thunder or a muted drum-roll. The feeble rattle of the parallel bars doesn't really sound like a puppet about to perform, let alone bones. Another set of fire doors brings me alongside the art room. Once I'm past I wonder what I saw in there: one of the paintings displayed on the wall must have made especially free with its subject—I wouldn't have called the dark blotchy peeling piebald mass a face apart from its grin, and that was too wide. As I hurry past classrooms with a glance into each, that wretched image seems to have lodged in my head; I keep being left with a sense of having just failed to register yet another version of the portrait that was pressed against the window of the door at the instant I looked away. The recurrences are progressively more detailed and proportionately less appealing. Of course only my nerves are producing them, though I've no reason to be nervous or to look back. I shoulder the next pair of doors wide and peer into the science room. Apparently someone thought it would be amusing to prop up a biology aid so that it seems to be watching through the window onto the corridor. It's draped with a stained yellowish cloth that's so tattered I can distinguish parts of the skull beneath, plastic that must be discoloured with age. While I'm not sure of all this because of the dazzle of sunlight, I've no wish to be surer. I hasten past and hear movement behind me. It has to be one if not more of the boys from Jack's party, but before I can turn I see a figure beyond the last set of fire doors. It's the headmaster.

The sight is more reassuring than I would have expected until he pushes the doors open. The boy with him is my son, who looks as if he would rather be anywhere else. I'm about to speak Tom's name as some kind of comfort when I hear the doors of the assembly hall crash open and what could well be the sound of almost a dozen boys charging gleefully out of the school. "I take it you were unable to deal with them," says Mr Holt.

"They were all hiding together," Tom protests.

Since Mr Holt appears to find this less than pertinent, I feel bound to say "They must have been well hidden, Tom. I couldn't find them either."

"I'm afraid Master Francis rather exceeded himself."

"I was only playing." Perhaps out of resentment at being called that, Tom adds "I thought I was supposed to play."

Mr Holt doesn't care for the addition. With all the neutrality I'm able to muster I ask "What did Tom do?"

"I discovered him in my passage."

Tom bites his lip, and I'm wondering how sternly I'm expected to rebuke him when I gather that he's fighting to restrain a burst of mirth. At once Mr Holt's choice of words strikes me as almost unbearably hilarious, and I wish I hadn't met Tom's eyes. My nerves and the release of tension are to blame. I shouldn't risk speaking, but I have to. "He wouldn't have known it was out of bounds," I blurt, which sounds at least as bad and disintegrates into a splutter.

Tom can't contain a snort as the headmaster stares at us. "I don't believe I've ever been accused of lacking a sense of humour, but I fail to see what's so amusing."

That's worse still. Tom's face works in search of control until I say "Go on, Tom. You should be with the others" more sharply than he deserves. "Sorry, head. Just a misunderstanding," I offer Mr Holt's back as I follow them both, and then I falter. "Where's—"

There's no draped skull at the window of the science room. I grab the clammy doorknob and jerk the door open and dart into the room. "Someone was in here," I insist.

"Well, nobody is now. If you knew they were, why didn't you deal with them as I asked?"

"I didn't see them. They've moved something, that's how I know."

"Do show me what and where."

"I can't," I say, having glared around the room. Perhaps the item is in one of the cupboards, but I'm even less sure than I was at the time what I saw. All this aggravates my nervousness, which is increasingly on Tom's behalf. I don't like the idea of his being involved in whatever is happening. I'll deal with it on Monday if there's anything to deal with, but just now I'm more concerned to deliver him safely home. "Would you be very unhappy if we cut our visit short?"

"I'm ready," says Tom.

I was asking Mr Holt, who makes it clear I should have been. "I was about to propose some non-competitive games," he says.

I don't know if that's meant to tempt Tom or as a sly rebuke.

"To tell you the truth"—which to some extent I am—"I'm not feeling very well."

Mr Holt gazes at Tom, and I'm more afraid than makes any sense that he'll invite him to stay even if I leave. "I'll need to take him with me," I say too fast, too loud.

"Very well, I'll convey your apologies. A pity, though. Jack was just making friends."

A hint of ominousness suggests that my decision may affect my record. I'm trailing after the headmaster, though I've no idea what I could say to regain his approval, when he says "We'll see you on Monday, I trust. Go out the front. After all, you're staff."

It feels more like being directed to a tradesman's entrance. Tom shoves one fire door with his fist and holds it open for me. It thuds shut behind us like a lid, then stirs with a semblance of life. Perhaps Mr Holt has sent a draught along the corridor. "Let's get out of his passage," I say, but the joke is stale. I unlatch the door opposite his office and step into the sunlight, and don't release my grip on the door until I hear it lock.

My Fiat is the smallest of the cars parked outside. I watch the door of the school in the driving mirror until Tom has fastened his seat belt, and then I accelerate with a gnash of gravel. We're nearly at the gates when Tom says "Hadn't I better go back?"

I halt the car just short of the dual carriageway that leads home. I'm hesitating mostly because of the traffic. "Not unless you want to," I tell him.

"I don't much."

"Then we're agreed," I say and send the car into a gap in the traffic.

A grassy strip planted with trees divides the road, two lanes on each side. The carriageway curves back and forth for three miles to our home. Tom doesn't wait for me to pick up speed before he speaks again. "Wouldn't it help if I did?"

I'm distracted by the sight of a Volkswagen several hundred yards back in the outer lane. It's surely too small to contain so many children; it looks positively dangerous, especially at that speed. "Help what?"

"You to stay friends with the headmaster."

This may sound naïve, but it's wise enough, and makes me doubly uncomfortable. As the Volkswagen overtakes me I observe that it contains fewer boys than I imagined. "I don't need to use you to do that, Tom. I shouldn't have used you at all."

"I don't mind if it helps now mother hasn't got such a good job."

The next car—an Allegro—to race along the outer lane has just one boy inside. He's in the back, but not strapped in, if he's even seated. As he leans forward between the young couple in front I have the disconcerting impression that he's watching me. I don't know how I can, since I'm unable to distinguish a single detail within the dark blotch of his face. I force my attention away from the mirror and strive to concentrate on the road ahead. Until I brake I'm too close to a bus. "Look, Tom," I hear myself say, "I know you mean well, but just now you're not helping, all right? I've got enough on my mind. Too much."

With scant warning the bus halts at a stop. The Allegro flashes its lights to encourage me to pull out. Its young passenger is unquestionably watching me; he has leaned further forward between the seats, though his face still hasn't emerged into the light. The trouble is that the man and woman in front of him are middle-aged or older. It isn't the same car. This confuses me so badly that as I make to steer around the bus I stall the engine. The Allegro hurtles past with a blare of its horn, and I have a clear view of the occupants. Unless the boy has crouched out of view, the adults are the only people in the car.

The starter motor screams as I twist the key an unnecessary second time. I'm tailing the bus at more than a safe distance while cars pass us when Tom says "Are you sure you're all right to drive, dad? We could park somewhere and come back for it later."

"I'll be fine if you just shut up." I would be more ashamed of my curtness if I weren't so aware of a Mini that's creeping up behind us in the inner lane. The old man who's driving it is on his own, or is he? No, a silhouette about Tom's size but considerably thinner and with holes in it has reared up behind him. It leans over his shoulder, and I'm afraid of what may happen if he notices it, unless I'm the only person who can see it. I tramp on the accelerator to send the Fiat past the bus, only just outdistancing an impatient Jaguar. "I mean," I say to try and recapture Tom's companionship, "let's save talking till we're home."

He deserves more of an apology, but I'm too preoccupied by realising that it wasn't such a good idea to overtake the bus. The only person on board who's visible to me is the driver. At least I can see that he's alone in the cabin, but who may be behind him out of sight? Suppose he's distracted while he's driving? A woman at a bus stop extends a hand as if she's attempting to warn me, and to my relief, the bus coasts to a halt. The Mini wavers into view around it and trundles after my car. I put on as much speed as I dare and risk a glance in the mirror to see whether there was anything I needed to leave behind. The old man is on his own. Tom and I aren't, however.

My entire body stiffens to maintain my grip on the wheel and control of the steering. I struggle not to look over my shoulder or in the mirror, and tell myself that the glimpse resembled a damaged old photograph, yellowed and blotchy and tattered, hardly identifiable as a face. It's still in the mirror at the edge of my determinedly lowered vision, and I wonder what it may do to regain my attention—and then I have a worse thought. If Tom sees it, will it transfer its revenge to him? Was this its intention ever since it saw us? "Watch the road," I snarl.

At first Tom isn't sure I mean him. "What?" he says without much enthusiasm.

"Do it for me. Tell me if I get too close to anything."

"I thought you didn't want me to talk."

"I do now. Grown-ups can change their minds, you know. This is your first driving lesson. Never get too close."

I hardly know what I'm saying, but it doesn't matter so long as he's kept unaware of our passenger. I tread on the accelerator and come up fast behind a second bus. I can't avoid noticing that the object in the mirror has begun to grin so widely that the remnants of its lips are tearing, exposing too many teeth. The car is within yards of the bus when Tom says nervously "Too close?"

"Much too. Don't wait so long next time or you won't like what happens."

My tone is even more unreasonable than that, but I can't think what else to do. I brake and swerve around the bus, which involves glancing in the mirror. I'm barely able to grasp that the Fiat is slower than the oncoming traffic, because the intruder has leaned forward to show me the withered blackened lumps it has for eyes. I fight to steady my grip on the wheel as my shivering leg presses the accelerator to the floor. "Keep it up," I urge and retreat into the inner lane ahead of the bus. "I'm talking to you, Tom."

I will him not to wonder who else I could have been addressing. "Too close," he cries soon enough. I scarcely know whether I'm driving like this to hold his attention or out of utter panic. "Too close," I make him shout several times, and at last "Slow down, dad. Here's our road."

What may I be taking home? I'm tempted to drive past the junction and abandon the car, but I've no idea what that would achieve beyond leaving Tom even warier of me. I brake and grapple with the wheel, swinging far too widely into the side road, almost mounting the opposite kerb. Perhaps the lumps too small for eyes are spiders, because they appear to be inching out of the sockets above the collapsed shrivelled nose and protruding grin. I try to tell myself it's a childish trick as the car speeds between the ranks of mutually supportive red-brick semis to our house, the farther half of the sixth pair on the right. As I swing the car into the driveway, barely missing one concrete gatepost, Tom protests "You don't park like this, dad. You always back in."

"Don't tell me how to drive," I blurt and feel shamefully irrational.

As soon as we halt alongside Wendy's Honda he springs his belt and runs to the house, losing momentum when his mother opens the front door. She's wiping her hands on a cloth multicoloured with ink from drawing work cards for the nursery. "You're early," she says. "Wasn't it much of a party?"

"I wish I hadn't gone," Tom declares and runs past her into the house.

"Oh dear," says Wendy, which is directed at least partly at me, but I'm busy. Reversing into the driveway would have entailed looking in the mirror or turning in my seat, and now I do both. I have to release my seat belt and crane over the handbrake to convince myself that the back seat and the floor behind me are empty. "Done your worst, have you?" I mutter as I drag myself out of the car.

This isn't meant for Wendy to hear, but she does. "What are you saying about Tom?" she says with a frown and a pout that seem to reduce her already small and suddenly less pretty face.

"Not him. It was—" Of course I can't continue, except with a frustrated sigh. "I was talking to myself."

The sigh has let her smell my breath. "Have you been drinking? How much have you drunk?"

"Not a great deal under the circumstances."

"Which are those?" Before I can answer, however incompletely, she says "You know I don't like you drinking and driving, especially with Tom in the car."

"I wasn't planning to drive so soon."

"Was it really that awful? Should I have come to support you?"

"Maybe." It occurs to me that her presence might have kept the unwelcome passenger out of my car, but I don't want her to think I'm blaming her. "I wasn't going to make an issue of it," I say. "You didn't seem very eager."

"I'm not completely terrified of school, you know."

Despite the sunlight and the solidity of our house, I abruptly wonder if my tormentor is listening. "Me neither," I say louder than I should.

"I hope not, otherwise we'll never survive. Come inside, Paul. No need for anyone to hear our troubles."

"All I was trying to say was I've already made one person feel they had to tag along with me that shouldn't have."

"I expect one of you will get around to telling me about it eventually." Wendy gazes harder at me without relinquishing her frown. "Taking him with you didn't put him at risk, did it? But driving like that did. He's the best thing we've made together, the only one that really counts. Don't endanger him again or I'll have to think what needs to be done to protect him."

"What's that, a threat? Believe me, you've no idea what you're talking about." The sense that I'm not rid of Jasper is letting my nerves take control of my speech. "Look, I'm sorry. You're right, we shouldn't be discussing this now. Leave it till we've both calmed down," I suggest and dodge past her into the hall.

I need to work out what to say to Tom. I hurry upstairs and take refuge in Wendy's and my room. As I stare at the double bed while Tom and Wendy murmur in the kitchen, I have the notion that my fate is somehow in the balance. Now there's silence, which tells me nothing. No, there's a faint noise—the slow stealthy creak of a stair, and then of a higher one. An intruder is doing its best not to be heard.

I sit on the bed and face the dressing-table mirror. It frames the door, which I didn't quite shut. I'll confront whatever has to be confronted now that I'm on my own. I'll keep it away from my family however I have to. The creaks come to an end, and I wonder if they were faint only because so little was climbing the stairs. How much am I about to see? After a pause during which my breath seems to solidify into a painful lump in my chest, the door in the mirror begins to edge inwards. I manage to watch it advance several inches before I twist around, crumpling the summer quilt. "Get away from us," I say with a loathing that's designed to overcome my panic. "Won't you be happy till you've destroyed us, you putrid little—"

The door opens all the way, revealing Tom. His mouth strives not to waver as he flees into his room. I stumble after him as far as the landing and see Wendy gazing up from the hall. "He wanted to say he was sorry if he put you off your driving," she says in a low flat voice. "I don't know why. I wouldn't have." Before I can speak she shuts herself in the front room, and I seem to hear a muffled snigger that involves the clacking of rotten teeth. Perhaps it's fading into the distance. Perhaps Jasper has gone, but I'm afraid far more has gone than him.

# Skeleton Woods

THEY WERE NEVER CALLED THAT, BUT THEY SEEM TO be now. When I manage to drag the warped sash high enough for me to lean over my old bedroom windowsill, I'm almost certain as I squint at the wooden arch daubed with moonlight that Skelton has acquired an extra letter. Under the moon the urban dell resembles a web that has caught the luminous worm of the stream. The woods look smaller than I remember, and even more secretive, no doubt because the trees have grown since I last took in the view. That's why the closest branches appear to be reaching for my attention until I back away and slam the window.

It's time to leave. I've seen all there is to see, which is virtually nothing. Every item of furniture has gone, even the lampshades and carpets. They were so faded they wouldn't have helped sell the house, but the stark rooms under the naked dusty bulbs feel stripped of all their memories. I switch off the lights on the upper floor and hurry past the rattling echoes of my footsteps in the darkened rooms as empty as my skull. Only the hall light remains to be extinguished, and I open the front door first so as not to feel

trapped in the damp stale gloom. I jab the switch and am heading down the passage that has yielded its drab colours to the moonlight when I'm reminded of trying to escape before our mother could issue her instructions. "Watch out for Tim," she would tell me. "Don't let him get in any trouble, Philip."

At first I was proud to be trusted to take care of my younger brother—and I'm overwhelmed by such a flood of memories that I have to grip the scaly doorframe for support. I remember wheeling him in his pram through the woods, which our mother believed was safer than pushing him through the streets—old houses on our side of the railway, a cheap new estate beyond—that enclosed the reserve. I wasn't meant to take him in the tunnel that led the footpath and the stream underneath the railway, but of course I did, talking to him in a voice overgrown with a giant one that amused him. Once he graduated to a buggy I made him promise not to tell our mother if he ever wanted to go through the tunnel again, and now I realise I was teaching him to be surreptitious with me as well. I'm even more responsible for events I don't want to remember.

The worst of it is that we didn't need to deceive her. She walked me to school over one or the other bridge across the railway, but once I started taking Tim she encouraged us to use the tunnel; it would keep us clear of the children from the estate, at least until we reached the only local school. Relying on me let her work longer at the hospital, and soon she could afford to buy me a bicycle. In two years this passed to Tim, which seemed fair to me; it and its upsized replacement had been second-hand when I was given them for Christmas. But he didn't take long to see that it gave him the chance not to do as I told him.

Wasn't our mother to blame? People weren't supposed to cycle in the woods, but she thought the route was safer for us than the roads or even the pavements. "Just be careful of the old folk" was her only warning. Tim was too intent on leaving me behind to bother about them or anyone else on the footpath. I gave up shouting "Wait for me on the other side," because it simply provoked him to race faster through the tunnel and out of sight, leaving behind a mocking laugh that seemed to scuttle all over the glistening bricks in the dimness. If the stream was low he might cycle along it, stirring up ripples that sounded as though a dweller in the mud was sniggering.

Was the water already tainted by then? Tim was about that age when he began to call the place Skeleton Woods. That needn't mean anything, but I'm so enraged by the rest of my memories that I slam the door behind me and tramp out of the wild garden. I want to see how the woods have grown.

The entrance is directly across the road. Four-year-old Tim used to call them our garden. Whenever he said anything that delighted her, such as that, our mother would clap her hands and sigh. The memory slips away, because I can't see the letter that was added to the name carved on the arch. It must have been the shadow of a twig. "Skelton Woods," I repeat as I stare at the thin arch until it appears to be exuding moonlit clouds. I shake my head to dislodge the impression and step onto the path beneath the arch.

Trees close over the path as it slopes down to the stream. It's ribbed with steps and imprinted with shadows like traces of roots about to break through the earth. Where it levels out, the shadows merge into a mass of blackness, solid except for the glimmer of fallen leaves. As I pad down the steps, something clatters fast between the trees across the stream. Since nobody could be so thin, I imagine it was a squirrel. I try to drive off any other lurkers by adding weight to my tread as I reach the foot of the slope.

It isn't as dark as it looked from above. Leaves colourless as scraps of paper glow among the shadows on the path and hide a secret pattern in the dimness. The November trees have fastened their claws in the sky, so that I could fancy they're bringing the luminous clouds to a standstill. Apart from the whisper of the milky stream, the woods seem as fixed as a memory. I stride along the path, through the tangles of shadows. Perhaps I'll find Tim's and my den.

I found it one Saturday while I was cycling by myself. He was watching television programmes for children younger than he was. If I'd changed the channel his screams would have given our mother one of her headaches. Besides, she'd said "Let him have his favourite, Philip. You used to like that show." I didn't want to be reminded, and tried to be an explorer several times my age as I cycled onto one of the side paths that led deeper into the woods. A cluster of bushes at the intersection put me in mind of a jungle hut. There was just one way in, so low I had to crawl, but the interior could have accommodated at least a dozen tribesmen, while the green ceiling was high enough for someone taller than me to stand up. As a man walking beside the stream wondered why his dog was straining to reach the bushes, I realised I could watch and not be detected. Even better, the entrance to my hideout wasn't visible from either path.

I thought of hiding there from Tim, and then I realised I could make him do my bidding. I told him I had a secret that he would never learn unless he promised not to leave me behind again. I had to threaten to tell our mother that he'd been disobeying before he would promise. He knew she would accuse him of resembling our father or, worse still, the woman he'd gone off somewhere with that we mustn't name. Even so, he had to be coaxed to walk. I didn't want our bicycles to betray our presence.

As soon as he saw a woman on the path by the stream he began to call "You can't see us. We're here." How wise of me was it to persuade him just to make noises at people instead? Once he discovered that if he dragged a stick across the slender trunks of the bushes nobody could identify the bony rattling, he would play for hours. Now I wonder when he decided that it sounded like a skeleton.

He was already calling the dell Skeleton Woods. Our mother applauded and told him to carry on being himself. When he did in the schoolyard I saw his classmates laughing at him. "He thinks they're called Skeleton Woods."

"They are," Tim protested, clenching his fists and his small thin face smaller. "There are skeletons in them."

"There's never," one girl scoffed.

"Go when it's dark and you'll see."

"What'll we see? You making a face like that? Doesn't scare us."

"They live in the trees and they'll jump on you. When you hear the clicky noise that's them laughing, it's their teeth. And you'll see their shadows and think they're just bits of trees till they grab you and make you into bones like them. That's how it works, there was only one at first and it caught people and made them stay down there with it."

I couldn't judge whether his audience was impressed by all this or by how his eyes had glazed as if he was gazing inwards at the scenes he was describing. I was simply glad our mother wasn't there to deliver his biggest round of applause. Did he mean to frighten his classmates out of the woods? He had the opposite effect. Before long we heard children in the woods at night, giggling and whispering, sometimes crying out and running away. Perhaps they were fleeing the screams, not knowing they were Tim's response to not being allowed to go out after dark. "You're all I've got," our mother said, presumably including me.

He managed to content himself with daylight once he found it offered victims. I remember how his features widened with delight when he saw from our hideout two of his classmates who were venturing along the path, not nervously enough for him. He rattled the bushes and watched the girls shriek and stare about and dash away, and then he dodged out of hiding and ran after them, shouting "The skeletons want you. They'll be waiting for you."

A man out walking from the old people's home that overlooked the woods pointed his stick at him. "Don't stir things up, son. You don't know what you're doing."

Tim stared at him as the girls were surrounded by their own cries in the tunnel. "You'll be one soon," he said and ran off, leaving the old man to lean on his shaky stick.

I can't locate the den. I've forgotten which side path it was closest to, and all the clumps of bushes by the main one are the wrong shape, just crouching huddles full of gaps. I mightn't be able to recognise how it's grown, if it has even survived. I lower myself onto a bench that's too damp for me to rest my hands on and fumble a bottle of water out of my quilted coat. As I drain the bottle the pale rushes bordering the path finger the dim air with their fattened tips, though I can't hear the ripples that must be stirring the fleshless stalks. I could almost imagine that the stream is keeping some activity to itself.

How much was the water to blame? Hardly anyone seemed to give it a thought except Tim. Of course we may have been the only ones who saw the dog. There was gossip about a leak from a medical factory, but that was beyond the horizon, past an underground section of the stream. By then I was too worried about Tim to take much notice of the rumour. He was thirteen and using drugs.

At first I hoped that someone else had started hiding in our den. More than once I'd found the stubs of scrawny cigarettes under the bushes, on the carpet of fallen leaves that lent the interior a special secret glow. When I asked Tim about them he stared at me. Silence was his new response to much that he was asked, either to do or to answer. Our mother had been unable to keep him in at night for at least a year, and was reduced to sending me after him while she tried to relax with a bottle of wine. "Don't let anything happen to him," she would plead. "He's still your little brother."

He didn't seem like it to me. I thought he was determined to act older than I was, to do things I wouldn't dare. I knew it the night I trailed him to the den and saw greyness drifting out of the bushes. I tried to believe it was mist until I smelled it, which made my head swim. I dodged around the bushes and crawled underneath, bruising my elbows as twigs scraped my back. I lurched upright to see Tim suck most of the last inch of a thin cigarette to ash, then lick the remains and his fingers before dropping the blackened scrap. "What do you think you're doing?" I gasped.

When this was met with a wordless stare I stood up as straight as the branches overhead would allow and leaned over Tim, who was squatting cross-legged. "Where did you get that?" I tried demanding.

"Want some?"

"I don't, and you certainly shouldn't. Don't ever do it again."

This time his silence didn't hold. "You're not my dad. I'll do what I like."

"Suppose I tell mother? What'll you do then?"

He glared at me so fiercely that even in the dimness I could see his eyes were red. "Go on, tell her. Like I care."

We both knew I wouldn't, and I wished I hadn't threatened to. "Why are you doing it at all? Don't you know what it can do to you?"

"Helps me is what." Before I was goaded to ask the obvious question, he answered it. "See things."

I attempted to laugh, though it made me feel like one of the scoffers in the schoolyard years earlier. "What things?"

"Like him."

Tim stared at the leafy canopy above me, which gave a loud creak. The next moment something clawed so viciously at my scalp it might have been eager to reach my brain. I ducked but managed not to cry out as I glimpsed a thin shape crouching on top of the branches. In an instant I couldn't distinguish it. I must have mistaken part of the tree above the bushes for a figure after I'd stood up too far and scratched myself on a twig. Its raggedly perforated head could only be a bird's nest. "There's nothing. You're just making yourself see things," I said.

His mouth twisted smaller as if locking up a secret, but then he spoke. "That's all you know. It makes them come."

"No, it made me," I said, feeling clever. I felt less so once I followed him out of the den and was unable to locate the nest I'd thought was a head or even the branches I'd taken for limbs. Apparently the incident satisfied him in some way, because he headed home, which meant I had to worry that our mother would notice his condition. I was relieved when he made for his room without speaking and shut himself in with his headphones. I was even able to convince our mother that he had only been out for a walk.

After that I had to chase him most nights, always in the woods. He found it easier than ever to outdistance me on the latest of my old bicycles while I cycled warily along the twisted flickering paths. Sometimes he would linger in the tunnel to leave pungent smoke waiting for me in the dark. I never overtook him before he finished what he'd brought, until the night I almost collided with him as I put on speed out of the tunnel. He was so immobile that I grew even more afraid for him. "What's wrong?" I cried.

"Shut up. I'm looking."

When I peered past him I was reassured to see there was something to look at: a more or less Alsatian dog that was drinking from the edge of the stream. At first I thought Tim was fascinated by the way the glimmering ripples crowded back across the water to splash the dog's muzzle as though impatient to be swallowed. Then the animal raised its head and turned it slowly to survey the woods in an entirely uncanine fashion. I found I couldn't breathe until it finished and plunged its whole face into the stream for another drink. I wanted to intervene somehow, but I hadn't moved when the dog backed away and trotted along the path, swinging its head from side to side with great deliberation. "It's the water," Tim whispered.

"Well, don't you try," I said more loudly, feeling too much like our mother.

"Who's going to stop me?"

"It's poisoned, don't you realise? Do you want to kill yourself?"

"Maybe."

Though I didn't believe him, his saying it dismayed me. I was wondering if I would have to fight him to keep him from drinking the water, and how I would explain any injuries to our mother, when he cycled off at speed. I almost screamed at him to wait until I realised from the way he was peering about that he wanted to observe the dog's behaviour. I would have helped him find it if it kept him clear of the stream. I cycled after him as fast as I dared, but there was no sign of the animal, either on the main route or on the paths that wound under the trees, not to mention those that bridged the stream. Eventually Tim scowled at me as if I'd chased the dog away, and then he sped home.

Neither of us had anything to tell our mother. I hid from her questions in my room and gazed from my window at the furtive obscure movements of the woods. What was ranging about under the trees as if searching for prey? Was it the dog? If I captured it I could take it to someone for examination, and then they would warn everyone about the water. I could save Tim.

The next day was Saturday. While our mother took him shopping for new shoes to replace a pair he'd trodden holes in, I found a length of old clothesline in the back yard and hurried down to the woods. I walked every path, some of them more than once at least, but couldn't see or hear the dog. I was trudging back to the tunnel when I heard something less than footsteps descending a side path towards me. Once I saw that the cause of the thin relentless sound was the stick an old man was clutching, I had to cover a nervous laugh.

He grabbed the back of a bench overgrown with initials so as to poke his stick at me. "You'll never catch them with a rope."

Politeness required me to ask "What?"

He hobbled around the bench, pivoting on his gnarled fist, and lowered himself to sit. "Dray's the name. Yours?"

I felt as if I was being set a test. "Philip."

As he lifted his long face his neck stretched so thin that it looked barely capable of supporting his pale puffy head. "Weren't you the lad that was going on about skeletons?"

"That was my brother." In defence of Tim I added "He was just making up stories."

"You don't make things like that up."

I couldn't tell if this was a statement or a warning. "Why not?"

"They're underneath everything. They're under us now. Don't they teach you anything at school any more?"

I managed not to resent this, because I thought I could impress him. "You mean fossils and all that? I know about those."

"Well, give him a trophy. I'll bet you don't know nothing wants to be dead. It wants to be more alive, just in another way. Some things get together and help each other to be. And telling stories like that does."

By now I was lost. I wasn't even sure if he meant Tim's stories or this one. As I tried to make out what his face would have looked like with less of a profusion of flesh he said "So what were you chasing after?"

"Have you seen a dog? I think it's drugged."

"Good God, things just keep getting worse. Who did it? You or your brother?"

"We wouldn't ever," I protested loud enough to send some eavesdropper and its lanky shadow scuttling away behind the bushes. "It's the stream. Some kind of drug has got into it."

Did I imagine that I could call on him to deal with this because he was an adult? I didn't want to trouble my mother. His response wasn't encouraging, however. "That's all it needs."

I was too nervous for politeness now. "What are you talking about?"

"If it's like that on the surface it'll reach down. There are things that haven't even been alive yet. It'll dredge up worse."

I was more than sorry to have asked. I would have retreated except for the need to learn "So did you see the dog?"

"I didn't, son. I've seen nothing you'd like to see." I was afraid he might expand on this until he said "I used to live round here, you know. It's all changed. I can't even find my home."

"You still live here, honestly. Keep looking and you'll find it." I couldn't take him—I was already responsible for Tim. I hurried away, and when I returned through the tunnel Mr Dray had gone. I never found the dog either, just as I haven't found the den, and now I wonder if that's on the far side of the tunnel.

I mustn't be nervous of going through. There never was a reason. I push myself up off the bench and do my best to stride along the path, which has begun to resemble a trail of mist. Has it always followed the course of the stream so closely? Except for the substance I could imagine they're identical. The water glows as whitely as the sky that trickles between the entangled branches, so that I feel in danger of forgetting which is reflecting which. I'm almost glad when the darkness grows more solid between the trees ahead.

It's the railway embankment. For a few yards I can distinguish the glistening outlines of bricks arched over the stream and the path, and then there appears to be blackness for hundreds of feet, leading to the huddle of tree-trunks framed by the end of the tunnel. I don't need to see in order to walk through, even if the path is slippery with mud. The trouble is rather that as I pick my way I'm more able to discern it than I ought to be. It's as though the stream is carrying the moonlight through the tunnel, but if the water's luminous that might be worse. Can I really see ripples settling into stillness beside me in the middle of the tunnel before they come back to life some yards further on? How can any of this be possible? I'm halted by the notion that something is about to rear up out of the stagnant stretch of water, unless the water itself is preparing to leap at me. That's the kind of thing Tim would have imagined, and perhaps Mr Dray as well. The thought releases me, and I flounder and skid to the end of the tunnel.

The bare trees open out to the sky above the stream. Between the branches that overtop the banks of the valley, a very few windows are lit. I can tell by their smallness that they belong to the new houses, and now I remember another time I did. It was the night I found Tim with a girl in our den.

He'd stopped smoking, as far as I could establish, which only aggravated my unease. What might he be doing to himself now? He often didn't speak for hours, and avoided me whenever he could. Although I disliked resenting how his state didn't affect his schoolwork, mine was suffering from my anxiety for him. Perhaps our mother was aware of some of this, because eventually she asked "Is everything all right between you two?"

We were sitting in the kitchen with the fluorescent tube glaring down at the remains of that night's burgers from the Turkish fish and chip shop. Tim barely even shrugged, but I thought the twitch of his shoulders looked nervous. The best I could manage and try to believe in was "We're still us."

"I hope so." She let her gaze trail over me and then Tim as she drained another glass of wine from the box. "I see enough bad things at work. I don't want to come home to them."

When Tim sat up out of his crouch I was afraid his interest had been caught too well. Was he thinking there were better things to see and how to do so? Suppose he hinted or more than implied as much? My head was throbbing with the search for some remark that would forestall his when he shoved his chair backwards. "I'm going out," he muttered.

"Oh, where are you going now? What did I say?"

All at once I'd had enough—too much to be careful any longer.

"That's right, Tim, where are you going? Why don't you say for once?"

He didn't bother looking at either of us. "I told you, out," he said and almost immediately was.

As the front door slammed I dashed into the front room, nearly tripping over his computer magazines strewn beside an armchair, and saw him making for the woods. Once his head dropped below the brink of the path I picked up a wineglass from the couch in front of the television and carried it to the kitchen. Perhaps I hoped the gesture would satisfy my mother in some way, but she was waiting with a question. "Do you think it's a girl?"

"I don't know," I said and tried to concentrate on clearing the table. I dealt with the washing-up as swiftly as I could, striving not to let her glimpse my concern for Tim. At least he wasn't cycling, and so I hoped he hadn't gone too far for me to find him. "I'll go out for a bit," I said.

"A bit of what, Philip?" Her smile couldn't keep up its slyness or even its shape. "Why don't you find yourself a girl too? I wouldn't mind."

I hurried out as much to escape her insistence as to discover the reason for Tim's eagerness. I'd followed the path beside the stream so frequently that by now it felt like a connection in my brain. I tried just to walk and ignore the surroundings. I tiptoed through the tunnel, and as I left the scrabbling of echoes behind I saw lit windows above the trees. They let me feel less apprehensive until I heard Tim's voice.

I don't know how far I'd walked—perhaps further from the tunnel than I have now. I sit on a bench anyway and close my eyes so as not to watch the stream groping at the darkness with its reeds, because it feels as though they're reaching to snag my mind. At first it seemed that the bony tangles of branches were muttering. "I made them up," Tim was saying. "Skeletons are for kids."

I'd begun to wonder if he was talking to himself when a voice so high it reminded me of how mine still leapt an octave said "So why do you still call them Skeleton Woods?"

"That's what they are. The skeletons are everything that's here.

Ordinary people just see them. When you know that's all they are you can start to see the rest. You're not just a skeleton, are you? Neither is this place."

I hoped the silence denoted boredom, but then the girl spoke. I heard admiration and apprehensive eagerness. "What do you see?"

I couldn't stand any more. I shouted into the bushes "Never mind what. Why are you seeing things, Tim? What have you been doing to yourself now?"

I thought I'd shocked him into some kind of awareness until they both laughed. "Is that him?" the girl said.

"That's him all right. Big fat Phil. Phil the mummy's boy. Doesn't dare do anything she wouldn't like him to, or maybe that's what he wants her to think. Wonder what he does to himself when he's in his room with nobody to see."

"Nothing," I shouted and tried to part the branches, but they were as immovable as ribs, between which the darkness allowed me no view. "I can see you," I lied. "Stop that now."

I heard a kiss that suggested the darkness had developed soft wet flesh. Once his mouth was free Tim said "He's mad because he thinks this is his place."

"I found it," I declared and dealt the roots a kick that shook the bushes, rattling twig after twig.

"It was here first. You didn't make it anything."

"I thought I made it ours."

"Well, it isn't any more," Tim said and scrambled out so fast I thought he was going to attack my ankles like a dog. "So piss off and play somewhere else."

"I'm not playing, you are." Perhaps that was his worst betrayal, to dismiss my concern like that. "He's always made things up," I called into the bushes. "They're just like the stories he used to tell when he started school. He likes people thinking he's got more imagination than them, that's all. It's rubbish, everything he told you. There were never skeletons here and there aren't now."

By now Tim was on his feet. He brought his face so close to mine I saw his eyes glitter like coal. "You'll see," he said.

"Keep people like that out of there in future."

When I heard his companion crawling towards us I retreated alongside the stream; I didn't want a confrontation with anyone else. I lingered at a bend in the path long enough to watch the two of them vanish into the dark towards the new houses. I considered following them to learn what else they did, but I felt I'd done enough for one night. I was in bed before I wondered what exactly Tim had meant by "You'll see."

Did he plan to make me if I wasn't careful? I didn't want to think so. Perhaps he was trying to work on my nerves by passing me drinks at dinner—glasses of water from the tap. At first I told him I could fetch them myself, and then not to bother, and eventually just not to. Once I knocked over a glass he'd insisted on filling, and our mother burst into tears. He took that as an excuse to leave, and by the time I'd calmed her down and assured her that nothing was really wrong I couldn't find him when I went out to check on him.

We were at a new school now. Tim had taken to its size at once, and soon to the ways the girls were also bigger. At least it didn't involve passing through the woods. Instead I tailed him along the edge of the new estate. Sometimes he lost me, but after the night I caught him with the girl in the den I succeeded in observing him several times with one, presumably the same girl. In the schoolyard he had to share her with her giggling friends, but I saw them walk to school together more than once. The last time I overtook them and was able to watch them arguing. When they noticed me the disagreement grew fiercer, and they hurried off before I could hear what they were saying. It must have come to an unpleasant end, because when I asked Tim that night why he was walking home alone he gave me a look bordering on hatred. "Because I am," he said.

I wasn't sure this meant he'd finished with the girl. Whenever he went out at night I couldn't find him, even if I was cycling while he was on foot. Eventually I couldn't stand it, and waited for him outside the front door after dinner. "What are you up to now?" I murmured.

"Only one way to find out. Still want to see?"

"You aren't frightening me, Tim. There's nothing to be frightened of."

"Come on then, if you can keep up," he said so fiercely I felt his words condense like mist on my face.

When he dodged I thought he meant to run into the woods. Instead he hurried around the side of the house, and I was afraid he'd brought something too close to home. He was only collecting his bicycle. As I sprinted across the yard to mine our mother cried from somewhere inside the house "Can't you stay in with me for once?"

Tim glared at me as if I was to blame, and then he cycled fast around the building. I was about to follow when I realised that in the confusion, if indeed he was confused, he'd taken my latest bicycle and left its predecessor. For years that one had been too small for me, but I mustn't let him elude me. I squatted on it as best I could and wobbled alongside the house towards the woods.

I nearly lost my balance as the front wheel jerked downwards beneath the arch. Descending the steps felt like cycling over a giant's ribcage almost buried in the earth. Even when I reached the level path I couldn't help veering back and forth on it. Twigs clawed at my splayed knees while tree-trunks lurched at me as if they were bent on clubbing my skull. I might have abandoned the chase if I hadn't been able to hear Tim.

I heard my bicycle rattling along the path before it set up echoes in the tunnel. I could have imagined they'd barely ceased when I arrived at the downturned mouth. As soon as I rode in, the clacking of my pedals was multiplied by chattering in the blackness. No wonder I was so distracted that halfway through I strayed off the slippery path into the shallow water. I almost sprawled headlong on the path as I dragged the bicycle free of the stream. "Tim," I yelled furiously, but the only response was my own voice.

I righted the bicycle and pedalled awkwardly out of the tunnel. Even once I emerged from beneath the twitching of faint ripples on the bricks, I felt as though the stream was clinging to my feet and ankles. I did my best to shake off the chill as it seeped up through me while I tried to speed along the path. Then my flailing legs snatched both feet off the pedals, and as I struggled to regain control the machine toppled over.

At least I didn't fall on the hard path or in the water. I ended up with one leg under the bicycle on the damp grassy bank of the stream. As the clicking of the rear wheel wound down I saw that I was opposite the den. I was almost certain that I'd heard another noise—a stealthy creak among the bushes. I opened my mouth to shout at Tim, but instead I lifted the bicycle and used it to lever myself to my feet before laying it down again. I could be as sly as Tim if I had to be. I tiptoed swiftly onto the side path and dropped to all fours on the grass. Crawling into the den, I felt as if I'd won a game of hide and seek. "Tim," I said triumphantly, and looked up.

I couldn't see much, either despite or because of the pallor of the fallen leaves, but I knew at once that the figure craning down towards me wasn't Tim. For an instant I thought it was Mr Dray—thought I heard the scraping of his stick over the scattered twigs. His condition must have worsened, since he had more than one stick now; indeed, he sounded built out of them. He creaked and rattled closer, so that I glimpsed dimness through more than one gap in the looming mass of his head, and I scrabbled backwards out of the den.

I was floundering to my feet when I heard a commotion among the bushes. Whatever was in there sounded impatient to claw its way out, unless the figure Tim had cobbled together from bits of the woods in an attempt to impress me had collapsed against the branches. By the time I managed to conclude the latter, I'd staggered away from the den. "It didn't work," I called, and then I saw his bicycle lying beside the stream—my bicycle, that was.

Where was the one I'd ridden? How far had I blundered before I could stop? All that seemed to matter was that Tim had to be nearby. I sensed that I was being watched. "Tim," I called and heard a surreptitious movement somewhere close. It wasn't among the huddles of bushes or in the gloomy labyrinth of trees; it was just the whisper of ripples around two small whitish rocks in the middle of the stream. In the moonlight they looked more than weathered. They looked—I searched for the word and grew dizzy with alarm as it came to me—scuffed. They were the toes of a pair of trainers, which led my gaze to the faint shape of a body in the stream.

"Tim," I cried and ran to the edge. The water was coated with moonlight, which virtually blotted out the figure lying on its back. I threw myself flat on the soaked grass and reached for its hands, but I couldn't find them in the unexpected depths. I was confused by an impression that the face was somehow wrong, though I couldn't distinguish its features, until I realised it must be upside down. I rolled up my sleeves and plunged my hands deeper but still found nothing to grasp. In desperation I lurched forward on the bank to immerse my arms all the way to the shoulders, and my head sank underwater.

A face rose to meet mine, but it wasn't Tim's face. It was too large, and luminous with moonlight or of itself. Its eroded piebald features reminded me of the moon too, except that they were blurred by an excess of flesh. I had a sudden suffocating notion that the figure I'd glimpsed in the den had swum or drifted to find me while putting on flesh. A drowned voice seemed to fill my ears. "Now you'll see," I thought it said. I was terrified that whatever the shape had for hands were about to seize mine and drag me into the impossible depths. I snatched my arms clear of the water and dug my fingers into the earth to haul myself away from the stream.

As I staggered to my feet and stumbled backwards onto the path I noticed that the objects poking up from the stream were only rocks whitened by lichen, and that's all I want to remember just now. Why did I come down here? I grip the bench, which feels spongy as a fungus, and stand up. When I hauled my face out of the water my surroundings appeared to have grown brighter—as bright as they've become. That's because my vision is feasting on the moonlight, and wasn't it then? All that matters is that there was nothing under the water or anywhere else, then or now. I simply want to leave because I've no reason to be here. I'm beginning to find the place oppressive, even the scent that looms out of the shadows. I plant one hand over my mouth and nose as I tramp along the twisting path.

The scent seeps between my fingers. It puts me in mind of an old woman's perfume in which she has doused her entire body to disguise the smell of burgeoning flesh. It's threatening to make me dizzy, which is why I'm confused by a movement in or on the stream. Either the insect was skimming the surface before I was aware of it or it has emerged from the water. It must be a kind of dragonfly, even if it's white as ice, with wings like traceries of crystal. It glides in my direction, and I lean towards it. So does a growth at the edge of the stream, a flower like puckered white lips on a stick. The plump wrinkled lips gape wide and close around the fly, and I seem to hear the faint fragile crunch of its wings as the swollen stem works throatily. Then I dash away along the path for fear of hearing the lips speak.

The scent keeps up with me. Perhaps it belongs to the flowers that pout at me alongside the stream, or perhaps the spiders in their cut-glass webs that span the bushes are exuding it. As I try not to watch, the spiders blossom, their luminous white bodies efflorescing with filaments and scaly petals while every leg twitches its web in such unison it might be a message. A chalky bird flaps out of a tree, and I hope I may be able to look at it instead, until I realise that although it's flying away above the stream, it's growing no smaller in my eyes, which has to mean that it's expanding with each beat of its wings. The trees are flexing their branches, drawing white flesh down from the bloated sky, slipping it on like fat gloves. I try to ignore the sight of the glowing tree-trunks as they writhe and gesture me towards them. I have to run in that direction, but only to pass them. I'll be safe as long as I stay on the path. Surely I'm not really feeling it stir like a cocoon about to crack open. At least nothing to either side of it can reach me if I keep to the middle—and then I hear something that can. There are footsteps ahead, around a bend in the path.

They're heavy and deliberate. They're coming for me. I know that before a voice calls my name. I stare about wildly, but there's nowhere to hide; even the shade under the trees is as bright as the clouds. Besides, I don't think I could bear treading on the restless white pelt that was the grass, never mind approaching the bushes that crouch forward to peer at me from beneath their pallid swollen convoluted fleshy scalps. I spin around again and almost fall against a tree, which is still trying to lure me with sinuous movements, although I can see it's old and cracked and scabby. Then the voice calls out again, too close. "Philip. Philip Dray," it insists, and the speaker strides into view.

For as long as he stands gazing at me I'm sure he's a total stranger. When he takes another step I realise that, despite the uniform, he's Tim. The recognition seems to bare everything at me—the litter caught in the broken trees, the avalanches of household rubbish on the slopes below the new estate, the objects like long whitish flattened glistening fingers under the bushes, a rusty bicycle in the stream. Perhaps the clump of splintered bushes beside us is the den, its branches charred, the ground beneath it glittering with syringes and glass. Is all this the skeleton? If that's the case, I don't want to know about it; I'd even rather listen to Tim. "Come on, old fellow," he says. "Let's get you home."

I'm not about to tell him I've forgotten where it is. I wait for him to take my arm and lead me along the path. I need some distraction from everything I won't look at, and so I say "How's mother?"

He doesn't answer until we're past the bend and I see the steps up to the road. "It all got too much for her, Phil," he says and seems to wonder if he should say any more. "She's gone. It was a long time ago."

I don't think his gaze is accusing me. It looks more like suppressed pity, but I don't want either. As he ushers me far enough to see his police car at the top of the steps I retort "You were the one who took drugs, you know. I don't care how you've changed."

He turns his eyes away from me. I don't know what they're withholding, and I'd rather not. I focus my attention on the path, and then I grin to myself so fiercely I can feel it hiding from him under my face. I'm looking at our shadows, and I see what he can't have noticed. At last I understand the real name of the place. He's holding me by the gap between the bones of my arm.

# Digging Deep

It must have been quite a nightmare. It was apparently enough to make Coe drag the quilt around him, since he feels more than a sheeted mattress beneath him, and to leave a sense of suffocating helplessness, of being worse than alone in the dark. He isn't helpless. Even if his fit of rage blotted out his senses, it must have persuaded the family. They've brought him home. There wasn't a quilt on his hospital bed.

Who's in the house with him? Perhaps they all are, to impress on him how much they care about him, but he knows how recently they started. There was barely space for all of them around his bed in the private room. Whenever they thought he was asleep some of them would begin whispering. He's sure he overheard plans for his funeral. Now they appear to have left him by himself, and yet he feels hemmed in. Is the dark oppressing him? He has never seen it so dark.

It doesn't feel like his bedroom. He has always been able to distinguish the familiar surroundings when any of his fears jerked him awake. He could think that someone—his daughter Simone or son Daniel, most likely—has denied him light to pay him back for having spent too much of their legacy on the private room.

However much he widens his eyes, they remain coated with blackness. He parts his dry lips to call someone to open the curtains, and then his tongue retreats behind his teeth. He should deal with the bedclothes first. Nobody ought to see him laid out as if he's awaiting examination. In the throes of the nightmare he has pulled the entire quilt under him.

He grasps a handful and plants his other hand against the padded headboard to lift his body while he snatches the quilt from beneath him. That's the plan, but he's unable to take hold of the material. It's more slippery than it ought to be, and doesn't budge. Did his last bout of rage leave him so enfeebled, or is his weight pinning down the quilt? He stretches out his arms to find the edges, and his knuckles bump into cushions on both sides of him. But they aren't cushions, they're walls.

He's in some kind of outsize cot. The walls must be cutting off the light. Presumably the idea is to prevent him from rolling out of bed. He's furious at being treated like this, especially when he wasn't consulted. He flings up his hands to grab the tops of the walls and heave himself up to shout for whoever's in the house, and his fingertips collide with a padded surface.

The sides of the cot must bend inwards at the top, that's all. His trembling hands have flinched and bruised his sunken cheeks, but he lifts them. His elbows are still pressed against the bottom of the container when his hands blunder against an obstruction above his face. It's plump and slippery, and scrabbling at it only loosens his nails from the quick. His knees rear up, knocking together before they bump into the obstacle, and then his feet deal it a few shaky kicks. Far too soon his fury is exhausted, and he lies inert as though the blackness is earth that's weighing on him. It isn't far removed. His family cared about him even less than he suspected. They've consigned him to his last and worst fear.

Can't this be another nightmare? How can it make sense? However prematurely eager Simone's husband may have been to sign the death certificate, Daniel would have had to be less than professional too. Could he have saved on the embalming and had the funeral at once? At least he has dressed his father in a suit, but the pockets feel empty as death.

Coe can't be sure until he tries them all. His quivering fists are clenched next to his face, but he forces them open and gropes over his ribs. His inside breast pocket is flat as a card, and so are the others in the jacket. When he fumbles at his trousers pockets he's dismayed to find how thin he is—so scrawny that he's afraid the protrusion on his right hip is a broken bone. But it's in the pocket, and in his haste to carry it to his face he almost shies it out of reach. Somebody cared after all. He pokes at the keypad, and before his heart has time to beat, the mobile phone lights up.

He could almost wish the glow it sheds were dimmer. It shows him how closely he's boxed in by the quilted surface. It's less than a hand's breadth from his shoulders, and when he tilts his face up to judge the extent of his prison the pudgy lid bumps his forehead. Around the phone the silky padding glimmers green, while farther down the box it's whitish like another species of mould, and beyond his feet it's black as soil. He lets his head sink onto the pillow that's the entire floor and does his desperate best to be aware of nothing but the mobile. It's his lifeline, and he needn't panic because he can't remember a single number. The phone will remember for him.

His knuckles dig into the underside of the lid as he holds the mobile away from his face. It's still too close; the digits merge into a watery blur. He only has to locate the key for the stored numbers, and he jabs it hard enough to bruise his fingertip. The symbol that appears in the illuminated window looks shapeless as a blob of mud, but he knows it represents an address book. He pokes the topmost left-hand key of the numeric pad, although he has begun to regret making Daniel number one, and holds the mobile against his ear.

There's silence except for a hiss of static that sounds too much like a trickle of earth. Though his prison seems oppressively hot, he shivers at the possibility that he may be too far underground for the phone to work. He wriggles onto his side to bring the mobile a few inches closer to the surface, but before his shoulder is anything like vertical it thumps the lid. As he strives to maintain his position, the distant phone starts to ring.

It continues when he risks sinking back, but that's all. He's close to pleading, although he doesn't know with whom, by the time the shrill insistent pulse is interrupted. The voice isn't Daniel's. It's entirely anonymous, and informs Coe that the person he's calling isn't available. It confirms Daniel's number in a different voice that sounds less than human, an assemblage of digits pronounced by a computer, and invites him to leave a message.

"It's your father. That's right, I'm alive. You've buried me alive. Are you there? Can you hear me? Answer the phone, you— Just answer. Tell me that you're coming. Ring when you get this. Come and let me out. Come now."

Was it his breath that made the glow flicker? He's desperately tempted to keep talking until this chivvies out a response, but he mustn't waste the battery. He ends the call and thumbs the key next to Daniel's. It's supposed to contact Simone, but it triggers the same recorded voice.

He could almost imagine that it's a cruel joke, even when the voice composed of fragments reads out her number. At first he doesn't speak when the message concludes with a beep, and then he's afraid of losing the connection. "It's me," he babbles. "Yes, your father. Someone was a bit too happy to see me off. Aren't you there either, or are you scared to speak up? Are you all out celebrating? Don't let me spoil the party. Just send someone who can dig me up."

He's growing hysterical. These aren't the sorts of comments he should leave; he can't afford to antagonise his family just now. His unwieldy fingers have already terminated the call—surely the mobile hasn't lost contact by itself. Should he ring his son and daughter back? Alternatively there are friends he could phone, if he can remember their numbers—and then he realises there's only one call he should make. Why did he spend so long in trying to reach his family? He uses a finger to count down the blurred keypad and jabs the ninth key thrice.

He has scarcely lowered the phone to his ear when an operator cuts off the bell. "Emergency," she declares.

Coe can be as fast as that. "Police," he says while she's enquiring which service he requires, but she carries on with her script. "Police," he says louder and harsher.

This earns him a silence that feels stuffed with padding. She can't expect callers who are in danger to be polite, but he's anxious to apologise in case she can hear. Before he can take a breath a male voice says "Gloucestershire Constabulary."

"Can you help me? You may have trouble believing this, but I'm buried alive."

He sounds altogether too contrite. He nearly emits a wild laugh at the idea of seeking the appropriate tone for the situation, but the policeman is asking "What is your name, sir?"

"Alan Coe," says Coe and is pinioned by realising that it must be carved on a stone at least six feet above him.

"And where are you calling from?"

The question seems to emphasise the sickly greenish glimmer of the fattened walls and lid. Does the policeman want the mobile number? That's the answer Coe gives him. "And what is your location, sir?" the voice crackles in his ear.

Coe has the sudden ghastly notion that his children haven't simply rushed the funeral—that for reasons he's afraid to contemplate, they've laid him to rest somewhere other than with his wife. Surely some of the family would have opposed them. "Mercy Hill," he has to believe.

"I didn't catch that, sir."

Is the mobile running out of power? "Mercy Hill," he shouts so loud that the dim glow appears to quiver.

"Whereabouts on Mercy Hill?"

Every question renders his surroundings more substantial, and the replies he has to give are worse. "Down in front of the church," he's barely able to acknowledge. "Eighth row, no, ninth, I think. Left of the avenue."

There's no audible response. The policeman must be typing the details, unless he's writing them down. "How long will you be?" Coe is more than concerned to learn. "I don't know how much air I've got. Not much."

"You're telling us you're buried alive in a graveyard."

Has the policeman raised his voice because the connection is weak? "That's what I said," Coe says as loud.

"I suggest you get off the phone now, sir."

"You haven't told me how soon you can be here."

"You'd better hope we haven't time to be. We've had enough Halloween pranks for one year."

Coe feels faint and breathless, which is dismayingly like suffocation, but he manages to articulate "You think I'm playing a joke."

"I'd use another word for it. I advise you to give it up immediately, and that voice you're putting on as well."

"I'm putting nothing on. Can't you hear I'm deadly serious? You're using up my air, you—Just do your job or let me speak to your superior."

"I warn you, sir, we can trace this call."

"Do so. Come and get me," Coe almost screams, but his voice grows flat. He's haranguing nobody except himself.

Has the connection failed, or did the policeman cut him off? Did he say enough to make them trace him? Perhaps he should switch off the mobile to conserve the battery, but he has no idea whether this would leave the phone impossible to trace. The thought of waiting in the dark without knowing whether help is on the way brings the walls and lid closer to rob him of breath. As he holds the phone at a cramped arm's length to poke the redial button, he sees the greenish light appear to tug the swollen ceiling down. When he snatches the mobile back to his ear the action seems to draw the lid closer still.

An operator responds at once. "Police," he begs as she finishes her first word. "Police."

Has she recognised him? The silence isn't telling. It emits a burst of static so fragmented that he's afraid the connection is breaking up, and then a voice says "Gloucestershire Constabulary."

For a distracted moment he thinks she's the operator. Surely a policewoman will be more sympathetic than her colleague. "It's Alan Coe again," Coe says with all the authority he can summon up. "I promise you this is no joke. They've buried me because they must have thought I'd passed on. I've already called you once but I wasn't informed what's happening. May I assume somebody is on their way?"

How much air has all that taken? He's holding his breath as if this may compensate, although it makes the walls and lid appear to bulge towards him, when the policewoman says in the distance "He's back. I see what you meant about the voice."

"What's wrong with it?" Coe says through his bared teeth, then tries a shout, which sounds flattened by padding. "What's the matter with my voice?"

"He wants to know what's wrong with his voice."

"So you heard me the first time." Perhaps he shouldn't address her as if she's a child, but he's unable to moderate his tone. "What are you saying about my voice?"

"I don't know how old you're trying to sound, but nobody's that old and still alive."

"I'm old enough to be your father, so do as you're told." She either doesn't hear this or ignores it, but he ensures she hears "I'm old enough for them to pass me off as dead."

"And bury you."

"That's what I've already told you and your colleague."

"In a grave."

"On Mercy Hill below the church. Halfway along the ninth row down, to the left of the avenue."

He can almost see the trench and his own hand dropping a fistful of earth into the depths that harboured his wife's coffin. All at once he's intensely aware that it must be under him. He might have wanted to be reunited with her at the end—at least, with her as she was before she stopped recognising him and grew unrecognisable, little more than a skeleton with an infant's mind—but not like this. He remembers the spadefuls of earth piling up on her coffin and realises that now they're on top of him. "And you're expecting us to have it dug up," the policewoman says.

"Can't you do it yourselves?" Since this is hardly the best time to criticise their methods, he adds "Have you got someone?"

"How long do you plan to carry on with this? Do you honestly think you're taking us in?"

"I'm not trying to. For the love of God, it's the truth." Coe's free hand claws at the wall as if this may communicate his plight somehow, and his fingers wince as though they've scratched a blackboard. "Why won't you believe me?" he pleads.

"You really expect us to believe a phone would work down there."

"Yes, because it is."

"I an't hea ou."

The connection is faltering. He nearly accuses her of having wished this on him. "I said it is," he cries.

"Very unny." Yet more distantly she says "Now he's aking it ound a if it's aking up."

Is the light growing unreliable too? For a blink the darkness seems to surge at him—just darkness, not soil spilling into his prison. Or has his consciousness begun to gutter for lack of air? "It is," he gasps. "Tell me they're coming to find me."

"You won't like it if they do."

At least her voice is whole again, and surely his must be. "You still think I'm joking. Why would I joke about something like this at my age, for God's sake? I didn't even know it was Halloween."

"You're saying you don't know what you just said you know."

"Because your colleague told me. I don't know how long I've been here," he realises aloud, and the light dims as if to suggest how much air he may have unconsciously used up.

"Long enough. We'd have to give you full marks for persistence. Are you in a cupboard, by the way? It sounds like one. Your trick nearly worked."

"It's a coffin, God help me. Can't you hear that?" Coe cries and scrapes his nails across the underside of the lid.

Perhaps the squealing is more tangible than audible. He's holding the mobile towards it, but when he returns the phone to his ear the policewoman says "I've heard all I want to, I think."

"Are you still calling me a liar?" He should have demanded to speak to whoever's in charge. He's about to do so when a thought ambushes him. "If you really think I am," he blurts, "why are you talking to me?"

At once he knows. However demeaning it is to be taken for a criminal, that's unimportant if they're locating him. He'll talk for as long as she needs to keep him talking. He's opening his mouth to rant when he hears a man say "No joy, I'm afraid. Can't trace it."

If Coe is too far underground, how is he able to phone? The policewoman brings him to the edge of panic. "Count yourself lucky," she tells him, "and don't dare play a trick like this again. Don't you realise you may be tying up a line while someone genuinely needs our help?"

He mustn't let her go. He's terrified that if she rings off they won't accept his calls. It doesn't matter what he says so long as it makes the police come for him. Before she has finished lecturing him he shouts "Don't you speak to me like that, you stupid cow."

"I'm war ing ou, ir—"

"Do the work we're paying you to do, and that means the whole shiftless lot of you. You're too fond of finding excuses not to help the public, you damned lazy swine." He's no longer shouting just to be heard. "You weren't much help with my wife, were you? You were worse than useless when she was wandering the streets not knowing where she was. And you were a joke when she started chasing me round the house because she'd forgotten who I was and thought I'd broken in. That's right, you're the bloody joke, not me. She nearly killed me with a kitchen knife. Now get on with your job for a change, you pathetic wretched—"

Without bothering to flicker the light goes out, and he hears nothing but death in his ear. He clutches the mobile and shakes it and pokes blindly at the keys, none of which brings him a sound except for the lifeless clacking of plastic or provides the least relief from the unutterable blackness. At last he's overcome by exhaustion or despair or both. His arms drop to his sides, and the phone slips out of his hand.

Perhaps it's the lack of air, but he feels as if he may soon be resigned to lying where he is. Shutting his eyes takes him closer to sleep. The surface beneath him is comfortable enough, after all. He could fancy he's in bed, or is that mere fancy? Can't he have dreamed he wakened in his coffin and everything that followed? Why, he has managed to drag the quilt under himself, which is how the nightmare began. He's vowing that it won't recur when a huge buzzing insect crawls against his hand.

He jerks away from it, and his scalp collides with the headboard, which is too plump. The insect isn't only buzzing, it's glowing feebly. It's the mobile, which has regained sufficient energy to vibrate. As he grabs it, the decaying light seems to fatten the interior of the coffin. He jabs the key to take the call and fumbles the mobile against his ear. "Hello?" he pleads.

"Coming."

It's barely a voice. It sounds as unnatural as the numbers in the answering messages did, and at least as close to falling to bits. Surely that's the fault of the connection. Before he can speak again the darkness caves in on him, and he's holding an inert lump of plastic against his ear.

There's a sound, however. It's muffled but growing more audible. He prays that he's recognising it, and then he's sure he does. Someone is digging towards him.

"I'm here," he cries and claps a bony hand against his withered lips. He shouldn't waste whatever air is left, especially when he's beginning to feel it's as scarce as light down here. It seems unlikely that he would even have been heard. Why is he wishing he'd kept silent? He listens breathlessly to the scraping in the earth. How did the rescuers manage to dig down so far without his noticing? The activity inches closer—the sound of the shifting of earth—and all at once he's frantically jabbing at the keypad in the blackness. Any response from the world overhead might be welcome, any voice other than the one that called him. The digging is beneath him.

# The Moons

I MIGHT HAVE SEEN THE CHILDREN ONCE AGAIN.

I never wanted to see them at all. I would have been happiest up in my room, but my mother said "You haven't seen your chums since Christmas."

She'd only taken to talking about chums since we moved house, as if she had to bring her language up in the world. She used to call my friends in our old neighbourhood a gang. "I saw Claude and Ludwig on Sunday," I tried saying.

"Only on their way to church. You know what I mean." I thought she was about to say I should follow their example until she added "You've spent no time with them since your party."

As far as I was concerned it hadn't been mine, and I didn't want to be blamed for it. She kept saying how polite all the guests had been, though I wondered if she knew. The party had been her idea for earning me new friends, and she'd served the kinds of refined sandwiches and cakes her parents used to dish out when they owned the house. I'd told her nobody would bring a present, but all four of them did, and to my hot-faced embarrassment she gave each of them an envelope containing a ten-pound note. They'd thanked her so profusely that I'd felt even worse. "I was going to write a story," I said. "Or I might read. Don't you want me to read?"

"Stories aren't the whole world, Stuart," she said, though she worked as a book bunny at the local branch of Texts. "You need to play out as well."

At thirteen I was far too old to do anything of the sort or at least to call it that. "Maybe they're out," I said. "Maybe they've gone to some church thing."

"Don't start taking after your father. He would never make an effort if he wasn't certain he'd succeed." She was searching the carpet for scraps of needles that the Christmas tree might have left behind. "Give them a ring if you can't just walk along the road," she said, "and then you won't be under my feet."

She was always cleaning in case any of the neighbours came to call. I hoped she might have cleared away the cordless phone somewhere we wouldn't find it, but it was among her mother's china cats on the granite mantelpiece. She'd stored the number for Claude's and Ludwig's house, and far too soon I heard the kind of music business phones put on while you wait for anyone to answer. It meant somebody at the house was listening to music. "It's Stu," I said.

"Don't say that, Stuart," my mother said. "You're not a plate of food."

"Stuart." Mr Smith might have been correcting me as well. "Did you have a splendid festival with all the trimmings?"

"It was good." When he didn't find this worth answering I had to say "Are Claude and Ludwig there?"

"Indeed they are, and their friends you so kindly invited to your celebration. Do give us our turn to play host." Before I could speak he called "Young Mr Armstrong is imminent, everyone" and was gone.

"I didn't even speak to them," I complained. "It was just their dad telling them I was going."

"Off you go where you're wanted, then."

I don't suppose she meant I wasn't wanted at home, but it gave me an excuse to flounce out of the room before snatching my padded anorak from the stag's horns her father had made into coat hooks. "Let me know when you'll be back," my mother said, having hurried to see me off.

The sun was just above the detached houses across the road, as high as it would rise this early in the year. The stone menagerie in our garden had shadows more than twice their size lying down behind them. I never knew if my mother kept the ornaments because she'd inherited them from her parents or in case the neighbours expected it of her. The shadow of her Mini on the drive was almost the size of the car I wished we had. The pines beyond the houses opposite clung to the roofs with dozens of shadowy fingers. A path between two houses led through the forest to the beach. The face of a ranger on the path was blurred by the low fierce light, but I thought he was watching me. I wasn't going to let a ranger make me feel out of place, and I stared at him before turning away from the path.

The Smiths lived in front of a magpie's nest a quarter of a mile away down the long straight road, past gateposts with marble bowling balls balanced on them and bushes politely clipped into sculptures. A Mercedes kept a Renault company beside the Smiths' weedless turfy lawn. A local artist had designed the ceramic plaque that said **WELL-TEMPERED** beside the solid oak front door. As I pushed the marble button in its shiny brass surround, all of which put me in mind of fingering the kind of nipple you saw on magazines, a magpie's chatter seemed to answer for the bell. I dragged a comb through my unruly hair and was about to thumb the button harder when Mr Smith opened the door. "Stuart," he enthused before he lowered his plump ruddy face on its swelling jowls towards me. "See if you can make a difference."

It sounded like a test, and I didn't know what kind. I kept my mouth shut as I followed him along the wide hall, which was panelled like an old museum and hung with paintings of naked people in groves. He opened a door at the end and announced "Ladies and gentlemen, the newcomer."

Sunshine through the windows that were most of one wall found me like a spotlight in an interrogation room. I had to narrow my eyes to see the boys and the Turner sisters, Verona and

Valencia, who lived halfway between the Smiths' house and mine. Besides the floppy suede chairs where everyone was sitting there was a jigsaw half made up, and an electronic keyboard, and a sketch pad on a table by the windows. I thought someone had drawn a cage on the pad until I saw it was the view of the pines beyond the back garden. For a moment I fancied a ranger was watching from the top of the slope above the garden wall, but I couldn't locate him, and the trees were too thin to hide a man. Mr Smith shut the door and went back to his music, and I realised that everyone was gazing not at me but at eight-year-old Valencia. "What's wrong?" I said.

The others stared at me in distaste, though I was only trying to fit in. "I lost my bracelet," Valencia wailed.

"It was only cheap." Verona was three years older and determined to show it. "It wouldn't have fallen off otherwise," she said.

"You bought it for me." Valencia blinked wet-eyed and said "It had all the moons."

This seemed to be my chance to join in. "All which?"

"The phases of the moon," Ludwig said with a fourteen-year-old's haughtiness. "They're what it was made of."

"For purgatory's sake," Verona said to her sister. "If it means that much to you I'll buy you another."

"It won't be the same. I coloured all the moons," Valencia said and burst into sobs.

Ludwig sighed like a parent. "Well, now nobody's going to be able to work."

"Not us." Claude seemed to think I needed to be put right, even though I was a year older than him. "Mother and father are writing their lectures," he said, "and Mr and Mrs Turner are doing their day with the homeless. And father's already asked Valencia if she could be quiet once."

"Does she know where she lost it?" I said.

Valencia stopped sobbing long enough to mumble "On the beach."

"Couldn't we go and see if it's there?"

Ludwig shoved himself off his chair and marched out to knock on a door. "Father?"

In a moment the door opened, spilling a wave of music. "What is it going to be this time?" Mr Smith seemed not to want to know.

"Stuart's proposing a search party to look for Valencia's jewellery."

"There can't be any harm in it if they take their phones," a woman said, "and see they're back well before dark."

"Mama has spoken," Mr Smith said. "Harmlessness is guaranteed."

Ludwig came back and stared at me before saying "We're to go down to the beach."

"What do you say, Valencia?" Verona said.

"Thank you, Stuart," Valencia said, which didn't seem to please anyone but me.

I was wearing my coat. While they all went to fetch theirs I remember wondering if I still felt watched because I was unwelcome—I'd decided that Mr Smith had meant I would make a difference by being out of place. Ludwig opened the windows and locked them again with a code on a keypad, but I didn't look in case anyone thought I was planning to rob the house. He keyed more numbers at the gate in the wall at the end of the long garden, and then he led the way up a slope so strewn with needles that I imagined my mother complaining if I brought any home on my shoes. A magpie uttered its rattling call, and Valencia laughed as it soared out of its nest. She'd stopped crying as soon as Ludwig said we were going to the beach. Now I wish that nobody had listened to me—that I hadn't been there at all.

Just then I was only uncomfortable with hearing Verona nag her sister. "Don't slide," she said as we went down the far slope, and "Don't kick the needles, you'll spoil your shoes." Once she'd been told not to run either, Valencia looked about for something else. "We're walking on a big tiger," she said.

"It's a bit like one, isn't it?" I saw she meant the shadows on the brownish slopes. "All the stripes," I said.

To my surprise she took my hand. Hers was hot despite the winter chill, and sticky as a sweet. "The trees," she said before she had to pause for thought, "they're insects standing up."

As I saw the stubby branches protruding like insect legs from all the pines Verona said "Who are you trying to impress, Valencia? Paul and Diana aren't here." Apparently those were their parents. "Hurry up if you're looking for your bracelet," she said without even glancing at me.

Perhaps she hoped her sister would leave me behind, but Valencia pulled me along with all her strength, to a road on which a ranger's truck was hauling a cart piled with used Christmas trees. Nobody else passed us on the road, where the trees on both sides put me in mind of a cage like the sketch on the pad. I could have imagined someone peering between the bars, waiting to be let out. Beyond the dunes at the end of the road rangers were using Christmas trees to build a barrier against erosion, and a few people were throwing sticks for dogs beside the sea. "Where are we supposed to be going?" Verona asked her sister.

"Where everybody is."

All our shadows helped Valencia point along the beach. Half a mile away a crowd was bunched together near a car park among the dunes. People were throwing balls or kicking them or riding fat-wheeled motor tricycles or trying to fly kites that soon fell flat as if their shadows had brought them down. "You don't imagine they'll have left it, do you?" Ludwig said.

He meant the people who used the other road. I felt Valencia's fingers struggling to make a fist. Her eyes were turning wet again, so that I was in a hurry to say "Why don't we ask if anyone's handed it in?"

"I'm asking," Claude declared and marched over to the rangers. "Excuse me, has a bracelet been given in?"

All of them shook their heads, and one said "Is it valuable?"

"It is to her," I said.

The ranger gave Valencia a sympathetic look. "Keep asking if you like, love, and we'll keep an eye out."

The last high tide had brought shells and seaweed almost to the edge of the dunes, and I was afraid it might have carried off the bracelet. As Valencia tugged me along the beach the crowd ahead receded like a mirage. The distance had made them seem closer together than they were, and the people with kites were leaving the beach in defeat. Once I fancied someone had carried off a recycled Christmas tree, but when I looked up at the dunes above us there was no sign of the green shape I'd seemed to glimpse. I could have thought Valencia was moving not much faster than the shadows of the dunes, except when she darted to pick up objects that always turned out to be shells. Her sister kept telling her to keep up but never spoke to me. She and Claude and Ludwig had almost reached the entrance to the car park when four boys who'd been chasing birds at the edge of the sea converged on them.

They wore track suits and trainers. Some of them might have been old enough for their tattoos, and even those who weren't had them. The oldest and bulkiest boy was about as old as Ludwig. "What you lost?" he said.

"Nothing that need concern you, thank you," Ludwig told him. "We'll manage by ourselves."

"Can't stop us looking," said a wiry boy in a baggy mauve suit. "Snot your beach."

Valencia hauled at my hand so fiercely in her haste to head them off that she almost pulled me over. "Don't let them get it, Ludwig," she cried.

Another stringy boy stared at him and laughed so hard he spat. "You called Ludwig?"

"Will you please leave us alone," Claude said. "You've been politely asked."

The boy wiped his mouth to some extent and looked ready for a bigger laugh. "What's your name, then?"

"It's of no possible interest to you," Ludwig said. "Now for the last time will you please be on your way."

The fourth newcomer said nothing, and I wondered if he was as beside the point as me. Ludwig glanced at the crowd, but there wasn't one; the tricycles had sped away, and the scattering of adults still on the beach were too distant to help. A truck started its engine near the Christmas trees, and then another did. Ludwig beckoned to the rangers, who must have thought he was waving, unless they found the gesture too presumptuous. The trucks vanished into the dunes, taking all the rangers with them, and Valencia yanked at my hand as if she wanted me to intervene. My only thought was that if I didn't try to sound like Ludwig he might think I sounded too much like the intruders, or even if I tried. I did my best not to make too much noise in clearing my throat, but everyone stared at me—everyone except Verona, who suddenly bent double. I thought nerves had made her sick until she straightened up and slipped an object into her pocket. "I've found it," she said.

"Oh, let's see," Valencia cried.

"Oh, do let's," said the boy with spit around his mouth.

"It's safe now," Ludwig told Valencia. "Let her keep it for you till we're home."

As soon as he made for the road where the rangers were, the boys in track suits followed him. He turned at once and headed in the opposite direction. "That's the wrong way," Valencia protested.

"It's where there'll be grown-ups," I said.

I thought my remark might drive away our unwanted companions, but it only earned a scowl from Ludwig. As they followed us Verona told them "You weren't going this way."

"Changed our mind," the bulky boy said.

Ludwig twisted around to confront them. "Would you like me to phone someone?"

"Go for it," the bulky boy said like a gunfighter. "Mobiles don't work down here."

"You don't know if ours do," Claude blurted.

"They'll be worth having, then," said the boy with the wet mouth.

Ludwig might have glared at Claude for giving them more reason to come after us, but he was striding to the car park. The boys fell behind as we hurried to keep up with him until he halted on the path between the dunes. Fewer than a dozen vehicles were parked in a gravelled area the size of a football field, and not a single human being was to be seen.

We were halfway across the car park when gravel clattered at our backs. While the boys weren't throwing it yet, they were following us at speed. As we carried on towards the road through the woods we heard a car on it. I hoped it was a ranger's truck, but it was a jeep full of more big dogs than people. Ludwig stood in its way and held up one hand like a policeman. "Will you tell these people to go away, please?"

"What's wrong with them?" the driver said. "They've as much right to be here as you, son."

"We live round here."

"We don't," the woman with the driver said, "so you'll just have to put up with us all."

"I shouldn't have expected any better," Ludwig said.

I wanted to tell the couple in the jeep that it was only how he'd been brought up, but I don't suppose it would have helped. The driver revved the engine to make Ludwig step aside, and as the jeep coasted alongside the boys I heard the driver say something to them. He sounded as though he was joking. Ludwig looked ready to remonstrate with him, but Claude said "Look, there's someone who'll help."

I was just in time to glimpse a figure in green who'd emerged from the pines at the bend. He vanished beyond it before anyone could attract his attention. "Quick," Claude said even more urgently and demonstrated how we should run.

Ludwig didn't quite, instead stalking after Claude with exaggerated strides that earned him sniggers from the boys in the car park. The rest of us followed, running whenever Verona told Valencia to keep up. We turned the bend to find Claude and Ludwig stranded in the middle of the road. "I saw him," Claude complained.

The road stretched straight for at least half a mile between mounds of sandy earth. There was no sign of anybody on it or among the trees that occupied the mounds. I heard footsteps leave the car park and start along the road. "This way," Ludwig said at once.

He stuck his arm out like a guard at a school crossing while we dashed up the nearest piny slope. From the top I saw pines beyond pines beyond pines, and hollows strewn with needles between the long high irregular mounds. The sun was so much in my eyes that I hardly noticed all the outstretched shadows until I slithered with Valencia down the further slope. For a moment I'd thought someone had abandoned a topiary sculpture in the woods, but when I looked for it I couldn't even locate the green shape. Ludwig tramped up the next mound, frowning to make everyone follow. As I helped Valencia down that one I checked my mobile for a signal. Because of the dazzle I had to hold the phone close to my eyes before I was certain it was useless. Everyone else's was more sophisticated, even Valencia's, but they had no signal either. By the time this was established we'd left several mounds behind, but we still heard the boys on the road. They'd stopped at the bend to wonder aloud where we were, and threateningly too. "Keep quiet," Ludwig muttered. "Keep down."

I don't believe I was alone in holding my breath. Valencia's fingers squirmed to take a firmer grip on mine. We heard no more from the direction of the road, and eventually Ludwig pointed downhill. He might have been playing a platoon leader in a war film. I thought he was enjoying himself, and even I began to until I heard a whisper in the chill piny silence. "They're there."

Whoever was speaking must have crept up on us. Ludwig brandished his hand at the platoon and stiffened into a crouch. Valencia was digging her small nails into the back of my hand by the time anyone relaxed. It seemed the boys hadn't found us after all. We stole down the slope and were equally careful about climbing another. From the top the road was entirely out of sight, and so were the boys. We were in the next hollow, where the shadows looked unnaturally pallid with the dazzle that stuck to my eyes, when the soft voice repeated "They're there."

It sounded secretive but also somehow lulling, so that I could have fancied it was saying "There, there." Claude sprinted up the next mound and grabbed a fallen branch. "Come on," he shouted.

He might have been challenging the boys or urging Ludwig if not me to do so—perhaps even all of that. "Stay with your sister," I whispered to Valencia and ran to join Claude as his brother frowned at both of us and then tramped after us. The sun glared into my eyes, and I was peering about not much better than blindly for a weapon when a voice said "Now who's this who's lost in my woods?"

At first I couldn't see him. His voice came straight out of the low sunlight that seemed to pinch the trees as thin as blackened matches. As I wiped my eyes he appeared between the trees and descended the mound opposite ours swiftly but silently. He was a ranger in uniform, taller and broader than he'd looked at first, with unexpectedly small and delicate features in a broad jowly face. His short black hair wasn't much less spiky than the pines, and his lips were almost as pale as his cheeks and ridged forehead. By the time he climbed up to us he'd developed a puckish grin. "Why, it's you," he said.

Ludwig's eyes narrowed. "Do we know you?"

"You're the Smith boys, aren't you? And these are the Turner girls." The ranger cocked his head and gave me a bright-eyed blink. "And here's Mrs Armstrong's lad."

"I'm sorry," Ludwig said, "we still don't know who you are."

"Don't I look familiar?" The ranger seemed disappointed. "Woodward by name and by nature as well," he said. "I'm just up the way from you."

"I've seen you," Valencia said and let go of my hand.

"There's one pair of sharp eyes for me," Woodward said and turned to Claude. "Who did you think you were going to fight?"

"Some boys are chasing us," Verona told him. "They want to steal our phones."

"And my bracelet," Valencia protested.

"Don't bother Mr Woodward with that now. You know it's safe."

"As safe as you all are," Woodward said. "Shall I show you the quickest way home?"

"We aren't supposed to go anywhere with people we don't know," Claude said and seemed unsure what to do with his stick.

"You won't be," Woodward told us. "I'll be busy making sure nobody finds you."

"Can't you come with us?" Valencia pleaded.

"Don't worry, they'll never know where you are." Woodward's voice was growing softer as if to ensure that the boys wouldn't hear. "Nobody can find my way if they're not shown," he said.

This sounded like a fairy tale to me, but it impressed Valencia. "Is it the rangers' special way?" she said.

"It's anyone's who belongs there. Straight through and carry on in that direction," he said, pointing all the long thin fingers of one hand at a gap between two mounds. "Just see you don't stray from the track if you want to be where you should be before dark."

I was wondering what accident had left him so little in the way of fingernails—not even indentations where the nails should be. When Ludwig tramped down to the gap we trooped after him, and Valencia took my hand again. I glanced back to see Woodward perched on the ridge, clasping his long hands together. "Homeward bound, the famous five," he said in a low voice that nevertheless reached us. "Leave everything to the lone ranger."

The path beyond the dunes wasn't quite as straight as he'd made it sound. It led between mounds several times the height of the tallest of us—Ludwig. Whenever it turned a bend it confronted us with the sun, which seemed to have grown even colder and fiercer as it sank. The mounds never cut off the sunlight long enough for my eyes to recover, but I glimpsed side paths wandering into the unnaturally pallid gloom. "We're in a maze," Valencia said.

She was trotting beside me, though there was barely room. "Just concentrate on keeping up," Verona told her if not me as well.

This silenced Valencia for a few turns of the path, and then she said "We're in his cage."

Perhaps not being able to see the way clearly had put her sister on edge. "What are you prattling about?" she demanded.

"The tiger's cage. See all the bars."

She meant the shadows, but perhaps Verona didn't care to understand. "Can't you just walk instead of trying to make things into things they aren't?" she said rather than asked.

Valencia stuck out her tongue at her sister's back as Ludwig led the way into a glade hemmed in by mounds. The sun was lying low among the trees and almost blotted out the ground we were walking on, where all the fallen needles glared like tinfoil. The trees framing the sun looked charred to the bone, except they weren't even that substantial—more like their own shadows standing on end. "It's scaly," Valencia whispered.

I supposed she meant the ground, but I wasn't especially anxious to know. Ludwig shaded his eyes and stared ahead. "Mr Woodward said straight on," he reminded everyone. "He must have meant there."

"It's the nearliest," Valencia said.

Neither of the gaps between the mounds on the far side of the glade was exactly opposite us. When we followed Ludwig through the right-hand gap it seemed not to matter that he'd chosen that path, since it soon veered left between the hillocks. The sun was beside us now, sending shadows even longer than the trees were tall down the slopes to mark the path like a board for some game. Valencia held my hand so that she could hop from patch to patch of the track boxed in by shadows. The path curved until the sun was at our backs, but she kept hopping as if she could still see the pattern. Her shadow hopped alongside Verona, who swung around. "Oh, it's you," she said with an odd edge to her voice. "Just try and walk like an ordinary person."

Valencia performed a defiant hop. "Give me my bracelet and I will."

"When we're home, so that's why you should hurry up."

"I want to see it," Valencia said, staying where she was. "Show me."

"There isn't time now," Verona said and turned her back. "Wait till we're home."

"You haven't really got it, have you? You just pretended so those boys would go away."

Ludwig glanced at Verona, and I saw he'd already known the truth. I was afraid that Valencia would burst into tears or run back the way we'd come, but she marched forward. "I don't care," she said. "I'll find it. We're going to the beach."

"We can't today," Claude told her. "It'll be dark."

"Well, we are," Valencia said not stubbornly but with satisfaction. "It's taking us."

I thought she meant the path, and I couldn't judge if she was right. I had no idea how long we'd been following it, and yet I felt we should have been home by now or within sight of home. "Of course it isn't," Ludwig said and tramped more purposefully along the path.

The sun was directly at our backs now. The shadows of the pines stretched ahead as if they were helping the mounds wall in the path. Every individual needle underfoot seemed to have its own shadow. The practically supine light emphasised the outline of each footprint, Ludwig's and Claude's and Verona's and whoever's had preceded them. "They're my stars," Valencia said.

Verona turned her head without looking around. "What are you making up now?"

"I'm not. I don't. They're my shoes." Valencia stood on one leg and tugged at my hand. "Aren't they, Stuart?"

She was showing me the sole, which bore a pattern of two large five-pointed stars. There was no mistaking the prints of her shoes, and they weren't only behind us; they extended out of sight ahead. "We've already come this way once," I had to admit.

"That's just—" Ludwig peered at the sole and the prints behind Valencia, and at last stared at the prints ahead. "That's—" he said before lurching up the nearest slope to shade his wincing eyes and narrow them. "I see where we must have gone wrong," he said. "Let's go back."

The sun was still glaring in our eyes when we came to a place where the path forked. I supposed I must have been too distracted by Valencia to notice it before. Ludwig took the right-hand path and we followed him almost blindly. On the mounds caged by shadows the lurid pines looked as artificial as Christmas trees, and too insubstantial with the dazzle that still lay across my eyes. All at once Ludwig halted in a gap between two mounds. "There's my stars again," Valencia said.

There were footprints on a track that crossed the one we were following, and some were unmistakably hers. Ludwig stared both ways along it and swung around. "We turned off too soon, that's all."

I felt as if the sunlight had blanked out my brain as I trudged after him. The path curved, and a mound cut off the light. The dazzle clung to my eyes, so that all I could distinguish were the huge recumbent shapes that loomed above the track. Around the bend I almost collided with Verona, who'd stopped because the Smith boys had. "This can't be right," Claude protested.

"I know that," Ludwig said more savagely than he might have liked their parents to hear.

We were back at the glade, and yet we hadn't passed the fork, unless we'd been too dazzled to notice. The glade was strewn with fallen needles and with footprints, which seemed so numerous that I could have imagined we'd crossed it more than once. Against the sun, which was only just above the mounds, the trees looked like sketches waiting to be filled in. I'd had enough of Ludwig's leadership; I was almost the oldest one there, after all. "Wait here, Valencia," I said and ran up the nearest mound.

I thought I'd find the way from the position of the sea, which had to be close. It was nowhere in sight, nor even audible, and I couldn't see or hear anything like a road. On every side mounds crowned with trees receded into an impenetrable distance. The forest seemed far larger than it ought to be, and it was as silent as a picture of itself. I couldn't panic when I'd taken the lead. "We'll have to phone," I said. "There must be a signal by now."

Ludwig gave me an unimpressed look. "Whom do you suggest calling?"

"Your parents will be closest, won't they? If they shout from the house we'll hear them."

"Maybe Stuart's right," Verona said.

Ludwig performed an extravagant shrug as if he was sloughing all responsibility. When he saw Claude reach for his mobile he snatched out his own, and then a voice intervened. "I didn't think you were the sort to make a noise in our woods."

Verona squealed and tried to look as if someone else had, while Claude and Ludwig stiffened to make sure nobody thought they'd been startled. Woodward was striding out of the sunlight across the glade, but I couldn't see where he'd come from; I hadn't even heard him until he spoke. It left me feeling useless as an observer or a pathfinder. Only Valencia seemed delighted. "How are you being so quiet?" she cried.

"You can be too. I'll show you how."

Valencia ran to take his hand. "Have you found my bracelet?"

"Don't bother Mr Woodward with that now," Verona said.

"The other rangers said we had to ask," Valencia protested with some pique.

"It wasn't there, Valencia," her sister said. "We all had a good look."

I didn't think I had, and I felt more excluded than ever. "Then someone must have taken it," Valencia said.

"Or something from the woods did," said Woodward.

"A magpie," Valencia cried.

"Something like that. They'll steal your eyes if you don't watch out. You won't believe what you find in the treetops."

"I'm sure it's very interesting, Mr Woodward," Ludwig said, "but we need to get home before dark."

"I'll take you. I'm going there now," Woodward said, and the sun went out behind him.

It felt as though the woods had swallowed the light. The sun was still behind the mounds, of course. At once the green of Woodward's uni-form was several shades darker. As he led Valencia to the next path out of the glade, her sister and the Smith boys trooped after him. It was the path Ludwig had rejected, which was the best reason I could think of to use it. The track snaked between mounds too high and too close together to see beyond. Darkness appeared to be seeping out of the mounds to creep up the spiky trees, which might almost have been glowing from within. Valencia gazed up at them and said "Are we going to find my bracelet?"

"I'll make sure it shows up for you," Woodward said and gazed at her. "There are jewels everywhere in the woods if you look."

When I glanced about I seemed to see what he had in mind. Patterns had begun to glimmer on the mounds that flanked the path. The fallen needles were spangled with frost and beads of icy dew. The more I looked, the more the glittering patterns grew visible. They might have composed a single design too vast and complicated to grasp, leading away into the darkness that was closing in. The impression made the woods feel boundless, and I couldn't help blurting "Are you sure we're going home?"

Woodward turned his head so smoothly that I was reminded of an owl, by his round-eyed gaze as well. "I'm seeing you do," he said.

Perhaps I was jealous because Valencia had so readily transferred her trust from me to him, but I no longer liked the look of him. His face seemed more heavily jowled, almost froglike, and his diminutive features looked somehow separate from it, as if they were emerging from a lair of flesh. I could almost have imagined that the dusk had added to his bulk. I was keeping up with him and the others only because I didn't want to lose sight of them. As I tried to concentrate on the path and ignore the patterns in the twilight I had the notion that although the shadows of the pines weren't visible, they were all around us—that we were walking into a cage we couldn't see. I couldn't have said so or anything like it, not least because I would have sounded like Valencia. There was silence except for muffled footsteps until a chatter as dry as a rattle of bones came from the treetops. "Magpies," Valencia cried. "Can we see if they've got my bracelet?"

The trees had given up their hold on the last of the light, and she peered towards the noise, looking for a side track. "Not there, Valencia," Woodward said.

I wasn't sure why I blurted "How do you know?"

Verona and the Smith boys scowled at me as if I'd betrayed how tactless I was. "That isn't the way home," Woodward said. "Come along, Valencia, or you won't see the secret way I take my friends."

"Do as Mr Woodward says," Verona told her.

Valencia raised her eyes to him and then turned back to the path. Everyone seemed relieved that she'd decided to go along with him—everyone except me. They must have been happy for him to say whatever might take us home quickest. As I watched the thickset figure lead Valencia along the twisted path between the looming mounds into the woods that appeared to be drawing the dusk towards us, I had the notion that his ranger's uniform was greener than it ought to be—as green as moss, and glowing like it in the dimness. I even thought his jacket had too much of the texture of moss. Suspicion or confusion made me call out "Aren't you supposed to have a badge?"

"Am I being questioned?" Woodward let go of Valencia's hand while he reached inside his jacket to lift out a rectangular plaque on a cord around his neck. "Here I am for all to see," he said.

I barely glimpsed the badge before it swung against his chest. All I'd seen was his last name and a blur where a photograph should be—a blotch like moss or fungus. "I didn't see that properly," I objected.

"We did," said Ludwig, "and we don't want any more delays."

He was making me sound as young as Valencia. I wasn't even sure that he'd had time to examine the badge or that anyone else had. Woodward recaptured Valencia's hand before he led the way beyond a mound. As the others followed him I noticed that the trees beside the path were carved with names. That ought to have made the path feel more frequently used, but then how could it be a secret route? I was about to draw everyone's attention when I heard Woodward say "There it is for you, Valencia. There, up high."

She cried out, and I ran around the hillock onto a crooked stretch of path. Valencia was clinging to Woodward's hand while she tilted her head to gaze into the treetops. "It's just like my bracelet," she cried.

The full moon was nesting among the highest branches ahead. It was as pale as Woodward's face but growing brighter, as though only the sun had held it back. At first I thought it was all Valencia meant, and then, as I followed the twisted path, I saw something that choked off my breath. Other shapes in the treetops had crept out of hiding. Lined up behind the silhouetted branches were all the phases of the moon.

There were crescents at each end of the pallid parade, and gibbous moons on either side of the full one, and every incomplete form of the moon in between. "Can you see?" Valencia urged everyone.

"It's the moon," Ludwig said, and Claude agreed with him.

"Don't stop," Verona told her. "You can look at it while we're walking."

I almost wished that I could borrow their unawareness if it would somehow keep me safe. I might even have tried to believe that Valencia's imagination had inflamed mine if Woodward hadn't murmured "Wait till they're up there, then they'll see."

While I didn't understand this, it disturbed me even more than the sight of all the thirteen moons. I was opening my mouth with no idea what to say when I heard a sound I would never have expected to welcome—a clash of glass. It came from the direction where we'd heard the chatter of the magpies, and it meant that the recycling bins full of Christmas bottles all along our road were being emptied. "We're going the wrong way," I said not as loud or as steadily as I would have liked. "There's home."

Everybody had to stop and turn to see where I was pointing, but Woodward only swivelled his head. It looked as if an extra moon had sunk to earth and was spinning slowly in the air beside Valencia. Nobody moved to join me, even when another clatter of glass came through the woods. "You can hear that," I almost begged. "They're collecting bottles on our road."

"Nothing of the kind," said Woodward. "They'll be boys like the ones who were chasing you, dumping rubbish in my woods."

"Then you'd better go and stop them," I dared to say. "We'll come too."

"I'll see to all of you first," Woodward said and turned towards the frieze of moons entangled in the branches. "Come along, Valencia. We don't want you anywhere near that sort of boy."

"Hold my hand, Valencia," I called in desperation if not panic. "You did before."

"Keep hold of Mr Woodward's," Verona said at once. "He's in charge."

She and the Smith boys gave me a backward glance that felt like a dismissal. Too late I realised that I should have taken Valencia's hand without announcing my intentions. "I'm going this way," I declared in the hope that my determination would infect the others, but I must have sounded childishly petulant. As I stalked off the path I was met by the chattering of magpies and the clash of a binful of bottles landing in a wagon. Behind me Woodward called "They're all waiting for you." I kept on and didn't look back, and then I heard no sound of any kind.

I told myself that if Valencia cried for help I would go back—

if anybody did—but I felt shamefully relieved when the woods stayed as silent as the moon. When I looked back at last I couldn't even see the path. The moon—just a full one—outlined the mounds and showed me the way ahead. Eventually I found that the rattle of bottles had brought me to the track that ended almost opposite my house. I sneaked across the road like a burglar. I was hoping to retreat to my room and put off any questions, but as I opened the front door my mother silenced the vacuum cleaner. "Did you have a good time with your chums?" she said.

"They went off in the woods with a ranger."

"Wipe your feet, Stuart." When she was satisfied at last she said "Why didn't you stay with them?"

"I didn't like him." My face felt capable of betraying my feelings, and my words almost let me down. "They didn't like me," I blurted on the way to my room.

Apart from the last remark, all this was some of what I told Mr Smith when he rang hours later, and Mrs Turner when she came to the house, looking like the headmistress she was and determined to establish the truth. At first she didn't seem to think it could be serious. The police did by the time they visited the house, because they interrogated me at length. I told them I'd been suspicious of Woodward and had tried to warn the others, who hadn't wanted to listen to somebody like me. I did my best to describe him, growing more nervous as I realised what I was describing—a face as jowly as the Smiths had but with features as small and delicate as Verona's and Valencia's. He didn't look like any of the photographs the police showed me. The sketch they made looked more like him, but it didn't help. Nobody called Woodward or of his description had ever worked as a ranger. The police never found a trace of him, nor any of the children who'd followed him into the woods at dusk.

For a while we had quite a few visitors, and then we had none at all, and nobody even spoke much to us. I felt blamed for returning alone from the woods, as if I didn't already blame myself enough, but what was I supposed to have done? I think everybody's mute reproof made my mother feel worse still, and by the summer she'd put the house up for sale. Before Christmas we were living in a house not much more than half the size in the next town.

She kept encouraging me to make new friends, but I was afraid to. I'd seen what happened when I tried. I did my best to lose myself in schoolwork instead, and aside from that I wrote stories in my room. I did well enough at my new school to come to university, hundreds of miles from the woods, but that hasn't helped me either. Everyone regards me as an outsider, because I've made sure I am. My room in the hall of residence is several storeys higher than my bedroom at home, but it makes no difference. It hasn't stopped the dreams, if that's all they are. I still hear the voice at night, just outside my window.

I want to think I never heard it, even on the day before we moved house—especially then. I don't know what I hoped to achieve by returning to the woods. I only knew I had to look, and I told my mother I was going for a last walk on the beach. I left her in the house so full of cartons that it felt as if she'd tried to box up every trace of clutter and only made another kind. I was glad nobody was in sight as I headed for the path.

I wandered through the woods for hours and found nothing at all. I couldn't even find the glade from which Ludwig had led us onto the path that turned back on itself. The woods were as silent as a secret waiting to be discovered. The only sign of humanity was the occasional name carved on a tree-trunk. The late October sun sank towards the mounds as if the pines were lowering it into its grave, and I turned homeward before nightfall. All that kept me peering about at the multitude of trees was the notion that I'd overlooked something in the dusk. Where had I seen it, or had I heard it? I could think of nothing I'd encountered that day—and then, with more unease than relief, I knew what I'd heard. It hadn't been that day, however. I was remembering Woodward's final words: "They're all waiting for you." At last I realised that he hadn't been talking to me.

As if the realisation had opened up my mind I glanced to the left and saw a path where I'd thought there were only random gaps between mounds. Names and dates were carved on the trees that flanked it, which seemed to prove that ordinary people used it. In any case it appeared to lead homeward. It took me around a series of hillocks, each one more steeped in darkness than the last. The declining light inked in the letters and numbers carved on the trees, and I saw that each name was followed by two dates—two years separated by a hyphen. Directly ahead of me were four names I knew all too well, the boys to the left of the path, the girls on the right. The second of their years was the same for everyone—that year.

As the sight held me as immobile as any of the trees I sensed that I was being watched. Perhaps my dread had brought him. He was almost hidden by a mound—I could have thought he was sprouting from it—but I saw enough of his greenish silhouette among the trees. This time he was only starting to have a face, and I guessed he still hadn't bothered with fingernails. I might have been forced to look closer if I hadn't heard a voice.

It wasn't his. It was Valencia's. "Up here," it called so softly that I might not have heard it except for the silence. I was afraid that if I raised my eyes I would see the multiplied moons, but what I saw when I couldn't keep my gaze down was yet more terrible. Valencia and Verona were there, and Claude and Ludwig too, in the midst of many other bodies turning sluggishly in the treetops. I didn't know if they were dangling like the contents of some creature's larder or hovering of their own unnatural accord. I couldn't grasp the expression that every face bore—in the gathering twilight I couldn't even tell whether they were blind. They were aware of me in some way, because as all the bodies swung in unison towards me they stretched out their arms to me. I was struggling to believe I'd seen none of this as I let out a savage cry and fled.

I don't know how I found my way to the road—perhaps because I'd been let go for the moment. I was able to take refuge in my room before my mother saw me, and I managed to pretend at dinner that nothing was wrong or at least not to say what was. The next day I started trying to forget, and years later I practically had until I heard that vandals had destroyed the woods—set fire to them during this summer's drought. None of the things I remembered were found, but where does that mean they've gone? The trees outside are as high as my room, and the wind in them sounds like a voice. If I look out, will I see the faces turning blindly in the air? "Up here," the voice whispers, but I already am. I would only need to step onto the sill and out of the window into the moonlight to be one of them at last. Perhaps then my mother would be proud.

IN LOVING
MEMORY

# Respects

By the time Dorothy finished hobbling downstairs, somebody had rung three times and knocked several more. Charmaine Bullough and some of her children were blocking the short garden path under a nondescript November sky. "What did you see?" Charmaine demanded at once.

"Why, nothing to bother about." Dorothy had glimpsed six-year-old Brad kicking the door, but tried to believe he'd simply wanted to help his mother. "Shouldn't you be at school?" she asked him.

Brad jerked a thumb at eight-year-old J-Bu. "She's not," he shouted.

Perhaps his absent siblings were, but not barely teenage Angelina, who was brandishing a bunch of flowers. "Are those for me?" Dorothy suggested out of pleasantness rather than because it seemed remotely likely, then saw the extent of her mistake. "Sorry," she murmured.

Half a dozen bouquets and as many wreaths were tied to the lamp-standard on the corner of the main road, beyond her gate.

Charmaine's scowl seemed to tug the roots of her black hair paler. "What do you mean, it's not worth bothering about?"

"I didn't realise you meant last week," Dorothy said with the kind of patience she'd had to use on children and parents too when she was teaching.

"You saw the police drive our Keanu off the road, didn't you?"

"I'm afraid I can't say I did."

At once, despite their assortment of fathers, the children resembled their mother more than ever. Their aggressive defensiveness turned resentful in a moment, accentuating their features, which were already as sharp as smashed glass. "Can't or won't?" Charmaine said.

"I only heard the crash."

Dorothy had heard the cause as well—the wild screech of tyres as the fifteen-year-old had attempted to swerve the stolen Punto into her road apparently at eighty miles an hour, only to ram a van parked opposite her house—but she didn't want to upset the children, although Brad's attention seemed to have lapsed. "Wanna wee," he announced and made to push past her, the soles of his trainers lighting up at every step.

As Dorothy raised a hand to detain him, J-Bu shook a fist that set bracelets clacking on her thin arm. "Don't you touch my brother. We can get you put in prison."

"You shouldn't just walk into someone else's house," Dorothy said and did her best to smile. "You don't want to end up—"

"Like who?" Angelina interrupted, her eyes and the studs in her nose glinting. "Like Keanu? You saying he was in your house?"

Dorothy might have. The day before the crash she'd come home to find him gazing out of her front room. He hadn't moved until she managed to fumble her key into the lock, at which point he'd let himself out of the back door. Apart from her peace of mind he'd stolen only an old handbag that contained an empty purse, and so she hadn't hurried to report him to the overworked police. If she had, might they have given him no chance to steal the car? As Dorothy refrained from saying any of this,

Charmaine dragged Brad back. "Come out of there. We don't want anyone else making trouble for us."

"I'm sorry not to be more help," Dorothy felt bound to say. "I do know how you feel."

Angelina peered so closely at her that Dorothy smelled some kind of smoke on the girl's breath. "How?"

"I lost my husband just about a year ago."

"Was he as old as you?" J-Bu said.

"Even older," said Dorothy, managing to laugh.

"Then it's not the same," Angelina objected. "It was time he went."

"Old people take the money we could have," said J-Bu.

"It's ours for all the things we need," Brad said.

"Never mind that now," said Charmaine and fixed Dorothy with her scowl. "So you're not going to be a witness."

"To what, forgive me?"

"To how they killed my son. I'll be taking them to court. The social worker says I'm entitled."

"They'll have to pay for Keanu," said Brad.

Dorothy took time over drawing a breath. "I don't think I've anything to offer except sympathy."

"That won't put shoes on their feet. Come on, all of you. Let's see Keanu has some fresh flowers. He deserves the best," Charmaine added louder still.

Brad ran to the streetlamp and snatched off a bouquet. About to throw them over Dorothy's wall, he saw her watching and flung them in the road. As Angelina substituted her flowers, Dorothy seemed to hear a noise closer to the house. She might have thought a rose was scratching at the window, but the flower was inches distant. In any case, the noise had sounded muffled by the glass. She picked up a beer can and a hamburger's polystyrene shell from her garden and carried them into the house.

When she and Harry had moved in she'd been able to run through it without pausing for breath. She could easily outdistance him to the bedroom, which had been part of their fun. Now she tried not to breathe, since the flimsy shell harboured the chewed remains of its contents. She hadn't reached the kitchen when she had to gasp, but any unwelcome smell was blotted out by the scents of flowers in vases in every downstairs room.

She dumped the rubbish in the backyard bin and locked the back door. The putty was still soft around the pane Mr Thorpe had replaced. Though he'd assured her it was safe, she was testing the glass with her knuckles when something sprawled into the hall. It was the free weekly newspaper, and Keanu's death occupied the front page. **LOCAL TEENAGER DIES IN POLICE CHASE.**

She still had to decide whether to remember Harry in the paper. She took it into the dining-room, where a vaseful of chrysanthemums held up their dense yellow heads towards the false sun of a Chinese paper globe, and spread the obituary pages across the table. Keanu was in them too. Which of the remembrances were meant to be witty or even intended as a joke? "Kee brought excitement into everyone's life"? "He was a rogue like children are supposed to be"? "There wasn't a day he didn't come up with some new trick"? "He raced through life like he knew he had to take it while he could"? "Even us that was his family couldn't keep up with his speed"? Quite a few of them took it, Dorothy suspected, along with other drugs. "When he was little his feet lit up when he walked, now they do because he's God's new angel." She dabbed at her eyes, which had grown so blurred that the shadows of stalks drooping out of the vase appeared to grope at the newsprint. She could do with a walk herself.

She buttoned up her winter overcoat, which felt heavier than last year, and collected her library books from the front room. Trying to read herself to sleep only reminded her that she was alone in bed, but even downstairs she hadn't finished any of them—the deaths in the detective stories seemed insultingly trivial, and the comic novels left her cold now that she couldn't share the jokes. She lingered for a sniff at the multicoloured polyanthuses in the vase on her mother's old sideboard before loading her scruffiest handbag with the books. The sadder a bag looked, the less likely it was to be snatched.

The street was relatively quiet beneath the vague grey sky, with just a few houses pounding like nightclubs. The riots in Keanu's memory—children smashing shop windows and pelting police cars with bricks—had petered out, and in any case they hadn't started until nightfall. Most of the children weren't home from school or wherever else they were. Stringy teenagers were loitering near the house with the reinforced front door, presumably waiting for the owner of the silver Jaguar to deal with them. At the far end of the street from Dorothy's house the library was a long low blotchy concrete building, easily mistaken for a new church.

She was greeted by the clacking of computer keyboards. Some of the users had piled books on the tables, but only to hide the screens from the library staff. As she headed for the shelves Dorothy glimpsed instructions for making a bomb and caught sight of a film that might have shown an equestrian busy with the tackle of her horse if it had been wearing any. On an impulse Dorothy selected guides to various Mediterranean holiday resorts. Perhaps one or more of her widowed friends might like to join her next year. She couldn't imagine travelling by herself.

She had to slow before she reached her gate. A low glare of sunlight cast the shadow of a rosebush on the front window before being extinguished by clouds, leaving her the impression that a thin silhouette had reared up and then crouched out of sight beyond the glass. She rummaged nervously in her handbag and unlocked the door. It had moved just a few inches when it encountered an obstruction that scraped across the carpet. Someone had strewn Michaelmas daisies along the hall.

Were they from her garden? So far the vandals had left her flowers alone, no doubt from indifference. As her eyes adjusted to the dimness she saw that the plants were scattered the length of the hall, beyond which she could hear a succession of dull impacts as sluggish as a faltering heart. Water was dripping off the kitchen table from the overturned vase, where the trail of flowers ended. She flustered to the back door, but it was locked and intact, and there was no other sign of intrusion. She had to conclude that she'd knocked the vase over and, still without noticing unless she'd forgotten, tracked the flowers through the house.

The idea made her feel more alone and, in a new way, more nervous. She was also disconcerted by how dead the flowers were, though she'd picked them yesterday; the stalks were close to crumbling in her hands, and she had to sweep the withered petals into a dustpan. She binned it all and replenished the vase with Harry's cyclamen before sitting on the worn stairs while she rang Helena to confirm Wednesday lunch. They always met midweek, but she wanted to talk to someone. Once she realised that Helena's grandchildren were visiting she brought the call to an end.

The house was big enough for children, except that she and Harry couldn't have any, and now it kept feeling too big. Perhaps they should have moved, but she couldn't face doing so on her own. She cooked vegetables to accompany the rest of yesterday's casserole, and ate in the dining-room to the sound of superannuated pop songs on the radio, and leafed through her library books in the front room before watching a musical that would have made Harry restless. She could hear gangs roving the streets, and was afraid her lit window might attract them. Once she'd checked the doors and downstairs windows she plodded up to bed.

Girls were awaiting customers on the main road. As Dorothy left the curtains open a finger's width she saw Winona Bullough negotiate with a driver and climb into his car. Was the girl even sixteen? Dorothy was close to asking Harry, but it felt too much like talking to herself, not a habit she was anxious to acquire. She climbed into her side of the bed and hugged Harry's pillow as she reached with her free hand for the light-cord.

The night was a medley of shouts, some of which were merely conversations, and smashed glass. Eventually she slept, to be wakened by light in the room. As she blinked, the thin shaft coasted along the bedroom wall. She heard the taxi turn out of the road, leaving her unsure whether she had glimpsed a silhouette that reminded her of stalks. Perhaps the headlamps had sent a shadow from her garden, though wasn't the angle wrong? She stared at the dark and tried not to imagine that it was staring back at her. "There's nobody," she whispered, hugging the pillow.

She needed to be more active, that was all. She had to occupy her mind and tire her body out to woo a night's unbroken sleep. She spent as much of Saturday in weeding the front garden as the pangs of her spine would allow. By late afternoon she wasn't even half finished, and almost forgot to buy a wreath. She might have taken Harry some of his own flowers, but she liked to support the florist's on the main road, especially since it had been damaged by the riots. At least the window had been replaced. Though the florist was about to close, he offered Dorothy a cup of tea while his assistant plaited flowers in a ring. Some good folk hadn't been driven out yet, Dorothy told them both, sounding her age.

She draped the wreath over the phone in her hall and felt as if she were bidding goodbye to any calls, an idea too silly to consider. After dinner she read about far places that might have changed since she and Harry had visited them, and watched a love story in tears that would have embarrassed him. She was in bed by the time the Saturday-night uproar began. Once she was wakened by a metallic clack that sounded closer than outside, but when she stumbled to the landing the hall was empty. Perhaps a wind had snapped the letterbox. As she huddled under the quilt she wondered if she ought to have noticed something about the hall, but the impression was too faint to keep her awake. It was on her mind when church bells roused her, and as soon as she reached the stairs she saw what was troubling her. There was no sign of the wreath.

She grabbed the banister so as not to fall. She was hastening to reassure herself that the flowers were under the hall table, but they weren't. Had she forgotten taking them somewhere? They were in none of the ground-floor rooms, nor the bathroom, her bedroom, the other one that could have been a nursery but had all too seldom even done duty as a guest room. She was returning downstairs when she saw a single flower on the carpet inches from the front door.

Could a thief have dragged the wreath through the letterbox? She'd heard that criminals used rods to fish property from inside houses. She heaved the bolts out of their sockets and flung the door open, but there was no evidence on the path. It didn't seem worth reporting the theft to the police. She would have to take Harry flowers from the garden. She dressed in her oldest clothes and brought tools from the shed, and was stooping to uproot a weed that appeared to have sprouted overnight when she happened to glance over the wall. She straightened up and gasped, not only with the twinge in her back. One of the tributes to Keanu looked far too familiar.

She clutched at her back as she hobbled to the streetlamp. There was the wreath she'd seen made up at the florist's. It was the only item to lack a written tag. "Earned yourself some wings, Kee" and "Give them hell up there" and "Get the angels singing along with your iPod" were among the messages. The wreath was hung on the corner of a bouquet's wrapping. Dorothy glared about as she retrieved it, daring anyone to object. As she slammed the front door she thought she heard small feet running away.

She had no reason to feel guilty, and was furious to find she did. She locked away the tools and changed into the dark suit that Harry used to like her to wear whenever they dined out. A bus from the shattered shelter on the main road took her to the churchyard, past houses twice the size of hers. All the trees in their gardens were bare now. She and Harry had been fond of telling each other that they would see them blossom next year. The trees in the graveyard were monotonously evergreen, but she never knew what that was meant to imply. She cleared last week's flowers away from Harry's stone and replaced them with the wreath, murmuring a few sentences that were starting to feel formulaic. She dropped the stale flowers in the wire bin outside the concrete wedge of a church on her way to the bus.

As it passed her road she saw the Bulloughs on her path. Charmaine and her offspring strode to meet her at the lamp. "Brad says you lifted our Keanu's flowers."

"Then I'm afraid he's mistaken. I'm afraid—"

"You should be," said Arnie, the biggest and presumably the eldest of the brood. "Don't talk to my mam like that, you old twat."

Dorothy had begun to shake—not visibly, she hoped—but stood her ground. "I don't think I'm being offensive."

"You're doing it now," Arnie said, and his face twisted with loathing. "Talking like a teacher."

"Leave it, Arn," his mother said more indulgently than reprovingly, and stared harder at Dorothy. "What were you doing touching Keanu's things?"

"As I was trying to explain, they weren't his. I'm not accusing anybody, but someone took a wreath I'd bought and put it here."

"Why didn't you?" demanded Angelina.

"Because they were for my husband."

"When are you going to get Kee some?" J-Bu said at once.

"She's not," Charmaine said, saving Dorothy the task of being more polite. "Where were these ones you took supposed to be?"

"They were in my house."

"Someone broke in, did they? Show us where."

"There's no sign of how they did it, but—"

"Know what I think? You're mad."

"Should be locked up," said Angelina.

"And never mind expecting us to pay for it," Arnie said.

"I'm warning you in front of witnesses," said their mother. "Don't you ever touch anything that belongs to this family again."

"You keep your dirty hands off," J-Bu translated.

"Mad old bitch," added Brad.

Dorothy still had her dignity, which she bore into the house without responding further. Once the door was closed she gave in to shivering. She stood in the hall until the bout was over, then peeked around the doorway of the front room. She didn't know how long she had to loiter before an angry glance showed that the pavement was deserted. "Go on, say I'm a coward," she murmured. "Maybe it isn't wise to be too brave when you're on your own."

Who was she talking to? She'd always found the notion that Harry might have stayed with her too delicate to put to any test. Perhaps she felt a little less alone for having spoken; certainly while weeding the garden she felt watched. She had an intermittent sense of it during her meal, not that she had much appetite, and as she tried to read and to quell her thoughts with television. It followed her to bed, where she wakened in the middle of the night to see a gliding strip of light display part of a skinny silhouette. Or had the crouching shape as thin as twigs scuttled across the band of light? Blinking showed her only the light on the wall, and she let the scent of flowers lull her to sleep.

It took daylight to remind her there were no flowers in the room. There seemed to be more of a scent around her bed than the flowers in the house accounted for. Were her senses letting her down? She was glad of an excuse to go out. Now that they'd closed the post office around the corner the nearest was over a mile away, and she meant to enjoy the walk.

She had to step into the road to avoid vehicles parked on the pavement, which was also perilous with cyclists taking time off school. Before she reached the post office her aching skull felt brittle with the sirens of police cars and ambulances in a hurry to be elsewhere, not to mention the battering clatter of road drills. As she shuffled to the counter she was disconcerted by how much pleasure she took in complaining about all this to her fellow pensioners. Was she turning into just another old curmudgeon weighed down by weary grievances? Once she'd thanked the postmaster several times for her pension she headed for the bus stop. One walk was enough after all.

Although nobody was waiting outside her house, something was amiss. She stepped gingerly down from the bus and limped through gaps in the traffic. What had changed about her garden? She was at the corner of the road when she realised she couldn't see a single flower.

Every one had been trampled flat. Most of the stalks were snapped and the blossoms trodden into the earth, which displayed the prints of small trainers. Dorothy held onto the gatepost while she told herself that the flowers would grow again and she would live to see them, and then she walked stiff as a puppet into the house to call the police.

While it wasn't an emergency, she didn't expect to wait nearly four unsettled hours for a constable less than half her age to show up. By this time a downpour had practically erased the footprints, which he regarded as too common to be traceable. "Have you any idea who's responsible?" he hoped if not the opposite, and pushed his cap higher on his prematurely furrowed forehead.

"The family of the boy you were trying to catch last week."

"Did you see them?"

"I'm certain someone must have. Mrs Thorpe opposite hardly ever leaves the house. Too worried that clan or someone like them will break in."

"I'll make enquiries." As Dorothy started to follow him he said "I'll let you know the outcome."

He was gone long enough to have visited several of her neighbours. She hurried to admit him when the doorbell rang, but he looked embarrassed, perhaps by her eagerness. "Unfortunately I haven't been able to take any statements."

"You mean nobody will say what they saw," Dorothy protested in disbelief.

"I'm not at liberty to report their comments."

As soon as he drove away she crossed the road. Mrs Thorpe saw her coming and made to retreat from the window, then adopted a sympathetic wistful smile and spread her arms in a generalised embrace while shaking her head. Dorothy tried the next house, where the less elderly but equally frail of the unmarried sisters answered the door. "I'm sorry," she said, and Dorothy saw that she shouldn't expect any witness to risk more on her behalf. She was trudging home when she caught sight of an intruder in her front room.

Or was it a distorted reflection of Keanu's memorial, thinned by the glare of sunlight on the window? At first she thought she was seeing worse than unkempt hair above an erased face, and then she realised it was a tangle of flowers perched like a makeshift crown or halo on the head, even if they looked as though they were sprouting from a dismayingly misshapen cranium. As she ventured a faltering step the silhouette crouched before sidling out of view. She didn't think a reflection could do that, and she shook her keys at the house on her way to the door.

A scent of flowers greeted her in the hall. Perhaps her senses were on edge, but the smell was overpowering—sickly and thick. It reminded her how much perfume someone significantly older might wear to disguise the staleness of their flesh. Shadows hunched behind the furniture as she searched the rooms, clothes stirred in her wardrobe when she flung it open, hangers jangled at her pounce in the guest room, but she had already established that the back door and windows were locked. She halted on the stairs, waving her hands to waft away the relentless scent. "I saw you," she panted.

But had she? Dorothy kept having to glance around while she cooked her dinner and did her best to eat it, though the taste seemed to have been invaded by a floral scent, and later as she tried to read and then to watch television. She was distracted by fancying there was an extra shadow in the room, impossible to locate unless it was behind her. She almost said "Stay out of here" as she took refuge in bed. She mouthed the words at the dark and immediately regretted advertising her nervousness.

She had to imagine Harry would protect her before she was able to sleep. She dreamed he was stroking her face, and in the depths of the night she thought he was. Certainly something like a caress was tracing her upturned face. As she groped for the cord, the sensation slipped down her cheek. The light gave her time to glimpse the insect that had crawled off her face, waving its mocking antennae. It might have been a centipede or millipede—she had no chance to count its many legs as it scurried under the bed.

She spent the rest of the interminable night sitting against the headboard, the bedclothes wrapped tight around her drawn-up legs. She felt surrounded, not only by an oppressive blend of perfume that suggested somebody had brought her flowers—on what occasion, she preferred not to think. As soon as daylight paled Keanu's streetlamp she grabbed clothes and shook them above the stairs on her way to the bathroom.

She found a can of insect spray in the kitchen. When she made herself kneel, stiff with apprehension as much as with rheumatism, she saw dozens of flowers under her bed. They were from the garden—trampled, every one of them. Which was worse: that an intruder had hidden them in her room or that she'd unknowingly done so? She fetched a brush and dustpan and shuddered as she swept the debris up, but no insects were lurking. Once she'd emptied the dustpan and vacuumed the carpet she dressed for gardening. She wanted to clear up the mess out there, and not to think.

She was loading a second bin-liner with crushed muddy flowers when she heard Charmaine Bullough and her youngest children outdoing the traffic for noise on the main road. Dorothy managed not to speak while they lingered by the memorial, but Brad came to her gate to smirk at her labours. "I wonder who could have done this," she said.

"Don't you go saying it was them," Charmaine shouted. "That's defamation. We'll have you in court."

"I was simply wondering who would have had a motive."

"Never mind sounding like the police either. Why'd anybody need one?"

"Shouldn't have touched our Kee's flowers," J-Bu said.

Her mother aimed a vicious backhand swipe at her head, but a sojourn in the pub had diminished her skills. As Charmaine regained her balance Dorothy blurted "I don't think he would mind."

"Who says?" demanded Brad.

"Maybe he would if he could." Dorothy almost left it at that, but she'd been alone with the idea long enough. "I think he was in my house."

"You say one more word about him and you won't like what you get," Charmaine deafened her by promising. "He never went anywhere he wasn't wanted."

Then that should be Charmaine's house, Dorothy reflected, and at once she saw how to be rid of him. She didn't speak while the Bulloughs stared at her, although it looked as if she was heeding Charmaine's warning. When they straggled towards their house she packed away her tools and headed for the florist's. "Visiting again?" the assistant said, and it was easiest to tell her yes, though Dorothy had learned to stay clear of the churchyard during the week, when it tended to be occupied by drunks and other addicts. She wouldn't be sending a remembrance to the paper either. She didn't want to put Harry in the same place as

Keanu, even if she wished she'd had the boy to teach.

Waiting for nightfall made her feel uncomfortably like a criminal. Of course that was silly, and tomorrow she could discuss next year's holiday with Helena over lunch. She could have imagined that her unjustified guilt was raising the scents of the wreath. It must be the smell of the house, though she had the notion that it masked some less welcome odour. At last the dwindling day released her, but witnesses were loitering on both sides of the road.

She would be committing no crime—more like the opposite. As she tried to believe they were too preoccupied with their needs to notice or at least to identify her, a police car cruised into the road. In seconds the pavements were deserted, and Dorothy followed the car, hoping for once that it wouldn't stop at the Bullough house.

It didn't, but she did. She limped up the garden path as swiftly as her legs would work, past a motor bicycle that the younger Bulloughs had tired of riding up and down the street, and posted the wreath through the massively brass-hinged mahogany door of the pebbledashed terrace house. She heard Charmaine and an indeterminate number of her children screaming at one another, and wondered whether they would sound any different if they had a more than unexpected visitor. "Go home to your mother," she murmured.

The police were out of sight. Customers were reappearing from the alleys between the houses. She did her best not to hurry, though she wasn't anxious to be nearby when any of the Bulloughs found the wreath. She was several houses distant from her own when she glimpsed movement outside her gate.

The flowers tied to the lamp-standard were soaked in orange light. Most of them were blackened by it, looking rotten. Though the concrete post was no wider than her hand, a shape was using it for cover. As she took a not entirely willing step a bunch of flowers nodded around the post and dodged back. She thought the skulker was using them to hide whatever was left of its face. She wouldn't be scared away from her own house. She stamped towards it, making all the noise she could, and the remnant of a body sidled around the post, keeping it between them. She avoided it as much as she was able on the way to her gate. As she unlocked the door she heard a scuttling of less than feet behind her. It was receding, and she managed not to look while it grew inaudible somewhere across the road.

The house still smelled rather too intensely floral. In the morning she could tone that down before she went for lunch. She made up for the dinner she'd found unappetising last night, and bookmarked pages in the travel guide to show Helena, and even found reasons to giggle at a comedy on television. After all that and the rest of the day she felt ready for bed.

She stooped to peer under it, but the carpet was bare, though a faint scent lingered in the room. It seemed unthreatening as she lay in bed. Could the flowers have been intended as some kind of peace offering? In a way she'd been the last person to speak to Keanu. The idea fell short of keeping her awake, but the smell of flowers roused her. It was stronger and more suggestive of rot, and most of all it was closer. The flowers were in bed with her. There were insects as well, which didn't entirely explain the jerky movements of the mass of stalks that nestled against her. She was able to believe they were only stalks until their head, decorated or masked or overgrown with shrivelled flowers, lolled against her face.

# PASSING THROUGH PEACEHAVEN

"WAIT," MARSDEN SHOUTED AS HE FLOUNDERED off his seat. His vision was so overcast with sleep that it was little better than opaque, but so far as he could see through the carriages the entire train was deserted. "Terminate" was the only word he retained from the announcement that had wakened him. He blundered to the nearest door and leaned on the window to slide it further open while he groped beyond it for the handle. The door swung wide so readily that he almost sprawled on the platform. In staggering dangerously backwards to compensate he slammed the door, which seemed to be the driver's cue. The train was heading into the night before Marsden realised he had never seen the station in his life.

"Wait," he cried, but it was mostly a cough as the smell of some October fire caught in his throat. His eyes felt blackened by smoke and stung when he blinked, so that he could barely see where he was going as he lurched after the train. He succeeded in clearing his vision just in time to glimpse distance or a bend in the track extinguish the last light of the train like an ember. He panted coughing to a halt and stared red-eyed around him.

Two signs named the station Peacehaven. The grudging glow of half a dozen lamps that put him in mind of streetlights in an old photograph illuminated stretches of both platforms but seemed shy of the interior of the enclosed bridge that led across the pair of tracks. A brick wall twice his height extended into the dark beyond the ends of the platform he was on. The exit from the station was on the far side of the tracks, through a passage where he could just distinguish a pay phone in the gloom. Above the wall of that platform, and at some distance, towered an object that he wasted seconds in identifying as a factory chimney. He should be looking for the times of any trains to Manchester, but the timetable among the vintage posters alongside the platform was blackened by more than the dark. As he squinted at it, someone spoke behind him.

It was the voice that had wakened him. Apart from an apology for a delay, the message was a blur. "I can't hear much at the best of times," Marsden grumbled. At least the station hadn't closed for the night, and a timetable on the other platform was beside a lamp. He made for the bridge and climbed the wooden stairs to the elevated corridor, where narrow grimy windows above head height and criss-crossed by wire mesh admitted virtually no illumination. He needn't shuffle through the dark; his mobile phone could light the way. He reached in his overcoat pocket, and dug deeper to find extra emptiness.

Marjorie wouldn't have approved of the words that escaped his lips. He wasn't fond of them himself, especially when he heard them from children in the street. He and Marjorie would have done their best to keep their grandchildren innocent of such language and of a good deal else that was in vogue, but they would need to have had a son or daughter first. He ran out of curses as he trudged back across the bridge, which felt narrowed by darkness piled against the walls. The platform was utterly bare. Did he remember hearing or perhaps only feeling the faintest thump as he'd left his seat? There was no doubt that he'd left the mobile on the train.

He was repeating himself when he wondered if he could be heard. His outburst helped the passage to muffle the announcer's unctuous voice, which apparently had information about a signal failure. Marsden wasn't going to feel like one. He marched out of darkness into dimness, which lightened somewhat as he reached the platform.

Had vandals tried to set fire to the timetable? A blackened corner was peeling away from the bricks. Marsden pushed his watch higher on his wizened wrist until the strap took hold. Theoretically the last train—for Bury and Oldham and Manchester—was due in less than twenty minutes. "What's the hold-up again? Say it clearly this time," Marsden invited not quite at the top of his voice. When there was no response he made for the phone on the wall.

Was it opposite some kind of memorial? No, the plaque was a ticket window boarded up behind cracked glass. Surely the gap beneath the window couldn't be occupied by a cobweb, since the place was staffed. He stood with his back to the exit from the station and fumbled coins into the slot beside the receiver before groping for the dial that he could barely see in the glimmer from the platform.

"Ray and Marjorie Marsden must be engaged elsewhere. Please don't let us wonder who you were or when you tried to contact us or where we can return the compliment..." His answering message had amused them when he recorded it—at least, Marjorie had made the face that meant she appreciated his wit—but now it left him feeling more alone than he liked. "Are you there?" he asked the tape. "You'll have gone up, will you? You'll have gone up, of course. Just to let you know I'm stranded by an unexpected change of trains. If you play me back don't worry, I'll be home as soon as practicable. Oh, and the specialist couldn't find anything wrong. I know, you'll say it shows I can hear when I want to. Not true, and shall I tell you why? I'd give a lot to hear you at this very moment. Never mind. I will soon."

Even saying so much in so many words earned him no response, and yet he didn't feel unheard. His audience could be the station announcer, who was presumably beyond one of the doors that faced each other across the corridor, although neither betrayed the faintest trace of light. "I nearly didn't say I love you," he added in a murmur that sounded trapped inside his skull. "Mind you, you'll know that, won't you? If you don't after all these years you never will. I suppose that had better be it for now as long as you're fast asleep."

He still felt overheard. Once he'd hung up he yielded to a ridiculous urge to poke his head out of the corridor. The platforms were deserted, and the tracks led to unrelieved darkness. He might as well learn where he'd ended up while there was no sign of a train. "Just stepping outside," he informed anyone who should know.

The corridor didn't seem long enough to contain so much blackness. He only just managed to refrain from rubbing his eyes as he emerged onto an unpromising road. The front of the station gave it no light, but the pavements on either side of the cracked weedy tarmac were visibly uneven. Beyond high railings across the road the grounds of the factory bristled with tall grass, which appeared to shift, although he couldn't feel a wind. Here and there a flagstone showed pale through the vegetation. A sign beside the open gates had to do with motors or motor components, and Marsden was considering a closer look to pass the time when the announcer spoke again. "Going to attract effect" might have been part of the proclamation, and all that Marsden was able to catch.

Some delay must be owing to a track defect, of course. Much of the voice had ended up as echoes beyond the railings or simply dissipated in the night, but he also blamed its tone for confusing him. It had grown so oily that it sounded more like a parody of a priest than any kind of railway official. Marsden tramped into the passage and knocked on the door beside the ticket window. "Will you repeat that, please?"

If this sounded like an invitation to an argument, it wasn't taken up. He found the doorknob, which felt flaky with age, but the door refused to budge. He rubbed his finger and thumb together as he crossed to the other door, which tottered open at his knock, revealing only a storeroom. It was scattered with brushes and mops, or rather their remains, just distinguishable in the meagre light through a window so nearly opaque that on the platform he'd mistaken it for an empty poster frame. Vandals must have been in the room; the dimness smelled as ashen as it looked, while the tangles of sticks that would once have been handles seemed blackened by more than the dark. That was all he managed to discern before the voice spoke to him.

Was the fellow too close to the microphone? If he was trying to be clearer, it achieved the opposite. Of course nobody was next to alive; a train was the next to arrive. "Speak clearly, not up," Marsden shouted as he slammed the door and hurried to the bridge, where he did his best to maintain his pace by keeping to the middle of the passage. If an object or objects were being dragged somewhere behind him, he wanted to see what was happening. He clumped breathlessly down the stairs and limped onto the platform. How could he have thought the windows were poster frames? There was one on either side of the exit, and although both rooms were unlit, a figure was peering through the window of the office.

Or was it a shadow? It was thin and black enough. There was no light inside the room to cast it, and yet it must be a shadow, since it had nothing for a face. Marsden was still trying to identify its source when he noticed that the door he'd slammed was wide open. It had felt unsteady on its hinges, and at least he had an explanation for the dragging sound he'd heard. He set about laughing at his own unease, and then the laugh snagged in his throat like another cough. The silhouette was no longer pressed against the window.

Had it left traces of its shape on the discoloured glass? As he paced back and forth, trying either to confirm or shake off the impression, he felt like an animal trapped in a cage and watched by spectators. He'd met with no success by the time the voice that might belong to the owner of the shadow had more to say. "Where's the party?" Marsden was provoked to mutter. "What's departing?" he demanded several times as loud. "It's supposed to arrive first," he pointed out, glaring along the tracks at the unrelieved night. The few words he'd managed to recognise or at least to guess had sounded oilier than ever, close to a joke. Why couldn't the fellow simply come and tell him what to expect? Was he amusing himself by spying on the solitary passenger? "Yes, you've got a customer," Marsden declared. "He's the chap who has to stand out here in the cold because you can't be bothered to provide a waiting-room."

The complaint left him more aware of the storeroom, so that he could have imagined he was being observed from there too. He would much rather fancy his return home to the bed that he hoped Marjorie was keeping warm for him. As he hugged himself to fend off the late October chill he wasn't too far from experiencing how her arms would feel when she turned in her sleep to embrace him. He couldn't help wishing that the tape had brought him her voice.

The only one he was likely to hear was the announcer's, and he needed to ensure he did. He lowered himself onto a bench opposite the exit and planted his hands on his knees. Though the seat felt unwelcomingly moist if not actually rotten, he concentrated on staying alert for the next message. His ears were throbbing with the strain, and his skin felt as if his sense of being watched were gathering on it, by the time his attention was rewarded.

Was someone clinking glasses? Had the staff found an excuse to celebrate? Marsden had begun to wonder if they were deriding his predicament when he identified the noise of bricks knocking together. The factory was more dilapidated than he'd been able to make out, then, and there was movement in the rubble. Perhaps an animal was at large—more than one, by the sound of it—or else people were up to no good. Suppose they were the vandals who'd tried to set fire to the station? Would the announcer deign to emerge from hiding if they or others like them trespassed on railway property, or was he capable of leaving his solitary customer to deal with them? Marsden could hear nothing now except his own heart, amplified by his concentration if not pumped up by stress. He wasn't sure if he glimpsed surreptitious movement at the exit, where he could easily imagine that the dark was growing crowded; indeed, the passage was so nearly lightless that any number of intruders might sneak into it unseen. He was gripping his knees and crouching forward like a competitor at the start of some pensioners' event while he strained to see whether anyone was sidling through the gloom when his heart jumped, and he did.

The voice was louder than ever, and its meaning more blurred. Even the odd relatively clear phrase amid the magnified mumbling left much to be desired. Marsden could have thought he was being warned about some further decay and informed that he had a hearing problem. The latter comment must refer to engineering, but wasn't this unreasonable too? How many hindrances was the train going to encounter? The reports of its progress were beginning to seem little better than jokes. But here was a final one, however inefficiently pronounced. It meant that the train was imminent, not that anything would shortly be alive.

Perhaps the man was slurring his words from drunkenness, and the clinking had indeed been glass, unless the contrivance of equality had reached such a pitch that the station was obliged to employ an announcer with a speech impediment. On that basis Marsden might seek a job as a telephone operator, but he and Marjorie were resigned to leaving the world to the young and aggressive. He peered along the railway, where the view stayed as black as the depths of the corridor opposite. All that his strained senses brought him besides a charred smell and a crawling of the skin was, eventually, another message.

"You won't be burying this old man," he retorted under his clogged breath. While the announcement must have referred to the train to Bury and Oldham, the voice had resembled a priest's more than ever. "And where's this train that's supposed to be arriving?" he demanded loud enough to rouse an echo in the exit corridor.

The next message was no answer. Presumably he was being told that unattended luggage would be removed without warning, but since he had no luggage, what was the point? Couldn't the fellow see him? Perhaps some legislation allowed him to be blind as well as largely incomprehensible. Still, here were another few words Marsden understood, even if he couldn't grasp where passengers were being told to change. "What was that?" he shouted, but the announcer hadn't finished. His tone was so ecclesiastical that for the space of an exaggerated heartbeat Marsden fancied he was being offered some kind of service, and then he recognised the phrase. It was "out of service".

He sucked in a breath that he had to replace once he'd finished coughing. "What's out?" he spluttered. "Where's my train?"

The only reply was an echo, all the more derisive for sounding more like "Where's my Ray?" He levered himself to his feet, muttering an impolite word at having somehow blackened the knee of his trousers, and hobbled to the bridge. An arthritic pang set him staggering like an old drunk, but he succeeded in gaining the top of the stairs without recourse to the banisters. He preferred to keep to the middle of the bridge, especially along the passage over the tracks. It was too easy to imagine that the darkness beneath the obscured windows was peopled with supine figures. Surely the humped mounds consisted simply of litter, despite the marks on a window about halfway along, five elongated trails that might have been left by a sooty hand as its owner tried to haul his body up. That afternoon Marsden had given a few coins to a woman lying in a railway underpass, but he hoped not to encounter anyone of the kind just now. He faltered and then stumbled fast to the end of the passage, mumbling "No change" as he clattered down to the platform.

"Here's your customer," he said at several times the volume, "and what are you going to do about it?" The question trailed away, however, and not only because the office was so thoroughly unlit from within. The imprint on the window had silenced him. He might still have taken it for a shadow if it weren't so incomplete. Just the top half of a face with holes for eyes was recognisable, and the bones of a pair of hands.

Some grimy vandal must have been trying to see into the room. Of course the marks weren't on the inside of the glass, or if they were, that was no reason to think that the figure at the window had stood in the same place. Nevertheless Marsden wasn't anxious to look closer, although he'd managed to distinguish nothing in the office. He made for the door with all the confidence he could summon up.

The storeroom distracted him. Even if his stinging eyes had

adjusted to the dimness, he couldn't understand how he'd failed to see that the room was more than untidy. It was full of burned sticks and bits of stick, some of which were thin as twigs. One charred tangle that, to judge by the blackened lump at the nearer end, consisted partly of a mop or brush came close to blocking the door. When he lurched to shut away the sight the edge of the door caught the object, and he glimpsed it crumbling into restless fragments before the slam resounded through the passage. He limped to the office door and, having rapped on a scaly panel, shouted "Will you come and tell me to my face what's happening?"

As far as he could determine, silence was the answer. He could have fancied that the station and its surroundings were eager for his next outburst. "You're meant to make yourself plain," he yelled. "I couldn't understand half of what you said."

If he was hoping to provoke a response, it didn't work. Had he offended the man? "I need to know where I'm going," he insisted. "I don't think that's unreasonable, do you?"

Perhaps the fellow thought he could behave as he liked while he was in charge. Perhaps he felt too important to descend to meeting the public, an attitude that would explain his tone of voice. Or might he not be on the premises? If he was beyond the door, what could he expect to gain by lying low? Surely not even the worst employee would act that way—and then Marsden wondered if he'd strayed on the truth. Suppose it wasn't a railway employee who was skulking in the office?

The kind of person who'd tried to set fire to the station would certainly be amused by Marsden's plight and think it even more of a joke to confuse him. Perhaps the indistinctness of the announcements was the result of suppressed mirth. Marsden shouldn't waste any more time if the information was false. He hurried to the phone and glared at the dim wall, which didn't bear a single notice.

No doubt vandals had removed any advertisements for taxis. At least the phone wasn't disabled. He fumbled the receiver off its hook and leaned almost close enough to kiss the blackened dial as he clawed at an enquiry number. He could have thought his hearing had improved when the bell began to ring; it sounded close as the next room. The voice it roused was keeping its distance, however. "Can you speak up?" Marsden urged.

"Where are you calling, please?"

This was sharp enough for a warning. Presumably the speaker was ensuring he was heard. "Peacehaven," Marsden said. "Taxis."

"Where is that, please?"

"Peacehaven," Marsden pronounced loud enough for it to grow blurred against his ear before he realised that he wasn't being asked to repeat the name. "Somewhere near Manchester."

In the pause that ensued he might have heard movement outside the passage. His hectic pulse obscured the noise, which must have been the tall grass scraping in a wind, even if he couldn't feel it. He was relieved when the voice returned until he grasped its message. "Not listed," it said.

"Forgive me, I wasn't asking for Peacehaven Taxis. Any cab firm here will do."

"There is no listing."

Was the fellow pleased to say so? He sounded as smug as the worst sort of priest. "The nearest one, then," Marsden persisted. "I think that might be—"

"There are no listings for Peacehaven."

"No, that can't be right. I'm in it. I'm at the railway station. You must have a number for that at least."

"There is none."

Marsden was aware of the dark all around him and how many unheard lurkers it could hide. "Is there anything more I can do for you?" the voice said.

It sounded so fulsome that Marsden was convinced he was being mocked. "You've done quite enough," he blurted and slammed the receiver on its hook.

He could try another enquiry number, or might he call the police? What could he say that would bring them to his aid yet avoid seeming as pathetic as he was determined not to feel? There was one voice he yearned to hear in the midst of all the darkness, but the chance of this at so late an hour seemed little better than infinitesimal. Nevertheless he was groping for change and for the receiver. He scrabbled at the slot with coins and dragged the indistinct holes around the dial. The bell measured the seconds and at last made way for a human voice. It was his own. "Ray and Marjorie Marsden must be engaged elsewhere…"

"I am. I wish you weren't," he murmured and felt all the more helpless for failing to interrupt his mechanical self. Then his distant muffled voice fell silent, and Marjorie said "Who is it?"

"It's me, love."

"Is that Ray?" She sounded sleepy enough not to know. "I can hardly hear you," she protested. "Where have you gone?"

"You'd wonder." He was straining to hear another sound besides her voice—a noise that might have been the shuffling of feet in rubble. "I'm stuck somewhere," he said. "I'll be late. I can't say how late."

"Did you call before?"

"That was me. Didn't you get me?"

"The tape must be stuck like you. I'll need to get a new one."

"Not a new husband, I hope." He wouldn't have minded being rewarded with the laugh he'd lived with for the best part of fifty years, even though the joke felt as old as him, but perhaps she was wearied by the hour. "Anyway," he said, "if you didn't hear me last time I'll sign off the same way, which as if you didn't know—"

"What was that?"

For too many seconds he wasn't sure. He'd been talking over it, and then she had. Surely it had said that a train was about to arrive; indeed, wasn't the noise he'd mistaken for thin footsteps the distant clicking of wheels? "It's here now," he tried to tell her through a fit of coughing. By the time he would be able to speak clearer, the train might have pulled in. Dropping the receiver on the hook, he dashed for the platform. He hadn't reached it when he heard a scraping behind him.

The storeroom was open again, but that wasn't enough in itself to delay him. His eyes had grown all too equal to the gloom in the passage, so that he was just able to discern marks on the floor, leading from outside the station to the room. Could someone not be bothered to pick up their dirty feet? The trails looked as if several objects had been dragged into the room. He didn't believe they had just been left; that wasn't why they made him uneasy. He had to squint to see that they were blurred by more than the dark. Whatever had left them—not anybody shuffling along, he hoped, since their feet would have been worse than thin—had crumbled in transit, scattering fragments along the route. He thought he could smell the charred evidence, and swallowed in order not to recommence coughing, suddenly fearful of being heard. What was he afraid of? Was he growing senile? Thank heaven Marjorie wasn't there to see him. The only reason for haste was that he had a train to catch. He tramped out of the passage and might have maintained his defiant pace all the way to the bridge if a shape hadn't reared up at the window of the storeroom.

Was the object that surmounted it the misshapen head of a mop? He couldn't distinguish much through the grimy pane, but the idea was almost reassuring until he acknowledged that somebody would still have had to lift up the scrawny excuse for a figure. It hadn't simply risen or been raised, however. A process that the grime couldn't entirely obscure was continuing to take place. The silhouette—the blackened form, rather—was taking on more substance, though it remained alarmingly emaciated. It was putting itself back together.

The spectacle was so nightmarishly fascinating that Marsden might have been unable to stir except for the clatter of wheels along the tracks. He staggered around to see dim lights a few hundred yards short of the station. "Stop," he coughed, terrified that the driver mightn't notice him and speed straight through. Waving his arms wildly, he sprinted for the bridge.

He'd panted up the stairs and was blundering along the middle of the wooden corridor when he thought he heard a noise besides the approach of the train. Was he desperate to hear it or afraid to? He might have tried to persist in mistaking it for wind in the grass if it weren't so close. He did his utmost to fix his shaky gaze on the far end of the corridor as he fled past shadow after crouching shadow. He almost plunged headlong down the further stairs, and only a grab at the slippery discoloured banister saved him. As he dashed onto the platform he saw that both doors in the passage out of the station were open. The sight brought him even closer to panic, and he began to wave his shivering arms once more as he tottered to the edge of the platform. "Don't leave me here," he cried.

The squeal of brakes seemed to slice through the dark. The engine blotted out the view across the tracks, and then a carriage sped past him. Another followed, but the third was slower. Its last door halted almost in front of him. Though the train was by no means the newest he'd ridden that day, and far from the cleanest, it seemed the next thing to paradise. He clutched the rusty handle and heaved the door open and clambered aboard. "You can go now. Go," he pleaded.

Who was the driver waiting for? Did he think the noises on the bridge were promising more passengers? There was such a volume of eager shuffling and scraping that Marsden almost wished his ears would fail him. He hauled at the door, which some obstruction had wedged open. He was practically deaf with his frantic heartbeat by the time the door gave, slamming with such force that it seemed to be echoed in another carriage. At once the train jerked forward, flinging him onto the nearest musty seat. He was attempting to recover his breath when the announcer spoke.

Was a window open in the carriage? The voice sounded close enough to be on the train, yet no more comprehensible. It was no longer simply unctuous; it could have been mocking a priest out of distaste for the vocation. Its only recognisable words were "train now departing", except that the first one was more like Ray—perhaps not just on this occasion, Marsden thought he recalled. He craned towards the window and was able to glimpse that both doors in the exit corridor were shut. Before he had time to ponder any of this, if indeed he wanted to, the train veered off the main line.

"Where are you taking me?" he blurted, but all too soon he knew. The train was heading for the property behind the station, a turn of events celebrated by a short announcement. There was no question that the speaker was on board, though the blurring of the words left Marsden unsure if they were "Ray is shortly alive." The swerve of the train had thrown open the doors between the carriages, allowing him to hear a chorused hiss that might have signified resentment or have been an enthusiastic "Yes" or, possibly even worse, the collapse of many burned objects into the ash he could smell. As the train sped through a gateway in the railings, he read the name on the sign: not Peacehaven Motors at all, or anything to do with cars. Perhaps the route was only a diversion, he tried to think, or a short tour. Perhaps whoever was on the train just wanted somebody to visit the neglected memorials and the crematorium.

# The Long Way

From an anecdote by Kim Greyson. Thanks, Kim!

It must have been late autumn. Because everything was bare I saw inside the house.

Dead leaves had been scuttling around me all the way from home. A chill wind kept trying to shrink my face. The sky looked thin with ice, almost as white as the matching houses that made up the estate. Some of the old people who'd been rehoused wouldn't have known where they were on it except for the little wood, where my uncle Philip used to say the council left some trees so they could call it the Greenwood Estate. Nobody was supposed to be living in the three streets around the wood when I used to walk across the estate to help him shop.

So many people in Copse View and Arbour Street and Shady Lane had complained about children climbing on trees and swinging from ropes and playing hide and seek that the council put a fence up, but then teenagers used the wood for sex and drink and drugs. Some dealers moved into Shady Lane, and my uncle said it got shadier, and the next road turned into Cops View. He said the other one should be called A Whore Street, though my parents told him not to let me hear. Then the council moved

all the tenants out of the triangle, even the old people who'd complained about the children, and boarded up the houses. By the time I was helping my uncle, people had broken in.

They'd left Copse View alone except for one house in the middle of the terrace. Perhaps they'd gone for that one because the boards they'd strewn around the weedy garden looked rotten. They'd uncovered the front door and the downstairs window, but I could never see in for the reflection of sunlight on leaves. Now there weren't many leaves and the sun had a cataract, and the view into the front room was clear. The only furniture was an easy chair with a fractured arm. The chair had a pattern like shadows of ferns and wore a yellowish circular antimacassar. The pinstriped wallpaper was black and white too. A set of shelves was coming loose from the back wall but still displaying a plate printed with a portrait of the queen. Beside the shelves a door was just about open, framing part of a dimmer room.

I wondered why the door was there. In our house you entered the rooms from the hall. My uncle had an extra door made so he could use his wheelchair, and I supposed whoever had lived in this house might have been disabled too. There was a faint hint of a shape beyond the doorway, and I peered over the low garden wall until my eyes ached. Was it a full-length portrait or a life-size dummy? It looked as if it had been on the kind of diet they warned the girls about at school. As I made out its arms I began to think they could reach not just through the doorway but across far too much of the room, and then I saw that they were sticks on which it was leaning slightly forward—sticks not much thinner than its arms. I couldn't distinguish its gender or how it was dressed or even its face. Perhaps it was keeping so still in the hope of going unnoticed, unless it was challenging me to object to its presence. I was happy to leave it alone and head for my uncle's.

He lived on Pasture Boulevard, where he said the only signs of pasture were the lorries that drove past your bedroom all night. The trees along the central reservation were leafy just with litter. My uncle was sitting in the hall of the house where he lived on the ground floor, and wheeled himself out as soon as he saw me. "Sorry I made you wait, Uncle Philip," I said.

"I'll wait for anything that's worth the wait." Having raised a thumb to show this meant me, he said "And what's my name again, Craig?"

"Phil," I had to say, though my parents said I was too young to.

"That's the man. Don't be shy of speaking up. Ready for the go?"

He might have been starting a race at the school where he'd taught physical education—teaching pee, he called it—until he had his first stroke. When I made to push the chair he brought his eyebrows down and thrust his thick lips forward, which might have frightened his pupils but now made his big square face seem to be trying to shrink as the rest of him had. "Never make it easy, Craig," he said. "You don't want my arms going on strike."

I trotted beside him to the Frugo supermarket that had done for most of the shops that were supposed to make the estate feel like a village. Whenever a Frugo lorry thundered past us he would mutter "There's some petrol for your lungs" or "Hold your breath." In the supermarket he flung a week's supply of healthy food from the Frugorganic section into the trolley and bought me a Frugoat bar, joking as usual about how they'd turned the oats into an animal. I pushed the trolley to his flat and helped him unload it and took it back to Frugo. When I passed his window again he opened it, flapping the sports day posters he'd tacked to the wall of the room, to shout "See you in a week if you haven't got yourself a girlfriend."

I had the books I borrowed from the public library instead, but I didn't need him to announce my deficiency. I knew he disapproved of girls for boys my age—they sapped your energy, he said. "I'll always come," I promised and made for Copse View, where the trees looked eager to wave me on. The wind gave up pushing me as I reached them, and I stopped at the house where the boards had been pulled down. As I peered across the front room, resting my fists on the crumbling wall, my eyes began to ache again. However much I stared, the dim figure with the sticks didn't seem to have moved—not in an hour and a half. It had to be a picture; why shouldn't whoever used to live there have put a poster up? I felt worse than stupid for taking so long to realise. My parents and the English teacher at my school said I had imagination, but I could do without that much.

Ten minutes brought me home to Woody Rise. "Well, would he?" my uncle used to say even after my parents gave up laughing or groaning. The houses on this edge of the estate were as big as his but meant for one family each—they looked as if they were trying to pass for part of the suburb that once had the estate for a park. My father was carrying fistfuls of cutlery along the hall. "Here's the boy who cares," he called, and asked me "How's the wheelie kid?"

"Tom," my mother rebuked him from the kitchen.

I thought he deserved more reproof when I wasn't even supposed to shorten my uncle's name, but all I said was "Good."

As my father repeated this several times my mother said "Let's eat in here. Quick as you like, Craig. We've people coming round for a homewatch meeting."

"I thought you were going out."

"Just put your coat on your chair for now. We've rescheduled our pupils for tomorrow. Didn't we say?"

She always seemed resentful if I forgot whichever extra job they were doing when. "I suppose you must have," I tried pretending.

"Had you found some mischief to get up to, Craig?" my father said. "Has she got a name?"

"I hope not," my mother said. "You can welcome the guests if you like, Craig."

"He's already looked after my brother, Rosie."

"And some of us have done more." In the main this was aimed at my father, and she said more gently "All right, Craig. I expect you want to be on your own for a change."

I would rather have been with them by ourselves—not so much at dinner, where I always felt they were waiting for me to drop cutlery or spill food. I managed to conquer the spaghetti bolognese by cutting up the pasta with my fork, though my mother didn't approve much of that either. Once I'd washed up for everyone I was able to take refuge in my bedroom before all the neighbours came to discuss watching out for burglars and car thieves and door-to-door con people and other types to be afraid of. I needed to be alone to write.

Nobody knew I did. My stories tried to be like the kind of film my parents wouldn't let me watch. That night I wrote about a girl whose car broke down miles from anywhere, and the only place she could ask for help was a house full of people who wouldn't come to her. The house was haunted by a maniac who cut off people's feet with a chainsaw so they couldn't escape. I frightened myself with this more than I enjoyed, and when I went to sleep despite the murmur of neighbours downstairs I dreamed that if I opened my eyes I would see a figure standing absolutely still at the end of the bed. I looked once and saw no silhouette against the glow from the next street, but it took me a while to go back to sleep.

For most of Sunday my parents were out of the house. As if they hadn't had enough of teaching at school all week, my mother did her best to coax adults to read and write while my father educated people about computers. They couldn't help reminding me of my school, where I wasn't too unhappy so long as I wasn't noticed. It was in the suburb next to the estate, and some of the boys liked to punch me for stealing their park even though none of us was alive when the estate was built, while a few of the girls seemed to want me to act as uncouth as they thought people from it should be. I tried to keep out of all their ways and not to attract any questions in class. My work proved I wasn't stupid, which was all that mattered to me. I liked English best, except when the teacher made me read out my work. I would mumble and stammer and squirm and blush until the ordeal was done. I hated her and everyone else who could hear my helplessly unmodulated voice, most of all myself.

I wouldn't have dared admit to anyone at school that I quite liked most homework. I could take my own time with it, and there was nobody to distract me, since my parents were at night school several evenings, either teaching or improving their degrees. It must have been hard to pay the mortgage even with two teachers' salaries, but I also thought they were competing with each other for how much they could achieve, and perhaps with my uncle as well. All this left me feeling I should do more for him, but there was no more he would let me do.

Soon it was Saturday again. I was eager to look at the house on Copse View, but once it was in sight I felt oddly nervous. I wasn't going to avoid it by walking around the triangle. That would make me late for my uncle, and I could imagine what he would think of my behaviour if he knew. The sky had turned to chalk, and the sun was a round lump of it caught in the stripped treetops; in the flat pale light the houses looked brittle as shell. The light lay inert in the front room of the abandoned house. The figure with the sticks was there, in exactly the same stance. It wasn't in the same place, though. It had come into the room.

At least, it was leaning through the doorway. It looked poised to jerk the sticks up at me, unless it was about to use them to spring like a huge insect across the room. While the sunlight didn't spare the meagre furniture—the ferny chair and its discoloured antimacassar, the plate with the queen's face on the askew shelf still clinging to the pinstriped wall—it fell short of illuminating the occupier. I could just distinguish that the emaciated shape was dressed in some tattered material—covered with it, at any rate. While the overall impression was greyish, patches were as yellowed as the antimacassar, though I couldn't tell whether these were part of the clothes or showing through. This was also the case with the head. It appeared to be hairless, but I couldn't make out any of the face. When my eyes began to sting with trying I took a thoughtless step towards the garden wall, and then I took several back, enough to trip over the kerb. The instant I regained my balance I dashed out of Copse View.

Perhaps there was a flaw in the window, or the glass was so grimy that it blurred the person in the room, though not the other contents. Perhaps the occupant was wearing some kind of veil. Once I managed to have these thoughts they slowed me down, but not much, and I was breathing hard when I reached my uncle's. He was sitting in the hall again. "All right, Craig, I wasn't going anywhere," he said. "Training for a race?"

Before I could answer he said "Forget I asked. I know the schools won't let you compete any more."

I felt as if he didn't just mean at sports. "I can," I blurted and went red.

"I expect if you think you can that counts."

As we made for Frugo I set out to convince him in a way I thought he would approve of, but he fell behind alongside a lorry not much shorter than a dozen houses. "Don't let me hold you up," he gasped, "if you've got somewhere you'd rather be."

"I thought you liked to go fast. I thought it was how you kept fit."

"That's a lot of past tense. See, you're not the only one that knows his grammar."

I was reminded of a Christmas when my mother told him after some bottles of wine that he was more concerned with muscles than minds. He was still teaching then, and I'd have hoped he would have forgotten by now. He hardly spoke in the supermarket, not even bothering to make his weekly joke as he bought my Frugoat bar. I wondered if I'd exhausted him by forcing him to race, especially when he didn't head for home as fast as I could push the laden trolley. I was dismayed to think he could end up no more mobile than the figure with the sticks.

I helped him unload the shopping and sped the trolley back to Frugo. Did he have a struggle to raise the window as he saw me outside his flat? "Thanks for escorting an old tetch," he called. "Go and make us all proud for a week."

He'd left me feeling ashamed to be timid, which meant not avoiding Copse View. As I marched along the deserted street I thought there was no need to look into the house. I was almost past it when the sense of something eager to be seen dragged my head around. One glimpse was enough to send me fleeing home. The figure was still blurred, though the queen's face on the plate beside the doorway was absolutely clear, but there was no question that the occupant had moved. It was leaning forward on its sticks at least a foot inside the room.

I didn't stop walking very fast until I'd slammed the front door behind me. I wouldn't have been so forceful if I'd realised my parents were home. "That was an entrance," said my father. "Anything amiss we should know about?"

"We certainly should," said my mother.

"I was just seeing if I could run all the way home."

"Don't take your uncle too much to heart," my mother said. "There are better ways for you to impress."

On impulse I showed them my homework books. My father pointed out where the punctuation in my mathematics work was wrong, and my mother wished I'd written about real life and ordinary people instead of ghosts in my essay on the last book I'd read. "Good try," she told me, and my father added "Better next time, eh?"

I was tempted to show them my stories, but I was sure they wouldn't approve. I stayed away from writing any that weekend, because the only ideas I had were about figures that stayed too still or not still enough. I tried not to think about them after dark, and told myself that by the time I went to my uncle's again, whatever was happening on Copse View might have given up for lack of an audience or been sorted out by someone else. But I was there much sooner than next week.

It was Sunday afternoon. While my mother peeled potatoes I was popping peas out of their pods and relishing their clatter in a saucepan. A piece of beef was defrosting in a pool of blood. My father gazed at it for a while and said "That'd do for four of us. We haven't had Phil over for a while."

"We haven't," said my mother.

Although I wouldn't have taken this for enthusiasm, my father said "I'll give him a tinkle."

Surely my uncle could take a taxi—surely nobody would expect me to collect him and help him back to his flat after dark. I squeezed a pod in my fist while I listened to my father on the phone, but there was silence except for the scraping of my mother's knife. My hand was clammy with vegetable juice by the time my father said "He's not answering. That isn't like him."

"Sometimes he isn't much like him these days," said my mother.

"Can you go over and see what's up, Craig?"

As I rubbed my hands together I wondered whether any more of me had turned as green. "Don't you want me to finish these?" I pleaded.

"I'll take over kitchen duty."

My last hope was that my mother would object, but she said "Wash your hands for heaven's sake, Craig. Just don't be long."

While night wouldn't officially fall for an hour, the overcast sky gave me a preview. I was in sight of the woods when I noticed a gap in the railings on Shady Lane. Hadn't I seen another on Arbour Street? Certainly a path had been made through the shrubs from the opening off Shady Lane. It wound between the trees not too far from Copse View. As I dodged along it bushes and trees kept blocking my view of the boarded-up houses. I couldn't help glancing at the vandalised house; perhaps I thought the distance made me safe. The scrawny figure hadn't changed its posture or its patchwork appearance. It looked as if it was craning forward to watch me or threatening worse. Overnight it had moved as much closer to the street as it had during the whole of the previous week.

I nearly forced my own way through the undergrowth to leave the sight behind. I was afraid I'd encouraged the figure to advance by trying to see it, perhaps even by thinking about it. Had the vandals fled once they'd seen inside the house? No wonder they'd left the rest of the street alone. I fancied the occupant might especially dislike people of my age, even though I hadn't been among those who'd rampaged in the woods. I was almost blind with panic and the early twilight by the time I fought off the last twigs and found the unofficial exit onto Arbour Street.

I was trying to be calmer when I arrived at my uncle's. He seemed to be watching television, which lent its flicker to the front room. I thought he couldn't hear me tapping on the pane for the cheers of the crowd. When I knocked harder he didn't respond, and I was nervous of calling to him. I was remembering a horror film I'd watched on television once until my mother had come home to find me watching. I'd seen enough to know you should be apprehensive if anyone was sitting with his back to you in that kind of film. "Uncle Philip," I said with very little voice.

The wheelchair twisted around, bumping into a sofa scattered with magazines. At first he seemed not to see me, then not to recognise me, and finally not to be pleased that he did. "What are you playing at?" he demanded. "What are you trying to do?" He waved away my answer as if it were an insect and propelled the chair across the room less expertly than usual. He struggled to shove the lower half of the window up, and his grimace didn't relent once he had. "Speak up for yourself. Weren't you here before?"

"That was yesterday," I mumbled. "Dad sent me. He—"

"Sending an inspector now, is he? You can tell him my mind's as good as ever. I know they don't think that's much."

"He tried to phone you. You didn't answer, so—"

"When did he? Nobody's rung here." My uncle fumbled in his lap and on the chair. "Where is the wretched thing?"

Once he'd finished staring at me as if I'd failed to answer in a class he steered the chair around the room and blundered out of it, muttering more than one word I would never have expected him to use. "Here it is," he said accusingly and reappeared brandishing the cordless phone. "No wonder I couldn't hear it. Can't a man have a nap?"

"I didn't want to wake you. I only did because I was sent."

"Don't put yourself out on my behalf." Before I could deny that he was any trouble he said "So why's Tom checking up on me?"

"They wanted you to come for dinner."

"More like one did if any. I see you're not including yourself."

I don't know why this rather than anything else was too much, but I blurted "Look, I came all this way to find out. Of—"

One reason I was anxious to invite him was the thought of passing the house on Copse View by myself, but he didn't let me finish. "Don't again," he said.

"You'll come, won't you?"

"Tell them no. I'm still up to cooking my own grub."

"Can't you tell them?"

I was hoping that my father would persuade him to change his mind, but he said "I won't be phoning. I'll phone if I want you round."

"I'm sorry," I pleaded. "I didn't mean—"

"I know what you meant," he said and gazed sadly at me. "Never say sorry for telling the truth."

"I wasn't."

I might have tried harder to convince him if I hadn't realised that he'd given me an excuse to stay away from Copse View. "Don't bother," he said and stared at the television. "See, now I've missed a goal."

He dragged the sash down without bothering to glance at me. Even if that hadn't been enough of a dismissal, the night was creeping up on me. I didn't realise how close it was until he switched on the light in the room. That made me feel worse than excluded, and I wasn't slow in heading for home.

Before I reached the woods the streetlamps came on. I began to walk faster until I remembered that most of the lamps around the woods had been smashed. From the corner of the triangle I saw just one was intact—the one outside the house on Copse View. I couldn't help thinking the vandals were scared to go near; they hadn't even broken the window. I couldn't see into the room from the end of the street, but the house looked awakened by the stark light, lent power by the white glare. I wasn't anxious to learn what effect this might have inside the house. The path would take me too close. I would have detoured through the streets behind Copse View if I hadn't heard the snarl of motorcycles racing up and down them. I didn't want to encounter the riders, who were likely to be my age or younger and protective of their territory. Instead I walked around the woods.

I had my back to the streetlamp all the way down Arbour Street. A few thin shafts of light extended through the trees, but they didn't seem to relieve the growing darkness so much as reach for me on behalf of the house. Now and then I heard wings or litter flapping. When I turned along Shady Lane the light started to jab at my vision, blurring the glimpses the woods let me have of the house. I'd been afraid to see it, but now I was more afraid not to see. I kept having to blink scraps of dazzle out of my eyes, and I waited for my vision to clear when a gap between the trees framed the house.

Was the figure closer to the window? I'd been walking in the road, but I ventured to the pavement alongside the woods. Something besides the stillness of the figure reminded me of the trees on either side of the house. Their cracked bark was grey where it wasn't blackened, and fragments were peeling off, making way for whitish fungus. Far too much of this seemed true of the face beyond the window.

I backed away before I could see anything else and stayed on the far pavement, though the dead houses beside it were no more reassuring than the outstretched shadows of the trees or the secret darkness of the woods, which kept being invaded by glimpses of the house behind the streetlamp. When I reached the corner of the triangle I saw that someone with a spray can had added a letter to the street sign. The first word was no longer just Copse.

Perhaps it was a vandal's idea of a joke, but I ran the rest of the way home, where I had to take time to calm my breath down. As I opened the front door I was nowhere near deciding what to tell my parents. I was sneaking it shut when my mother hurried out of the computer room, waving a pamphlet called *Safe Home.* "Are you back at last? We were going to phone Philip. Are you by yourself? Where have you been?"

"I had to go a long way. There were boys on bikes."

"Did they do something to you? What did they do?"

"They would have. That's why I went round." I wouldn't have minded some praise for prudence, but apparently I needed to add "They were riding motorbikes. They'd have gone after me."

"We haven't got you thinking there are criminals round every corner, have we?" My father had finished listening none too patiently to the interrogation. "We don't want him afraid to go out, do we, Rosie? It isn't nearly that bad, Craig. What's the problem with my brother?"

"He's already made his dinner."

"He isn't coming." Perhaps my father simply wanted confirmation, but his gaze made me feel responsible. "So why did you have to go over?" he said.

"Because you told me to."

"Sometimes I think you aren't quite with us, Craig," he said, though my mother seemed to feel this was mostly directed at her. "I was asking why he didn't take my call."

"He'd been watching football and—"

I was trying to make sure I didn't give away too much that had happened, but my mother said "He'd rather have his games than us, then."

"He was asleep," I said louder than I was supposed to speak.

"Control yourself, Craig. I won't have a hooligan in my house." Having added a pause, my mother turned her look on my father. "And please don't make it sound as if I've given him a phobia."

"I don't believe anyone said that. Phil's got no reason to call you a sissy, has he, Craig?" When I shook or at least shivered my head my father said "Did he say anything else?"

"Not really."

"Not really or not at all?"

"Not."

"Now who's going on at him?" my mother said in some triumph. "Come and have the dinner there's been so much fuss about."

Throughout the meal I felt as if I were being watched or would be if I even slightly faltered in cutting up my meat and vegetables and inserting forkfuls in my mouth and chewing and chewing and, with an effort that turned my hands clammy, swallowing. I managed to control my intake until dinner was finally done and I'd washed up, and then I was just able not to dash upstairs before flushing the toilet to muffle my sounds. Once I'd disposed of the evidence I lay on my bed for a while and eventually ventured down to watch the end of a programme about gang violence in primary schools. "Why don't you bring whatever you're reading downstairs?" my mother said.

"Maybe it's the kind of thing boys like to read by themselves," said my father.

I went red, not because it was true but on the suspicion that he wanted it to be, and shook my head to placate my mother. She switched off the television in case whatever else it had to offer wasn't suitable for me, and then my parents set about sectioning the Sunday papers, handing me the travel supplements in case those helped with my geography. I would much rather have been helped not to think about the house on Copse View.

Whenever the sight of the ragged discoloured face and the shape crouching over its sticks tried to invade my mind I made myself remember that my uncle didn't want me. I had to remember at night in bed, and in the classroom, and while I struggled not to let my parents see my fear, not to mention any number of situations in between these. I was only wishing to be let off my duty until the occupant of the derelict house somehow went away. My uncle didn't phone during the week, and I was afraid my father might call him and find out the truth, but perhaps he was stubborn as well.

I spent Saturday morning in dread of the phone. It was silent until lunchtime, and while I kept a few mouthfuls of bread and cheese down too. I lingered at the kitchen sink as long as I could, and then my mother said "Better be trotting. You don't want it to be dark."

"I haven't got to go."

"Why not?" my father said before she could.

"Uncle Phil, Uncle Philip said he'd phone when he wanted me."

"Since when has he ever done that?"

"Last week." I was trying to say as little as they would allow. "He really said."

"I think there's more to this than you're telling us," my mother warned me, if she wasn't prompting.

"It doesn't sound like Phil," my father said. "I'm calling him."

My mother watched my father dial and then went upstairs. "Don't say you've nodded off again," my father told the phone, but it didn't bring him an answer. At last he put the phone down. "You'd better go and see what's up this time," he told me.

"I think we should deal with this first," said my mother.

She was at the top of the stairs, an exercise book in her hand. I hoped it was some of my homework until I saw it had a red cover, not the brown one that went with the school uniform. "I knew it couldn't be our work with the community that's been preying on his nerves," she said.

"Feeling he hasn't got any privacy might do that, Rosie. Was there really any need to—"

"I thought he might have unsuitable reading up there, but this shows he's been involved in worse. Heaven knows what he's been watching or where."

"I haven't watched anything like that," I protested. "It's all out of my head."

"If that's true it's worse still," she said and tramped downstairs to thrust the book at my father. "We've done our best to keep you free of such things."

He was leafing through it, stopping every so often to frown, when the phone rang. I tried to take the book, but my mother recaptured it. I watched nervously in case she harmed it while my father said "It is. He is. When? Where? We will. Where? Thanks." He gazed at me before saying "Your uncle's had a stroke on the way home from shopping. He's back in hospital."

I could think of nothing I dared say except "Are we going to see him?"

"We are now."

"Can I have my book?"

My mother raised her eyebrows and grasped it with both hands, but my father took it from her. "I'll handle it, Rosie. You can have it back when we decide you're old enough, Craig."

I wasn't entirely unhappy with this. Once he'd taken it to their room I felt as if some of the ideas the house in Copse View had put in my head were safely stored away. Now I could worry about how I'd harmed my uncle or let him come to harm. As my father drove us to the hospital he and my mother were so silent that I was sure they thought I had.

My uncle was in bed halfway down a rank of patients with barely a movement between them. He looked shrunken, perhaps by his loose robe that tied at the back, and on the way to adopting its pallor. My parents took a hand each, leaving me to shuffle on the spot in front of his blanketed feet. "They'll be reserving you a bed if you carry on like this, Phil," my father joked or tried to joke.

My uncle blinked at me as if he were trying out his eyes and then worked his loose mouth. "Nod, you fool," he more or less said.

I was obeying and doing my best to laugh in case this was expected of me before I grasped what he'd been labouring to pronounce. I hoped my parents also knew he'd said it wasn't my fault, even if I still believed it was. "God, my shopping," he more or less informed them. "Boy writing on the pavement. Went dafter then." I gathered that someone riding on the pavement had got the bags my uncle had been carrying and that he'd gone after them, but what was he saying I should see as he pointed at his limp left arm with the hand my mother had been holding? He'd mentioned her as well. He was resting from his verbal exertions by the time I caught up with them. "Gave me this," he'd meant to say. "Another attack."

My parents seemed to find interpreting his speech almost as much of an effort as it cost him. I didn't mind it or visiting him, even by myself, since the route took me nowhere near Copse View. Over the weeks he regained his ability to speak. I was pleased for him, and I tried to be equally enthusiastic that he was recovering his strength. The trouble was that it would let him go home.

I couldn't wish he would lose it again. The most I could hope, which left me feeling painfully ashamed, was that he might refuse my help with shopping. I was keeping that thought to myself the last time I saw him in hospital. "I wouldn't mind a hand on Saturday," he said, "if you haven't had enough of this old wreck."

I assured him I hadn't, and my expression didn't let me down while he could see it. I managed to finish my dinner that night and even to some extent to sleep. Next day at school I had to blame my inattention and mistakes on worrying about my uncle, who was ill. Before the week was over I was using that excuse at home as well. I was afraid my parents would notice I was apprehensive about something else, and the fears aggravated each other.

While I didn't want my parents to learn how much of a coward I was, on another level I was willing them to rescue me by noticing. They must have been too concerned about the estate—about making it safe for my uncle and people like him. By the time I was due to go to him my parents were at a police forum, where they would be leading a campaign for police to intervene in schools however young the criminals. I loitered in the house, hoping for a call to say my uncle didn't need my help, until I realised that if I didn't go out soon it would be dark.

December was a week old. The sky was a field of snow. My white breaths led me through the streets past abandoned Frugo trolleys and Frugoburger cartons. I was walking too fast to shiver much, even with the chill that had chalked all the veins of the dead leaves near Copse View. The trees were showing every bone, but what else had changed? I couldn't comprehend the sight ahead, unless I was wary of believing in it, until I reached the end of the street that led to the woods. There wasn't a derelict house to be seen. Shady Lane and Arbour Street and, far better, Copse View had been levelled, surrounding the woods with a triangle of waste land.

I remembered hearing sounds like thunder while my uncle was in hospital. The streets the demolition had exposed looked somehow insecure, unconvinced of their own reality, incomplete with just half an alley alongside the back yards. As I hurried along Copse View, where the pavement and the roadway seemed to be waiting for the terrace to reappear, I stared hard at the waste ground where the house with the occupant had been. I could see no trace of the building apart from the occasional chunk of brick, and none at all of the figure with the sticks.

I found my uncle in his chair outside the front door. I wondered if he'd locked himself out until he said "Thought you weren't coming. I'm not as speedy as I was, you know."

As we made for Frugo I saw he could trundle only as fast as his weaker arm was able to propel him. Whenever he lost patience and tried to go faster the chair went into a spin. "Waltzing and can't even see my partner," he complained but refused to let me push. On the way home he was slower still, and I had to unload most of his groceries, though not my Frugoat bar, which he'd forgotten to buy. When I came back from returning the trolley he was at his window, which was open, perhaps because he hadn't wanted me to watch his struggles to raise the sash. "Thanks for the company," he said.

I thought I'd been more than that. At least there was no need for me to wish for any on the walk home. I believed this until the woods came in sight, as much as they could for the dark. Night had arrived with a vengeance, and the houses beyond the triangle of wasteland cut off nearly all the light from the estate. Just a patch at the edge of the woods was lit by the solitary intact streetlamp.

Its glare seemed starkest on the area of rubbly ground where the house with the watchful occupant had been. The illuminated empty stretch reminded me of a stage awaiting a performer. Suppose the last tenant of the house had refused to move? Where would they have gone now that it was demolished? How resentful, even vengeful, might they be? I was heading for the nearest street when I heard the feral snarl of bicycles beyond the houses. Without further thought I made for the woods.

Arbour Street and Shady Lane were far too dark. If the path took me past the site of the house, at least it kept me closer to the streetlamp. I sidled through the gap in the railings and followed the track as fast as the low-lying darkness let me. More than once shadows that turned out to be tendrils of undergrowth almost tripped me up. Trees and bushes kept shutting off the light before letting it display me again, though could anyone be watching? As it blazed in my eyes it turned my breaths the colour of fear, but I didn't need to think that. I was shivering only because much of the chill of the night seemed to have found a home in the woods. The waste ground of Copse View was as deserted as ever. If I glanced at it every time the woods showed it I might collide with something in the dark.

I was concentrating mostly on the path when it brought me alongside the streetlamp. Opposite the ground where the demolished house had been, the glare was so unnaturally pale that it reduced the trees and shrubs and other vegetation to black and white. A stretch of ferns and their shadows beside the path looked more monochrome than alive or real. My shadow ventured past the lamp before I did, and jerked nervously over a discoloured mosaic of dead leaves as I turned my back on the site of the house. Now that the light wasn't in my eyes I could walk faster, even if details of the woods tried to snag my attention: a circular patch of yellowish lichen on a log, lichen so intricate that it resembled embroidery; the vertical pattern on a tree trunk, lines thin and straight as pinstripes; a tangle of branches that put me in mind of collapsed shelves; a fractured branch protruding like a chair arm from a seat in a hollow tree with blanched ferns growing inside the hollow. None of this managed to halt me. It was a glimpse of a face in the darkness that did.

As a shiver held me where I was I saw that the face was peering out of the depths of a bush. It was on the side of the path that was further from Copse View, and some yards away from my route. I was trying to nerve myself to sprint past it when I realised why the face wasn't moving; it was on a piece of litter caught in the bush. I took a step that tried to be casual, and then I faltered again. It wasn't on a piece of paper as I'd thought. It was the queen's portrait on a plate.

At once I felt surrounded by the deserted house or its remains. I swung around to make sure the waste ground was still deserted—that the woods were. Then I stumbled backwards away from the streetlamp and almost sprawled into the undergrowth. No more than half a dozen paces away—perhaps fewer—a figure was leaning on its sticks in the middle of the path.

It was outlined more than illuminated by the light, but I could see how ragged and piebald the scrawny body was. It was crouching forward, as immobile as ever, but I thought it was waiting for me to make the first move, to give it the excuse to hitch itself after me on its sticks. I imagined it coming for me as fast as a spider. I sucked in a breath I might have used to cry for help if any had been remotely likely. Instead I made myself twist around for the fastest sprint of my life, but my legs shuddered to a halt. The figure was ahead of me now, at barely half the distance.

The worst of it was the face, for want of a better word. The eyes and mouth were little more than tattered holes, though just too much more, in a surface that I did my utmost not to see in any detail. Nevertheless they widened, and there was no mistaking their triumph. If I turned away I would find the shape closer to me, but moving forward would bring it closer too. I could only shut my eyes and try to stay absolutely still.

It was too dark inside my eyelids and yet not sufficiently dark. I was terrified to see a silhouette looming on them if I shifted so much as an inch. I didn't dare even open my mouth, but I imagined speaking—imagined it with all the force I could find inside myself. "Go away. Leave me alone. I didn't do anything. Get someone else."

For just an instant I thought of my uncle, to establish that I didn't mean him, and then I concentrated on whoever had robbed him. An icy wind passed through the woods, and a tree creaked like an old door. The wind made me feel alone, and I tried to believe I entirely was. At last I risked looking. There was no sign of the figure ahead or, when I forced myself to turn, behind me or anywhere else.

I no longer felt safe in the woods. I took a few steps along the path before I fought my way through the bushes to the railings. I'd seen a gap left by a single railing, but was it wide enough for me to squeeze through? Once I'd succeeded, scraping my chest and collecting flakes of rust on my prickly skin, I fled home. I slowed and tried to do the same to my breath at the end of my street, and then I made another dash. My mother's car was pulling away from the house.

She halted it beside me, and my father lowered his window. "Where do you think you've been, Craig?"

His grimness and my mother's made me feel more threatened than I understood. "Helping," I said.

"Don't lie to us," said my mother. "Don't start doing that as well."

"I'm not. Why are you saying I am? I was helping Uncle Phil. He's gone slow."

They gazed at me, and my father jerked a hand at the back seat. "Get in."

"Tom, are you sure you want him—"

"Your uncle's been run over."

"He can't have been. I left him in his flat." When this earned no response I demanded "How do you know?"

"They found us in his pocket." Yet more starkly my father added "Next of kin."

I didn't want to enquire any further. When the isolated streetlamp on Copse View came in sight I couldn't tell whether I was more afraid of what else I might see or that my parents should see it as well. I saw nothing to dismay me in the woods or the demolished street, however—nothing all the way to Pasture Boulevard. My mother had to park several hundred yards short of my uncle's flat. The police had put up barriers, beyond which a giant Frugo lorry was skewed across the central strip, uprooting half a dozen trees. In front of and under the cab of the lorry were misshapen pieces of a wheelchair. I tried not to look at the stains on some of them and on the road, but I couldn't avoid noticing the cereal bars strewn across the pavement. "He forgot to buy me one of those and I didn't like to ask," I said. "He must have gone back."

My parents seemed to think I was complaining rather than trying to understand. When I attempted to establish that it hadn't been my fault they acted as if I was making too much of a fuss. Before the funeral the police told them more than one version of the accident. Some witnesses said my uncle had been wheeling his chair so fast that he'd lost control and spun into the road. Some said he'd appeared to be in some kind of panic, others that a gang of cyclists on the pavement had, and he'd swerved out of their way. The cyclists were never identified. As if my parents had achieved one of their aims at last, the streets were free of rogue cyclists for weeks.

I never knew how much my parents blamed me for my uncle's death. When I left school I went into caring for people like him. In due course these included my parents. They're gone now, and while sorting out the contents of our house I found the book with my early teenage stories in it—childish second-hand stuff. I never asked to have it back, and I never wrote stories again. I couldn't shake off the idea that my imagination had somehow caused my uncle's death.

I could easily feel that my imagination has been revived by the exercise book—by the cover embroidered with a cobweb, the paper pinstriped with faded lines, a fern pressed between the yellowed pages and blackened by age. I'm alone with my imagination up here at the top of the stairs leading to the unlit hall. If there's a face at the edge of my vision, it must belong to a picture on the wall, even if I don't remember any there. Night fell while I was leafing through the book, and I have to go over there to switch the light on. Of course I will, although the mere thought of moving seems to make the floorboards creak like sticks. I can certainly move, and there's no reason not to. In a moment—just a moment while I take another breath—I will.

# Never to be Heard

As the coach swung into the drive that led to the Church of the Blessed Trinity, Fergal jumped up. He would have reached Brother Cox before the coach gasped to a halt except for tripping over lanky Kilfoyle's ankles in the aisle. Boys of all sizes crowded to the doors ahead of him, waving their hands in exaggerated disgust and denying they'd farted and blaming red-faced O'Hagan as usual, so that by the time Fergal struggled down onto the gravel Brother Cox was playing doorman outside the arched stone porch, ushering in each of his favourite choirboys with a pat in the small of the back. "Sir?" Fergal said.

The choirmaster gave him a dignified frown, rather spoiled by an April wind that, having ruffled the trees around the church, disordered the wreath of red hair that encircled his bald freckled scalp. "Shea, is it, now? O'Shea?"

"Shaw, sir. Sir, is it true Harty's mum and dad won't let him sing at the concert?"

"I believe that may turn out to be the truth of it, Shaw, yes."

Fergal found his eyes wanting to roll up, away from the choirmaster's inability to talk to him straight that was bad even by the standards of most adults, even of most teachers. If he looked above him he would see the pointed arch that reminded him uncomfortably of the naked women in the magazines making the rounds of the dormitory. "Sir, so if they're stopping him—"

"I'm not about to discuss the rights or otherwise of their decision with a choirboy, Shaw."

Fergal didn't care about their decision, let alone their objections to the music. "No, sir, what I meant was we'll be a tenor short, won't we? Sir, can I be him? My voice keeps—"

"Don't be so eager to lose your purity." Brother Cox was no longer speaking just to Fergal, who felt as though he'd been made to stand up in front of the whole of the choir. "You'll grow up soon enough," said the choirmaster with a blink of disapproval at the single hair Fergal's chin was boasting. "Sing high and sweet while you can."

"But sir, I keep not being—"

"March yourself along now. You're holding up half my flock."

Fergal bent sideways in case the choirmaster found his back worth patting, and dodged into the church. More than one window was a picture of Christ in his nightie, a notion Fergal wouldn't have dared admit to his mind until recently for fear of dying on the spot. Not only was the building full of pointed arches to inflame Fergal's thoughts, the broad stone aisle was an avenue of fat cylindrical pillars altogether too reminiscent of the part of himself that seemed determined to play tricks on him whenever and wherever it felt inclined. Choirboys were streaming down the aisle as their echoes searched for a way out through the roof. In front of the choirstalls on either side of the altar, a conductor was pointing his wand at members of an orchestra to conjure a note from them. Between him and the orchestra a woman was typing on a computer keyboard, and Fergal's interest nearly roused itself until he remembered why she was there—the stupidest aspect of the entire boring exercise. The computer was going to produce sounds nobody could hear.

When the Reverend Simon Clay had written the music there had been no computers: no way of creating the baser than base line he wanted for the final movement. The score had been lost for almost a century and rediscovered just over a year ago, not by any means to Fergal's delight. Even its title—*The Balance of the Spheres: A Symphony for Chorus and Large Orchestra*—was, like the music, too long to endure. Last year, when the choir had won a choral competition, some of the boys had sneaked away afterwards for a night in Soho, but now that Fergal felt old enough to join them, everyone was confined to quarters overnight and too far out of London to risk disobeying. He'd given up on that—he only wished he were anywhere else, listening to Unlikely Orifices or some other favourite band—but all he could do was take his place among the choirboys with hairless baby chins and wait for the orchestra to be ready. At last, though not to his relief, it was time to rehearse.

Brother Cox insisted on announcing the title of each movement, no matter how high the conductor raised his eyebrows. "The Voice of the Face That Speaks," said the choirmaster, all but miming the capital letters, as the stout radiators along the walls hissed and gurgled to themselves, and the choir had to sing a whole page of the Bible while the orchestra did its best to sound like chaos and very gradually decided that it knew some music after all. "The Voice of the Face That Dreams," Brother Cox declared at last, after he and the conductor had made the choir and orchestra repeat various bits that had only sounded worse to Fergal. Now the choir was required to compete with the orchestra by yelling about seals—not the sort that ate fish but some kind only an angel was supposed to be able to open. The row calmed down as the number of seals increased, and once the seventh had been sung about the brass section had the music to itself. The trumpeting faded away into a silence that didn't feel quite like silence, and Fergal realised the computer had been switched on. "We shall carry on," the conductor said in an Eastern European accent almost as hard to grasp as his name.

"Best take it in stages, Mr..." said Brother Cox, and left addressing him at that. "This is the hardest movement for my boys. Quite a challenge, singing in tongues."

Fergal had already had enough. Even if he'd wanted to sing,

his voice kept letting him down an octave, and singing in the language the Revolting Clay had apparently made up struck him as yet another of the stupid unjustifiable things adults expected him to do. Brother Cox had acknowledged how unreasonable it was by giving each choirboy a page with the words of the Voice of the Face That Will Awaken to use at the rehearsal. Whenever Fergal's voice had threatened to subside during the first two movements he'd resorted to mouthing, and he was tempted to treat all of the Reverend's babble that way rather than feel even stupider.

It looked as though that was how he was going to feel whatever he did. Keeping a straight face at the sight of Brother Cox as he opened and closed his mouth like a fish gobbling the gibberish was hard enough. The choir commenced singing what appeared to have been every kind of church music the Reverend could think of, the orchestra performed a search of its own, and Fergal was unable to concentrate for straining to hear a sound he couldn't quite hear.

He felt as though it was trying to invade everything around him. Whenever the choir and orchestra commenced another round, more than their echoes seemed to gather above them—perhaps the wind that flapped around the church and fumbled at the trees. Shadows of branches laden with foliage trailed across the windows, dragging at the stained-glass outlines, blurring them with gloom. Once Fergal thought the figure of Christ above the choirstalls opposite had turned its head to gaze at him, but of course it was already facing him. His momentary inattention earned him a scowl from Brother Cox. Then the choir climbed a series of notes so tiny it felt like forever before they arrived at the highest they could reach, while the orchestra contented itself with a single sustained chord and the computer carried on with whatever it was doing. Well before the top note Fergal did nothing but keep his mouth open. The conductor trembled his stick and his free hand at them all, and when at last there came a silence that appeared to quell the trees outside, he let the baton sink and wiped his eyes. "I believe we have done it, Brother," he murmured.

"If you say so."

Either the choirmaster objected to being addressed like a comrade or resented not having had his well-nigh incomparably straightforward name pronounced. His dissatisfaction was plain as he gestured boys out of the stalls row by row. Fergal was among the last to be marched past the amused orchestra, who were within earshot when Brother Cox caught up with him. "O'Shea," the choirmaster demanded, and even louder "Shea."

"It's Shaw, sir."

"Never mind that now. You've little enough reason to want anyone knowing who you are when you can't keep your eyes where you're told. Maybe you were dreaming you'd be singing low tomorrow, so let me tell you a boy from this very church will be taking Harty's place. A prize soloist, so don't you go thinking you're the equal of him."

On the coach he renewed his disapproval. "I want every boy's eye on me tomorrow from the instant he opens his mouth. There'll be no sheets for you to be consulting. After your dinners we'll spend all the time that's needed till every single one of you is letter perfect."

The choir groaned as much as they dared, and some of the boys who'd heard Fergal being told off glared at him as if he'd brought this further burden on them. The coach wound its way through the narrow Surrey lanes to the school where the choir was suffering a second night. The boys who ordinarily put up with it had gone home for Easter, but the monks they'd got away from had remained, prowling the stony corridors with their hands muffled in their black sleeves while they spied out sinful boys or boys about to sin or capable of thinking of it. The choir had hardly taken refuge in the dormitories when they were summoned to dinner, a plateful each of lumps of stringy mutton that several mounds of almost indistinguishable vegetables applied themselves to hiding. The lucky vegetarians were served the same without the lumps but with the gravy. Some of the resident monks waved loaded forks to encourage their guests to eat, and the oldest monk emitted sounds of what must have passed in his case for pleasure. After the meal, even the prospect of rehearsal came as almost a relief.

Brother Cox made the choir sit on benches in the draughty bare school hall and repeat the stream of nonsense Simon Clay deserved to be cursed for, and then he collected the pages with the words on and mimed trying to lift an invisible object with the palms of his hands to urge the choir to chant the whole thing again, and yet again. He mustn't have believed they could have learned it so perfectly, because he tried requiring each boy to speak it by himself. When it came to Fergal's turn the boy felt as though all the echoes of the repetitions were swooping about inside his head, describing the patterns of the absent music, and he only had to let them become audible through his mouth. "Nac rofup taif gnicam tuss snid..." He didn't even realise he'd finished until Brother Cox gave him a curt nod.

By the time Brother Cox dismissed the choir they were so exhausted that hardly anyone could be bothered with horseplay in the communal bathroom. As Fergal crawled under the blankets of the hard narrow bed halfway down the dormitory, a long room with dark green glossy walls as naked as its light bulbs, he wondered if anyone else was continuing to hear the echoes of the last rehearsal. There was only one kind of dream he wanted to have in the intimate warmth of the blankets, but the echoes wouldn't let it begin to take shape. They seemed to gather themselves as he sank into sleep—seemed to focus into just three voices, one to either side of him and one ahead. That in front of him began to lead him forwards while the others were left behind. Soon he was outside time and deep in a dream.

He was trudging towards a mountain range across a white desert that felt more like salt than sand. He'd been in the wilderness, his instincts told him, for three times thirteen days. He was bound for the highest mountain, a peak so lofty that the river which rushed down its glittering sheer slopes appeared to be streaming out of the bright clouds that crowned it. He thought he might never reach the water that would quench his thirst and lead him to the mystery veiled by the shining clouds, but in a breath the dream brought him to the river. It darkened as he drank from it and bathed in it, because he was following it downwards through a cavern he knew was the mountain turned inside out and upside down. Surely it was only in a dream that a river could run to the centre of the world, which would show him the centre of the universe, the revelation he'd journeyed so far and fasted so long to reach. Now, at the end of a descent too prolonged and frightful to remember, he was there, and the blackness was glowing with an illumination only his eyes could see. Around him the walls of the cavern were fretted like jaws piled on jaws, ridged as if the rock might be the skeleton of the world. Ahead was a pool so deep and dark he knew it was no longer water—knew the river was feeding a hole so black it could swallow the universe. A figure was rising from it, robed in rock that flowed like water. Was the universe creating it just as it had created the universe? Its eyes glinted at him, more than twice too many of them, and he struggled to awaken, to avoid seeing more. But he could hear its voices too, and didn't know whether his mind was translating them or trying to fend them off. In its image, he found himself repeating, in its image—

Brother Cox wakened him. "Get up now. Sluggards, every one of you. Rising bright and early is a praise to God."

He sounded so enraged that at first, bewildered by apparently having dreamed all night, Fergal thought the choirmaster was berating him for the dream. At breakfast, chunks of porridge drowning in salt water, it became clearer why he was infuriated, as the head monk flourished a newspaper at him while trying to placate him. "I just wanted to be certain you're aware what you and your charges will be involved with, Brother Cox."

"I'm aware right enough, aware as God can make me. Aware of how the godless media love to stain the reputations of the saints and anybody with a bit of holiness about them." Brother Cox said no more until he'd gulped every chunk of his porridge, and then he sprang off the bench. "If you'll excuse me now, I've a coach driver needs phoning to be sure he presents himself on time."

After a few moments of staring at the abandoned newspaper Kilfoyle ventured to say "Sir, can I read it?"

The head monk pursed his thin pale lips. "Perhaps you should."

Since Kilfoyle was by no means a speedy reader, when he didn't take long over it Fergal knew he'd given up. The newspaper was passed along the table, making increasingly brief stops, until it arrived in front of Fergal. Of course the article was about Simon Clay—all the stuff Harty's parents had objected to. Fergal was making to pass the paper to O'Hagan when the headline stopped him. **CLAY'S FIRST SYMPHONY: WHAT KIND OF PILGRIMAGE?** The question reminded him of his dream, and he read on.

It was mostly information he couldn't have cared less about. Simon Clay had revived the classical church symphony, starting with his Second... He'd composed nothing but religious music... During his lifetime he'd maintained that his first symphony was lost... Before he was ordained a priest he'd been a member of the Order of the Golden Dawn, and the original score had recently been discovered among the papers of a fellow occultist, Peter Grace... It hadn't previously been identified as Clay's work because he had signed it with his occult name, Indigator Fontis, Seeker of the Source... Grace had scrawled a comment on the first page: "fruit of the secret pilgrimage"... One wonders (wrote the critic) whether Clay's subsequent output was a prolonged attempt to repudiate this score and its implications. Yet the issues are less simple than has been stridently suggested by some members of the press. Underlying Clay's determination to outdo his contemporary Scriabin in terms of passion and ecstasy writ large and loud (Fergal no longer knew why he was bothering to read) is a radical attempt, so harmonically daring as almost to engage with atonality, to create a musical structure expressive of the cosmic balance to which the title alludes, a structure to which the sub-audible line of the third movement is crucial. Given that Clay wrote above this line the comment "Never to be heard"—

The newspaper was snatched away from Fergal. "Heavy reading, is it?" roared Brother Cox. "Let's try the weight of it." When he eventually finished slapping Fergal about the head with the paper truncheon he turned on the rest of the choir. "Eat up your breakfasts, all of you, that our hosts were so kind they provided us. And just you keep your minds on what you have to sing today instead of filling them with nonsense."

Fergal might have retorted, if only to himself, that nonsense was the word for what they'd learned, except that he was no longer sure it was. The ache Brother Cox had beaten into his head prevented him from thinking as he trudged away from breakfast and eventually to the coach, which threw his head about as it rewound yesterday's journey. Amid the chatter of his schoolmates he kept thinking somebody was practising the words of the last movement on either side of him. His mind was trying to retrieve the sentences he'd glimpsed as Brother Cox had snatched the newspaper. Had Simon Clay meant that the symphony never would be heard, or that it never should be? A more insistent question was why Fergal should care, especially when attempting to think sharpened his headache.

Cars were parked along the quarter-mile of lane nearest the church. Members of the audience for the world premiere that would be broadcast live at noon that Saturday were strolling up the drive while a small group of protesters flourished placards at them over the heads of several policemen who would clearly have preferred to be elsewhere. **GIVE EASTER BACK TO GOD**...**KEEP THE DEVIL'S MUSIC OUT OF GOD'S HOUSE**...**RAISE YOUR VOICE TO GOD, DON'T LOWER IT TO SATAN**...As the coach drew up beside the porch a man stalked out, pulling at his hair to show that he worked for the BBC. He wasn't happy with the cawing of rooks in the trees, nor the noises the doves made that put Fergal in mind of old women around a pram. He was especially distressed by the chorus of "Onward Christian Soldiers" outside the gates, and flounced off to speak to the police.

Fergal was trapped in the choirstalls when he heard the protesters being moved on. As a verse of "Nearer My God to Thee" trailed into the distance, his urge to giggle faltered, and he realised he'd been assuming the protesters would ensure that the premiere didn't take place. There was plenty to be nervous of: the audience and the conductor and Brother Cox, all of whom were expecting too much of him; the BBC producer darting about in search of dissatisfaction; the microphones standing guard in front of the performers; his sense that the church and himself were liable to change, perhaps not in ways to which he'd begun to grow used; the imminence of an occasion he was being made to feel the world was waiting for…As the conductor and Brother Cox took up their positions, Fergal gave the stained-glass window opposite him a look not far short of pleading. What might his old beliefs have been protecting him from? "It doesn't look like a nightie really," he almost mouthed, and then he heard a bell start to toll.

It was noon, even if the sky beyond the stained glass appeared to be getting ready for the night. The twelfth peal dwindled into silence not even broken by the hissing of the radiators, which had been turned off, and then the echoes of the footsteps of an announcer dressed like a waiter in an old film accompanied him to a microphone. "We are proud to present the world premiere of Simon Clay's *The Balance of the Spheres*. Despite the controversy it has engendered, we believe it is a profoundly religious and ultimately optimistic work…" All too soon the conductor raised his baton and Brother Cox, as though gesturing in prayer or outrage, his hands, to let the music loose.

Fergal managed to sing about the creation without dropping any notes, and could hear Harty's replacement was equal to the task. If Fergal started to be less than that he could always mouth—except the notion of leaving the choir short of a voice made him unexpectedly nervous, and he sang with such enthusiasm that Brother Cox didn't glare at him once during the first movement. He felt pleased with himself until he wondered if he was using up too much of his voice too soon.

Why should it be crucial to preserve it for the final movement—above all, for the last and highest note? He set about appearing to sing with all his vigour while employing only half. The display seemed to fool Brother Cox, but was it the choirmaster he had to deceive, and if not, wasn't his attempt to play a trick worse than ill-advised? As the last seal was opened he sang as hard as he could, and was able to rest his voice while the trumpets blared. They fell silent one by one, and as the seventh prolonged its top note he saw the woman at the computer reach for the keyboard. The incongruity made him want to giggle: how could they broadcast a sound nobody could hear? Then the fragile brass note gave way to that sound, which crept beneath him.

He might have thought he was imagining the sensation—it made him feel he was standing on a thin surface over a void—if all the birds hadn't flown out of the trees with a clatter that was audible throughout the church. The conductor held his baton high and stared hard at the windows as the computer sustained its note. Was he waiting for the branches to stop toying with the stained-glass outlines? Freeing himself from a paralysis that suggested the sound under everything had caught him like quicksand, he waved his wand at the forces he controlled.

The words of the last movement filled Fergal's head and started to burst from his mouth. Even if he didn't understand them, they were part of him, and he felt close to comprehending them or at least to dreaming what they meant. He had to sing them all or he might never be free of them. He had to reach the highest note, and then everything would be over. He had to sing to overcome the sound that was never to be heard.

Or could the choir be singing in some obscure harmony with it? He was beginning to feel as if each note he uttered drew the secret sound a little further into him. He tried not even to blink as he watched Brother Cox, whose scowl of concentration or of less than total contentment was in its predictability the nearest to a reassurance he could see. His breaths kept appearing before him like the unknown words attempting to take shape, and he told himself the church was growing colder only because the heating was off. He tried to ignore the windows, at which the darkening foliage had still not ceased groping minutes after the birds had flown, unless the trees had stilled themselves and the glass was on the move. The thought made the robed figure at the edge of his vision seem to turn a second face to him, and then another. He almost sang too loud in case that could blot out the impression, and felt his voice tremble on the edge of giving way, dropping towards the cold dark hollow sound that underlay everything, that was perhaps not being performed so much as revealed at last, giving voice to a revelation Simon Clay had spent his life trying to deny he'd ever glimpsed. Fergal didn't know where these thoughts were coming from unless they were somehow in the music. The choir and the orchestra had begun to converge, but they had minutes to go before they reached the final note that was surely meant to overcome the other sound. If he was failing to understand, he didn't want to—didn't want to see the stealthy movements in the window opposite. The choir had arrived at the foot of the ladder of microscopic notes, and he had only to sing and watch Brother Cox for encouragement—not even encouragement, just somewhere to look while he sang and drew breaths that felt as if he was sucking them out of a deep stony place, precisely enough breath each time not to interrupt his voice, which wasn't going to falter, wasn't going to let him down, wasn't going to join the sound that was invading every inch of him—

When Brother Cox's face twisted with rage and disbelief Fergal thought the problem was some fault of his until he saw movement beyond the choirmaster. A man had darted out of the audience. With a shout of "Grant us peace" he seized two power cables that lay near the broadcasting console and heaved at them. The next moment he tried to fling them away while, it seemed to Fergal, he set about executing a grotesque ritual dance. Then the computer toppled over and smashed on the stone floor, and every light in the church was extinguished.

The orchestra trailed into silence before the choir did. Fergal was continuing to sing, desperate to gain the final note, when a cello or a double bass fell over with a resonant thud. He was singing not to fend off the darkness that filled the church but the sight it had isolated opposite him. That was no longer an image in stained glass. The window had become a lens exhibiting the figure that was approaching while yet staying utterly still, its three faces grim as the infinity it had lived and had yet to live, its eyes indifferent as outer space, the locks of its multiple scalp twisted like black ice on the brink of a lake so deep no light could touch it. The figure hadn't moved in any sense he could grasp when it entered the church.

In the instant before the last glimmer of light through the windows went out, Fergal saw the three faces turn to one another, sharing an expression he almost understood. It was more than triumph. Then he was alone in the blind dark with the presence, and he struggled to hold every inch of himself immobile so as not to be noticed. But the presence was already far more than aware of him. For a moment that was like dying and being reborn he experienced how he was composed of the stuff of stars and the void that had produced them, and of something else that was the opposite of both—experienced how he might be capable of partaking of their vastness. He hadn't begun to comprehend that when his mind shrank and renewed its attempt to hide, because the presence had unfinished business in the church. Even if it had taken the man's dance of death as a tribute, that wasn't enough. Fergal felt it draw a breath much larger than the building so as to use every mouth within the walls to give itself a voice.

"I want to praise the choir for their self-control and their presence of mind at the concert on Easter Saturday. As the rest of you boys may be aware, a gentleman under the mistaken impression that the music was sacrilegious interrupted the performance but was unfortunately electrocuted. Some of the orchestra and some members of the public were injured in the panic, but our school can be proud that its choir kept their seats and their heads. It is regrettable that the effects of the technology used at the concert apparently damaged the building. I believe that is all that requires to be said on the matter, and I shall deal harshly with anyone who is caught circulating the superstitious rumours that have been invented by some of the gutter press. Let your minds remain unpolluted by such rubbish as we start the summer term."

As the headmaster's complexion began to fade from purple to its customary red, Fergal glanced at the choirboys seated near him. None of them seemed inclined to disagree with the headmaster's pronouncements. Perhaps they were cowed, or perhaps they preferred to forget the events at the church; perhaps, like all the members of the audience Fergal had seen interviewed on television, they actually believed that nothing more had taken place than the headmaster had said. For the moment Fergal was content to pretend he agreed. As the row of boys including him filed out of the school hall under the frowns of the staff, his fingertips traced like a secret sign the outline of the folded page hidden in the pocket against his heart.

It was from the newspaper the headmaster had condemned. Fergal didn't care what it said, only what it showed: the lopsided church in the process of twisting itself into a shape that seemed designed to squirm into the earth; the distorted stained-glass figure of Christ, an expression hiding in its eyes, a broken oval gaping above each shoulder. Fergal shuffled after the rest of the procession into the classroom and cramped himself onto the seat behind his desk, and put on his face that looked eager to learn. Of course he was, but not at school. The weeks to the next holiday seemed less than a breath he'd already expelled, because then he would return to the church to discover what was waiting, not just there but within himself. If Simon Clay had been unable to cope with it, he must have been too old—but Fergal had been through the fear, and he vowed to devote the rest of his life to finding out what lay beyond it. As the first teacher of the day stalked into the room, Fergal was on his feet a moment before the rest of the class. Pretending only promised a future reward. "Good morning, sir," he said, and sensed his other voices holding their tongues until he was alone with them in the dark.

# Double Room

"YOU AREN'T WITH US, ARE YOU?"

"I'd like to be."

"What's your name?" the other girl said, looking impudently quizzical. "You've seen ours."

He was glad if they assumed he'd been squinting in the dimness of the hotel bar only at the badges pinned above their long slim thighs. Each badge bore the image of a winged young woman dressed in a chain-mail bikini and a virtually transparent robe, an outfit both girls had copied apart from the wings. The sword in her hand indicated their names, Primmy and Barbaria. "Edwin Ferguson," he said.

"That's an old name," Primmy commented.

"You need to be old to know all the tricks."

"I like a good trick, don't you, Primmy? Are you going to show us yours, Edwin?"

However guilty he couldn't help feeling, he thought he might feel worse if he let the opportunity pass. "I only give private performances," he said.

"Is it going to be all for us?" Primmy cried.

Barbaria bent her head and an eyebrow towards her,

prompting Ferguson to assure the girls "It's all right, I didn't think you were angels."

"Why not?" Primmy demanded.

He pointed at her badge—at least, he hoped it was clear that was where he was pointing. "No wings."

"Sometimes we are," Barbaria said. "We can be all kinds."

"Depends who we're with."

"I'm looking forward to finding out. What roles you like playing, I mean."

He made the sudden silence the occasion for a sip of Scotch followed by a larger one. "You're looking at them," Barbaria said.

"And they're all you'll be seeing," Primmy said.

He was able to mistake this for a promise until they turned away as a man strolled into the bar. He was at least as old as Ferguson and even stouter, with greying hair that Ferguson thought far too long for his age. Nevertheless the girls stood up eagerly, although Primmy lingered to say "Thanks for the fun."

"Is that all?" When she tried to appear prim instead of primitive Ferguson was provoked to add "Maybe you shouldn't come out in public dressed like that. You might give some people the wrong idea."

"We were at the masquerade."

"You've been doing some of that all right." Loud enough for her to catch he said "And what do you get up to the rest of the time?"

Barbaria turned long enough to inform him "We're social workers."

"Is that what they call it these days?" he might have retorted except for feeling obsolete. As the girls each took the newcomer by an arm Ferguson saw that the man's badge depicted a bronzed bruiser in sandals and loincloth and crown, who was brandishing a blade at a lengthy name Ferguson felt expected to recognise. He drained his Scotch and murmured to the barman "Who's he?"

"One of their writers."

In his sleeveless denim outfit the fellow didn't look much like one, or his age. Was being a writer all it took to have girls hanging on your arms? Perhaps now Ferguson had time to write the book he imagined he contained, the rest would follow. The idea seemed so variously disloyal that he felt his face glow like the light of a brake he'd applied too belatedly to himself, and he hurried not much better than blindly out of the bar.

He hadn't reached the lifts when the lobby grew loudly crowded with people emerging from the conference suite. While a few were fantastically costumed, most struck him as not much less anonymous and awkward than himself. The hotel notice-board identified their event as a Fantasy Weekend, but it didn't mean the kind of fantasy he'd yielded to imagining. At least, it certainly didn't for him.

He kept his back to the mirror in the lift once he'd jabbed the button. On its way the lift opened to admit a view of the second-floor corridor, where badged individuals and their noise and drinks were spilling out of a room. For a moment he wished he were in there, but the room sounded too small for the revellers who were. That was one reason why the wish fell away before the corridor did.

The adjacent lift had just delivered someone to the third floor. Ferguson glimpsed their shadow vanishing around the corner ahead as he made for his room. From the corner he saw the door next to his standing ajar. "Good night," he called as it shut, because the clinically pallid corridor with its equally colourless doors separated by timid abstract pastels felt like losing all sense of himself. His last word was echoed in such a muffled voice that he couldn't be sure of its gender.

Once the lock on his door had given his card the green light he left the card in a slot inside the stubby vestibule to drape the room with indirect lighting. The word flat might have been invented for the accommodation: the boxy wardrobe and dressing-table, the single angular nominally padded chair, the double bed tucking nothingness up tight. Perhaps the midget television might provide some company—distraction, at any rate.

A fat old man with a threadbare grizzly scalp met him in the bathroom. The sight fired up his Indian dinner, the taste of which rose in a volcanic belch. "Pardon," he said almost as inadvertently, rousing a muffled echo. He wasn't apologising to his reflection; he didn't even watch the old fool mouth the syllables. He lifted the toilet seat and its lid with the toe of his shoe, and the plastic ovals rapped the tiled wall. The small room seemed to have an echo for everything. He dragged his baggy zip down to fumble himself forth, and had hardly started pouring when the noise became a duet. The other performer was in the adjoining bathroom.

Urinating in company always made Ferguson feel like a shy child, and he faltered to a dribble that trailed off to a drip. Was his neighbour suffering from the identical problem? Straining never helped, and the silence aggravated his inhibition just as much. He could only hum to lessen his awareness or pretend it wasn't troubling him. "Let's Do It" always came into his head on these occasions, and he might have added words—one of his rhymes for bees, "People who have finished having pees" or "Women who are down upon their knees", that used to amuse Elizabeth whenever he sang them at random—if his neighbour hadn't joined in.

He still couldn't identify the gender from the voice. His own was shriller than it had any right or need to be. Perhaps his fellow guest was borrowing his solution to the urinary annoyance; they hummed louder once Ferguson did. He squeezed his eyes shut and then managed to relax them, and was rewarded with activity where it mattered. Something had worked for his neighbour as well. The streams dwindled and fell silent simultaneously, and he was shaking himself dry when he heard a clink through the wall.

His neighbour had put a glass down, but it was ridiculous to fancy they'd been using a glassful of water to imitate his sounds. He pulled a tissue out of the box by the sink to blow his nose. As he dropped the wad in the toilet he heard a nasal trumpeting in the adjacent bathroom.

If it sounded very much like his, did it have much leeway to sound different? Hooking the toilet seat with the side of his shoe, he let it drop along with its lid on the pedestal, and was unsurprised to hear an echo through the wall. Both toilets flushed while he turned back to the sink. He had barely started brushing his teeth when the sound was imitated in the other bathroom.

The old wreck in the mirror let his wrinkled mouth hang open, displaying all his front teeth and the gap one had left last month. How could such a tiny noise be audible through the wall? How could his? He decided he'd heard an echo until another bout of brushing was copied beyond the mockingly blank wall. His neighbour must be making the noise in some other way, unless they were attacking their teeth with a savagery that sounded demonic. "Hope they all drop out of your head," Ferguson spluttered and spat in the sink. The answering spit was fierce enough for an insult. The words that followed were repeated in exactly Ferguson's tone, as far as he could distinguish the qualities of the voice. Was it deliberately muffled? Perhaps the speaker was obscuring it with a hand, hiding their ruined teeth from the other mirror, a notion that prompted Ferguson to blurt "What must you look like?"

Although he thought he'd only muttered it, the question came back through the wall. The idiotic trick must be affecting him more than he realised. "I know how I look," he couldn't help retorting as he wiped foam off his lips. "I think I'm better off not knowing how you do."

He was unable to imagine a sufficiently grotesque costume for them. Perhaps they passed for normal until an event like this weekend's gave them licence not to be. Well before they finished echoing his latest remarks he was sick of the joke, if it could be called one. "Very funny," he responded, wondering why he'd waited for the mimicry to finish. "Thanks for the laugh. Just what I needed. I haven't been so entertained since—"

He didn't know. When the partial sentence came back neutered through the wall, he had the uneasy idea that the imitator was about to complete it for him. It faltered as he had, but he wasn't about to finish it off. He couldn't just blame the clown beyond the wall for the whole asinine situation; there was a clown in here too, looking foolish and pathetic, not to mention incapable of controlling his own behaviour. If he didn't make any more noise, the other would have nothing to mimic. He turned off the light, muting the switch with his hand, before tiptoeing out of the room.

For the duration of a couple of prolonged but silent breaths he was able to enjoy the possibility that his neighbour might be lingering in the bathroom for another noise to echo, and then the enforced hush set about troubling him. It emphasised the anonymity of the bedroom, which felt close to empty even of him. He wasn't going to be forced to act as if he weren't there. Grabbing the remote control from the shelf that enthroned the dwarf television, he threw himself on the bed.

Did he just hear the springs yield beneath him, or was there an answering twang in the adjacent bedroom? He supported his shoulders with a pillow and awakened the television with a shrill whisper of static. Dismissing the Frugotel information menu, he began to search the channels: a comedy film teeming with teenagers even louder than the party he'd seen from the lift, a report of a polo game where all the players were in wheelchairs, a documentary about a drug that was meant to retard ageing, an episode of a reality series called *Fostered for a Fortnight*, another by the name of *From a Previous Relationship* . . . He hadn't reached the second channel when, with barely a second's delay each time, a television beyond the wall behind his head commenced dogging his progress.

His neighbour was entitled to watch television too. The order of the browsing needn't be significant, since it was the obvious one. Ferguson felt irrational for wondering what would happen if he reversed it—at least, until he did so and heard the other television copy him. Changing channels at random produced the same result, and he had to struggle not to shout at the wall. How could he watch the programme he'd been tempted to? Without the sound, of course.

He buttoned it before poking the keys to summon the Frugrownup channel, where he came in some way through an act of the kind the channel offered the no doubt solitary members of its audience. The rhythmic activity was as noiseless as it was vigorous, so that he couldn't help fancying that the participants were all straining to produce a sound. At least he'd called up silence in the next room too, and his body had begun to show signs of emulating that of the man on the screen by the time he heard a noise through the wall.

Somebody was panting. It grew louder and more dramatic, keeping pace with the efforts on the television. His neighbour had given in to the same temptation, Ferguson tried to think, but weren't the gasps too theatrical even for this sort of film, and oddly androgynous? Was the other guest producing them to taunt him? Without question there was just a solitary voice, and he could hear faint laughter too. It was muffled by distance, unless there were more people in the next room, covering their mouths so as to titter at his situation. That was beginning to seem as contemptible as his attempts to pick up the girls in the bar. He switched off the television, and the panting stopped at once.

He lurched away from the bed and stumbled to the window. The hotel was indeed reflected across the deserted downtown street, where the front of a building was largely composed of glass. He could see his room and his faint self in the elongated window of an unlit office, but no sign of the next room. Could its occupant really have seen the reflection of the programme Ferguson had been watching? Perhaps they were using binoculars, or their eyes were keener than his. He dragged the dun curtains together, to be rewarded by a clash of curtain rings on the far side of the wall. "Show's over," he mouthed and saw the old man beyond the dressing-table risk a triumphant grin. "Try and get to me now," they both said silently as he began to undress. He heard no further sound through the wall as he dumped his clothes on the chair and wriggled under the sheet and the dishevelled quilt before darkening the room. The silence in the other one felt so frustrated that he nearly laughed aloud, but he wasn't about to invite an imitation. He closed his eyes and edged the quilt over his exposed ear and sought the dark. It swarmed with thoughts, of which the most bearable was the book he'd imagined writing. Even this seemed potentially troubling now—the idea of a couple who fell in love at first sight only to be separated for the rest of their lives. When at last they met again they would be too changed and too senile to recognise each other. In their final moments one would regain the memory, which would seem to keep them together for eternity. Who would have it, or could it somehow be granted to both? The more Ferguson worried the idea the less likely it felt, and he was glad when the Scotch and the bottle of wine he'd had at dinner conspired to sink him in the dark.

A voice wakened him. He thought it was his own, despite its lack of shape. "Elizabeth," it repeated, or more accurately "Livadeth." It was talking in its sleep—no, replicating how he must have talked in his. "Weary of you," it said.

He wouldn't have said that, ever. He must have been asking where she was. "I bloody am of you," he informed his imitator. As soon as the remark started to be echoed he thumped the wall above the rudimentary headboard. "Enough," he yelled. "Enough."

The thumping was mimicked, and so was every repetition of the word. He might have been competing for the last one. He groped for the light-switch above the ledge that was Frugotel's version of a bedside table, and was marching or at any rate limping at speed towards the corridor before he grasped that he shouldn't leave the room while he was naked. Grabbing his trousers, he danced an ungainly impromptu hornpipe to don them, accompanied by echoes next door of the thuds of his bare feet. This enraged him so much that he almost forgot to retrieve his key as he stalked into the corridor.

It was deserted. If there was muffled laughter, surely it was downstairs. He pounded on the next door with both fists, so hard that the plastic digits of its number seemed to tremble. No doubt that was partly because of the pounding that answered his. "Stop this bloody game right now," he shouted. "Normal people need their sleep."

He was echoed so closely that they might as well have been speaking in chorus. "That's all. You've had—" he said and felt idiotic for attempting to catch the imitator out by stopping unexpectedly, all the more so when it didn't work. "You've had your chance," he declared and shoved his face at the spyhole in the door. The darkness beyond it only convinced him that he was being observed. Having dealt the door a final thump, he tramped to grab the phone from the ledge by his bed.

The receptionist hadn't finished announcing herself when he said "Can you do something about whoever's next door?"

"What seems to be the problem, sir?"

"They're—" He might have demanded whether she could hear the echo of his side of the conversation, but he didn't want to seem irrational. "They're making all sorts of noise," he said. "I've asked them to stop but they won't."

"Which room is that, sir?"

"They're in 339."

"Just a moment." After several of those the phone rang in the next room. It was answered immediately, but only by a childish imitation. "Ring ring," the voice said in falsetto. "Ring ring."

The phone fell silent, and so did the mimicry. As he strained to hear more than the labouring of his heart, the receptionist said "Is that Mr Ferguson?"

"There's just me here, yes. Why?"

"I'm afraid you're mistaken."

"What do you mean?"

"We've got nobody in 339."

"Don't give me that. You told me you were full. You couldn't change my booking."

"It was a late cancellation."

"Well, someone's in there. I can hear them. I've heard them all the time we've been talking. Maybe some of this weird lot you're full up with have managed to get in." The muttered repetition of his protests had begun to madden him. "Don't take my word for it," he urged. "Go and see."

There was silence at his ear and beyond the wall. Eventually the receptionist said "Somebody will come up."

Ferguson replaced the receiver and was devoting his energy to making no further sound when he wondered if his complaints might have warned off his tormentor. Suppose the person fled and left him looking like a fool? He sprinted to the door despite the twinges of his heart and leaned into the corridor. It was empty, and his neighbour hadn't had time to dodge out of sight along it. He glared towards 339 until he heard a lift hum and stop humming, and a large man in the yellow Frugotel uniform appeared around the corner.

Other than frowning at Ferguson, he refrained from any

comment. Once he'd finished peering through the spyhole he rapped on the door of 339. "Staff," he called. "Can I have a word, please."

Ferguson wouldn't have been surprised if the man had received every one of them back, but apparently the prankster wasn't so easily tempted. The man knocked harder and then slid a card into the lock. Brandishing the card like an identification and a threat, he advanced into the room. Ferguson mostly heard his own heart, but there were also the click of a light switch and the scrawny rattle of a shower curtain. He waited for the sounds to be followed up, and then he snatched his key card out of the slot on the wall and padded heavily into the corridor. "What's the hold-up? Who—"

He faltered, not just because the next room was almost indistinguishably similar to his. The Frugotel employee was staring at him across the tucked-in bed. "It's like Reception told you, sir. Nobody's in this room."

"You are," Ferguson thought of retorting, but demanded "Have you looked in the wardrobe?"

The man lingered over looking at him, so that Ferguson wasn't far from opening it by the time the employee did. "Nobody," he said at once. "Nobody's been here. Now if you wouldn't—"

A woman's peevishly sleepy protest interrupted him. "What's going on now?"

She was in the room opposite Ferguson's. From the threshold her husband or a man performing some of the functions of one informed her "It's the old hooligan that was making all the row out here before."

Ferguson was sure he recognised one of the rowdy drinkers from the floor below. "That's more your style, isn't it? I thought people were meant to keep their drinks in the bar."

He wouldn't have minded if the hotel employee had asked what he meant, but it was the man across the corridor who spoke. "You know, he looks like the old reprobate Primmy said was trying to get off with her and Barbaria when they just wanted a quiet drink."

"I don't think any of you know how to be quiet," Ferguson retorted and might have said more if the man hadn't called

"Good God, he's showing everyone what it sounded like he wanted to show them."

Ferguson glanced down to find his flies gaping wide. While his member had the grace to hide its head, its mat as grey as dust was well in evidence. "Forgive me," he gasped, yanking up the zip so fiercely that it came close to scalping his crotch. "I'm a bit distracted. It's not long since I lost my wife."

"Then what are you staying here for?" the offstage woman across the corridor wanted everyone to know.

"We'd already booked. I didn't want to let the hotel down. I thought it'd be better than staying at home by myself. We often used to come here," Ferguson added as best he could for a nervous belch, which he tried to explain by saying "It was one of our favourite towns to eat in."

None of this seemed adequate, but before Ferguson could think of a further excuse the man said "We can tell."

"We're sorry to hear of your tragedy. Please accept our sincerest condolences." It was unclear whether the employee was speaking for Frugotel or on behalf of the couple opposite. Having locked 339, he said "Will you be all right now?"

"I haven't been hearing things, if that's what you mean. That's to say I have. I certainly have." Ferguson folded his arms in case this lent him some authority and to hide his hirsute obese breasts. "I've lost my wife," he said, "not my mind."

He had time to interpret the awkwardness of the silence in various ways before the uniformed man said "We don't want any more of a disturbance. Most of our guests are asleep."

"I don't. I'd like to be," Ferguson said and backed into his room. He'd managed not to slam the door when he wished he'd left his listeners a better image of Elizabeth. Perhaps they imagined an old woman as overfed as he was, not the girl he'd carried over a stream and to a gate a quarter of a mile up the sunny slope beyond it, or the mother who'd perched their daughter on her shoulders when they'd returned for the same hillside climb, or the grandmother who'd continued to outdistance him on their countryside walks even once those had grown shorter and more effortful. He bruised his forehead against the door as he peered through the spyhole. If anyone was out there he was going to let them know that he and more importantly Elizabeth had come here for the countryside, not just the food. The corridor was deserted and silent, however. "It's all your fault," he almost yelled at the next room, instead mouthing the words. He tiptoed across the prickly carpet to stand by the bed, where he unbuttoned his trousers and eased the zip down and stepped clumsily but silently out of them. Once they were heaped on the floor he sat so gradually on the bed that the springs stayed as quiet as he was. He inched under the bedclothes and stood a pillow on end to support his raised head while he waited for some sound from the next room.

Could the imitator have gone away? Might they have fled as soon as he'd had the receptionist phone the room? He was convinced that he'd heard them imitating his subsequent protests, but if he was left alone at last, surely it was all that mattered. He listened to the hush until it let him breathe freely and slowed his heart, and then he reached to lay the pillow down. His knuckles bumped the headboard, and he heard an answering rap through the wall.

He might have grabbed the phone to demand another visit from the staff or, better, have dashed into the corridor to cause uproar outside 339, ensuring that the intruder couldn't escape unseen this time. Instead he spoke, quite conversationally. "I know you're there."

"I loathed her hair."

He wanted to believe he'd misheard or imagined the voice, which was more muffled than ever. Even when Elizabeth's hair had grown so thin her scalp showed through, he'd stroked it in the hope she would forget about its state. He hardly knew whom he was addressing as he objected "I never said that."

"I never said fat."

"That's right, I didn't."

"That's right, I did it."

"No, not that either."

"Oh, what a liar."

"That's just not true."

"That just stopped you."

Ferguson had begun to feel trapped in an infantile game by someone who'd succumbed to their second childhood if not worse. He could hardly wait for them to finish echoing or rather misrepresenting him before he responded—he was becoming desperate to think of an answer they couldn't turn into a gibe. He might have imagined he was being tricked into selecting words his tormentor found it easy to mishear. Although he tried to take his time, the best he could produce was "What a lie."

The indefinite voice didn't bother imitating his pause. "Watched her die."

While there was no denying this, he didn't need to admit "That's true."

"Not you."

He was afraid his words might take him unawares. "All right," he mumbled, "let's have silence."

"All right, let's have slyness."

He found his mouth with a hand, flattening his lips to keep in any further inadvertent speech. He ached to sleep, but suppose it released his voice? Even the notion of dozing made him feel threatened by a dream—an ill-defined image of somebody wakening in a dark place and struggling to communicate by whatever clumsy methods they still had. His mind recoiled, but staying awake was no refuge. Soon the voice in the next room began to speak.

He bore it mutely as long as he could, and then he tried to deny all it said. No, he hadn't ever even slightly wanted her to die. No, he hadn't grown tired of holding her hand as she lay in bed open-mouthed as a stranded fish. No, he hadn't wished as her hand grew slack yet again that this time it had slackened for good. No, he hadn't been disgusted by having to dab at her drool and deal with her other secretions. No, he hadn't sneaked out of their room to pray for an end to it all. By now he was striving to blot out the voice, but it went inexorably on until he lost any sense of which of them was trying to contradict the other. "All right," he cried at last. "I did, but only for her sake."

If this was echoed, it was by the flatness of the hotel room. He felt abruptly far too alone in the dark. When he switched on the light, the room looked as impersonal as a hospital ward—the kind of ward where Elizabeth hadn't wanted to spend her last weeks. His scattered belongings were at best pathetic attempts to make some kind of claim for his presence. "I shouldn't have come," he whispered. "There's nothing here."

He didn't know who was supposed to overhear this, or perhaps he did. "It didn't mean anything with those girls," he tried saying. "They wouldn't have wanted me. Nobody would."

He was hoping to be contradicted, but the only sounds were his—the creak of the bed as he shifted his weight, the intermittent urgency of his heartbeat. "You're still there, aren't you?" he said louder. "Say you're there. Say anything you like."

His voice made the room sound as small and flatly featureless as a cell. So did his rapping and then knocking on the wall. It was too late to wonder what he'd done to earn the answering silence. If he caused much more noise the hotel staff might intervene again and drive away for good whoever had been there. He could still use the phone, and he keyed 339, though his fingers were so unsteady that their fat tips almost added extra numbers. He heard the other phone ring in the dark, and continue ringing and at last fall silent, because he'd laid the receiver to rest in its cold plastic trench. After that there was silence—for all the long night, silence.

# At Lorn Hall

Randolph hadn't expected the map to misrepresent the route to the motorway quite so much. The roads were considerably straighter on the page. At least it was preferable to being a directed by a machine on the dashboard, which would have reminded him of being told by Harriet that he'd gone wrong yet again, even when he knew where he was going. Although it oughtn't to be dark for hours, the April sky beyond a line of lurid hills had begun to resemble a charcoal slab. He was braking as the road meandered between sullen fields of rape when he had to switch the headlights on. The high beams roused swarms of shadows in the hedges and glinted on elongated warnings of bends ahead, and then the light found a signpost. It pointed down a lane to somewhere called Lorn Hall.

He stopped the Volvo and turned on the hazard lights. The sign looked neglected except by birds, which had left traces of their visits, but Lorn Hall sounded like the kind of place he liked to wander around. The children never did, complaining to Harriet if he even tried to take them anywhere like that on the days he had them. They loved being driven in the rain—the stormier the better, however nearly blind it made him feel—and so he couldn't help feeling relieved that they weren't with him to insist. He could shelter in the mansion until the storm passed over. He quelled the twitching of the lights and drove along the lane.

Five minutes' worth of bends enclosed by hulking spiky hedges brought him to a wider stretch of road. As it grew straight he glimpsed railings embedded in the left-hand hedge, rusting the leaves. Over the thorns and metal spikes surrounded by barbs he saw sections of an irregular roof patrolled by crows. Another minute brought him to the gateway of Lorn Hall.

He couldn't have given a name to the style of the high broad house. Perhaps the stone was darkened by the approaching storm, but he thought it would have looked leaden even in sunlight. At the right-hand end of the building a three-storey barrel put him in mind of a clenched fist with bricks for grey knuckles. Far less than halfway from it on the unadorned frontage, a door twice as tall as a man stood beneath a pointed arch reminiscent of a mausoleum. Five sets of windows each grew smaller as they mounted to the roofs, where chimneys towered among an assortment of slate peaks. Even the largest of the ground-floor windows were enmeshed with lattices, and every window was draped with curtains that the gloom lent the look of dusty cobwebs. Apart from an unmarked whitish van parked near the front door there was no sign of life.

The signpost had surely been addressed to sightseers, and the formidable iron gates were bolted open, staining the weedy gravel of the drive. One of the gateposts in the clutch of the hedge had lost its stone globe, which poked its dome bewigged with lichen out of the untended lawn. Ivy overgrew sections of the lawn and spilled onto the drive. The shapes the topiary bushes had been meant to keep were beyond guessing; they looked fattened and deformed by age. If Harriet had been with him she would have insisted on leaving by now, not to mention protesting that the detour was a waste of time. This was another reason he drove up to the house.

Did the curtains stir as he drew up beside the van? He must have seen shadows cast by the headlamps, because the movements at all three windows to the left of the front door had been identical. Nobody had ducked out of sight in the van either. Randolph turned off the lights and the engine, pocketing his keys as he turned to face the mansion. The sky had grown so stuffed with darkness that he didn't immediately see the front door was ajar.

To its left, where he might have looked for a doorbell, a tarnished blotchy plaque said **LORN HALL**. The door displayed no bell or knocker, just a greenish plaque that bore the legend **RESIDENCE OF CROWCROSS**. "Lord Crowcross," Randolph murmured as though it might gain some significance for him if not summon its owner to the door. As he tried to recall ever having previously heard the name he felt a chill touch as thin as a fingernail on the back of his neck. It was a raindrop, which sent him to push the heavy door wide.

The door had lumbered just a few inches across the stone flags when it met an obstruction. Randolph might have fancied that somebody determined but enfeebled was bent on shutting him out, perhaps having dropped to all fours. The hindrance proved to be a greyish walking boot that had toppled over from its place against the wall. Several pairs grey with a mixture of dried mud and dust stood in the gloomy porch. "Don't go any further," Harriet would have been saying by now, "you don't know if you're invited," but Randolph struggled around the door and kicked the boot against the wall. As he made for the archway on the far side of the porch, light greeted him.

Little else did. His approach had triggered a single yellowish bulb that strove to illuminate a large room. Opposite the arch an empty chair upholstered in a pattern so faded it wasn't worth distinguishing stood behind a bulky desk. Apart from a blotter like a plot of moss and earth, the desk was occupied by a pair of cardboard boxes and scattered with a few crumpled pamphlets for local attractions. The box that was inscribed **HONESTY** in an extravagantly cursive script contained three coins adding up to five pounds and so thoroughly stuck to the bottom that they were framed by glue. The carton marked **TOUR** in the same handwriting was cluttered with half a dozen sets of headphones. As Randolph dug in his pockets for change, his host watched him.

The man was in a portrait, which hung on the grey stone wall behind the desk it dwarfed. He stood in tweed and jodhpurs on a hill. With one hand flattened on his hip he seemed less to be surveying the landscape in the foreground of the picture than to be making his claim on it clear. The wide fields scattered with trees led to Lorn Hall. Although his fleshy face looked satisfied in every way, the full almost pouting lips apparently found it redundant to smile. His eyes were as blue as the summer sky above him, and included the viewer in their gaze. Was he less of an artist than he thought, or was he meant to tower over the foreshortened perspective? Randolph had guessed who he was, since the **C** that signed the lower left-hand corner of the canvas was in the familiar handwriting. "My lord," Randolph murmured as he dropped coins in the box.

The clink of metal didn't bring anyone to explain the state of the headphones. They weren't just dusty; as he rummaged through them, a leggy denizen scrabbled out of the box and fell off the desk to scuttle into the shadows. "That's very much more than enough," Harriet would have said to him in the way she did about as often to their children. If you weren't adventurous you weren't much at all, and the gust of wind that slammed the front door helped Randolph stick to his decision. Having wiped the least dusty set of headphones with a pamphlet for a penal museum, he turned them over in his hands but couldn't find a switch. As he fitted them gingerly over his ears a voice said "You'll excuse my greeting you in person."

Nobody was visible beyond the open door beside the painting, only darkness. The voice seemed close yet oddly distant, pronouncing every consonant but so modulated it implied the speaker hardly cared if he was heard. "Do move on once you've taken in my portrait," he said. "There may be others awaiting their turn."

"There's only me," Randolph pointed out and stared with some defiance at the portrait. If Lord Crowcross had taught himself to paint, he wasn't the ideal choice of teacher. The landscape was a not especially able sketch that might have been copied from a photograph, and the figure was unjustifiably large. The artist appeared to have spent most time on the face, and

Randolph was returning its gaze when Crowcross said "Do move on once you've taken in my portrait. There may be others awaiting their turn."

"I already told you I'm on my own," Randolph protested. The headphones must be geared to the listener's position in the house, but the technology seemed incongruous, as out of place as Randolph was determined not to let the commentary make him feel. "I'm on my way," he said and headed for the next room.

He'd barely stepped over the stone threshold when the light went out behind him. "Saving on the bills, are we?" he muttered as he was left in the dark. In another second his arrival roused more lights—one in each corner of an extensive high-ceilinged room. "This is where the family would gather of an evening," Crowcross said in both his ears. "We might entertain our peers here, such as were left. I am afraid our way of life lost favour in my lifetime, and the country is much poorer."

The room was furnished with senile obese sofas and equally faded overweight armchairs, all patterned with swarms of letters like the initial on the portrait. A tapestry depicting a hunt occupied most of the wall opposite the windows, which Randolph might have thought were curtained so as to hide the dilapidation from the world. Several decanters close to opaque with dust stood on a sideboard near a massive fireplace, where cobwebbed lumps of coal were piled in the iron cage of the hearth. Had the place been left in this state to remind visitors it had fallen on hard times? Everyone Randolph knew would be ashamed to go in for that trick, whatever their circumstances. Quite a few were desperate to sell their homes, but all his efforts as an estate agent were in vain just now. He turned to find his way out of the room and saw Lord Crowcross watching him.

This time his host was in a painting of the room, though this was clearer from the positions of the furniture than from any care in the depiction. Sketchy figures sat in chairs or sprawled languidly on the couches. Just enough detail had been added to their faces—numerous wrinkles, grey hair—to signify that every one was older than the figure in the middle of the room. He was standing taller than he should in proportion to the others, and his obsessively rendered face appeared to be ignoring them. "Do make your way onwards whenever you're ready," he said without moving his petulant lips. "I fear there are no servants to show you around."

"No wonder the place is in such a state"—or rather the absence of servants was the excuse, and Randolph was tempted to say so. By now Harriet would have been accusing him of risking the children's health. He loitered to make the voice repeat its message, but this wasn't as amusing as he'd expected; he could almost have fancied it was hiding impatience if not contempt. "Let's see what else you've got to show me," he said and tramped out of the room.

All the lights were extinguished at once. He was just able to see that he'd emerged into a broad hallway leading to a staircase wider than his arms could stretch. He smelled damp on stone or wood. By the dim choked glow through doorways on three sides of the hall he made out that the posts at the foot of the steep banisters were carved with cherubs. In the gloom the eyes resembled ebony jewels, but the expressions on the chubby wooden faces were unreadable. "Do continue to the next exhibit," Crowcross prompted him.

Presumably this meant the nearest room. Randolph paced to the left-hand doorway and planted a foot on the threshold, but had to take several steps forward before the light acknowledged him. Fewer than half the bulbs in the elaborate chandelier above the long table lit up. "This is where the family would dine in style," Crowcross said, "apart from the youngest member."

The table was set for ten people. Dusty plates and silver utensils stained with age lay on the extravagantly lacy yellowed tablecloth. Like the upholstery of all the chairs, every plate was marked with **C**. Doilies to which spiders had lent extra patterns were spread on a sideboard, opposite which a painting took most of the place of a tapestry that had left its outline on the stone wall. Although the painting might have depicted a typical dinner at Lorn Hall, Randolph thought it portrayed something else. Of the figures seated at the table, only the one at the head of the table possessed much substance. The familiar face was turned away from his sketchy fellow diners to watch whoever was in the actual room, while a servant with a salver waited on either side of him. "Subsequently the situation was reversed," Crowcross said, "and I made the place my own."

Was the painting meant to remind him of the family he'd lost—to provide companionship in his old age? Randolph was trying to see it in those terms when the pinched voice said "By all means make your way onwards." He could do without a repetition, and he made for the hall. As the chandelier went dark he glimpsed somebody turning the bend of the staircase.

"Excuse me," Randolph called, moving the earpiece away from his right ear, but the other didn't respond. If they were wearing headphones too they might not have heard him. He'd only wanted to ask whether they knew what time the house closed to the public. At least he wasn't alone in it, and he picked his way along the hall to the kitchen, where part of the darkness seemed to remain solid as the weary light woke up.

It was a massive black iron range that dominated the grey room. A dormant fragment of the blackness came to life, waving its feelers as it darted into one of the round holes in the top of the range. How long had the kitchen been out of use? Surely nobody would put up with such conditions now. Chipped blotchy marble surfaces and a pair of freezers—one a head taller than Randolph, its twin lying horizontal—might be responsible for some of the chill that met him. A solitary cleaver lay on a ponderous table, which looked not just scored by centuries of knife strokes but in places hacked to splinters. Randolph looked around for a portrait, but perhaps Crowcross felt the kitchen was undeserving of his presence. "My father enjoyed watching the maids at their work," he said. "Red-handed skivvies, he called them. I did myself. Since then the world has changed so radically that their like have been among the visitors. Perhaps you are of their kind."

"Not at all," Randolph objected and felt absurd, not least because he suspected that Crowcross might have disagreed with him. He was searching for some trace of the people who'd worked here—initials carved on the table, for instance—when Crowcross said "There is no more to see here. Let us move on."

He sounded like a parody of a policeman—an officious one used to being obeyed. Randolph couldn't resist lingering to force him to say it again, and might easily have thought a hint of petulance had crept into the repetition. The light failed before Randolph was entirely out of the kitchen, but he glimpsed a door he'd overlooked in the underside of the staircase. As he reached for the heavy doorknob Crowcross said "Nothing of interest is kept down there. I never understood its appeal for my father."

Perhaps Randolph did, assuming the servants' quarters were below. He wondered how his guide's mother had felt about the arrangement. The scalloped doorknob wouldn't turn even when he applied both hands to it. As he looked for a key in the thick dust along the lintel Crowcross spoke. "I have told you nothing has remained. Let us see where I was a child."

His petulance was unmistakable. No doubt the basement rooms would be unlit in any case. Randolph was making his way past the stairs when he heard whoever else was in the house shuffling along an upper corridor. He wondered if there was more light up there, since the footfalls were surer than his own. They receded out of earshot as he pushed open the door of the turret room.

The room was lit, though nothing like immediately, by a single bare bulb on a cobwebbed flex. The round aloof ceiling caught much of the light, and Randolph suspected that even with the curtains open the room might have seemed like a cell to a child. It was furnished with a desk and a table in proportion, each attended by a starkly straight chair. While the table was set for a solitary meal, it had space for a pile of books: an infant's primer on top, a children's encyclopaedia many decades old at the bottom. Even when Randolph made the children read instead of playing, Harriet rarely agreed with his choice of books. The stone floor was scattered with building blocks, a large wooden jigsaw depicting a pastoral scene, an abacus, a picture book with pages thick as rashers, open to show a string like a scrawny umbilical cord dangling from the belly of a pig spotted with mould. The desk was strewn with exercise books that displayed the evolution of the omnipresent handwriting; one double page swarmed with a C well on its way to resembling the letter that seemed almost to infest the mansion. "This is where I spent the years in growing worthy of my name," said Crowcross. "In our day parents hired their delegates and kept them on the premises. Now the care of children is another industry, one more product of the revolution that has overtaken the country by stealth."

Above the desk a painting showed the room much as it was now, if somewhat brighter and more insubstantial. Crowcross stood between rudimentary impressions of the table and the desk. His arms were folded, and he might have been playing a teacher, except that nobody else was in the room—at least, not in the picture of it. "If you have learned everything you feel entitled to know," he said, "let us go up."

Did Randolph want to bother going on, given the condition of the house? Harriet certainly wouldn't have, even if the children weren't with them. He'd had nothing like his money's worth yet, unless he retrieved the payment on his way out. Perhaps the person upstairs might know more about the history of Lorn Hall, and Randolph didn't mind admitting to a guilty fascination, not least with the companion at his ear. "If you have learned everything you feel," Crowcross said and fell silent as Randolph left the room.

He was on the lowest stair when he noticed that the cherub on the banister had no wings. Somebody had chopped them off, leaving unequal stumps, and he couldn't help suspecting that the vandal had been Crowcross, perhaps since he'd found himself alone in Lorn Hall, the last of his line. He had the uneasy notion that Crowcross was about to refer to if not justify the damage. "If you have learned," the voice said before he could let go of the shaky banister.

From the bend in the stairs he saw the upper corridor, just about illuminated by the dimness beyond several doorways. Whoever he'd glimpsed on the stairs wasn't to be seen, and no light suggested they were in a room. Presumably they were at the top of the house by now. Barely glancing at a second mutilated cherub, Randolph made for the nearest room along the corridor.

Its principal item was an enormous four-poster bed. Burdened by plaster sloughed by the ceiling, the canopy sagged like an ancient cobweb. More plaster glistened on an immense dressing-table and an upholstered chair that must once have looked muscular. Most of the light from the few live bulbs in the chandelier fell short of a side room, where Randolph was just able to distinguish a marble bath with blackened taps and a pallid hand gripping the side to haul its owner into view, but that was a crumpled cloth. "You are in the master bedroom," Crowcross said tonelessly enough to be addressing an intruder. "Would you expect the master to have left more of a mark?"

His portrait showed him gripping the left-hand bedpost. As well as declaring ownership he gave the impression of awaiting a companion—watching with feigned patience for someone to appear in the doorway at Randolph's back. His imperiousness was somewhat undermined by crumbs of plaster adorning the top of the picture frame. "Will you know what robs a man of mastery?" he said. "Pray accompany me along the corridor."

Randolph couldn't help feeling relieved not to be given the tour by his host in the flesh. He suspected the commentary had been recorded late in the man's life—when he was turning senile, perhaps. The chandelier in the next room contained even fewer bulbs, which faltered alight to outline another bed. Its posts were slimmer than its neighbour's, and the canopy was more delicate, which meant it looked close to collapsing under the weight of debris. Had a fall of plaster smashed the dressing-table mirror? Randolph could see only shards of glass among the dusty cosmetic items. "Here you see the private suite of the last Lady Crowcross," the voice said. "I fear that the ways of our family were not to her taste."

He held a bedpost in his left fist, but it was unclear which bedroom he was in. His depiction of himself was virtually identical with the one next door. A figure identifiable as a woman by the long hair draped over the pillow lay in the sketch of a bed. Randolph couldn't judge if Crowcross had given her a face, because where one should be was a dark stain, possibly the result of the age and state of the painting. "Please don't exert yourself to look for any signs of children," Crowcross said. "They were taken long ago. My lady disagreed with the Crowcross methods and found another of our fairer counterparts to plead her case."

"I know the feeling," Randolph said, immediately regretting the response. There was no point in being bitter; he told himself so every time he had the children and whenever he had to give them up. As he caught sight of the bathroom shower, which was so antiquated that the iron cage put him in mind of some medieval punishment, Crowcross said "You'll have none of the little dears about you, I suppose. They must conduct themselves appropriately in this house."

While Randolph thought his and Harriet's children might have passed the test, at least if they'd been with him, he was glad not to have to offer proof. As he made for the corridor he glimpsed a trickle of moisture or some livelier object running down a bar of the shower cage. "That's the style," said Crowcross. "There's nothing worthy of attention here if you've taken in my work."

It almost sounded as though the guide was aware of Randolph's movements. To an extent this was how the commentary operated, but could it really be so specific? He was tempted to learn how it would react if he stayed in the room, but when the lit bulbs flickered in unison as though to urge him onwards he retreated into the corridor.

The adjacent room was the last on this side. Shadows swarmed and fluttered among the dead bulbs as the chandelier struggled to find life. All the furniture was stout and dark, the bedposts included. One corner of the laden canopy had almost torn loose. The room smelled dank, so that Randolph wouldn't have been surprised to see moisture on the stone walls. "This was the sanctum of the eldest Crowcross," the voice said. "His wife's quarters were across the corridor."

Presumably the portrait was meant to demonstrate how the room had become his. He was at the window, holding back the curtain to exhibit or lay claim to a version of the landscape in summer. His eyes were still on his audience; Randolph was beginning to feel as if the gaze never left him. He was meeting it and waiting for the next words when he heard a vehicle start up outside the house.

The bedposts shook like dislocated bones as he dashed across the room, and debris shifted with a stony whisper. The gap between the curtains was scarcely a finger's width. They felt capable of leaving handfuls of sodden heavy fabric in his grasp, and he knew where at least some of the smell came from. As he dragged them apart the rings twitched rustily along the metal rail. He craned forward, keeping well clear of the windowsill, which was scattered with dead flies like seeds of some unwelcome growth. The grid of cramped panes was coated with grime and crawling with raindrops, so that he was only just able to make out the grounds. Then, beyond the misshapen bloated topiary, he saw movement—the van near which he'd parked. Its outline wavered as it sped along the drive and picked up speed on the road.

Was Randolph alone in the house now? In that case, how had the driver sneaked past him? As the van disappeared into the rainswept gloom Crowcross said "Will you see the woman's quarters now? Everything is open to you, no matter what your pedigree."

How distasteful was this meant to sound? Randolph might have had enough by now except for the weather. He felt as if he was ensuring he outran the voice by hurrying across the corridor. A few bulbs sputtered alight in their cobwebbed crystal nest to show him yet another dilapidated bed. A hole had rotted in the canopy, dumping plaster on the stained bedclothes. Crowcross was holding a bedpost again, and a careless scribble behind him suggested that someone had just left the sketched bed. "Any little treasures would be barred from all these rooms," he said. "Have any found their way in now? Do keep an eye on their behaviour. We don't want any damage."

"I think you're having a bit of a joke," Randolph said. How senile had the speaker been by the time he'd recorded the commentary? Had he been seeing his home as it used to be? The light stuttered, rousing shadows in the bathroom and enlivening a muddy trickle on the initialled tiles above the marble trough. "If you have had your pleasure," Crowcross said, "the eldest breathed their last next door."

"My pleasure," Randolph retorted, and it was a question too.

The chandelier in the adjacent room lacked several bulbs. In the pensioned light a pair of four-posters occupied much of the cheerless space. Although the canopies were intact, the supports showed their age, some of the thinner ones bowing inwards. "They came here to grow as old as they could," Crowcross said. "Tell any little cherubs that, and how they had to stay together while they did."

Randolph thought the commentary had turned childish in the wrong way, if indeed there was a right one. He'd begun to feel it was no longer addressed to him or any listener, especially once Crowcross muttered "And then older."

The beds were flanked by massive wardrobes almost as dark outside as in. Both were open just enough to let Randolph distinguish shapes within. The figure with a dwarfish puffy head and dangling arms that were longer than its legs was a suit on a padded hanger. Its opposite number resembled a life-size cut-out of a woman drained of colour—just a long white dress, not a shroud. Nobody was about to poke a face around either of the doors, however much Randolph was reminded of a game of hide and seek. He'd never prevented the children from playing that, even if he might have in Lorn Hall. As he did his best to finish peering at the wardrobes Crowcross said "Are you still hoping for diversions? They await your judgement."

Randolph was starting to feel like the butt of a joke he wasn't expected to appreciate, since Crowcross didn't seem to think much of his visitors, let alone their views. When a pair of the lamps in the next room jittered alight, a ball on the billiard table shot into the nearest pocket. Of course only its legs had made it look as large as a billiard ball. Packs of battered cards were strewn across a table patched with baize, and cobwebs had overtaken a game of chess, where chipped marble chessmen lay in the dust beside the board. "This is where games were played," Crowcross said, "by those who had the privilege. Mine was waiting, and in the end I won."

He might have been talking to himself again, and resentfully at that. "We haven't seen your room yet," Randolph said and wondered if all of them had been. "You aren't ashamed of it, are you? It's a bit late to be ashamed."

He was heading for the turret room when Crowcross said "Eager to see where I was visited by dreams? Since then they have had the run of the house."

After a pause the room was illuminated by a stark grubby bulb. A bed with no posts and less than half the size of any of the others stood in the middle of the stone floor. The only other furniture was a wardrobe and a comparably sombre dressing-table with a mirror so low it cut Randolph off above the waist. Perhaps the soft toys huddled on the pillow had at some stage been intended to make the room more welcoming, but that wasn't their effect now. The pair of teddy bears and the lamb with boneless legs had all acquired red clownish mouths that contradicted their expressions. So much paint had been applied that it still resembled fresh blood.

They were in the portrait, where their sketched faces looked disconcertingly human. Perhaps the alterations to the actual toys had been a kind of preliminary study. Crowcross stood at the sunlit window, beyond which a distant figure stooped, hands outstretched. "I used to love watching the keepers trap their prey," Crowcross said. "They are put here for our pleasure and our use."

As Randolph turned away he saw what the painting didn't show. The toys on the pillow almost hid the clasped pair of hands protruding from beneath the quilt, which was blotched with mould. No, they were wings, none too expertly severed from the body—a pair of wooden wings. "This could have been a child's room," Crowcross mused. "We always raised our children to be men."

"Don't we talk about girls? I thought I was supposed to be unreasonable but my dear lord, my wife ought to listen to you," Randolph said and seemed to hear a confused violent noise in response. The window was shuddering under an onslaught of rain. He turned his back to all the eyes watching him—the portrait's and those of the disfigured toys, which were exactly as blank—and heard soft rapid footfalls on the stairs above him.

They were shuffling along the top corridor by the time he reached the staircase. "Excuse me, could you wait?" he shouted, raising the other headphone from his ear as he dashed upstairs so fast that he couldn't have said whether one cherub's face was splintered beyond recognition. Whenever he grabbed the banister, it wobbled with a bony clatter of its uprights. In a few seconds he saw that the top corridor was deserted.

None of the rooms showed a light. Perhaps whoever was about was trying to fix one, since otherwise their presence would have triggered it. Perhaps they were too busy to answer Randolph. Had the driver of the van been in the house at all? Presumably the person Randolph had glimpsed earlier was up here now. They couldn't have gone far, and he made for the turret room in the hope of finding them.

He saw he was alone once the meagre light recognised him. A lectern stood beside an imposing telescope that was pointed at the window. Astronomical charts—some crumpled, others chewed or torn to shreds—lay on the floor. "I never saw the appeal of the stars," Crowcross said, more distantly now. "I've no wish to be reminded of the dead. They say that's how old their light is. I preferred to watch the parade of the world. The glass brought it close enough for my taste."

He could have used the telescope to spy on the grounds and the road. Beyond the blurred fields Randolph saw an endless chain of watery lights being drawn at speed along the horizon. It was the motorway, where he promised himself he would be soon, but he could finish exploring while he waited for the rain to stop, particularly since the family wasn't with him. He left the turret room with barely a glance at the portrait in which Crowcross appeared to be stroking the barrel of the telescope as if it were a pet animal.

The next room was a library. Shelves of bound sets of fat volumes covered every wall up to the roof. Each volume was embossed with a **C** like a brand at the base of its spine. More than one high shelf had tipped over with the weight of books or the carelessness with which they'd been placed, so that dozens of books were sprawled about the floor in a jumble of dislocated pages. A ladder with rusty wheels towered over several stocky leather armchairs mottled with decay. "This might be tidier," said Crowcross. "Perhaps that could be your job."

What kind of joke was this meant to be? Randolph wondered if the last lord of Lorn Hall could have pulled the books down in a fury at having nowhere to hang his portrait. He couldn't have done much if any reading in here unless there had been more light than the one remaining bulb provided. It was enough to show that Randolph was still alone, and he dodged across the corridor.

An unshaded bulb on a cobwebbed flex took its time over revealing a bedroom. All four bedposts leaned so far inwards that they could have been trying to grasp the light or fend it off. The canopy lay in a heap on the bed. Although Randolph thought he'd glimpsed clothes hanging in the tall black wardrobe as the light came on, once he blinked away the glare he could see nothing except gloom beyond the scrawny gap—no pale garment for somebody bigger than he was, no wads of tissue paper stuffed into the cuffs and collar. "This could be made fit for guests again," Crowcross said. "Would you consider it to be your place?"

He sounded as furtively amused as he looked in his portrait, which showed him standing in the doorway of the room, gazing at whoever was within. It made Randolph glance behind him, even though he knew the corridor was empty. "I wouldn't be a guest of yours," he blurted, only to realise that in a sense he was. Almost too irritated to think, he tramped out of the room.

Next door was a bedroom very reminiscent of its neighbour. The fallen canopy of the four-poster was so rotten it appeared to have begun merging with the quilt. The portrait beyond the bed was virtually identical with the last one, and the light could have been competing at reluctance with its peers. Nothing was visible in the half-open wardrobe except padded hangers like bones fattened by dust. Randolph was about to move on when Crowcross said "This could be made fit for guests again. Would you consider it to be your place?"

The repetition sounded senile, and it seemed to cling to Randolph's brain. As he lurched towards the corridor Crowcross added "Will you make yourself at home?"

It had none of the tone of an invitation, and Randolph wasn't about to linger. Whoever else was upstairs had to be in the last room. "Have you seen all you choose?" Crowcross said while Randolph crossed the corridor. "See the rest, then."

The last room stayed dark until Randolph shoved the door wider, and then the lights began to respond—more of them than he thought he'd seen during the rest of the tour. The room was larger than both its neighbours combined, and graced with several chandeliers that he suspected had been replaced by solitary bulbs elsewhere in the house. They were wired low on the walls and lay on the floor, casting more shadow than illumination as he peered about the room.

It was cluttered with retired items. Rolled-up tapestries drooped against the walls, and so did numerous carpets and rugs, suggesting that someone had chosen to rob Lorn Hall of warmth. Several battered grandfather clocks stood like sentries over wooden crates and trunks that must have taken two servants apiece to carry them, even when they were empty of luggage. Smaller clocks perched on rickety pieces of furniture or lurked on the floorboards, and Randolph couldn't help fancying that somebody had tried to leave time up here to die. Crouching shadows outnumbered the objects he could see, but he appeared to be alone. As he narrowed his eyes Crowcross said "Here is where I liked to hide. Perhaps I still do."

"I would if I were you," Randolph said without having a precise retort in mind. He'd noticed a number of paintings stacked against the wall at the far end of the room. Were they pictures Crowcross had replaced with his own, or examples of his work he didn't want visitors to see? Randolph picked his way across the floor, almost treading on more than one photograph in the dimness—they'd slipped from unsteady heaps of framed pictures which, as far as he could make out, all showed members of the Crowcross family. Even the glass on the topmost pictures in the heaps was shattered. He'd decided to postpone understanding the damage until he was out of the room when he reached the paintings against the wall.

Though the light from the nearest chandelier was obstructed by the clutter, the image on the foremost canvas was plain enough. It portrayed Crowcross in a field, his arms folded, one foot on a prone man's neck. He looked not so much triumphant as complacent. The victim's face was either turned away submissively or buried in the earth, and his only distinguishing feature was the **C** embossed on his naked back. It wasn't a painting from life, Randolph told himself; it was just a symbol or a fantasy, either of which was bad enough. He was about to tilt the canvas forward to expose the next when Crowcross spoke. "The last," he said.

Did he mean a painting or the room, or did the phrase have another significance? Randolph wasn't going to be daunted until he saw what Crowcross had tried to conceal, but as he took hold of a corner of the frame the portrait was invaded by darkness. A light had been extinguished at his back—no, more than one—and too late he realised something else. Because the headphones weren't over his ears any more he'd mistaken the direction of the voice. It was behind him.

The room seemed to swivel giddily as he did. The figure that almost filled the doorway was disconcertingly familiar, and not just from the versions in the paintings; he'd glimpsed it skulking in the wardrobe. It wore a baggy nightshirt no less pallid and discoloured than its skin. Its face was as stiff as it appeared in any of the portraits, and the unblinking eyes were blank as lumps of greyish paint. The face had lolled in every direction it could find, much like the contents of the rest of the visible skin—the bare arms, the legs above the clawed feet. When the puffy white lips parted Randolph thought the mouth was in danger of losing more than its shape. As the figure shuffled forward he heard some of the substance of the unshod feet slopping against the floor. Just as its progress extinguished the rest of the lights it spoke with more enthusiasm than he'd heard from it anywhere else in the house. "Game," it said.

Printed and bound by CPI Group (UK) Ltd, Croydon, CR0 4YY
09/01/2026
02032387-0005